The Fallen Blade

The palaces lining the Canalasso were the grandest in the city. The buildings were rich, decorated with carvings and tiny squares of coloured glass. Many palaces painted. The carvings and the varied stones and the paintings like nothing he'd ever seen. In his fractured mind buildings were wood or earth.

The walls of a great hall, double-skinned with logs filled with pounded dirt. A turf roof over crude beams. In winter, snow kept warmth in the hall. The snow in Venice was so thin Tycho barely recognised it.

How could his home be burnt for a hundred years? Bjornvin was there in his memory now. Not perfect, certainly not that, but real and recent.

After that . . . ?

He could remember an axe cutting into a ship's hull. His brief blindness as someone thrust a lamp into his prison. Until the light reached him he hadn't known how his eyes had changed. And until he threw himself backwards off the little boat he hadn't realised he moved faster than other people. Everyone here seemed to move clumsily, stumbling through dark alleys, barely seeing what was there.

At first, he'd wondered what was wrong with them. Who these clumsy people were. Now he had fragments of memory back, and Maître Thomas's memories too, he was coming to wonder if he was *people* at all.

By Jon Courtenay Grimwood

The Assassini
The Fallen Blade
The Outcast Blade

The Fallen Blade

Act One of THE ASSASSINI

Jon Courtenay
GRIMWOOD

www.orbitbooks.net

ORBIT

First published in Great Britain in 2011 by Orbit
This paperback edition published in 2012 by Orbit

A CIP catalogue record for this book
is available from the British Library.

ISBN 978-1-84149-846-1

Typeset in Adobe Garamond by Palimpsest Book Production Limited,
Falkirk, Stirlingshire
Printed and bound by CPI Group (UK) Ltd, Croydon CR0 4YY

Papers used by Orbit are from well-managed forests
and other responsible sources.

MIX
Paper from
responsible sources
FSC
www.fsc.org FSC® C104740

Orbit
An imprint of
Little, Brown Book Group
100 Victoria Embankment
London EC4Y 0DY

An Hachette UK Company
www.hachette.co.uk

www.orbitbooks.net

For Sam,
who found Venice stranger than she imagined . . .

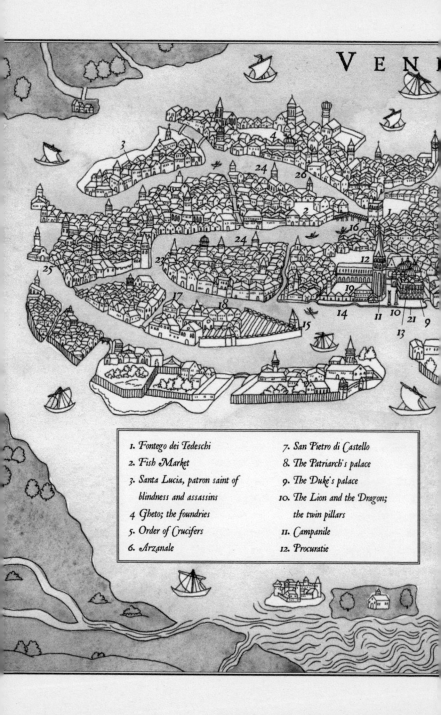

VENI

1. Fontego dei Tedeschi
2. Fish Market
3. Santa Lucia, patron saint of
   blindness and assassins
4. Gheto; the foundries
5. Order of Crucifers
6. Arzanale

7. San Pietro di Castello
8. The Patriarch's palace
9. The Duke's palace
10. The Lion and the Dragon;
    the twin pillars
11. Campanile
12. Procuratie

I A

22

6

8

20

The Millioni family tree

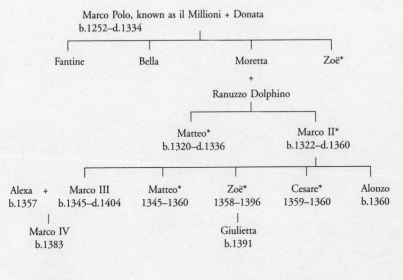

Marco Polo, known as il Millioni + Donata
b.1252–d.1334

Fantine   Bella   Moretta   Zoë*

+

Ranuzzo Dolphino

Matteo*   Marco II*
b.1320–d.1336   b.1322–d.1360

Alexa +   Marco III   Matteo*   Zoë*   Cesare*   Alonzo
b.1357   b.1345–d.1404   1345–1360   1358–1396   1359–1360   b.1360

Marco IV   Giulietta
b.1383   b.1391

* Murdered

First Republic
1336 –1348

Second Republic
1360–1362

Dramatis Personae

Tycho, a seventeen-year-old boy with strange hungers

The Millioni

Marco IV, known as Marco the Simpleton, Duke of Venice and Prince of Serenissima

Lady Giulietta di Millioni, the fifteen-year-old cousin of Marco IV

Duchess Alexa, the late duke's widow, mother to Marco IV, sister-in-law of Prince Alonzo

Prince Alonzo, Regent of Venice

Lady Eleanor, Giulietta's cousin and lady-in-waiting

Marco III, known as Marco the Just. The late lamented Duke of Venice, elder brother of Alonzo and godfather of Lady Giulietta

Members of the Venetian court

Atilo il Mauros, ex-Lord Admiral of the Middle Sea, adviser to the late Marco III, and head of Venice's secret assassins

Lord Bribanzo, member of the Council of Ten, the inner council that rules Venice under the duke. One of the richest men in the city

Lady Desdaio Bribanzo, his daughter and sole heir

Sir Richard Glanville, Cypriot envoy to Venice and knight of the Order of White Crucifers

Prince Leopold zum Bas Friedland, the German emperor's bastard. Secret leader of the Wolf Brothers

Patriarch Theodore, Archbishop of Venice and friend of Atilo il Mauros

Dr Hightown Crow, alchemist, astrologer and anatomist to the duke

A'rial, the Duchess Alexa's *stregoi* (her pet witch)

Atilo's household

Iacopo, Atilo's servant and member of the Assassini

Amelia, a Nubian slave and member of the Assassini

The Customs Office

Roderigo, Captain of the Dogana, penniless since he refuses to take bribes

Temujin, his half-Mongol sergeant

Street Thieves

Josh, fifteen-year-old gang leader

Rosalyn, his thirteen-year-old companion

Pietro, Rosalyn's young brother

PART 1

"...what a hell of witchcraft lies
In the small orb of one particular tear..."

A Lover's Complaint, William Shakespeare

1

Venice, Tuesday 4 January 1407

The boy hung naked from wooden walls, shackles circling one wrist and both ankles. He'd fought for days to release his left hand, burning his skin on red-hot fetters as he worked to drag his fingers free. The struggle had left him exhausted and – if he was honest – no better off than before.

"Help me," he begged, "I will do whatever you ask."

His gods stayed silent.

"I swear it. My life is yours."

But his life was theirs anyway; even here in an enclosed space where his lungs ached at every breath and the air was sour and becoming sourer. The gods had abandoned him to his death.

It would have helped if he could remember their names.

Some days he doubted they existed. If they did, he doubted they cared. The boy's fury at his fate had become bitterness and despair, and then turned to false hope and fresh fury. Maybe he'd missed an emotion, but he'd worked his way through those he knew.

Yanking at his wrist made flesh sear.

Whatever magic his captors used was stronger than his will to be free. The chains with which they bound him were new, bolted

3

firmly to the wall. Every time he grabbed a chain to yank at it, his fingers sizzled as if a torturer pressed white-hot irons into his skin.

"Sweet gods," he whispered.

As if flattering the immortals could undo his earlier insults.

He'd shrieked at his gods, cursed them, called for the aid of demons. Begged for help from any human within earshot of his despair. A part of him wanted to return to shrieking. Simply for the release it would bring. Only he'd screamed his throat raw days ago. Besides, who would come to his grotesque little cell with no doors? And if they did, how would they enter?

Murder. Rape. Treason . . .

What else merited being walled up alive?

His crime was a mystery. What was the point of punishment if the prisoner couldn't remember what he'd done? The boy had no memory of his name. No memory of why he was locked in a space little bigger than a coffin. Not even a memory of who put him here.

Earth strewed the floor, splattered with his own soiling.

It was days since he'd needed to piss, and his lips were cracked like dry mud and raw from where he tried to lick them. He needed sleep almost as desperately as he wanted to be free, but every time he slumped his shackles burnt and the pain snapped him awake again. He'd done something wrong. Something very wrong. So wrong that even death wouldn't embrace him.

If only he could remember what.

You have a name. What is it?

Like hope and freedom, this too remained out of reach. In the hours that followed, the boy hovered on the edges of a fever. Sometimes his wits were sharp, but mostly he inhabited a blasted wasteland inside his own skull where his memories should be.

All he saw in there were shadows that turned away from him; and voices he was unable to hear clearly.

4

Pay attention, he told himself. *Listen.*

So he did. What he heard were voices beyond the wooden walls. A crowd from the sound of it, arguing. And though what he heard was little louder than a whisper it told him they spoke a language he didn't recognise. One voice snapped out an order, another protested. Then something slammed into the wall directly in front of him.

It sounded like an axe or a hammer.

The second blow was even harder. Then came a third, his wooden world splintering as sweet air rushed in and fetid air blew out. The light through the narrow gap was blinding. As if the gods had come for him after all.

2

Late Summer 1406

Almost four months before the boy woke to find himself trapped in an airless wooden prison, a young Venetian girl hurried along a ramshackle *fondamenta* on her city's northern edge. In some places in that strange city the waterside walkways were built from brick or even stone. The one here was earth, above sharpened logs driven into the silt of the lagoon.

After sunset everywhere in Venice was unsafe, particularly if you were fifteen years old, unmarried and out of your area. But the red-haired girl on the *fondamenta* hoped to reach the brine pans before then. She planned to beg passage on a barge carrying salt to the mainland.

Her burgundy gown was already dusty and sweat stained.

Despite having walked for only an hour, she'd reached another world entirely. One where silk dresses attracted envious glances. Her oldest gown was still richer than the *campo gheto*'s best. Her hopes of passing freely ended when a small group of children stepped out of the shadows.

Opening her cloak, Lady Giulietta yanked free a gold locket from around her neck. "Take this," she said. "Sell it. You can buy food."

The boy with the knife sneered at her. "We steal food," he said. "We don't need your locket for that. Not from round here, are you?

Giulietta shook her head.

"You Jewish?"

"No," she said. "I'm—"

She was about to say . . . something stupid, knowing her. It was a stupid kind of day. Being here was stupid. Stopping was stupid. Even treating his question seriously was stupid. "I'm like you," she finished lamely.

"Course you are," he said. On either side, others laughed. "Where did you get this anyway?"

"My m . . ." She hesitated. "Mistress."

"You stole it," a smaller boy said. "That's why you're running. Nasty lot, the Watch. You'd be better coming with us."

"No," Giulietta said, "I'd better keep going."

"You know what happens if the Watch take you?" a girl asked. She stepped forward to whisper in Giulietta's ear. If even half were true, someone of Giulietta's age would be better killing herself than being captured. But self-murder was a sin.

"And if the Watch don't get you, then . . ."

The youngest shut his mouth at a glare from their leader. "Look around," he snapped. "It's getting dark. What have I said?"

"Sorry, Josh."

The older boy slapped him. "We don't use names with strangers. We don't talk about . . . Not when it's almost nightfall." He switched his glare to the girl who stood beside him. "I'm going to cut him loose. I swear it. Don't care if he is your brother."

"I'll go with him."

"You'll go nowhere," Josh said. "Your place is with me. You too," he told Giulietta. "There's a ruined *campo* south of here. We'll make it in time."

"If we're lucky," the girl said.

"We've been lucky so far, haven't we?"

7

"*So far, and no further,*" said a shadow behind them.

Old and weary, the voice sounded like dry wind through a dusty attic.

Unwrapping itself, the shadow became a Moor, dressed in a dozen shades of grey. A neatly barbered beard emphasised the thinness of his face and his gaze was that of a soldier grown tired of life. Across his shoulders hung a sword. Stilettos jutted at both hips. Lady Giulietta noticed his crossbow last. Tiny, almost a toy, with barbed arrows the size of her finger.

With a sour smile, the Moor pointed his crossbow at Josh's throat, before turning his attention to the young woman he'd been following.

"My lady, this is not kind . . ."

"Not kind?"

Bunching her fists, Lady Giulietta fought her anger.

She'd become used to holding it in in public, screaming about her forthcoming marriage behind closed doors. She was two years older than her mother was when she wed. Noble girls married at twelve, went to their husband's beds at thirteen, sometimes a little later. At least two of Giulietta's friends had children already.

She'd been whipped for her refusal to wed willingly.

Starved, locked in her chambers. Until she announced she'd kill herself. On being told that was a sin, she'd sworn to murder her husband instead.

At that, Aunt Alexa, the late Duke Marco III's widow, had shaken her head sadly and sent for hot water to which she added fermented leaves to make her niece a soothing drink. While Uncle Alonzo, the late duke's younger brother, had taken Giulietta aside to say it was interesting she should mention that . . .

Her world became a darker, more horrid place. Not only would she marry a foreigner she'd never met. She'd be taught how to kill him when the bedding was done. "You know what they expect me to do?"

"My lady, it's not my place . . ."

"Of course not. You're just the cur sent to round up strays."

His eyes flared and she smiled. He wasn't a cur and she wasn't a stray. She was Lady Giulietta dei San Felice di Millioni. The Regent's niece. The new duke's cousin. Duchess Alexa's goddaughter. Her whole life defined by how she was related to someone else.

"Say you couldn't find me."

"I've been following you since I saw you leave."

"*Why?*" she demanded. Only in the last half-hour had she felt herself watched. She couldn't believe he'd let her travel right across Venice by herself, knowing he would stop her before she could escape to the mainland.

"I hoped you might turn back."

Rubbing her temples, Giulietta wished they'd sent a young officer she could shout at, or beguile with her charms, meagre though they were.

"How can I marry a man I haven't even met?"

"You know . . ."

Giulietta stamped her foot. She understood. All daughters were assets. Princely daughters more than most. It was just . . . Maybe she'd read too many poets. What if there was someone she was *meant* to marry? She regretted her words the moment they were spoken. The Moor's quiet contempt for her question ensured that.

"And what if he lives on the world's far edge or is not yet born? What if he died centuries ago? *What if he loves someone else?* Policy can't wait on a girl's fantasies. Not even for you . . ."

"Let me go," Giulietta begged.

"My lady, I can't." He shook his head sadly, never letting his crossbow's aim stray from Josh's throat. "Ask me anything else."

"I want nothing else."

Atilo il Mauros had bought her her first pony. Dandled her on his knees. With his own hands he carved her a bear fighting a woodcutter. But he would return her to Ca' Ducale because that was his duty. Atilo did his duty without fear or favour. It had made him the late duke's favourite. And earned him Alonzo, the new Regent's, hatred. Giulietta had no idea what Aunt Alexa thought of him.

"If you loved me . . ." Her voice was flat.

Lord Atilo glanced at the bow he held, looked at the ragged thieves and shifted Giulietta out of their hearing, without letting his aim waver.

"My lady."

"*Listen to me.*" She felt sick in her gut. Tired and fed up and close to tears. "King Janus was a Crucifer. A Black Crucifer."

"I know."

"And I had to learn it from servants' gossip. They're going to marry me to an ex-torturer, who broke his vows of poverty and chastity. Who abandoned *the purity of pain.*" Her lips curled in disgust at the words.

"To become king," Atilo said simply.

"He's a monster."

"Giulietta . . . The Germans want Venice. The Byzantines want it too. The Mamluks want your colonies. Even my people, the Moors, would happily see your navy sunk. King Janus was Black only briefly. Cyprus is an island we can use."

"*Use?*" she said in scorn.

"Venice's strength rests on its trade routes. It *needs* Cyprus. Besides, you have to marry someone."

"It might as well be him?"

The Moor nodded, and she wondered if he could read the fury in her eyes. Anger kept her fear at bay. Her fear of what being bedded by a Black Crucifer might involve.

"My lord," Josh interrupted.

Atilo raised his bow. "Did I tell you to speak?" His finger began tightening on the trigger.

"*Let him speak.*"

"My lady, you're in no . . ."

". . . position to demand anything?" said Lady Giulietta bitterly. She'd never been in a position to demand anything as far as she could see. At least not since her mother was murdered. Giulietta was a Millioni. A princess. She had one of the most gilded childhoods in Venice. Everyone envied her.

She'd swap all of it for . . .

Lady Giulietta bit her lip so hard it bled. There were days when her self-pity nauseated even herself. This was turning out to be one of them.

"Let's hear what he has to say," she suggested.

Atilo lowered his tiny crossbow. A nod said the boy was reprieved, for now. "This had better be good."

"We should get off the streets, my lord."

"That's it?" Atilo sounded astonished. "That's your contribution? You're a split second away from death. And you think we should get off the streets?"

"It's almost dark."

"They're afraid of the Watch," Giulietta said.

She wasn't surprised. *Beat you and violate you, smash your face and twist your arms if you don't do everything they want.* That sounded as if the girl spoke from experience.

"Not the Watch," the younger boy said dismissively. "We ain't afraid of them now. They don't go out after dark."

"They're the Watch," Giulietta said.

"Got more sense," he told her. "Not with what's out there."

"And what is out there?" she asked. Perhaps the small boy didn't see Atilo's warning scowl. Perhaps he wasn't bothered.

"Demons."

"No," his sister said. "They're monsters."

"Atilo . . ." She shouldn't be using his name like that. Not without "my lord" or whatever title he held since the Regent had stripped him of Admiral of the Middle Sea, which had been his position

11

under Marco III . . . The late and very lamented Duke Marco III. Since his son, Marco IV, her poor cousin, was a twitching simpleton.

"What?" His tone was sharp.

"We can't just leave them."

"Yes," he said. "We can." Atilo stopped at an owl's hoot, his shoulders relaxing slightly. When he hooted back, the owl hooted in return. "It's you we can't leave." There was bitterness in his voice.

"But you would if you could . . . ?"

"I have fifteen blades out there. The best I've trained. My deputy, his deputy, thirteen others. Good soldiers. If half come through this alive I'll be grateful."

Giulietta didn't recognise him as the old man who had carved her a wooden toy as a child. This was the Atilo people saw in battle.

"Are we heading for safety?"

He turned, looked at her. A hard glare that softened slightly. "There is no safety tonight, my lady. Not here and not now. The best I can do is hope to keep you alive."

"And the children?"

"They're dead already. Leave them."

"I can't . . . We can't . . ." She plucked at his sleeve. "Please."

"You want them saved?"

"Yes," she said, grateful. Thinking he'd changed his mind.

"Then let them be. They stand a better chance of living if they hide now. Not much, admittedly. But staying with you will certainly get them killed."

Lady Giulietta looked sick.

"It's you our enemies want. Well, it is now."

Taking a stiletto from his hip, he reversed it fluidly, offering her its handle over the edge of his forearm. *Sweet Lord*, she thought. *He's serious.* From the knot in her guts, her body was ahead of her brain. She was afraid the knot would let go and she'd disgrace herself in front of the old man.

"Find a tanner's pit," Atilo snapped at Josh's group. "Shouldn't be hard round here. Squat in it up to your necks. Don't move. Keep silent until morning."

"The demons hate water?"

"They hunt by smell. You stink of piss already. Find a tanner's pit and you might get lucky." Atilo turned without further thought. They were gone already as far as he was concerned.

"Stay close," he told Giulietta.

Atilo used a *sottoportego*, an underpass beneath a tenement building, to reach a tiny square. At its far edge, the square was prevented from crumbling into a narrow canal by oak stakes along its bank. Slicing a rope to a shabby gondola, Atilo kicked it away from the side to make a makeshift bridge. Once Lady Giulietta was over, he cut the remaining rope and jumped for safety as the boat drifted away.

"Where are we going?"

"I have a house," he said.

"Ca' il Mauros?" Her heart sank. To reach there from here, they'd need to cross the Grand Canal by gondola twice, or walk round it, which would double the distance and take them down one of the most dangerous streets in Venice.

"A different house," he told her.

When he reached for her hand, it was not to comfort her, but to grip her wrist and start dragging. He wanted her to walk faster.

"Atilo, you're . . ." Giulietta shut her mouth. The old man was trying to save her. He was furious, in a way she'd never seen, his face a battle mask, his eyes hard in the darkness.

"I'm sorry," she said.

He stopped, and Giulietta thought . . . For a second, she thought he'd forget himself and slap her. Then there was no time to think more of that, because a grotesque figure watched them from a square ahead.

"This way."

A yank on her wrist hurled her towards an alley. Only that

way out of the new square was blocked as well. As were the other two exits.

"Kill yourself," Atilo said.

Giulietta gaped at him.

"Not now, you little fool. If I'm dead, and they're dead . . ." He pointed to silhouettes appearing in the shadows. Some stood near the grotesques who blocked the exits, others stood on rooftops or balconies. "Don't let yourself be taken."

"They'll rape me?"

"You can survive that. What the Wolf Brothers do you don't survive. Although you might be more use to them alive and unharmed. Which means you must definitely kill yourself."

"Self-murder is a sin."

"Letting yourself be captured is a worse one."

"To God?"

"To Venice. Which is what matters."

Serenissima, the name poets gave to the Serene Republic of Venice, was an inaccurate term. Since the city was neither serene nor, these days, a republic.

In Atilo's opinion, it was most like a bubbling pot into which some celestial threw endless grains of rice. And though each morning began with the bodies of beggars against walls, new born infants in back canals, paupers dumped to avoid the inconvenience of burying them – those unwanted, even by the unwanted – the city remained as crowded, and as packed, and as expensive, as he remembered it ever having been.

In summer the poor slept on roofs, on balconies or in the open air. When winter came, they crowded squalid tenements. They shat, copulated, fought and quarrelled in public, seen by other adults as well as by their own children. The stairwells of the tenements had a permanent odour of poverty. Unwashed, unloved, stinking of sewage, and a greasy misery that oiled the skin until it looked and smelt like wet leather.

A dozen scholars had drawn maps of Venice. Including a Chinese cartographer sent by the Great Khan, who'd heard of this capital with canals where roads should be and wanted to know how much of it was true. None of the maps were accurate, however, and half the streets had more than one name anyway.

Running through what he thought of Venice, Atilo il Mauros wondered, in retrospect, why he felt reluctant to leave it and the life he'd made here. Was it simply that this was not the way he'd intended to die? In a squalid *campo*, near a ramshackle church, because every *campo* had one of those. Although not usually this run-down. A church, a broken wellhead, ruined brick houses . . .

He'd hoped to die in his bed years from now.

His wife, beautifully stricken, backlit by a gentle autumn sun; a boy at the bed's foot, staring sorrowfully. To have this, of course, he'd need a wife. A wife, a son and heir, maybe a couple of daughters, if they weren't too much trouble.

After the siege of Tunis, Duke Marco III had offered him a deal. The duke would spare the city and Atilo would serve Venice as Admiral. If Atilo refused, every man, woman and child in the North African city would be slaughtered; including Atilo's own family. The great pirate of the Barbary Coast could turn traitor to those he loved and save them, or stay loyal and condemn them to death.

Bastard, Atilo thought with admiration.

Even now, decades later, he could remember his awe at the brutality of Marco's offer. In a single afternoon Atilo uttered the words that divorced his wife, renounced his children, converted his religion and bound him to Venice for life.

In taking the title of Lord Admiral of the Middle Sea, he had saved those who would hate him for the rest of their lives. In public, he'd been Marco III's adviser. In private he'd been the man's chief assassin. The enemy, who became his master, ended as his friend. Atilo would die for that man's niece.

15

This was the biggest gathering of Wolf Brothers in Atilo's life-time – and he was shocked to discover so many in his city. Well, the city Atilo he'd come to love. Atilo knew what this battle meant. To fight *krieghund* in the open like this would destroy the Assassini, quite possibly leave him without an heir. Destroying the Assassini would leave Venice without protection.

Was her life worth that much?

He knew the girl behind him had caught the moment he wanted to slap her. Fifteen-year-old princesses were not meant to run away, unhappily betrothed or not. They were not meant to be *able* to run away. A savage whipping would await her if she lived; assuming Atilo told the truth about her flight. Alonzo would see to the whipping even if her aunt objected. For a woman so fond of poisoning her enemies Alexa could be very forgiving where her niece was concerned.

"My lord . . ."

A black-clad man appeared out of the darkness, sketched a quick bow and instinctively checked what weapons his chief was carrying. He relaxed slightly when he saw the little crossbow.

"Silver-tipped, my lord?"

"Obviously."

The man glanced at Giulietta, his eyes widening when he realised she carried Atilo's dagger.

"She has her orders," Atilo said. "Yours are to die protecting her."

There were twenty-one in the Scuola di Assassini, including Atilo. In the early days he'd given his followers Greek letters as names, but he drew his apprentices from the poorest levels of the city and many had trouble with their own alphabet. These days he used numbers instead.

The middle-aged man in front of him was No. 3.

No. 2 was in prison in Cyprus on charges that couldn't be proved; he would be released or simply disappear. Knowing Janus it would be the latter. No. 4 was in Vienna to kill Emperor

Sigismund. A task he would probably fail. No. 7 guarded their headquarters. No. 13 was in Constantinople. And No. 17 was in Paris trying to poison a Valois princeling. In theory, only one of them needed to survive to ensure the *scuola*, the Scuola di Assassini, continued unbroken.

Sixteen Assassini against six enemies.

With those odds victory should be certain. But Atilo knew what was out there: the emperor's *krieghund*. His blades would die in reverse order. The most junior trying to exhaust the beasts so their seniors had a chance of success. Atilo was arbiter of what success entailed. Tonight it meant keeping Lady Giulietta out of enemy hands. "Go die," he ordered his deputy.

The man's grin disappeared into the night.

"Numerical," Atilo heard him shout, and hell opened as a snarling, silver-furred beast stalked into the square, leaving a screaming, vaguely man-shaped lump of meat in an alley mouth behind.

"What is it?" Giulietta asked, far too loudly.

"*Krieghund*," Atilo snapped. "Speak again and I'll gag you." Sighting his crossbow, he fired. But the beast swatted aside the silver bolt and turned on an Assassino approaching from its blind side. The kill was quick and brutal. A claw caught the side of the boy's skull, dragging him closer. A bite to the neck half removed his head.

"I thought they were a myth," Giulietta whispered, then clapped her hand over her mouth and backed away from Atilo.

The Moor grinned sourly. She was learning. Give him the girl for a few months and he'd give her aunt and uncle something worth keeping, and not just keeping alive. But they didn't want something to keep. They wanted something unbroken they could trade.

In a miracle of luck and poor judgement the third most junior Assassino hurled himself at the creature in front of him, ducked under a claw and managed to stab his sword into the beast's side before the *krieghund* struck. The young man died with his neck broken and his throat spraying blood.

"Kill the beast," Giulietta begged.

"I don't have arrows to waste." Sweeping his gaze over the small, dark square, Atilo concluded fifty people must be watching from behind shutters. Houses this poor lacked glass. So they could hear as well.

None would help. Why would they?

"Look," he told her, pointing at the *krieghund* on its knees. As she looked, the beast began to change, its face flattening and its shoulders becoming narrower. Giulietta took a second to understand what she was seeing. A wolfthing becoming a man, who stopped howling and started trying to shovel loops of gut back into his gaping stomach.

"Now we kill him."

Out of the darkness came an Assassino, his sword already drawn back to take the dying man's head. Blood pumped in a fountain and fell like rain. The battle was ferocious after that. Beasts and men hacking at each other. And then men lay dead in the dirt. Most in riveted mail, a few naked.

"My lord . . ."

Giulietta was finding her nerve, addressing him politely now. She still looked pale in the moonlight. They all looked pale to him. At least she'd stopped shivering and now held his dagger more confidently. There was an old-fashioned Millioni princess in there somewhere.

"They're advancing . . ."

"I know," he said, raising his bow.

The officer who took orders originally glanced over, bowing slightly in reply to Atilo's nod, to acknowledge whatever passed between them. He signalled to those of the Assassini who remained and they attacked as one.

The last stages of the fight were brief and brutal.

Swords slashing, daggers sliding under ribs, blood spraying. The stink was the stink of the abattoir; of shit and blood and open guts. The men died well, but they died, and, in the end, most corpses were clothed, a handful were naked and one furred half-corpse lurched towards Atilo, a dagger jutting from its ribs.

"Kill it," Giulietta begged.

Sighting his crossbow, Atilo fired for the creature's throat.

The beast staggered, but kept coming. Straight into a second arrow. Hooking back his string, Atilo slotted a third, and would have fired had the *krieghund* not slashed the bow from his hand.

Never thought I'd die like this.

The thought came and went. There were worse ways to go than facing a creature from hell. But he had Marco III's niece behind him and he couldn't just . . . "Don't," he shouted. He was too late, however.

Stepping out from behind him, Giulietta rammed her stiletto into the *krieghund*'s side, twisting hard. She went down when the creature cracked its elbow into her head. It was stooping for the kill, when a piece of night sky detached itself, dropping in a crackle of old leather and dry clicks. Atilo took the opening. Stabbing a throwing knife into the beast's heart.

"Alexa . . . ?"

The square of leather bumped into ground-floor shutters, crawled between rusting bars and hung itself upside down. Wings folding to a fraction of their previous size as golden eyes glared from a face disgusted with the world.

"Giulietta's still alive?"

Kneeling, Atilo touched his fingers to the girl's throat. "Yes, my lady."

"Good. We'll need her now more than ever." The bat through which Giulietta's aunt had watched the battle turned its attention to the *krieghund*'s death agony. "You've upset him." The words were thin. A whisper of wind forced from a throat not made for speech.

"He's dying."

"Not him, fool. His master. Leopold will try stealing her again."

Atilo considered pointing out that the German prince hadn't stolen her this time. Lady Giulietta had stolen herself.

"Then we hunt Leopold down and kill him."

"He has protection," whispered the bat. "He will be more cautious now. He will move more carefully. And he will rebuild his Wolf Brothers. And then all this will start again. Slaughtered children and the Night Watch too scared to do their job. Until we grow tired and beg for the truce he keeps offering us."

"This is our city."

"Yes," said the bat. "But he's the German emperor's bastard."

The second time someone didn't come when he knocked, Atilo kicked the door off its hinges and entered with a throwing dagger in his hand.

"Boil water," he ordered. "And fetch me thread."

A combination of the blade he carried, his air of command and his absolute certainty he would be obeyed was enough to make the householder put down an iron bar, bow low and order his wife into the kitchen at the back.

"Who sleeps above?" Atilo pointed over his head.

"My daughter . . ."

"Bring her down."

"My lord."

Atilo caught fear in his voice. "I don't want your damn daughter," he said brusquely. "I want her bed, and privacy. Leave hot water, a needle and thread outside her door."

"Thread, sir?"

The Moor sighed. "Find a horsehair, boil it in the water, and the needle while you're at it. Knock when they're ready." Disappearing into the night, he returned carrying Giulietta, her legs hanging over his arms, her head thrown back to reveal blood in her hair.

"You know who I am?"

The man, the woman and their newly arrived daughter shook their heads. The daughter was about twelve, wrapped in a blanket, and flinched when he turned his attention to her. "Did you see the battle?"

"No one here saw anything, my lord."

"Right answer," said Atilo, pushing past towards the stairs.

3

New Year 1407

In the days then weeks and finally months that followed that autumn's pitched battle between the Assassini and the Wolf Brothers – a battle known only to a few – plans went forward for the marriage of Lady Giulietta to Janus, King of Cyprus.

As the year dragged towards its end and another was born, on 25 December, the same day as the Christian Lord, Atilo il Mauros – who wasn't quite sure which god he acknowledged – licked his wounds and wondered how to keep the destruction of his Assassini secret.

The girl they'd died protecting simply waited to meet her new husband. Although she should have realised he wouldn't come himself. Instead, he sent an Englishman, Sir Richard Glanville, as his envoy.

Arriving in mid-December, the envoy spent Christmas at the ducal palace, while terms were negotiated and arrangements made for Lady Giulietta's departure. When these were agreed, Sir Richard celebrated by offering a hundred gold coins as the prize for a gondola race. A foreign noble's traditional way of ingratiating himself with the Venetian public.

However, his generosity failed to impress Lady Giulietta, who resented having to leave her warm quarters for the chill wind of a winter afternoon, and made little attempt to hide it. She had no idea that Monday 3 January would change her life. As far as she was concerned, it was the day sleet frizzed her hair as she turned out to watch the end of another stupid race.

"They say Crucifers prefer men."

Sir Richard's simple breastplate was half hidden by the cloak of his order. His only jewellery was a ring marrying him to his priory. By contrast, the captain of Giulietta's escort wore red hose, scarlet shoes and a brocade doublet short enough to show his codpiece. Both men were watching a merchant's wife.

"My lady. Are you sure about that?"

"Eleanor . . ." Giulietta started to reprimand her lady-in-waiting and then shrugged. "Perhaps Sir Richard's the exception."

"Perhaps the rumour is wrong."

"You like him!"

"*My lady.*"

"You do!"

Eleanor was thirteen and Giulietta's cousin. She had the dark eyes, black hair and olive skin of those who mix northern blood with blood from the south. She was loyal but quite capable of answering back. "He's a White Crucifer."

"So?" Giulietta demanded.

"Crucifers are celibate."

"Supposedly."

"What do you think they're discussing?" Eleanor asked, trying to change the subject. Although all that happened was that Giulietta's scowl deepened.

"My engagement. All anybody talks about."

"She's interesting."

Captain Roderigo regarded the merchant's wife with surprise. She was certainly blonde, and pink-skinned, big-breasted and big-boned. With thighs made to cushion a man's head. But interesting?

"I meant your Lady Giulietta."

Both men glanced towards the Millioni princess.

Her family had worn the *biretum*, that oddly shaped cap adopted by the doges of old, for five generations. Earlier dukes were elected, however corrupt that election. Marco Polo's descendants claimed it by birth. Their palace was grander than the Medici's. Their mainland estates wider than the Pope's own. They were aggressive, avaricious and scheming. Essential qualities for a princely family. To these they added a fourth, *murderous*. Their arm was long. The blade it held sharp.

"The Millioni have kept us free."

"From whom?" Sir Richard asked, sounding surprised.

"Everyone. Venice balances on a rope, with predators waiting in the pit below. They see us dance elegantly, pirouette daintily; dressed in our gaudy clothes. And never ask the reason we stay high on our rope."

"And who are the predators?"

Roderigo regarded him sharply. "We have the German emperor to the north. The emperor of Byzantium to the south. The Pope has declared the Millioni *false princes*. Making them fair game for any penitent with a sharp dagger and a guilty conscience. The Mamluks covet our trade routes. The King of Hungary wants his Schiavoni colonies in Dalmatia back. Everyone offers to protect us from everyone else. Who do you think the predators are?"

"So you marry Giulietta to Janus because it will help protect those trade routes? Poor child . . ."

Finding them watching her, Giulietta turned away.

"She makes no pretence to be pleased," said Sir Richard, then shrugged. "Why would she? Janus is years older. I imagine she dreams of the Florentine."

"Cosimo?"

"He's . . . what? A few years older than her? Educated, loves music, dresses well. He's even said to be handsome."

"She fancies no one," Roderigo said. "Not even," he said, trying

24

to sweeten the truth, "a ruggedly handsome, war-hardened veteran like me."

Sir Richard snorted.

"Anyway, she can't marry the Medici. Florence is our enemy."

"So were we until your ambassador proposed this match at the funeral of our late queen. Janus was surprised by your timing."

Roderigo wasn't.

Venice's ambassador to Cyprus had the patience of a baited bear and the subtlety of a rampaging bull. He'd been given the post because Duchess Alexa couldn't stand his presence in her city any longer.

"Look," said Roderigo. "You should tell Giulietta that Cyprus is beautiful. That Janus is struck dumb by the beauty of her portrait."

"I'm a Crucifer." Sir Richard said ruefully. "We don't lie."

"You have to entice her."

"You've visited Janus's island? Then you know the truth. The summers burn, the winters are bleak. The only thing he has in abundance are rocks and goats. I won't embellish the truth to impress her."

Roderigo sighed.

"On to other matters," Sir Richard said. "Who takes the tenth chair?"

Glancing round, as if to indicate that simply asking was unwise, Roderigo muttered, "Impossible to say. No doubt the decision will be a wise one."

"No doubt."

The city's inner council had one seat vacant. Obviously enough, that seat was in the gift of Marco IV, reigning Duke of Venice and Prince of Serenissima. Unfortunately, Marco had little interest in politics.

"Surely you have some idea?"

"It depends . . ."

"On what?"

After another quick glance, Roderigo said, "Whether the Regent or the duchess get to choose." They walked on in uneasy silence after that. Until Sir Richard stopped at a proclamation nailed to a church door.

Wanted.
Axel, a master glass blower.
Fifty gold ducats to anyone who captures him. Death to anyone who aids his escape. This is the judgement of the Ten.

The glass-blower was described as thickset, heavy of gut and white at the temples, with a lurid scar along his left thumb. If he had any sense, he'd crop his hair. Moreover, skulking in fear for his life should shrink his gut. The scar would be harder to hide, however.

"Will you find him?"

"We usually do."

"What happens to his family?"

Roderigo checked that his charges were walking arm-in-arm ahead; one sullen, the other watchful. Being Giulietta's lady-in-waiting was an honour, but not an easy one. "They'll be questioned obviously."

"They haven't been already?"

"Of course they've . . ." Roderigo's voice was loud enough to make Lady Eleanor look back. "Yes," he hissed. "They've been questioned. One son-in-law and a grandchild are dead. The Council examines the others tomorrow."

"And then . . . ?"

"Death between the lion and the dragon."

Two columns marked the lagoon edge of the *piazzetta*, a small square attached to San Marco's much larger one. One topped by a winged lion, the other by Saint Todaro slaying a dragon. It was here that traitors died.

"Why kill them if they know nothing?"

"What do you know about Murano?"

"Little enough. You don't encourage strangers."

"The glassmakers' island has its own courts and cathedral, its own coinage, its own bishop. It even has its own Golden Book. A good portion of Venice's wealth comes from its secrets."

Captain Roderigo paused to let that sink in.

"It's the only place in the world where artisans are patrician and skill with your hands earns you the right to wear a sword in public."

"This comes at a price?"

Honesty kept Roderigo from lying. Glass-blowers couldn't leave Murano without permission and the penalty for a Muranesq caught trying to abandon Venice was death. "Didn't you need your Prior's permission to leave Cyprus?" he added, refusing to concede the point entirely.

"I'm a Crucifer." Sir Richard's voice was amused. "I wake, sleep, piss and fight on the orders of my Prior. And we should stop talking. Ignoring Lady Giulietta makes it hard for her to ignore us."

Roderigo laughed. "She's young," he said. "And Janus has . . ." He hesitated. "A strange reputation."

"For liking boys?"

"Also pain."

"The last is a lie."

"Yet he married his late wife for love?"

"Bedded her once. And was stricken when she died. Your Lady Giulietta will not have an easy time of it."

First out of the Grand Canal and already speeding towards the *piazzetta*, a curly-haired boy and his Nubian companion were far enough ahead to have a length between them and the first of those behind.

Maybe the lightness of their boat made up for the slightness of its crew.

Two boys rowing, where others had three, five or even seven working an oar. All stood, using a single oar each. There were ten thousand *gondolini* in Venice and each was taxed yearly. That was how their number was known.

A hundred and fifty craft had set out, hoping to race round the city's edge, before returning along the reversed S of the Canalasso, as the Venetians called their largest canal. Although most were *gondolini*, the boat in front was not.

"What is it?" Sir Richard asked Roderigo. Then, remembering his manners, added. "Perhaps her ladyship knows?"

"Eleanor?"

Her lady-in-waiting didn't know either.

"A *vipera*," Roderigo said. "Mostly used for smuggling."

"It's a *vipera*," Giulietta said flatly. "Mostly used for smuggling."

"Equally pointed at both ends?"

Roderigo nodded. "Instead of turning his boat, the oarsman turns himself, while my men are still turning their *gondolini*. It's rare to see one used openly."

"And the name is from *viper*?"

"Because they strike fast."

"Smugglers who strike fast. Or maybe such boats have other uses?"

Roderigo smiled at the dryness in Sir Richard's voice. Venice was known as the city of gilt, glass and assassinations. The whole of Italy knew why the boats racing towards the finish were black.

Eleven years earlier, in the year of Our Lord 1396, a gondola had drawn alongside the ornately painted craft carrying Giulietta's mother, Zoë dei San Felice. The crossbow bolt that killed her passed through her oarsman first. When the oarsman crawled to her side, the late duke's only sister was dead.

A sumptuary law passed that evening instructed that all *gondolini* be painted black. This was not death's colour in Venice, that was red. But in honour of Zoë's elegance, all vessels would be her favourite colour. The truth was that Marco III had wanted the safety *gondolini* looking alike would bring his family.

The boys in the *vipera* were extending their lead when the boat closest behind rocked suddenly and tipped, losing its crew with a splash. Glancing back, the curly-haired boy shouted something and his Nubian companion started to laugh.

"That was Dolphino taking a ducking," Roderigo said, as if this explained everything. "He can't bear losing."

"You mean . . . ?"

Lady Giulietta curled her lip. "That was no accident."

"By tonight," added Roderigo, "Dolphino will have been closing the gap and about to win. And the boys who just stopped will have sacrificed their second place to help a friend."

"Let's get this over with," Giulietta said

Gathering her gown, she stepped from a wooden walkway on to slippery brick and headed for the finish line. Sir Richard followed, wondering how King Janus would deal with his strong-willed bride.

"Your names?" Roderigo asked.

"Iacopo, my lord." Cheaply dressed but freshly razored, the curly-haired boy bowed with lazy grace, as if born to court rather than the poverty his jacket suggested. "And this is . . . a slave." The slave bowed low in the Eastern style, silver thimbles dancing at the ends of a dozen tight braids.

"Well done," Sir Richard said.

The curly-haired boy smiled.

A wide face and brown eyes. Strong arms and . . . His virility made obvious by the tightness of his hose and the salt spray that soaked them.

"Eleanor," Lady Giulietta said. "You're staring."

The girl flushed with embarrassment.

"The distance?" Sir Richard asked quickly.

"Nine *mille passum*, my lord. Seven thousand paces around

the edge, and two thousand back through the canal. The waves were tough to the north, but she's good . . ." He nodded to the *vipera* in pride.

"Yours?"

"My master's."

Realising the silence following was a question in itself, the boy added. "Lord Atilo il Mauros. He's . . ."

Sir Richard knew. "Your winnings," he said, offering a purse.

The young man bowed again, and couldn't resist weighing the purse in his hand. His grin showed white, and crinkled the edges of his eyes.

"Eleanor . . ."

"I'm not the one gawping."

Giulietta glanced sharply at her lady-in-waiting.

"And have this," Roderigo added hastily, shucking himself out of his brocade doublet. It was outdated and darned, but the victor's eyes widened and then he scowled.

"Silver thread, my lord."

Tattered brocade he might get away with. However, silver thread, like gold thread, fur, enamel, silk and embroidery, was denied to servants by law.

"I doubt the Watch will arrest this afternoon's winner before nightfall and you can have your woman pick it clean by tomorrow."

"I don't have one, my lord."

"You will tonight," Sir Richard promised.

4

Grateful to be free of the wind in their faces, Lady Giulietta's party were walking away from the salt spray and the bobbing boat of the victors when Roderigo became aware of footsteps behind him.

"My lord . . ."

Turning, he found the curly-haired boy. "Iacopo, isn't it?"

The young man was pleased the captain remembered his name. "Yes, my lord. Forgive me. You know Lady Desdaio, I believe?"

Roderigo nodded.

"Intimately, my lord?"

The captain's scowl was so fierce Iacopo stepped back.

"I have no doubt of Lady Desdaio's honour," Roderigo said fiercely. "*No one* has any doubt about her honour. Understand me?"

Nodding, Iacopo bowed low for causing offence. After which, he chewed his lip and shuffled his feet like the street urchin he'd probably been. His was a face found everywhere in Venice. A curving mouth and knowing eyes framed by curls. His straight, unbroken nose was less usual. It said that either he disliked fights or fought well.

"What about her?"

"She is betrothed to my master."

Roderigo was not a man of tempers.

He did his job well and both the Regent and duchess used him when they needed a good officer. He'd reached his post as head of the Venetian customs by hard work, having entered as a junior lieutenant. All the same, there was a blackness to his gaze as it swept the herringbone brick of the *piazzetta* that made people look away.

"When did this happen?"

"Yesterday, my lord . . . I learnt this morning when preparing for the race. Lord Atilo came to wish me luck."

"I see," Roderigo said tightly.

Full-breasted, plump and buxom, Desdaio Bribanzo was his ideal of beauty. Hell, she was the city's ideal. Only her hair let her down. This was chestnut rather than the reddish blonde Venice favoured.

Unlike other girls, she refused to dye it.

At twenty-three, Desdaio combined huge eyes, a sweet face and sweeter smile with being heiress to a vast fortune. Her father imported more pepper, cinnamon and ginger than any other noble in the city. Obviously enough, she had more suitors than any of her rivals. One of whom was Roderigo. They'd known each other since childhood. He'd thought they liked each other well enough.

"Why tell me this?"

"I'd heard . . . Your kindness. The coat . . ." Iacopo stuttered to a halt and went back to shuffling his feet.

"Lord Bribanzo approves?"

"He's still in Rome, my lord."

"In which case we'll see what he says. She wouldn't be the first to give her heart to one man while her father gives her body to another."

"This case is complicated." Iacopo chose his words carefully, keeping his face neutral as he waited for the captain to ask why.

"So tell me," Roderigo growled.

"She has moved herself into Ca' il Mauros."

"My God. Her father will . . ."

"Be furious, my lord. None the less, if she stays even a single night there unchaperoned. No parental fury can undo the damage that does her."

"She has gold." Roderigo said flatly. "It will be enough."

Iacopo sucked his teeth, as if to say the ways of women, particularly noble and rich ones, were beyond him. And if the brave captain said this was the case, who was he to disagree?

The Ca' Ducale was built using pillars, window frames and door arches looted from other cities. Its style, however, was unique. Round arches from the Orthodox East combined with mauresque fretwork and pointed windows from Western Gothic; mixed in a fashion only found in one city in the world: this one.

This theft of materials was not the insult.

Nor was the fact that the palace and its basilica both used materials stolen from mosques, synagogues and even churches. How could one expect better of a place where *Venetian first, Christian second* was said daily?

The insult was more subtle.

The palace said to foreign princes, You hide behind fortified walls in ugly castles. I live on islands in the sea. My power is so great I can afford to live behind walls so thin they could be made from glass. That fact had not occurred to Captain Roderigo until Sir Richard pointed it out to him.

"Sir Richard, perhaps you could . . ."

Indicating Giulietta discreetly, and then the nearest palace door, Roderigo said, "I have official matters waiting."

"You're not dining with us?"

"As I said, duty calls."

Sir Richard scowled. "I don't suppose . . ."

"Me," said Roderigo, "the duke can manage without. You, he

is expecting for supper. Well," he added, more honestly, "I'm sure the Regent and Duchess Alexa expect you. His highness . . ."

There was no need to say more.

"This business had to do with the customs office?"

Roderigo jerked his head at a dozen ships moored on a stretch of lagoon reserved for those in quarantine. Since God's wrath killed half of Venice sixty years before ships now waited offshore to make certain they carried no disease.

"We think one of those might already have taken the glass-blower aboard. We'll be boarding the ship tonight."

"Which one?"

"See the last?"

Sir Richard peered into the sleet. After a second, Roderigo realised that Giulietta and her lady-in-waiting had joined them.

"Moorish," Eleanor said.

Giulietta shook her head. "Mamluk," she corrected. Seeing Sir Richard's surprise, she added tartly, "When there's nothing to do but watch ships you learn their flags quickly enough. Any fool can work it out."

Sir Richard's face went blank.

He had to confirm a treaty, collect his king's new wife and escort her to Famagusta, where she could watch ships headed north for the Venetian ports strung like pearls between Rhodes and the city itself. After this, Giulietta's temper was the king's business. Sir Richard didn't look upset at the thought.

"What did the ship do wrong?"

"Absolutely nothing," Roderigo told Lady Eleanor. "It arrived, waited as told, and followed our pilot without arguing the price . . ."

"That's it?" Giulietta's lady-in-waiting sounded surprised.

"Paid harbour dues, bought fresh water. They didn't even try to bribe their way out of quarantine . . ."

Lady Giulietta snorted. That was suspicious indeed.

5

Inside the customs house, Venice's famous Dogana fortress, men had been gathering since sunset. Roderigo was the last to arrive.

"Hey, chief . . ."

The man who spoke was shorter than his commander and half as broad again. He had the wide face, Mongol eyes and tallow skin of his father. After fifty years on God's earth, he still spoke like his mother, a Rialto fishwife.

"What?"

"Guess that answers that."

"Answers what?"

"I was going to ask if you were all right."

Roderigo had found Temujin drunk in the street begging for alms. In two years he'd gone from mopping floors to sergeant. He fought dirty, drank hard and paid his debts; and the troop respected him for it, or had the sense to keep any doubts to themselves.

"Everyone here?"

"One's ill. I've borrowed him instead."

Temujin pointed to a rat-faced man in a Castellani smock, overlaid with a leather jerkin so filthy he could pass unseen on a moonless night. The composite bow over his shoulder fired arrows of a kind the captain hadn't seen in years. Taking another look, he noted the shape of the man's eyes.

"I can find someone else."

"No need." The Mongols kept a *fontego* in the city. A trading post where Mongol law applied. Like every other race, they left their bastards.

Taking another salted fish, Roderigo chewed it until it was just about soft enough to swallow. He wanted wine to remove the aftertaste, but once ordered the temptation to drink would be impossible to bear.

Atilo il Mauros had to be sixty-five at the least. His name wasn't in the Golden Book, the list of noble families with a right to sit in Council. Worse, he wasn't even from Serenissima. He spoke Italian with an Andalusian accent.

"Find me wine," Roderigo demanded.

Temujin looked at him, but sent a trooper for a fresh jug and a squat tumbler on which fading saints stared ghost-like. Having filled his glass, Roderigo returned the jug. "Tip the rest away."

"Chief . . ."

"All right. All right. Share it around. But if one man gets drunk I'll have him whipped. If someone dies through his folly I'll have him hanged. Make sure they know that."

The men filled their mugs anyway.

"The boats are ready?"

Of course the boats were ready. The boats were always ready. But Temujin made do with a brief nod before asking if there was anything else his captain wanted.

Other than the head of Atilo on a spit?

The upstairs office to which the Captain of the Dogana took himself had a fire laid, and a stout woman knelt before it. Who, Roderigo suspected, could be laid with little enough trouble herself. Maria was Temujin's woman and the customs house's unofficial maid.

36

She had an almost full set of teeth, wide hips and low breasts that shifted as she moved to light his fire. Still crouching, she turned and he saw darkness between her thighs. "Is there anything, my lord . . . ?"

"*No*," Roderigo said.

He wanted Desdaio. Who didn't?

In the corner stood a pair of grinding wheels.

One was coarse, the other so fine he'd never seen another like it. Their combined weight was hard to start rolling but they kept revolving longer than a single stone. Sharpening his sword with casual competence, Roderigo honed edge and point until both could slice leather, this being what most sailors wore as armour.

Temujin knocked as midnight struck.

"Ready when you are, chief."

The sergeant had checked his men's weapons but Captain Roderigo rechecked them anyway. Temujin would be disappointed otherwise. After the fug inside the fortress, the night felt colder than it was. Drizzle coming in sheets on the wind. With luck, it would turn to sleet and fling itself in Mamluk faces, providing cover and allowing Roderigo's men to approach less carefully.

Staring into that wind, Roderigo felt tears fill his angry eyes and cursed himself for stupidity, glad of the darkness. He'd watched Desdaio grow from pampered child to a young woman desperate for the freedom her young cousins still had.

Of course, her fortune would have helped his. His own house was a ruin, his salary from the Dogana less than he spent. All the same, Roderigo hadn't lied when he told Desdaio he loved her. For her to sneak into another man's house . . .

Into another man's bed.

"Chief . . ."

"*What?*"

His two boats had drawn together in the swell, and Sergeant

Temujin was gripping the sides of both to keep them steady. At his anger everyone froze. Now was the time Roderigo was meant to say some words. Choose who boarded first. Tell them what he expected to find.

"Any special orders, chief?"

He and Temujin had searched a hundred ships before. Everything from visiting Moorish galleys and trade ships from Byzantium to Rus boats and even a felucca that sailed all the way from the mouth of the Nile. Why should this one be any different? Roderigo felt he owed his sergeant some explanation.

"A girl I know is getting married."

"That's it?" Temujin looked disgusted.

"There's red gold," Roderigo replied. As if his last words were unspoken. "Also Mamluk silver. They're on the manifest. Three leopard skins, sky stone for hardening steel and a box of rubies. All declared. It's what they're hiding that worries me. I mean, for a Mamluk not to try to barter . . ."

"Chief, can I say something?"

"I don't have to like it."

"You won't. Whoever she is. Forget it. She's just a slit, pretty or not. You can't go into a possible battle moping. It's the quickest way to die."

He hated it when Temujin was right.

As the boats separated and one headed into the wind bound for the far side of the *Quaja*, which was the Mamluk vessel's name, Sergeant Temujin kept up a count as steady as the Watch's steps on Piazza San Marco at midnight.

"Fifty," he said.

Pulling a wide sash from his pocket, Roderigo draped it over his shoulder and adjusted the weight that kept it at his hip. A Venetian officer boarding a foreign vessel had to wear a city sash. It made an insult to the officer an insult to the city. An insult to the city was an insult to the duke.

This simplified matters.

"One hundred," Temujin said.

"Take us in."

A swirl of oars carried them close, the *Quaja*'s side looming so large it threatened to crush their lugger in the swell. An anchor rope hummed with tension above them. That was where they would board.

"I'll go first."

"Chief . . ."

"You heard me."

Even Temujin, sworn to protect Roderigo, knew better than to query an order given in the field. When the captain reached deck, he found a man from his other lugger already standing over a dead Mamluk.

"Sweetly done," Roderigo said.

At his gesture, others climbed aboard.

"Right," Temujin said, keeping his voice low. "You and you by that cargo hatch, and you by that door . . . *And you, why isn't your crossbow loaded?*" This last hiss because a string wasn't ratcheted back.

"Give me a . . ."

One second the sergeant was glaring, the next shock replaced anger in the hiss of an arrow from high overhead. Temujin stared at the shaft in his chest.

"Rigging," Roderigo said.

As Temujin fell to his knees, blood running between his fingers, the troop's newcomer planted his feet, raised his own half bow and hesitated.

"Dead or alive?"

"Kill him."

The man put an arrow between crows nest's boards, through the Mamluk archer's foot and into his groin. The lookout fell with a thud. He should have fired the moment they appeared or held his element of surprise.

"Alive was better." Temujin's words came from between blood-frothed lips. "So any bastards we leave living could kill him for being useless. Good job he was, though. We'd be fucked otherwise."

"Help Temujin up."

Two soldiers did as ordered. The arrow was a yard long, with its point exiting from Temujin's lower back. Sighing with relief, Roderigo confirmed the point was unpoisoned and snapped the feathered end without saying what he intended to do.

"Bind the arrow in place," he told a guard.

"Sir . . ."

"Seen it." A door was opening. As half a dozen crossbows shifted in that direction, Roderigo said, "Wait on my order."

Opening a little more, the door suddenly started closing and then stopped. The man behind must know it offered minimal protection. Steel-tipped quarrels would rip straight through.

"In the name of Marco IV," Roderigo said. "Show yourself. We search for a missing glass-blower. And have reason to suspect he may have come aboard. Any attempt to hinder us will be regarded as an act of war."

The door shut with a bang.

"My God," one of the men muttered. "We've found him."

It looked that way. Roderigo hoped it was true. Although the glass-blower would die horribly, his children and grandchildren – those left living – would be spared a similar fate.

Strange words came from behind the door.

Guttural and impassioned, the man speaking sounded young to captain a ship, never mind a vessel as large as the *Quaja*. When Roderigo didn't reply, the sentence was repeated, as far as Roderigo could tell word for word. Problem was, Roderigo had no idea if it was a question, a statement or a boast that the *Quaja*'s crew would fight to the death. "Anyone understand that?"

The newcomer nodded.

"What are you called?"

Bato sounded like a nickname.

"Tell him I'm looking for a glass blower. We think he might have been smuggled aboard this ship."

"They haven't got him," Bato said eventually.

"What's the language?"

"It's Turkic. Good Turkic. Formal. Very proper."

"Tell him I'm Dogana chief and I *will* search his ship. If what he says is true, he can wait out his quarantine, or sail on tomorrow's tide. We will count his dead and my sergeant's injury as the cost of a misunderstanding."

The answer when it came was calmer.

No glass-blower was aboard the ship. The manifest of goods given to the Dogana was accurate. All the same, they would let the Venetians search where they liked. Since they had nothing to hide.

"Tell him, if it was up to me I'd take his word and leave now."

Untrue, of course, but any honeyed words that helped get this over with, and Temujin to Dr Crow, were fine with Roderigo. As he watched, the door opened and a fine-featured Mamluk stood blinking in the moon's rays. His robe was rich with silver thread and a scarlet turban wrapped his skull.

He looked little more than a boy.

Identifying Roderigo by his sash, the Mamluk touched his hand to his heart, mouth and forehead in formal greeting and gestured the Dogana captain inside.

The vessel's layout was like dozens of others he'd searched before. A captain's cabin at the stern and quarters for crew below deck. Half of that area being put aside for cargo. Below this was a crawl space where the hull curved towards the keel. Under that, a stinking slop hole filled with stones for ballast.

Roderigo checked the lot. All the time carrying the weight of Desdaio's betrayal like stones in his own heart. Two of his troop were helping Sergeant Temujin towards the upper deck when

Roderigo stopped. At a growled order, his men did likewise and a flicker of blind panic filled the Mamluk's face.

The crawl space was twenty-one steps long. The cargo deck nineteen. Had it been reversed Roderigo could have dismissed the difference as loss for the curve of the prow. But that way round?

"Tell the man we're going to break this down."

Roderigo pointed at the bulkhead of the stern. A torrent of impassioned Turkic greeted this news. And the Mamluk went to stand in front of it.

"He says his ship will sink and we'll die. It will be your fault and his country will go to war with Serenissima. A thousand ships will sail up the Adriatic sacking every Venetian colony on the way."

"Tell him it's a risk I'll take."

It took five minutes to find a large enough axe. In which time the Mamluk's crew gathered, silent ghosts watching uneasily. Only the loaded crossbows of Roderigo's men kept them from attacking.

"Now," he ordered.

Bato swung the axe.

"And again."

A second blow widened the crack.

"No water yet," Temujin growled.

The planks were too thin to be the *Quaja's* outer skin and their timber too green. Venice's own shipwrights used wood from trees stored for at least two years before cutting planks that had to dry in their turn.

"Hack the lot down."

Planting his feet, Bato swung a blow to behead a horse. His next opened darkness. And a tanner's stink of shit and stale piss hissed through the gap. Not waiting for more orders, Bato gripped one edge of the planking and tugged. Wood split and a plank creaked free from battens behind.

Another plank followed just as noisily.

"Light," Roderigo demanded.

Stepping between the wreckage of Bato's handiwork, he entered a fetid compartment behind the wall. A moment later, the Mamluk followed.

Roderigo was thirty years old. He'd fought his first battle at fourteen and taken his first girl a year earlier. He'd lived through cities sacked, and seen a Florentine spy torn apart by wild horses. He expected the missing glass blower. He got . . .

The captain crossed himself.

A naked boy hung in chains, his wrists raw from fighting shackles. In life, the boy must have been about seventeen. Nineteen at the most. Long silver-grey hair half hid a face so beautiful it belonged to an angel. The corpse had the sheen of wet marble. Almost alabaster in its translucence.

Black earth strewed the deck beneath him.

Lurching past his commander, Sergeant Temujin lifted the boy's head to the light.

Amber-flecked eyes snapped open.

As the foreign captain shouted a warning, the sergeant drew his dagger, and turned to slash the Mamluk's throat, drenching himself in blood.

"*Temujin . . .*"

"Kill them all," Temujin shouted.

Outside, his troop obeyed without question. Crossbows snapped, arrows flew, daggers found hearts. Fifteen seconds of hellish slaughter ended in the stink of blood, Mamluk corpses, and Bato leaving, bow in hand, to hunt down stragglers.

"Burn this boat."

Roderigo stared at his sergeant.

"Chief . . . Steal what you need to keep the Regent and duchess sweet and burn everything else. Him included. Because I know what *that* is and it cannot be tamed. The Khan owned one in my grandfather's time. It killed him."

"*Sergeant.*"

Temujin stopped talking.

His eyes were bright with the onset of fever, and the crude bandage around his ribs dark with blood. Only willpower and his need to convince Roderigo kept him conscious.

"You want to tell me why you killed that man?"

It hurt Temujin, probably more than it hurt to drop to a crouch, but he did it anyway. Opening buttons at the dead Mamluk's neck he revealed the swell of breasts, and said, "She's got to be someone, chief. To command this ship and carry that."

Temujin meant her prisoner.

"We can't let anyone find her. And, believe me, you don't *want* anyone to find that. Kill it, fire this damn ship and get us out of here."

"I wish it was that simple."

"It is."

Roderigo shook his head.

Halfway across the lagoon, while the Dogana troop concentrated on getting their badly wounded sergeant to Dr Crow for treatment, the boy made his move. He simply stood, and tipped backwards into the water with a splash.

"Kill him," Roderigo shouted.

Not a single man had his crossbow cocked.

By the time Bato slotted an arrow, his target was being swept away by the cross-currents that made Venice's lagoon so unpredictable. Had the burning Mamluk ship been close enough to light the scene Bato might have had a better chance. He fired anyway.

6

The shock of an arrow striking blew breath from the boy's body. And the pain in his shoulder opened the boy's mind to a vision that swept in like smoke.

In the smoke a veiled woman smiled, then scowled and began to protest as her image blew away, leaving him spitting water. When she reappeared, she was sitting on a squat throne with a thin young man in black clutching her knees.

"Join us."

"Where am I?" he asked.

She looked puzzled, as if this was not what he was meant to say.

But already he was thinking other things. Clutching at passing fragments of memory, he tried to recall why he'd been locked behind the false bulkhead of a ship. *Fire and ice, earth and air.* Fire started this. A blaze swept through some building. A man killed another. A sour-faced woman hated him worse than ever. He fought to remember who she was.

Who he was.

But the foul-tasting lagoon swallowed the boy before he could remember more than a single word: *Bjornvin.* The word made no more sense to him than his vision of the veiled woman. Since the men who hacked him free were heading in one direction, the boy let cross-currents sweep him in the other.

He wondered what would happen. He'd die, he supposed. Perhaps he should stop swimming to see how sinking felt?

Stopping kicking, the boy let his shackles pull him under.

And, tasting salt, let himself sink further. Opaque above, darkness below. His toes squelched on soft mud in a channel. Minor canals in Venice were cleared every ten years, waterways and large canals whenever necessary. He knew nothing of this. He simply felt softness beneath his toes.

Sinking deeper, he felt gravel.

His lungs pulled life from the water rushing into them.

Flickers of lightning twitched his limbs as fire lit behind his eyes and he felt his body fight itself, without understanding how it won the battle for life. Slamming into an ancient wreck, which crumbled as he snatched for it, he let a brutal undercurrent sweep him sideways before kicking for the surface.

The burning ship was far behind and buildings lined the horizon ahead of him. Above, in gaps between the clouds, was a bowl of stars. More stars than any man could count. Should he be able to count beyond his fingers.

The boy had reached the Grand Canal without knowing where it was, what it was or anything about it. As his eyes struggled to focus and his body shivered, and his guts retched filthy water, he accepted the embrace of an incoming tide. Then a spasm locked his stomach, and the sky became purple, the moon hurt his eyes, and bitterness filled his throat.

"*There you are . . .*"

The words were not his.

They came uninvited into his mind. With them an image of the woman he'd seen in his head earlier, when he was drowning. An old woman with a young woman's smile. A young woman with an old woman's eyes. Thin wisps of smoke across her face like a veil, which blew away as he stared harder.

"Alexa?" he said.

"Who told you my name?"

Having no answer, he felt her try to pull clues from his ruined memories. All she found were the names others had once called him.

"*White hair* is descriptive. *You* is a pronoun. *Tadsi* is an Old Norse pun on shit, and *Tychet* means idiot. Here we've Latinised it to *Tycho*." She sounded darkly amused. "Keep the last. It suits you."

Tycho forced her voice away.

7

Moonlight glimmered on the Canalasso, the elegant waterway bisecting the city to which the burning ship had delivered Tycho. It glimmered in blanket-sized scraps of silver leaf. And the reflection this glimmering created lit the walls of a fish market opposite. But the three children staring down the slimy steps at the edge of the Grand Canal saw none of this beauty.

They were concentrating on a tidal area, beside the steps, where flotsam gathered. Tonight's catch was a drowned girl, long silver hair rippling in the gentle waves.

"Get her then."

Rosalyn guessed Josh meant her. Since she was the one he glared at. Hooking her smock to her hips, she stepped into the filthy water. "It's cold."

"Just do it."

Corpses could be sold, Josh said.

Necromancers, probably. Rosalyn couldn't see who else might want one. She gasped as the water climbed her thighs, realised she still couldn't reach the floating girl and stepped down again, grabbing hair. "Give me a hand then," she protested.

When Josh didn't move, her brother Pietro did, wading into the canal to help her drag the body nearer the steps.

"My God," Rosalyn said.

Scowling, Josh came to take a look.

A boy, his genitals flopping sideways, his chest entirely flat, his belly button an intricate coil. If not for the belly button, he could have been an angel with his wings cut off. She'd never seen anyone so beautiful.

"He's been shot."

"As if that matters."

She yanked the arrow free anyway.

"We can't sell that," Josh snapped. "What's round his wrist?"

Rosalyn dropped to a crouch, seeing her moonlit reflection in the metal's surface. "A shackle, some of it's silver."

"Don't be stupid. No one would . . ."

Shuffling closer, Rosalyn snapped her knees shut. She didn't like the way Josh was leering at her. After a second, she knelt.

His temper had never been good. After that night in Cannaregio, when they hid in a tanner's pit while demons fought, it was worse. He was less forgiving each day of what had happened to her with the Watch. Maybe, her gut relaxed slightly at the hope, this would keep him happy. The dead boy was pale and very dead, with a ring of ruined flesh where his shackle scraped bone.

"What's so interesting?"

Her guts locked again. "Look," she said. The blood trickling from his arrow wound was blackish, its exact colour hard to determine in the darkness.

"So he's foreign." Turning to Pietro, Josh said, "Give her your knife . . . And you, stop pissing around and chop off his hand."

This was a test, Rosalyn knew it was. Josh spent most of his time telling her she was too stupid to live on her wits like him. Her brother was coming to believe it too. "I'll cut off the shackle."

There, she'd failed. As he expected her to.

"Rosalyn . . ."

Now was when he'd order her to remove it at the wrist, like they'd split a pig's knuckle they stole. Surprisingly, he just sucked his teeth in disgust. "Hurry it up."

Bending the corpse's elbow, she gripped the shackle. It was hard wood, inlaid with bands of silver wire, and it was hinged, clasped and soldered, instead of locked, which was even stranger. In the end, she hacked at the solder wondering why he hadn't done that himself. Maybe he lacked a knife.

Shouldn't be here, she told herself.

Shouldn't be with Josh.

Rosalyn was cold, sodden from the canal, dressed in rags that clung to her legs, hips and buttocks, and scared. Her bladder hurt, her guts said she'd bleed soon, which was a blessing. "Almost there."

"About time."

Dragging her blade, Rosalyn freed the weld and sliced her finger to the bone, feeling instantly sick. She rocked back on her knees, but not before blood splashed on to the dead boy's face.

"What now?" said Josh, as she gasped.

She'd jumped back when dark eyes, tinged with amber flecks, flicked open to glare at her. She felt her stomach turn over as the dead boy examined her face. Then he shut his eyes again. "Cut myself," she said weakly.

"Kick him back in then."

"Someone's coming," Rosalyn said. "We've been lucky so far. Let's just leave." Fortunately, Josh agreed with her.

8

Street children. She should feel sorry for them, Maria knew that. Instead, they simply made her nervous. Listening carefully, she heard them arguing as they moved further away from her towards a warren of alleys.

Ahead was another shrine. This was not good. Five shrines in the last few minutes meant this parish was dangerous and the patriarch wanted to remind everyone that God watched everywhere. In Serenissima, he'd probably gone beyond shocked by what he saw. That naked body by the water steps for a start.

Just another murder the Watch would ignore.

Stranglings and suffocations were rare in Venice. Because Venetians believed a curse passed to the murderer if flesh touched flesh. Knifings were common, however. Why risk throttling someone when a dagger could keep their ghost at bay? So many in Venice believed this, that to beat someone to the edge of death and then knife them was regarded as simple common sense.

Pausing at a statue of the Madonna, Maria the cordwainer's wife muttered a prayer for the dead boy she'd just seen. And finishing, turned to find him standing behind her, water still dripping into the dirt at his feet.

She couldn't help yelping.

Although her yelp ended as he spun her round, fixed one hand over her mouth and dragged her to a doorway. One second, she stood at the Virgin's shrine, the next she and the youth she'd thought dead watched a drunk wander from a tavern, stare around him and disappear the way he'd come.

The strange-looking youth didn't have Mongol eyes. He was far too pale for a Moor, and he wasn't Jewish, although she'd be embarrassed to admit how she knew. If Maria had to describe him, she'd say his cheekbones were Schiavoni, those incomers from Dalmatia colonising her city. Reaching out, he took her face and turned it to the shrine's light. Amber-flecked eyes gazed into hers.

"Doesn't that hurt?" she asked, touching her finger to the wound in his shoulder. And suddenly she was held from behind, his face nuzzled her neck. He removed his hand from her breast the moment she burst into tears.

"Don't hurt me."

". . . hurt me." His voice echoed her plea.

Maria – who had no last name, because people like her didn't – was fifteen and a half, being born in high summer. She was in a parish she barely knew, long after she should be home, in an alley with more shrines than a single street should need. As she registered this, Maria finally realised where she was.

Rio Terra dei Assassini.

I should concentrate, she decided.

Not least because the strange youth now stood in front of her again. She was a married woman out after dark and he was obviously foreign. When she tried to step around him, his face tightened, and she remembered his nakedness, the speed at which he moved, and how her father scowled before he lost his temper.

"You should let me go now."

Releasing her, he watched her hurry away.

She kept her panic in check until she believed herself safe. Then her sobbing began, so loud and so open, the boy almost missed the point at which other steps began to follow her. Since most of those crowding the alley around him seemed to be ghosts – hollow-eyed and helpless, waiting to see what he would do – and this woman was undoubtedly alive, he decided to follow her too.

9

"Captain . . . over here." A young whore shushed the voice, shocked at its impudence.

Roderigo recognised its owner despite his gaudy mask. The whore on his arm and the flagon he waved suggested Atilo's servant had spent his prize money with glee. Like most Venetian men, Roderigo used whores. This one was shapely, only half drunk and grinned prettily.

"Iacopo."

"My lord . . ." Turning, Iacopo said, "This is Captain Roderigo. He's head of the Dogana."

The whore shot a glance to say, *Don't be stupid*. Then realised her client meant it and curtsied deep enough to reveal her breasts, which improved Roderigo's temper slightly.

The Riva degli Schiavoni lined Venice's southern shore.

It was the quay where captains sought supplies for their ships. There were food stalls, rope chandlers, and barrel-laden carts with water from the cisterns that collected the city's rainfall. Slaves were sold, crews recruited. It was to the Riva that sailors went to find whores. Here was where Atilo's handsome servant had come to celebrate his victory in the previous day's regatta.

In the course of the night just gone, he'd lost Roderigo's doublet and the hat Sir Richard gave him. In their place, he sported a black eye and an ornate dagger that undoubtedly broke the sumptuary laws. Also two whores.

Although the second, arriving as Roderigo noticed the dagger, proved Iacopo hadn't lost the doublet at all. It was draped over the shoulders of his friend, who needed it against the cold, since her breasts were bare.

"Did you see that ship's fire, my lord?"

"Yes," Roderigo said. "I saw it."

"They say Mamluk spies burnt a Cypriot ship."

Did they now? Roderigo smiled grimly. He'd told his men to say nothing of what had happened, but this was better than expected.

"Why so?"

"Well . . ." said Iacopo. "Lady Giulietta's marrying Cyprus." His elbow missed a ledge, almost tipping him to the ground. "And Cyprus," he added heavily, "is Byzantium's ally. And ours, now, of course."

Byzantium and the Mamluks were enemies, as expected of neighbouring empires. And Venice was Byzantium's ally, theoretically. At a push, if drunk, you could build a plot from that.

"Almost right. But it was a Mamluk ship and I'd put my money on the Moors." Why not? They were the Mamluk sultan's other enemy.

"I heard . . ."

"Believe me. Moorish spies."

Opening his mouth to disagree, Iacopo shut it when one of the whores dug her elbow in his ribs. He was very drunk indeed. "I'll buy you a drink."

"Another time . . ."

"You off to bed?"

Captain Roderigo nodded.

"Then you need help to heaven, don't you?"

It was too late to stop Iacopo's recitation and after the first line the whores joined in. *"He who drinks well sleeps well, he who sleeps well has no evil thoughts, he who has no evil thoughts does no evil, he who does no evil goes to heaven. So drink well . . ."*

"And heaven will be yours," Roderigo finished for them.

After five minutes of one-sided conversation, Roderigo knew that Iaco had been in Atilo's service for eight years. He wanted a promotion. He deserved promotion. There were days – and this was secret – he felt little better than a slave. Atilo's people had slaves. He was sure the captain knew that.

So do we, Roderigo thought. Half the men working cranes outside were indentured to Schiavoni gang masters. The peasants on the mainland were bound to their lords. Did Iacopo think the whore on his arm worked freely? Taking a gulp from his glass, Roderigo winced at its bitterness.

Halfway down the jug, Roderigo realised why the wine was so bad.

If his mind had not been on last night's disaster he would have realised men came here with other things on their mind. To share taverns was a Serenissiman tradition. The rules governing brothels were more complicated. In being here he was breaking half a dozen laws.

"I should leave . . ."

"You sent my whore to check on your sergeant."

So he had, Roderigo remembered.

Taking his hand from between her thighs, Iacopo patted the remaining whore's knees. Her shrug making it clear that losing his attention meant little.

What am I doing here? Roderigo knew the answer the moment the question entered his head. He was behaving as any Venetian noble would when invited by the victor of the previous day's race to have a drink.

"My lord. You look as if the wine doesn't agree with you."

"It doesn't," he said flatly.

When Iacopo returned it was with a different flask. "Frankish," he promised. "The best they have. I'm sorry, I should have realised."

"Realised what?"

"That a nobleman would not have the stomach for the wine we drink. It was thoughtless of me."

Feeling shamed, Roderigo said, "It's not your wine. Yesterday's news about Lady Desdaio has unsettled me . . ." Toasting Iacopo, he discovering the man was right: this wine was better.

Raising his head from the table, Roderigo watched a serving girl approach. Did she work the stalls? He decided he didn't care. She'd come to his bed right enough. He was a patrician with a palace on the Grand Canal.

A small one, admittedly. A thin, three-storey building between two fat ones. But still a palace and still overlooking the Canalasso, that watery road Venice chose for its heart. There were times he didn't like himself and this was one of them.

Last night had begun well enough, only turning sour when Temujin took an arrow. Turning sourer still with his discovery of that boy.

Who knew where he was now?

Drowned, with luck . . .

Early morning sun crinkled on the lagoon and the tide flowed as sluggishly as molten lead. Somehow, without Roderigo noticing, the room had emptied and his companion was gone.

"*Iacopo?*"

"A girl is murdered. Iaco went to look."

In a city where passers-by stepped over bodies most mornings this sounded passing strange. "What makes this killing different?"

"The murderer. A boy was seen nearby. Naked, with silver-grey hair. The Watch believe he was her attacker."

10

Tycho woke with his bladder full, his penis hard and his balls so tight they ached. And when he pissed against a wall his urine was so rank it shocked him into wondering if the stink was something else.

Until he realised everything smelt extreme.

The smoke from fires banked low for the night, the smell of pies and casseroles baking in the public ovens that dotted every other street. This new world was a mix of opulence and filth. And people, thousands of strangely dressed people, living their lives to rules denied him.

Here the horizon was flat, when it could be seen beyond the mist. Because there was always mist. So these might be the last islands in the world. Or the only islands in the world. Or perhaps all the world there was.

The roof above him leaked, and half of the warehouse where he slept was full of rubbish. The other half was piled with drying wood. A side canal, which once served its landing stage, was silted and stale. A bridge across its mouth, blocking entry, was old, the decaying warehouse older.

On the fourth night after Tycho found this hiding place – the sixth night of the city's rioting, and the first of the snows – he headed south, driven across the roofs by hunger, and a realisation he needed more than one bolt hole in this city.

He learnt to use the shadows, his breath never disturbing falling snow. Men, youths and older boys let him pass unseen. He was the dagger over their heads and the silence above. Girls, cats and old women were less easy, but everyone knew they saw things anyway.

The Nicoletti were at war with the Castellani.

If the ship-workers had guild pride, the Nicoletti prided themselves on being from San Nicolò dei Mendicoli, the toughest parish in the city. No one really knew what had started their hatred, but the street battles it spawned had simmered for four hundred years. And the dukes, while not actively approving, did not disapprove. Should parishes one side of the Canalasso rise, parishes the other side could be relied on to crush them.

The cause of tonight's fight was real, for once.

The red-clad Castellani accused the Nicoletti of the slaughter of Maria, a cordwainer's wife. The black-clad Nicoletti accused their enemy of trying to extract blood money they couldn't afford and didn't owe.

And so, at midnight, with snow falling so fast rioters lost sight of the canal edges, the battle resumed. At midnight, because that was tradition. And it began, as tradition also demanded, with the previous night's champions meeting on a bridge, scraping away snow to reveal footprints carved into the bridge's floor, and tossing a coin to chose who threw the first punch.

In the hour before midnight, while those preparing to fight were finding their courage in alcohol, and refuelling their anger with tales of how virtuous Maria had been, or how wicked it was to demand blood money falsely, Tycho reached a chimney on the roof of the Fontego dei Tedeschi north of the Rialto bridge. For company he had a dead pigeon and a live cat, the pigeon having died to keep the cat alive for another few days.

Around him were a dozen chimneys, twice his height, and topped by fluted stone funnels from which warmth drifted. He'd been drawn here by a noise he'd heard on his first night in the city. A mechanical heartbeat.

Unthreatening but steady, it drew him to the far edge of the *fontego* roof, on to icy tiles two floors below and into an alley where frozen mud cut his feet through a covering of snow. The heartbeat was loud as it echoed off the alley walls. Opening a door without thinking, he stepped through. The machine shop was in darkness, except for a candle in the far corner. A question came from behind the candle.

The voice of the man asking was proud and old. He sounded not at all worried by the arrival of a stranger, where no stranger should be. Tycho knew later what he asked, regretting how he came to know.

"My machine prints."

The book master had the belly of a man who ate well and walked little. His cheeks flapped, as if he'd once been larger, and his eyes were pale and watery. His hair was thick, though, for all it was grey.

"The only printing press in Serenissima."

Tycho looked at him.

"You don't understand?"

He didn't. Although he would reconstruct the conversation in flashes and slivers, as he fled the building. But that came later.

"The Chinese invented this. I changed it to harness water power." The man indicated a moving belt that vanished through a slit in the floor and reappeared a pace later. It turned a wheel, which worked gears that shuttled sheets of paper under a falling square. This was what Tycho had heard outside.

"The future. That's what this is. We can print fifty pages of Asia Minor as the tide rises, change the plate and print fifty copies of China as it falls."

There was pride in his voice. A pride Tycho was to understand later, when the old man had no further use for it. Having explained what it was in Venetian, and seen how hard Tycho struggled to understand, the old man tried mainland Italian, German, Greek and Latin. Finally he shrugged and reverted to his original choice.

"Engraved by a Frank, printed on a Chinese press, adapted by a Venetian. Based on the best facts of Portuguese, Venetian and Moorish navigators. I'm hoping Prince Alonzo will buy my first atlas."

Next to the press was a trestle holding a title page. A fish, that was what its picture looked like. A fish, with a canal's northern opening as its mouth, the sweep of the canal, and the southern exit as its gills.

"San Polo," the man said, pointing to its head.

Cannaregio was the spine.

Dorsoduro, San Marco and Arzanale its belly. The island of San Pietro made its tail. It took Tycho a while to realise he was looking at this new world in which he found himself. And the hope flooded his heart and his face softened.

"*Bjornvin . . . ?*"

Watery eyes examined Tycho. The book master made him repeat the name. Then, turning to the end of an atlas, where a dozen printed lists crossed the page like prison bars, the old man ran one finger down its list of tiny names . . .

He shook his head.

"*Bjornvin.*"

"All right, all right . . ." Pulling down a book so old its cover flaked under his fingers, he ran down a different list, this one handwritten. The third book was no better. The fourth gave an answer.

"A town in Vineland. It burnt a hundred years ago."

The man read the entry, read it again and shook his head. "There's a record of finding ruins." Shuffling across to a collection of manuscripts, he unrolled one. "Sir John Mandeville writes

61

of meeting a merchant who saw them. That would be fifty years ago. It had been burnt to the ground."

His words meant nothing to Tycho.

"*Bjornvin.*"

The old man sucked his teeth. "Why would you be interested?" He stopped to examine Tycho, suddenly noticing how strange he looked. "Impossible. You'd have to be . . . ? What, eighteen now? Plus a hundred."

For the first time he looked worried.

"Buy yourself food," he insisted. "Find somewhere to sleep out of the cold." Digging in his pocket, he found small coins and folded them into Tycho's hand, jumping back as Tycho hurled his offering to the floor.

One had been silver.

As Tycho broke Maître Thomas's neck, the old man's memories flowed into Tycho's mind. And with them language, a sense of where Venice was, and knowledge of what had just happened, seen from the other side.

11

The snow along the *fondamenta* had the feel of marble polished by the feet of others and was so cold and hard it burnt Tycho's bare toes.

He hardly noticed.

Maître Thomas's memories filled his head. And the knife he'd grabbed escaping the print shop was forgotten in his hand. He found himself on the edge of a street fight by accident.

That night in January was the night Tycho met three women who'd change his life forever. If you could count an eleven-year-old, red-haired *stregoi* as a *woman* . . . At eighteen, the Nubian slave counted. So did the fifteen-year-old Giulietta di Millioni, but Tycho met her last and only briefly.

"No blades . . ." The voice was outraged.

A girl black as a moonless night, her braided hair ending in tiny silver thimbles, stood glaring. She had the eyes of a predator and the stare of one too. One hand rested on her hip, the other gripped a frosted tree on a *fondamenta* edging the canal. Nodding at the knife in Tycho's hand made her silver-tipped braids dance some more. Blood oozed from above her eye.

"What?" she said. "Never seen a Nubian before?"

"No, never."

Even though touching a silver-tipped braid would burn him, Tycho lifted his thumb to her eyebrow and touched the blood. A steel grip stopped his thumb from reaching his mouth. "Don't," she said.

Her braids swayed like poisoned weed in the canal, holding him back as her scent drew him in. He could smell wine, garlic and a stink rising from her. Despite her filthy feet, and a dress hacked to the knees, she looked dangerous and elegant. Mostly dangerous.

How old was she?

Old enough to be in a street brawl, obviously. Lifting the knife from his fingers she tossed it casually into the canal beside them.

"You know the law."

He did, because Maître Thomas had known it. And the book master's memories were now his, transferred in the moment he broke the man's neck. Although many of them had already begun to fade. When Tycho glanced up he found the Nubian watching him, her eyes glittering in the starlight. She thought him Castellani because of his stolen tunic.

"Which is your parish?"

All and none. He lived everywhere and nowhere. Out of the way of strangers and the Watch and those who'd hurt him or needed hurting. Probably not the answer she was looking for. "What's your name?" he asked instead.

"Amelia," she said, grinning at his change of subject.

"And where do *you* live?"

"Near here. I'm a lady's maid. Well, since Lady Desdaio moved in." The girl didn't look like a lady's maid to either of them. Although Tycho only knew what one was because of fragmenting memories.

"Lady . . . ?"

"Desdaio, my mistress."

"What's she like?"

Amelia gave a huge sigh. "Sweet," she said, "with added honey, and an extra spoonful of sugar. I'd hate her, but that's impossible."

"Sounds hideous."

"Should be," Amelia said. "But she isn't. Big eyes and big tits. I get scared for her. She's also a walking mint. Although, obviously enough, men don't simply want her money and body . . ."

"She's rich?" Tycho interrupted.

Amelia rolled her eyes. "Of course she is. She's old man Bribanzo's heir. Boxes of jewellery, chests full of coins, endless velvet dresses, bolts of shot silk, paintings . . ."

"What else do the men want?"

"You know what happens to innocence?"

"It dies?"

"Someone kills it."

"That what happened to you?"

"Shit," she said. "What kind of question's that?" Lifting her face, she grinned at him. Her eyes glittering in the light of a flaming brand fixed to an arch behind him. The pulse of blood in her neck clearly visible. "Kiss me then."

He fled her. Outrage following him in shouted insults as he lost himself in a nest of serpentine backstreets, ducking through an underpass to find a wide alley beyond. As he fled, the night sky changed from the red it had suddenly become to a more normal blue-black, the houses lost their glittering edges and the tightness in his gut released slightly.

He had enough sense to know the anger and his hunger were interchangeable; different ways to describe what soured his mouth when the Nubian girl raised her head to expose her throat.

Statues, and frescoes and marble inlay.

The palaces lining the Canalasso were the grandest in the city. The buildings were rich, decorated with carvings and tiny squares of coloured glass. Many palaces painted. The carvings and the varied stones and the paintings like nothing he'd ever seen. In his fractured mind buildings were wood or earth.

The walls of a great hall, double-skinned with logs filled with pounded dirt. A turf roof over crude beams. In winter, snow kept warmth in the hall. The snow in Venice was so thin Tycho barely recognised it.

How could his home be burnt for a hundred years? Bjornvin was there in his memory now. Not perfect, certainly not that, but real and recent.

After that . . . ?

He could remember an axe cutting into a ship's hull. His brief blindness as someone thrust a lamp into his prison. Until the light reached him he hadn't known how his eyes had changed. And until he threw himself backwards off the little boat he hadn't realised he moved faster than other people. Everyone here seemed to move clumsily, stumbling through dark alleys, barely seeing what was there.

At first, he'd wondered what was wrong with them. Who these clumsy people were. Now he had fragments of memory back, and Maître Thomas's memories too, he was coming to wonder if he was *people* at all.

"Who goes there?"

Tycho fell into the darkness. He could feel it shimmer, and colonnades lighten as the darkness closed around him. Conical steel caps, straw-stuffed jerkins with scales of cheap steel. There were five guards, two of them carried daggers and two had pikes, their sergeant had a war hammer hanging from his belt. All wore boots studded with rivets against the ice underfoot.

"I saw someone."

"Where?" The question was dismissive.

"Over there," insisted a youth, pointing to where Tycho stood in the shadows. Their sergeant peered into the darkness.

"Boss?" one said.

"Nothing," he replied. Cuffing the boy across the back of his head, the sergeant said, "Scared of his own shadow."

Tycho trailed them around the expanse of a snow-skimmed square, moving silently and unseen behind them, and keeping his steps within the slush their boots churned from the virgin snow. He would have completed the circuit had he not looked up and seen horses.

Four of them.

Striking the air with their hooves as they leapt from the balcony of the Basilica San Marco. He knew the horses instantly. Because Maître Thomas had known them. How could he not? Looted from Byzantium, who stole them from Athens, where they'd decorated the original Hippodrome. He'd never seen a horse close to.

Thanking the masons who carved the basilica's façade, Tycho used one foothold after another to scale a column and roll himself on to the balcony's balustrade. Behind him he left stone angels with muddy toe prints on their heads. The four bronze horses he expected. The red-haired child sat beneath he didn't.

Looking up, she grinned.

"Well," she said. "What a surprise."

The child huddled over a fire, which flickered in the night wind. Its flames were trapped in her cupped hands and burnt nothing, unless it was the empty air between them.

Her hair was greasy, her green eyes unreadable as he hesitated, half over the balustrade, one foot still on the halo of a stone angel. "Impressive, aren't they?" She patted a stallion's leg. "Stolen from Greece by the Romans, stolen from Rome by Romanised Greeks, stolen from them by us . . ."

"Us?" Tycho asked.

"Well, them really." The girl looked at him, hanging half on and half off the balcony, and raised her eyebrows. "Afraid of witches?"

When Tycho scowled, her grin widened. So he rolled himself over the balustrade wishing he'd kept the printer's knife.

"Strange city," she said. "Strange hungers you didn't know you had . . . You're right to be scared. I don't blame you."

"I'm not scared."

"Of course you're not."

Closing her hands to quench the flame, she pulled a scrap of bread from her smock, revealing ribs like twigs as her smock fell open. Eleven, he thought, maybe twelve if starved. "Take, eat," she said, mockingly. "Or is it a different kind of salvation you're after?"

He grabbed the bread, stuffing it into his mouth. Its crust was old leather, the middle sawdust. It tasted of ashes and coal.

She laughed. "Apparently so."

Climbing to her feet, the girl scooped slush from the balcony floor and offered him that instead. He drank from her hands, wondering why. The slush was fresh, if gritty, but it didn't change the taste in his mouth.

"You shouldn't be here," she said.

"Nor should you."

She laughed. "You should go home."

Tycho's eyes filled with snow. Snow and fire and ashes.

"Ahh," she said. "You remember that much." She paused, and for the first time looked uncertain. "Alexa thinks you drowned. Should I tell her you didn't?"

He didn't know the answer. But then he didn't really understand her question. Or how she'd moved from offering him water to standing there. All he knew was she moved as swiftly as he did. Maybe sunlight hurt her too.

"I've tamed death walkers." Her words were bitter. "Seljuk mages, *krieghund* even. A skill much needed last autumn, I gather. But you . . ." Without hesitating, she bit her wrist deep enough to draw blood. Then she took a deep breath and held it out to him.

"Bind yourself."

The world turned red.

Bronze horses leapt through scarlet mist. Hunger hollowed out his guts, his throat tightened at the taste of blood flowing from broken gums where his dog teeth lengthened. As his senses heightened, Tycho rocked back on his heels. Stunned by the onslaught of what he suddenly saw, heard and smelt.

"You stop when I tell you. Or else."

Tycho's intuition said she doubted she could deliver on that threat. A hundred thousand rivers of blood flowed beneath her filthy skin and he could sense them all, for a second they were all he could see of her.

Grabbing her arm, he suckled at her wrist. A second later, he was spitting at the floor, scrubbing his lips with his hand. Curdled milk barely described the taste of her blood. Nothing he'd eaten came close. The red mist was gone, swept away by shock, and the night was dark around him. He felt like crying.

The girl sighed.

Blood ceased to well as she licked her wrist, scabs closing over bite marks. She dipped her chunk of stale bread into a puddle and tore half free, offering it to him. "Sometimes one magic doesn't like another."

Tycho nodded, not trusting himself to speak.

He was still chewing the last of the bread when she walked to the edge of the balcony, and stared over the darkened expanse of Piazza San Marco. "Dawn soon," she said. "We should both go."

"Tell me your name."

She grinned. "I offer you my blood. You want my name as well? It's A'rial, I'm Alexa's *stregoi*. Her pet witch."

Before he could answer A'rial was gone.

12

Patting his stallion's neck, Tycho slid from its bronze back to stand at the balcony's edge, with the wind in his face. Below him, a chair waited, its link men shuffling against the cold. In the distance, the Watch still scuffed their way round the piazza, while cutpurses slunk behind its colonnades, hidden by black cloaks and masks.

Out on the lagoon half-furled sails snapped in the wind. Five men approached the *piazzetta* in a low, lean *gondolino*, saw the Watch and changed their minds. The slight splash of their retreat muted by falling snow.

Tycho listened harder.

Concentrating, he caught a sound from within the basilica itself. A young woman crying, and, tied to her sobs, a scent so compelling it hooked him through the guts. He'd turned towards her before he realised. Desperate to make his way inside the building.

Ducking under a lintel, he found a locked door beyond. The door was solid and the lock firm. So, without thinking, he slid his fingers under the door and lifted it off its hinges. Leaving it against a wall, he entered an attic beyond.

Stones stairs were blocked by a wrought-iron gate, with a better lock and hinges. So he took a corridor that led to an internal balcony high above the basilica floor. A rat paused in its scavenging, only to resume when he moved on.

The balcony stank of dust, damp wood and sweet smoke from a censer hanging over the darkened nave. Below it, mosaics swirled away in patterns that mimicked a Persian carpet, unless it was the other way round.

Christ, his mother and apostles whose names Tycho struggled to place watched from the domed ceiling. Their faces stern, their noses aquiline and their resemblance to long dead Roman emperors unmistakable. Every one of them stared at a girl kneeling below.

Tycho understood why.

She was beautiful, her hair as red as her dress. The Virgin she knelt before stood silent, as stone virgins do, but the supplicant's shoulders heaved with anguish, her sobs rising to heaven. From the desolation on her face she doubted the Virgin would help. It was a low, urgent and very one-sided conversation.

"Please, my lady," she begged. "If you don't . . ."

A heart-shaped face looked up, blue eyes fixing on heaven. Tycho had no idea what she looked for, but he saw a desperate girl pull a knife from her cloak. Gripping its handle, she folded her fingers over the pommel as if this was something she'd been taught and put the point to her chest.

When she lowered the knife, Tycho felt his heart restart.

Only to stop again when she undid a gilded clasp on her cloak and let the garment slide from her shoulders. Next she undid her dress, exposing a white shift beneath. A bow at the neck undid this. Regaining her knife, she slid the dress and shift from one shoulder to reveal a breast.

He didn't know whether to watch the blade or the girl as she put the knife to her heart. He saw her hesitate, watched her wince as she jabbed slightly, blood tricking down her ribs.

"Sweet God," she whispered.

And Tycho's senses exploded, hunger overflowing desire as his world narrowed to the half-naked girl, and her alone. The nighttime nave was daylight bright, the smell of incense viciously cloying. Meltwater dripping overhead was loud enough to startle. The gap between him and the censer vanished in a single leap, its chain swinging wildly, until he dropped and its swing ended.

Only when he reached the censer did the girl look up.

Some fifth sense where Tycho now had a dozen. One hand rose to hide her breast and she opened her mouth to scream. Before she could, Tycho dropped, closing the gap between them. Grabbing her knife, he tossed it away.

"*Don't*," he snarled.

He wanted . . . her, but how?

His dog teeth ached, sweetness flooded his mouth. Her neck was freckled and perfect, her exposed nipple pale and pink, the breast it tipped small but ripe. She wore rose petal scent. *That* was what hooked him.

Not just her nakedness. Not just her beauty.

The combination of roses and blue eyes reminded him of . . . Who? Because they reminded him of someone. Shuddering, he traced one finger up the trickle of blood on her ribs, only stopping when he reached the underside of her breast.

"Do you know who I am?" she demanded.

How would he? All he knew was that sucking her blood from his finger sent shivers up his spine. Blood must be what he wanted. Blood must be what he hadn't allowed himself since arriving in this strange city.

"Well . . . ? Do you?"

Furious eyes glared from a heart-shaped face as she freed her wrist, and Tycho let it happen. As he watched, dumbstruck, she raised her shift to hide her breast, blood blossoming in a run of roses across its surface.

"Do you know what my uncle will do to you?"

No, and he didn't care either. He caught her wrist before she could slap him for lowering her shift again. He wanted to hurt and protect her. Strip her naked, take her screaming on the cold floor. And die keeping her from harm. Just looking at the trickle of her blood made him drunk.

"Did you hear what I said?"

"What's your name?"

She glared, convinced he was mocking her. But he wasn't. He wanted to know her name. Needed to know it more than anything he'd ever needed to know.

"I'm Lady Giulietta di Millioni."

"Giulietta?"

"My uncle will flay you."

"I don't care . . ." That was the truth. He didn't.

Outside, guards stamped their feet against the cold, and an oxcart rumbled and creaked over melting snow. Daybreak was near, and Tycho needed to hide. But he stayed instead. "I saw a man flayed once," he said, remembering.

Lady Giulietta scowled ferociously.

"I mean it. He'll have you nailed to a door. Or boiled in oil." She glared at Tycho. "Maybe you've seen a man boiled in oil?"

"No," he said. "Does it last long?"

She hissed in fury. "How would I know? I haven't seen a man flayed either. I'm barely allowed out of the palace." She caught herself. "This is ridiculous. I don't know why I'm even talking to you."

"Because you can't help it."

"That's . . ."

"True," Tycho said. He let her raise her shift again.

Blood still seeped from her slight wound, darkening cloth where it trickled down to her red velvet dress. Giulietta did nothing when he touched the largest stain, though she froze as he lifted her breast, finding the source beneath her shift with his thumb. Carrying her blood to his mouth, he sucked until the ball of his

73

thumb was clean. Then he brushed his thumb across the stain again, and watched in surprise as the trickle lessened and stopped.

Behind him, a door began to open.

"Go," Giulietta begged.

He went, taking the scent of roses, the memory of her heart-shaped face and the taste of her blood with him.

13

When she looked the boy was gone. Despite herself, Lady Giulietta glanced at a huge marble pillar, seeing movement where it met a balcony. But the light in Basilica San Marco came from candles or oil lamps, and she couldn't be sure it wasn't just shadows shifting.

"My lady . . ."

Captain Roderigo looked tired, and worried at how he found her. Since his scars said his courage wasn't in question, she assumed he hung back to give her time to pull up her dress. He said nothing as she fixed her cloak and bent for the dagger, sliding it into a secret hiding place.

"What?" she demanded.

"I have a message for you."

Lady Giulietta sighed. "So?" she said flatly, and watched the captain's eyes tighten at her rudeness. As if she'd care.

"The Regent is asking where you are."

"What did my aunt tell him?"

"My lady, I wouldn't . . ."

"Of course you would," Giulietta said crossly. "Everyone in the palace knows everything. They just pretend they don't. It's a prison."

It wasn't. She'd been inside a prison.

As a child she'd been taken to see a toothless and naked patrician, who huddled in a freezing cell, filthy with his own faeces and sitting in a puddle of his own piss. Nicolo Paso led a rebellion in his youth. The so-called Second Republic, which lasted three years and saw a hundred senators beheaded in a single day when it fell. Paso was spared.

His condition an object lesson in what awaited those who challenged the Millioni dynasty. She'd heard the Byzantine empire funded Paso's treason. But then she'd heard the German emperor was to blame. And the Hungarian king, and the Mamluk sultan . . . Clearly, no one considered Paso might have thought of the rebellion himself. She kept that opinion to herself.

"I've seen Paso's cell," she said, by way of apology. She couldn't help being rude. Well, she probably could, but she wouldn't know where to start or why she would . . .

"Bother," Giulietta said, fumbling a button.

Roderigo's apparent fascination with her face obviously turned on the fact that her fingers struggled with buttons at the neck of her dress, and her hands wouldn't stop shaking. "My lady," he said. "Lord Paso's conditions are good." Before she could disagree, he added. "There are far worse . . ."

"Worse than that?"

"Much worse," Roderigo said. "The Ca' Ducale is *not* a prison. In comparison with the worst this city has, Lord Paso's cell is almost a palace."

"As I would know if I'd need a *real* prison?"

"Yes, my lady."

Giulietta hated being patronised. "Tell me the worst then."

Roderigo considered her demand, then shrugged and obviously decided he had nothing to lose in answering. "The pit of the Black Crucifers. It fills with water each tide and requires hours of labour to empty. Prisoners work in shifts to remove the water before the next tide comes."

"And if they don't succeed?"

"They drown."

"Well," she said, fastening her last button. "I'd still rather pump water there than be here talking to you." Captain Roderigo looked as if he wanted to slap her. That was fine; most days she wanted to slap herself.

Smothering a shiver, Giulietta ordered him to escort her back to the palace. Where she discovered Aunt Alexa and her uncle now separately abed, and retired to her own chambers on the palace's family floor. Dismissing Lady Eleanor, who'd stayed awake to help her undress, she struggled out of her blood-stained dress, pulled off her undergown and changed it for a fresh one, hiding her bloodied shift under her mattress. Falling into bed, Giulietta dragged a heavy fur over her and dreamed of snows and wooden buildings burning.

Next morning she woke, pissed in a cold pot and dressed as quickly as her buttons and ribbons and Lady Eleanor's slowness allowed.

"Eleanor."

"My fingers are frozen."

Her lady-in-waiting was fumbling the ribbons on the sleeve of an overgown when she stopped, with the ribbon half tied. Pulling back the sleeve she revealed a bruise on Giulietta's wrist.

"My lady."

"What?"

"It looks . . ." Eleanor hesitated.

"Well?" Giulietta said crossly. "What does it look like?"

"Finger marks"

Lady Giulietta slapped her.

And having slapped her, she sent Eleanor to her room and tied the ribbons herself, pulling them too tight and making a mess of the bows. She considered recalling her lady-in-waiting to tell her she was dismissed for good. But Giulietta couldn't face that, and Eleanor probably didn't want to go to Cyprus anyway and would only be glad of the news.

So she said nothing and kicked her heels in the map room, endlessly examining a fresco of Cyprus, which showed pitiful little ships sailing in all directions. The artist depicted her future home as rocky and barren, with few towns and fewer cities. This made her no happier than arguing with Eleanor.

It was absurd and ridiculous. It made her sound like a maiden in a troubadour's song, but Giulietta couldn't shake the feeling that the touch of the boy in the basilica had set hooks into her soul. As if he'd stolen a part of her and left a part of himself in its place. A part that tasted bitter, unforgettable.

Aunt Alexa was too busy to be disturbed.

So Giulietta spent the rest of the day practising her harpsichord with fearsome intensity, until the guards in the corridor winced at every repetition. It was next morning before the girls spoke, and three days before they made up their quarrel. Without discussing it, both avoided mentioning the bruises again.

14

"Where is my aunt?"

Roderigo looked into Lady Giulietta's anxious face and opened his mouth to say he didn't know.

"You don't know, do you?"

"No, my lady."

"Idiot," she said crossly. "Everyone's an idiot this evening. I know she's not with the duke, because he's in his room." Permission was needed to visit Marco after dark, even for Giulietta, so Roderigo avoided asking how she knew.

"Have you asked the Regent?" he said instead.

Giulietta turned on her heel.

Wrong suggestion, obviously. "My lady," he called after her. "Shall I mention your wish to see her should I meet the duchess?"

"Yes," came the answer. Although Lady Giulietta didn't bother to stop or turn and thank him for the thought. *Why would she?* he thought. She was a Millioni. A member of the richest family in Europe. And he . . . ? A minor patrician, who squatted one room of a ten-room palace because the other nine were colder, damper and even more disgusting than the one he used.

His meeting that afternoon with her uncle had been worrying. There was something not being said. Something that had Prince Alonzo trapped between fury and worry, with the Mamluk ambassador's reactions almost identical. The men were sparring nervously. Roderigo would have been happier, and more secure, if he had known about what.

The Mamluk ambassador demanded the Ten investigate the burning of his master's ship, and refused to accept the ship hadn't been ransacked and its cargo stolen before being set on fire. He refused, flatly, to accept it was an accident.

"Mamluks don't drink wine," he said crossly, when Duchess Alexa suggested a drunken crew member tripped over an oil lamp and brought disaster. There were just enough drunk Mamluks, Arabs and Moors in the taverns along Riva degli Schiavoni to give that the lie. But in general it was true.

The ambassador's position was firm.

His master did not take kindly to his trade ships being burnt. Nor would the sultan take kindly to the Ten's refusal to investigate. The duchess hoped that wasn't a threat. The ambassador, with the cold pride for which he was famous, declared it a warning, nothing more. Although he suggested Venice take his warning seriously.

"You already know," Alonzo said, "my respect for your master."

"The sultan has been your friend in the past."

Maybe Roderigo was the only one who read *but that is now over* into this sentence. "I would hate to be disappointed," Prince Alonzo said. "To feel my overtures, my offers of friendship were being rejected."

"Disappointment is a fact of life."

Prince Alonzo looked at the ambassador in shock. "Both our countries will lose if this is not resolved smoothly."

"As God wills," the ambassador said.

At this, Prince Alonzo seemed to regain his temper. He repeated that the fire aboard the Mamluk ship had been an accident. Captain Roderigo was certain of this, wasn't he?

"Of course," Roderigo had said.

"My lady . . ." The voice behind her was oily. *Unctuous*, Lady Giulietta decided, shivering at the word's suggestion of greasy ointment. She increased her pace towards the stairs.

"His highness is looking for you."

"The duke?" she said, spinning round.

The Regent's secretary swallowed, and shot a nervous glance at a nearby guard. "Forgive me," he said. "I meant, his excellence, Prince Alonzo . . ."

She knew her uncle was looking for her. That was the reason she was looking for her aunt. Lady Giulietta had begun to fret about the way Uncle Alonzo eyed her. And his constant suggestions that they have a quiet talk soon, alone. Her worry wasn't helped by her aunt's reply when told this earlier.

"We must talk too," Alexa said. "In the meantime, light a candle for your mother, every night. You can rely on her to guard you."

Everyone wanted to talk. No one specified when and time was running out. Sir Richard left on tomorrow's tide and took Giulietta. The treaties were signed, the banquets were over. The courtiers wanted her gone. She could see it in their eyes. They wanted her moping, and her anger and her misery, out of their lives.

Aunt Alexa was so elusive that Giulietta now wondered if she also wanted her gone. The duchess knew how she felt about this marriage, because everyone at court knew how she felt, even those who usually found safety in knowing nothing. So why was Alexa refusing to see her? *If you had any guts you'd kill yourself.*

The voice was small, still and her own.

"My lady."

"*What?*" Her uncle's horrid little secretary was still there. Looking like a weasel, with his watery eyes and balding head.

"I really think, my lady . . ."

"Well, don't." He'd never dare express an opinion if she wasn't leaving tomorrow. But she'd be gone by the following noon, so what did he have to fear from her now? Her aunt was nowhere to be found and she could hardly complain to . . . "Where is my uncle?"

"Della Tortura."

"He's torturing someone?" She wouldn't put it past him. He often claimed to miss the mud, blood and brutality of the battle-field. *So much cleaner than politics.* You were meant to believe he was a reluctant ruler. But he plotted and schemed and lied with the rest of them.

The Sala della Tortura was on the fourth level, below the roof and above the armoury and chambers of government. Since she was on the second level she had two sets of stairs to climb and a dozen or so guards to pass. No doubt each would sneak a look at her face, wondering what was wrong this time.

The stairs were cold and wind rippled the tapestries ordered by the last duke. These were French and showed the highlights of his reign. The first outlined Marco III's overthrow of the Second Republic as a young god, with his enemies crabbed and bitter. The second his marriage to the Khan's granddaughter, who became Alexa di San Felice il Millioni. She arrived with three boxes of gold, a case of black tea and a dozen imperial pigeons. Her grandfather relied on the breed to carry messages about his conquests, issue orders to his armies and send to the rear for supplies or rein-forcements. Tīmūr, the new khan of khans, did the same.

The third and final tapestry was divided into Heaven, Hell and Earth. On Earth, Marco III sat with Alexa and his son. In Heaven, Princes Matteo and Cesare, murdered by the Second Republic, smiled on their brother's new family. And below, in the bowels of Hell, republicans were tortured by demons, while their sons and daughters were violated with spits or hung like joints of meat.

That one gave Lady Giulietta the creeps.

The stairs to the next floor were narrower and far less grand. Flaking murals no one cared about lined the walls. The tapestries had holes. She liked these stairs better. Neither of the guards by the Tortura door readied to open it.

Giulietta was about to be furious when she remembered she'd told them she could open doors for herself the last time she came here. She decided to be furious anyway.

"*Open it, then.*"

They did as ordered.

A fire burnt in a brazier and sweet smoke filled the air. The room was double height. A balcony ran down both sides, with wooden chairs for councillors who wanted to watch a questioning. A single rope dangled from high above. It was the rope from which suspects were suspended. The Sala's walls were bare wood, darkened with smoke and age. The floor was old stone. An incongruous leather bed was pushed into one corner, covered with a Persian carpet. Next to it stood a portable desk, overflowing with papers and cut quills, while an ink pot had its lid open. The man sat at the desk was sketching a horoscope with confident strokes.

"You're here at last," Dr Crow said.

"Where's my uncle?"

"Busy." Alonzo's voice came from an alcove behind curtains.

"I'll come back later."

"No," he crossly. "You'll wait. I sent for you an hour ago. Your lateness could have made matters . . ."

"What?"

"Unnecessarily complicated."

Hearing the door open behind her, Giulietta glanced back, expecting her uncle's secretary or one of the guards. A sour-faced *abadessa* in the white wimple of her order stood there instead. And next to her, a drunk so blowsy she could have been scooped from the stalls of the nearest brothel. Sweat and alcohol rose from her filthy skin.

"*You*," she hissed, seeing the alchemist.

Dr Crow smiled. "Mistress Scarlett." The air crackled with the early stirrings of a storm. Only to settle when the nun glared between them.

"We're all here, then."

Dropping the curtain behind him, Prince Alonzo stepped out of the alcove holding a goose quill. It looked like a pen, except it was missing a cut nib and lacked the feathers usually left to balance a pen's upper end. "You're certain the time is propitious?"

"A day off the new moon," Dr Crow said. "No time better."

"What about her?"

"If what her linen maid says is true. Scarlett can check."

Stepping towards Giulietta, the blowsy drunk scowled when the young woman backed away from her. "This will be easier with your help."

"What will?"

"Everything," Prince Alonzo said heavily. "Believe me. It will be easier for everyone if you cooperate. *Abadessa* . . ."

Grabbing Giulietta, the abbess spun her round and dug a thumb into the soft flesh of Giulietta's arm, shocking her into stillness. "Struggle, and I'll press harder."

Piss spread in a puddle around Giulietta's feet.

"With the Regent's permission," said the abbess. "We'll begin. Mistress Scarlett, if you'll confirm we're not wasting our time?"

Lifting Lady Giulietta's gown and undergown, the wise woman pushed her hand between the girl's thighs and sniffed her fingers. "Close enough. The quill's fresh?"

"What do you think?" Alonzo said, lacing his codpiece.

"It would be surer to . . ."

The Regent's face darkened. "Do you *want* me damned?" he snarled. "It's against the rules of consanguinity. I might as well burn churches and eat meat on a Friday."

"*You can't* . . ."

And then Giulietta said no more, because the sharp-faced nun dug her thumb so savagely into Giulietta's arm she wet herself again, shame spreading in a growing puddle across the floor.

"Stop snivelling," the abbess told her.

"I'm not sure," Dr Crow said, "that was necessary. And I'm not sure," he added, looking reproachful, "you mentioned your niece was unwilling."

"If she'd bothered to answer my summons we'd have had time to discuss this. As she didn't . . ." Alonzo let his comment hang. He obviously considered Giulietta's ignorance of his plan her fault. "And I don't explain myself to my mage."

"Duke Marco's mage," Dr Crow said quietly.

Lady Giulietta thought her uncle would strike him. When the Regent held his tongue she knew it meant one of two things. The alchemist was more powerful than she suspected. Or her uncle wanted this over, whatever *this* was. Neither choice made her happy.

"Put her on the divan," Mistress Scarlett said.

It didn't matter that Giulietta struggled. On her back, with her dress and undergown round her waist was where she ended. Although it was only when she began to scream that the Regent lost his temper. "Fetch the bitch a gag."

"We don't have time."

"Deal with it," Prince Alonzo ordered Dr Crow.

"As you wish." Touching both sides of Giulietta's jaw, he whispered, "Silence." And that was that. Lady Giulietta's jaw locked and her tongue froze in her head. When Mistress Scarlett began to force her knees open, the alchemist looked away, then headed for the alcove where the Regent had been earlier.

"Where do you think you're going?"

"To get wine. You do have wine, don't you . . . ?" Dr Crow muttered something about bloody well hoping so. And then he was gone, the curtain was in place and Mistress Scarlet was raising the girl's ankles while the abbess held her wrists.

"This will happen," the wise woman said, apologetically.

"Struggling only makes things worse. So be kind to yourself and behave."

Although she hated her own cowardice Giulietta did as she was told. Mistress Scarlett spoke the truth. All Dr Crow had to do was pass his hands across her hips and those would be out of her control as well.

"Do it," the Regent ordered.

Taking the quill, Mistress Scarlet pulled a fish bladder from her sleeve, blew into it and pushed it on to one end of the quill. The other, she slid between Lady Giulietta's thighs, cursing when the young woman began bucking hard enough to free one wrist.

"*Hold her.*"

The grip on her captive wrist grew savage. "Such a fuss," the nun said. "You'd think you were the only girl to do her city a service."

Repositioning the quill, Mistress Scarlet squeezed the bladder to free its contents. "See," she said. "Not so bad. And you're as intact as the day you were born." She smiled, as if this should make the difference.

"*Alchemist.*"

"It's Dr Crow to you, woman."

"My part's done," Mistress Scarlett said. "I'll be taking my money and going."

The Regent opened his mouth.

"I'll take my money and go," she repeated.

Prince Alonzo threw a purse at her. "Witch," he muttered, as the door shut behind her.

"If you will," said Dr Crow, moving the *abadessa* back from the divan and indicating that Giulietta should remain where she was. Since the nun blocked her escape Giulietta did as ordered.

"A son," the Regent said tightly. "You understand? She's to bear Cyprus a son. If she fails I'm going to be angry. In fact, you'll find I suddenly agree with the Pope in Rome's opinion that you're a heretic."

Dr Crow ignored him.

"My lady," he said. "First babies are often late. Cyprus will never suspect your child is not his. And you will never tell him. In fact . . ." The alchemist glanced at the Regent, who nodded. "You will never talk of what happened here."

The mage held Giulietta steady until she stopped shivering and then touched her face, letting his fingertips brush her jaw.

"How could you?" she demanded.

"I need corpses to dissect, my lady. The Regent provides those and keeps me safe from those who regard my work as abomination."

The *abadessa* left next. And Giulietta was made to lie for half an hour with her knees up and a cushion under her hips. Although the nun's contemptuous parting gift, which was to rearrange Giulietta's gown, at least meant she had her decency. But when Giulietta was at last allowed up, and turned for the door, her knees weak, her guts vomitous and her bowels on the edge of emptying, her uncle called her back. Her job was more than simply giving Cyprus the son his first wife had not. There were other considerations, matters of policy. He wished to explain exactly what was required of her when she arrived at her new kingdom.

15

Stumbling from the room, Giulietta heard footsteps and walked faster, but her stomach was water, the hem of her dress stank of piss, and vomit filled her throat. She refused to believe Aunt Alexa knew of what had just happened. But if she didn't, why had her aunt been unwilling to see her?

It was, Giulietta knew, only a matter of time before her guts released at one end or the other. And when they did, she wanted to be anywhere but on cold stairs watched by needlepoint demons.

"Wait," Dr Crow called.

Lady Giulietta increased her speed.

He caught up with her at the end of stairs leading to the loggia. This was easy, since by then, she was on her knees outside the Sala dei Censoi, vomiting up her supper. All Dr Crow had to do was walk up to her and wait.

"It's the shock," he said.

She stood slowly. Slapped him hard.

"You didn't see that," Dr Crow told a guard coming towards them. The man carried a halberd and wore a thick cloak, as befitted someone whose duties involved walking down an open-sided corridor in mid-winter.

"Saw what, sir?"

"Good man. Now, get me drinking water."

The guard wanted to say fetching water wasn't his job. He was right, his job was patrolling the loggia. But Dr Crow had turned an enemy to a black cat, and drowned him. Added to which, he treated the new duke in his moments of madness. About which nobody was meant to know . . .

"My lady."

Taking the cup from the guard, Giulietta sipped slowly. A second later she remembered to dismiss the man with a nod. Turning, he marched into the wind, his cloak billowing like a shroud. So much in this palace had to be kept secret. No doubt he'd seen worse.

"Chew this, my lady."

She looked at the sticky pill Dr Crow offered.

"It will settle your stomach and balance your humours." Dropping the pill into her palm, the alchemist folded her fingers around it. "You should sleep, get your strength for tomorrow."

"I can't. Not yet."

The mage had an old man's eyes, clouded and watery. But Giulietta felt, as she always did, that he could read her thoughts. And she couldn't shake the feeling he knew what she'd say before she did. If so, he must realise how furious she was. How revolted. He must also know what else she had to do.

"I need to light a candle for my mother."

"In the morning, my lady."

"There won't be time," she said bitterly. "Sir Richard, Lady Eleanor and I board at noon, and sail on the tide. There will be farewells first. A formal breakfast in the state room. I will need to say my . . ."

She fought back tears.

"Your own goodbyes?"

Lady Giulietta's nod was abrupt.

"My lady, this is not . . ."

"Don't you dare," she shouted. "Don't dare say I'll see the city again. That this is for everyone's good. That what you did to me in there . . ." Her voice folded into sobs and hiccups.

"It would be the truth."

"That this is for everyone's good?" Lady Giulietta said through tears.

"No. You will leave this city and you will return. Both will be hard but the second will be harder than the first . . . Now, think about going to bed. Your uncle will be unwilling to provide guards for a journey at night. You know they'll not stir without a signed order."

"It's not a *journey*," she said. "It's a hundred paces. And they're not his guards. They're Marco's."

"You'll still need them."

"No, I won't." Opening his mouth to say she would, he shut it when she said, "I'll use the way into the Lady chapel."

Dr Crow looked shocked.

Because she knew about the passage, Giulietta realised. He knew obviously enough. She was meant to be ignorant of it.

"The door will be locked."

"You can open it."

"My lady . . ."

"Or shall I tell everyone in Cyprus you cut up bodies?"

Apart from locking her jaw, for which she'd never forgive him, this was the first time she'd seen him perform magic. The first time she'd ever seen anyone perform magic. If one ignored producing fire from your fingers, because every mountebank in Piazza San Marco could do that.

The door was behind a tapestry at ground level in a wall that adjoined the basilica. Kneeling, the old alchemist rubbed his hands together. Then he placed his fingers on the key plate, while Giulietta kept watch for guards.

"Hurry up," she whispered crossly.

There was a sharp click as a spring let go and a bolt ratcheted back. Opening the door, Dr Crow put his hand on the far side of the lock and muttered under his breath. "Shut it when you leave," he said. "It will lock itself."

With that he was gone, in a shambling shadow of grey velvet and the mustiness of an old man with no one to wash his clothes.

Basilica San Marco, the most beautiful basilica outside Byzantium itself, was the duke's personal chapel. Open on saints' days and high holidays, it was reserved for the Millioni at all other times. It was begun when Venice was still an imperial city and the mainland beyond owed its loyalty to the Eastern emperor.

At that time, there was no emperor of the West. At least none Byzantium was prepared to recognise. So, for a while, the Eastern emperor was simply, *the emperor*. This changed with the rise of the Franks who founded the Tedeschi empire, otherwise known as the Holy Roman empire. The Franks were French and the Tedeschi were German, so Lady Giulietta wasn't sure how this worked. But Fra Diomedes used his cane willingly and she'd learnt not to interrupt his lessons with questions.

And so Venice, trapped between two powerful rulers, became sly. She became sly because only this kept her safe. Having changed her saint to one not claimed by the Tedeschi, the Papacy or the emperors in Byzantium, she announced she owed loyalty to no one and would trade with all.

And so matters remained.

The same slew of glass stars circled the Virgin's head, and the same soft smile greeted Giulietta as she bobbed a curtsy, before heading towards a jewelled screen that hid the high altar from public view. She wanted Fra Zeno, one of the few Mamluk converts allowed into the priesthood. Fra Zeno was young, and smiled when he saw her. He would listen without getting cross. But she found the patriarch instead. Or, rather, Patriarch Theodore found her.

"My child . . ." His quavering admonition from the darkness made her jump. "What," he asked, "are you doing here at this hour?"

"I . . ." She was about to say looking for Fra Zeno, when she realised that was tactless, open to misunderstanding, and it didn't matter which priest she talked to. And Theodore was patriarch, after all.

If he didn't know what she should do . . .

"Seeking help."

The old man looked around him and smiled. "There are worse places to seek it," he agreed. "And a troublesome mind is no respecter of the hour." Taking an oil lamp from a shrine, he turned and Giulietta realised she was meant to follow him into the area beyond the altar.

"That's . . ."

"The warmest place here."

In a tiny sacristy she'd never seen stood a gold chalice, deco-rated with emeralds and rubies. Slabs of lapis were set into the bowl and its rim was ringed with sapphires. The cup rested on a chest containing priestly vestments. An old Persian carpet covered half the floor, and a tattered battle flag hung from one wall. In the bowl of the chalice was a wedding ring.

She knew it instantly. It was the ring with which the Duke of Venice married the sea each year to calm the waters and give fair wind to her ships. Not a year had passed since the city was founded without the marriage taking place. That was what she'd been told by her tutor anyway.

"How old is the ring?"

"How old is an axe if you keep replacing handle and blade? The ring's been repaired this year. And the chalice has had a new base, a new stem and new stones in my lifetime alone. The orig-inals would be six centuries old. Perhaps less. Records undoubtedly lie about which duke first married the sea."

The old man laughed at her shock. "You didn't come here for

history lessons. So tell me why you're here and by a secret entrance. I didn't realise you knew about that door."

"I discovered it."

She wondered why he smiled.

"The devil makes work for idle hands. And between them, Aunt Alexa and Uncle Alonzo have kept you idle for longer than is wise. Still, there are worse things for girls your age to discover than secret doors."

For a moment, Giulietta thought he'd lean forward and ruffle her hair, but he simply sighed and balanced his stolen lamp beside the chalice, looking round for a chair.

"So," he said, finding one. "Tell me what upsets you."

Maybe he expected doubts about her wedding; God knows she had enough of them. Or maybe doubts about leaving Serenissima, because she had those too. But his smile died and the twinkle left his eyes within seconds. By the end he watched with the stillness of a snake. Although his fury was not for her. Giulietta realised that when he did his best to paste a smile into place.

"Let me think for a moment."

She'd avoided all mention of Mistress Scarlett, the hatchet-faced *abadessa* and the goose quill, fearing Dr Crow told the truth. To speak of them would steal her voice forever. But what she said was bad enough.

"Perhaps you misunderstood?"

"No," she said firmly. "Uncle Alonzo's orders are clear. Once an heir is born I must poison my husband and rule as Regent until he is old enough to rule for himself. My uncle will tell me what decisions to make."

"And how are you . . . ?"

"With these." Giulietta produced two tiny pots from beneath her dress. One was small, the other smaller; no bigger than a thimble. "This," she said, holding up the larger, "has three hundred fly specks of poison."

"To kill your husband?"

"No. To *habituate* myself from the poison in this one."

She stumbled over Dr Crow's strange word and Archbishop Theodore looked thoughtful. Maybe he heard the alchemist's echo in her voice. The patriarch always greeted Dr Crow with a steely politeness Giulietta now recognised as hatred.

She watched the patriarch unscrew the smaller pot. The paste inside was sealed against the air with wax set in a swirl. "Rose balm to colour your lips. When you're certain the baby is healthy, you simply . . ." He mimed applying balm to his lips. "And then you greet Janus warmly for a week?"

Lady Giulietta nodded.

"It's slow-acting?"

"Mimics plague . . . I'm to be his food taster, with Eleanor to taste mine, and a taster to test hers before that." Giulietta's gaze was bleak. "I will remain healthy, so no one will suspect poison. Particularly if I insist on nursing Janus." Dashing tears from eyes, she asked. "What should I do?"

"Stay here."

"In Serenissima? But my ship leaves tomorrow. Sir Richard will never stand for it."

"No. Stay here now. Don't move until I've talked to Alexa. I can't believe she knows about this. And I'll be taking these." The patriarch took the tiny jars of poison, then paused. "You don't think Alexa knows, do you?"

Considering how hard it had been to find her aunt, never mind talk to her, Giulietta thought she might. Although she hoped she didn't. Every time she'd gone looking Aunt Alexa was busy or not where her servants said she would be. There had been wariness in her aunt's eyes the last few times they'd met.

"I'm not sure."

"You're not . . ."

Taking a deep breath, Giulietta said, "Aunt hates Uncle Alonzo as much as you hate Dr Crow, maybe more. He wants the throne.

She wants the throne for Marco. All Marco wants, of course, is to be allowed his toys. So if Alonzo wants this, I'd expect her to object."

"But . . . ?"

Giulietta hesitated. "It was Aunt Alexa who suggested I marry Cyprus in the first place." The thought of it made her want to burst into tears again.

"How old are you?"

An odd question, Giulietta decided, from the man who presented her to the crowds gathered in Piazza San Marco on her naming day. "Fifteen."

Archbishop Theodore smiled sadly. "And already you know how Venice works. You should have been . . ."

"What?" she demanded.

Sent to a nunnery, whipped more often, drowned at birth like a kitten? Those were her uncle's usual suggestions. She'd survived her share of whippings. It was the Regent's contempt she found harder to take. Aunt Alexa wished she'd been Marco's brother. That way, two Millioni would stand between Prince Alonzo and the throne, two heirs being harder to murder than one.

Giulietta simply wished she'd been a boy.

She'd wanted to be one for so long she'd forgotten when it started. Certainly before Aunt Alexa suggested marrying her off. And long before Uncle Alonzo decided she should murder her husband.

"I wish," the patriarch said. "Your mother had lived. *Do* you think Duchess Alexa knows about this?"

"It's possible."

As the clock in the south tower struck one, and their stolen lamp continued to gutter, its flame always on the edge of dying, but struggling back to life, Patriarch Theodore sighed. "Then I'd better start with your uncle. Maybe Aunt Alexa knows, maybe she doesn't. But talking to Alonzo is where I'll start."

16

The first time the beggar girl nodded to him Tycho thought it was an accident, the second he knew it was intentional. She glanced from beneath lank hair, nodded and kept walking.

The night streets were full of those who caught each other's glances and looked away. A quick glance and a slight nod. He'd acquired membership of a clan for whom this was enough. No one tried to talk, no one *wanted* to talk. The nod simply meant, *I'm not your enemy.* He knew, looking at the girl, that she wasn't his enemy. Her spirit was too thin to make her anyone's enemy but her own.

He wondered, however, how she knew he wasn't hers.

The third time they crossed she smiled. A fragile flicker, demanding he comfort her in some way, maybe simply by returning her smile. The days were far too bright for him, the light too dangerous for his eyes. He wondered what her excuse for living in the night world was. This city was full and it was empty. That thought led to separate iterations of *empty*.

Back from the busy thoroughfares were other, emptier streets in this city of the living; because although the obvious places were crowded, there simply weren't enough of the living to crowd the edges. There was, however, *another* city. Really empty, behind this one. It shared identical streets and brick-floored squares, identical churches and squat fortified towers. When Tycho entered it the living disappeared and the sky became silvery. The world in the empty city looked solid close to, but thinned and became translucent immediately beyond. Those in the city of the living showed in the streets of the other city like shadows.

Tycho had reached a point of wondering if all this had some deeper significance; or if was simply how this world was. For days dead children had followed him, shouting pleas he couldn't hear. And then one night they were gone. He had another memory, of a Nubian with silver snakes for hair. Unless she'd been one of the ghost children. And now most of that memory was gone too.

She was young, the beggar girl on the night street. With a filthy smock and bare legs and rags wrapped round her feet and tied at her ankles with twine. Sometimes she was alone, at others with a glowering older boy. Occasionally, a younger boy was there too.

The time she smiled she was alone.

In the time it took the moon to swell from new to quarter full Tycho had discovered how to move between cities, hide himself in the shadows and steal all the food he needed. This would have been something if he'd been able to enjoy it.

Everything he ate tasted like ash.

He drank water from habit, fed when he remembered. But his piss was almost black and it was days since his bowels had worked. He should be starving to death. Instead, he simply felt hungry. If only his stomach knew for what . . .

"You," he said.

She stopped, turned herself and smiled.

"You know me?" he demanded, and watched the smile drop from her filthy face. Without knowing it, she looked around her. Checking for exits. The alley behind the fish market was long and narrow, and more of the crowd were moving against them than going their way. She tried to shrug his hand from her shoulder, then let herself be gripped by the arm and dragged to a doorway.

"So," he said. "Do you?"

"Yes . . ." His expression must have scared her, because she began shaking her head almost immediately. "I mean no. I mistook you for someone else."

"How do you know me?"

She looked at him, debating her answer. In the end she told the truth, perhaps because she was scared by now. Of what he was. Of what he might do to her. Or of the fact he might know the truth already.

"I pulled you from the canal."

He stared at her.

"Don't you remember? I thought you were dead. And then you opened your eyes and looked right at me . . ." She blushed, the change to her skin unseeable in the darkness for anyone but him. Not that there was anyone wanting to see.

"*You* pulled me from the canal? The night I . . ."

Turning her face to the fragile moonlight, he stared into her eyes and watched her blush deepen. A salt mix of fear and arousal rose from her body. When he sniffed, her blush deepened again. Only his grip kept her in place.

Her breasts were tiny beneath her thin smock. Its hem showing more leg than was decent in a girl of her age. Tycho tried to imagine her naked, or half exposed with one breast visible and a trickle of blood beneath.

"You're hurting me."

No, if he was hurting her she'd know.

"Your name?" he demanded.

The girl hesitated, wincing as his fingers gripped tighter. "Rosalyn," she said. "And I'm sorry about your shackle . . . Josh sold it," she added. "I stole it, but Josh sold it. I'm sorry."

"What shackle?"

She really looked at him then.

Tycho knew there had been chains. They trapped him in darkness and held him fast. He had fleeting memories of those chains. Fire, then chains.

"The shackle that was hurting . . ."

Reaching his wrist, Rosalyn lifted it into the moonlight, gaping at the perfect skin where scars should be. The shock in her face was enough to make Tycho remember scars should be there too. He would have said so, but she had already dragged herself from his grip, and was pushing through the crowd, with her head down and her shoulders hunched, careful not to look back.

Tycho let her go.

17

The lamp was about to burn out when Giulietta heard footsteps beyond the sacristy door. Warmest room in the basilica or not, she was frozen and fed up with waiting. Her fingers were so cold her knuckles ached, and she'd been reduced to folding her arms over her chest and tucking her fingers into her armpits.

"Well. What did Uncle Alonzo say?"

She didn't expect the patriarch to have much success. He was allowed into San Marco at will and his unofficial palazzo, behind the basilica, shared a small garden with the ducal palace; but those were concessions Marco Polo offered for acceptance of his family's legitimacy. San Pietro di Castello, Venice's official cathedral, and Theodore's formal palace, were on the city's edge for a reason.

Mostly Uncle Alonzo got what he wanted. Unless, of course, Aunt Alexa objected strongly. If she did, she'd have stopped this already. That was the conclusion Giulietta had reached as she nursed her frozen fingers, shuffled her feet and wished she'd thought to visit the privy before this.

Here came Theodore to give her the bad news. Only the hooded figure in the doorway was not the patriarch. For a second, Giulietta believed that the silver-haired boy was back. But he wasn't this tall.

Other hooded figures appeared behind the first.

Wolf Brothers, she thought, feeling her guts lurch. Then she heard a clang as the man in the doorway turned and his dagger hilt hit the arch, and knew she was wrong. *Krieghund* went unarmoured. At least the ones that inhabited her nightmares did. When the man drew his dagger, Giulietta grabbed an altar cross, muttering an apology to God as she reversed it to use as a weapon.

The man laughed.

So she swung the cross hard, its base denting his vambrace as he threw up an arm to protect herself. The blow rang like a bell. His dagger landed on the sacristy floor.

"Laugh at that," she said.

When he retreated, Giulietta saw his face in the lamplight. A hooked nose, a sharp beard and a smile so cruel she shivered. "You burnt our ship," he said over loudly. "So now we kill you. Or you come with us . . ."

A man behind raised a crossbow.

"First," she said. "I must replace this."

Replacing the silver cross, Giulietta lifted the chalice from where it rested on the vestment chest, kissed it as if obeying some obscure rite and put the chalice carefully on the altar beside the cross. As she did, she palmed the wedding ring it contained.

"You're sure she's the right one?"

Grabbing her, their leader wrapped his fingers in her hair, and yanked back her head to take a better look. She would have tripped if his grip hadn't kept her upright. She found herself staring at a man with a golden earring.

"Oh yes," he said. "This is her."

Oars slapped against water and Lady Giulietta felt the boat rock as it drew away from a jetty. A man spoke once, his words guttural and only half heard through the darkness of the rug wrapped around her. All she could hear after this was the creaking of the boat which stole her away.

Later she realised her hand was still clenched. Pins and needles stabbed it, but clutching her fingers confirmed something she hadn't dared hope. She still had the ring she'd grabbed from the altar.

Uncle Alonzo might have spent his life demanding demons take her. But he'd come after the sacred ring, Giulietta had no doubt of that. Without it, how could Marco marry the sea?

18

"*Well?*" The Regent's fury could be heard through the door of the Sala Scarlatti. In fact it could be heard down the corridor outside. And since the corridor was open to the courtyard, it could be heard by the stair guards, servants in the kitchen and a cat crossing snow-smattered flagstones in the courtyard.

Only the cat reacted, twitching in irritation. The guards and kitchen servants knew better. They heard nothing and saw nothing. "*Well?*" Prince Alonzo's voice was quieter this time. Hardly more than a bellow.

"My lord . . . We are searching."

"Search harder."

Captain Roderigo withdrew, risking a sigh as the door shut behind him. It could have gone worse. He'd walked out with his life. Something that had been by no means certain when he walked in. He would issue orders that his men should search ships faster. It would make little difference. They were searching as hard and as fast as they could.

In San Nicolo and Castello, the Watch swept through parishes that had hardly been policed in fifty years. Rookeries scattered, child brothels shut their doors, hazard dens threw loaded dice into canals. The frenzy lasted until the beggar kings, panders and den owners realised they weren't the target.

The Watch were both frenzied and tight-lipped. The whole city, from lowest to highest, knew they searched for something. Only a handful knew what. Some imagined the Ten had news of the missing glass-blower. Others insisted a philosopher's stone had been hidden in the city. A monk caused a riot by announcing Dr Crow had disappeared, having spent the city's treasure trying to create an elixir of life. Cooler heads suggested the Watch hunted a spy.

Many wondered why the Watch hunted where it did. In the foreign sections of the city. Among the Mamluks, the Seljuks, the Moors and the Jews. Among those who kept their women's faces covered, and their mothers, sisters and daughters locked behind doors. Captain Roderigo could have told them. But he kept his secrets, and hoped this would be enough to let him keep his life.

"We should have moved them . . ."

Antonio Cove was a black beetle. A small, old and hunch-backed one. If dung beetles became human this was how they would look. In his defence, the count was rich, and knew where most of the bodies were buried, having helped Duke Marco III, and lately Prince Alonzo, bury many of them himself. He was the oldest member of the Council of Ten, who controlled Venice under the duke. As such, his opinions had to be respected. No matter how hard that sometimes proved.

"Moved whom?" Alonzo asked.

"The Jews. The Schiavoni. The Mamluks. The leather-boiling workshops. Those stinking urine pits their tanners use. Why don't we just banish them all to the mainland? We could . . ."

"*Count.*"

The man stopped talking.

"We have more important things to discuss."

"Yes," said Duchess Alexa. "We have. Explain again why my niece Giulietta was hiding in the basilica. While you met the patriarch here? And how you came to escort Archbishop Theodore back to his palace in San Pietro with a troop of your own guard? I'm sure my son would love to know."

Duke Marco IV, theoretical head of the inner council, looked more interested in his fingernails.

"It's a spiritual matter," the Regent said.

"Which is why Theodore has taken to his bed?"

"He's old. The shock of hearing about Giulietta." Prince Alonzo looked thoughtful. "I wouldn't be surprised if it kills him. We should be concentrating on getting her back."

"First we need to know who stole her."

"Indeed," said Alonzo. "I was going to ask you if you had an opinion on that." He held Duchess Alexa's gaze.

"The Abrahams," Count Cove's voice was bitter. "Who else? I dread to think what those fiends . . ."

Foam flecked the corners of his mouth.

"I doubt it," Duchess Alexa said. "This is one of the few cities where they're allowed to live in peace. Why foul their own nest? There has to be a better answer. Remember what Marco always said?"

Prince Alonzo's scowl showed what he thought of dragging his brother into this. Since this was who she meant. No one was about to start quoting the thumb-sucking fool kicking his heels in her late husband's place.

"No doubt you'll tell us."

"*Who gains?*" Duchess Alexa said calmly. "That was always Marco's question after an attack or murder. "Who gains from this?"

"No one," the beetle said triumphantly. "That's why it has to be . . ." A hard knock at the door stopped Count Cove before Alexa had to.

Kneeling to the duke, Roderigo bowed to Prince Alonzo and Alexa, and nodded to the rest, his apology for interrupting their meeting. His face was pale beneath his curling hair. He had trouble meeting anyone's eyes.

Marco IV, Duke of Venice, stopped kicking his feet. A beautiful smile spread across his face. "Y-y-you've found my butterfly?"

"No, your highness."

Everyone was so shocked Marco had spoken, they almost forgot to listen to Roderigo's answer. "But we found this." Producing a dagger from under his cloak, he placed it carefully at the duke's feet.

As guards hurried forward, Alexa waved them back.

"You know the law," Prince Alonzo said. "No weapons in this chamber."

"Yes, sir. I thought . . ."

Duchess Alexa was out of her chair, the others standing as she rose. Dropping to a crouch she flicked back her veil to examine the weapon. "Mamluk," she said. "Maybe Seljuk or Moorish. Where was this found?"

"Below the Riva degli Schiavoni."

She waited for him to explain the significance.

"If Lady Giulietta's abductors headed north, through the patriarch's garden, then chose Zalizzada San Provolo, they would have been able to cut south and reach the Riva without raising suspicion. At that time of night . . ." Everyone knew. At that time of night the Riva would have been filled with drunken crews from ships anchored in the lagoon.

"Anything else?" Alexa asked.

"An unflagged ship slipped through the sandbanks before dawn. Its oarsmen rowing against the tide."

"Galley slaves, you mean," Alonzo said crossly.

Serenissima's galleys used freemen. The Mamluks and Moors, Byzantines, Cypriots and Genoese used slaves. Some Venetians captured at sea served the Barbary pirates. But they were few.

Marco III had extracted such revenge for attacks on his fleets that fewer Venetians now languished under the whip than ever before.

"How could you let this happen?"

A question on which Roderigo's life hung.

Although Roderigo knew it was already lost if anyone discovered what had really happened out on the lagoon the night the Mamluk ship burnt. A Mamluk princess killed. Now a Millioni princess abducted in revenge. A new ship slipping away at night. Roderigo needed to avoid laying these strands at Duke Marco's kicking feet. Only to have Prince Alonzo tie them neatly into a knot.

"You saw this ship leave yourself?" Duchess Alexa sounded acid.

"No, my lady. I was told."

"What nationality?"

"We don't know." Roderigo swallowed.

"Why not?" the Regent demanded. "What's the point of a Dogana chief who doesn't register vessels as they arrive in our lagoon?"

"My lord, there are five hundred ships out there. It often takes us more than a day to give them a place in the quarantine line."

"I'm not interested in excuses."

"We can deal with details later." Duchess Alexa was firm. "If Captain Roderigo has been lax he will be fined. If his men have failed they will be flogged. If treason is involved people will die. That is not the issue. Assume the Mamluks took Giulietta. Now ask, *why?*"

"W-w-why why?" Duke Marco asked. "Even, w-why why why?"

"Because," his mother said patiently. "If we don't know *why* they've taken her. How will we know what they want to give her back?"

"She's nice. Perhaps they'll keep her."

"Does he have to be here?" Prince Alonzo hissed.

"Without him there is no Council."

"Enter," the duke shouted. "Sweet bird."

Prince Alonzo and the duchess were still glaring when a guard suddenly knocked and the door was thrown open. In bustled a soft-faced man in scarlet, dragging a dark-haired girl behind him. She dressed as one might for walking. Since she was plump, pink and healthy – and he was old – she obviously allowed herself to be dragged. Her embarrassed yet defiant expression suggested to Duchess Alexa that this was her father. She had some experience in such matters.

"Lord Bribanzo . . . ?"

The old man let go long enough to bow, turning back as if expecting his captive to be sprinting for the door. "I'm sorry to be late." He hesitated. "I have family problems of my own. Of course, if now is an inopportune time . . ."

The smile Prince Alonzo fixed into place belonged to a man who had borrowed fifty thousand gold ducats from Lord Bribanzo and had yet to repay them. "For you, we always have time."

"And this is your daughter?" Alexa said.

"It is, my lady."

Yes. She rather thought it was.

"She's joined our Council without my being told?"

There was an edge to the duchess's question. Even a man as distracted as Bribanzo understood that. "No, my lady. Of course not . . ."

"But you consider her a matter for the Ten?"

Being a matter for the Council was two-edged. They were the law in Venice, and in the city's fiefs on the mainland and in her colonies beyond. They found in your favour. Or they found against you. There was no appeal.

"I have been wronged," Bribanzo said.

"An unwelcome suitor, perhaps?"

"*That's one way to put it . . .*" Catching his temper, Bribanzo spread his hands apologetically. "This has political implications for the city, my lady. I've been in Milan, with Prince Alonzo's permission."

Have you now?

Alexa scowled "The Duke of Milan is our enemy."

"Alliances change." said Alonzo. "Milan needs access to the Adriatic. We could use an ally in the north. The ill will between our cities makes little sense. To me it never has." This was as close as he'd come to outright criticism of his late brother's policies.

"So you approved Lord Bribanzo's journey?"

"We gain an ally and lose an enemy. In Desdaio, Milan gains a duchess. A Venetian-born duchess," Alonzo stressed. "Whose father is a member of the Ten."

And Duke Gian Maria Visconti gains Desdaio's dowry?

Nothing else would persuade Milan's new duke to agree. Gian Maria had just fought a ruinously expensive war. So Bribanzo's gold would be welcome. His daughter's links to Venice less so.

"Months of negotiation," Bribanzo protested. "Weeks on the finer points." He meant how much Gian Maria wanted for making Desdaio a duchess. "All wasted unless we can hush this up."

"Hush what up?" asked Alexa.

"A heathen has ruined her. Stolen the flower of my pride and . . ." Bribanzo stopped, unable to finish.

"Wronged her? Or wronged you?"

The young woman was staring at the floor, blushing to the roots of her curling chestnut hair. She was pretty in a lush way. Breasts young men would like, full and firm. Wide hips and a soft stomach. Alexa had no doubt her bottom wiggled as she walked.

"They are betrothed," her father said furiously.

The duchess could see how that might upset him. Lord Bribanzo's strongroom was apparently so stuffed with gold ducats that his palace had needed new foundations. As well gold didn't tarnish in salt water. Since Ca' Bribanzo was as prone to flooding as the next house.

"Gian Maria Visconti was your idea?"

"Or Cosimo de' Medici. He'd do."

Someone snorted and Bribanzo's chin went up. He was unapologetic about his ambition. How had Cosimo's father secured Florence if not by being rich and ruthless?

"You don't think Venice has young men to offer?"

Lord Bribanzo knew he'd strayed on to treacherous ground. This time he took longer to answer, and his voice was calmer when he did. "My lady, many worthy Venetians have wished for a union. Any one of them would have been preferable to this . . . Mamluk."

"*He's not a Mamluk.*" These were the first words Lady Desdaio uttered. "And I'm not ruined . . ."

"What is he then?" Alonzo asked.

She dropped the Regent a curtsy. "A Moor, my lord."

Alonzo snorted. "Not much difference. They're all more trouble than is wise. It's time we reminded the heathens of our power. Venice is a great city. A kind city. A good city . . ." He glanced round, checking he had the court's attention. Bribanzo and Count Cove were nodding. Even the guards at the door looked attentive. Despite tradition demanding they hear nothing. "But we don't want our kindness mistaken for weakness." Opening her mouth to refute him, Alexa decided not to bother. She'd heard it all before.

"You'll punish him?"

Lord Bribanzo wanted more than his daughter back. He wanted his pound of flesh for the insult to his ambitions. He wanted a warning issued to anyone else who thought they could trick their way to his fortune. "A public flogging at the least?"

"Guards," Alonzo said. "Fetch this man!"

"My lord . . ." Bribanzo was meant to look grateful not embarrassed by this gesture of support from the Regent. "I've already sent for him."

The Regent considered this. Lord Bribanzo was within his rights. Any member of the Ten could demand the attention of anyone in the city.

"Then we wait," Alonzo said.

The grounding of spears on marble outside the chamber announced that guards had crossed their halberds, barring entrance to the prisoner and his escort.

Alexa heard one demand their business.

The answer had metal creaking, as a guard turned the huge handle of the council chamber door. That was when Alexa realised her son was grinning. Sprawled like a skinny black spider across his throne, Marco had one leg dangling over its gilded arm, his shoulder twisted at an ugly angle, and was grinning fit to burst.

When his mother looked worried, he winked.

"Marco . . . ?"

The duke nodded towards the door.

The old man entering wore a Moorish gown, a turban round his head, and turned-up leather slippers. A silver sheath jutted from his belt, but its blade was gone, removed on his arrest. His beard was dyed, although grey flecked his temples.

"*Atilo* . . ."

The duchess was on her feet before common sense kicked in. Sitting, she gripped her chair.

Prince Alonzo smiled.

"You knew about this?" she asked angrily.

"About what?" Turning to Bribanzo, he said, "Are you saying this is the villain responsible . . . ?"

Atilo stepped forward.

"Later," Prince Alonzo snapped. "You will be told when to speak. I am addressing Lord Bribanzo. Well?"

"It is, excellence."

"Then the betrothal is void. You cannot have a betrothal where marriage is banned. Suitable candidates for Lady Desdaio's hand

111

include foreign princes and families in the Golden Book. Lord Atilo is neither a recognised prince nor in the Book. We do not grant permission."

By *we* he meant the Ten. At least, Alexa hoped he did.

"However," Alonzo added. "My brother, the late duke, had faith in this man's abilities. Because of that he will be spared public punishment."

Lord Bribanzo scowled. A quick scowl, speedily swallowed. "No punishment at all, my lord?"

"He has done my city some small favours."

Your city? Small favours?

The duchess was glad to have a veil to hide her anger.

Atilo had won a dozen battles. Never mind the services he rendered as head of the Assassini. And hadn't he sacrificed almost every one of his men to keep Giulietta out of the hands of the Wolf Brothers? What more did Alonzo want?

Alexa wished she'd followed her instincts the morning the late duke died, and had Alonzo killed immediately. If only her husband hadn't made her promise to let him live. Marco III had been known as the Just and the Wise. In this, she doubted both his justice and wisdom.

"I *am* right," Alonzo was saying. "Your name isn't in the Book?"

"No, my lord." Atilo shook his head, his face tightening behind his beard.

"Then this matter is done. Lord Bribanzo may take his daughter. And you can be grateful for our mercy. Now let the Ten consider more important business."

"You can't make me."

Desdaio's protest echoed off wood-panelled walls. Both her father, and Atilo, moved to comfort her and stopped, glaring at each other. While Desdaio stood uncomforted between them, her shoulders shaking with sobs.

Little idiot, Alexa thought.

But a buxom little idiot. Of the kind Venetians find irresistible, burning themselves like moths against her need. Looking into the eyes of her late husband's favourite, the duchess saw real pain. Atilo il Mauros, the man who turned back German cavalry on the marshes of the Veneto, had fallen for the ephemeral charms of a woman a third his age.

Duchess Alexa sighed.

Throwing herself at the feet of Duke Marco's throne, Desdaio gripped its carved legs as if guards were already trying to drag her free. "*Please*," she begged. "*Help me.*"

The duke kicked his heel hard. He glared at his mother. He glared at Atilo. He glared at a spare chair. An empty, gilded chair. Sitting back, he rammed his thumb into his mouth, scratched his crotch openly and scrunched his eyes.

"I think . . ." Alonzo began to say.

But the duchess was standing. Moving swiftly, she stopped opposite Atilo as the court pushed back their chairs, hurrying to stand in their turn. Pausing just long enough to heighten their expectations, she clapped Atilo on the shoulder.

"There is my choice," she said loudly. "My husband's old adviser, this city's faithful servant for the Tenth Chair."

Utter silence filled the room.

"Alexa . . ." Prince Alonzo hesitated. Obviously choosing his words with care. "This is not wise. You know there are reasons why . . ."

"It's my turn."

"No," said Bribanzo. His fleshy face red with the effort of controlling his temper. "You can't."

"My lord . . ." Alexa's voice was icy. And Bribanzo went stock still. He might only be five years older than Atilo, but there the likeness ended. Lord Bribanzo was a coward, albeit an ambitious one.

"You presume to tell me what I may do?"

After Bribanzo had grovelled, Alexa glared round the room, daring anyone else to disagree and, for a second, her gaze halted at the sight of her son smiling sweetly. She could swear he blew Desdaio a kiss.

"Do you accept the chair?" Alexa asked Atilo.

"My lady . . ."

"*Do you?*"

Sinking to his knees, Atilo il Mauros kissed the ring her husband had placed on her finger on their wedding day years earlier. "As always, I am yours to command." Amending this, he said. "As the duke, the Regent and you command."

"Delighted to hear it," Alonzo said.

Turning to a scribe, Alexa said. "Have Lord Atilo's name entered in the Golden Book immediately. He will lead the hunt for my niece."

"Roderigo will accompany him." Prince Alonzo's voice was firm.

To Bribanzo, the duchess said, "Make your peace. My niece must be found and this seat needs filling. Atilo is a trusted servant. As are you." The compliment sounded hollow even to her.

It would help if she could put warmth in it. Give Bribanzo a smile he could interpret as the promise of her future favour. Unfortunately, she loathed the man. Alexa liked her favourites lean and hungry.

"My daughter?"

"Milan will not take her now," Alexa said flatly. "As for other suitors . . ." If they have any sense, she thought, they'll accept defeat to avoid upsetting the Ten's newest member; a man dangerous in ways most didn't know.

An ignorance that came close to bliss.

"You may g-g-go," the duke said. He'd taken his thumb out of his mouth and was pointing at Bribanzo. "N-n-now."

At the door, Lord Bribanzo turned, and his words were heard by those in the chamber, and by those in the corridor outside. By nightfall, they were known everywhere in the city. A declaration of hatred for Atilo, although he directed his venom at his daughter.

"You, I disown."

His voice was the hiss of a snake. His eyes flat, beyond fury, in a state where he would kill her without regret. "You were never mine. It is not that you died for me this day. You were never born."

19

News of Bribanzo's feud with Atilo was overshadowed by rumours that the Mamluks had abducted Lady Giulietta il Millioni to prevent her marrying King Janus, because an alliance with Cyprus would have given Venice the mouth of the Nile. Rumours that grew from abducting, to abducting and probably raping, and then to abducting undoubtedly, raping and probably murdering, as days turned into weeks.

The Cypriot ambassador said goodbye.

Regretful but implacable, Sir Richard Glanville boarded his ship and hoisted his king's colours, and the colours of his Priory, and slipped through the sandbanks at the mouth of the lagoon into the Adriatic beyond.

His was the only vessel allowed to leave.

The ship that had sneaked from the lagoon was chased, stopped and boarded. It turned out to be Mamluk, but Lady Giulietta was not aboard. And its crew swore they had not put ashore since leaving Venice. Their captain died under questioning, still protesting he knew nothing about an abduction. He was a simple smuggler.

Trade ceased on the lagoon for the first time since Marco the

Cruel overthrew the Rebel Republic fifty years earlier. Gulls still swept the waves, cormorants dived from posts holding fishing nets. They were the only movement. Food piled up on the mainland. Night soil was not collected. *Cittadini* made deputations citing loss of profits. Leaving shocked by Prince Alonzo's contempt for their worries.

The city's fishing nets, as famous as San Marco itself, hung from crossed poles, dry and unused. The small boats that should have collected the dawn catch remained beached on Venice's mudflats. Ships at anchor remained there. Those waiting to enter stayed beyond the lagoon or found another port. Salt barges were refused leave to set out for the mainland. New barges, loaded with dried fish, salted beef and wizened fruit stored the previous summers remained on their mainland moorings, their produce slowly rotting.

"You must show yourself," Duchess Alexa told the Regent. "Let the people see you. Reassure them."

"You show yourself."

"I'm in mourning."

"It's three years," he said crossly. "Enough of the hiding in darkened rooms and refusing to appear in public. Take Marco and let the city see you."

"Impossible," the duchess said. "You know . . ."

"He can't be let out in public?"

"*Alonzo* . . ."

"It's the truth. And, speaking of truth, are you behind this?"

"Behind what?"

"Giulietta's abduction?"

"Why would I do that?"

"*Answer me.*"

"If you remember," Alexa said tightly. "I suggested her marriage to Janus. We need Cyprus to secure our trade routes. In fact, our future wealth depends on it. You seem over-friendly with the sultan's ambassador. Should I be asking you the same?"

"Believe me, that's changing.."

Stamping to the balcony, Alonzo glared through fretted shutters at a crowd on the Molo, the palace's water terrace. Beyond them, to his left, the Riva degli Schiavoni was equally thronged. Most of those gathering were Arsenalotti. "Venice needs a duke who can control it," he said.

"You, you mean?"

"It can't be you."

"Because I'm a woman?"

"And a Mongol. You know how they feel about that."

The deal Marco Polo had struck with Kublai Khan to import goods from China made the city richer than ever before. Gratitude from the richer merchants had secured Marco the throne. The doge became a duke in power as well as name. The Council became the duke's servant and not his master.

The price Kublai extracted was twofold. A *fontego di khan* near the Rialto from which to trade. And a guarantee that Khanic law would apply to all Mongols in Venice, whatever their crime and wherever that crime was committed. Marco III's marriage had sweetened the deal on both sides. But Marco's grip had been iron for all he claimed it velvet.

"They need a real duke," Alonzo said.

"They have one."

"Whom they see once a year. Heavily sedated. Painted white like some whore, drugged with opium, with his hands twitching like broken wings."

"My son will never abdicate."

"You mean," Alonzo said, "you will never let him . . ."

It was what his niece's absence represented, not the abduction itself, which drove the Regent to fury. All his plans, all his brilliance, simply wasted. He wouldn't put it past the little bitch to get abducted on purpose . . .

20

Rolling over, Giulietta scooped up a blanket and stood. Only to sit back down when the little room began to spin. Hunger hollowed her guts. It stopped her sleeping. Today she would make herself eat.

A fire already burnt in her grate, a large bowl of warm water stood on a stand, ready for her to wash her face. A smaller bowl would be waiting on the table at breakfast so she could wash her hands. As one had been waiting on the table at supper. This was not what she expected captivity to be like.

The first day she'd refused help dressing.

But the old woman in the doorway looked so forlorn that yesterday Giulietta relented and let her help a little. Of course, Giulietta still only had the one dress. And that now looked tired, although still cleaner than it had that night in the basilica when she *got blood on it*.

That barely came close to describing what happened when the strange grey-haired boy dropped from the basilica ceiling and found her half naked. Perhaps, she thought, he would have let her kill herself if he'd known what Uncle Alonzo intended to do to her.

Feeling her eyes fill, Giulietta rubbed them angrily.

The chamber in the Ca' Ducale had been well named. What they did to her in her in the Sala della Tortura *was* torture. The memory of having her knees forced apart filled her with helplessness. She couldn't bear to think about it and she didn't know how to stop herself thinking about it. Every time she recalled the violation she felt sick. And Dr Crow's magic had worked; she couldn't even talk to herself about it.

At least not aloud.

But since the old woman who looked after her now was deaf as well as dumb it made no real difference. Her husband was the same. It was hard to put an age on them. To Giulietta everyone older than her looked old.

The old woman dried Giulietta's tears carefully, washed her face with a damp cloth and helped her dress, tying the ribbons with shaking hands. Giulietta did the buttons herself. Otherwise the food would be cold.

Her breakfast today was fresh bread, cheese, a wizened apple, a slice of warm sweetmeat tart, and hot wine with nutmeg to keep out the chill. Her wine tasted heavily watered. To the old couple she was obviously a child. The apple was already cut and the pie sliced. Knives had not been laid today.

"I'd like a walk," Giulietta said.

The man looked at the woman, who was the one who made all the decisions. The woman tipped her head to one side, considering. So Giulietta went to stand directly in front of her, and said, "please".

Both of them could read her lips, which told her they understood Italian. She'd already decided they'd once been able to speak or hear, or both. That made her wonder who they were. She was a prisoner. There was little doubt about that.

A prisoner in a warm, sweetly decorated prison in the middle of . . .

And that was where Lady Giulietta's knowledge fell apart.

Obviously, she was somewhere. Since she had yet to go outside, and the shutters were locked, and the skylight showed only cloud, how could she escape if she didn't know what she was escaping from?

"Please," she said. "Let me take a walk."

Maybe it was the *please* that did it.

They must have known it was not a word to drop easily from the lips of a Millioni princess. Because the old man looked at the old woman and something passed in the silence between them. The woman nodded, and the old man fetched a coat of purest white fur. And this puzzled Lady Giulietta more than ever. Because a coat that rare must be priceless.

All she'd seen of her prison was her bedroom and the little room where they ate. But then the woman reached into her pocket for a key, glanced at the old man for reassurance and unlocked the world beyond.

The small hall was so full of furniture Giulietta had to turn sideways to slide between a wooden chair and a chest on her way to the door. Unhooking a heavy key from a nail, the man unlocked the front door and stepped back.

She was imprisoned in a tiny temple.

A tiny wooden temple surrounded by a walled garden run to seed, snow-flecked and stripped bare by winter. Half the trees seemed desolate, the other half looked dead. Giulietta wasn't sure she recognised any of them. The wall enclosing this desolation was higher than she was. Much higher.

"Where am I?"

The old man looked at her.

"Tell me." Since he was dumb, Lady Giulietta wasn't sure how she expected him to answer. Then she noticed him glance towards a post and she wondered if this was her answer. Two horsetails hung from a pole jammed into the snow. Since the silver decorating the pole was black she guessed it had been there for a while. The sky looked familiar and the air smelt as salt as it should.

"Am I still in Venice?"

When the old man turned away, she walked round to the other side of him and he sighed. Giulietta decided a straight question might be better.

"I *am* in Venice, aren't I?"

The old man shook his head, then nodded.

"What's that meant to mean?" she demanded. His smile was kind, but no more use than his conflicting shake and nod. So she headed towards the wall, hearing him hurry to keep up. There was a single door. Needless to say it was locked.

"Open this for me."

The old man shook his head.

"Please," Giulietta said. "Let me see what's on the other side."

To escape she needed to know exactly where she was. And for that she needed him to open the gate. But he simply shook his head when she asked. Lady Giulietta quickly realised he could shake his head as often as she could ask. It made no difference if she begged, wheedled or commanded as a Millioni princess. He wasn't prepared to unlock the gate.

"Has someone ordered you not to open it?"

The old man nodded.

"Who ordered you?" she demanded.

It seemed he could shake his head equally well for every name she offered. Although whether that was because she suggested the wrong names or he had no intention of telling her, she had no way of knowing. So her day dragged to an end, with her feeling scarily like she was trapped in a fairy tale. One of those her mother had told her when her mother was alive. After an early supper, Giulietta decided she needed another walk.

"Please," she said.

The old man looked at the old woman, who shook her head.

"It will help me sleep later," Giulietta persisted. "You want me to be able to sleep don't you?"

At the old woman's sigh, the old man smiled. He collected

the key from the wall by the door, while the woman fetched the fur coat. Once they had her safely wrapped, the old man opened the door to let in the darkness.

And a demon entered with it.

21

The Regent's temper when he showed himself to the people by walking the streets at dusk was worse than ever. Fierce enough for Roderigo to fear still for his own future. Prince Alonzo held Roderigo responsible for the delay in finding Giulietta. If he'd done his job properly, the unflagged Mamluk vessel would never have been allowed to leave port. Days would not have been wasted chasing it. The real search for Giulietta could have begun earlier. How he squared this with the fact that the Watch had turned the poor parishes of the city upside down was a mystery.

The mood in the taverns was ugly. The Nicoletti claimed the Castellani helped Mamluks carry out Lady Giulietta's abduction. The Castellani declared they would die to the last man before letting Nicoletti scum accuse them of treason.

Unofficial chains had gone up across canal mouths to lock parishes off from each other. Barricades were being erected. Bricks being prised from *campi* floors as street gangs began to stockpile ammunition.

"So," the Regent said. "How would you suggest we handle this situation?"

"Call out the Watch, my lord."

"There are going to be riots, Roderigo. Do you consider the watch is sufficient?" Prince Alonzo looked from under lowered brows. "That was a question, Captain. Do you think the Watch will be sufficient?"

"No, sir."

"The Watch, plus your men?"

The Dogana guard were few in number. But well-armed, well-disciplined and regarded with a certain fear by the city's poor. They'd provide a backbone, but Roderigo couldn't pretend their spine wouldn't be broken eventually. Even adding the palace guard to the mix would be insufficient. And Roderigo doubted the Regent was prepared to leave Ca' Ducale undefended anyway.

"You could hire mercenaries, my lord."

"They cost, Roderigo. And finding good ones takes time."

"What do we do, my lord?" It turned out to be the right question. Prince Alonzo's shoulders straightened and he glowered, as if he was already on a battlefield viewing enemy deployments.

"We give them an act of utter brutality."

"*My lord . . . ?*"

The parishes had long memories, and memories festered into open wounds in this city in a very Venetian way. Money might keep the *cittadini* sweet. And the Castellani hatred of the Nicoletti, and the Nicoletti's hatred of everyone else, keep the parishes of the poor at each other's throats. But an act of brutality by the Millioni would be remembered. More than one patrician had died for the sins of his ancestors.

"Not the parishes, you idiot."

Alonzo's father, grandfather, one brother and his sister had fallen to the dagger. Both Republics began and ended with murder. In Rome, they joked that assassins were more common in Venice than canals. The Regent obviously had no desire to inspire a third republic. What little remained of his good temper was gone.

"Have you searched the Fontego dei Mamluk?"

"Yesterday, my lord."

125

"We'll do it again. Properly this time."

Roderigo bowed, without bothering to say it was searched properly last time. If Prince Alonzo wanted the Mamluk warehouses re-searched that was his business.

Near la Volta, on the left bank of the Grand Canal, dangerously far into Nicoletti territory, they found an armed band of Castellani mixed with Arsenalotti. "You," Prince Alonzo said. "With me."

The mob fell in, nudging one another when they realised who the barrel-chested man in the breastplate was. Some carried swords, others daggers, one had a shipwright's adze. When they met a gang of Nicoletti, battle was averted. The black caps being stunned to a sullen truce by the Regent's presence.

There was a growing sense of excitement. No one knew what was going to happen. But everybody knew that something was. And Roderigo began to realise it was more than a simple search Alonzo had in mind for the Mamluk *fontego*. His suspicion proved right when they stopped in front of the building.

"Break down its door," the Regent ordered.

Half the black-clad Nicoletti rushed round to the *fontego*'s *porta d'acqua* to make sure nobody escaped via one of the side canals. The red-capped Arsenalotti fanned out around Alonzo. If the Regent wanted to be seen, it was working. As a mason with a sledgehammer stepped up to the land door, the street behind began filling with spectators.

"Shouldn't we announce ourselves, my lord?"

"If the sultan's subjects do not want to be a friend to me, then they will find I am not a friend to them, or their master. If they wanted to welcome me, Roderigo," the Regent said, "those doors would already be open."

Only, thought Roderigo, *if they want to die.*

The Mamluk merchants had probably hoped they could remain unobtrusive until the city's temper cooled. It had taken courage to open their *fontego* to Roderigo's guard yesterday. But they knew

Roderigo and had dealings with the Dogana. The arrival of Prince Alonzo with a crowd meant only one thing.

Lady Giulietta had not been found.

Now the mob wanted revenge. Personally, Roderigo doubted the Mamluks had done it. The sultan might be ruthless – he'd strangled his elder and younger brothers, after all – but everyone said he was a brilliant tactician. Surely a strategist of his ability would be ashamed of such a clumsy move? What could he gain from making an open enemy of the Venetians?

The Sultan's *fondak* was huge. Built around three sides of a central courtyard, it had one side open to the Grand Canal, where a small *riva* let Mamluk barges unload with trade goods for selling. Some of the mob – Nicoletti, probably – were already launching luggers. They claimed they wanted to prevent the barges escaping. It was more likely they intended to loot them later.

Faced with Istrian stone, the *fontego*'s endless rounded arches lightened its façade. Most large buildings in Venice used colonnades to lighten their weight. Otherwise the wooden pilings of their foundations simply sunk into the mud.

The secrets of such work were jealously guarded and patricians and *cittadini* who ignored advice from the Masons' Guild found themselves owners of expensive piles of rubble. It was a huge man in a mason's leather apron who stepped up to the iron-bound door of the *fontego* and raised a sledgehammer.

Prince Alonzo nodded at Roderigo, who nodded at his sergeant. Leather and horn scales hid Temujin's half-healed shoulder. His pain was obvious, however, in the sweat beading his forehead. "Do it," he ordered.

Spitting, to make clear what he thought of being bossed around by someone half Mongol, the mason pounded his hammer into the stone arch, about three-quarters of the way up.

"Attack the door," Temujin growled.

"No," Roderigo muttered. "He knows what he's doing."

The third blow cracked stone.

So the mason pounded again and the block shattered, leaving an iron bolt jutting from broken stone. It looked almost as new as the day it was fitted. A crack of his hammer drove the bolt inwards, creating a gap at the edge of a huge door.

"Arrows ready."

At Temujin's order, eight Dogana guard ratcheted back their crossbows and slid quarrels into place. Without being told they fanned out, providing cover. Their weapons pointed slightly downwards.

"Now," said Roderigo. "He'll break the lock."

As if to prove him right, the mason swung his hammer into the key plate. Metal rang and the door rattled. A second blow buckled the iron plate and inside someone shouted a warning.

"Should have opened it earlier," Alonzo spat.

Around him the mob nodded, as if the prince might require their agreement. His voice sounded fired up with passion, fury and outrage at his niece's disappearance. His eyes, however, were ice. When he glanced at the captain, Roderigo looked away.

"Stay watchful," Roderigo hissed.

A moment later, Roderigo's sergeant relayed the order, his version centring on what he'd do to their daughters if they failed. When the mason swung his sledgehammer one final time, the lock broke free. For a second the door remained upright, supported on its remaining hinge, and then it toppled. Metal screaming as the hinge tore itself free.

The first arrow from inside hit the mason.

I'd do the same, Roderigo thought.

Dropping his hammer, the mason touched the arrow in disbelief, not daring to pull it from his throat. The Mamluks would die. Shooting the mason ensured it would be fast. At least, Roderigo hoped so. After the siege of Luca he'd seen what happened when angry men decided to kill slowly. That he'd been in the mob and the Lucans its victims made no difference in his dreams.

"Sack this place," Alonzo ordered.

His supporters didn't need telling twice. Swarming past the Regent, they charged the archway. At a nod from his captain, Temujin let them go. The first three through the arch stumbled back with arrows in their chests.

A single archer from the look of it.

Mamluk bows were half as long as English, made from layers of hardwood and horn. Their arrows had three flights and barbed points to make freeing them more dangerous than pushing them through.

"You want me to deal with their archer, boss?"

Roderigo shook his head. Let the crowd do it. That the Venetian mob pushed forward had little to do with courage. The weight of those at the back made it inevitable, whether the front wanted to advance or not.

"We keep the Regent safe."

Temujin nodded.

Not that Prince Alonzo faced much danger. A breastplate covered his chest, while a gorget protected his throat and a crested helm was crammed on to his skull. Vambraces protected his forearms. Across his shoulders hung his broadsword. A dagger sat at his hip. With his beard and armour he looked like a *condottiero*.

Intentional, no doubt.

Grabbing a fisherman's gaff, a squat man hefted it, found its balance and threw with the casual skill of an old soldier. His makeshift spear arcing above those ahead of him to hit its target. Temujin grunted his approval. "Now we go in!"

Since the Regent was freeing his sword and loosening his dagger it looked like the sergeant was right.

"Let me through," Alonzo growled.

One Castellani pushed back, until he glanced round and realised who his rival was. Grabbing the man's red scarf, the Regent tied it to his arm, grinning at the man's shock and the crowd's roar. *I'm like you*, Alonzo's expression said.

Apart from the palace, obviously. The Millioni millions. The fact the law was blind when those who angered the Regent disappeared.

"Boss . . . ?"

"Nothing," Roderigo said.

A merchant in a striped robe barred their way.

Behind him stood half a dozen Mamluk soldiers. The maximum a foreign *fontego* could keep to protect itself from thieves. Six for a foreign *fontego*. Eleven for a Venetian one. Thirteen for a patrician. The rule was clear and ruthlessly enforced.

"Planning to shoot me too?" Alonzo demanded.

"My lord . . ." The merchant bowed, decided his greeting wasn't reverential enough and adjusted it. "Your highness."

The hunger those words fired in the Regent's eyes was frightening. For a moment, Roderigo thought the Mamluk had bought himself life, maybe even freedom. His next words ruined it.

"Could your niece have run away?"

A growl of anger rolled through the mob as those in front carried his comment to those behind them. She was a Millioni princess, about to become a queen, how ignorant could the Mamluk be. Not ignorant, *insulting*.

The Regent dealt with the insult himself. Drawing his great sword, he stepped forward as the merchant began to plead for his life. The sword slashed down anyway.

"Now," Temujin ordered, and his troop cut down the Mamluk soldiers before they could begin to fight back. High above, Roderigo saw two boys manoeuvre a money chest on to a balcony's balustrade, their bodies foreshortened as they struggled to push it over the edge.

"*My lord . . .*"

Flinging himself forward, Roderigo shoulder-slammed the Regent so hard that Alonzo staggered, dropping his bloody sword. And then the flagstones exploded behind them. The chest landing where Alonzo had stood. As one, the mob began chasing the rolling coins across the hall floor, stuffing their pockets with silver dirham. The chest had been the heaviest object the boys could find.

"You saved my life," Alonzo said.

Perhaps Roderigo only imagined he sounded surprised. Although Roderigo was shocked himself, when the bear of a *condottiero* grabbed him, hugging him close.

"Name your reward," Alonzo said.

"My lord, about Lady Giulietta. That Mamluk vessel . . ."

"God's sake, man," the Regent said. "Ignore it." They were talking about different ships. "Your mansion is falling apart?"

"There's not a room that doesn't leak."

"Then it's settled. Two thousand ducats. Tell the treasury I order them to release that amount. What's your rank?"

"Armiger, my lord."

"I make you a baron. Subject to Marco's approval, obviously."

While the crowd scrabbled for dirham, and the Mamluk boys stood frozen on the balcony above, too scared to move, Roderigo bowed low. He bowed low to stop Prince Alonzo from seeing his face.

As Roderigo followed the Regent up the stairs, he considered the implications of accidentally choosing sides in the feud between Alonzo and Alexa. He now had money enough to mend his roof, and a title. One alone would improve his chances of marrying well. Two made it a certainty. Although Desdaio would always be beyond him. Roderigo hadn't intended to choose one faction over another, however. Something he doubted the duchess would believe.

The Fontego dei Mamluk had three levels. At ground level, cargo was unloaded, goods were stored and deals made. An area of hall behind them held booths selling spices and scarlet leather. The booths were kindling now.

The floor they approached had family rooms. A library, most

likely. But it was the floor above the mob wanted to reach. The kitchens were on the top floor, so oven smoke could escape through *fumaioli* to the sky. Here, too, valuables were kept, both living and non-living. The doe-eyed beauties of rumour.

So beautiful they had to be kept veiled like novice nuns, unable to stand temptation. It was this thought that carried Alonzo's followers up two flights of stairs. Behind them they left the Mamluk boys dead on their balcony.

"You cannot enter."

A fat man waddled towards them. He was bald, hairless and wearing scarlet silk pantaloons and a sleeveless jacket, embroidered with peacocks picked out in blue and silver thread. A gold ring hung from his ear.

"A eunuch," Temujin whispered.

Roderigo had worked that out for himself.

"My lords." Planting his feet apart, the eunuch tried to block Prince Alonzo's entrance to the harem. "This is not fitting. Please . . ."

He died. An arrow in his throat.

"Not ours, boss."

A Castellani had helped himself to a Mamluk hunting bow. Roderigo imagined the Regent knew he'd have to disarm the mob once this was over. But for the moment Prince Alonzo flattered them. "Help yourselves," he said.

Did he mean, help yourselves to the women? To the food in the kitchens? Or to the gold hidden in the strongrooms beyond? The crowd decided he meant all three.

Roderigo wondered if they realised Venice had just declared war.

22

"You got Mamluk blood?"

Tycho shook his head.

"Told you," Pietro said triumphantly. He swept straggles of black hair from his childish face, spreading the dirt more evenly. "They're killing Mamluks," he explained. "Rosalyn thought . . ."

He glanced across.

"Well, the City Watch want you. And a black girl with braided hair. So Rosalyn thought you must be Mamluk . . ."

"If he's not," said Rosalyn, "he must be a slave."

"That's it." Josh nodded. "Your master's important enough to use the Watch." He looked suddenly worried. "He's not Ten, is he?"

Rosalyn scrambled to her feet.

She bared her teeth when Tycho stopped her. Behind him, Pietro grabbed half a brick. "*You hurt my sister . . .*"

"I won't." Tycho put his fingers to Rosalyn's head and saw Josh's eyes narrow and his face harden at the sight.

"*I mean it,*" Pietro said.

Tycho nodded, but kept his fingers in place.

I can do this, he told himself. *If it can happen by accident, it can happen intentionally.* He let the question trickle through his body, feeling how it flowed from his fingers to her mind. The black girl she talked about was the Nubian he'd seen earlier. The Watch looked like thugs everywhere.

"Witchcraft," Rosalyn said, stepping back.

Pietro raised his brick and Josh reached for a dagger in his belt.

Tycho might have had to fight them, maybe kill one, but the moon stopped the fight before it began. Sliding from behind cloud, it lit the door of his ruined wooden warehouse. It also lit his face, although Tycho only realised this when Rosalyn's own softened and she shifted, almost unknowingly, to put herself between Josh and Tycho.

"Wait," she said.

They stood as they were. Pietro with his raised brick, Josh scowling and Tycho swaying on his feet. Rosalyn looked into the bleakness in his eyes. "Are you a slave?" she demanded. "Is that why they're hunting you?"

"I was," he admitted. "But that was before here."

"And I suppose your mother was a princess?" Josh said spitefully. "Your father was captured in battle? No doubt your grandfather lived in a palace." He rolled his eyes derisively. "Never met an escaped slave who didn't claim he was a prince."

Tycho wondered how many he'd talked to. And then, wondered how many escaped slaves there were in Venice. A dozen, a hundred, more? What happened when they were caught?

"Were you a prince?"

"*Rosalyn . . .*" Josh sounded exasperated.

"Just asking. *Did* you have a palace? *Was* your mother a princess?"

"My mother died when I was born. She was a slave before that. I don't know, maybe she was a princess before she was a slave. No one ever said. The woman who brought me up called her, *Lady . . .*"

Rosalyn tipped her head to one side. "Maybe that's the truth," she said. "Otherwise he'd say his palace was huge."

"And perhaps he's just being clever," Josh said flatly. "He looks clever. Maybe he's a Jew. His hair is strange enough."

"Jews aren't slaves."

Josh spat. "They should be."

Rosalyn flushed, her face darkened and she bit her lip, hugging herself. This only made her small breasts jut. And that only made Josh smirk. There was a tension and strangeness to the night. A chill wind holding scents that demanded Tycho find their origin even as they told Rosalyn to flee.

"You hungry?" she asked him.

Tycho shook his head.

"*Rosalyn.*"

"What?" The girl looked nervously at . . .

Who? Tycho wondered. *Her brother? Her lover?*

Strays, thrown together by chance? He looked more closely, seeing if he could guess which. Siblings, perhaps. There was a family likeness. Unless that was simply the hunger in their eyes and the dirt.

As if hearing his thought, Rosalyn said, "Josh is my boss. Pietro my brother. We're going to San Michele. You should come."

"It's an island," Pietro added.

"He knows that . . ."

"How would he?" Josh demanded. "He's foreign. He doesn't know anything." Jerking his head at Tycho, he said, "I say we leave him."

Tycho thought of telling them that crossing water made him feel sick. That even crossing bridges made him uneasy. But he didn't want them to know that. So he watched them go instead, seeing Josh snarl when Rosalyn looked back.

The sacking of the sultan's *fondak* lasted until daybreak. A stranger would have thought one house on a canal was attacked by all the others. That was wrong. The area inside the walls was

Mamluk. As foreign as France or Byzantium itself. Just easier to sack, with less distance to carry the spoils.

Screaming told Tycho he was near.

He could feel lightning in the air. Looking up, he expected thunderclouds, but found a sliver of moon that tugged at his mind.

Hunger was the missing fact of his life.

Around Tycho, Venetians slurped stolen pomegranates, licked their lips and looked satisfied. Beggars hunched over dried figs like misers over gold. Dogs fought for pastries looters had taken, half eaten and discarded as too strange for their tastes. It made Tycho certain something was missing in himself.

He could no longer distinguish flavours. Eating or not eating made little difference to his happiness. It didn't even seem necessary to keep him alive. And yet, he'd lied to Rosalyn about not being hungry. He had a hunger no food could fill. A hunger he dragged after him like a shadow, always half seen and oblique to the world in which he lived.

The dead were dead to him now. Either they'd abandoned him or he'd abandoned them. The empty city, below this one, he tried to avoid revisiting. It was too strange, too lonely, too much like him. The beasts roaming it terrified him. He was beyond being able to meet his fears in its distorting mirror.

The empty city called him, of course.

But not as fiercely as the women's screams from up ahead. He was almost at their source when a Nubian with silver-tipped braids stopped him. "So are you going to kiss me this time . . . ?" She smiled. "I didn't think so."

He flinched as she reached for him, scared of the silver thimbles glittering in the moonlight. "Don't reveal your weaknesses," she said. "Only your strengths. And if you don't yet know what those are, keep silent."

Tycho tried to say he was silence's closest friend, but she hadn't finished. "Change is painful," she told him. "But not to change is . . ."

"To die?"

"You don't have that option. The longer you fight against who you are the harder your transformation will be. Believe me," she said. "We are different enough to be alike." The closer she stood the more scents Tycho recognised. Sweat and shit and garlic and cloves, and something else.

The Nubian laughed softly. "What drives your hunger?"

"I don't know."

"Most boys want this." Slipping her hand under her skirt, she touched herself. Smearing her finger across his face, she laughed. "Trust you to be different."

"I'm not," Tycho lied.

"You want . . . *What?*" Looking up, she found the moon. "Not the Goddess exactly. Although your hunger grows as she does. But her blood tides are not the blood you need . . ." Her voice sounded as if it belonged to someone older. And there was a strangeness in her eyes that made him shiver.

"You will feed," she said.

"I've tried eating . . ."

Her slap snapped his head sideways. "Listen to me," she hissed. "Twice I've helped you now. Once kindly, this time not. When we meet again it will be as strangers. Understand me?"

Tycho didn't. "Where am I?"

"Here," she said. "As opposed to there. *Dust and ashes, dead and done with. Bjornvin spent what Bjornvin earned.* You will never go back. No one does. No one can. There is nothing to go back to. Go now, feed."

23

Had there not been snow, and had the *fontego* been built around a proper courtyard it might have held out for longer. But the Canalasso side made it vulnerable to attack from water as well as land. And three luggers filled with Castellani bobbed offshore to make certain no Mamluk barges tried to escape. The barges were burning, and the screams from inside said their crews burnt too. The snows simply meant no one watching this happen worried about accidental fires starting elsewhere, since the embers from the barges landed in the water or sizzled out on slush.

The building itself was intact. Sacked and savaged, shit-smeared and pissed in, but still standing and unburnt. It would be sold by the city to the highest bidder and the buyer could hire men to clean up what this night had done.

In the central courtyard, overlooked by the colonnades of its three sides, a young woman was backlit by burning barges. She looked to Tycho the same age as the girl in the basilica, but there the likeness ended. This girl had dark skin, and hair cut from the night, perfectly black and waterfall straight. Where the earlier girl had been thin this one was not. Her hips were full, her breasts fuller. The anger in her eyes was as fierce as any Tycho had seen.

"*Little bitch*," a man said. Wiping spittle from his cheek, he flicked it to the ground. "Have your men hold her, Roderigo. And make sure they bend her right over. We'll see how she likes this."

Two guards grabbed the girl, who visibly flinched when the man with the steel breastplate began untying the laces to his codpiece.

"Strip her, then."

A squat man stepped forward.

The same man who'd helped free Tycho from the ship, only to make him a prisoner again. Pulling down his cap, Tycho wrapped a filthy scarf around his neck and backed into the crowd.

"Hurry it up . . ."

Grabbing her collar, the squat man yanked so hard he pulled the young woman free from the two holding her. As the guards reached for her, she spun round and spat full into the face of the man in the breastplate. This time her spittle hit his lips and he didn't flick it nonchalantly away; he scrubbed his lips with the back of his hand instead. And Tycho watched the smoky evil he felt around him enter the man's eyes. Pointing at Roderigo, the man snarled, "Nail her to that tree. Flay her."

"My lord?"

"You heard me, Roderigo."

"She's barely a child, my lord. And the building is yours. Cut her throat and be done with it. Take her first if you must."

"Kindness is a weakness. Tell your man to flay her and do it fast. I'm due at prayers in an hour. You'll be coming with me."

As one guard went to fetch nails and a hammer, another disappeared looking for a kitchen knife and steel. His face relaxed when Roderigo ordered him to give both to Sergeant Temujin. The sergeant swore.

"What did he say?"

Roderigo looked uneasy.

"What did your man just mutter?"

"If it takes a Mongol to do the job, my lord. He's happy to serve."

Tycho doubted these were the exact words. So did Roderigo's master, from his scowl. Although the words obviously hit home, because he shot the sergeant a glare and stared round the mob-filled courtyard, his gaze alighting on Tycho. "You," he said. "Come here."

The man behind pushed Tycho forward.

"I'm Prince Alonzo, Regent of this city. You hear me?"

Tycho nodded slowly.

"Typical," the Regent muttered. "The village idiot. Give him the knife, explain what he's to do. And hurry it up."

It had been dark in the boat and Tycho's face was now filthy, framed by a stolen cap and what showed of his hair was matted and greasy. All the same, the sergeant stood on the edge of recognition.

"*Buonasera*," said Tycho, sounding like the Nicoletti's son the dead printer had been. Temujin shrugged.

"Cut her a bit. Kill her soon after. Only not too soon . . ." Jerking his head towards Prince Alonzo, he added. "He needs to hear her scream. His type always does. Right, you two, wrap her arms around that tree."

Temujin's knuckles were white as he put a nail to her wrist, drew back his hammer and slammed it down so hard its crash almost drowned her cry. She howled again when the second nail went in. Thrashing as Tycho stepped up behind her with his knife.

"Please," she begged. Her voice guttural, her Italian so thick he barely recognised the words. "Don't."

She knew he was there to hurt her.

Into Tycho's mind came memories of a flaying. *Bloody Boot* stripped the ankles, *Red Gauntlets* the hands and wrists. *Raw Saddle* flayed the . . .

"Get on with it," Temujin hissed.

Slicing fast, he outlined her spine, adding a second cut beside the first, slashing a third at the top and scooping under to give him something to grip. It was over in a second, maybe less. When he ripped, the young woman screamed so hard her voice broke. Behind Tycho someone vomited.

"*Please . . .*" The word was in his head.

A child's whisper behind her animal howl. Pain spread like angel's wings from her body, feathered and bright. Brighter than his eyes could stand.

"*Please,*" she begged. "*Make it stop . . .*"

He did as she asked, taking the brightness into himself. Feeling her shock as her mind abandoned the bleeding meat nailed to the tree. She was two people now. One silent, inside him. The other loud and bestial.

Such as it was her life lay open. The taste of food he'd never eaten, and memories of a rambling family home in Egypt, seen through her eyes as a child. Snatches of her language. Memories of a happy childhood turning sour as a father's love hardened to anxiety. And the *fontego* that had been her world became her prison.

Tycho felt his dog teeth extend.

The night was his. The night, the city, the world . . . Everything was his and he moved freely through it. The water under the bridges barely troubled him as he flowed through the city at impossible speeds, streets unravelling as he printed them on his memory. Giving names to places he knew, learning locations for which he'd only known names. Behind him he left a crowd shocked into silence. Stunned guards and a prince open-mouthed with horror.

Tycho's body hummed with power, his hearing was so sharp he surprised a hunting tom before the cat was aware of him. Time stretched and twisted and became malleable. Eventually moving so slowly he owned the spaces between seconds as well as the seconds themselves. He knew the stars for tiny suns lighting a night sky to the brightness of day. Except this sky was red.

As was the rest of his world.

Red walls and water held within red canal banks. The underworld and the overworld and the world of the dead were finally one. To look at somewhere was to be there. He could kill, he could observe, he could touch. Drunken couples fucked in doorways, feet slipping on slush and snow. Masked thieves waited to rob elegant *cittadini*. Old men staggered halfway across the city with goods from the sacked building that they didn't really want anyway. And light to their darkness, children played marbles by candlelight on dusty floors. A boy stroked the face of a girl and ventured a kiss, feeling daring. Little knowing how long she'd been waiting for him to make this move. The air stank of sweetness. It smelt sweetly of dung. He was God and the Devil in one.

It was close to dawn before his euphoria faded. Dangerously close.

Too late to return to his lair, he found an empty attic above a goldsmith, with tiles new enough to keep out sunlight and settled himself into one corner, folding one arm under his head to make a pillow and folding his knees to steady himself.

He felt stronger than before, no longer hungry. But he also remembered how he'd earned this God-like happiness. Opening his mouth, Tycho ran a finger across his teeth, finding them normal. The creature that moved so confidently through the night was gone. But memories of the creature's power, speed and glory remained. He'd thought his greatest challenge was to remember who he was. And had been wrong, almost childishly so. Who he was paled before tonight's slaughter. What he was . . . That was the real question.

24

The carved face of a lion between bat's wings decorated the keystone of an arch over an old palace door. On the left bank of the Canalasso, below la Volta, to the left of San Gregal, the palace was being restored. Its position almost opposite the sacked Mamluk warehouse was a coincidence.

The bat-winged face was carved into a roundel.

A patera, of which there were several thousand in Venice, featuring hundreds of separate insignia. Everyone in the city could identify the lion reading a book. The lion was Venice, the book Saint Mark's gospel. San Marco being their patron saint. So the patera *was* Venice, which was why it could be seen everywhere.

It marked the Dogana di Mar, the Palazzo Reale on one side of Piazza San Marco, where the city authorities gathered, and the Orseolo Hospice opposite. It marked the Zecca, which minted ducats, and the campanile, which doubled as a lighthouse, and a place from which traitors' bodies could hang.

It practically smothered the *bucintoro*, Marco IV's ceremonial barge. A vessel so impractical it could barely navigate the Grand Canal and so top heavy it could not survive open sea.

Palaces sported the badges of their owners.

The almshouses and guild schools had symbols of their own. As did the Arsenalotti, and even the Nicoletti and Castellani, whose patera became accepted simply through frequency of use. In a world where few could read, and churches used murals to tell improving tales, most Venetians could identify at least a dozen patera. Slightly fewer could identify two or three dozen. A handful of scholars could identify sixty or so without effort.

In the Street of Scribes, where Jewish letter writers mixed ink and sharpened quills and kept secret the letters they read in whispers for a single grosso, was a rabbi who could identify at least two hundred. But there were patera – flaking and rotted by wind, rain and sea salt – which remained obscure because the last scholar to know the answer was dust.

The bat-winged mask was one of these, supposedly.

The Moor who waited for his *gondolino* that Friday afternoon in January knew what it represented, and was glad others didn't. He'd purchased the palace, which was near the Dogana, because it amused him that the house now called Ca' il Mauros exhibited one of only two examples of the Assassini's patera. At least, examples that could be publicly seen. The Assassini master who'd had that patera carved was long dead, and his descendants had struggled down the generations, without knowing what it represented. Only selling up, reluctantly and with bad grace, when repairs became too expensive for their pocket.

"You'll be safe?"

"My dear . . ." Gathering his robes, Atilo kissed his beloved on both cheeks and smiled. "I'll be fine." When Desdaio raised her face, he let his lips touch hers before stepping back. "I'm going to the palace for a few hours. Nothing important."

"You're Ten, now . . ."

Atilo regarded his victory over the German fleet as far more important than anything that might come from talking with nine other men. But this was Venice. Although Duke Marco IV owned the Istrian coast from Austria to Byzantium, his court looked inwards instinctively, being interested in their own reflection. The briefest glimpse of lovers, seen through the window of a candlelit room overlooking the Grand Canal, carried more interest than princes murdered on Venetian orders miles away. The world outside existed only as a place from which the city could make money. If a deal was good, that was enough. The circumstances, Venice regarded with mild curiosity at best, maybe not even that.

"I'll be back for Compline."

"You'll eat then?"

Atilo sighed. There would be food at Ca' Ducale should he be hungry, but Desdaio obviously wanted them to eat together. "Something light."

"I'll make something."

"Desdaio. We have a cook."

"It's not the same . . ." Lord Bribanzo's daughter had discovered the joy of dressing herself, brushing her own hair, washing her face and preparing food. Chores that had plagued Atilo's mother, the unlucky bride of a star-gazing poet who wasted his money on instruments while his children ran wild and his estate ran to ruin.

Atilo found it strange and oddly touching. "Eggs, then."

Despite the January cold she remained on the steps, splashed by spray, and with the occasional rough wave soaking her shoes, while Atilo settled back and Iacopo bowed low to Desdaio, his eyes sweeping her body. Then he grabbed his oar with a flourish, untied the ropes holding the *gondolino* steady, and pushed off into those tides that made steering difficult in the mouth of the Grand Canal. That young man appeared to have focused on crossing the choppy water as swiftly as possible, but Desdaio couldn't shake the thought he was still watching her.

If Iaco continued to make her uneasy, she'd ask Atilo to find him another job. Either that, or get rid of him altogether. Amelia, however, she liked. Not beautiful but striking. That black skin, lean figure and braided hair with silver thimbles. She wondered if Atilo had . . . Feeling her stomach knot, Desdaio refused to finish the thought. Her future husband was known to have lived like a monk before he courted her. Everyone said so. She was sure they were right.

"Amelia, I need your help in the kitchen."

"My lady?"

"Chopping things."

The young Nubian's eyes flicked to the window, where late afternoon had turned to early evening and the outlines of a dozen *gondolini* had blended so far into darkness as to become almost invisible. All she said was, "I thought you told me Lord Atilo wanted eggs, my lady."

"I'll include eggs."

"If you make me chop things . . ." The girl hesitated, and then turned away, deciding her words best left unspoken.

They hadn't really talked, Desdaio realised. A few hellos, the occasional good morning, and pretence at a curtsy from Amelia. Desdaio had no idea where her slave was born. Not even if she was Christian.

"Where are your parents?"

Amelia's mouth shut with a snap. Muttering an apology, she turned away . . . And Desdaio grabbed her, feeling Amelia struggle, only to fall still when Desdaio pushed her cheek against the other girl's face and refused to let go.

"Stupid," Desdaio said. "That's me. I'm sorry."

Amelia laughed through her tears. "My lady. Iacopo and I . . . We're orphans. All of the Admiral's servants are."

"Even Francesca the cook?"

"Yes, my lady," Amelia nodded.

"What were you going to say? About chopping things?"

"Francesca lets you in the kitchen, because . . ."

"She can't refuse?"

"Yes, my lady. You are the mistress of this house. Me, I'm not welcome in her kitchen. No one is. Francesca's been with Lord Atilo for a long time. Even he knocks before he enters."

"Then we'll knock too," Desdaio said brightly.

25

For the second time in days Giulietta felt smothered by the Persian rug in which she'd been rolled. She'd never felt so helpless. Not even when the *abadessa* held her wrists, Dr Crow froze her tongue and Mistress Scarlett forced her knees apart . . .

Hot tears filled her throat. All that did was make it hard to breathe when her nose started running. And it was hard enough to breathe wrapped in a carpet anyway. She tried to concentrate on what was happening outside. She was in a boat of some kind. But whether it was a small boat or a large galley . . .

How would she know?

When she heard the keel grate on gravel she realised they'd reached land and she had her answer. A small boat and a short ride. Having been carried ashore, her smothering prison was tossed down and picked up just as quickly when someone hissed with anger. "It's Persian. I'm not paying you to get shit on it."

The men answering sounded Schiavoni.

Hoisting the carpet on to their shoulders, they began to carry her up a slight incline. While inside, now gagged, and with her hands trapped by the carpet's tightness, Giulietta heard the curses of men struggling through mudflats. Her journeys had been so

148

brief she suspected she was back where she had started. In Venice, or on the Venetian mainland. But not, it seemed, near the Riva degli Schiavoni.

Uncle Alonzo? Aunt Alexa? Patriarch Theodore?

Who would do this to her and why?

Were the men who stole her from the basilica the ones who delivered her to the little temple in the walled garden? If so, who were these? And why were they in league with *krieghund*?

Lady Giulietta had wanted excitement her entire life. She'd wanted it through Fra Diomedes's lessons, Sunday services in San Marco, formal meals with her family. Something more real than ritual and gossip. Now that she had it, she wanted her own boring life back.

Somewhere behind her . . . In the ruined furniture of a little temple's hallway, on a leather divan in the Sala de Tortura, on a stinking road through Cannaregio, in a throwaway comment that she'd kill her husband if not allowed to kill herself, were the pieces of her broken childhood.

Unable to help herself, Giulietta started sobbing.

The old man had died instantly. His throat torn out in a sweep of claws from the monster in the doorway. The *krieghund*'s second blow removed his head, the squelch of it landing still sounded in her ears. The old woman had clapped hand to her own mouth, looking hideously sick. Then turned abruptly to Lady Giulietta.

"*Hide . . .*" The word was silent. When she didn't move, the old woman pushed Giulietta towards her bedroom.

You can survive rape.

You can't survive what krieghund *do to you.*

The old man's death, Atilo's brutal words and her own terror made her scrabble as she grabbed the key from the lock, slammed her bedroom door behind her and locked and bolted it from inside. She dragged a chest in front of the door, then her bed in front of that. And, finally, she looked round her.

She had her bed, her blanket, her mattress. A bowl of water

to wash her face, which would do for drinking. A bucket for pissing. And a thick door between her and the danger beyond. Nothing she could use as a weapon.

Hammering began at the door.

"Go away," she shouted. "Go away . . ."

By then there was no one left to hear but the monster outside.

A night of sobbing, raging and promises to God on Lady Giulietta's part gave way in the morning to surprise when, after an hour or so's silence, someone knocked softly at her bedroom door. The voice accompanying the knock was also soft, and very human. The man on the other side offered her safety. All she had to do was turn the key and undo her bolts, lie face down on the floor and shut her eyes.

"What about the monster?"

The silence was eloquent, followed by a deep sigh. "What choice do you have?"

"And if I don't trust you?"

"The *monster* will be back."

He was right, of course. What choice did she have? What choice had she ever had? Lady Giulietta's whole life was one of duty and demands. Why should today be any different? On the plus side, she was alive, which was surprising. And she wasn't on her way to marry King Janus . . . Patriarch Theodore always said concentrate on life's goodness. And being alive after being abducted was good, wasn't it?

So Giulietta unblocked her door, half expecting the monster to burst in immediately. And then she lay face down and closed her eyes, keeping them tightly shut when the door began to open. The man who came in, gagged her, blindfolded her and used the rug from the sacristy to roll her tight.

And, following a short boat trip, she found herself here. Wherever that was. "My lord," she heard a Schiavoni whisper.

"Not far now," someone whispered in return. "Not far at all."

26

"Wait here," Atilo ordered.

Iacopo bowed, checked the knots holding the *gondolino* were secure enough to defeat the waves washing over the Molo, and glanced longingly towards the food stalls lining the muddy start of the Riva degli Schiavoni.

Darkness came early in winter. But the city still ate late.

The Riva looked crowded; with sailors seeking employment most likely, and captains seeking new crews. A tenth of the hiring was paid in advance and went just as fast on one of the whores plying their trade along its length. Another fifth was collected on boarding, and the rest paid at the journey's end.

"I mean it," Atilo said.

Iacopo looked up, surprised.

"Wait *here*. Buy yourself a pie if you want." Atilo tossed a coin, watching in amusement as Iacopo checked if it was bronze or silver. "But no taverns and no brothels. I expect to find you here when I get back."

Iacopo's bow was even lower. So low Atilo didn't see his face.

Leaving his servant beside the black *gondolino*, Atilo stepped between a captain and an Arab who was insisting he knew every sandbank in the mouth of the Nile. When he looked back, Iacopo was staring longingly at three nuns leaving a convent where the novices were known to be young, beautiful and friendly.

Sucking his teeth, but not crossly, Atilo changed direction.

A guard stepped aside at that night's password, and the Moor swept through an open door, turned right immediately and negotiated the benches of an empty audience room. Well, its lobby. That particular audience room was now locked for the day. Checking the corridor beyond was empty, he slid behind a tapestry. The ducal palace was riddled with secret doors. Listening posts, too, recesses hidden by panels or wall hangings where spies could note what was said that shouldn't be said. Most secret doors led from one floor to another, as hiding a spiral of stairs was easier than building a passage down which a man might walk.

Such passages existed, however.

It was along one of these that Atilo strode, his outstretched fingers dusting cobwebs from brickwork. Touch told him how far he'd gone, since every ten paces or so the walls were marked with the bat-winged patera. If only two patera were visible in Venice, there were ten hidden in this corridor alone.

Behind him Atilo dragged five centuries of history, the names of the twenty-seven previous Assassini masters, and the worry he could offer no name to follow his. Every master proposed his successor. The final choice was the duke's, but in five hundred years no recommendation had been refused.

Iacopo hid ambition behind a smiling face. Some masters believed this was an essential quality. An assassin with a smile could open doors shut to those who frowned. Atilo was unconvinced. To his eyes – old as they were – the essential quality was an ability never to reveal your calling.

On the Canalasso this night, the old-House patricians – those whose families had graced the Golden Book five centuries before Ca' Dolphini was built – would flatter their host, whose grandfather bribed his way on to their company. The Dolphini fortune was one reason. The other, that Lord Dolphino – by nudges and winks, sly boasts and strategic silences – claimed, without claiming, to be the duke's Blade. His son Nicolò had bedded more than one virgin from a family in trouble enough to believe the Assassini could help.

Since the new duke could not give orders, the real Blade obeyed instructions from both Alexa and Alonzo. The ground rules were simple. Neither would order the other's murder, nor a murder within the other's immediate entourage. Their individual orders would remain secret from each other. Atilo's duty was to say if this agreement was broken. A responsibility he could do without.

He was getting old. Well, older.

Old enough to know the Angel of Death was watching and would add tonight's business to the scroll. Atilo wondered if those he killed in battle would count against him in the final weighing. Or only those murdered in cold blood on his master's orders. He also wondered, and despised himself for this, if the old duke had already taken some of that weight on himself.

It would have been quicker to reach where he wanted to go by walking through the small garden behind Ca' Ducale, which each new duke threatened to destroy by extending the Rio di Palazzo side of the palace, and no duke had yet been able to bring himself to do.

Cutting through the first, to a second garden beyond belonging to the Patriarch's city residence would have been simpler. But then he might have been seen entering the Patriarch's little study, and that was not Atilo's plan.

A city limited to sandbanks, surrounded by sea and supported on thousands of piles driven into the underlying sand and clay could not afford the waste of space that large gardens represented. A single poplar in a private *cortile* might form a patrician's entire garden. Three trees in a *campo* were as close as many Venetians got to nature. At least at ground level. Many houses had *altane*, roof gardens decorated with flowerpots where women could sit and sun-bleach their hair.

For the Ca' Ducale to have gardens was a matter of pride. Although the patriarch only had one because Marco I's respect for the Church made him divide the strip along Rio di Palazzo in two, and give the smaller section to the Church.

The fact Patriarch Theodore had been called from his sickbed in San Pietro di Castello by a message from the Regent made the night's work easier, sparing Atilo the burden of having to visit the eastern edges of the city.

"My old friend." Laying down a tiny pair of pliers, the patriarch started to stand, then sat down again. "You know I've been ill?"

"Nothing serious, I hope?"

"Old age. A sickness of the heart. You know how it is."

Atilo did. Picking up the ball hammer, he examined it. The hammer was too small to use on nails, even small ones.

"For beating metal," Theodore said, although this was obvious. The top of a hollow censer was crushed out of shape, the filigree twisted. "The provost says my altar boy dropped it. The boy denies it."

"If it had been dropped it would be crushed at the base."

"That's what the boy says. The provost whipped him. I wish he wouldn't. It'll only make him more nervous. But, of course, I can't really . . ."

"Of course not."

To treat this altar boy differently was to recognise him as the Patriarch's bastard. A brief moment of loneliness, several years ago. When the palace at San Pietro was cold and the Patriarch's bed had looked warm to a novice newly arrived from the mainland. Not Theodore's only moment of loneliness. Although his other bastards had reached maturity without their father having to protect them.

Theodore had several nephews and nieces. Most bishops did.

Looking round the small room, with its old manuscripts, most in Latin and Greek, the patriarch said, "I'm not sure he's suited for the Church. I was wondering. If anything were to happen to me. Perhaps you . . . ?"

Atilo looked at him.

"I'm not saying it will," Theodore said sadly. "Just, if it does. You're known for your kindness to orphans. I've always wondered," he added, "if that was penance of some kind. If you were, perhaps . . ." He looked embarrassed. "We're all atoning for something."

Did he know? Atilo wondered.

"Have a look at this," said the patriarch. He lifted a lamp so its light fell across the table, before removing a cloth with a slight flourish. Under it was the chalice the duke used to marry the sea.

"Damaged?"

"Yes," Theodore said. "So much is these days."

The rim was dented, two precious stones missing from the base. A third stone cracked across its surface. A scratch on the bowl looked deep enough to need filling rather than simply polishing out.

"You know I trained as a jeweller?"

Yes, Atilo knew. The story was famous. As a young man, the patriarch heard God's call while helping repair the rood screen in front of San Marco's altar. He threw away the money his father had spent buying an apprenticeship. Entering the White Crucifers, he found himself making swords instead. When not giving last rites to those who died of fever and battle.

Theodore tapped the damaged censer.

"This, my old friend, I can mend. A little hammering, some soldering, not difficult, even with these old hands. That, however . . . needs someone better than me. Someone better than I would have been had I stayed a jeweller."

"What's so difficult?"

The patriarch had Atilo stand behind him, then adjusted the

lamp so it threw more light. "See?" A bas-relief of vine leaves and grapes in gold and rubies circled the base, and Atilo realised they were cracked where three stems wove an intricate plait. "You think I should try," said Theodore. "Or leave it for someone else?"

"Someone else."

He nodded sadly. "You don't mind if I say something?"

"No," Atilo said.

"You should ask yourself why the chalice was left. If her abductors took the ring and took her why did they leave this?"

"The Mamluks?"

"If it was them."

"What have you heard?" Atilo's voice was sharp.

"I've heard nothing," said Patriarch Theodore gently. "And what I suspect cannot be revealed without breaking the seal of confession. You would not expect me . . ." Turning down the lamp slightly, Theodore suggested they take the night air and talk further, if talking was why Atilo was here. He made no attempt to take his lamp with him, and Atilo didn't suggest it. When he knelt on damp grass to tie his laces, holding the position longer than necessary, Atilo knew Theodore knew. Whatever had happened, Alonzo could not allow him to live.

He cut the man's throat fast, yanking back his head and dragging a blade through gristle until it hit bone. And in the final moment, Atilo could swear the patriarch smiled.

"Thank you, my dear . . ."

Atilo finished washing his hands in a bowl and took the towel Desdaio offered, drying his fingers carefully. Like everyone in Venice, he washed his hands before and after every meal. As surely as he washed his face each morning and before going to bed each night. As surely as he'd washed his hands before returning to Ca' il Mauros.

His thoughts were on what came after the murder.

A noise . . . ? That must be what made him go back. Most

likely he'd heard a noise without realising it. He'd just entered Theodore's study, with the study's owner lying in the damp garden behind him, when he stopped, turned and hurried back. Taking the handful of steps that would change his life.

Complimenting Desdaio on a dish involving eggs, noodles and salted mutton, Atilo took another glass of wine, and wished the storm in his head would subside; only then would be able to unpick what mattered from the rest. He'd turned back. And a boy was there.

That was the nub of it.

A boy had knelt over Theodore, cradling him.

For a moment Atilo thought the figure listened to some final words. But dying men don't speak with their voice boxes cut. They gasp air, bleed to death, and die. That didn't stop the boy asking his question. "Tell me where she is."

Theodore gurgled.

"In the basilica," the boy hissed. "That girl. Where is she?"

When Theodore still didn't answer, the boy bent his head and bit, adding another wound to the ruined flesh of the Patriarch's throat. Although Atilo drew his knife, he never came close to frightening the unwelcome witness.

Instead, the moon slipped from behind cloud to light a creature with the face of an angel and the eyes of a demon. Its hair was silver-grey, braided into snakes. Blood dripped from its open mouth. Its dog teeth were unnaturally long.

Instinct made Atilo flip his dagger so he held it by the point. And he threw hard, allowing for where the creature would be when he realised a blade was coming. The blade still passed through empty air.

"Fine," the creature said. "I'll find her myself."

It sounded like a boy and it looked almost like a boy, but nothing human moved that fast. Flicking its gaze from Atilo to the wall, from the garden wall to the Patriarch's little palace. Its calculations were swift. Its answer unexpected.

One second it stood there.

The next? Atilo looked round. A scraping behind him made him look back, and the creature was halfway up the Patriarch's palace, clinging to the carved balustrade of a balcony. The wall was too smooth to be climbed. The balcony far too high to reach by any other means.

As Atilo watched, the creature rolled itself on to the balcony, jumped up on to the balustrade, crouched like the wild animal it was and unleashed a bound that carried it to the roof's edge above. Finding an impossible foothold, it disappeared.

Fifty years as a soldier. Twenty-six as the duke's Blade. A lifetime staying alive against the odds. Not a single missed kill. In less than twenty seconds Atilo had been bested by *what*? An angel-faced thing that made impossible jumps. A creature, God help Atilo, who fed on the dying.

So be it.

Atilo had made his choice. That creature would be the next master of the Assassini. But first it must become an apprentice. Atilo just needed to hunt it down.

27

The Moors, Mamluks and Seljuks make their first call to prayer in the moment a single black thread can be distinguished from pre-dawn darkness. It had a name few Venetians knew. Anyone looking out of their window on the second to last Sunday in January, in the fourth year of Marco IV's reign, would have assumed it was still night. Yet day and night balanced on the cusp. And though the moon, two days from being full, was cloud-shrouded, and the sun still to rise, the nature of the darkness changed. In this black-thread moment three things happened.

The least of these was that a silver-haired boy discarded his Arsenalotti tunic and cap and wound himself in rags, like a leper. Protection against the city, other beggars and the coming sun. Had he known better, he would have protected himself from the moon, because it was the moon that drove his hunger, and his hunger that drove him to trace a scent on the wind to a square south of San Polo, where the alleys led nowhere and the only way out was back the way he'd come.

The second thing, more important by far, was that Atilo dragged himself from his knees, having spent the night praying for Archbishop Theodore, whose murder had so shocked the city.

After five days of masses and mourning, the patriarch was to be buried that day in the nave of San Pietro. Newly elected to the Ten, his election unopposed following Duchess Alexa's nomination, Atilo was expected to attend. But then, as an old friend of Theodore, he'd have been there anyway.

Iacopo and Amelia were out scouring the city for the boy Atilo had seen in the Patriarch's garden. Amelia's final test before ending her apprenticeship. So she negotiated unnamed streets, arm in arm with Iacopo, dressed as Arsenalotti or Nicoletti or Schiavoni from Dalmatia. Whatever it took to enter the areas they were searching. Another half-dozen of Atilo's orphaned ex-apprentices, now found safe jobs as cooks, stallholders and fishermen, had orders to report what they saw.

One of these, Junot, who fished off della Misericordia, that square-shaped bite out of the northern shore, sent news of the third, most important event of that morning. Junot's brother-in-law had a good night's fishing. Or so he thought, until he drew his net higher and found his catch human.

Catching one bloated corpse was unlucky. Two was simply life being cruel. Junot's brother-in-law knew he could not simply return them to the tides. At least, he knew that once he saw the bodies wore sleeveless mail under Mamluk robes. Had he known the mail was Milanese, he might have tipped them back anyway.

As it was, he brought them ashore and sent word for the Watch, whose captain went cap in hand to the duchess later that morning. By noon the following day Archbishop Theodore was buried. Tycho was safely back under his *sottoportego*, having survived another round of fever. And Junot's brother-in-law confessed, under torture, to killing two soldiers and dumping their bodies in the sea. For which he was swiftly executed. The Captain of the Watch, being of use to the city, was simply ordered to forget everything he'd seen.

The fisherman had *not* found Milanese mercenaries dressed in Mamluk clothes, possibly similar to those worn by Lady Giulietta's captors. There was *no* suggestion that anyone other than Mamluks was behind her disappearance.

The Watch captain took those words away with him. It was, he told his men, a misunderstanding. They valued their lives enough to nod.

The fourth and final thing was that, a few nights later, having listened to his Nubian slave's report, Atilo decided to use the street children who told Amelia where the boy was as bait. So, as night fell, he and Roderigo headed for an underpass south of Campo San Polo; one of his bait boastful, one silent, one in tears.

"Told you," Josh said. "Didn't I? He's hunting for someone. He stands and sniffs the night wind like some dog. Said I knew. Here is where he comes most nights. Would I lie?" He turned to Rosalyn. "Would I lie to them?"

She turned her head away.

Josh scowled. "You'll keep your promise?"

"Not to kill you?"

The youth glared. He knew, from that night in Cannaregio, this was a great lord, and so he had to tread carefully. But he was still alive, which was more than he'd expected that night last year. And much more than he'd expected when the old man appeared, just before tonight's sunset, and reintroduced himself by putting the edge of his dagger to Josh's throat, wrapping his fingers into Josh's hair and dragged him from between Rosalyn's sullen thighs.

"To let us go," Josh said. "That's what you promised." In the moonlight, the boy looked slightly younger than Atilo remembered. Small, narrow-faced and tricky, with a thin nose. His shoulders hunched round some slight he employed to justify using the other two as he wanted. The hierarchy of the dirt poor.

"You three stay quiet, right? Otherwise . . ." Temujin mimed cutting their throats. "And don't run, little rat." He grinned at Pietro, and lifted his bow slightly. "Cos no one outruns this."

"Sergeant."

"It's true," Temujin told Atilo. "A galloping horse can't outrun this. How do you think my people conquered half the world?"

"And lost it again."

That wasn't strictly true. The Golden Horde *had* conquered lands stretching from China to Western Europe, including India. They still owned much of their empire. But until recently it had been divided between the Great Khan's descendants, who fought each other as bitterly as they fought outsiders. Now Tīmūr, known as Tamberlaine, at most a bastard of a minor branch, for all he claimed the heritage, was busy being Khan of Khans.

"Down here, you say?"

Josh nodded.

"Go ahead," Roderigo told Temujin, having checked that this met with Atilo's approval. He followed after, leaving Atilo where he was. The Moor's gaze never leaving the roof line above.

"Shoot to wound," Atilo said. "I want him alive."

A flick of Roderigo's hand in darkness acknowledged this order. All might have gone well if not for Rosalyn; who took a deep breath as Roderigo and Temujin headed towards the *sottoportego*, opened her mouth and screamed words guaranteed to wake the entire area. "Fire. Fire. Fire . . ."

"Shit," Roderigo said.

Flipping his knife, the old man hammered its hilt into her head. "Stop him," he snapped.

Stop who?

And then Temujin and Roderigo knew.

In the mouth of the underpass stood a gaunt silhouette, lit by pale moonlight and framed against the blackness of the passage behind. The figure glanced from Temujin to Atilo and grinned. Then it saw Rosalyn in the dirt.

And stopped grinning. He'd hunted the scent this far. A faint trace on the night wind that pulled him here, and then left him here, unable to trace the scent further. He was stupid to have stayed in one area for so long. Tycho had known that, even as he found himself unable to leave. And now his nightmares had caught up with him.

The old man from the garden. The soldier who cut him free. And the squat Mongol who ordered him to flay the dark-skinned girl, whose memories still haunted his head. To make it worse, at the old man's feet lay the girl who'd dragged Tycho from the canal, the one who'd smiled at him in the night alleyways.

He could run, of course.

The ruined *corte*, with its broken well and collapsed buildings, was behind him. Its walls were unsafe, its floors unsteady. He could climb faster than them, jump further. "He's going to run," the sergeant said.

"Where?" The one they called Roderigo was contemptuous.

Raising his bow, the sergeant said, "Straight through us. If I don't get the order to fire."

"*Temujin.*"

"You know I'm right, boss."

People in this city used their real names, not knowing the danger they put themselves in. To know a real name was to own a sliver of that person. All the great shamans used this knowledge in their magic. Tycho couldn't believe people would waste their strength so freely.

"My lord Atilo?" Roderigo said.

Tycho moved.

"Boss . . ."

Ducking a grab, Tycho elbowed Temujin hard, fast and brutally, finding himself facing Atilo a second later. Atilo dropped to a fighting crouch and lifted his knife. Did the old man think him a fool? That order to take Tycho alive was Atilo's mistake, his weakness. He should want Tycho dead.

Spinning round Atilo, Tycho stopped in front of Josh.

"I had no choice," Josh's voice was desperate. "He made me."

And Bjornvin made me, Tycho thought; and look what it made

me into. Grabbing the back of Josh's head, he put his other hand to Josh's chin and twisted savagely. A sudden shit stink rose from his falling body.

"Impressive," Atilo said.

Tycho had the old man, his other hand reaching for his neck when Roderigo threw. Dodging cost Tycho his kill and almost his life. Because Atilo jabbed at Tycho's throat. If he hadn't ducked fast enough for the blow to pass through air he'd be dead.

"You're enjoying this," Atilo growled. "Aren't you?"

Someone was.

Tycho just wasn't sure it was him.

He had the *sottoportego* behind him now. Atilo still holding a dagger. Roderigo undecided. Temujin climbing to his feet. Of the other three players, Josh was dead, Pietro standing petrified in a puddle of his own piss, and Rosalyn . . .

Moving.

"She dies," the old man said. "If you don't surrender."

How had the old man identified her as his weakness? Was it even true . . . ? Atilo looked cool now, almost amused as Temujin notched an arrow to his bow and aimed at the girl on the ground.

"All it takes is my order."

What should Tycho do? Let her be killed? Let himself be captured? The triumph in the old man's eyes decided him. Grabbing Atilo's wrist, not to snap, but to freeze his dagger and put the old man in the way of Temujin's bow, Tycho brought their foreheads so close he and Atilo touched.

Kill Rosalyn, he thought. *And I flay your woman.*

Shock and fear. The last quickly brought under control. Unease that Tycho might actually harm the soft-faced girl he'd sensed earlier. The one the old man had yet to bed. The inside of Atilo's mind was a charnel house of whispering secrets. Bat's wings and lion's faces. A thousand corpses silhouetted in almost military neatness against a horizon that went back years.

And three girls. Two dead, Tycho knew immediately.

The other waiting at home, not knowing why he wouldn't come to her. Didn't simply marry her and take her to his bed as she expected the man who loved her to do.

Ask the Mongol. He's seen me do it already.

The wind was in his face, the city's scents intense and cloying, disgusting and exhilarating at the same time. Someone shouted in an attic below, but he was gone before they could open their shutters. A shadow among shadows, faster than thin clouds scudding across a night sky.

He leapt without looking; laughing as he dropped two floors and rolled to his feet, his sinews stretching with the shock. His fever was gone, unless it was simply lost beneath his exhilaration. Jumping another canal, he landed at ground level, looked around him and decided he preferred the roofs. So he scrabbled the wall of a palace, leapt an alley and climbed higher. Until he stood on the very top of a bronze cupola, with Venice spread below him and an unclaimed night ahead.

Atilo would come looking.

As would Roderigo and his Mongol sergeant. They would not forget and they would not forgive. He held their secrets, and knew their failures. Maybe he should be worried. But worried about what? He was here, with the night creatures. They were down there in the dirt.

28

Everyone in the palace slept except the night guard, and those in beds not belonging to them, who'd creep back to the stillness and silence of pretend slumber before next morning. Alexa was alone, her bed unoccupied behind her. She was less cross than Atilo expected about being woken. Maybe it was the fact he couldn't stop his hands shaking.

"So, did you find him?"

"We did, my lady."

Duchess Alexa put down her tea, pushing the tiny porcelain cup away from her. Sitting back, she said. "I'm not going to like this, am I?"

"We lost him."

"You woke me to tell me this?" Amusement lightened her voice, as if the guard's shock, and her lady-in-waiting's outrage at his arrival, requesting an audience, was an elegant joke.

"It's the nature of our loss."

"The nature of our loss." She smiled. "You would have made a poet. They say the Maghreb is a land of poets. Of fountains and palaces, stark mountains and lush orange groves . . ."

"And beggars," said Atilo. "Braggarts, brothers who kiss publicly and hate in private. Much like everywhere else. Except," he hesitated. "Maybe more beautiful."

"Why leave?"

"I had no choice." Atilo waited for her to nod before realising she didn't know his early history. "I always assumed you . . ."

"My husband was discreet. Sometimes I suspect no one in his council knew all there was to know. He arranged matters to make this so."

Their discussion about the escaped boy was suspended, apparently. Since Alexa did little from chance she would have her reasons. They would involve thwarting her brother-in-law or protecting her own son, which often turned out to be the same thing. And if not these directly, then increasing her own power or binding Atilo to her camp to balance Roderigo's decision to support the Regent; a blow, since the Captain of the Dogana controlled the money coming into Venice, theoretically at least. Clearly, Atilo already belonged to her, since he was her choice for the Council. Whichever mix of these, it would boil down to the same thing. She would move heaven and earth to protect Marco, since the young duke could not protect himself.

"What drove you out of your homeland?"

Taking the tiny porcelain cup she offered him, Atilo sipped fermented leaves soaked in boiling water. The duchess drank the mixture several times a day, her cups so fine candlelight shone through them. They had been part of her dower. As had the first crate of fermented tea. When the crate was half empty, Marco III sent orders for another. This arrived the month the first crate ran out.

Duchess Alexa cried at his kindness. So it was said, anyway.

"Well? A love affair gone wrong? Gambling debts? A wish to explore the world? An overbearing wife . . . ?"

Giving up his battle to like tea, Atilo put his cup down carefully. "Those are very Venetian reasons," he said lightly.

"A matter of honour then?"

Atilo smiled. Without saying it, the duchess was admitting non-Venetians thought Venice a city without morals. But then you didn't become the Middle Sea's richest city by behaving nicely. "My father remarried."

"You hated your stepmother?"

"I liked the first. I mistrusted the second."

"The second?"

"The first died shortly after the second arrived as her lady-in-waiting. We lived in glorious squalor while my father searched the heavens for new stars. Emirs came to ask their futures. Princes sent gifts from Frankish lands. It would have made more sense to send us food."

"He was a scholar?"

"A hoarder of knowledge. Perhaps it's the same."

The duchess greeted this with a nod. Candlelight softened her nightgown, and though its shadows shifted in the night wind, it couldn't reveal her face behind the veil. Mostly, Atilo had to guess her thoughts from gestures. The fact her head was slightly to one side said she listened intently.

"You were afraid?"

Atilo considered denying it. "Yes," he admitted finally. "I was thirteen. A bitter, unruly child. My half-brother eleven. The grain house rats started dying shortly after she became my new stepmother. The cats came next. Then my hunting dog. I fell ill that winter and she insisted on nursing me. I knew then it was time to leave. So I crawled from my bed, and hid in a culvert until night."

"Poison, cruelty, betrayal. Sounds pretty Venetian to me."

"You're probably right."

"So why did you wake me at this hour?"

"You said you wanted to know about the Patriarch's murderer. That you were to be the first to know if I captured him." Did she tense suddenly, Atilo wondered. As if sensing he'd lied? *Or is that me?*

"But you didn't capture him."

"No, my lady. I failed."

"Ahh . . ." The duchess clapped her hands to summon a girl with a silver jug of boiling water, and a squat iron teapot, already warmed. As Atilo watched, the duchess sprinkled leaves into the pot and added water. "You don't like my tea?"

"I've drunk it half a dozen times. Always in your company. I'm sure I'll learn to appreciate it eventually."

"Bring Lord Atilo wine."

He nodded gratefully.

"So," she said, when they had the room to themselves again. "It is how he escaped that will interest me."

"My lady . . ."

"I know you, Atilo. When they fail most men hide the fact. You drag me from my bed to tell me you failed. I should be cross. But something tells me you believe his escaping is more important than your failure. Am I right?

"As ever, my lady."

"Don't try to flatter me." Her voice was sharp, the atmosphere between them suddenly colder.

"I'm not," Atilo said simply. "And I need your advice."

"About this?"

"Which would be easier to control? An angel fallen to earth? Or a demon escaped from hell? Because that boy isn't human."

"*Krieghund?*"

Atilo shook his head. "Not *were*, not a night walker." Finishing his wine, he sat back in his seat, feeling every one of his years. "My lady, what else is there?"

Duchess Alexa took longer than usual over her next sip. She considered her answer as carefully as Atilo had considered his. And this, he knew, as she knew, was answer enough.

"You ask me why?"

"Captain Roderigo of the Dogana di Mar has . . ." Atilo shrugged, apologetically. "A half-Mongol sergeant who was with us when the creature escaped. He fired an arrow . . ."

"That fell magically to the ground?"

"No, my lady. He plucked it from the air, flipped it round and threw it back."

"And this sergeant?"

"Would be dead. If not for a boiled-leather tunic with buffalo-horn scales. The arrow hit his chest."

"My father had such a tunic," said the duchess, sounding almost wistful. "He had another made for my brother. Although riveted mail was common by then. A tunic and a laminate bow. This sergeant, he uses a proper bow?"

Atilo described Temujin's weapon.

"That's the one," she said. "So, this *thing* caught an arrow, and returned it hard enough to split horn scales. It did split the scales, didn't it?"

"Yes, my lady."

"Tell me more . . . No." She shook her head crossly. "Tell me everything. Especially the things you don't think important."

So Atilo did, from beginning to end, admitting finally that the boy, the creature, whatever this thing was, might not have killed the patriarch after all. He might simply have seen the murder. At which, Alexa said she could see how that might make Atilo want to find him. A point to which he had no answer.

"And it killed the beggar who led you there?"

"Broke his neck. Almost broke mine."

The duchess looked thoughtful. "To kill without spilling blood even when the moon is fat, while sparing the beggar's girl and her brother. That shows . . ."

"What, my lady?"

"Self-control."

"It twisted the boy's head half round."

"Believe me, it could easily have ripped his head right off."

"You know what it is . . . ?" *Stupid comment*, Atilo told himself. Her words made it obvious she did.

"It's our answer to the *krieghund*."

170

Alexa laughed at Atilo's shock.

"We've been losing the secret war for too long. It's about time we found a way to fight back. You think I didn't notice when you changed *killed Archbishop Theodore* to *might have witnessed his murder*? You hate my brother-in-law . . . No, don't bother denying it. Yet you let his captain help your search. Admittedly, Theodore was a friend of yours. But you're not sentimental. Certainly not enough to hunt down this boy for him. I doubt you're sentimental about anything. Except, perhaps, that little chit you plan to marry."

Atilo shivered, remembering the boy's threats.

"So why all this effort? The answer is you think this creature useful. Am I right?"

"He's my heir."

Duchess Alexa froze. "Everyone desires old magic. No one really knows what it will do when it arrives. Catch it, train it. We can talk about it being your heir later. Meanwhile, I'll write to my nephew . . ." She meant Tīmūr, newly created Great Khan of Khans and conqueror of China.

"I'll ask what his librarians know of creatures like this. It will take a year for my request to arrive, be deciphered and his answer to return."

Duchess Alexa hesitated. Whatever doubts she had about what she wanted to say, they lasted long enough for Atilo to fill a glass of wine and empty it in slow sips, while looking around at her room. It was small, but its paintings, statues and tapestries would buy a city. He'd just realised every single thing here once belonged to her husband when Alexa leant forward, her decision made.

"Once upon a time," she said, "angels fought. They fought high up in the wastes of space, where the stars are. This was long ago. When the gods still walked the earth openly and the oldest of the old kings ruled. When power meets power terrible things happen. The gods died, the kings died, the angels died . . . Whole forests burnt in the blink of an eye."

Atilo stared at her.

"This is a tale from my childhood. How the gods became the sky god, who watches everything but interferes little. A handful of angels escaped to wander, bitter and alone, in the wilderness. They moved like lightning. Killed without thought. Regarding us as we regard the animals."

"As food?"

"Among other things. But the last of them died in the year Kublai Khan was born. My nephew's librarians will know if it is otherwise. That's why I will write to him. You have the year it takes."

"To capture this creature?"

"No, Lord Atilo. To capture it, break its spirit, and make it our answer to the *krieghund*. If that can't be done, kill it. However, I would regard that as failure."

Discovering her water jug was empty, the duchess reached for a bell to summon a servant, then changed her mind. "Marco, my husband, believed talking of demons brought bad luck. That evil comes at the sound of its own name. He was wrong. It enters when invited. So, the real question is . . . Who invited it?"

Atilo had never heard her talk like this.

He had never heard her refer to the late duke by his first name or call him simply *my husband*. And he had never, in the times they'd met in public or private, heard her talk about her childhood, about being Mongol, about being foreign in how she thought. It made him uneasy.

"Come here," she said, patting her seat.

He could obey, or find a reason to leave. The first might make her an enemy, eventually. The second would make her one now. When Duchess Alexa lifted her veil she was smiling. And, Atilo couldn't answer anyway. Her face's beauty stole his breath away. *Words for a poet*, he told himself crossly. *I'm not one of those.* But it was the face of a girl a quarter her real age. Bright-eyed and innocent, knowing and inviting. Atilo shivered.

"Come on," she ordered.

He did.

If her face was flawless and her eyes undimmed, her body belonged to the daughter she never had, if not that daughter's daughter. Alexa di Millioni's skin was the yellow of fresh vellum and soft as Moroccan leather. With her head thrown back and her face safely veiled she rode him to some place he could never reach. And Atilo realised there *were* more things in heaven and earth than dreamt of in anyone's philosophy, and he was looking at one of them. "Your turn," she said.

Feeling every ache in his spine, Atilo wrapped one arm about her waist and twisted them both round, so she lay flat and he rested above.

"You've done that before."

"My lady, I'm sixty-five. I've done everything before."

"I'd tell you my age," she said lightly, "but you wouldn't believe it. And I'd tell you what I've done. But it's best you don't believe that either."

Then she said nothing much, because Atilo shifted his position and she gasped and grabbed his hips, forcing herself against him savagely. He ploughed her with an intensity that surprised him, collapsing on top of her when it was over. But felt his pleasure was more ordinary, less unknown.

"I take it you haven't bedded that chit of yours yet."

Raising himself on to his elbows, Atilo glared at the woman sprawled naked beneath him. Her voice was mocking enough to make him grab her upper arms. He rode her harder this time. Knocking gasps from her body. Until he collapsed breathless across her, his forehead pressed into the pillow.

"I guess not," she said.

In the early hours, after a maid arrived to take that day's orders, replace the tea and trim the wick, without once appearing to notice anyone else slept in her mistress's bed, Alexa woke Atilo with the sound of pissing in a pot.

"Have you met my *stregoi*?" she asked, dropping her gown.

He shook his head groggily. Alexa had a *stregoi*?

A wild witch child . . .

"You should," Duchess Alexa said. "In fact, you must. Send word to Desdaio that you've been detained by Council matters. And order your household to continue as normal. It's time we came up with a plan."

"For tonight?"

"No," said Duchess Alexa, kissing Atilo's cheek lightly. "We have a month to lay our trap. Requisition silver from the treasury and have it made into wire. Send the wire to the rope walk at Arzanale. I'll give orders that it be woven into a net. You can leave the rest to me."

Atilo tried not to shiver.

29

Velvet soiled. How easily Giulietta never realised, not having had to wear any garment for more than one day at a time. Locked in a cold attic, she still wore the red *houppelande* gown and fine woollen chemise she'd worn the night she was abducted. Which was, it happened, what she'd worn that time with the boy in the cathedral.

A tiny slit in the *houppelande* showed where she'd put the dagger to her chest, unwittingly ruining embroidery her mother had sewn. And she could still remember her trembling hands undoing mother-of-pearl buttons and slipping aside her chemise to put the point to her skin. Giulietta blushed.

The memory of that silver-haired boy refused to leave her. It left her troubled, sleeping badly and waking early. Part of her had always believed he was searching for her. There had been other fondnesses, of course. Other crushes. No matter what her aunt and uncle thought. A lute player, chestnut-haired and slight, with soft brown eyes that captured everything in their gaze. His fingers held her shoulders as he kissed her lightly on the lips. A sweet sin that would have seen them both whipped had she told anyone. Which she hadn't, except Eleanor, who could keep a secret.

The eyes she thought of now were not soft. Their owner not slight . . . Wiry, maybe. She could imagine his fingers on her shoulders. Elsewhere too.

A single look, and his memory burned.

Giulietta shook herself crossly. Of all things to think about, a boy had to be the most stupid. So she thought of her mother instead. More stupid still, since her eyes backed up with tears, overflowed against her will and kept falling long, long after she willed them to stop. Her mother was even less able to help her than a stranger seen across a darkened nave.

Wishes granted kill you. Her mother had whispered that.

Curling up on the floor, Giulietta tried to sleep; but the memories of her mother were too strong. She'd been assassinated three days after that whisper, at the age of thirty-six. Her marriage to a Visconti had been unhappy.

Her death a release.

The old duchy included Venice itself, and the towns, villages and estates on the mainland inland for a day's ride on a fast horse. The estates boasted fortified houses, built of brick and limed with stucco. Those towns not built with limestone-faced defensive walls had made good their lack in the last few generations.

By accident, long before returning merchants brought Chinese cannon to Serenissima, the creators of the first town walls provided protection against not-yet invented weapons. The stone-faced walls split, but the compacted earth inside withstood the impact of a cannonball.

The young woman curled on the attic floor – hips stiff, swelling breasts pressed against cold boards – owned two estates, three towns and more villages than she'd bothered to count. She could recall, if she tried, the names of the ones she'd ridden through as a child, when they still belonged to her mother.

At dawn, she gave up trying to sleep and went as close as she dared to her only window. It was locked and shuttered and, from what she could see, looked out on broken roofs and a part of the city she didn't recognise. A church tower in the distance looked ready to topple. The houses opposite were ruined, or near-ruined. None of them seemed occupied.

Unbuttoning her gown, the girl weighed one breast as a cook might examine a plump capon. It was definitely bigger. This would have delighted her a year ago. Now she was simply scared. Her nipples, usually pale, were puppy-tongue pink and hurt to touch. She prodded one all the same.

"You're safe," said the note she'd found on waking.

She didn't feel safe, and she didn't understand the bit about not stepping outside the circle until she realised it meant an oval of salt trickled round the edges of the room. That amount of pure salt was expensive. So she obeyed, being as yet too afraid of what might happen if she broke the command.

Her breasts ached, her flux had stopped its tides and her belly, she could swear it was swelling. Added to which, she'd worn the same gown for days. In a world where poor women wore rags that rotted with sweat under the arms, beneath the breasts or across their buttocks that would be unremarkable. But Giulietta changed her dress regularly, washed daily and bathed weekly.

At least she had, until that night in the cathedral.

Now she stank like a servant. And her food would disgrace an almshouse. Bread so stale it needed soaking. Rancid cheese that clogged her nails as she picked free the mites. Always served on a filthy pewter plate.

In one corner a bucket was hidden under her discarded chemise. She could wear the chemise and suffer the stink of her own shit. Or cover her bucket and freeze. From the scratches on the wall, she'd covered the bucket and been frozen for the best part of six weeks.

"You're a fool," she told herself.

It made a change from her uncle being the one to tell her. So many memories and so few of them good. "You have your health,"

Giulietta snapped. Something her nurse used to say. It made little enough sense then. She had her health, and her life.

Didn't expect that, did you?

She'd taken to talking to herself. There being no one else to talk to. This made her think of Lady Eleanor, her long-suffering lady-in-waiting . . .

Well, Giulietta didn't think she was long-suffering. But she'd heard it said, more than once, and been so offended she slapped Eleanor next time they met, and demanded to know what she'd been saying. The memory made her ashamed. At least, she assumed that was the feeling. It made a change from rage, and fear and despair. These being her usual responses to waking in this attic.

She never saw who collected her bucket. She never saw who delivered her food. The one time she stayed awake to find out, her slop bucket went unemptied and her plate unfilled. No one arrived to clean the mess when she kicked her bucket over in fury. Only the memory of cleaning it herself stopped her from doing so again.

Damn it . . .

She could scream and shout for help. But what was the point? The last time she tried she screamed herself to a frog's croak and damaged her throat so badly it hurt to swallow. Her nails not encrusted with rancid cheese she'd broken scraping mortar from around the door that kept her prisoner. Someone had thought about this. Her prison was filthy, its floor splattered with pigeon shit, its ceiling sticky with cobwebs, in which dead flies and desiccated spiders mixed equally.

Only the door was new, its hinges freshly oiled. When she woke, still rolled in the carpet, it was the hinges she noticed after struggling free. Now she wondered if the carpet was more significant. Still here, looking rich and out of place.

Like me, Giulietta thought.

Except she and squalor were proving to be closer bedfellows

than she liked. The dirt troubled her less than it did. Her bucket's stink was bad, but she was close to choosing warmth over her sensibilities. And she was regarded as having delicate sensibilities indeed. She was changing, and that scared her too. Because the change that scared her most was the one she didn't dare think about.

A vicious wave of fear broke over her, tumbling her emotions in its wake, and then swept back, threatening to drown her altogether. *What*, she wondered, feeling tears fill her eyes again. *What if it was even worse than she thought?* People said Dr Crow called up demons, captured djinn in bottles.

What if she carried a monster?

30

Men were watching for Tycho's return. A collection of restless Dogana guards, changing every few hours and all grateful to be relieved. Who knew what the captain told them? That they faced a demon, probably.

On the wind was the scent he hunted.

So slight and fragile he heard it as a perfect chord, a single bell-like note in the silence of his mind. He could not ignore its call. He could not stay away. Nothing in his life came close to how the scent made him feel. Hollowness and hunger ate away at him, bringing him to the edge of despair.

Above him, the sky was piled high with cloud. The full moon a sullen circle behind this masking. A fact for which he felt grateful. The sunlight burnt him, but the full moon hurt in other ways. So he stood in the squalid cave of an upper room, staring at the *campo* floor through broken shutters, and tried to master his emotions as he sought the scent he was tracking.

Red hair, blue eyes and a defiant glare. He could smell her, only too aware her scent might be in his head, with no right to compete with the stink of this world.

Eyes glared from under rotting floorboards and Tycho glared back.

The cat blinked first. Tycho wasn't the only predator in these ruins, simply the largest. The tom was sandy, little more than skin over bone. An Egyptian desert cat, from a ship that abandoned it by accident. The home-grown Venetian ignored them both. The lesser animals stayed away. When mice scattered below him, Tycho knew people were coming.

Few people were stupid enough to wander this way by accident. And fewer still came to ruined squares like this one by choice. So he knew the hesitant steps belonged to someone who had none.

Sharpening his senses, Tycho let go the scent that brought him back here and concentrated instead on who was approaching. He did this from instinct. Unaware he had until the rotten doors and broken shutters of the square became so clear he could see beetles scurrying, and hear the nervous breath of a girl entering the square, loud as shingle on a beach.

She was naked. A black tangle of hair between her thighs.

Rosalyn, shivering with fear. Her emotion so extreme fear barely began to describe it. Instantly he could taste her terror. Like the promise of rain before a thunderstorm.

Up here, Tycho thought, stepping from the shadows.

As she looked for him, something clattered from her fingers to the *campo* floor. Its loss dragging a swallowed sob from her throat. Falling to her knees, she scrabbled with her fingers, searching frantically.

She's blind in the dark.

Of course she is. How could he forget that being blind in the dark was normal ... ? It had been normal for him too once. Now he had trouble knowing the normal from the passing strange.

Let me help you.

Dropping three flights, Tycho landed on heaped rubble, sliding the final stage to stop a dozen paces from the girl. She was sobbing openly now. Her shoulders quivering and her face twisted in misery.

"I won't hurt you."

You will. Tycho heard the words clearly in his head. He was trying to pin down how that worked when her fingers found the dagger and she stood, facing him as heavy clouds finally parted and moonbeams lanced down.

"Don't," he said.

But she did it anyway.

Raising her blade, Rosalyn put its point to her shoulder. And before he could stop her, hacked diagonally across herself from collarbone to hip, the blade negotiating the valley of her breasts. Skin peeled, blood flowed.

Hunger hit.

So hard Tycho rocked on his heels.

Narrowing his eyes against the moon's flaring brightness he closed the gap in a blur, ending on his knees in front of her. All thoughts of being able to control his hunger forgotten. His dog teeth sharp as he bit into the wound and her body went rigid with shock. Grabbing her hips, he held her in place. She moaned and he fed, blood dripping down his face until the red mist faded and the ruined courtyard around them lost its hard edges and the sky paled to a watery pink.

Lifting his head, Tycho took another look at Rosalyn and discovered her mouth wasn't twisted in misery. It was sewn shut.

Scrambling up, he slashed it open. His fingernail growing from nothing. The action leaving her lips untouched.

"Behind you," Rosalyn whispered.

Every strand of the net burnt, searing his skin as silver weights fixed to its corners wrapped round his body, trapping him in its agonising embrace. His scream made rats scatter and sleeping pigeons swirl into the air from their roosts on the ledges. He fought the mesh, burning himself with every move he made, as he searched for the net's edges and tried to free himself from pain. He might have made it too. So desperate he was to escape. But the blood in his mouth soured, and the pink sky swirled and he felt himself fall, wrapped in fire and still screaming.

Within a minute his screams had turned to whimpers, turning to silence shortly afterwards. No Nicoletti came to see what was happening. The *campo* was ruined and unsafe, and no one they knew lived there. Some of them had seen a veiled chair being carried by guards from their windows. The rest simply had more sense.

"Wash him well," Duchess Alexa said.

A'rial scowled.

As the red-haired little witch broke the seal on a bottle and splashed purple liquid over weeping burns that stopped oozing and began healing before she had time to find a stopper, Duchess Alexa unwound a strand of horsehair and threaded a needle, the one she'd used to guarantee the beggar girl's silence.

"Stand up," she barked crossly.

The beggar girl continued to crouch, in blood and piss, swaying backwards and forwards, until the duchess grabbed her hair and dragged her up.

"It's not deep," she said. "At least you got that right. But it'll heal faster if you stand still yourself and we do this properly. What's your name?"

"Rosalyn, lady . . ."

"Jewish?" Duchess Alexa sighed. "Not sure why I'd expect you to know. It's like expecting you to know your age or your father's name. Your mother's too, probably."

"She was called Maria."

"Of course she was," Alexa said. "Mother of God. The inviolate. Amazing how many whores have her name in this city."

"*She wasn't a whore.*"

183

A'rial looked round, grinning.

Then hastily went back to dressing Tycho's wounds when her mistress raised her veil to give her a look anyone watching would have thought mild.

"And you," Alexa said. "Are you a whore?"

Rosalyn shook her head indignantly.

"So, little not-a-whore, what are you?"

"I'm Rosalyn," she said, trying not to cry as the duchess dug a needle into her shoulder, hooked it through flesh and tied off the knot with the ease of someone who'd done the job before. The pain from the stitching was worse than the pain when Rosalyn cut herself, unless one had simply caught up with the other.

She looked to where the red-haired child had Tycho laid out like a corpse, stripped of his clothes as she finished wiping his face and moved on to cleaning the rest of his body. "He's dead?" Rosalyn asked, her bottom lip quivering.

A'rial grinned.

"He's drunk," the duchess said. "On blood and opium, moonshine, a little antinomy, some henbane." She sounded amused. "And mandrake, obviously. To muddle his wits. Not that his wits needed muddling. Sadly . . ."

"Lady?"

"You're not the one."

"I'm not the one what?" asked Rosalyn, unconsciously mirroring the thoughtful tilt of Duchess Alexa's head.

Tying off the final knot, the duchess leant back to examine her handiwork. Her nod was satisfied. She was happy with the result. Pulling a tiny jar from her pocket, Duchess Alexa prised off its lid and stopper.

Rosalyn was staring at it transfixed.

"Would you like a look?"

"Please, lady."

The duchess scooped up a little ointment, then replaced the

lid and handed the jar to Rosalyn, while she smoothed the odd-smelling mix along the stitches. "Camphor," she told Rosalyn. "That's what you can smell."

But Rosalyn was turning the jar in her hand. Her fear, the pain and her stitches forgotten as she traced the path of a twisting, seven-toed dragon that chased itself around the rim. "*It's beautiful.*"

"From my grandfather's grandfather's days. It belonged to a Ming empress. And was found in the ruined gardens at Chang gan . . ."

That was when Rosalyn realised she should know who this woman was. She was rich, obviously. Rich enough to be carried in a chair and have guards. Powerful enough to talk openly about her witch when witches were to be executed. And foreign enough to go veiled and talk with an accent Rosalyn didn't recognise.

"Lady. Who are you? Can I ask?"

The woman smiled beneath her veil. "I am the weeds in the rubble. The bricks in that . . ." She nodded at a ruined warehouse. "The women bedded and children born in those broken tenements behind you. I am the hammering in Cannaregio's forges. The sweat of artisans boiling hides for cheap armour."

"Lady?"

"Call me *my* lady," she said, almost kindly.

The woman traced the stitching down Rosalyn's chest and sighed. Then she pulled back her veil to show her face in the moonlight. "I am Alexa di Millioni, and my son should be those things, not me. Be faithful and my favour is yours. Betray me and you will wish you died here tonight."

Looking into her cold eyes, Rosalyn believed her.

In the days when Venetians wore rags and Venice was a collection of fishermen's huts on stilts in the middle of a muddy lagoon, where inhabitants worried more about staying alive than building palaces, invaders threatened and the last imperial fragments of

Western Rome broke up around them, salt and fish were what they traded. Back then, salt was scraped from the rocks. Now the sprawl of low-walled tidal pools beyond Cannaregio produced salt for export in industrial quantities. Which was just as well, as a month's production of a single pool seemed to have been used to redraw the oval around the edge of Giulietta's attic.

If she hadn't been upset enough to kick it away to see what happened – the answer being nothing – she would never have seen tonight's gruesome little moonlit masque. And her dull despair at imprisonment, and her fear of what might happen, if she stepped over the salt circle would never have been burnt away in her anger that the silver-haired boy had come so close to finding her. Only to be stopped by the very aunt who had promised to protect Giulietta after her mother died.

It look Lady Giulietta forty minutes to climb down from the roof. And before she could do that, she had to cut her way through bottle glass. The house she was in was a ruin, but once it had been rich enough to have glazed windows.

The actors in that night's masque were gone.

She was grateful for that.

Using the stairs at first, she navigated in darkness, feeling her way from rotten step to rotten step, each slimy with frost and wood canker. She'd believed exiting her attic window was hard, as was crawling over tiles and tumbling through a skylight to hit the floor below. That was not the hard part.

Finding the second set of stairs broken and the floor so soft one heel tore wood as if it was paper was not the hard part. Not even doing this while shaking with fear and struggling to stop her teeth chattering in case anyone heard. (Since her bucket had still to be emptied and her platter refilled.) The hard part, she realised, was what came after she escaped.

Her uncle had betrayed her and so had her aunt. Even if her aunt had not, what could Giulietta say? Nothing, since she could barely form the words in her head to describe what Dr Crow had done to her and forcing them from her mouth was impossible. Giulietta knew. She'd tried . . .

I can't go to a physician, she realised in horror. He'd examine her, find her maidenhead intact, and proclaim a miracle, or damn her as bewitched. A wise woman? Mistress Scarlet was one of those. What if wise women talked to each other? They were out, priests were out, Dr Crow was definitely out. Uncle Alonzo would kill her before she could betray him.

And the woman she'd always turned to . . . ?

On whose lap she'd rested her head and poured out childish woes. Giulietta barely recognised Aunt Alexa in the terrifying being who stalked after that naked girl, and later sewed the girl's wounds shut. Her face, when she pulled back her veil. So beautiful lit by moonlight. So unbelievably cold.

It took Giulietta twenty minutes to crawl through a jagged hole in the floor, hang by her hands from splintery boards and drop on to rubble, twisting her ankle in the fall. Nineteen of those were spent summoning her courage. Unless, she thought bitterly, it was desperation that finally forced her through.

The blood on the *campo* where the girl cut herself had frosted like expensive icing. A scuff showed where the silver-haired boy had fallen to his knees, and buried his face in the naked girl's stomach. Of all the things she should be thinking, Giulietta was certain jealousy shouldn't top the list.

31

A thousand events happened next morning. Fishing boats docked on Venice's northern edge, their nets safely reset. That day's catch would go to feed the city, since it was Friday and eating meat that day invited the fires of hell.

Since none of the three corpses caught in the nets belonged to anyone who mattered, no fisherman was dragged to the leads, made to confess sins belonging to someone else and executed.

Master shipwrights scrambled from their mattresses, having bedded their wives for warmth in the minutes before the Arzanale bell rang. Apprentices and journeymen tumbled their women and left them with half promises of marriage, and a newly made brat to widen their wombs, as like as not.

The rope walkways, dry docks and shipyards of Arzanale were the source of Venice's power. The older men still called it Darsina, from the Arabic *Dar-al-sina*, and a few even called it that. Across the city, foreigners – including those from the countries that gave the city that word – finished their prayers and rose to stock their stalls or unload boats or carry goods through alleys more complex than any minotaur's maze. White men, black men, yellow men. A dozen face shapes and twice as many languages. Their laws did not require Friday fish but most ate it out of expediency. Although they called it politeness.

Night soil men carried waste to barges bound for the mainland. Butchers slaughtered pigs, working under canvas to protect them from the drizzle. The Church might forbid eating pork on Friday, but it allowed the butchering of swine and the preparation of tomorrow's meat. Awnings or not, the dirt beneath the butchers' feet still turned to slop from the blood, guts and excrement that spilled from the swine, along with their lives.

Whores swore, splashing water between sore thighs as brothels closed or shifts changed. Losers staggered from gaming houses, having mortgaged already mortgaged houses, as card sharps shook aces from their sleeves, and rolled loaded dice for that day's luck, knowing that it was already secure.

Hearths were swept. Kindling chopped.

In the hours either side of the black thread moment Venice changed her masks like a gambler hoping to avoid his creditors as he heads for a new *casa chiusa*.

The sun rose cold and pale over the lagoon's edge, where the first villages stood. A starving memory of the previous summer's sun, which had glowed like slowly falling iron shot. And along the Riva degli Schiavoni, fighting memories of that summer sun, walked a young woman in a half-mask of her own.

The mask was cracked, found in the mud a minute earlier. Her shoes were filthy. Her velvet *houppelande* gown squalid enough to suggest she earned her living on her back. Lady Giulietta di Millioni was used to seeing Venice from the canals. Her Venice was ornamental and gilded, and glimpsed through the fringes of her gondola's scarlet curtains. The rare times she'd left Ca' Ducale, it was to walk Piazza San Marco. This Venice was unknown to her.

Stinking and strange and badly dressed. It didn't help that her gown, as well as being filthy, was cut lower than it need be. A dozen men mistook her for a whore between the Rialto and the start of Riva degli Schiavoni. And Moorish sailors leered openly as she dodged between carts, calling out offers for her service she wouldn't toss to a beggar. The sailors guarded women chained at the ankle. *Criminals*, Giulietta decided, then noticed their cheekbones and dark hair. Captured on the wild plains beyond Dalmatia, they were headed for slave markets in the Levant.

Fifteen ships lay close to shore between Ponte della Paglia, just beyond Ca' Ducale and the bridge before Arzanale. French, Tedeschi, Byzantine, Andalusian and English . . . Lady Giulietta identified as many of the eagles, lions, fleur-de-lys and leopards as she could. Maybe, if she'd been looking where she was going, instead of playing herald, she wouldn't have walked into a French officer, negotiating for a dozen large barrels of fresh water.

He swung round, hand on his sword hilt.

The Schiavoni laughed as Giulietta jumped back. And the French officer's face darkened, thinking she mocked him. There was little doubt the merchant was. The Schiavoni were the largest group in the city after the Venetians. When Serenissima claimed the Dalmatian coast it gave the inhabitants trading rights. The new stone quay along the city's southern edge became home to Slav traders. They built churches, *scuole* and hospitals, founded charities and supported monasteries with their tithes. They also built the largest water cistern in the city. It gave them, their competitors claimed, unfair advantage. But then Venetians widely believed anyone who came between them and a greater profit had to have an unfair advantage one way or another.

"Look where you're going . . ."

Lady Giulietta glared back. When the young Frenchman scowled deeper, she made to walk round him and froze in shock when he thrust his arm out to stop her. He caught her wrist just ahead of her slapping him. Gripping it, he slapped her arse hard. "Sauce for the goose," he said.

"*How dare you?*"

"Dare I what?" he asked, grinning. "Object to you slapping

me. Or object to you trying to walk off without apologising?" He realised he still held her wrist when she did. Stepping back, he let his eyes flick to the Schiavoni, and Giulietta realised, belatedly, he was simply trying to regain his pride.

Men was her first thought. Her second was to say sorry. So she did, realising that was probably the first time she'd said it. *Do I mean it?* Giulietta ran back through not looking where she was going, running into him, and being cross. "Yes," she added. "I mean it."

Uncertain how to answer, the Frenchman turned to the Schiavoni merchant instead. "We have a deal, right?" Taking five grosso and two ducats from his belt pocket, he double-counted them, tipping the gold and silver into the man's hand. "Deliver them there." He pointed to a tired-looking lugger.

Surely he knew enough to make sure the casks were full? And was he really going to walk away without checking his supplier delivered the number of casks just paid for? How did she, who'd never paid for anything in her life, know he should do when the Frenchmen didn't? Because she was Venetian, and he wasn't, obviously enough. Nor was the water seller, but a hundred years of Venetian rule rubbed off on people. There was a joke about Schiavoni men. How can you profit from one? Buy him for what he's actually worth. Sell him for what he says he's worth. Buy a house with the difference . . .

"You," she said.

The Schiavoni looked at her strangely.

"Deliver the right number of barrels. And make sure they're full." His scowl said he'd been planning to do neither.

She walked on. Head up, shoulders back. Doing her best to hold her misery at arm's length. Squeezing between carts carrying swine, Giulietta stepped under a hoist lifting pigs into a boat, and only just missed being showered with the terrified animal's excrement. Someone laughed. Laughing louder when Giulietta turned her head aside to hide her tears.

Beyond the Riva degli Schiavoni and Arzanale gates was San Pietro di Castello, the island housing Venice's main cathedral. It was here Giulietta was headed, because when she'd summoned her courage to try the Patriarch's little palace by San Marco, announcing she was a friend of his, she'd been sworn at, called a grasping little whore and damned for her impiety. When she insisted she needed to see him, she'd been told with a sneer to try San Pietro.

Despite taking her two hours to walk there, this being further than she'd ever walked before – certainly alone – and discovering an unknown city in the space occupied by one she knew; even though she crossed a rickety bridge to discover her confessor was dead, his body having lain in state in San Pietro, before being buried under the nave; and a sour-faced, wimpled nun, looking too much like another sour-face wimpled nun, had rolled her eyes at Giulietta's sudden sobs, and sent her packing, with threats of a whipping, this was not the important part of Giulietta's story that day.

This came shortly afterwards.

Her return from San Pietro di Castello was quicker, in the way such walks always are. On a mudbank before Arzanale two vessels rested on their sides; one was being caulked with twists of rope dipped in tar. The other had a hole in its side large enough to ride a horse through. Two men stood beneath, arguing.

By skirting the shipyard's gate, Giulietta avoided being whistled at a second time. She avoided hoists lifting hog-tied swine, although excrement still splattered her as she waded, ankle-deep, through Judas-soft mud.

"My lady . . ."

She turned, surprised.

Her admirer was broad, high-cheeked and darkly bearded. Dressed in a scarlet doublet, tight black hose and a floppy hat. His codpiece was more prominent and more highly decorated than she'd seen. Eyeing the sailors watching her, he smiled lazily. "*Eggs*," he said. "*Have no business dancing with stones.*"

"You know me?"

"I know quality."

Her eyes tightened at his mockery.

"Believe me," he said. "I mean no insult."

And then, strangely, he leant close and inhaled her scent, as if smelling new-mown grass or some expensive perfume. And taking her hand, he opened her fingers to reveal a ring turned so its stone was hidden from view. The stone was priceless. The setting so old that much of its decoration had worn away.

He smiled and shrugged. His smile was easy and the shrug elegant. "I have . . . a certain *facility* for reading situations. And you, being beautiful, caught my eye. A second glance and I knew . . ."

"What?" she demanded.

He pointed to the chaos of the quayside. The penned pigs and sullen slaves. The whores stumbling from doors and blinking at the sunlight. The Schiavoni, the Mamluks, the Greeks. "That you don't belong here. You belong in a palace."

Maybe bursting into tears wasn't her wisest reaction. Alternatively, it was exactly what was needed. Either way, she found herself in his arms, held tightly until the crying fit passed.

"Prince Leopold zum Bas Friedland," he said, introducing himself. "The German emperor's envoy to Serenissima."

"Sigismund's . . . ?"

"Yes," he said. "The emperor's bastard." Leaning forward, he kissed her carefully on the brow and she felt herself shiver. A part of her did more than shiver. It began to melt.

"I'm Lady Giulietta San Felice di Millioni."

"I know," he said. "All things come to those who wait."

It was later, walking north, through alleys that Giulietta barely knew existed but which Prince Leopold seemed to navigate as if he'd lived his entire life in the city rather than it being the other way round, that she vomited. She did it guiltily. Turning aside and spewing against a wall, kicking dirt over her mess.

"Are you sick?" Prince Leopold asked.

She shook her head, face miserable and mouth turned down. Tears began to back up behind her eyes and she turned away again, unable to stop their fall and not wanting him to see her cry twice.

"What is it then?"

Maybe he read the answer in her silence, because he stepped forward to put his hand softly on her lower gut, feeling Giulietta freeze at his touch. And then, she felt a flutter beneath his fingers and his face turned white.

32

Situated in Dorsoduro, between the Grand Canal to the north and the wide expanse of the Giudecca Canal to the south, Atilo's palace occupied half of what was once a small mudflat before it was reclaimed from the lagoon. The ankle-deep channel between it and the next mudflat had been dug out to make a usable canal. The edges staked with oak pilings, lined with stone and turned into *fondamente*, those inland quays that ran along many canals. Although the house was brick it was faced in stone. Elegantly open galleries overlooked a red marble fountain dominating its central *cortile*, the private courtyard beloved by patrician families. Fretted boxwork balconies hid its public windows from the world.

Marble columns, supporting arches carved with flowers and plants and animal faces, ran around the *cortile*. A narrower row supported the trefoil windows of the floor above. The whole effect was of an elegant lace knit from stone.

There were two *porte d'acqua*. An ornate one on the Grand Canal and a slightly less grand, but more often used, one on Rio della Fornace. While the land door was close enough to Dogana to be walked in minutes. Of course, everywhere in the city was within walking distance of everywhere else.

Since Atilo didn't trade, which made him rare in Venice, his colonnaded *cortile* was empty and his servants few. He entertained in the piano nobile, a wood-panelled first-floor reception room with alternating black and white tiles, huge fireplace and long windows stretching from floor to high ceiling. Furniture was sparse but the walls had Murano mirrors. And a painting of Atilo as a young admiral, by Gentile da Fabriano, held pride of place among round-faced madonnas and anguished saints.

A huge Persian carpet covered much of the tiling.

Directly above one corner of the piano nobile were the separate chambers where Atilo and Desdaio slept. A strongroom and chambers for guests took up the rest of that floor. In one of these, Desdaio's possessions waited to be unboxed.

On the floor above was the kitchen, with an iron range venting to the sky. That floor also had servants' quarters, additional storage rooms and attic space never used by anything other than pigeons, mice and rats. When Atilo summoned labourers to dig a cellar in the weeks before Tycho joined his household, Desdaio was puzzled. No one had cellars. In a city like Venice they were an absurdity.

But the labourers arrived towards the end of spring.

They dug where Atilo ordered, and an intense young Sicilian with greasy hair, sucked his teeth and talked to himself, before sketching plans that he scrawled over and crossed out and scrawled over again. And though the men mocked his twitch and his accent behind his back, and sometimes to his face, they dug where he told them, dug as deep as he demanded, and built a double-skinned cellar without windows. The underfloor and the cavity between the first wall of brick and the second had to be filled with fiercely puddled clay to keep water from flooding the room.

In the Griffin and the Winged Lion and the Whore's Thighs, which is what the labourers called the Aphrodite, men drank and squabbled and talked of the strange strongroom Atilo il Mauros was building. It was agreed it must be to house Lady Desdaio's fortune. Since he'd never bothered with such a room to protect his own treasure. Had they looked closely, they might have noticed the clay they puddled with bare feet contained finely powdered silver. Enough of it to pay them all several times over. And they left before a door was installed at the bottom of a short run of steps leading from the *cortile*. Its handles, hinges and locks were also silver.

"Why keep him in a cellar?" Desdaio asked.

"For his own good."

"In the darkness?" she said. "Locked in."

Atilo took a deep breath, wondering what reason would convince her. He could say his new slave was so dangerous it was for her own good. But then she'd want to know why he'd brought Tycho into his household.

"It's only temporary. Until he gets over his fear of daylight."

Desdaio looked doubtful. "You're not punishing him?"

"I'm helping him," Atilo promised. And he was, in his way. The alternative to Atilo's training was death. Duchess Alexa had made her position clear. Atilo had wanted this boy, not just as his apprentice but as his heir. It was up to Atilo to make him fit for both positions.

He had a year.

Atilo suspected the time limit was arbitrary. A way of reminding him he might share her bed but she still held his life in her hands. With Alexa it was almost impossible to know. "What are you thinking," Desdaio suddenly demanded.

"Nothing," Atilo assured her, wishing his thoughts had been about something else. She'd heard the rumours. The whole city had heard the rumours.

There was a distance growing with every conversation he refused to have. Already he could see unhappiness in Desdaio's eyes. This was why he'd long avoided remarriage, bedding only women he would never love. Now he had a lover who haunted his dreams, and a wife-to-be who haunted his daylight thoughts.

"My father used to lock me in the dark."

He looked at her, wondering. All he remembered was how cosseted she'd been. How surrounded with servants and toys and nurses.

"He's not who you think," she said. "He's vain and ambitious and a coward . . ."

A dangerous mixture. The fact she could say it made Atilo take another look at the young woman he'd asked to marry him. She was as clear-eyed, attentive and gentle as ever. But he couldn't shake his feeling that her wits were sharper than he first thought.

"We live in dangerous times."

As they stood in the piano nobile, looking down from an arched window on to the *cortile*, where the artisan who fitted the cellar door was packing his work tools, Desdaio nodded to show she was listening.

"Sometimes it's necessary to make difficult alliances."

She went very still and he watched her glance from the corner of her eye. Her hand shifted and one finger touched his as if by accident, remaining there. Although she gave no hint that she was aware of this. "Alliances you might not make in other circumstances?"

"Yes," Atilo said.

"I see," she said. "I think."

Picking up a small wooden box, Atilo opened it. Watching as she shook out an ornate collar and held it up, letting the last rays of that day's light play across overlapping scales of filigreed silver tied with twists of gold wire. At the bottom, a heavy pear-shaped pendant was set with rubies, pearls and squares of mutton-fat jade.

"Silver?" Desdaio sounded surprised.

"I have one too." Atilo opened his cloak to show a new chain where his gold one usually hung. "I know silver's for *cittadini* here but in my country it's lucky. And it suits you better than gold. Silver sets off your eyes and hair."

198

Desdaio smiled. "I'll put my gold away."

"No," said Atilo. "Wear it. But wear this as well."

When he looked, her eyes were bright and her chin trembled with unspilt tears and unexpressed emotion. Taking her hand, he kissed it. Seeing tears spill down her cheeks as she turned away from him. A rustle of silks, and the click of a door handle said she was returning to her chamber.

She did so in silence.

Unquestionably more intelligent than people supposed. She'd understood instantly his comment about alliances, and believed his answer about their being necessary. Whether he believed it was another matter.

33

The craft Atilo arrived home in that evening was larger than a *vipera* and smaller than a *sandolino*. It had been designed to Dr Crow's specifications and built in half a day by a master shipbuilder and his apprentices. The fact the shipbuilder had been given his orders by Duchess Alexa ensured the man worked hard and asked no questions.

The vessel featured a small cabin, no windows.

Atilo was uncertain what brief Dr Crow had given the master of the Arzanale. As a member of the Ten he could find out. As head of the Assassini he should probably know already. To say Atilo lived between those two roles was simplistic. His fame as Venice's old Lord Admiral, his new position with the Ten, and his duties as head of the Assassini were three strands of poison ivy strangling each other. How he could support a fourth as Duchess Alexa's lover was beyond him.

"Ready that rope."

The mage's vessel powered itself. Although Dr Crow claimed a dwarf hid in a compartment at the rear, turning a handle to drive infinitely complex gears that drove a screw that forced the craft through the waves.

Atilo thought that unlikely.

Twisting the rope back on itself, Iacopo dropped the noose he'd made over a bollard, holding the rope's free end while the vessel's forward momentum narrowed the gap and brought the strange craft to rest.

"Neatly done, Iacopo."

Iacopo lost his smile as the cabin creaked open, revealing darkness.

Eyes shielded behind smoked glass peeked through a narrow gap and vanished just as quickly. Hightown Crow had told Tycho daylight was now safe for short periods. He obviously doubted it. Braided to snakes, even the boy's hair was oiled against sunlight. His braids being all Atilo could see above the arms Tycho had crossed over his face to protect him from the day.

"It's safe," Atilo said gruffly. "Now hurry it up."

He'd asked for this *thing* as his heir. Now he had to train it. Atilo's job was to make sure Tycho didn't disappoint. *Be careful what you wish for.* The old man's guts twisted with doubts he couldn't risk showing, least of all to Duchess Alexa.

Moonstruck poets were the mainstay of fable.

But a moonstruck assassin? One the duchess half believed a fallen angel? Assuming Atilo had the point of her wilfully oblique fairy story. Stepping on to dry land, Duchess Alexa's protégé sniffed the air, his shoulders sagging a second later. Whatever scent he was after he'd failed to find it.

The boy was dressed in a flowing leather coat over a doublet of silk, both black and both oiled. His hose was also silk, also oiled. Boots and gloves matched. Cut from black Moroccan leather so fine it stretched like skin. He was undoubtedly the most expensively dressed slave in the city.

Hightown Crow's choice.

From his belt hung a pocket. Inside it, a purple-glazed ceramic dragon curled around a pot of ointment mixed by Hightown Crow himself. Duchess Alexa defined what it should do. He chose the zinc-white, camphor, pounded silica and grape-seed oil needed to achieve that. The mixture stopped the sun from burning Tycho for up to an hour at a time. The alchemist was proud of this. Proud enough to tell Atilo twice what the mixture did. The leather coat and oiled silk might protect Tycho's body, the gloves his hands.

But the ointment was Tycho's mask.

"Shall I tell Lady Desdaio we have a new member of the family?" Iacopo asked, stepping back at a growl from Atilo.

"He's a slave."

Iacopo bowed deeply, and then turned to enter the *porta d'acqua* to Ca' il Mauros, leaving his master with the newcomer still peering at the ghostlike sun hiding on the far side of drizzling clouds.

"I own you," Atilo said. "Do you understand that? Whatever you are, wherever you come from doesn't matter now. You live and die by my rules."

Tycho shrugged.

"Do you understand?"

The boy's shoulders straightened at Atilo's tone. *He's taken orders before*, Atilo thought. *That's good.* Also bad. Most of those who passed through Ca' il Mauros arrived young and unformed. Eleven or twelve, homeless, unprotected and hungry.

Their gratitude carried them through early weeks of brutal training. The girls, less likely to be vicious, let their gratitude overwhelm their scruples about violence. Dragged from the streets to the palace of a strange patrician, one obviously rich and powerful, most girls thought they knew what awaited them. That Atilo proved them wrong bound them tight. The boys had less awareness of their possible fate.

Atilo put that down to lack of imagination. "Well?" he said.

"I understand." Something about the boy's tone worried his new master.

"What do you understand?"

"That you believe what you say."

Atilo stared at him. "Tomorrow we begin training," he said. "It will be brutal. You will be punished if you fail." The Moor kept his sentences simple, still not certain how much of what was said Tycho understood. He expected the boy to nod his agreement, to show some gratitude. Gratitude and respect. If needed, gratitude, respect and fear. Those bound an apprentice to his master.

Instead Tycho shook his head. "Tonight would be better."

"What?"

Touching his glasses, the boy said, "I see best in the dark." He weighed his words and obviously found them wanting, because he added, "Probably kill better too. If that's what this is about."

34

"He's a strange one," Desdaio said.

Taking another spoonful of venison from the pie in front of him, Atilo felt rather than saw her smile. She'd trimmed the meat herself, chopped root vegetables, ground Indian pepper and cut stale bread to serve as plates. He had a cook to do all that. Just as he had a serving woman to stand behind his chair and top up the glass Desdaio refilled from a jug.

He sat at the head of his long oak table in the piano nobile, with Desdaio at his right. Although light from a candelabrum made his glass sparkle, it barely reached the high-beamed ceiling overhead, and he sat with her in a puddle of brightness surrounded by shifting shadows. Both of them ate using forks. A habit Byzantium had adopted from the Saracens, its enemies. A princess brought the fashion to Venice two centuries before when she married the doge.

"Maybe three," Atilo admitted.

Desdaio nodded to indicate she was listening.

The rest of Italy still ate with knives and their fingers and regarded Serenissima's use of the two-pronged forks as proof the city was corrupted by its links with the Levant. As Gian

Maria of Milan jeered, "What needs man with a fork when God gave him hands?" He would have been even less impressed to know the implement's heathen origins.

"I have to go out later," said Atilo, putting down his silver fork and wiping his mouth with his hand. Desdaio would be disappointed. She'd found a harpist from Brittany. On the run from something, Atilo imagined. He was to play for them that evening. It was meant to be a surprise.

"Can't it wait?"

"Probably not," Atilo said. "Council business."

Desdaio's face fell. Nothing came before the Ten. The daughter of a Venetian lord, the great-granddaughter of a rich *cittadino*, she understood that.

"You're taking Iacopo?"

"Tycho," Atilo said. "I'll be taking Tycho."

"He's a strange one," Desdaio said. As before, Atilo said nothing, simply waited for Desdaio to put her thoughts in some sort of order. People thought her beautiful but simple. She was not. She simply thought slowly. "He scares me," she admitted finally.

"Why?" Atilo was interested.

"Something about him." Desdaio bit her lip. She hesitated, considering her words. "He could be a prince," she said finally. "When he's not sulking in corners like a beggar. I'm not saying he is. Just sometimes, when he looks at us . . ."

"He seems . . . princely?"

"Don't laugh at me. He eats *castradina* with his fingers, but stands up when I enter a room. And he watches always. I find him in rooms and don't know how he got there. He's like a shadow. Always there, except when he's not."

"And Iacopo doesn't scare you?"

"That's different."

"In what way?"

Desdaio blushed, looking towards the fire as if shifting logs had suddenly caught her attention. All men looked at her, Atilo knew that was what she wanted to say. Iacopo was simply one of those.

"Should he scare me?" she asked instead.

He's knifed a dozen men and cut a child's throat without hesitation, simply because those were my orders. He uses his fists freely on whores, and more often than not takes them and forgets to pay. When he thinks I'm not looking, he leers at you as if he would deflower you on the spot if not for me.

And, God forbid I was to order it. But if I did, he would knife you now, weight the sack containing your body with stones and row it beyond the Giudecca himself, returning for breakfast with his appetite intact.

"That was just an example."

"Something about Tycho is wrong."

"He's been living on the streets," Atilo said. "We don't know what's been done to him."

"It's what he's done to others that worries me. Oh, I don't *know* he's done anything. It's just . . . The way he barely speaks."

"Give me a month," Atilo said. "If he still worries you the Black Crucifers can have him." It was a lie, of course. He could no more give him to the Crucifers than he could tell Duchess Alexa he'd changed his mind and he no longer wanted the boy as his heir. And that would be a lie in its turn. He wanted the boy, just on his own terms.

"You'd let Crucifers torture him?"

"My dear," Atilo began, and changed his mind. Let her think that was what he meant, rather than what he *had* meant. That Tycho could join the Order, being darker in temperament than even them.

She'd let him stay now. She'd probably have let him stay if the alternative was Tycho being accepted as an order acolyte. Desdaio hated the Black, not understanding the purpose they served. The White Order protected Cyprus and guarded caravans in the Middle East. The Black extracted every last sin with torture, before forgiving the lot. The Black Order's purpose was to ensure no prisoner faced God with crimes on his conscience.

"Can you row?" Atilo asked, when he and Tycho stepped on to the landing beyond the watergate of Ca' il Mauros.

No, of course I can't . . . The boy shook his head.

"Then learn quickly," Atilo growled, settling himself into a *vipera* and sitting back. The night was clear and full of stars, an old moon hung above the city, already tired in that way fading quarter moons are. "And when I ask you a question you answer. And you call me *my lord*. Understand?"

Tycho nodded, too nauseous to speak.

Atilo hissed in irritation.

Their trip across the mouth of the Grand Canal was a vomit-inducing nightmare. One that took five times longer than necessary according to Atilo. Glowering at his master, Tycho wondered if he knew the only thing standing between him and drowning was Tycho's fear of being left alone on the water. Although he had been told what would happen if he rebelled. He would be given to the Black Crucifers. An order so fearful Desdaio crossed herself when he asked what they did.

Jumping from the *vipera*, Tycho slipped and fell, hitting his face on the slippery boards of the new jetty. Dark water taunted him through its gaps. So he rolled sideways a couple of times to reach land, lying there gasping, while stars left trails in a spinning sky.

Having tied the boat for himself, Atilo stamped over to Tycho and kicked him. "You're afraid of *water*?" Tycho's reply that water made him sick earned another kick. "This is ridiculous."

"Not at all." Stepping out of the shadows, Hightown Crow yanked Tycho upright before swinging round to face Atilo. "Did I or did I not fashion boots he was to wear? And did I or did I not ship him to you in a cabin floored with earth?"

The fat little man with his absurd beard and wire spectacles glared at the Moor who towered over him like a wooden carving of a hard eyed god. And all the while Tycho knelt by the jetty, hands pressed to the dirt as he willed the sky to stop spinning. A dozen late-night revellers staggered by, ignoring the little tableau as if such things happened every night.

"We train in bare feet."

"He wears what I provide. Unless you want this to happen every time you take him across the lagoon? God knows, he gets sick simply crossing the Rialto bridge. How can you be so stupid?"

Atilo glowered. "Why are you here?"

"To watch him train."

Atilo wanted to say no one watched. But since the only other person to know where Tycho trained tonight was Alexa, Dr Crow's presence meant she'd sent him. Which meant he stayed. Atilo was wise enough not push the point.

They woke a cobbler at random in a tiny alley to the west of Piazzetta San Marco, a stone's throw before la Volta. Once he recovered from his fright, and realised he'd been selected not for his sins, such as they were, but because his was the first sign they'd seen, he vanished into his shop and returned with second-hand boots and shoes. Many were simply heels designed to be sewn to leggings. More than a few were designed for women. It looked as if the man had simply obeyed Dr Crow and brought every piece of footwear in his shop.

"Try these ones," Dr Crow suggested.

Having selected the softest and most worn pair, these being the ones least likely to rub, Dr Crow ordered the cobbler to rip free their soles and heels. Then he went into a nearby *campo*'s church, unlocked the crypt by passing his hand over the key plate and scraped dirt from the lid of an old coffin.

The cobbler was ordered to trim a new sole from the best leather he had, cut away its centre and sew what remained to the boot. He was to fill the cutaway space with the dirt before fixing the original sole over it.

"My lord . . ."

Taking the shoes, Dr Crow gave them to Tycho, saying, "These will also make it easier to cross bridges." To the cobbler, he said. "This never happened. Understand?"

"I understand, my lord."

"Good," said Dr Crow, tossing him silver.

They were fifty paces beyond the shop when Atilo vanished. A few minutes later he caught them up again, tossing the alchemist his coins. "There are better ways to buy silence," he said, wiping his blade on a scrap of leather.

35

Tycho recognised the place immediately. The Patriarch's little gardens, adjoining the gardens of the ducal palace. Ca' Ducale showed lights. The Patriarch's palace, however, was in darkness. According to Atilo, Gregory XII, the new Pope in Rome, was too busy trying to negotiate a union of the two papacies with his rival, anti-Pope Benedict XIII, to appoint a new Venetian archbishop, and, besides, he didn't like the Venetians, few people on the mainland did, so he felt they could wait . . .

A very slight wind rustled the branches of the poplars; bushes looked uncared for. But staff had taken the trouble to scatter earth across any stains that might remain from Archbishop Theodore's murder. Unless that was simply the rain, sleet and snow that had filled the last few weeks.

A girl, a young boy and a dead-eyed man stood beneath the garden's single oak. Their hands were tied, and a noosed rope around each neck threaded over the lowest branch and was pegged into the dirt behind. Tycho recognised two of the three immediately. Rosalyn and Pietro, last seen the night he was captured. The third was a broken-faced man who watched Atilo approach with the stare of someone who's seen violence before, much of it of his own making. Anger burnt off him like steam.

Did the others know how dangerous he was? Tycho wondered briefly. He imagined they must. As he moved forward, Tycho felt fingers on his shoulder lock him to the spot. Whatever nerve Atilo squeezed cost Tycho his ability to move.

"Look around you. Always look around you."

An archer with a three-quarter bow stood behind another tree. An arrow already notched, his bow drawn and his fingers curled around the string.

"Poisoned," Atilo warned.

Where Rosalyn's hands were secured with a single rope, the man's were double tied, his ankle fixed to an iron ball by a fat chain. If he tried to run, unwise as that seemed, a second archer waited to make sure he didn't get far.

"The garden is secure?"

"Yes, my lord." A sergeant nodded.

"Then give me the key," Atilo said. "And go."

If the sergeant's gaze stopped on Atilo's apprentice it was simply his strangeness. From the speed at which the man hurried off he had little stomach for what was about to happen. Letting go of Tycho, Atilo said, "Lesson one. You have no friends." He jerked his head towards Rosalyn. "Punch her."

"No," Tycho said.

"You refuse to punch her?"

"Yes, I refuse."

Atilo pulled a dagger from his belt and reversed it across his wrist. "Then you cut her face," he said. "And if you won't do that, you'll take an eye. If you won't take an eye, then you'll take both ears and her nose. If you won't do that, the archer will shoot you . . ."

"Please," Rosalyn said. "Do what he says."

"Never." Tycho shook his head.

"More fool you," Dr Crow muttered.

Atilo's dagger slashed once and the ropes binding the wrists of the broken-faced man fell away. A second slash severed his overhead rope, leaving its noose dangling like a scarf. Lobbing him a key, Atilo said, "Free your feet . . . Right, now we trade." He caught the key and tossed the man a blade in return.

"You know what to do?"

The man's eyes slid to Rosalyn. And Tycho saw her skull beneath the skin. Her eyes hopeless in hollow sockets.

"Don't," he yelled. As he lunged for Atilo something hit the side of his head. Turning, he saw Hightown Crow raise his walking stick. It came down a second time so hard the boy fell. When he tried to stand, Dr Crow hit him again.

"Stay there, damn you."

"Make it fast," Atilo told the freed prisoner.

Without needing to be told again, the man grabbed Rosalyn by her throat, rammed Atilo's blade between her ribs. Her little brother's scream ended when Atilo punched him in the stomach.

"Slow is better," the flat-eyed man said.

"How many women now?"

"Eight, my lord."

"Our friend tortured the last he killed. Slit her from sex to throat. The Watch captain said it took her an hour to die."

"Longer," the man insisted. "Much longer."

Standing over Tycho, Atilo said, "Punching her would have saved her. Cutting her face would have saved her. *You* could have saved her. *You didn't.* Learn from your mistakes."

Ignoring him, Tycho crawled to where Rosalyn lay dying.

And, blood falling from his wounded scalp across her face like tears, he watched life leave her eyes. Bile filled his mouth. The smell of her blood made his jaws ache so badly he felt punched on both sides at the same time.

Above him the moon's normal hue was gone, replaced by a blood-red filter between the world and his anger. And something else . . . For the first time Tycho *felt* his body begin to change.

Something black slithered inside him, strengthening his muscles, heightening his senses.

Dragging Tycho to his feet, Atilo said, "Are you listening?"

"No," Tycho said.

His entire anger went into the blow that crushed her killer's voice box. Lacking a blade, Tycho dug his thumbs into the man's eyes until yolk ran down his wrists. When Atilo reached for his dagger, Tycho went for his eyes instead. He missed because Atilo blocked with the speed of a man half his age.

"Don't," Hightown Crow ordered.

And Tycho felt the point of a blade burn his neck. It felt colder that the coldest ice. Dr Crow had drawn a sword from his stick.

"Silver. From the court of the Khan," he said. He was talking about the blade. "Not pure, of course. That's too soft to take an edge."

"*Dr Crow.*"

"He must learn," Hightown Crow said, lowering his weapon.

"Metallurgy?"

"Everything. Those are Alexa's orders. Anything else she will regard as failure. *Your* failure," the alchemist added, in case this wasn't obvious. "So, now you've cleverly killed the only person he trusted, I suggest you work out other ways to influence our little friend."

36

Desdaio was the one who half tamed him, and asked diffidently if Atilo could stop referring to Tycho as *that creature*. She was the one to suggest, since daylight scared him, magic ointment or not, perhaps he should be reserved for duties that needed to be done at night.

And Atilo, who considered every word he spoke, and judged others by what they meant rather than what they said, weighed her words and realised she meant precisely what she said; astounded by how that realisation touched him.

Sentimentality and ruthlessness were the prerogative of old age. Sometimes he wondered if they were all he had left.

She would never have unlocked Tycho's door had she known he intended to kill her in revenge for Rosalyn's death. And Tycho would never have found himself with the opportunity. Only to discover he lacked the desire.

His war, Tycho's war, was with Atilo, who was away doing whatever he did when he locked Tycho in the cellar and left Desdaio alone with her tapestry.

'My lord Atilo says I should be wary of you . . ."

"Of me?" Tycho asked, bowing his way into the high-ceilinged piano nobile of Ca'il Mauros and realising she was the only other person there. Alone, defenceless, wearing a gown that barely covered her breasts. She sat near a huge fire, a scrap of embroidery on her lap. Wine, glasses, bread and cheese rested on a table next to her bench. Her face was flushed from the fire and too much red wine.

"And I am a little afraid," she said. "Is that silly of me?"

Tycho waited to discover what Desdaio wanted. It turned out she'd like to make friends. Since he was a slave and she was rich beyond his imagining, he wondered why he was the only one of them to see the stupidity of this.

"What did you do this morning?"

Stabbed corpses in a morgue until the knife was blunt and the corpses mince . . . Almost worth telling her to see how she'd react. Hours spent learning *where* to stab, followed by hours practising on the bodies of beggars, criminals and foreigners. People without friends.

"Well?" she asked.

"I studied with Lord Atilo."

Desdaio sighed. "I know that. What did you study?"

"Ask him, my lady."

"I'm asking you." It was rare for her to frown. So rare her face looked wrong. Her nostrils flared and her lips thinned, lines appearing at the side of her mouth.

"My lady," he said carefully. "I'm not allowed to tell you."

"My lord Atilo said that?"

"Yes, my lady." He'd told Tycho exactly what would happen if Desdaio discovered through him about the Assassini. Although that was something else Tycho was not allowed to say.

"Why are you here?" Desdaio asked.

Tycho was about to say, "You ordered me," when he realised this was not what she meant. "Because I can't leave."

"You could run away," she said, as if discussing a game. "Steal a boat and row to the mainland. Or escape on a ship." Glancing towards a window, she said, "There are always ships."

"Water hurts me."

"Hurts?"

"It tried to kill me once. And I have other reasons."

"Really," Desdaio said. "What are they?"

"I'm looking for a girl . . ."

Laughing, Desdaio reached to cut cheese and tear a loaf to pieces. When she filled two glasses with wine from a jug in front of her, Tycho realised she intended to feed him. "My lady, I've eaten already."

Her glance was sharp. "Amelia says not."

Ah yes, Amelia of the silver braids and the double life. They were strangers to each other these days, as Amelia had said they must be.

"I ate with Lord Atilo, my lady."

"Drink, then. Drink, and tell me your life. Who are your family? Where did you live before this? I want to know these things . . ."

"My lady, I'm a slave." Tycho wondered if she knew he'd used a whole fifth of his precious pot of Dr Crow's ointment protecting himself from the weak sunset dribbling through her window. Of course not. And she knew next to nothing of her husband-to-be's life, even less about his training methods.

Masters beat servants, journeymen beat apprentices; such was the nature of training. Atilo had shown him the whip he used to beat Amelia and Iacopo. Then the whip he would use on Tycho. This was leather and silver wire. The single lash he'd slashed into Tycho's naked back that morning made Tycho piss himself with agony.

"I know all about Amelia," Desdaio said brightly.

What could she know? He wondered how close it was to the truth. Reaching absent-mindedly for a glass, he looked up to find Desdaio smiling. She tapped the double seat in which she sat.

"Come here. And tell me all."

The rule, *don't show what you feel*, had kept him alive. But with Desdaio the temptation to tell her how he found himself here was overwhelming. And she might know who the girl in the basilica was.

That would be worth discovering.

"I don't know my name," Tycho said. "Not my real name. And what I remember changes. But I know I was born in a rotting town. With little food in summer and less in winter. Beyond the walls lived demons. Inside, a crippled lord and his drunken brother, their guards, their women and us. Their slaves."

"You were a slave before?"

"I believe so . . . Until Duchess Alexa trapped me this may be the only time I've been free."

"What does Alexa have to do with this?" A sudden bleakness wintered in Desdaio's eyes.

"I was born a slave," Tycho said quickly. "And became a dog. That much I've remembered."

His words did what he wanted. The trouble fled her eyes. She smiled, laughed, wondered if he was serious and smiled again. "A dog?"

"A wolf dog . . . Wolf dogs kill wolves."

Desdaio leant closer. The fire was warm, her face flushed. Leaning forward shifted her breasts under silk. Tycho watched them try to overspill the embroidered scoop of her gown. "How many wolves did you kill?"

"It's hard to remember . . . I mean it," he added, when Desdaio rolled her eyes. "I was . . . ill, when I arrived here. Remembering is hard."

"Maybe you simply want to forget?"

"That's possible."

Atilo was away on Council business, Iacopo with him. Amelia? Who knew where she was? Fighting Nicoletti, probably. The cook was up in her kitchen, glad to have it to herself. There were only three people in the whole of Ca' il Mauros, and one of those was pounding dough a floor above.

"Tell me about the wolves," Desdaio said impatiently.

*

Lord Eric's wolf dog was old, its temper erratic. Tycho remembered that much. And in remembering this, remembered more . . .

Since there were no sheep left, owning a wolf dog was pointless. But the lords of Bjornvin arrived with wolf dogs and sheep, not to mention cattle, horses and slaves and their brats. All the things needed to settle a new land. Lessons had been learnt from earlier colonies. The lesson from Iceland was that, if you want families to come, don't name it after the cold. So Greenland, which had far more claim to be *Iceland* than that country ever did, was named to sound welcoming.

Vineland had vines. It had green fields and clear streams and less harsh winters than either Greenland or Iceland, for all its winters turned brutal in later years. But after Greenland no one trusted settlers. So the Vikings and their families who should have come never did. And the founding families slowly lost land and the will to fight the wilderness. Bjornvin was the last town. When it fell, and no one but Lord Eric and his cousin Leif doubted it would, Vineland would be no more.

This is what the thralls whispered.

Silent and watchful, silver-haired even as a child, Tycho grew up among truths that couldn't be said. Lord Eric was unable to father children but his bard still sang of glorious generations to come. Lord Leif fought drunk, because fear made him vomit when sober. But poems celebrated his battles with the Skaelingar . . .

"The wolves," Desdaio demanded.

"First the wolf dog. Which was old, its temper erratic . . ." Realising he should have started somewhere else, Tycho stopped. "First me. A thrall the others avoided. For the first seven years I ran naked. I did so because my mother hated me too much to clothe me. At least, I thought she was my mother. Maybe she hoped the cold would kill me."

It almost had. One winter he'd been saved by a drunken house carl who staggered from the great hall, found Tycho curled in a little ball by an outhouse door locked against him, and thought it funny to piss on a sleeping child. A dozen other house carls staggered out to join the fun. He woke crusted in yellow slush and heaped with snow where they'd buried him. But he woke. Having been saved by the casual contempt of others.

He was three at the time.

The memory hurt less now Tycho knew Withered Arm wasn't his mother. Back then, he believed if she hated him the fault was his. And his brothers followed her lead. Afrior, though, never hated him. She saved his life.

Half starved, his ribs sticks and hair so filthy house carls stopped calling him silver hair and simply started calling him *you, thing, shitface*, he'd been combing through a rubbish pile, searching for anything edible, food being scarcer than ever, when Afrior screamed his name. Looking up, he saw his brothers grinning.

The wolf dog's chain was fixed to its post. The collar was fixed to the chain. The wolf dog wasn't fixed to its collar. In that split second, Tycho understood what his brothers' look meant. He dropped as the beast leapt from behind him, splattered by the creature's drool as it passed overhead. Scrambling up, he ran. Cunning and hatred made him head straight for his brothers, who scattered. The wolf dog went after one of them instead.

Grabbing Afrior, he threw her through a gate.

The gate was huge, at least for him. But he pushed it shut anyway, heels dug into the dirt, expecting at any time to hear snarling behind him and feel jaws close on his hip. When he looked round, the dog had his eldest brother cornered by the log pile. The best anyone could say for what came next was that it was quick. Leaping, the beast bit the boy's neck to bring him down, and ripped out his throat.

Throwing a stone at the dog was stupid. His other brother did it anyway.

And the beast would probably have killed again if Tycho –

aged seven, and naked – hadn't grabbed a pottery shard from the rubbish and intercepted the beast. He didn't do it to save his brother. He did it because Lord Eric was back from hunting, and Afrior had entered the gate behind him.

Driving the shard between the beast's teeth, Tycho's blow cut into its jaws until his shard hit bone with a jolt. The dog tried to bite but its jaw muscles were severed and the shard stopped its teeth from closing.

"You, step back . . ." Lord Eric's shout brought all noise to a halt.

He should have obeyed. He should have let go of the shard, leaving it lodged in the dog's jaws, and stepped back. Instead, he pulled the shard free and slashed it hard across the beast's throat, feeling hair drag and flesh open. It was blind luck that he found an artery and bled the dog out.

Grabbing the boy's shard, Lord Eric looked at it.

It was a quarter of a broken bowl, with the bowl's rim making a handle and the break and glaze creating a razor edge. Even so, the shard had chipped where it crunched into the bones of the wolf dog's jaw. For a moment, it looked as if Lord Eric would use it on him. Instead, he pointed at the collar in the dirt.

"Fetch that," he ordered.

The boy did so.

"Who undid this?" Lord Eric demanded, his face hard and his eyes furious. Afrior glanced at her middle brother, and the boy saw Tycho notice.

"My brother did," the boy said, pointing to the corpse by the log pile.

Lord Eric grunted.

When Withered Arm arrived she began keening for her eldest son, until the master glared at her and she felling into hiccupping silence and swallowed sobs instead. The look she shot Tycho was brutal.

"This is your boy?" said Lord Eric, pointing at him.

She stayed silent until the Viking grabbed her and twisted her face to look into his. "When I ask you a question you answer." His voice was quiet and dangerous. "Is he your son?"

"Yes, my lord."

There was something unnerving in Lord Eric's gaze. When he released her face, Withered Arm stared at the ground.

"Well," Lord Eric said, buckling the collar round Tycho's neck. "Now he's my wolf dog . . ."

"And what happened to Afrior?" Desdaio asked.

She looked at Tycho's drained face and his barely drunk glass of wine. When she touched his hand, he flinched. "Another time," she agreed. "You can tell me about it another time." Hesitating on the edge of saying something, she shrugged. "I think you're better off here. Such things could never happen."

Remembering Atilo's silver whip, his warning of what would happen if Tycho was ever sent to a Venetian prison, and the Mamluk girl nailed to a tree in the *fondak* garden, Tycho kept his silence. On the way out, he suggested Desdaio lock him back in and not tell Atilo they'd talked. It would upset him.

Tycho took back to his cellar the thought that Atilo now owed him two lives: Rosalyn's, and the one he'd just refused to take.

37

There were a dozen pig shambles in Venice. The one Tycho was delivered to by Amelia on a hot summer night was on the city's northern edge; ten minutes west of della Misericordia and almost opposite the island of San Michele. Like all slaughterhouses it was as far away from human habitation as possible. Which translated as far away as possible from anyone rich.

So it stood on the lagoon's edge, with a gently sloping floor that let the bricks be sluiced and the filth be washed into the sea. Although little was left after butchering. Outside, in a stinking pen, pigs milled and snuffled and slopped up to their knees in their own dirt, or the dirt of meat before them. They were jointed according to Guild rules; not to be sold within twenty-four hours of slaughter or longer than ten days after. Their blood, guts and viscera made sausages. The skin became leather, and the hooves and long bones, once split for their marrow, boiled down to glue.

Even individual vertebra provided soup. The method used by Master Robusta involving two cuts, one either side of the backbone, instead of the more common single cut that split the spine down the middle.

Most of the pork was salted and sold to ships moored in the

Bacino di San Marco, since they needed to revictual for their journeys south. The better cuts ended up on stalls in the Rialto market, and pork sausages fed the poor across the city. Master Robusta's place stank. It was a shambles after all. But it stank no worse than other slaughterhouses and smelt far better than the tanneries. And, unlike the iron foundries to the west, it was unlikely to kill you with air poison while you slept.

"What brings you back here . . . ?"

Amelia jerked her thumb at Tycho, scowling as Master Robusta grinned at his silvery braids and white skin. "Don't say it."

"You have a letter?"

She gave him Atilo's note, waiting while he broke its seal, read the contents and held the single sheet of paper over a flame, letting it burn to his fingers before letting go and watching embers dance away.

"Every month?"

Amelia shrugged. "I don't read. Anyway, it wasn't shown me." Glancing at Master Robusta, she added, "I'll be accompanying him." Her tone said how much she liked that idea.

"We kill, gut and joint every minute of every day, except those forbidden by the Church. These days we use cleavers. Your master has asked you be taught the old ways first." Walking to the back, Master Robusta chose a knife from a rack. "Use this," he said. "It's too old to damage."

It might be old but it was sharp. The edge so honed it curved like a sickle moon. That upset the balance.

"Good enough for you?" Master Roberto and Amelia were watching him. The butcher's look was half amused. Amelia's harder to read.

"May I?" Tycho nodded to a sharpening wheel.

"It's sharp already."

That was when Tycho knew he was expected. The business with the sealed letter was play-acting. At least on the butcher's part. Amelia had probably been told after Tycho, which was less than an hour before. Walking to the wheel, he set it spinning and ground wood and slivers of tang from the handle, until the knife balanced properly.

"Where did you learn to do that?" The first words Amelia had spoken to him since they left Ca' il Mauros. Since he could hardly say, *Watching Lord Eric's armourer*, he shrugged her question away, watching her mouth tighten.

"Through here," Master Robusta said.

A dozen men looked up but it was Amelia they watched as she moved among them like a black lynx jostling a herd of something too stupid to know just how dangerous the newcomer was.

"Take a bench each."

Amelia shook her head. "I'm just here to watch."

The master butcher looked as if he might disagree. Instead he shrugged and told her to keep out of the way if she couldn't be useful. Point made, he nodded to an oak frame hung with two pulleys. "I'll show you once only."

A small boy dragged in a pig, which he trapped between his knees, before fixing two slipknots round its hind legs and yanking on a rope that ran between three pulleys. In no time at all he had his victim hanging upside down.

Kicking a tub into place, Master Robusta took the knife, yanked back the squealing pig's head and slit its throat. He began cutting immediately, ripping down the animal's belly to drop pulsing guts into the tub. They landed with a splash he ignored. The butchering was brief and brutal, two slashes down the spine, forelegs, shoulders, flanks, saddle . . . He stripped meat from bone and severed joints with a ruthless efficiency that spoke of thousands and thousands of animals before this one. When he looked up, he found Tycho watching with a fierce intensity.

"Think you can do that?"

Tycho nodded.

"Then show me."

A boy dragged in a second pig and looped its legs, hoisting

the shrieking beast into the air and wrapping its rope briskly around a hook. Then he vanished, one of a dozen junior apprentices, to do the same for another butcher.

Gripping the animal's snout, Tycho slashed.

He expected red mist and shifting shadows. A fear his dog teeth would descend had travelled with him across the Rialto bridge to the doors of the shambles. He felt nothing. Without considering, he dipped his hand into the blood flowing from the animal's slit throat and drank. It tasted mud-like and flat. The fierce flame that heightened every sense was missing.

In the moments following he repeated Master Robusta's movements exactly. Splashing viscera in the blood-filled tub, slashing parallel lines either side of the spine, and butchering the animal with cold efficiency that left him time to think about the slaughterhouse around him.

Amelia was scowling. Master Robusta's gaze was keen.

Other butchers stopped to watch until Master Robusta's glare returned them to their duties. Fresh pigs were dragged in and hoisted, gutted and killed, often in that order. The shrieking was hideous, sometimes unbearable. And the iron stink of blood, and the smell of shit, and the heat released from the butchered pigs, joined to that of the summer night outside, filled Tycho's hairline with sweat.

"You've done this before."

Tycho shook his head.

"But you've killed?"

"Wolves," Tycho said. "People." He looked at the one-sided battle around him, the slick of spilt blood and the twitching bodies. "Although killing pigs doesn't seem that different."

38

A roof tile slid beneath his feet, skating towards the roof's lip, and Tycho followed it over the edge, pushing off from the overhang and catching it on the way down, to land silently in the tiny garden of an insignificant palace in San Polo.

A scrap of black leather followed him.

He ignored the scrap. Since magic was best ignored in his opinion.

A leap for the garden wall, a roll over the top and he was in a private alley, with a wrought-iron gate at one end. Beyond the alley was an underpass. And since he couldn't leap over the iron gate he lifted it off its hinges, as silently as rust and age allowed, then replaced it.

Unless the palace's owners looked carefully for prints in their overflowing flower bed they would never know he'd passed through there.

Two down, three to go.

He scrabbled to the top of the first church he found beyond the *sottoportego* and found the scrap of black leather already waiting. It stared at him with amber eyes. "Are you going to follow me all night?"

It opened its mouth, displaying tiny needle-like teeth.

So Tycho ignored it again, inhaled the wind, and searched for the scent he was after. In there, like a missing note, was a gap where the scent he'd been hunting the night Duchess Alexa trapped him should be. He missed finding it, but ignored the hollowness this opened in his belly. The hardest lesson in a hard year of training. One that had seen spring turn to summer and leaves finally begin to fall.

This test mattered, which was not to say others didn't. Simply that Atilo placed a greater value on this one. He'd tried not to let Tycho know, but the youth had become expert at reading the emotional currents swirling through Ca' il Mauros. So he breathed deep, filtering out bass notes of sewage and tanneries.

Five prisoners from the pit released, one deserving to die. The others mere prisoners. Kill the right one and the others went free. Kill the wrong one and everyone died. That was meant to be his incentive. A call on his sympathy. But up here in the wind, on the tower of a San Polo church, Tycho had no sympathy for those sleeping below while the night crawled around them.

He wanted to get it right because he wanted to get it right.

Quickly, in the early days he'd reached a point where he judged himself only against what Atilo could do. Even Amelia, better than Iacopo, couldn't move as silently as Tycho could. And a handful of months after that, he'd stopped judging himself against Atilo and started judging himself only against himself.

He was his own competition. The only person he was interested in beating was himself. It made the world a private place and most of Tycho's life was lived inside his head. This, he suspected, suited everyone just fine.

Atilo, he knew, expected him to try to escape. That he didn't worried the old man far more than Tycho trying to escape would have done. Another reason he kept his own company, retired to his cellar and sat out the full moons to keep his hunger manageable. Rosalyn's murder was walled around with ice; Afrior's death; his other fragments of memory from Bjornvin. He could consider his losses. Examine them without feeling the hurt that should go with them. His was a life of stale pig's blood, and an iron control that filed each new skill he learnt as he waited for Atilo to admit what Tycho already knew.

He was the old man's heir.

A slave would become the duke's Blade. Chances were, he'd be freed first, but even that wasn't necessary. The Seljuks had generals who were born and died slaves, the property of their sultan. It made no difference to him. Maybe he could, as Desdaio once suggested, escape the city. But why would he bother?

When the only life he wanted was closed to him?

Venice was as good as anywhere in this world. Maybe better. Since it sat in the middle of its richest trade routes. And a job was waiting for which he was suited. For which his nature could have been . . .

He caught it then.

A scent of fear, an echo of feet as they left dirt and hit herring-bone brick in a street three blocks beyond. He caught it, and he followed it. If he was those he hunted he'd use canals, take to the water and rely on it to hide his stink. They'd been ordered to keep to dry land. One reason to do the opposite.

A skinny whore of fifteen, maybe younger. Dressed in rags and with a desperate look in her haunted eyes. Even beggars had more sense than to push through a late-night crowd around the Rialto bridge. A *cittadino* turned on her, expecting a clumsy pick-pocket. And met fear and a gabble of prayers.

The Rialto bridge was not yet closed for the night.

On the bank she'd abandoned, porters sluiced the floor of the covered fish market and the guard changed shift outside the state prison. On the one she wanted, stevedores emptied ore from Tedeschi barges along the Riva del Ferro, despite the late-ness of the hour. The ore was loaded on to carts headed for the foundries.

Tycho let her begin to cross. Watching from his fish market roof.

Only to beat her to the other side. Having run fleet-footed over the bridge's wooden roof, jumped the gap where drawbridges raised to let masts through, and leapt from the bridge beyond into the mouth of a passageway she entered, thinking it empty. Her scream died beneath his fingers as he brought his forehead close to hers.

A theft, a little whoring, a murder not reported. Her sins were minor in a city where most people like her would have regarded that as innocence. He could see her face but not the skull beneath.

"Make it to the end," Tycho said. "Stay safe."

The whore gaped at him. "I'm not the one?" she asked. He knew then she knew the rules but not the reasons.

"Go. Before I change my mind."

It was enough. She vanished into the darkness.

A hired thug; a discarded catamite; a little part-time whore, who did no more or less than half the patrician women he'd come across in his year in the city, but paid a price no one demanded of them. In the Corte Seconda Millioni, Tycho stopped to gaze at the house where Marco Polo was born. It was grand, but not that grand. If it had belonged to a *cittadino* he wouldn't have been surprised. No one lived there now, although the Millioni still owned it. Marco III brought his mistress there. Duchess Alexa accepting a duke must have mistresses, while refusing to have them in the palace.

Its walls were old, mortar crumbling beneath Tycho's fingers as he climbed. In the distance, beyond the dry docks, walkways and factories of Arzanale, was the squat cathedral tower of San Pietro di Castello. It was here the prisoners must reach.

Two more to go.

He ran the roofs, barely entering Sestiere di San Marco before leaving it for Sestiere di Castello, avoiding loose tiles, skirting *campi* and jumping canals rather than cross bridges at ground level, which, more often than not, were guarded by informal militias or taxed by local thieves who regarded whichever parish as their own. Only once did he hesitate.

On a roof in Santa Maria dei Miracoli a clawed and shaggy figure was changing against the half-moon. As Tycho approached, the creature twisted, moaning softly as its limbs straightened, joints shifted and flesh remade itself, leaving a naked man in the creature's place. He turned to watch Tycho approach, dipping to wrench free lead piping at his feet. Nothing in his expression suggested he intended to offer a reason for being there.

Tycho hesitated. Shocked to find this creature from the silent city so at home in the noisy one above. Tycho had settled into this world, the one around him. Although it made sense the dead should seem real on his arrival and fade first. And the silent city fade next. At least, he supposed it did.

"Think you can take me?" The man's accent was strange.

Tycho nodded.

"Then do it."

Atilo's orders were firm. Tycho must kill his target before the first prisoner reached San Pietro di Castello. "I don't have time."

He watched the man's eyes narrow. The mouth that had been mocking settled to a thin line and his stance became less easy. Anger was always a waste of emotion unless converted to something useful. Maybe he intended to fight. Tycho couldn't afford time to find out.

"Later," he promised.

The *krieghund* followed, his breath animal and rasping. And then Tycho was gone, in a leap that crossed both the Fondamenta di San Lorenzo and the *rio* beyond, landing him on the flagstones of Corte Maltese, where a crumbling palazzo slipped by beneath his fingers as easily as if someone had fixed handles to its walls.

The meeting with the *krieghund* sharpened his senses.

So when Tycho stopped, a few minutes later, to check the

krieghund wasn't following, he'd found both his targets by the time he spotted the naked man watching from inside a bell tower three or four minutes away.

Two prisoners, one little more than a youth.

Both better fed and healthier-looking than the others. This suggested families rich enough to bribe prison guards or have food sent in. Maybe even money enough to guarantee a daylight cell. Since it hadn't been one of the first three, his target had to be one of these. Tycho wondered how apprentices without his abilities made the call. By seeing who panicked? By who blustered or begged?

Atilo had taught him to read men's faces for lies. How to listen for telltale weakness in their words. How to count the pulsing of blood in a guilty man's temple, wrist or throat. He hardly needed to tell Tycho to watch for this. There were times when he found it hard to watch anything else.

To go through Arzanale would be stupidity for the prisoners.

The great dockyard worked day and night and was guarded by Arsenalotti militias who assumed, probably rightly, that anyone found in the dockyard who didn't belong was a thief. The prisoners he chased would go south of Arzanale's walls. This meant navigating a strip barely three houses deep, between the dockyard walls and the lagoon's edge.

Tycho let the first three through the strip without stopping them.

They skulked so obviously when they were forced briefly on to the open quayside of Riva Ca' di Dio that lookouts on ships half a mile away would have been able to spot them. Should the lookouts be able to see in the dark.

The last two came together.

They had a dagger, at least one did. Since it looked new and lacked a sheath they must have robbed a drunk. Weapons were forbidden, like entering the water. But the smugness on their faces said rules were not for them.

"*Stop*," he said, dropping from a window ledge. A scrap of black leather remained behind. The two men looked at each other, then rushed him at once. Their blade flashed and Tycho dropped under it, his movement a blur as he grabbed the knifeman's wrist and twisted, breaking half a dozen bones.

Tycho caught the knife before it hit brick. His victim would have screamed but the dagger to his throat persuaded him otherwise. Abandoning his friend, the other man made a run for San Pietro di Castello, hoping for sanctuary. Not knowing Atilo, Iacopo and Amelia waited at the church door. So accurate was Tycho's throw that it cut the tendon in the running man's heel.

"I'll give you money," he promised. "More than you can imagine. You name it, I'll give it to you." His voice was raw, his fear real. But his eyes betrayed him as they focused beyond Tycho, who ducked as a stone hissed past where his skull had been.

He stabbed the runner in the leg and twisted the blade. Not caring if the man's yell brought the Watch. And then Tycho returned his attention to the stone thrower and knew suddenly why he should die.

"God's name," Iacopo said. "What happened to you . . . ?"

Blood dripped from Tycho's mouth. He was shaking, his whole body humming with energy, as if it was fighting itself. He had taken his reward for success and taken it without thought.

"I was attacked."

"And your attacker?" demanded Atilo, his voice flat.

"Is dead." Tycho shrugged. "And his friend. I was forced to bite out the first's throat. And break the neck of the second."

Having laughed, Amelia apologised.

Atilo waving her apology away as he told Tycho to clean his face. In the time it took the boy to swill lagoon water around his mouth and spit, his breathing steadied and the shakes subsided. So he knew what to say when he got back. Although first Atilo had to say what Atilo needed to say.

"You failed." The words brought glee to Iacopo's eyes.

"No," Tycho said. "I didn't."

"You killed two when you should have killed one. And you didn't even kill the one you should have killed. You had a one in five chance of getting it right by luck. And even taking two chances you failed."

"You think it should have been the girl?"

Atilo's face went still.

"Do you? Because of what she saw?"

"Who told you of that?" Atilo's voice was dark and dangerous. Coming from a cold and distant place. And his own hands twitched towards his dagger before he brought his reactions under control.

"She doesn't even understand what she saw."

"You know this?"

"Yes," Tycho said. "I know this."

"And why did you kill the others instead?"

"Because they ordered the murder she saw. You said the Blade was justice in action. Where would be the justice in killing the innocent?"

The old man wondered if he was being mocked.

39

Looking up from her pillow, Lady Giulietta asked the question that had been troubling her for months. Certainly since Prince Leopold had moved her into a house on a small estate on the mainland. "Will you kill me when my baby's born?"

Prince Leopold wiped sweat from her brow with a vinegar-soaked rag and wrinkled his nose at the smell. "Why would I do that?"

"That's not an answer."

Taking her hand, Prince Leopold waited until she looked him in the eyes. "I won't," he said. "I can't believe you'd think I would."

"You hate Venetians. Remember?"

He looked apologetic.

And then she swore. "Shit. Shit, shit, shit . . ."

"*I'll get the midwife.*"

Face screwed in agony, her hands gripping her gut, Giulietta cursed as a second contraction hit. And then she drew breath, air rushing into her lungs as the muscles in her abdomen unlocked. It was an hour since Leopold had arrived. Five hours since this torture began.

"Answer my question first."

Watching him look around her room, an upper chamber in a near-ruined farmhouse near Ravenna, she wondered what Leopold saw.

A sweating prisoner with distended stomach and swollen and aching breasts, screaming in pain? A young woman terrified of what came next? A child who'd already caused him endless problems?

She should never have sent for him.

In dismissing the midwife and demanding they let Leo in, she'd doubled the rumours. The guards below already said he was the father of her child. This would simply confirm it for them.

"My love," said Leopold.

She felt tears fill her eyes, and was too exhausted to stop sadness spilling over and running down her cheeks. Instead, she turned away.

"What?" he said, turning her face back.

"You called me . . . You've never called me . . ."

As he stroked her face, she felt him scoop up a tear and trace it back to the corner of her eyelashes. He was smiling. "I never dared."

She looked at him. "You're scared of nothing."

"I'm scared of losing you."

"Why would that happen?"

"Because you love that boy you talk about."

"*Leopold!*"

"It's true," he said. She was still crying when her maid, his doctor and the midwife returned.

In the hours that followed, the pain became so fierce that Giulietta barely stopped screaming. She had never imagined, had never dared imagine, such pain existed outside a torture chamber. Each contraction was fiercer than the one before. But the baby inside her showed no sign of being born. When she begged for the shutters to be opened to cool her room they were for a while. Until the doctor ordered them shut again. Giulietta thought stuffiness was part of her treatment. Then she realised the shutters were kept closed to keep in her cries.

She pushed until she could push no more.

As the afternoon wore on the encouragements of the midwife and the platitudes of the doctor faltered and finally faded. When Leo's doctor went to the door, shouted for Giulietta's maid, and told her to find the master and tell him to come at once, Giulietta realised he thought she could no longer hear them. And inside the tight red swirl of her pain there were times when she couldn't. Although this wasn't one of them. And then it was, and she was lost in memories.

Leopold's words hurt.

His sadness that she had loved someone before him, and better. She wanted to say . . . If she lived through this, she would say, it was untrue. And it was, she told herself, even as she knew it wasn't. The fierce-faced boy in the basilica had set his hooks in her flesh with a single touch and his was the scowl she now saw.

Silver-grey hair. Amber-flecked eyes that looked right through her. Shivering, Lady Giulietta felt a little warmth leave her body.

"She's going," the midwife said.

"Why hasn't someone found the prince yet!"

"He's outside, sir."

"Gods, woman. Ask him to come in."

"I was riding," Prince Leopold said, shutting the door behind him. "I couldn't stand . . ." His voice was a whisper that Giulietta heard from miles away. The rustle of wind through the grass. She was beyond pain now. Floating in a red warmth far removed from her body.

"You have a choice," the doctor said.

"What choice?" Leopold said.

"I can try to save my lady but you will lose her child for certain. Or I can save her child, and you will lose her. If it's a boy, God willing he will live. My lady's ability to live is less certain . . ." To Giulietta, it sounded as if the doctor had already made his own choice.

"Save both," Prince Leopold said.

"Your highness. That's not possible."

"You don't have the skill?"

"No, sir. No one could . . ."

"Then find someone who can," Leopold said, not letting the man finish his protest. "*And do it now.* I will not accept the death of either." His voice held an anger that threatened bloodshed if he was disobeyed. Even Giulietta, cocooned in her red warmth, and wondering if it wouldn't simply be best to let sleep take her, flinched at his fury.

"Highness," the doctor said, his voice tight from the fear of being asked to do the impossible. "I beg you to . . ."

"There's a man in the next town," the midwife interrupted. "He cut a baby from a slave, and a pup from a hunting dog. All lived."

"He's a heathen." The doctor sounded outraged.

"Yes," she said. "A heathen who dislikes losing his slaves."

"The man's a Jew?" Prince Leopold asked.

"Calls himself a Saracen, my lord." The midwife sound scared to be addressing the prince directly.

"Send for him."

"Your highness, consider . . ."

"You know who this is?" Prince Leopold asked the doctor.

"No, my lord. They said she was . . ."

"My woman?"

The doctor nodded.

"God willing she'll be my wife. If she dies I will have you hanged."

The Saracen was sent for.

Having cleared the little room of people, he opened the shutters and announced that if the screams of a birthing woman were bad luck then people should go elsewhere. Since it was the nature of women in childbirth to scream. Even Christians should be able to accept that.

Water was brought.

Cold water for drinking. Warm water for washing. And boiling water for cleaning his implements. And having sharpened his knives, and knelt at Lady Giulietta's side and whispered his apologies, the doctor removed her sweat-soaked sheet and washed between her legs before feeling for the child.

"As I thought," he said. "The baby has turned."

Since she hovered on the edge of the red darkness, and the room was empty apart from the two of them, he had to be talking to himself.

"It cannot be turned back. So it is best if you sleep. Either you will wake or you will not. Mostly that is in God's hands. And a little bit in mine."

Opening a wooden box, he found black paste wrapped in oiled silk, and unstoppered a small bottle of spirits, the only spirits he ever let himself touch. Mixing the paste with the spirits he dribbled the mixture between Lady Giulietta's lips and waited for her to settle. Once she had, he began to cut open her abdomen.

The newborn boy issued his first cry ten minutes later.

Although it was a day and a half before Lady Giulietta was awake enough to realise she lived and her child already suckled for milk, his face against the ring she kept on a chain between her breasts. By then, Prince Leopold had named the boy Leo, claiming him as a son.

PART 2

"May the winds blow till they have waken'd death!"
Othello, William Shakespeare

40

Easter 1408

"If an angel can fall a demon can rise . . ."

Nothing in the books Desdaio used to teach Tycho to read suggested this was true. But she said it the evening he told her about the Skaelingar attack, Bjornvin burning and Withered Arm ordering him to make a fire circle. An evening when the waxing moon above Venice was near enough full to fire his hunger.

He'd told her about elk horns over the great doors. About red-painted naked Skaelingar flinging themselves on to sharpened palisades so that those behind could climb over. Red bodies and red weapons and a red world. Everything the Skaelingar owned was painted with ochre and oil, even their canoes.

Desdaio had been seated on a bench in the piano nobile, talking about the winter just gone, about the snows that had fallen, the fires that had warmed them. That was how their conversation started.

With snow and fire.

Iacopo was with Atilo, Amelia in bed, monthlies so fierce Desdaio fed her poppy seeds in wine. The cook was making pies for a party, and her scowl said no interruptions.

Tycho was there because Desdaio had summoned him.

She was lonely and cold and scared, her happiness draining day by day as her husband-to-be spent ever more time with his duchess. She didn't say this. Desdaio didn't need to. Tycho could feel her sadness. She was wondering if those who shunned her were right. She'd made a mistake.

Her grief was revealed in talk of flowers, and memories of summer barley on the mainland, the counterpoint to her forced brightness. A shadow to the wideness of her smile. "Aren't you cold?" she asked suddenly.

Tycho shook his head.

Somehow this led to him talking about Bjornvin and the snows he remembered from childhood.

"Bjornvin?" said Desdaio, tasting the name.

Then she shuffled up on her bench and patted the cushion beside her. Frowning when Tycho didn't immediately abandon his place to join her. He could smell oil in her hair, the orange-blossom scent she often wore, and the gunpowder she was using for toothache. And beneath these a smell that hooked him brutally. So that his jaws throbbed, his throat dried and he couldn't keep his eyes from her when she adjusted her shawl, her breasts spilling against her gown's low front.

"Tell me about Afrior," she demanded.

So he did. Talking fast and desperately. Aware of the tightness behind his eyes and a growing ache in his groin he hunched to hide. He talked of the Skaelingar, of Bjornvin, Lord Eric and Withered Arm. Of the day he took Afrior swimming. He told Desdaio everything he remembered. And in telling her he came face to face with the shame and regret he'd spent so long denying. From which he'd been running so unsuccessfully for what seemed like so long . . .

Afrior of the golden hair, sweet smile and soft curves was Bjornvin's most beautiful girl. She was also a slave and the youngest of

Withered Arm's children. Peering from under her long eyelashes, she'd smiled, her modesty at war with her lips.

To Tycho, her blue eyes held the sky and her smile his heart.

"See," he said. "I came after all."

"I thought . . ." She stopped, not wanting to finish.

People said Afrior was simple. That she had to be to befriend him.

If Lord Eric discovered them together, he'd beat them. Tycho was meant to be guarding goats against the wolves, Afrior grinding rye. But it was nothing to what their mother would do. Withered Arm might be old, but she was vicious with it.

"Come here," Tycho said, grounding his spear.

She stepped away. "We're . . ."

"No," he said. "*We're not.*"

No brother could want his sister the way he wanted her.

Wanting Afrior was more important to Tycho than hunting. More important than his mother's lack of love. More important than Lord Eric's hatred. And Tycho and Afrior *did* look different. Her impossibly blue eyes against his own's amber-flecked darkness. Her hair sun-yellow. His wolf-silver, as if he'd been born old. He had sharp cheeks and not a sliver of fat. She was all curves.

For a second Afrior fought him, and then her mouth opened and his tongue touched hers. She was shaking when he pulled back.

"This is wrong."

"It's not," he said.

But her gaze was firm. "We can't. You know that." Lord Eric would expect her untouched and know if her maidenhead was gone.

Afrior was thirteen. Maybe fourteen.

Her mother said thirteen, but Lord Eric and his warriors had been away fighting red-painted Skaelingar when she was born. Whispers said she lied to allow her daughter a few months' extra happiness. Given Lord Eric's temperament, it was a miracle he hadn't taken Afrior already.

"He'd know," Afrior said.

Tycho had tried not to let glee show in his eyes. Until that moment she'd never admitted she wanted to. *He'd know* was close to admitting she might if not for that.

"Let's swim."

Her scowl said she suspected a trick. All the same, she followed him through the speckled alder and showy mountain ash, using a path the deer cut back when they still came this way. The herd was gone these days, eaten or too sensible to venture closer. Finding a dip in the river bank hidden by wild roses, he told Afrior to turn her back and stripped off his rags. The day was hot, the sun bright on his skin and the air rich with scents of roses and grass, life's freshness and tumbling water.

"And you," he said, not giving her time to argue.

He went into the water fast, fighting the shock that diving into icy currents tightened around his ribs. And Afrior was crouched naked in the shallows when he turned. Lord Eric, his warriors and body slaves were raiding a Skaelingar village. That was what they called it, *raiding*. Mostly it meant killing women while the savages were away fighting each other.

No women meant no babies, no babies meant fewer warriors in years to come. It was more effective to kill those who would deliver the unborn than fight those already living. "Come here," Tycho said.

"You think I'd trust you?"

There was humour in her voice, and enough truth to make him glance away. So he missed her edging closer.

"You really believe we're not kin?"

Feeling full breasts brush his chest like the touch of tiny fish, he nodded. "I'm sure," he said, banishing doubt from his voice. "We don't even look alike."

Kissing her deeply, he registered the moment she felt him go hard. The sudden wariness that had her stepping back. So he used the gap to cup one breast, finding her nipple already erect from the coldness of the river.

She let his hand wander until . . .

"No," she said, grabbing his wrist.

They wrestled, until she found his thumb and twisted.

He ignored the pain for as long as he could, then stopped fighting and dipped his head to recognise her victory. She was staring at him. "I thought you were going to let me break it."

"So did I," he said.

Afrior's face softened. Taking his hand, she kissed his thumb, which ached with a dull pain that would last for days. And, having kissed it, she replaced his fingers between her legs. Tycho knew then he would never understand women.

Her insides were more mysterious than he expected. Afrior moaned, her mouth nuzzling as her sounds got louder. When she froze, mid-moan, he thought he'd been too rough. But her eyes watched the bank behind him.

"Stop," she said.

Turning, he felt piss leave his body before his mind caught up with what he saw. A row of five Skaelingar warriors, bright red in their mixture of oil and ochre. They were naked, flint knives hanging on sinews from their shoulders. Some had sycamore bows already drawn. A sixth man stood between them. A half-Skaelingar slave who'd escaped Bjornvin the year before.

"How interesting," he said.

The Skaelingar chief snapped out a question, and the ex-slave's smirk closed down. His reply was humble. Whatever he said, it wasn't that this was a brother and sister. That would have earned more than the growl he got in return.

"You're to come here."

Afrior looked doubtful, but then she was a girl and naked. Looking at her, one man muttered and a second laughed. Both silenced by a snarl from their chief. At his command, they grabbed Afrior the moment she climbed from the water.

Tycho attacked on instinct.

And fell to a blow to his head. Having kicked the air from his lungs, and what was left of the piss from his bladder, the chief stopped when Tycho shat himself. It wasn't a serious beating. More a warning not to be stupid.

Then another Skaelingar picked him up and turned him to face Afrior, who was struggling with her own captors. When one dug his thumb into her elbow, she started to cry instead.

"I am to translate," the half-Skaelingar said. "Have you seen what we do to your women? Yes, or no?"

Tycho hadn't. But he'd heard it whispered.

"We take these," the translator said.

Their chief gripped Afrior's breasts, lifting slightly.

"Cutting like this."

The chief's hand traced a circle, sloping in so that Tycho understood they cored a pit to take what was behind as well. Afrior might have been an animal for all the attention the man paid her.

"And we take this."

She screamed when the chief dropped his hand. Tycho didn't think he hurt her; it was the shock of having him grip her there.

"And, finally, we slit from here to here." The chief traced from blonde body fur to the arch of Afrior's ribs. "And pull out what we find." He stepped back, offended, as she soiled herself.

"You understand?"

Tycho nodded dumbly.

"There is another choice," the chief said, his words translated through the half-Skaelingar. "Would you like to know it?"

"Yes," he said. "I would."

Having glared, to make sure Tycho paid attention, the chief unslung his flint knife, grabbed Afrior between her legs and cut. She jerked in her captor's hands. And then the chief scattered pale hair at her feet.

"This is all that will happen."

Tycho looked in disbelief at the man translating, then at the chief whose words these were. He wondered if the ex-slave translated right.

"No harm will come if you do what we ask." And then the Skaelingar told him what was wanted. Since it seemed the two Viking slaves should not be out together, their chief would not find it strange if one returned alone. Sometime tonight Tycho would unlock Bjornvin's gate. If it was not unlocked, his lover's mutilated body would be left at the gates at dawn. If it was, both would have safe passage through Skaelingar territory to the lands beyond.

"The next tribe will kill us."

"What you should consider," the chief said, "is that we will not."

Tycho could have let Afrior die. With her would have died the risk of anyone finding out what had happened. He could have return to his life as Lord Eric's wolf dog, continued to ignore the hard-faced bitch he called mother.

He was a slave. Lord Eric said *do this*, he did it.

Running faster than the others, jumping higher, hunting swiftly and silently didn't make him valuable. It simply made him hated. Most days, he got up at daybreak, obeyed orders till nightfall, then slept. Saving Afrior meant betraying everyone else. How could that be right?

He could tell Lord Eric what had happened.

The beating would be terrible but he'd survived others. But Afrior would die and Tycho wanted her. So he killed the gate guard instead. Hitting the man clumsily, clubbing him from behind. When the guard was dead, Tycho lifted the bar to Bjornvin's gate.

The first thing the Skaelingar chief did on entering Bjornvin was yank back the head of the naked, bound and gagged Viking girl in front of him, spit into her face and rip his blade across her throat.

Afrior bled out before she hit the dirt.

Tycho's attack would have made him a hero had any lived to sing of it. Grabbing the fallen gate guard's sword, he flung himself at the chief and plunged the blade in the man's guts, twisting in his fury.

Then Lord Eric was there, broad-shouldered, more grey than red in his beard. A bloody battle-axe in hand. He believed his slave was guarding Bjornvin's gate. In three blows Lord Eric killed another three Skaelingar. Then he turned, clapped Tycho on the shoulder. "Wake everyone," he ordered.

Tycho would have done.

But his mother grabbed him before he reached the great hall. The first thing she told him was that she wasn't his mother. The next, that he was neither Viking nor Skaelingar, but *Fallen*. She said this through gritted teeth, hatred in her face. "Where's my daughter?"

"Dead. The Skaelingar killed her."

Withered Arm slapped him. "*You* killed her. You think I didn't know?"

Her eyes were hard, her voice cold as winter. Tycho had no doubt she wanted him dead. Would like to kill him herself. Instead, with battle raging, she hurried him to her quarters, and told him to spread the straw from her mattress in a wide circle.

"Do it now," she ordered.

Outside the slaughter continued.

Individually, Lord Eric's warriors were better armed. Their swords, chain mail and the helmets brought from Greenland gave them an advantage. But they were outnumbered. The Skaelingar had been closing on the village for years. When Withered Arm returned it was with a flaming brand.

"My mistress told me how to do this before she died. Maybe she knew . . ." Withered Arm stopped, face bitter. "Oh, she knew all right. She died in birth so you could live. And I knew it for a bad bargain then. Now we die so you . . . Who knows what? Who will be left to even care?"

Pushing him into the middle of the circle, Withered Arm set

fire to the straw, stepping back as flames crackled around him. And then he felt ice instead of flames, and a rushing like wings, and a vicious wind as if he was falling from a great height. The last thing he saw was the hatred in her face.

"That's true?" Desdaio asked. She was blushing furiously. At the things he'd said about Afrior and the river, Tycho realised.

"It's what I remember."

"Does Atilo know?"

"No, my lady. He never asked."

"You stepped into the flames of where you came from. To find yourself in my world?"

Tycho nodded.

Crossing herself, Desdaio scrambled to her feet and returned staggering under the weight of a leather-bound Bible. "This was my mother's," she said. "Take it from me. Use both hands."

He did as she demanded. Watching her chew her lips.

"What did you think would happen?"

"I thought you'd go up in flames."

"Why would I . . . ?"

"If you were a demon you would catch fire. I thought . . ." She looked embarrassed. "It sounds as if you came from hell."

"I thought *this* was hell," Tycho told her truthfully. "When I first arrived. All these people crowded on to misty little islands. And the water here . . . In Bjornvin I'd swim when I could and it always made me happy. Here, simply crossing the canals sickens me. The air stinks of smoke and shit."

"But you were starving. You said so. We have food here."

"Some people have food here. And why shouldn't there be food in hell for some. Do you think Satan lives in squalor?"

They sat in silence on a bench after that. Desdaio fed him wine and cake, which he barely drank and didn't touch respectively. And, finally, she asked him where he went at night, on the occasions he accompanied my lord Atilo.

"Council meetings," Tycho lied.

Dog days, full moons, his training kills. Tall scratches for men, shorter ones for women. A single dot for an infant, all that stood between Venice and an estate on the mainland, a dying count's new grandson. The truth was scratched on his cellar wall. All of it, apart from Atilo's visits to Duchess Alexa.

There were too many of those.

Nine deaths in total. Fewer than he expected. Lord Eric had killed more than that in a single battle. A dozen Skaelingar, their guts steaming and their eyes fresh for the crows. Almost all of Tycho's kills had been clean. Atilo was impressed at first, worried later. More worried still when Tycho's final kill in San Pietro di Castello proved so much bloodier than his previous eight.

41

During the year that Tycho trained Iacopo grew a beard. A soldier's beard to make him look older, fiercer. He used masks less these days. No longer needing to hide his youthful softness in the company of others.

A tumbler of wine sat in front of him. The last of this year's wages glinted on his chest. A steel breastplate in the Aragonese style. A scratch below its left armhole suggested its previous owner died in battle or was knifed in his sleep.

Iacopo wasn't superstitious, and that sign of ill luck was enough to bring the armourer's price down to something he could almost afford. Although it had taken a dagger borrowed from Atilo's collection to seal the deal. The Schiavoni claimed the scratch was simply where the breastplate fell and the piece was worth double Iacopo's final offer. But he spat on his hand and shook on it just the same.

"New?" someone asked.

Looking up, Iacopo saw Captain Roderigo. So he smiled modestly, and let the captain believe that if he wished. The last year had seen Venice split between Prince Alonzo and Duchess Alexa's factions. Almost by accident, Roderigo found himself on one side. And Atilo found himself on the other. Positions worsened after last week's incident with Tīmūr bin Taragay's messenger.

A minor prince from Tīmūr's wife's family, the Mongol refused to deliver his message to the Ten, talking only to the duchess and leaving immediately. No one knew what Tīmūr's message said. The duchess simply burnt it after reading and refused to say. So now, Prince Alonzo found himself trapped between caution and fury. Never a good place for someone like him to be.

"Captain." Iacopo raised his glass. He saw no point in making unnecessary enemies. Life at Ca' il Mauros was complicated enough. Lord Atilo and his betrothed keeping separate quarters. Everyone knew they would marry. No one knew when. Some said not until Atilo left the duchess's bed. Others, that the Moor would be stupid to exchange vows if he had any chance of marrying Alexa instead.

And then there was the freak, with his strange spectacles, priest-coloured doublet and hateful silences. Tycho didn't talk to Iacopo, he didn't not talk to Iacopo. He barely noticed Iacopo's existence. Desdaio and Amelia, on the other hand . . .

Iacopo sucked his teeth.

"Problems?" Captain Roderigo asked.

"Such is life," Iacopo replied. Realising the captain was about to move on, he found his smile. "Let me buy you a drink, my lord."

"It must be my turn."

Iacopo looked surprised.

"After you won last year's race. We drank at the Griffin behind St Bartholomew, remember?"

"How could I forget, my lord. I'm simply surprised you remembered yourself." He'd overdone it. The captain was glancing round the tavern, not finding who he'd come to see, and framing reasons for refusing the offer. Iacopo could see it in his eyes. Although why a man like Captain Roderigo would bother to excuse himself to a servant like him . . .

Because that's what he was, Iacopo thought bitterly.

A servant, for all he owned a breastplate and greaves and a sword. His training was secret, the tasks he performed for his master equally so. No one knew the secrets he carried. No one was allowed to know. There were days he found this harder to bear than others. "An honour to buy you a drink," he said, forcing a smile. "An even bigger honour to leave you with a hangover."

Captain Roderigo laughed.

"Who were you looking for, my lord?"

"My sergeant. He's off duty but we have business tomorrow that needs discussing today."

Iacopo nodded sagely.

He had an idea what that business might be and had sense enough to say nothing. Today was Maundy Thursday, one reason the tavern was full. Obviously enough, tomorrow was Good Friday, when the devout flogged themselves through the streets, and the rest avoided sex and gambling, and a long list of other vices the new patriarch had recently read from the pulpits.

It was to be the day of Tycho's testing. Just as it had been the day of Iacopo's testing. And Amelia's, and all those who went before. All those who died nearly two years back in the slaughter at Cannaregio.

"Perhaps I will have a drink," Captain Roderigo said.

"This might even be the real thing," Iacopo said, wiping blood-like drops of wine from his beard. The tavern keeper claimed it was Barolo and it looked dark enough.

"I agree," Roderigo said.

Iacopo had never tasted Barolo in his life.

"So," Captain Roderigo said. "How are things with you?"

"Much the same. His lordship attends Council. Dotes on Lady Desdaio. Visits Duchess Alexa for advice."

The captain grinned.

Iacopo thought he might.

"And how is Lady Desdaio?" Even if Iacopo hadn't known the

captain for an ex-suitor, the careful nature of his question would have announced it.

"As sweet as ever."

Roderigo took a sip of wine. "It's none of my business, obviously. But what news of their marriage?"

"None I would know."

"No," Roderigo admitted. "I don't suppose you would." Holding his glass to the light, he examined the contents critically. "I'm not sure this is Barolo after all." But he emptied it quickly enough. And Iacopo was careful to demand Barolo when he bought the next jug.

"Yes, my lord."

Iacopo checked the tavern keeper wasn't mocking him, but the man seemed serious enough. "Open a tab," Atilo's servant ordered. "I'll send my man to settle tomorrow."

"That's Good Friday, my lord."

"Maybe so. You'll still want paying, won't you?"

The tavern keeper nodded and filled a jug to the brim from a barrel apart from the others. Even if it wasn't Barolo, it was obviously special enough for him not to want jugs given away by accident.

"What is it really?" Iacopo demanded.

The tavern keeper glanced round. "It really is Barolo," he whispered. "Just not a very good one."

Iacopo laughed loud enough to make the hazard players look over. He met their gaze and they saw a stranger with a sharp black beard, wearing a stylish breastplate, taking a jug of the best wine. A couple of them nodded, one even smiled.

"Friends of yours?" Roderigo asked.

"Not really," Iacopo answered, leaving it understood he knew them, just not very well. His embroidering was interrupted by the tavern keeper, who carried a bowl of stewed mutton, which he ladled in heaped spoonfuls on to thick slices of stale bread. The captain ate his mutton and left the bread. So Iacopo did the same.

"I should go," Roderigo said. "Temujin's probably drunk by now." He stood unsteadily, appeared on the edge of saying something about his own state and shrugged. "Bloody man," he muttered. "Always causing trouble."

Iacopo hoped he was talking about the sergeant.

"About Desdaio . . ." Roderigo said a few minutes later.

"My lord?"

"Is she happy?"

"Oh yes, she's . . ." Iacopo stopped. "Well, as happy as can be expected. It must be hard to be disowned. And she . . . My lord, may I speak plainly?"

"Feel free."

Roderigo waited.

"What," he asked finally, "did you have to say?"

Iacopo sucked his teeth. "Maybe she's not that happy," he said. "She expected to be wed by now. But my lord Atilo is always busy. And it must be a lonely life for a healthy young woman . . ."

"You have her confidence?"

"No, my lord. She confides in Amelia, her maid. And . . ." Iacopo hesitated again. "Atilo has a slave."

"The blind boy?"

"He's not blind, my lord. But light does hurt his eyes. So he wears strange spectacles and avoids daylight whenever he can."

"So I gather," Roderigo said shortly.

"My lord, if I've offended you . . ."

"I've had dealings with the boy."

Iacopo caught himself and kept drinking. Something in the captain's voice was too casual. If Iacopo hadn't known better, he'd say Captain Roderigo feared Tycho. "My master intends to release him."

"So soon?"

"Soon, my lord?"

"I heard Atilo kept his slaves and bondsmen for three to five years before releasing them. To release them at all is ridiculous. No offence, of course. But to get only one year's work." Captain Roderigo shrugged. "How long before he freed you?"

"I was not a slave or bondsman."

"Really? I thought . . ."

"I was an orphan, true enough. My father died on the galleys."

Iacopo had no proof of this, since his father was unknown. But Venice held a special place for freemen who died in battle protecting the city's trade routes or opening other avenues of trade. And Roderigo's approving nod said this mythical father counted in his favour.

"Why is Atilo freeing this one so soon?"

"He learns fast," Iacopo said flatly. "Table manners. Italian. All that Desdaio teaches him. He's even starting to learn to write."

"You don't like him." Captain Roderigo said this as a fact.

"I don't trust him, my lord. And Desdaio watches him," he said carefully. "I used to think she was afraid of him. Now I'm not sure. They spend a lot of time together."

"Desdaio and the slave?"

"Lady Desdaio, the slave, sometimes Amelia," said Iacopo, forcing a worried smile. "Hours alone in the piano nobile while Atilo is away. And the slave accompanies them on evening walks. Sometimes they go for hours. I'm sure nothing happens . . ."

"He's a slave."

"Indeed, my lord."

Captain Roderigo looked disgusted.

42

"Iacopo?" asked Tycho, hearing his door begin to open.

Desdaio peered into the cellar. "Are you expecting Iacopo?" she asked, sounding surprised.

"He was moving about earlier."

Slipping inside, she left the door open and moonlight flooded in from above. The moon was full tonight, the sky bright with stars.

"My lady, shut the door."

"We can't all see in the dark."

More moonlight filled the room as Desdaio obstinately opened it a little wider. Turning, she found Tycho facing the wall. "Leave," he said. "Or close it."

"Tycho . . ."

"Do it now."

She shut the door with a bang.

"Go to that corner. Don't come any closer . . ."

Kicking a wooden wedge under the door, Tycho found a candle, kindling and flints. The kindling was rag, the flints dropped by a *cittadino* too spoilt to retrieve them. "Candles cost," said Desdaio, with the fervour of a rich woman who believes she is now poor.

"Moonlight hurts me," Tycho said.

"That's the sun."

"A different kind of pain."

Desdaio looked at him doubtfully. Moving closer, she seemed surprised he kept the candle between them. "I have things to tell you. And I want to sit."

"On my mattress?"

"Do you see a chair?"

She smelt of roses and sweet wine, an undertaste of sweat, and a musk Tycho loved, loathed and found addictive. Every woman in the city between fifteen and thirty smelt the same.

"Are you all right?"

"No," he said harshly. "I'm not."

Desdaio was so shocked she stepped back. And for that Tycho was grateful. Her body still called to him, the pulse in her throat the beat of a drum summoning him to disaster. The skin of her neck glowed with youth and candlelight.

"Leave," he told her. "Just go."

"I thought you were my friend," she said. "And then you talk to me like this." Her eyes were huge with unspilt tears. "You can't. It isn't allowed."

"Because I'm a slave?"

"It's rude."

"Some days," he said, "I hate you."

She sobbed. A single gulp in the back of her throat. "I thought if I was kind it might help. They say all slaves want to kill their owners. You're meant to be different. You have a good heart," Desdaio said fiercely. "Inside all your hate."

Tycho's smile made her shiver.

"You're wrong, my lady. I doubt I have a—"

The knock interrupting his boast was abrupt and Desdaio's eyes widened. Being found here was bad enough. To be found in her nightdress, a woollen shawl thrown over her shoulders and her feet bare . . .

"Maybe it's Amelia. I'll explain."

"It's Atilo," said Tycho, as the knock repeated.

It came again, angrily. Atilo now knew the door was jammed, from trying its handle when his second knock wasn't answered.

"How do you know?"

"His footsteps."

Pulling aside his mattress, Tycho revealed a hole in the floor. An early and abandoned attempt to tunnel out. When Desdaio hesitated, Tycho lifted her – one hand under her knees, the other round her ribs – and dropped her in, before dragging his mattress back into place. From the look on her face she'd felt his hand come to rest under her breast too.

"*Open this door.*"

"My lord, if you could stop pushing."

The pressure ceased and Tycho pulled away the wedge, moving just fast enough to avoid having his fingers crushed by Atilo's furious entry. The old man glanced at the offcut in Tycho's hands, then glared round the cellar, his eyes alighting on the candle. "Why do you need that?"

"My night sight's not perfect," Tycho lied.

"Where is she?" he demanded.

"Who, my lord?"

"Amelia."

"Asleep in her bed, I imagine."

The old man scowled. "She was meant to come to me tonight." He sucked his teeth, deciding he'd said too much. "Iacopo is also missing. If they're up to mischief together . . ."

"He returned a little earlier."

"How do you know?"

"I heard him, my lord. His new breastplate scraped the wall above and he swore loud enough for me to hear."

"Drunk, I imagine." Dark eyes above a sharp beard watched Tycho. "You don't miss much, do you?"

"I try not to, my lord."

"And your locked door?"

"You know there are no bolts inside. But I found this above." Holding up his offcut, Tycho said, "It keeps my door secure. You say we should secure our entries and exits. I'm simply obeying orders."

The old man snorted. "Get some sleep. Wake early, rested and ready, with your wits sharp. Much turns on tomorrow. Don't let me down."

"My lord?"

"Pray to your gods for success."

There are no gods, Tycho almost said. *Not for the likes of you and me.* "I will, my lord. Goodnight."

Kicking his door jamb back into place, Tycho dragged the mattress aside and hauled Desdaio from the hole beneath. She shook him off when he tried to brush earth from her gown. "That's what I came to tell you. Atilo has a special job for you tomorrow. And I should have known . . ."

She hiccuped.

"Known what?"

"Amelia goes to his bed. I thought . . ."

That he confined himself to the duchess? That he kept his whoring for brothels? She couldn't really believe that a man as powerful as Atilo il Mauros slept alone under his own roof? Even Desdaio wasn't that naive.

Holding her tight as she cried, Tycho folded her in his arms, feeling her breasts press against him and her nipples harden. Her eyes went wide when he kissed her and for a second she responded. Then he was blocking a slap.

"You kissed me back."

"I did not."

"My lady . . ."

"Enough." Her voice was furious. "We won't talk of this again."

43

"This had better be good . . ."

Atilo stood in his chamber door in a long-sleeved woollen robe, with scarlet slippers that curled at the toe. Even though Iacopo had given his name when knocking, the old man had a stiletto in one hand and a lamp in the other.

Oil thrown at an attacker was everyman's mage fire. Ten years earlier a patrician died after a lamp was hurled by a servant whose daughter he'd raped, with the girl tossing a flaming torch after. Duke Marco let the two hang. He forbade the slitting or castrating, gutting and burning tradition demanded. A popular decision with everyone except the noble's wife. And she was Genoese anyway.

"Well?" he demanded.

"May I enter, my lord?"

Atilo stepped aside grudgingly.

"Forgive my intrusion . . . You intend to test Tycho tomorrow?"

The old man's face hardened and he sat on a wooden stool without inviting Iacopo to do the same. His eyes fixed on Iacopo's face and held his gaze until the young man looked away. "Jealousy gets you killed."

"I'm not jealous, my lord." The young man shrugged. "Although I envy the speed with which he learns. And his night sight is useful. Guard dogs ignore him also. As if he wrapped himself in magic."

"It's not magic," said Atilo. "He has no smell."

Iacopo's mouth fell open.

"You should have worked that out. Whatever sickness makes him day-blind denies him a scent. That's why hounds never find his tracks. They've nothing to follow . . ."

A season's lessons in how to double back, lay false scents and hide in water had been abandoned after a week. Tycho couldn't hide in water even if he wanted to. And, since the dogs couldn't find his scent in the first place, the rest of the lessons were irrelevant.

"No smell," Iacopo said. "That must be useful."

Atilo looked on him more kindly. "You're drunk. Get some sleep and you'll feel better. And make friends with him . . ." Atilo held up his hand, admitting the obvious. "Not easy for you, I know. But make the effort. Because he will join us if he passes tomorrow's test."

"You're freeing him?"

"Separate the two," Atilo said. "Training takes five years. He's a slave. I free slaves when they complete training. If he succeeds tomorrow I free him. One follows the other."

"No one can train in a year."

"Are you saying I'm wrong? That I don't know when an apprentice is ready to become a journeyman?" There was ice in the old man's voice.

"No. Certainly not, my lord."

"What are you saying?"

"He was trained already . . ." Iacopo considered his suggestion, obviously liked it. "He must have been. He came here to kill someone. To betray us. He could be working for the emperor."

"Which one?"

"Either," Iacopo said, warming to his theme. "German or Byzantine, it doesn't matter. They both want Venice. How better to . . ."

"Iacopo!" Atilo's tone was sharp.

"Sir?"

"Why don't I let you street-brawl? Why aren't you allowed to compete in sword competitions? Because you'd pick up bad habits. If Tycho had trained do you think I wouldn't know? Every sword school boasts of a move – elegant or deadly – that only they teach. All lies, of course. Sword schools have styles. So do assassins. I'd *know* if Tycho had been trained. He has amazing reflexes and reactions. But he was untaught when I first met him . . ."

And there things might have remained if Atilo hadn't stood, patted Iacopo on the shoulder and said, "He's not here to betray us, my boy."

"Not me certainly," Iacopo agreed, turning for the door.

Fingers like claws locked him into place. He tried to twist free but he might as well have fought a gaff through his flesh. The old man's fingers were immoveable. The utter stillness Atilo exhibited before a kill was in place.

"Explain yourself."

"My lord . . ."

"Forget politeness."

That in itself was warning. Atilo believed in the art of manners, because manners opened more doors than a crowbar. Just as a smile could kill more easily than frontal attack. Although it might hurt less to begin with and take the victim longer to die. Atilo was smiling.

That was the second warning.

I should have stayed silent, thought Iacopo, the truest thought he'd had all day. *I should have stayed silent. I should have left when I could. Then I could have dealt with this in my own way.*

"My lord, I'm sorry. But I saw Lady Desdaio leave Tycho's cellar. She was dressed . . ." Iacopo bowed his head. "In

263

nightclothes. A gown covered by a shawl. Her hair was down, my lord." As an unmarried woman, Desdaio was allowed her hair down. She'd taken to pinning it up, however, the morning she joined Atilo's household. None of his staff had seen her since with her hair untied.

"Really? When did you see this?"

"Just now, my lord. A few moments ago."

"You swear this?"

Iacopo gulped. "Yes, my lord."

Atilo moved so fast that no one, no matter how good, could have blocked him.

One second his stiletto was on a table beside him, the next its blade had slithered up Iacopo's nostril and a single drop of blood ran down its edge.

Iacopo could feel the knife *behind* his face. To move was to slice the cavities of his face open. If Atilo pushed further Iacopo was dead. It would take little pressure to ease a blade that thin into his brain.

"Then you're foresworn. A moment ago I was *in* Tycho's room and he was alone. If you'd said Amelia, an hour ago." When Atilo shrugged the trickle of blood from Iacopo's nose grew thicker. "I'd have had Tycho whipped. But that wasn't enough. You want me to sell him. And so you're prepared to *blacken* . . ."

Iacopo thought the old man would kill him.

"Take it back," Atilo snapped. "Withdraw your accusation. Admit you are forsworn and tried to blacken her name."

"I would never . . ."

"You just did," Atilo said coldly.

"My lord, I'm sorry. I must have misunderstood what I saw."

The blade edged higher. He was standing on tiptoe, Iacopo realised. Drunk, with a stiletto nestling in one nostril. As if standing on tiptoe could keep the blade from entering his skull.

"I lied," he said hastily. "I'm sorry."

Atilo withdrew his stiletto. The next moment saw him slash

it forward to open Iacopo's cheek. Scarring him for life. "Everytime you look in a glass, remember you risked a woman's good name to further your ambition."

Stumbling, Iacopo turned for the door.

"Iacopo . . ."

He turned back.

"You sew that yourself, understand? You don't wake Amelia. You do it yourself. And you will behave around Tycho."

A knock at her door woke Desdaio to shame and spring moonlight. A single knock, almost hesitant. Amelia was out of her truckle bed within seconds, pulling a shawl around her and looking sleepily for orders.

"I'll go," Desdaio said.

She approached slowly. Her anger bright and with it her shame. He'd told the truth, damn him. She, Desdaio Bribanzo, had melted in the arms of . . . a strange and beautiful slave admittedly. One who read her thoughts and seemed to know her mind and understand the nature of her unhappiness.

"My lady, would you prefer . . . ?"

"I said I'll go," Desdaio snapped. "*Who is it?*"

"Me," said a deep voice. "Atilo."

She opened her door slowly, knowing he'd never visited her chamber before. It was her demand that Amelia slept in a truckle at the end of her bed. A demand Desdaio made when she understood her wedding would not be immediate. A way of saying Atilo could not come to her bed without a marriage contract. Except he'd never even tried to come to her bed.

Amelia's late nights looked like the reason why.

"My lord?"

He looked like a man undecided what to say. One whose ideas and actions and words had fallen out of step with each other.

"Is there trouble?"

"That's it. I thought I heard someone on the stairs."

"Iacopo, perhaps?"

"No," said Atilo. "We've been talking."

"I heard nothing, my lord."

He was still apologising when Desdaio shut the door firmly.

Amelia had simply come in later than expected, Atilo decided, listening to bolts slide into place. Any suggestion Desdaio had been with Tycho was unworthy. Yet he was troubled by the anger in her eyes.

44

Tycho drank small beer for breakfast in a shuttered house in Cannaregio, in the hour before daylight. The last intoxicating drink he'd touch all day. Small beer was only intoxicating in the way a blunt knife was dangerous. You could do yourself damage if you tried hard enough. But everyone would think you a fool and it would take weeks to live down.

Cutting a small chunk of bread, he trimmed rind from a ewe's cheese before slicing himself a waxy sliver. It looked like wax, and smelt and tasted only marginally better. Hunger for food was not something he recognised any more.

A locally made candle burnt in front of him.

The buildings around here were greasy with smoke from tallow vats that boiled day and night, rendering fat for cheap candles. White candles, the expensive ones used in churches and the ducal palace, were made elsewhere. These were candles that cobblers used to do their work. Which burnt in brothels and taverns and the hovels of the almost poor.

Beer, cheese, bread, candle and flint . . .

All had been waiting in the upstairs room of a deserted leather boiler's shop north of the Grand Canal's upper entrance. A

hundred paces from the church of Santa Lucia, patron saint of
assassins and the blind. The table on which these sat was wooden
and old. As were the floor, the shutters, the walls and the roof.
All of them were old, and wooden. Except for two upstairs
windows, which were both shuttered and lined with waxed paper.
It was a while before Tycho realised how quickly the building
would burn. Perhaps that was the point. A single flame to one
of the waxed windows would reduce all this to ash.

His heart had sunk on entering. All this wood reminded him
of Bjornvin.

Most buildings in Venice were brick or stone. Even huts with
wooden frames or wattle and daub walls were plastered. This was
bare wood, except for a chimney rising three floors to exit from
a small *fumaiolo*, one of those conical flues common in this city.
The chimney was brick. The fire in it had heated the shop's cauldron, the one used to boil and shape leather.

Over the fireplace a lion's face was flanked by bat's wings.

This said he'd come to the right place. If that wasn't enough,
the weapons on the table told him anyway. A Florentine stiletto,
thin enough to slide from armpit to heart, or enter the anus and
destroy vital organs without leaving a mark. The sword Dr Crow
gave him, not seen since the day Tycho arrived at Ca' il Mauros.

Climbing hooks, which Tycho didn't bother to examine. He
wouldn't be taking or needing those. Rope, which he also ignored.
Focusing instead on the steel span, wooden stock and intricate
trigger of a tiny hand-held crossbow.

Assembling it quickly, without mistake, he wished Atilo was
there to see it. Time and again he'd fumbled slightly when watched
by the man. Five silver-tipped arrows came with the bow and
these made him shudder.

The silver would hurt if he touched it. Tycho knew that well
enough. He also knew Atilo reserved this crossbow for *krieghund*.
And most of those were meant to have been driven from the
city. It made him wonder about that night's assignment.

The final gift was three throwing blades.

Lifting one, Tycho flicked his wrist and put the blade between the teeth of the lion mask across the room. Five other knives had found its mouth over the years. Several dozen had missed. He hoped this was a good omen, and forbore to throw again in case he risked his luck.

Tycho oiled the little bow, checked the edge of his sword, which was sharp enough to shave him, and carefully wrapped the silver arrows. The balance of the stiletto was faultless. Pivoting on his first finger at the point where the blade met the handle.

Having chosen his weapons for the evening, Tycho found the darkest corner of an already dark room and folded his cloak into a crude pillow, closing his eyes and imagining water flowing through him as Atilo had taught.

"Your face?"

"Attacked, my lady. Three robbers." Iacopo smiled modestly. "I managed to fight them off."

Desdaio looked at him. "I heard you were drunk."

"You heard?"

"I mean . . ." She blushed. "I heard you come in last night, and thought you were drunk. I didn't realise," she looked at the crude stitches on his cheek, "you'd been injured."

"It's a dangerous city, my lady. Particularly for those who wander where they shouldn't at night. No one remains lucky forever."

Nodding, Desdaio glanced at the cages making up the duke's zoo. The morning air was chill enough for her to see her breath, but warmed by the scent of caged animals. The smell reminded her of stables. Although it was obviously ranker. "You are clever. How did you get permission?"

Iacopo sketched a bow to acknowledge the compliment, and smiled for the first time that morning. "A friend's father."

The truth was he'd blackmailed the son of an official in the Office of the Duke's Animals, who couldn't afford to pay the sum

Iacopo won from him an hour earlier at breakfast. A game where Iacopo supplied the dice. That Desdaio Bribanzo was Iacopo's guest made the visit easier to arrange. And brought a warning. Don't let her near the tyger. Iacopo grinned when he learnt the reason why, almost hearing the final part of his revenge fall into place.

Three clerks from the zoo sat on a wall, smirking at the infamous heiress. Iacopo cursed them and himself. He should have insisted he, Desdaio and Amelia had the place to themselves. Preferably without Amelia, who was relieving herself after accompanying her mistress on the walk from Ca' il Mauros.

"Iacopo . . ." Amelia had just noticed his face. "What happened?"

"Cutthroats. You know what this city is like."

"He fought them off," Desdaio said.

As Amelia tipped her head to one side the silver thimbles on her braids clattered. "Looks professional to me. Unlike the stitching."

"*Amelia* . . ."

"Not that I'd know, my lady."

"I was attacked," Iacopo said stiffly. His beloved beard was gone, with the lower end of the livid cut extending far below the shaving line to the edge of his jaw.

"And you fought them off?"

"Obviously," Desdaio said. "Since he's here. Now let's all look at the animals." She refused to think about bad things today. Sometimes she thought it was all Atilo could talk about. Politics, violence, old wars, and . . .

The duchess.

That was his other topic. Alexa's name slipped in and out of conversation like that of an old friend. Or an old lover, Desdaio thought bitterly. The rumours were impossible to miss, even for her. Old *friends* who hadn't talked to her in a year went out of their way to make sure she knew. And Amelia . . . Maybe Desdaio had misunderstood what Atilo meant. And maybe not.

"A tyger, you say?"

"Yes, my lady. To go with the camel bird."

"I thought Marco had a rhinoceros?"

"It died. They say it mourned the old duke's passing and refused to eat."

"Probably ill," Amelia said. "Ill and bored. It probably died of being ill and bored. If it didn't simply die of boredom."

"What's wrong with you today?" Desdaio's words were sharp.

"Look around you, my lady." She indicated the iron bars, the walls edging deep pits, the fishermen's mesh overhead that kept exotic birds from flight. "This place is a prison. It's loathsome," said Amelia, loudly enough to make Desdaio turn to see if anyone had heard. The only people who might were the clerks and they were too busy giggling.

"You can wait outside then."

"Thank you," Amelia said, although Desdaio meant this as punishment. Sneering at the clerks, Amelia nodded to a caged leopard as she passed. Its eyes followed her to the gate, and seemingly beyond.

"Really! I don't know what's got into her . . ."

"I'm glad we're alone," Iacopo said.

She blushed prettily. If he'd been Atilo he'd have taken her to bed a year ago. She was a rose, perfect in every way. But he'd have taken the bud before it had fully opened. Not waited 'til the bloom risked being blown. And that magnificent figure. There wasn't a woman in Venice half so fine. An opinion shared by the clerks, who kept staring. But it wouldn't last. Women's figures never did.

If she lived through childbirth, he could see her with half-Moorish brats, feeding and spanking and cajoling and spoiling. Employing a wet nurse and day nurse and then refusing to let them do the jobs they were paid to do. Iacopo had fantasised after the slaughter at Cannaregio of becoming the Blade. Maybe even becoming Atilo's adopted son. It would never happen. Desdaio would give him heirs. And if she didn't, the old man's favourite was now his white-haired freak.

"You're scowling, Iacopo."

"Thinking, my lady." He swept a low bow. "I'll try not to do it again."

Desdaio laughed. "Think away."

When he offered his elbow, Desdaio looked surprised, but threaded her arm through his all the same, and headed for the camel bird's cage. Passing an empty enclosure on the way.

"What lived here?"

"Duke Marco's unicorn, my lady. It was the last living example in existence. So I've heard said."

"Really?" said Desdaio, wide-eyed. "What happened?"

"Died of old age is one version."

"And the other?"

"Butchered and wind-dried on the new duke's orders. Marco wanted to know if unicorn tasted like horse. I'm sure that's a lie . . ."

So shocked was Desdaio, she let him wrap his arm round her for comfort, pulling away a few seconds later. As she did, his hand grazed her buttocks, which felt as plump as they looked. She flushed, and he said nothing.

Merely smiled.

The camel bird was huge and grey, with short body feathers and absurd little wings. Its feet were turkey-like but fifty times bigger. Its neck stretched so high its tiny head reared above them.

"It doesn't have a hump."

It did. Albeit a small one. But Iacopo had more sense than to point this out. "They live in the desert," he told her, having learnt this at breakfast that morning. "Hence the name. They can go for a month without water."

Desdaio was impressed.

"And the tyger's over here," said Iacopo, steering her to a brick hut where one wall was replaced by bars. A new ditch surrounded it. "Poor Marco," Desdaio said, as they were approaching.

Iacopo raised his eyebrows, languidly he hoped.

"I imagine that's to keep him away. He probably wants to feed the beast by hand."

"You've met the new duke?"

"Yes," said Desdaio, her voice neutral. "My father hoped . . ."

Of course he did. What Venetian father wouldn't want to marry his virgin heiress to a duke, insane or not? A small sacrifice, when the reward was birthing the next heir to the ducal throne. Access to the Millioni millions. Trade routes to the East. And Khan Tīmūr bin Taragay's protection to use them.

"You refused?"

He'd offended her. So much so, Desdaio stopped dead, twenty paces from the hut. Sweeping a low bow, Iacopo smiled his apologies. "Forgive me. I've upset you." Smiling hurt him, but he needed her favour.

"I'm a good daughter."

Really? Iacopo thought. Then why are you living with a Moor who isn't your husband? Why did your father disown you? And how come I have this . . . He touched his new scar, feeling its crude stitches. When all I did was tell the truth about seeing you leave Tycho's cellar?

"Let's see the tyger," he said brightly.

A scowling white face greeted them. The beast barely bothered to sneer as it turned tight circles, the straw beneath its feet marked by endless pacing. The stink was incredible for all that it was only spring, the sky was overcast, the sun on the far horizon and the air cold.

"I thought tygers had stripes."

"She's a snow tyger," Iacopo said. "The rarest type in the world. Even the Mamluk sultan doesn't have one."

Desdaio looked at the beast with new respect.

"Beautiful, isn't she? said Iacopo, as Desdaio edged closer. He stepped behind her, feeling her shift forward. Another tiny nudge put her nearer the bars.

"My god," Desdaio said. "She's magnificent."

Even away from her high mountains and the snows that gave her that colour, the tygress was impressive. Also unhappy and crowded. Turning, she lifted her tail, as Iacopo had been warned she might, and squirted rank-smelling urine across Desdaio's fur-edged cloak. A little hit Desdaio's hand.

"*My lady.*"

"Oh my God . . . Foul creature."

Desdaio was already wiping her fingers, tears of mortification filling her eyes. As she glanced back to check if the clerks had noticed it happen, Iacopo grinned.

"I want to go *now*."

"Of course, my lady. Let me take this." Unclipping her cloak, he folded it to hide stinking velvet and tucked it under her arm. "There's a trough by the gate where you can wash . . ."

The trough was stone. Used to water horses that brought food for the duke's animals from the Riva degli Schiavoni. Desdaio washed her hands so thoroughly in the freezing overspill that she made her fingers red.

As the late afternoon sky filled with clouds and the air prickled with unused lightning, Atilo retreated to his study with plans for the Rialto bridge. The old duke had wished to replace the existing wooden bridge with a stone one. His bridge was to have shops down both sides. Since Marco owned the bridge the rents would be his. More importantly, his new bridge would be defensible, with arrow slits, and floor gratings through which burning oil could be poured.

His plan called for ten thousand larch piles, cut by hand and hammered into the sand, clay and gravel to support the foundations at either end. The corpse of an entire forest would be compressed into a tiny area and covered with oak beams, on which rubble from Istrian stone would rest. Only then could the new bridge be built.

Three things worked against this.

Two solvable, one not. The current bridge was loved by all. This was solvable. The duke announced that San Domenico Contarini, one of Serenissima's greatest doges, came to him in a dream to say Venice deserved a stone bridge . . .

The changing of the date of the duke's marriage to the sea, from Epiphany to Easter, and the fact the dukedom should become hereditary, had both been announced to the Millioni in dreams, backed by saints. San Marco was always a good choice. Unfortunately, he'd approved the duke's previous plan.

But if San Domenico demanded a stone bridge, then the second problem could be solved. Houses both sides of the Canalasso would have to be pulled down for a hundred paces inland to allow those foundations to be built. There would be protests. It was hard to argue, however, with a saint.

The unsolvable problem was that Marco III joined San Domenico Contarini in Heaven before the old bridge could be ripped down and the new one begun. So the wooden bridge remained while the Ten argued about the cost of replacing it.

"Come," he said, hearing a knock at his door.

Iacopo opened it and waited until Atilo gestured him coldly inside. Iacopo's plan, Atilo decided sourly, was obviously to bow and apologise enough to irritate Atilo into forgiving him.

"What do you want?"

"I thought . . . perhaps . . ." Iacopo took a deep breath. "Perhaps I could take tonight's orders to Tycho? Then I could wish him luck." The young man's usual bravado was gone in the face of last night's tongue-lashing. His cheek was livid, his face raw from where his beloved beard had been hacked away.

"I've given the job to Tomas."

A quiet and unassuming man, quite unfit to lead, Tomas had trained with Atilo before Iacopo. He baked cakes, these days, in Campo dei Carmini, his bakery famous for pastries in the French style. His other skill, poisoning people, went unremarked upon and unadvertised. On the night of the *krieghund* he'd been in

Paris introducing a Valois prince to God with a succession of tartlets that, if eaten alone, had no effect whatever.

Atilo's troops might have been reduced to a shell, but Tomas's work in Paris had saved their reputation. He did more than kill a Valois. He gave Marco's enemies something to fear. None of them yet understood how weak this city was. The average training for a member of the Assassini was five years. No empire could afford to employ so few blades. And those still living, those away that night, were ragged from moving city to city enforcing the Ten's silent will.

Looking up, Atilo realised Iacopo still waited for an answer.

"Go," he said. "Make your peace. Never bring Lady Desdaio's name into your disputes again."

Spinning, knife in hand, Tycho found Iacopo behind him.

"Don't," Iacopo said.

Tempting, Tycho couldn't deny that. His rival framed in the open window of a room two floors up in a parish the Night Watch avoided. Who would know? Well, Atilo for a start. If his servant was found skewered in the dirt outside a house the Assassini owned.

"I could claim it was an accident."

Tycho didn't realise he'd said it aloud until Iacopo's eyes widened. And the man glanced down and behind him, judging the drop to a muddy alley below.

"I have your orders."

"Tomas was meant to bring those."

"Atilo asked me. He wants us friends." Iacopo's scarred face and twisted smile said he knew it wasn't that simple. But their master's name was enough. Tycho gestured him into the room.

"What have they told you?" Iacopo asked.

"Nothing." Surely that was the point? Orders were given and obeyed without notice. No one knew when an order would be passed or by whom. He was to wait in this room until told otherwise. Tycho guessed Iacopo was telling him now.

"Find the Golden Horse behind San Simeon Piccolo . . ."

That meant crossing the canal near its mouth.

"Buy a jug of wine and insist on Barolo." Iacopo placed two gold ducats, three silver grosso and five tornsello on the table, arranging them in piles. Nudging them slightly until they were neat.

"Il Magnifico died years ago," said Tycho. "But the ducats are new."

"Magnificos are still minted. The Moors and Mamluks won't take anything else. And Byzantines give a better rate for these than their own bezants."

"Why?"

"They're purer," Iacopo said as if it was obvious. "The emperor can cheapen bezants if he has to. Venice can't cheapen ducats. If we did, trade would fail."

"And what does a jug of Barolo cost?"

"A tornsello. A tornsello and a half at most."

Nodding to say he understood, Tycho scooped up the coins and thrust them into a leather pocket on his belt.

"Let me help you." Pulling a scrap of fur from his boot, Iacopo thrust it quickly into the pocket and folded the leather top. "It'll stop the coins from jangling," he said. "One of my own tricks."

Tycho nodded.

"I'll go now," Iacopo said. "You'll need time to prepare. But let me have some of that small beer first." Taking the jug, he began filling a rough-blown glass, his grip suddenly slipping and the glass crashing to the floor to roll away unbroken.

"Shit," he said. "I'm sorry."

"No matter. The glass isn't broken."

"That's not what I'm worried about." Producing a scrap of velvet, Iacopo wiped beer from the back of Tycho's boots. "That's more like it," he said.

45

The carving above the door of the Golden Horse, a narrow tavern between narrow houses in a street south of the Grand Canal's northern mouth, looked more like a donkey. Once cheaply gilded, it now peeled in patches. The bits not peeling were the hue of rancid fat. Tycho wasn't surprised to hear a man pissing outside call it the Mouldering Mule. The man stank, as did the tavern and the street in which he pissed. Anywhere near a tannery always stank.

Shit shovellers and tanners' boys bathed daily. Probably the only people in the city to do so. Except for the very rich, for whom bathing was an expression of power. The difference was that the rich bathed inside, sitting on huge sponges, their baths shrouded by tents to preserve the heat. While the shit shovellers and tanners boys bathed in canals that were frozen in winter and rancid in summer. So rancid that their sole virtue was that they stank less than those bathing.

The man leaving the Mouldering Mule worked a shit boat. From the smell of him he'd decided to have a drink or three before facing the waters of the canal.

"What are you looking at?"

Ignoring him, Tycho turned to go in. He wore his black leather coat, collar turned up. Black doublet, black codpiece, black hose, black boots. Maybe these made customers stare when he began to push his way through. Many glanced up, most glanced away. A human response to seeing someone pass.

A few kept staring.

He could stare back or look away. The first a challenge, the second surrender. So he glanced away, heard a snort and glanced straight back, hardening his gaze. It left his mocker uncertain. Shouldering him aside, Tycho found a table near the back. A one-eyed ex-soldier sat with a heavy glass in front of him.

"This stool free?"

The man spat into the sawdust. "What do you think?"

Tycho sat himself and smiled at the man's scowl. After a moment, the soldier went back to examining his mug of wine. The woman who came over to take Tycho's order was Schiavoni, large and busty. In a Venetian her tied-up hair would make her married. With the Schiavoni who knew?

Apart from another Schiavoni, obviously.

"Well?" she demanded.

"Barolo . . . A jug."

She scowled. "Red, white, strong beer, small beer. You want anything else go somewhere else."

"Barolo."

The soldier laughed. "Your red's shit," he told her. "Your white's worse. As for the beer, you should pay us to drink it. Tell Marco to give him a jug of the good stuff."

When she came back, she banged Tycho's jug down hard enough to make her breasts bounce and wine slop across the table. Running his finger through the puddle, Tycho licked it. When he looked up, she was blushing. He gave her a tornsello and a half coin and watched her flounce away. At the counter, she looked back and flounced some more.

"Too bad you'll never get to explore what's in that blouse . . ."

279

Pushing a folded note around the newly made wine puddle, the soldier said, "Can you read?"

"A bit." Tycho said.

"More than I can."

Along the Fondamenta delle Tette, the bare tits and rouged nipples that gave the brothel canal its name were on display. In a hundred and fifty pairs of chilly flesh, and an endless choice of shapes from barely there to pendulous. The patriarch owned this area. The Church having decided that making whores cheap, available and frequent would cut down on sodomy, at least between men.

"You're no fun . . ."

The half-naked girl in a tavern full of sailors and off-duty soldiers scowled at Tycho, who shrugged and didn't bother to disagree.

"I'm cheap," she said. "And good."

He could see why she might be proud of the second. But being proud of the first was odd. Unless he misunderstood her.

"And I'm here on business."

Turning away, she threw her arms around the neck of a passing Schiavoni bosun, who nodded at her whispered price and thrust his hand up her skirt; unable to wait until he reached the stalls before beginning to toy with his purchase.

Although Tycho drank as little as he could get away with at each stop his head was still spinning, and his thoughts wandering by the time he reached the Alexandrian, his fifth destination. A single-storey building leant against the side of a palace, with the fish market downstream on the Canalasso's far side. He approached it along a narrow alley, and found himself facing an original palace, which was halfway through being rebuilt. Bamboo scaffolding rose in the darkness.

Slick with rain, the rope lashing the lengths together was dark and swollen. A vicious-looking guard dog turned to watch Tycho approach. And for the first time since he'd arrived in Venice a dog raised his hackles and launched an attack. Only to be brought up short by its chain.

Picking itself up, it bared its fangs and tried again.

"Easy," said Tycho.

This only drove the beast into a frenzy of snapping teeth. Until saliva flew and the beast's eyes looked ready to roll in its head. *Dogs ignore me*, Tycho thought. It wasn't that they liked him or disliked him. They simply behaved as if he didn't exist, until now. He hoped it wasn't an omen.

The club's owner obviously had permission from the palace's new owner to keep trading, because nothing looked temporary. The Alexandrian was as far from the Mouldering Mule as two drinking dens could be. Far further than the thousand steps it would take to walk from one to the other. Above this door stood a gilded warrior, dressed in a battle skirt and holding a sword. "Iskander" said a carving on its base. "Conqueror of the Known World."

The room was narrow but deep, with a painted ceiling. The floor paved in Istrian stone that was almost clean. A carpet hung on one wall, its reds and browns matched by smaller carpets on other walls. Marble-topped tables matched stools that didn't wobble. Candles burnt in candelabra.

And the air stank of beeswax, incense, expensive wine and perfume so heavy Tycho thought he'd wandered into another brothel by mistake. According to Atilo, brothels existed in Venice for every taste. Young women, older women. Whores who would hurt you. Whores who liked to be hurt. Whores who didn't like to be hurt, but, for extra, you could hurt them anyway. The best provided food, usually at a loss. Food and drink and hazard tables and areas for conversations best not overheard. According to Atilo brothels were for more than fucking.

A dozen masks looked across. None looked away and Tycho could feel their hunger. Languidly pushing back his chair, a figure in a white mask, red silk gown and golden shawl came to drape one arm around Tycho's shoulders.

"First time?" Before Tycho could respond, a waddling doll propelled herself to her feet, and hurried over.

"He's with us."

"I saw him first."

"Allophone, you'd be wise . . ."

The first figure dropped his arm from around Tycho's neck and left hurriedly, muttering apologies and protests that he hadn't realised who he'd been talking to.

"He's a little idiot," Hightown Crow said, pushing back his gilded mask and smoothing the front of a purple gown. "But a *pretty* little idiot. Who will get himself into trouble. Probably serious trouble if we're lucky."

Tycho gaped at him.

"Welcome to the Alexandrian," said Dr Crow. "I have two patrons who want to meet you." He pointed to a door at the back.

"You're grown," Duchess Alexa said. She looked at Tycho thoughtfully. "Into what is another question. In height, certainly. Atilo tells me you're ready for testing . . ."

"Yes, madame."

She laughed at his flatness of tone. "Still hate me, do you?"

"I'd kill you."

"What prevents you?"

Something did. His fury at seeing the woman who used Rosalyn as bait to catch him burnt like flame. And that Rosalyn had died that night should have . . . But the flame shrank and shrivelled, leaving only regret. Blinking, Tycho claimed back a little of his anger. "Magic."

Alexa smiled. "Close enough."

"I'll kill you though, eventually."

"When you're able to kill me you'll no longer want to . . ."

"Don't count on it."

"I won't," she promised. "You should know I count on

nothing." Tiny octopuses filled a plate on a table in front of her. They were dressed with oil, large flakes of pepper and sprigs of some dried herb. "Try one," Duchess Alexa said.

Tycho shook his head.

"I insist." Tycho popped a tiny octopus into his mouth, feeling it wriggle briefly as he crunched. "Did you taste it?"

He nodded, swallowing his mouthful.

"Now eat another."

This time he felt a tiny spark and watched the duchess smile at the surprise in his eyes.

"Finish the plate."

By the time he bit into the last wriggling morsel the spark was obvious. A flicker of tiny lightning as the creature died. Wiping the platter clean with a sliver of bread, Tycho was surprised to find himself happier.

"You know why you're here?"

"For the testing."

"In the old days my husband would give your master the name of someone he needed dead. A foreign prince. A troublesome priest. Your job would be to make that happen. Tell me what *deniability* is."

"I know you did it. You know you did it. I can't prove it."

She laughed. "The basis of a *perfect kill*. No one can prove a thing. A *trick kill* blames someone else. A *non-kill* looks like a suicide. A *possible kill* looks *almost* like an accident. That's its subtlety. Since doubt enters our enemies' hearts like a blade. I can see from your face Atilo has taught you this. So, another question. Why do we allow this club to exist?"

"It keeps Dr Crow happy."

She clapped her hands. "Marco would have loved you," she said. "So young, so cynical. What else?"

"It gives you his friends to blackmail."

"So astute. If I told you to kill Dr Crow, would you?"

"Happily, my lady."

"I almost want to make him your target. Sadly, this comes first." Unrolling a piece of paper, she revealed an ink drawing. Somewhat between man and wolf, with sharp ears, shaggy fur, pointed snout and long claws. Tycho felt his throat tighten.

"You recognise it?" Alexa asked.

"No, my lady."

"Would you lie?"

"Of course not, my lady." Tycho glanced round the room. A raised divan covered with a silk carpet was visible behind her chair. More carpets draped the walls. A tiny single window was leaded with small circles of glass. The room's only real oddity was its smell. A mix of smoke and something sharper. Tycho had been catching traces of the latter all night.

"Hashish," said Alexa, "the poor man's opium." She nodded to a fretted brass dish, which dribbled smoke. "Your nose wrinkled."

"And you read my thoughts?"

"Not easy. In fact, surprisingly hard. But tell me first how you got here . . ." She waited expectantly.

Tycho opened his mouth to say he walked from behind San Simeon Piccolo, along the edge of the Rio Marin, and Rio di San Polo, then cut between the churches of San Aponal and San Silvestro to the Rialto bridge. The way anyone Venetian would describe his walk. Only, he realised, as he prepared to answer, this was not what she meant. "I don't know."

His words tasted bitter as ink.

"Ragnarok," she said. "I see more than you think."

"Not my beliefs." He said it without thinking, but it was true. Lord Eric and his followers believed in flames and fire at the end of time. Tycho's mother was not Viking, nor Skaelingar. That much Withered Arm had told him.

Duchess Alexa seemed strangely pleased with his answer. "That's Prince Leopold zum Bas Friedland." She gestured at the drawing. "His father's emperor, his mother's French. He's a *krieghund*. As

284

the German's bastard, a *krieghund* and the German envoy, Leopold is protected. In all senses . . ."

Tycho should ask what the duchess meant.

She sighed when he stayed silent. "Officially, we can't touch him. No matter what he does." Tycho *shouldn't* ask what that meant. This was not his to know. Assassini orders existed to be obeyed, without question and without thought. Thought limited action in the happening, according to Atilo, and destroyed the chance of rest afterwards.

"What's he done?"

"None of your business." Duchess Alexa tipped her head. "Surely you were told that?"

"It's almost the first lesson."

She laughed, reached for her glass of wine and sipped it, careful not to stain her gauze veil. "He murdered fifteen women over the course of five months. Well, his men did. Only three of the deaths mattered. The third, the seventh and the last. There's a subtlety in that. Killing at random so his target kills appeared also to be by chance. And then, to finish, he destroyed the Assassini. In a single night, a year and a half ago, his Wolf Brothers killed most of Atilo's men. They crippled Venice's reach and left us open to threats."

"Why not act before now?"

"So," she said. "You can think as well as look pretty. In which case, answer your own question . . ."

"The time wasn't right?"

"You weren't ready."

Tycho looked at her and knew his mouth hung open. So he shut it smartly and smoothed the shock from his face. More rested on tonight than he first thought.

"How could so many Assassini be killed?"

Duchess Alexa took a deep breath. Such a deep one that her breasts rose beneath her dress, and she saw him notice . . . "Concentrate," she snapped, and Tycho knew she intended to tell him.

Lady Giulietta had been abducted twice.

Most recently by the Mamluks. There was something about the way Duchess Alexa said this that troubled Tycho. But by then she'd returned to talking about Prince Leopold. He'd been behind the first abduction. And Alexa and the Regent hadn't even known about it until Atilo returned Giulietta, distraught and in tears, to the palace and reported his losses to . . .

"The Council," Prince Alonzo said, shutting a door crossly behind him. "You should have waited."

"I did . . ."

"And yet here the two of you are." His gaze swept the room, the carpeted bed and single glass of wine before finally reaching Tycho and dismissing him. "I guess I should be grateful talking's all I find you doing."

"Is there a point to this?" Duchess Alexa demanded, sliding the freshly rolled scroll discreetly into her pocket. The Regent and his sister-in-law faced each other, both on their feet and leaning forward. The difference was that Alonzo was blind drunk.

"We agreed to do this together."

"I was simply awaiting your arrival."

"Of course you were. You . . ." Alonzo glared at Tycho. "What do you know so far?"

"Nothing, my lord."

"Good. Your job is to kill a German princeling. He means nothing. It's a test. That's all you need to know." Leaning forward, he emptied Alexa's wine glass, either forgetting or not caring it wasn't his. "Kill the bastard, kill his sister, kill everyone in the house . . ."

"*Alonzo* . . ."

"You have a problem with that?"

"This isn't what we agreed."

"We didn't agree you'd see this brat first, either. Do you see me complaining? He kills Leopold, end of story. Let your Moor prove he hasn't lost his grip." Refilling Alexa's glass from a jug,

Alonzo emptied it again. Only to look up and appear surprised Tycho was still there. "You," he said. "Go make yourself useful."

At the door, Tycho was stopped by a question. "How old are you?" asked Duchess Alexa.

Prince Alonzo snorted.

"Seventeen winters. Maybe eighteen."

And maybe more, if the fact that Bjornvin burnt a century before meant anything. And there were his dreams of slaughter, of light and ice.

Ca' Friedland was ten minutes' walk from the Rialto bridge, north along the right bank of the Canalasso, at the corner with Rio di San Felice. A once unfashionable area that was obviously being redeveloped. Prince Leopold's palace was a huge waterside mansion in the old style, its grey façade black with age. A single lamp burnt in an upstairs window and an ordinary looking *gondolino* was moored by its watergate. Tycho had assumed a prince's *gondolino* would be grander.

Tycho would have liked a house like this. One that rose five storeys, with endless arched windows. A house with columns and statues, and probably carpets and tapestries.

"*No you don't,*" said a voice.

A beggar squatted on the quayside. Rat eyes bright in the night as he curled a turd into the dirt. He was squinting to see more of Tycho than shadow.

"Fuck off now. This is my patch."

Closing the gap, Tycho killed. Simply shifting from there to here to break the man's neck and lower him silently, before life left his eyes. A splash, and the current carried a new corpse. The kill was instinctive, unpremeditated.

Tonight he'd discovered Atilo's truth. A truth Tycho doubted Amelia and Iacopo had worked out. The Assassini's greatest weapon was currently their name, backed up by the occasional murder, and the fact no one had yet discovered how weak they really were.

It would take years to rebuild the group. Atilo didn't have years. He was an old man busy making a fool of himself with a younger woman. And looked – more so every day – to be regretting it.

The Assassini were there for Tycho's taking.

Atilo insisted belief made fools of men. Tycho had started to wonder if lack of belief wasn't more crippling. Tycho didn't believe in anything. Not really. He might do if he knew how. But, most days, the hole where his heart should be felt too huge to fill. Being the duke's Blade might fill it.

Get to it, he told himself.

The walls were built from crudely cut Istrian stone, and rotting brick held by mortar that had soured years earlier. Cracks meant handholds were easy. All the same, Tycho made himself edge round to Rio di San Felice, and scale the side of Ca' Friedland that rose from the narrow canal, using the shadows to hide himself. Tycho had no wish to be spotted by the Watch, another beggar or some passing drunk.

Idle thoughts filled his climb.

Another handhold and he'd be outside the only lit window. A balcony called him from above and Tycho reached for it, hooking one hand over a decorative detail made from a single run of bricks, before stretching for the balcony's floor.

He should concentrate but the climb was easy. Not suspiciously so. Simply easy. A climb that would have left Iacopo exhausted barely troubled him. His heartbeat as slow as ever. His skin cool to the touch.

No sweat, no sign of fear.

Listen, he told himself sharply. *Do this properly.*

The problem was he *knew* three drunks were leaving a tavern in Campo San Felice. He'd *already noticed* the splash of oars from an unlit *vipera* in the *rio* below. The law forbade unlicensed movement on the side canals after dark, and sluice gates blocked many of the smaller intersections, but gates could be raised if smugglers offered enough.

A clipclop of hooves came from the street.

To ride like a Venetian was an insult. For all stables existed in the city, the standard of horsemanship was appalling, according to Atilo. Anyway, riders had to dismount before crossing the Rialto bridge, and horses couldn't be brought into Piazza San Marco, but had to be tethered next to the Mint. So the only point of owning one was show.

And from inside the Ca' Friedland?

The sound of a harpsichord. An instrument he recognised because Desdaio had one at Atilo's house. Hers was Flemish, as were most in Venice. Whoever was playing was good. Desdaio simply managed basic tunes.

See who was in there or keep climbing? The question answered itself when the music stopped, a stool scraped back and he heard a woman grunt gently as she lifted a heavy lamp. Behind the shutters the room dimmed to darkness.

Tycho kept climbing.

Grit rattled beneath his boots and fell with the sound of rats scuttling as it trickled down the wall to patter lightly on a balcony below. Too much noise, he thought, listening to falling dust settle and wondering why it didn't worry him.

Because he was drugged.

The twist of Iacopo's body as he picked the glass from the floor. Iacopo's sudden decision not to drink small beer after all. Tycho using the glass, to drink down the last of the water before leaving for the Mouldering Mule. It all made sense. He'd been feeling strangely relaxed since.

One chance, Atilo said.

That was what everyone got. No exceptions.

Failure would see him sold as a slave, supposedly. Although Tycho suspected, given his recently learnt skills, failure would see him dead. Which was fine, he didn't intend to fail. He intended to kill the German and return to Ca' il Mauros to rip out Iacopo's throat.

Levering himself over a parapet, Tycho dropped to a crouch and discovered he wasn't alone. A dark-haired man waited five or six paces away, lazily elegant in an open shirt; his crouch a mocking mirror of Tycho's own. He was grinning behind his beard. "I hope you realise you stink like a polecat? And – I have to admit – I thought you planned to hang on the edge of that balcony all night."

"Leopold Bas Friedland?"

"Prince Leopold zum Bas Friedland." His eyes slid over Tycho's costume. "Is that how Atilo dresses his bum boys these days? And that sword . . . I thought a dagger in the back was more the Venetian style?"

"You're not an assassin?"

The German flushed at Tycho's jibe. Much of the humour going out of his face. "I'm a soldier in a secret war. A peasant like you wouldn't understand what that means."

Tycho snorted.

"Took you long enough to get here."

"A few minutes to climb your crappy wall."

"Eighteen months to pluck up the courage." Prince Leopold saw Tycho's scowl. "Oh, not you. You're the disposable bit in this. The Regent, Duchess Alexa, that raddled Moor she's fucking. Perhaps you should tell me before you die . . . What took them so long?"

Tycho drew his sword.

In the muted light of a cloud-shrouded moon he saw Prince Leopold's eyes narrow. Tycho's blade glittered like water reflecting sunshine. And then Prince Leopold's gaze flicked upwards, and a patch of black detached itself from the night's upturned bowl with a creak like old leather.

"Six months to make the sword," it said. "A year to turn this boy into your death. Another five minutes for that to become a reality. Emperor's bastard or not, Prince Leopold, you've plagued this city too long."

"Alexa, and I thought you didn't care."

Rolling the sword across his hand, Tycho swept a figure of eight. It felt like any sword to him. For all that its blade . . . Stepping closer, Tycho saw the blade brighten. So he stepped back quickly and saw it dim.

"Well I never," the prince said. "A mage sword matched to a boy who doesn't quite know how to use it. This should be interesting."

He drew and lunged in the same second.

His lunge changing direction. Tycho was so busy blocking he almost missed the dagger in Leopold's other hand. It would have killed him had it pierced his side. Instead it ripped his doublet and drew blood.

Both men stepped back.

Your job is to kill a German princeling. He means nothing. That's all you need to know. The Regent's words rang sour in Tycho's memory.

In a year, Tycho had swapped a crude knowledge of axes for swordplay, knife work and unarmed combat. But he'd also half-learnt to read, studied poisons, and discussed politics. He felt spread thin in the face of a man who held a sword like an extension of his own arm.

"Ready to die?" Prince Leopold asked.

Dropping his dagger, the prince raised his sword. As if intentionally opening himself to attack. But he could sweep his weapon down to either side or straight ahead. He could block every stroke Tycho offered with a single move. So Tycho raised his blade in turn, and waited.

Overhead, cracking leather circled.

Dipping and swooping and offering dry clicks that sounded like falling dust. When it swooped close, Tycho realised it was large. As large as his doublet given the power to fly. Prince Leopold snorted, flicked his gaze at the clicking darkness, and struck as Tycho's gaze followed, swinging his blade in an arc brutal enough to lop a man off at the knees.

Metal met metal. Sparks flying as shock numbed their arms.

Tycho had no idea how he blocked the blow. From the look on Prince Leopold's face he had no idea either. Sweeping the man's sword aside, Tycho went for his throat. Almost losing his own entrails as Leopold ducked beneath the strike and spun, his sword passing a hair's breadth from Tycho's belly.

The princeling changed styles three times in seven moves. Switching again for the three strikes after. Blocking a skull strike, Tycho jumped a Sicilian sweep, just avoiding a backslash to his Achilles heel. Tycho's arm was already dead to the shoulder. His fingers gripped his sword from instinct.

When he stepped back, Prince Leopold was also gasping, sweat running down his face. The veins in his neck standing out like hawsers. His scowl said Tycho shouldn't have been able to survive that rally.

His next attack came so fast it drove Tycho to the parapet.

Risking a glance, Tycho saw a low wall stretch away on both sides behind him. Beyond his attacker, a roof rose steadily. On that slope's far side would be another slope falling gently to a gutter cutting across the roof's middle. A second slope would rise and fall beyond that, ending above the land gate.

It was a traditional design.

Ducking a blow, Tycho tried to spin past Prince Leopold, risking death to reach the slope. Had he succeeded he'd have had the roof's height on his side and room to fight freely. But Prince Leopold's sword caught his above the hilt and took the blade from Tycho's hand.

The princeling's smile was gone.

Opening his mouth, he bared teeth in a grin that narrowed his eyes to slits. A trickle of drool ran down his beard and Tycho felt his stomach lurch. Lord Eric's brother had been berserker. They lived outside pain. Died outside it too. They'd crawl up a sword to gut the man who stabbed them.

As Tycho waited, night clouds parted.

A full moon nailed Tycho to the spot, fever waterfalling through his body as the sky went red around him and the city acquired hard edges and the water in its canals glowed like molten steel. For the first time ever, he let the moon's rays take him and felt his dog teeth descend.

Opposite him, Prince Leopold raised his face to the blood moon and howled, his body arching as his shriek split the air. Behind him the stars distorted, and the shimmering air ripped as worlds fought each other.

The stronger of the worlds won.

Peeling back, the skin of Prince Leopold's chest split to reveal blood, raw flesh and fur beneath. His ribcage cracked. Muscles tearing and ribs breaking as unseen hands racked him, dislocating his joints and twisting him to a newer shape. Prince Leopold's clothes tore too. Rags he ripped away to stand naked. His fingers turning to claws and black fur flowing in a wave across his reformed body. Blood dripped from his jaws where his teeth had extended.

Sex erect, head back, Prince Leopold screamed at the moon.

When his gaze flicked to Tycho it was animal.

The sword he'd been wielding fell from his claws and clattered to the lead of the roof. The prince barely noticed. He was too busy completing the changes that made him *krieghund*.

Tycho moved.

He moved so fast the roof blurred as he reached the sword he'd dropped, grabbed it up and adopted the stance Prince Leopold had used earlier. Legs apart, blade held high above his head.

"Ready to die?" he asked.

The *krieghund*'s eyes blazed as it dropped to a crouch and sprang. Leaping high over Tycho, it twisted on landing, claws raking down Tycho's spine. Blood rose black and sticky through torn leather, pain hitting Tycho a moment later. So shocking, he dropped to his knees.

The red sky faltered.

A second later, Tycho realised he'd dropped the sword.

The creature reached it before him.

It stood on Tycho's blade, jaws so wide its tongue lolled from one side. While Tycho stood in a puddle of his own blood watched by the grinning monster. Stepping sideways, Tycho saw the *krieghund* do the same.

So he did it again and again.

Always moving closer to Prince Leopold's own sword. Until he was close enough to grab it from lead flashing at his feet. And the creature howled with laughter as Tycho let go, clutching his fingers.

The sword was bewitched in some way.

Magic was all Tycho needed.

He reached for Prince Leopold's sword again, his fingers blistering. The prince was judging distances and Tycho only just ducked in time to avoid claws jagging for his throat. He was about to retreat, when crackling blackness eclipsed the moon and Prince Leopold leapt high, trying to hook the irritation from the air.

And in that moment the red sky steadied.

"Become yourself," the bat said.

To do so was to ignore every rule Atilo had taught him about remaining in control. But Tycho obeyed anyway, embracing the moonlight. Across his back cuts began to mend. The pain in his fingers vanished. The city became as clear as day. Stretching out around him with a shocking clarity. Light scribbled bright lines around the buildings. He had the secrets and the scents of the city in an instant

He discovered how both Leopold zum Bas Friedland and the guard dog from the Alexandrian knew he was coming. His boots stank. It should be unmissable. And then Tycho identified the drug in his blood dulling his senses, and felt the effects wither as whatever made him who he was swept it swiftly away.

Standing on Prince Leopold's blade, Tycho snapped it in two and hurled handle and hilt, seeing it scour a line in the wolfthing's cheek. His blade might be magic. The handle was common metal. Stepping back, Tycho swallowed the roof's layout in a single glance. He felt . . .

Good came in there somewhere.

Good, and *focused*. And *here*, and *now*. He belonged inside his own skin for the first time ever. Looking at his fingers, he realised they were longer. His skin whiter. When he raised a hand to his mouth his fingers came away bloody. His dog teeth had grown. Not like this creature's. His face hadn't twisted and become animal, it had refined.

This was what being *Fallen* meant.

His speed and strength were simply side effects. Good ones, but side effects as surely as his hatred of sunlight. "You die here," Tycho said.

And the *krieghund* feared him.

They met in the middle of a leap. Crashing into each other so hard a human's bones would have broken. Tycho landed three paces away, spinning sideways as the *krieghund* used the parapet for leverage and leapt straight back. Tycho swept one foot under the creature as it landed, sending it rolling towards a corner.

As he grabbed the creature's hips to hurl it to the canal below, it twisted and sank claws into his shoulders, dragging him close. Tycho could smell the *krieghund*'s fetid breath. Feel dog-like heat rise from its body.

Struggling would bury those claws in his flesh. Pulling away wouldn't free him. Going close put him within jaw reach. The *krieghund* was strong but Tycho was faster. That had to count for something.

He kneed the *krieghund* from instinct and heard the creature gasp. So he kneed it again, and as its grip faltered, put his elbow into its throat.

The beast stumbled. Clawed hands clutching for its neck as it fell to its knees, rocking backwards and forwards. As if keening in silence. Maybe it was, Tycho thought, not caring either way.

46

This time he could clearly see magic rippling along his sword blade. Flecks of fire brightening as he approached his target. Hightown Crow had designed the weapon for one purpose only. Killing *krieghund*.

"Any last words?" Tycho demanded.

Prince Leopold looked up dumbly.

"I guess not." Drawing back his sword, Tycho found its balance. "Quite sure about those last . . ."

"*Don't. Please don't.*"

The words came from behind him.

Tycho froze. He refused to turn. Refused to admit what his senses told him. Instead he watched the wolfthing's eyes focus beyond him and something human slip back into them. Prince Leopold shook his head very slightly.

"Anything," the voice promised, closer now. "We'll give you anything. Leopold has estates. He'll pay a ransom. Please."

Kill Friedland. Kill his *sister*. All Tycho had to do was obey those orders and the Assassini would be his eventually. He didn't dare turn around.

"I have my orders."

He could prove himself worthy to be Blade. Assassini killed with no more thought or conscience than a dagger. They existed to be wielded by the duke and his Council. Who they killed was not their concern.

"Stay back," he warned.

The young woman sobbed as Tycho's sword reached tipping point. Already the *krieghund* was changing. Its limbs straightening. Blood running down its face as its jaws retracted. A near-human head would roll across that roof.

He chose a point behind the prince's skull.

As his sword readied for the kill, a young woman flung herself across Prince Leopold's naked body. A black scrap of sky detached, falling fast. And Tycho only just managed to pull his blow, shredding the bat instead. Wheeling away, the dying animal tumbled dirtwards.

A tear-stained face looked at Tycho.

Huge eyes widening as she recognised him. He felt unable to breathe, unable to do anything but stare back. He had hunted for over a year to find her and now she had found him. It was the girl from the basilica.

"You won't kill Leopold?"

Tycho shook his head mutely.

Putting his sword down, he stepped back from temptation. How could he not let the prince go? The sight of Lady Giulietta stole his will to act. He could *feel* the hairs on her arm as they rippled in the wind. Her scent was a drug far stronger than whatever Iacopo used. A golden heat haze danced around her. He felt awe. An awe so absolute it left him barely able to function.

"Your price?" she whispered.

Touching her lips, he smoothed his fingers down her cheek and rested them lightly on her throat, feeling her pulse flutter. She blushed, and then caught herself. Making herself meet his eyes.

"Me?" she asked.

"Yes," he said. "You."

Lifting her to her feet, he looked deep into her eyes and saw himself silhouetted against a night sky. Her eyes were blue and he saw in them things no one would see. A thousand specks of light arranged around darkness. A flotilla of ships drawing in on an island.

"In the basilica," she whispered. "I almost . . ."

I know.

The memory of her, with a dagger to her breast, remained undimmed. The taste of a single drop of blood from the slightest of wounds had changed him forever. She had locked him to this absurd city.

"Will you let Leopold rise?"

He let her help the German princeling to his feet. If the man attacked Tycho would kill him. But Leopold simply stood there, swaying. His gaze met Tycho's own, and then Leopold zum Bas Friedland looked at Giulietta and tried to speak. No words came from his ruined throat.

"It's all right," she promised.

He was objecting to her offering herself. All three of them knew that from the anguish on his eyes.

Lady Giulietta had a chamber of her own. On the third storey, above the piano nobile and overlooking Rio di San Felice. It was ringed with salt, enough salt to leave a clear trail around the edge of the room. All the passages were lined with salt, even the stairs. Every room in Ca' Friedland had salt around it.

"Leopold's idea," she said. "It's there to keep me safe."

"From what?"

"You," she said, tears filling her eyes.

Shuttered windows led to a tall and narrow balcony with a tiled overhang supported by elegant pillars. Tycho opened the windows slowly, already knowing no enemy waited beyond. In time he would learn to trust his instincts. For now it felt arrogant simply to believe he was right.

Caution made him lock her chamber, sliding its bolts, before checking outside. If you wanted to reach her balcony you would have to climb from the canal, using cracks in the outside walls and the stone ribs of the window arches. Anyone trained by Atilo could do it. That was what made him nervous.

"What are you doing?"

Tycho stopped lugging an old iron chest by its handle. "Blocking that." He pointed at balcony doors. She nodded mutely, perched on her bed, its curtains down, except the side she'd tied back earlier.

"He won't try to come in."

"It's not Leopold I'm worried about."

Her eyes went huge in the darkness. She was the girl he'd seen in the basilica. And yet she looked different. As if life had not been kind. "He hurts you?"

She flushed angrily. "Never. Not once."

His fingers were steady as he slid her undergown over her shoulders, exposing her breasts. They were full, fuller than he expected. Tipped with dark nipples that looked engorged. He lowered her gown further, letting it drop and tugging her hand to show she should step out of it.

Small, but swollen breasts, narrow hips, and flame-red pubic hair.

"What's that?" A scar crossed her abdomen, and she shivered as he traced its length with one fingertip, halting at the end.

"You can see in the dark?"

He nodded, realised that wasn't much use, and said, "Yes, but not in the light. Tonight my sight's clearer than ever." Why did he tell her that?

"That scar," he said.

Instead of answering, she slid from his fingers, disappearing behind a curtained arch. When she returned it was with a baby swaddled in bandages so tight it could barely move. Tycho felt constricted just looking at it.

"Yours?"

She nodded defiantly.

"Someone cut a baby out of you?"

"A Saracen surgeon," she said. "Cut Leo free to save my life. He sewed me up with a tail hair from a white stallion. Said he always knew he'd need it one day." There was awe in Giulietta's voice. Women died in childbirth every day. Even a good birth held risks and offered pain.

"It's Prince Leopold's child?"

"Leo's not an it," she said crossly. "He's a he. My son . . . Our son." She stood naked. Slight hips and soft belly. Milk oozing from her nipples like tears, to trickle along the under slope of her breasts.

"Feed him."

"Now's not appropriate."

She tried to meet Tycho's eyes, but her room was in near darkness and he had the advantage. She reminded him of the stone mother in Pio Tera dei Assassini, his first night in this hellish city. The one the woman prayed to.

"Lie down," he told her. "And do it."

When she continued to stand there, he edged her towards her bed, pushed her on to her side, told her to stay there and took her child, unswaddling it before placing it at her breast. And then he stripped off his doublet, boots and hose. Most of his remaining weapons he put in one corner.

A single stiletto went under her pillow.

Lying behind her, he folded one arm across her stomach and shaped himself around her, feeling the curve of her buttocks, the line of her back and the slope of her shoulders. In the silence that followed he heard her crying.

"Is this so bad?" He knew it for a stupid question even as he asked it. She tensed, with him curled there. Although her child simply guzzled.

"You're young," she said eventually.

"You're younger."

"Only in years. You know he'll kill you afterwards?"

"Leopold?"

Lady Giulietta sighed. "My uncle."

"I'm not here to kill you. I'm here to kill your lover, surely you realise that? Anyway, why would I murder you? How would I even know you were here?"

She opened her mouth to say something, and closed it again.

"Leopold's *krieghund*," Tycho said. "You saw what he became."

"It's a curse," she protested. "You can't hold being cursed against him. And he told me about it, right at the beginning. He kept nothing back."

"Can I ask you something?"

"You half killed Leopold. You're naked in my bed. My baby lies defenceless beside me. Do you think I'd risk refusing?"

"I don't know. Would you?"

"Depends," she said.

"Why don't you go home?" It seemed an obvious question. At least, obvious to someone who didn't have a home. Who'd been born a slave, grown up a slave, and would likely die one now, probably soon.

"This is my home," Giulietta said. "Well, it was. The Ca' Ducale is simply where Uncle Alonzo and Aunt Alexa live. Plus, my cousin, of course. Poor Marco, always condemned to being mentioned last."

"He's mad?"

"They're all mad. I could join them. Or leave."

"You believe that?"

"Oh yes. Who knew being abducted from your abductors was lucky?" There was a mix of bitterness and resignation in Giulietta's voice. She understood the irony. "Let Leopold go and take the baby. Kill me, if someone has to die. It will be enough for my uncle."

"Go where?"

She shrugged. "France's out; he's not safe there. And the Byzantines would torture him both for every secret he knows."

"What about if it was all of you?"

"Cathay maybe. In the long term."

"And in the short term?"

"Cyprus. If Janus will take us."

"Won't he mind that you were meant to marry him?"

Lady Giulietta sighed. "Is this nerves? Do you always talk so much in . . . When forcing yourself on a woman."

"My first time."

"Your first rape. How sweet."

"My first anything."

"You're like Leopold," Giulietta said, turning to face him and using the baby to hide her breasts. "A beast inside a man. And a man inside the beast."

"No," Tycho warned her. "I'm nothing like him."

Wrapping one hand into her hair, he dragged back her head until her throat was exposed.

"You are," she whispered.

He bit her neck savagely, blood flowing into his mouth, across the baby and on to the sheets. As she screamed, and Prince Leopold began to hammer at the door, Tycho bit deeper, tasting the sweetness her life had to offer.

He'd done what he did. While the baby howled and Prince Leopold beat at the door, Tycho walked Giulietta to the very edge of death's precipice. The *krieghund* had known what Tycho's feeding meant even if Tycho hadn't.

When Tycho opened the door the German wanted to kill him. Only Leopold was weak and wounded, and Tycho was more alive than he'd ever been. Aware of every movement in the city outside. And there was another reason for Prince Leopold's fury. One Tycho learnt when the man's anger ebbed through livid recriminations to tears and guilt. He would rather have died on the roof himself . . .

Tycho's kind no longer . . . Nephilim were . . .

"Save her," he demanded.

"How?" Tycho asked.

"Don't mock me."

"I'm not."

Tears rolled down the *krieghund*'s face, his voice reduced to a grating whisper. "Your blood," he begged. "Smear it on her wounds. You can have this palace. My gold. Anything you want. Just save her."

Biting into his wrist – watched by Prince Leopold, whose gaze never left the child at his lover's breast – Tycho dripped blood into Giulietta's mouth and on to her ravaged neck, which began to heal, almost as if a saint touched her.

In place of Tycho's hunger came stillness. The wild fever that the full moon had summoned withdrew like surf on shingle now the storm was over. As Tycho stroked Giulietta's face, watching her cry wide-eyed and silent on the blood-soaked bed, he knew he loved her.

As did Leopold zum Bas Friedland, lord of the Wolf Brothers and the German emperor's envoy to Serenissima. Who loved so unwisely both her family and his would kill him without thought if they knew about it.

"Go," Tycho told her. "Get out of here. Take money, weapons, whatever your lover doesn't want found." Tycho stopped, remembering something. "Where's Leopold's sister? Atilo told me he lived with his sister."

"Atilo il Mauros?" Giulietta said. "What has he got to do with this?"

"I killed fifteen of his men." Prince Leopold's voice was flat. "About a year and a half ago. In Cannaregio. We were hunting someone and his men ended up hunting us. It was a bloodbath. He killed my men and I killed his."

"Leopold, that was . . ."

"Yes," he said. "We were hunting you."

"You wanted to kill me?" Lady Giulietta's voice was a whisper.

303

"Capture you. And I didn't know you then."

"That isn't an answer." Shrugging on to an elbow, she realised she was still half naked and wrapped her blanket more tightly around her, completely covering her child. "Throw me that," she ordered, pointing to a robe.

Both men stood. Prince Leopold fetched the blanket, letting his fingers brush hers as he handed it over. She appeared not to notice. Tomorrow would bring fear, anger and anxiety. For the present she seemed to take almost dying in her stride.

"Tell her why you fought."

Prince Leopold glared at him. He wanted to say this was none of Tycho's business. In the end he shrugged. "Atilo heads the Assassini."

"You're wrong. That's Lord Dolphino."

"No," Tycho said. "It's not."

"Duke Marco had my father assassinated," Prince Leopold said, his voice heavy.

"My cousin?"

"Your late uncle. When they offered me Venice, how could I refuse? The German emperor's envoy by day. Leader of the Wolf Brothers by night. We were to terrify you into loving us. Terrify you into signing a treaty of friendship." Leopold scowled. "I begged for the job."

"For the chance of capturing me?"

"I didn't know you," Prince Leopold said desperately. "When I received news you'd fled Ca' Ducale I couldn't believe my luck. Every Wolf Brother in the city was called to track you. When we realised Atilo had Assassini tracking us it was too late to back down. My friends died trying to reach you."

"To capture me?"

"Or kill you if we couldn't do that." Leopold looked ashen in the candlelight. "I'm glad we failed," he said. "I couldn't bear . . ."

"You'd never have met me. You would never have known."

"No," he said. "I never would."

47

Atilo stood in the silence of the early morning gloom trying not to let his gaze slide beyond the palace balcony to the mist on the lagoon. Today's mist was so thick he could barely see the monastery at San Giorgio.

"You failed . . ." The Regent's voice was icy and his face white with fury. The cold flame of his anger was far more dangerous than his usual red-faced bluster. Prince Alonzo was afraid.

He believed Prince Leopold was alive.

Krieghund healed quickly. Leopold zum Bas Friedland had been an implacable enemy before this. As the German emperor's envoy to Serenissima he'd been bound, at least in appearances, by diplomatic niceties. Any such restraint would now be gone.

"Do you have an excuse?"

In Atilo's head were Desdaio's words.

"If you love me you'll save him." How much did Atilo love her? Enough to be cuckolded? Enough to live with the fact that Iacopo spoke the truth, later denied. Desdaio had been seen coming from Tycho's cellar.

That's what Atilo was starting to believe.

"Nothing to say?"

"My lord?"

"Don't you *my lord* me. You have told us *that* was ready. That it had the necessary skills to . . ." Prince Alonzo waved his hand dismissively. The Moor knew exactly what was wanted. That was what his wave meant.

"I was wrong, my lord."

"Yes, you were. Weren't you?"

That knelt silently at the feet of the throne. Blood glued his braids to his skull. Atilo's beating of the boy had been brutal, his most brutal yet. The old man couldn't work out if stupidity, ignorance or courage made the boy return to announce his failure. That was all Tycho said. He'd failed.

Behind the kneeling boy stood Captain Roderigo, looking bleary-eyed and furious. He'd been to Ca' Friedland and waited to make his report.

"We'll give him to Black Crucifers for public torture."

"Alonzo," said a voice from the doorway. Alexa's tone was surprisingly mild. Clearly, she realised how close the Regent was to doing something stupid.

"*What?*" Prince Alonzo demanded.

That Alexa let his rudeness pass said it all. Pointing out the obvious in front of servants to a drunken prince who should have realised it already was a delicate task. "Perhaps that's not fitting."

"Why not?"

"He's young."

"What's that got to do . . . ?"

Children were frequently tortured. Sons required to condemn their fathers. Daughters their mothers . . .

"Ahh," Alonzo said, stumbling over the answer for himself.

Tycho's age was an irrelevance. Alexa simply wanted him to pause long enough to think. The torturer would discover every detail of Tycho's training. He would know about Prince Leopold's true nature. Who knew the complications that would bring?

"Wine," the Regent demanded.

The steward's eyes flicked to Alexa. The little man wouldn't dare refuse Alonzo but he could have his staff dilute the wine. He'd served the old duke and served him well. He'd have done the same for the new duke, if the young man hadn't been sitting there watching mist slowly burn off the lagoon.

The duchess nodded. Alonzo tight was easier to handle.

"You said he was *ready*," the Regent insisted, grabbing a goblet and emptying it in one gulp. "You said he was up to the task."

As well Roderigo was loyal. In the old duke's day Assassini matters were not discussed openly. Then, in Marco III's day, all decisions were taken by the duke, who was not given to discussion. Except, occasionally, with his duchess. And Atilo only knew that because she'd told him. They'd been in bed at the time. Glancing across, he saw her watching him.

"Well?" Alonzo said. "Are you going to answer?"

"I'm sorry, my lord."

"Sorry isn't good enough. You should pick your people better."

"The mistake is mine."

"I'm glad you admit that. We wouldn't want you wriggling out of your responsibilities. Would we, Alexa? Roderigo, tell us what you found."

"Blood on the palace's roof, my lord. Discarded weapons. A broken blade." He opened his right hand, unfolding a cloth to reveal burns. "Enchanted. It took Dr Crow to make it safe. A woman's chamber exists on the third floor."

"His sister?" Duchess Alexa's voice was tight.

Atilo hadn't even known Prince Leopold had a sister. And Alexa's voice was much too tight for a woman of her subtlety. Now that he thought of it, she seemed less shocked than Alonzo at Tycho's failure. Though she'd been careful to glare at the boy fiercely.

"I would imagine so, my lady," Roderigo said.

"What about servants?"

"No sign of servants, my lord."

"You checked?"

"Yes. I checked. The attics were derelict." Attics were where servants slept. Hot in summer and freezing in winter, they were shared with mice, rats, pigeons and old furniture.

"Leopold zum Bas Friedland and his sister, alone together. That sounds suspicious to me." Prince Alonzo's eyes gleamed at the thought. When he waved his goblet a woman hurried forward. His gaze as he watched her pour was hungry. "Describe the state of her chamber."

"The bed had been slept in, my lord. The sheets were . . . in need of laundering."

"You mean what I think?"

"Possibly, my lord."

"Then say it clearly," Prince Alonzo snapped.

"The sheets were stained, my lord. With blood, urine and shit. Either she was murdered there by . . ."

"Her brother?"

Captain Roderigo winced. "Or Atilo's apprentice violated her first."

Prince Alonzo looked at Tycho with new interest. His eyes glancing at Atilo's impassive face. "Roderigo. Do you believe they're dead?"

The captain shrugged. A mistake.

"The mattress was drenched with blood," he said hastily. "There were also splatters of blood on the roof, and signs of a struggle and the broken sword . . . But no bodies anywhere. They could have been removed." They could also be alive. The more he drank, the easier the Regent was to read, and Roderigo knew his master was scared, and furious.

"Death," Alonzo said. "That's my verdict." When Duchess Alexa opened her mouth, he snapped, "You disagree?"

"This needs discussion."

"No, it doesn't . . . Let the Black Master extract every last secret in private. Although I've a mind to do it myself." For a second it looked as if the Regent was serious. "Go," he said, glaring at Roderigo. "Take him away."

"Where, my lord?"

"The Crucifer pit, obviously."

48

"Strip him . . ."

Tycho struggled to locate the speaker. His gaolers had him blindfolded with his hands tied behind his back tight enough to make his fingers distant memories. Shackles locked his feet. He was ungagged. Perhaps they expected him to plead.

"Get on with it."

Rough hands yanked his doublet; when the buttons failed to rip free, someone punched him and Tycho fell to the floor.

"*That's enough.*"

A different voice this time. Behind him.

"Maybe you'd like to tell me what's going on?" There was a smoothness to the words that set Tycho's teeth on edge. A reasonableness that grated.

"Sir, we're preparing him."

"What day is it?"

"Saturday, sir." The man sounded afraid.

"And why is preparing him like this a bad idea?"

"We're not torturing him, sir. We just need to remove his clothes. It's not like . . ." The voice trailed into gurgling, followed by a thud. Pushing his foot to the side, as far as his shackles allowed, Tycho felt another body.

"Pick him up."

Hands hauled Tycho to his feet.

"Right," the voice said. "Free his hands, unbutton his doublet properly, throw him naked into the pit. Leave the shackles. I begin torturing him on Monday. Understood?"

"Yes, sir. Sorry, sir."

"My lord." Tycho's throat was dry. Partly fear, partly that he hadn't drunk anything since the previous night, and his head ached from Atilo's beating.

"You speak."

"Sunlight, my lord. It . . ."

"Burns you. So I've been told. An interesting fact, don't you think? What kind of sinner is burnt by God's own light? Only the worst, I suspect. The Regent has instructed me to question you myself. An unpleasant task, but one I shall undertake to the best of my abilities. And I wouldn't worry. Where you're going now has no sunlight, nor any other kind most of the time."

Footsteps climbed stairs.

"I can open it myself," he said.

A second later hinges creaked, then the door shut again. Every gaoler listened to check the man was gone. And then a punch to the kidney dropped Tycho to the floor. A vicious kick took air from his lungs and filled his throat with bile. "You cost me a man," a voice snarled.

"Boss . . ."

"*What?*"

"He comes back and sees this we're all in trouble."

"You afraid?"

"Of course I'm shitting afraid. I almost piss myself every time the Black Master enters a room. You want him angry, fine. I want to keep living." There was muttered agreement.

"Throw him in the pit then," the boss said.

The gaolers freed Tycho's hands but left him blindfold, his feet shackled by a short chain joining two crude iron fetters, with a single silver wire welded to the inside. The fetters tore at his ankles, which was the point. There was no space to run where he was going.

"Too pretty for his own good," a gaoler laughed. "Dee, then Blue. After that Federico. The others later."

"He's only there two days."

"Long enough," the voice said. A fist caught Tycho in the back and he stumbled, ankles burning as he took three quick steps to regain his balance.

"Here we go."

A clang told Tycho a hatch was opening.

"Don't fight it," a voice muttered in his ear, sounding almost sympathetic. "It's going to happen anyway. So soak it up, and work out who you can take your revenge on later."

"*What are you telling him?*"

"That he's going to get his good."

"Damn right. All that sweet flesh. Too bad I only like slit . . ."

"And this one's so pretty," said another voice. "Put him in a dress and you couldn't tell the difference." The man guffawed. "Like to try it. Dee would be good for gold." He stopped, realised what he'd said. Waited for the inevitable question.

"You saying Dee's still got coin?"

"He's got friends. They've got coin."

Hands gripped Tycho's shoulders and walked him to the edge. A gaoler dragged free his blindfold and Tycho twisted, avoiding a vicious jab to his side. He'd seen someone liver-punched. If all you did was vomit, shit yourself and black out briefly you were doing well.

"Slippery bastard, isn't he?"

"Yeah," said Tycho, juggling numbers. Three gaolers here, four guards at the top of the stairs, two levels and three doors between him and freedom. Acceptable odds, if he could change. Against that, he was shackled with silver wire, stark naked and it was daylight if he made it as far as outside.

And he deserved to be here. All the same, he planned on evening the odds. Grabbing a rusting dagger from a gaoler's belt, Tycho stepped backwards and dropped into hell, falling for two seconds before hitting something soft, which swore, and dislocated.

"Fuck," it snarled.

Tycho had landed in an oubliette.

Flooded, except for a tiny island on which three men huddled. Half of the remaining prisoners crouched in stinking water, some of them up to their waists, others to their necks. Against a wall, a huge treadwheel was turned by the rest, who swore and whimpered as they worked. A single torch lit the fetid pit from the far side of a grate high above. That was the trapdoor.

"Which one's Dee?" Tycho demanded.

"I am, you fuck. And you're going to die hideously."

If Prince Alonzo got his way Tycho's death would undoubtedly be hideous. Since he mended fast and died slowly it would be more hideous than the Regent realised. The man with the dislocated shoulder intended to get there first, however . . .

"And Blue?"

"What's it to you?" said a man behind Dee, answering Tycho's question anyway.

"I guess that makes you Federico?"

The third man scowled in the half darkness. Instinctively, he'd shifted into a street fighter's stance. He was younger than Dee and Blue, his muscles less wasted and his skin healthier.

"Keep the wheel turning, you bastards . . ."

Dee's order had the pump working again. Prisoners climbing from step to step, their chains clanking as the wheel kept the water from rising further and the small island from being drowned.

"I'll fix your shoulder, boss," Blue told Dee. "Then you should get some rest. Give your muscles a chance to mend."

"If you think," Dee said, "I'll fall for that. *You get some sleep and I'll just break him in for you.* You think I'm shitting stupid?"

"Don't think you're stupid at all, boss."

"No," Federico said. "We don't think that." The slipperiness in his voice suggested others did.

"Bugger this." Slamming his palm into his twisted shoulder, Dee grunted as his arm slid into its socket. "That's better. Now bring him here. I'll show you who's stupid."

The *bucintoro*, Marco's ceremonial barge, was scrubbed, painted and newly gilded. Its hull was free of barnacles, the caulking between its planks freshly tarred. New-woven ropes guided its triangular sail, and the lion flag of Serenissima flapped high above. The flag was the height of a man, with St Mark's winged lion picked out in gold on a white background.

When not flying above the *bucintoro*, the flag lived in a jewelled case behind the altar of San Marco. The duke's annual marriage to the sea, and his leading an army into battle, were the only reasons to remove it.

On the black throne of the Millioni, Duke Marco IV hummed softly, watching the seagulls that followed his barge. The gulls were hungry for the scraps and fish guts usually found in the wake of fleets this size.

For once the Regent was not centre stage.

He had no right to marry the sea. And Alexa, being a woman, could not. Marco IV would marry the sea for them, and for the whole city and its empire beyond. His mother doubted her son even realised the ring on his little finger, the one he would toss into the Adriatic at a nod from her, was fake.

A good fake, of course.

The lapis was real and the gold pure. The design exact. Even the scratches around the old-fashioned Byzantine setting and across the shank were lovingly recreated. Fake only in that it wasn't the original. Alexa regretted having to kill one of Venice's finest jewellers but regarded it as a price worth paying. Her only worry about offering the sea a perfect replica was that the sea might reject it.

The problem with Westerners was that they fulfilled their rituals carefully, without understanding the reasons behind them. Half of the nobles thought this day stupid superstition. The other half imagined it a gaudy display designed to overawe the *cittadini* and keep the Arsenalotti in their place. None considered what the sea's rejection of this marriage might mean . . . Fierce storms at the very least. Ships lost at sea and fishermen returning with their nets empty.

At the lagoon's mouth, the surrounding flotilla slowed its pace and came to a halt, the oarsmen holding their place against the pull and push of the tide. Only the *bucintoro* went on.

"You have the list of prisoners?" Alonzo asked.

"Yes, my lord." Roderigo's voice rang clear across the deck. Tradition demanded Marco free one prisoner in honour of his marriage. Vast sums changed hands, with families desperate to buy freedom for one of their own. Sometimes the money went to someone who could actually influence the choice. More often than not, it made no difference.

"Read it, then."

The captain bowed. Being one of the Regent's favourites was a double-edged sword, and sometimes even the handle was too dangerous to hold.

"Federico, an expert forger and murderer. Who claims to have sometimes given aid to this city . . ." As close as anyone would get to admitting he was a spy. "Giovanni Cisco, salt dealer. Murdered his wife, wrongly. She was not cuckolding him as he suspected. Lord Gandolfo, accused by his enemies of false witness."

Captain Roderigo's money was on Gandolfo.

Not literally. He was too close to the Regent to find anyone willing to take his bet. Even old friends assumed he knew something they didn't.

"Those are the names?"

Tradition demanded three. So three was what they got. Tradition also demanded that question. And that Captain Roderigo answer it. "Those are the names, my lords."

"Then let our duke show justice."

Roderigo was thinking how hard Alonzo found it to say those words, acknowledging his nephew's rule as they did. And wondering whether Marco would be able to repeat the name his mother had just whispered to him, when a sob broke the uneasy silence.

"You have something to say?"

Everyone looked at Duke Marco in shock. Their gazes flicking to the sobbing Desdaio a moment later. Every patrician there knew who she was. Not one had acknowledged her on arrival, although they'd all been careful to recognise Atilo. He was one of the Ten. And, quite possibly, Duchess Alexa's lover. A fact that might help explain the stiffness between Atilo and the woman beside him.

"Well?" Alexa said.

"Tycho should be included."

Prince Alonzo raised one eyebrow. "*Who?*" he said.

"The boy you sent to . . ."

"Do what? We sent where?" Duchess Alexa's gaze settled on Atilo. He shook his head slightly.

"I don't know."

"Atilo's slave is charged with treason." Alonzo's voice was firm. "The sentence for treason is death. It cannot be revoked."

"Slaves can't commit treason."

Someone gasped. Technically, it was true. Slaves could commit murder, rape and steal. All of these counted as treason against their master. But they could not commit treason against the state. This was the act of freemen. Such acts belonged to their masters.

"Do you understand what you're saying?" Alexa asked.

If treason was proved and the penalty was death, and Atilo's slave could not be held responsible, then the only person who could was Atilo.

"Yes," Desdaio said.

As Federico and Blue advanced, Tycho glanced behind to see a squat man reach for his ankle. Kicking back, he broke the dwarf's nose and heard a splash. Next time he risked a glance two boys were holding the dwarf underwater, while bubbles rippled the water's dark surface.

"Look," said Dee. "Fighting just makes it harder."

"Depends how well you fight." Whipping the blade from behind his back, Tycho slashed it across Blue's throat, stabbed Federico in the guts and threw it at Dee in a single moment. Dee had a hand to his eye, already sinking to his knees, when Tycho stepped forward and drove the dagger home.

He wiped his blade on Dee's face for effect, though he doubted many could see, the light being so bad. Hooking his toe under Dee's body, he rolled it into the water. The other two he simply picked up and threw. Those in the shallowest water were obviously stronger or meaner than those behind. So they were his greatest threat. Letting them see his contempt was simple common sense.

"Anyone else want to fight?"

There were growls of anger and snarled insults, but no one stepped up to the challenge.

"Well?" Tycho said.

In the shallows the dwarf stopped struggling. An old man who'd tried to save him was being shuffled into deeper water, while the boys moved forward to take his place. "Wait till you're hungry," someone muttered.

Tycho looked for the voice.

"And then?"

"We'll see how tough you are."

A bear of a Mamluk with a matted beard and a belly that

jutted like a boat's prow. He was chest deep in water, but only because he crouched down.

"Man's got a knife."

The Mamluk snorted. "He's gotta sleep sometime. We'd all be tough if we had a knife."

"He's tough without, believe me." A boy's voice came from deep water. "You ain't seen nothing like it. Moves like lightning. Kills just as fast."

"You," Tycho said. "Come here."

"He's just a kid," a voice hissed.

"Like that ever stopped Dee and Blue," someone else answered.

Hands bundled the boy towards the island. Where he stood naked, hands clenched into fists, his ribs thin as twigs. His eyes never left Tycho's face in the half-darkness. "It's you," Tycho said.

Pietro nodded.

"I'm sorry . . ." Tycho made himself say it. "I'm sorry about your sister."

"Not your fault," Pietro said flatly.

Tycho wished he could agree with him. "Here," he said. "Hold the knife for me."

The small boy gaped, then grabbed the dagger by its hilt and stepped back. He swung the blade at the first man to grab for it.

"Anyone tries to take that from Pietro they answer to me."

Heads turned to fix on Tycho in the darkness. He pointed to the barrel-chested Mamluk, gesturing him closer. "The island's his if he can take it."

The challenge was enough. The treadmill stopped. Only starting when people began shouting. "It's time to change shifts," whispered Pietro. "Only Dee's dead. Maybe you'd better tell them?" He made the last part a question. In case Tycho grew angry.

"Change shifts," Tycho ordered.

The wheel worked a pump that stopped the pit from drowning

its inhabitants. As long as people worked the wheel every hour of every day, the level stayed low. At least, low enough for the island to remain visible and the slopes to be shallow enough for most to stand and a few to kneel.

"Right," Tycho said. "Want to try your luck?"

"I'll be having that knife," the Mamluk warned Pietro. "If you've got any sense you'll give it up without fuss."

Stepping forward, Tycho kicked the man in the balls.

There was nothing subtle about his move. He waited until the Mamluk was ashore, stepped forward and kicked hard. The shackle around his ankle crushed the man's bollocks. Both of Tycho's ankles ripping as the linking chain snapped tight. His curse was lost under the Mamluk's scream.

Breaking the man's neck with a twist, Tycho kicked his body into the shallows. "The knife," someone begged. "Lend me your knife."

"Why?"

"So I can fillet him quickly. Please. In this heat he'll be rotting by tomorrow. Believe me, I know. I used to be a butcher."

"How long?" Tycho asked.

"Months," the man said. "Years, tens of years. How can one tell time in hell? Will you lend me your knife?"

"No," Tycho said.

The man sighed, dragged the Mamluk towards the shallows, and collected Dee, Blue and Federico as well. He left the dwarf floating. "We'd better eat what we can then."

Everyone fed.

The deck of the *bucintoro* remained in silence except for sails creaking, the hum of the hawsers and slap of the waves. Even Duke Marco stopped drumming his heels, mesmerised by the twisted expression on Atilo's face.

Lords who hadn't met her gaze in a year, their ladies, who'd spent time looking through her, stared openly at Desdaio. And the young woman stood there, wide-faced and innocent, her body soft, her breasts heavy and her smile gentle. But there was steel in her eyes.

Duchess Alexa was impressed.

"Let me get this right." The Regent's grin was that of a cat that had got both the cream and the canary, and had just discovered seconds. His hatred of Atilo was well known. "You're accusing your lover of treason?"

"He's not my lover," Desdaio snapped.

Atilo stared at his feet.

"Really?"

"We're to be married. Sometime." There was a world of bitterness in Desdaio's last word and her eyes filled. Raising her chin, she ignored them. "Until then I remain a virgin. I swear it."

The duchess smiled behind her veil. "If," she said, "you're accusing your beloved of treason I doubt there will be a wedding or a bedding."

"I'm not, my lady."

"That's what it sounds like to me."

"I'm not saying Lord Atilo is guilty. I'm saying his slave is innocent. Tycho wouldn't commit treason any more than my lord would. There must be a mistake. What can he have done that is so bad?"

The nobles began looking at their wives.

Everyone knew patrician women sometimes had affairs with servants. Young wives with old husbands had to find comfort somewhere. As did women married to men more interested in men. Sometimes the wives were simply bored, or married to weak men who accepted it. A few women ended poisoned, returned to their fathers or locked in their rooms. Mostly, the servants were found floating with their throats cut.

But this young woman had just publicly sworn herself a virgin.

"*You* don't believe he's guilty, do you?"

Iacopo shuffled his feet, obviously stunned to be thrown so

publicly to the lions by Desdaio's question. He was only there as Atilo's bodyguard. It might be Easter, a day of peace and celebration, but nobles still took sensible precautions.

"My lady," he said. "I'm hardly in a position . . ."

"Yes, you are." Atilo's voice deep and slow. He was, those who knew him realised, in battle mode. His face was stern, his eyes steady. "And I'm interested to know your answer. Tell me. Do you believe my slave guilty of any treason?"

Maybe Alexa imagined the stress on *any*.

"How can I . . ." Iacopo stumbled to a halt. "I'm a servant. If I say no the lords think I lie. If I say yes, the lords might think I lie anyway. These are matters far above . . ."

"Your highness." Desdaio's voice cut through the excuses. "May I have leave to talk privately with my lord Atilo?" It took Alexa a second to realise she was talking to the duke. Marco stopped looking at the seagulls.

"I don't see why not," he said.

Nicolò Dolphino gasped, and then flushed under Alexa's glare. It didn't matter that the duchess wore a veil, she was obviously glaring. And it didn't matter that most days Duke Marco could barely string two words together. Everyone was to pretend he ruled. Expressing surprise that he'd managed two sentences in one day slighted that.

Desdaio walked Atilo to the stern of the *bucintoro*. Ahead of her, podgy wooden cherubim, painted gold rather than gilded, gambolled and rolled and exposed tiny genitals and even more unlikely wings. She dismissed a year of a master carver's life with a single sniff.

"Do you love me?"

Hard eyes looked at her. She'd never seen his face so cold or severe. He wore his age and experience like armour. She felt stupidly young and not worthy of him.

"Answer me," she demanded crossly.

He let his silence stretch to the point of cruelty.

"I love you," she said, feeling her eyes fill. She was furious with herself, furious with him. Furious that fifty people who'd spent a year ignoring her were now openly staring. "I love you more than life."

"I'll ask you again," Atilo said. "Did you go to his room?"

"That's what this is about? You're accusing me of . . ." She glared at him. "What are you accusing me of?"

He just looked at her.

His answer was in his silence and the stillness of his stare. She knew he could outwait her. He'd done it before over lesser things. Things that didn't matter. Not in the way this mattered. Although they'd felt important at the time.

"Well?" he said.

"No," Desdaio said. "I didn't."

She saw doubt in his eyes, and grabbed his hand before it could grow greater. He was stronger than her, experienced in battle as well as the ways of the world. He could free himself easily. But she held his wrist so tight, and looked so frightened at where she found herself, he didn't break her grasp.

Instead he waited for her to say more.

Desdaio breathed a sigh of relief. She couldn't say why but he smiled slightly, and some of the warmth came back into his eyes. "A little guilt," he said. "But only a little. I've judged people," he added, as if she didn't know. "People have hung on my assessment of their innocence or guilt."

That she didn't know.

She wanted to tell him the truth, and she wanted him to respect her. She couldn't have both, and she was a coward. Desdaio knew that. To risk everything on a simple statement of the truth. *I went, nothing happened.* She lacked the courage, the certainty he loved her enough to believe and forgive. Her life was full of the little truths she'd never managed to say. How could she start with a truth so big?

Atilo was staring at her, she realised.

322

"Tell me what happened."

"I entered his room. Nothing happened."

Atilo's gaze sharpened. "Why?" he demanded.

"I asked Amelia if you'd free him. She said maybe. Some you did. Others you sold. It depended on a test . . . No," Desdaio said, seeing him frown. "She didn't say what the test was. I asked, she refused."

"We come back to, *Why?*"

"I like him." Desdaio said, risking a little truth. Maybe she shouldn't have said that. But Atilo simply nodded.

"Do you like Iacopo equally?"

"No." Desdaio shook her head. "I don't trust him," she said. "Iacopo gives me the creeps. Always watching. Always so polite it feels like mockery. And he . . . he lusts after Amelia." She blushed at her own words.

Then blushed again at what she saw in Atilo's eyes.

He wanted to tell her everyone lusted after Amelia. With her long legs and narrow hips and black skin she was an exotic gazelle. Maybe even a tyger. As fierce as anything in the duke's zoo. If Amelia was a tyger, Desdaio didn't want to think what animal that made her.

"I swear on my life nothing happened."

"Should I be worried that you like him?"

Desdaio hesitated. "I know what he is," she said. "He's never said. But I've worked it out. And it must be so sad . . ." Stepping close, she whispered in Atilo's ear. Hearing his hiss of surprise.

"Desdaio."

"What?" she asked. "Am I wrong?"

"A fallen angel exiled from hell . . . Because his enemies paint themselves red? And his house burnt down? And he fears daylight?"

"Don't laugh at me."

"I'm not." Atilo cupped her chin in his hands and raised her face to smile at her. "You're beautiful," he said. "Rarer than gold.

Far sweeter than honey. I'm sorry things have been," he glanced towards Alexa, "complicated . . . We'll marry this summer, I swear it."

"You'll save him then?"

Atilo's smile faded slightly.

"You believe me? That I'm not wicked? That nothing happened. That I would never do that to you?"

"Yes," Atilo said. "I think so."

"Then prove it. Save Tycho."

Atilo's face set hard. It was the face of a general weighing his choices before battle. Considering what price he was prepared to pay for victory. And as Desdaio decided she'd asked too much, that she should take her words back, he nodded . . .

"This should be interesting," Alexa said.

49

Steam from the heat of a hundred bodies sweated the dungeon's stone walls and rose from the water's filthy surface in a parody of lagoon mist. It swirled through rotting tread steps, disturbed by the wheel's movement. Settling only when a shift changed, breaking into fresh flurries as soon as the wheel resumed turning.

The faces around him were also parodies. Deprived of light, bleached by the mist. Skin withered and puckered and rotten from years of immersion.

Sometime later, the flickering torch visible through the grating burnt out to leave the pit in darkness. It had to be late, because the gaolers barely bothered to rattle the grating as they passed. Contenting themselves with pissing through the grill, or defecating and kicking their shit on to the prisoners below.

Tycho slept in shallow five-minute naps.

A skill he'd developed in childhood, when not rushing to answer Lord Eric's call meant a beating and even less food. He could flash from slumber to fully awake in an instant.

"Why did they put you in here?" Tycho asked Pietro.

"Didn't want me to talk about that night, did they?" he replied with the certainty of an eight-year-old who'd thought it through.

"When Rosalyn died?"

Tycho held Pietro by his shoulders while the small boy fought bitter sobs and won. He felt embarrassed comforting the boy. When Tycho held it was to kill, or take. But the boy mourned his sister. And Tycho having killed Rosalyn's murderer was not enough to make that good. Not even close.

"Found yourself a friend?"

Spinning, Tycho saw a red-headed girl in rags.

A'rial was older than Pietro by a few years. Her hair tied up in a clumsy knot and fixed with a raven's bone. She stank like a fox. A purple light shimmered around her. When Pietro crossed himself, she grinned, her teeth glowing white.

"No one else can see us," she said.

Sure enough, a translucent haze enclosed the three of them and the pump's noise had faded.

"I've come with an offer."

"For me or him?" Tycho said, nodding towards the boy.

"You, *obviously* . . . The duchess knows."

He'd upset A'rial with his flippancy. Because she stopped there, leaving him to imagine what Alexa knew. That Prince Leopold was alive? That Tycho let him get away. That Lady Giulietta also lived . . . ?

"Yes," A'rial said. "That one."

Pietro was staring at the oubliette beyond the edge of A'rial's magic. He'd moved as far from her as he could without actually touching the shimmering bubble that contained them.

"Go," A'rial told him, tearing a gap in the haze.

Tycho grabbed the boy. "He stays."

"Collecting pets?"

"Is that what the duchess does?"

Tycho's blow struck home, because flint entered A'rial's eyes. Thinning the haze, she pointed to the relentless wheel and the oubliette's dripping walls. "You want to stay here?"

Even inside her magic the air was fetid, hot and stinking.

"Except you can't, can you?" she said. "At one minute after midnight the Black Master arrives to question you himself."

Pietro gasped. "Kill yourself while you can. Use the knife."

"What knife?" A'rial's gaze sharpened.

"This one," said Tycho, putting his blade to her throat. What Pietro saw was Tycho face one direction, then suddenly face another. But Tycho knew he'd moved the way a normal person moves, simply faster. Much faster. A'rial's fingertips lit and Tycho twitched his hand. "I can strike faster than you."

"Impossible."

"You willing to risk being wrong?"

Tension drained from A'rial's body and she smiled. He waited for her to try to trick him but she kept smiling. Looking for all the world like an eleven-year-old told to deliver a message by her mother or mistress.

"The duchess watched you fight Prince Leopold. She says you were magnificent. But you can be more. Embrace your nature. Complete the . . ."

Tycho wasn't listening. He was more concerned with another question. How could she have watched? His guts churned. What had she seen? The start of the battle? He could handle that. Giulietta's sudden appearance? The girl offering herself in return for Prince Leopold's life?

"Yes," A'rial said.

"Stop that." Tycho raised his blade.

A'rial shrugged. "I'll try, but it takes effort. And you do the same, don't you? You do it all the time."

"I need touch to sense thoughts."

"No. You just think you do," she said crossly. "You're your own worst enemy. My mistress can save your life."

"And in return?"

The small girl sighed. Reaching for Pietro, she wrapped her arm round his shoulder, and drew him close. For a second, the small boy rested his head against her, believing the embrace

327

genuine. But the face she showed Tycho was distant and strange. "Make Alexa an army of immortals."

"No," Tycho said, stepping back.

Pietro looked between them, his face puzzled.

"He's going to die anyway. After you've gone, they'll kill him simply because you favoured him. So what difference does it make? Come to that, why this fuss about feeding. You've done it before. And beggar children? A dozen die every week of cold or hunger. Do you try to save them?"

"That's different."

"No," A'rial said. "It isn't. Claim him. Save yourself."

The calm of feeding on Giulietta was beginning to fade, and Tycho's hunger was tiny threads of twisting smoke looking for a way into his mind. With A'rial's words came knowledge that there was a step beyond where he was. There would always be another step until he was no longer human.

If he'd ever been human.

Remembering Prince Leopold's agony as his muscles ripped and tendons broke, and his body became wolf, Tycho said, "I won't."

If he closed his eyes he could see it happen. Skin splitting, flesh tearing and bones being twisted into new shapes by invisible hands. Bad enough the Black Crucifers would torture him. Why would Tycho do it to himself?

"That's twice," A'rial said. "I won't offer a third time. But you call, I'll come to you then."

"Never." Tycho was firm.

"Don't count on it," A'rial said.

There were two tides a day. A low and a high. The first mattered neither here nor there to those in the pit, who were removed from the festering mud banks of Venice's edges, and the stink of sour water, as backstreet canals revealed rubbish, puddles and the occasional corpse with every ebbing tide.

The second did concern them.

At high tide, lagoon water flowed along ditches, for a few minutes to as much as an hour, and splashed into the oubliette below. One day's tide left half the central island still exposed. Two days' drowned it, but left prisoners able to stand. Three days' killed those unable to swim. Only by constantly working the pump could everyone stay alive. Exquisite cruelty. Hard work for the sake of it. More than this, it stopped prisoners trying to escape. You worked the wheel; slept, woke and worked again. No one was allowed to slack. The oubliette was self-controlling, self-containing.

In it, Tycho saw Serenissima.

The varied councils, the courts within courts, the Arsenalotti at war with the Nicoletti, the *cittadini* jealous of the patricians, the patricians divided into old house and new, rich and poor. No one in Venice got off the wheel.

Beyond the city, Serenissima's colonies fed the capital, the Venetian navy fought the Mamluk pirates; the Moors allied themselves with whoever the Mamluks opposed. The Germans offered support, claiming Byzantium was Serenissima's greatest threat. The Byzantines claimed the German emperor's ambition was a greater threat and offered support in turn. Tīmūr's Mongols conquered ever larger slices of the world, threatening to recreate the sprawling empire of his hero Genghis Khan.

And the wheel went round and round and round . . .

"What did she mean *save yourself*?" Pietro said. The first words he'd spoken since A'rial vanished.

"It doesn't matter."

The boy looked embarrassed to be caught asking. But he continued watching Tycho with concern. High above them guards arrived, bringing fresh torches. "If you can save yourself, you should." Pietro sounded far older than his age.

"How did you first get involved in this anyway?"

Pietro told him.

Being hunted by Wolf Brothers sounded terrifying. And listening to the boy's tale of street rumours and outright lies, Tycho realised this was an old battle, one begun long before he reached the city. Maybe before Atilo even controlled the Assassini.

"We should have hidden," Pietro admitted.

That was what he'd been told to do. And that's what he'd done, as had his friends, until the battle was almost over. They had seen only the end. Admitting it, after Tycho had been captured, was their mistake.

"*Tycho* . . ." a guard yelled.

Pietro grabbed him. "It's the Black Master," he whispered. "Into the water. Hide now."

The grate clattered as it was thrown back. Crossbowmen pointed their weapons into the pit and a long wooden ladder dropped, squelched into the mud and sank several inches. This was enough to stop those on the wheel. For a second, total silence filled the pit, then a voice shouted, "Tycho, move yourself." Captain Roderigo stood lit by torchlight. He had his hand to his nose to shield himself from a rising stink Tycho had already forgotten existed.

"I said no," Tycho protested.

"No what?" Roderigo shouted down.

Tycho couldn't remember the *stregoi*'s name. He knew it once but he'd forgotten; perhaps that was part of her magic.

"The duchess's . . . girl," he finished lamely. "That red-headed one. She asked . . . She said . . ." He didn't know how to finish that sentence.

"Up here now," Roderigo barked. "Stop wasting my time."

Tycho pushed Pietro ahead of him, jeers and sneers following after. Pietro refused to climb. Tycho made him. And faced with Tycho armed here, and crossbowmen above, Pietro chose to avoid the here and now. Atilo would cure him of that weakness, Tycho was sure.

Roderigo stood beside the Black Master, who wore nightclothes.

His lips were thinned to a slash of fury. Behind him waited a gaoler and a turnkey, in a uniform of filthy silk with a tatty and sad-faced winged lion embroidered on his chest.

"Who's this?" Roderigo demanded.

"Atilo's new apprentice."

"My lord ..." The turnkey said. "Your order specifies one only."

Until then, Roderigo intended to toss the boy back. Now his pride refused. The turnkey opened his mouth to insist and shut it at a snarl from the Black Master.

"The *duke* is waiting."

50

Marco IV sat on his black throne gripping its arms like a sailor holding a rail in fear of being thrown overboard in a storm. His grip was hard enough to turn his knuckles white. Ignoring the unshackled child who shuffled ahead of Tycho, Duke Marco said, "Behold, the Grievous Angel."

Shackles made Tycho's answering bow clumsy.

Standing to one side, Atilo saw the duchess smile at her son. The Regent simply sighed. "Didn't it occur to you to wash him first?" he demanded of Roderigo, finding somewhere to aim his anger.

"My orders said bring him straight here, my lord."

"You always obey to the letter?"

The captain nodded.

"How admirable." The bite in Alonzo's voice ensured everyone knew he meant the opposite. "You," the Regent said. "Step forward."

Tycho did. A second later, Pietro did the same.

Atilo stood to one side of the throne. Desdaio's father and a handful of other inner council members stood to the other. Lamps flared and guttered, the night air was heavy with burning fish oil, and most of those in the chamber looked surprised, irritated or slightly scared to be dragged from their beds.

This was the Ten, Tycho realised.

He counted off those either side of the throne, realised that Hightown Crow was amongst them, and wondered who outside the Ten knew an alchemist was a member of the inner council. A small girl half hid behind Alexa's chair. When she met Tycho's gaze, she smiled. A cold and cruel and brilliant smile.

"You know why you're here?" Alonzo asked.

"No, my lord."

"Nor do I," the Regent said.

"Alonzo . . ." Duchess Alexa's rebuke was gentle.

"This is ridiculous," he said. "The Ten called for a matter that should be decided in private."

Alexa's voice hardened slightly. "My lord Atilo has a right to be heard . . . So," she said, looking at Atilo, "say your piece."

Stepping forward, Atilo dropped to his knees in front of the throne. "The city has proclaimed me *fidelis noster civis*. A faithful servant of Venice. Grant me a life," he said. "For the services I have done."

Marco IV picked his nose.

"I counted your father as my friend . . ."

Atilo's words were measured, his voice deep and serious. No one listening could doubt the thought he'd put into his plea. "I have served Venice well. Been both Admiral and commanded your land forces. And I have," he hesitated, "performed other tasks to keep this city safe."

"What do you actually want?" Marco asked.

Atilo blinked.

Alexa and Alonzo usually decided affairs between them. But no one could speak when the duke spoke, and his decisions were law. Those were the foundations on which his mother and uncle built their power. The duke's outbreak of sanity upset the balance.

"Well?" he demanded.

"Give me the prisoner's life. Please."

"There are two of them," Duke Marco pointed out reasonably. "You mean the one who scares you? The one you fear fucked your beloved? Or the one who knows you lied about Lady Giulietta's abduction?"

The chamber was already quiet. But in the seconds following the duke's question it was utterly silent. And then Desdaio stepped forward, her face red and tears of frustration welling in her eyes.

"I would never . . ."

"You would," Marco said. "You simply don't know it. He scares you too. That's why you like him."

"What's this about Lady Giulietta?"

The duke turned to face his uncle, who blushed and found himself apologising for his interruption. So the duke told him it was all right, just not to do it again. "Tell them the truth," Duke Marco ordered Atilo.

"That first time. She simply ran away."

"And you simply returned her?" Alonzo asked. "And forgot to mention the circumstances?

"Yes, my lord."

"That was the night . . ."

"Alonzo," Duchess Alexa said.

"The Regent is right," said Marco, smiling sweetly. "That was the night the Blade was broken." Seeing the blood drain from Atilo's face, he smiled. "Well, cracked certainly. You admit it's cracked?"

The kneeling man nodded.

"And my mother is right. *Krieghund*, mages, death walkers, now this." Marco IV, Prince of Serenissima, stared round the chamber, nodding to each of the Ten in turn, before finally blowing Desdaio a kiss. "It's best to be discreet. We have so many enemies one can never tell who's listening."

Standing up, he descended the steps in front of his throne and dragged Atilo from his knees. Standing him straight. "You know what saves him?"

"No, your highness."

"I will not offend heaven. And I will not risk offending hell. Tycho's life is spared. So is that of your next apprentice. Though I'm not sure my uncle will let you keep the demon."

These were the last coherent words Duke Marco IV was to say for three months. No one knew that then, obviously. Except, perhaps, Hightown Crow, who hurried forward to help the duke back to his seat.

Gripping its arms, Marco clung tight as if his life deepened on it. Relaxing seconds later, and kicking his heels against its base. A little while after that, he became lost in watching a moth circle a lamp. When Atilo was certain the duke's attention was elsewhere, he glanced from Alonzo to Alexa.

"Do I have the throne's permission to withdraw?"

"No," Alonzo said. "You don't."

Alexa looked across. "Marco has given him their lives."

"Their lives," the Regent said heavily. "He said nothing about the slave's freedom. The beggar brat means nothing. Atilo can keep him. But the other *is* a slave. He now belongs to the city. The city will dispose of him."

"Let me buy him," Desdaio said.

The Regent grinned. "I'm sure your beloved would love that. No, the slave will be sent south and sold. With those looks . . ."

With those looks he'd command a premium in the slave markets of Constantinople, Alexandria or Cyprus. The matter of his clothes, his fear of daylight, and the whiteness of his skin would merely add to his exoticism and increase his price. If he died there who could blame Venice? And if he didn't, well, he'd probably come to wish he had, given time.

"How many galleys leave harbour tomorrow?"

"A dozen, my lord."

"And where's the first headed?"

"Dalmatia, Sicily and then Cyprus."

"Make sure he's on it. As a galley slave. Give orders he's to be sold at the journey's end and any money sent to our agents. He may wear his ridiculous clothes. Be coated with whatever repellent unguent our alchemist recommends. And an awning can be used to stop our merchandise being damaged. Other than that, he's to be treated like any other slave."

51

A knock at the door made Giulietta look up from the baby at her breast.

When she didn't answer, the door opened slowly and Prince Leopold put his head round. "May I come in, my lady?"

"I've told you," she said. "You don't need to knock."

"You might have been feeding Leo."

"I was," she said. Smiling, she folded back her gown and stroked her child's cheek until his mouth opened and he returned to his hungry nuzzling. When Giulietta returned her gaze to Leopold, he was staring pointedly through a window at red-earthed Cypriot fields outside.

"Something interesting?"

"Farmers cutting barley on the upper slopes."

Their friendship was sometimes fragile. So much now unspoken.

Leopold and she shared a bed, sleeping together when the baby let either of them sleep, which was more often now than in the first few months following his birth. She could have had a wet nurse; in fact, Leopold offered to have one found for her. He seemed resigned to the fact she refused. Yet he knocked at the door before entering and looked away when she fed her child.

Such delicacy was at odds with the cursed thing he'd become on the roof of Ca' Friedland. And at odds with the savagery of the battle she'd witnessed in Cannaregio.

The fight against the Assassini was more than a year gone, but its memory still made her shiver.

"What are you thinking?

"Nothing," she promised.

"About that boy," Leopold said sadly.

"Leopold . . . I swear. He doesn't even enter my head."

It was a lie. There were moments, usually on the far side of midnight, when she woke certain the silver-haired boy from the basilica was in her room, watching her as she slept. He never was, of course.

"I saw how you looked at him."

"That's not true."

"Yes," Leopold said. "It is. And I saw how he looked at you. You think he let us go because of me? If you hadn't appeared I'd be dead. He let *you* go, and he let me go with you."

"I love you."

Tears were building in Giulietta's eyes.

"And I love you," he said. "In my way. But you dream of him. It's as if you had one soul between you, and someone cut it down the middle. Remember, you told me how the child wasn't Marco's . . ."

"Leo, please stop."

"Is the baby his?"

Giulietta's mouth shut in misery.

Prince Leopold returned that evening carrying a Maltese lace shawl, half a dozen early figs and a bowl of sorbet – white wine mixed with lemon juice and crushed ice – as peace offering and apology. "I'm sorry," he said, placing his presents on a table and turning to go.

"You can stay."

"I'll only say something else stupid."

"All the same . . ." Giulietta patted the seat beside her. "You know," she said, "at the court in Venice they talked of your silver tongue. My aunt was furious at the number of her ladies-in-waiting . . ."

"Whose heads I'd turned?" Leo said, offering her a fig.

"Although maybe she was cross about other things," Giulietta admitted. "But I didn't know about you being *krieghund* then. But your reputation . . ."

"Around you, my tongue turns to lead."

She smiled. "Not always." Leaning her head against his shoulder, she let him fold his arm around her. Their companionable silence lasted for the time it took a candle to burn out. And then, when Leopold stood to light another from the guttering wick of the first, Giulietta rearranged her gown. "So it's true about the Mamluk sultan gathering a fleet?"

"What makes you say that?"

"The barley. They're gathering it against a coming siege."

"Possibly."

"Leopold, where did you get the ice for the sorbet?"

"From the last of the king's own supply."

"Exactly," Giulietta said. "I hear he's also drinking his best wine and sharing out the pickles the kitchens usually keep for banquets."

"What are you saying?" Leopold asked, fixing the candle into a holder and turning to face her.

"What will happen if the sultan does attack?"

"We'll fight."

"And will we win?"

When he came to sit beside her, wrapped his arm round her shoulder and kissed her gently on the forehead, she knew the answer was no. Instead of protesting or asking Leopold to lie, she snuggled against him and tried to frame the question she wanted to ask. The fact he said nothing meant he knew ... If not that she was wondering about a question, then that she was thinking.

Thinking time when you had a new baby was rare.

Well, it was if you insisted on feeding the child yourself and letting it sleep in the same room. A decision so odd, Giulietta knew she'd become a talking point among the ladies of the court. If she hadn't been one already.

"Leopold."

"Yes?" he said, sounding ready for whatever she wanted say.

He really did know her, Giulietta realised. Their shared time here meant he knew her better than any man had. Maybe better than any other would. Leopold knew her weaknesses. These, he insisted, were fewer than she imagined. And her strengths, which, he told her she underestimated daily. He knew her so well she wondered if he knew what was on her mind.

"If we lose ..."

"Yes," he said. "I promise."

She kissed him on the cheek. Not knowing the right response to a man you've just asked to kill you rather than let you be taken prisoner. When the man promising loves you, despite the fact, if you're honest, you dream of someone else.

52

Thunderclouds filled the far horizon. The light was a sullen grey, as if malign angels flew between the setting sun and the swollen sea, casting shadows over everything below. Tycho would vomit, but had nothing to throw up.

So, he hunched in his oil-silk doublet on a dirt-filled bag and hoped the rotten canvas of a makeshift awning would protect him while he waited for orders.

Everyone was waiting for orders.

The *Seahorse* was a small galley. One captain, the owner's son, one drummer, one slave master and fourteen rows of slaves. Tycho wasn't sure what she carried. Nothing heavy from the way she tossed on the swell.

The wind was rising. Ominously cool.

In other circumstances he might have welcomed it and been refreshed. But he learnt what it brought when Adif, the Mamluk next to him, began to count the gaps between lightning and thunder. The strikes were close and coming closer.

A wall of rain headed for them, hiding the distant lines between sea, land and sky. Behind them, night had arrived already, constellations visible and the ocean dark and flat where it met the night's edge.

"We must go north."

"Sir, that's impossible."

The galley owner's son stamped his foot. He was young, rich and afraid. If his father had been there to control him it might have been different. The boy wanted to be on land. In storms, orders said head for the nearest port.

But it was the storm that stood between them and the Dalmatian coast, with its cliffs, endless small islands and rocky shoals. Italy's own coast was a day in the other direction given wind and luck, much longer if luck was bad and the wind against them.

Captain Malo had offered two alternatives.

Hack down the mast and ride out the storm or run before it. That had been before he took another look at the wall of rain and declared he now lacked enough time for the first. So he suggested the second.

Fat-bellied, old and tired, the Greek was resigned to lugging his ship up and down sea lanes that faster vessels used daily. The *Seahorse* had been modern once. Now she was a patchwork of replaced planks. Her caulking needed redoing and she required new tree nails, those thin lengths of dowel holding her sides in place. Most days it a miracle she still floated.

He'd like to keep it that way.

Ruined galleys were found after every storm. So were dead slaves. Chained to their oars and floating or washed up on beaches among driftwood and splintered planks from the ships they'd served.

Running from the Dalmatian coast meant trying to outrun the storm, and widening the violent and nasty seas between the *Seahorse* and those cliffs. The odds weren't great. But they were better than trying for port.

"Find land," the boy said. "That's an order."

"I'm captain."

"Not much longer if you don't do as I say." The boy's words carried over a lull in the wind. "We return to port now."

Beside Tycho, the Mamluk hawked on the deck and spat words in his own language. Tycho didn't need a translator to know it was a curse.

"That's bad?"

"He's going to get us killed, snow djin."

Adif had taken to calling him that on the first day. After Tycho unhooked his makeshift awning as night fell, and let the doublet drop from his shoulders to reveal snow-white skin.

"If they unchain us, grab an oar and kick for land."

"Water will kill me."

The Mamluk hissed and then nodded. Cross with himself for expecting anything else. "Then I wish you a quick death."

Tycho and Adif sat either side of an aisle on the last bench of all. Ahead of them sat the other slaves. Immediately behind, an open-fronted shelter of canvas over wooden hoops was where Captain Malo and the owner's son slept.

Like everyone else on the ship, they shat over the side.

The difference was they did so at will. Adif and Tycho were restricted to pissing themselves where they sat, and shitting each morning, when their hands were briefly unchained. Not all of the slaves could wait that long.

"Arnaud, make him."

The slave master was midway in age between the boy and the captain. His face once handsome but his eyes hard and his temper brutal.

"You heard the boss," he said.

"He's not the boss," Captain Malo said. "I am."

The whip cracked and Tycho heard the captain stagger back, hissing in pain and outrage. "Return to harbour," the slave master ordered.

"If we try, we'll die."

"What's your plan then?" the boy demanded.

"Outrun it," Captain Malo said. "While we can. If we can."
He spat, angrily. "Which I now doubt. We could head south,
maybe. See if we can edge past it. But in the dark . . ."

"The storm's too big," said Tycho, without thinking.

"Who asked you?"

He heard a whip crack a split second after pain ripped across
his shoulders, tearing oiled silk and skin. And then Arnaud was
on the raised walkway that ran along the aisle. His boot scraping
down the side of Tycho's cheek.

A slave on the row ahead turned round to see what was
happening and took the rest of the slave master's anger.

"Enough," Captain Malo snapped.

The slave master raised his whip, and gasped as Adif suddenly
slammed his unchained hand into Arnaud's knee. An awkward
blow, but it struck lucky, dropping the man to his knees. When
he came upright he was holding a knife.

"This is where you die."

There was a dignity to Adif's face as he braced himself to face
the blade. And Tycho suddenly understood that the man had
forced the quarrel, seeking a quick death instead of drowning.
"Good choice," he said.

"*Wait.*"

Anger fought obedience as Arnaud hesitated at the boy's order.

"We've had nothing but shit since we took that thing on
board." The owner's son meant Tycho. "Kill him after that one."

The slave master was readying his blade, Adif still waited, refusing
to show fear. Captain Malo's face said he knew it ended here.

"Die well," Adif said.

"No," said Tycho. "It doesn't work like that."

Gripping silver-topped spike that nailed him to his oar, he
screamed as he ripped it out, feeling flesh sizzle. And then
standing, he blocked Arnaud's dagger with his forearm, and
jammed the nail under the man's chin. Slamming it into his skull
with a slap of his burning hand.

The slave master tumbled sideways.

As the slave opposite grabbed the owner's son by one ankle, Captain Malo elbowed the boy hard in the throat, ordered the slave to let go, and flung the boy overboard to drown. "Idiot," he said.

"*Right*," shouted Tycho. "*Turn her to the storm.*"

"Reckon you're a sailor now?" Captain Malo snarled.

"I intend to live," Tycho said, surprising himself when he realised it was true. "At least, I don't intend to die drowning. Tried it once. Never again."

"He's a djinn. Listen to him."

"Well," Captain Malo said, "he's sure as shit not human. My lord Atilo warned me of that."

Tycho felt his guts knot. He'd hoped Atilo felt some affection. Something behind the coldness in his face as he'd hammered the silver-topped spike in place himself.

"*Turn her. Then lose the oars.*"

"What?"

"Lose them."

"We can stow them," Captain Malo protested. Iron rests either side let the oars be lifted when the galley was under sail.

"It won't be enough."

The sea terrified Tycho. The thought of being swallowed was unbearable. He'd died, and still survived the canal in Venice. What if he sank, died and lived now? Water took his strength. Only the earth bag beneath him kept him sane. He'd be trapped in a watery half-life forever.

"You want to die?" he shouted. The silver-topped spike still jutted from Arnaud's skull, but Tycho had the man's dagger.

Captain Malo shook his head. "I'll get the key."

"No time."

Oars were removed in harbour to stop slaves rowing away when the crew were ashore. At sea, oars were chained in place. "Turn into the storm," Tycho ordered.

"Do it," Captain Malo shouted.

Slaves churned oars in the gravid waves. Those on one side rowing forward. Those on the other rowing back, until the *Seahorse* turned into the wind just as the rain arrived in a rushing wall.

"Hold her steady . . ."

Grabbed Adif's oar chain, Tycho snapped it and pushed the oar through the galley's side. He managed to clear two thirds the *Seahorse*'s length before a huge wave struck, breaking over them. It hit straight on, half lifting the galley, but catching the still-chained oars of those at the front.

The *Seahorse* screamed, wooden ribs twisting and dowels shrieking as they were dragged from their holes. Oak splintered and split. The noise as she fought the sea for the right to stay in one piece was unbearable.

It was a battle between shipwrights now dead and the sea, who wanted their handiwork to join them. Mixed in with the rage of the ship, the howl of the wind and the drumming of the rain were the screams of slaves nursing broken limbs or shouting prayers.

No god would lower his hand to pluck them from the storm. Endless promises might be made. Debts racked up. They meant nothing. The only thing that could save the *Seahorse* was blind luck and the skill of those long dead.

"I'll take it," Tycho said.

Captain Malo glanced from the tiller to the strange youth in front of him.

Rain glued Tycho's braids to his skull. His ghostlike flesh glowed every time lightning flickered. His eyes . . . Tycho could see from the captain's face that something about his eyes terrified the man.

He hadn't time to work out what.

Stepping forward, Tycho grabbed the rudder bar.

Fighting it, he kept the *Seahorse* into the wind. Muscles locked, sinews popping. It was touch and go if the tiller or his wrists broke first. He felt sicker than ever, numb with shock as a wall of water the height of San Marco raced towards him. And then the second wave struck.

53

"You've heard the news from Cyprus?"

"How could I . . ." When the news is so fresh a scroll lies curling in your desk and the wax from its broken seal still sticks to your gloves? "No, my lord," Atilo said. "I haven't."

Alonzo sighed, more heavily than he needed. "You're our spymaster within the city. Our Blade within and without. We should be able to rely on you for knowledge like this."

"My apologies."

"I know," said Alonzo, "life has been tricky for you recently. That failure with your apprentice. The disappearance of Prince Leopold's body. Those men you lost last year. Unless it was the year before. If you feel the burden of your job is too heavy. That perhaps old age is . . ."

"My lord."

The Regent paused expectantly.

"I work for this city day and night. All my energy goes tracking its enemies; recording what happens on the streets; gathering information on those who pretend to be one thing but are another . . ."

Atilo stopped, cursing that he'd walked straight into that one.

"And you must be tired," Alonzo said. "Rightfully exhausted by your burden. This is why important news slipped past you. As I said, if you wish for the freedom to take life more easily at your advancing age . . ."

"All I wish, my lord, is to be allowed to continue."

He could remember what his own father, the idiot astronomer, said. Young men fantasise about death and fear life. Old men fear death and fantasise about youth. Atilo had dismissed it fiercely, then not so fiercely, right up to the day he discovered it to be true. He sighed.

"You're certain? That you simply wish to do your duty?"

"Absolutely certain."

The Regent smiled happily. "I can't tell you," he said, "how glad I am to hear it. That new boy of yours settling in all right?"

A little dig. Just enough to let Atilo know Alonzo had no plans to let Tycho's reprieve go without mention.

"He has potential."

"That's what you said about the last one."

"My lord, whatever I failed in, I stand by my claim he had potential."

"To be the greatest assassin of all time? To be your chosen successor as the duke's Blade itself. Yes, I've heard of your plans for that troublesome young man. I must admit to being surprised."

Heard from whom? From the duchess . . . ?

Surely not. Alexa might have banished Atilo from her bed, but not so far from her favour that she'd share secrets with her hated brother-in-law. There had to be a spy in Atilo's household. Amelia was possible. Iacopo? He wouldn't want to think that likely.

"My lord, may I ask how you know?"

"Of course you may," Alonzo answered. Obviously delighted at the thought of Atilo, Serenissima's spymaster and chief assassin, asking him how he'd discovered such secrets. "Lady Desdaio told me."

"She . . . ?"

Atilo shut his mouth, wondering where Alexa was and why he was alone with the Regent, without even the duke swinging his feet and humming to provide legitimacy for this meeting.

"Not in so many words," Alonzo added. "She said you seemed surprisingly fond of him for you. I simply read between her words. Although your response confirms it." The Regent beamed, pleased with his cunning.

"My lord . . . The reason I'm here?"

"All in good time," Alonzo said, picking a honey-glazed almond from a Murano glass salver and sucking off its sweetness. "The duchess would be upset if I started without her."

As if on cue, halberds slammed on the marble outside as guards came to attention and a door swung open. Duchess Alexa took one look at Alonzo behind the table and Atilo standing there in front of it and scowled.

"I thought the meeting was at six."

"Did we say that?" The Regent sounded surprised. "I confess, I thought it was half an hour earlier. That was the time my lord Atilo arrived."

"Having been called by your guards."

Prince Alonzo smiled. "Perhaps we should start," he said. "Now that you are here at last."

The Regent pretended not to notice the tightness of Alexa's shoulders, or her awareness that, in choosing the desk, he'd left her to stand or take one of the lesser chairs. "My lady."

Alexa took the chair he suggested.

There were servants there, of course. There were always servants. As tradition demanded, they were treated as invisible, only obeying or reacting if spoken to directly. Nothing said here would be repeated. They had families: wives, children, parents . . . Silence was assured.

"Atilo has been telling me he's keen to help any way he can. He has no intention of refusing any task we'd like him to undertake."

The duchess relaxed. "Atilo?"

The Regent was luring him into a trap. No, Atilo shook his head. Far worse. He'd trapped himself already and left no retreat. All he could do was discover how serious it was and what room he had left for manoeuvre.

Easy to forget Alonzo had been a *condottiero*. No, even that was wrong. It was easy to remember, since he mentioned the fact constantly. What was easy to forget was that his fame was deserved. In the days before Alonzo became a drunk he was the best strategist in Italy. Atilo should have realised the Regent's current sobriety was significant.

"Obviously," Atilo said, "I will do what you command. Although my lord Alonzo expressed worries about my age . . ." He knew the Regent wouldn't let him get away with that and he was right.

"Worries now assuaged," Alonzo said smoothly. "Atilo is firm in his belief he's the best man for this."

Best man for what, damn it?

Unrolling a map of the Middle Sea, with red crosses against three Mamluk ports, Alonzo added another at the mouth of the Nile, near Alexandria, and a final cross halfway along the African coast to indicate Tunis or Tripoli. Quickly sketched arrows followed, converging on Cyprus.

Atilo's heart sank. "The sultan?"

"His fleets launched over a week ago." For once Alonzo's voice was flat, his tone matter-of-fact. "He accuses us of burning a Mamluk ship in the lagoon. He refuses to believe otherwise. If he takes Cyprus . . ."

The Regent didn't need to finish that sentence.

If the Sultan took Cyprus, Venice would lose a major ally, a way station between the Nile and Europe, and be disgraced. More than this, if Cyprus fell the Order of Crucifers would be root-less. Bad enough having their embassy in Venice. The idea that the whole Order might need a new base . . .

"Cyprus must be saved." Alexa's voice was brittle.

"My lady?"

"My favour depends on this. What we have in Cyprus is . . ." If Atilo didn't know better, he'd swear she cried beneath her veil. "It's priceless. It must be defended to the death."

Alonzo looked surprised.

"You don't agree?" she demanded.

He shrugged. "I didn't realise you felt so strongly."

"My lord, my lady . . . can we put a fleet together in time?"

"It's done," Alonzo said. "Such as it is. All ships have been ordered to gather at Cyprus. And we've kept a small fleet there since the new year. We simply didn't expect the sultan's own fleet to be this size."

"How many does he have?"

"Two hundred war galleys."

"And how many are we?" Atilo wasn't sure he wanted the answer. Two hundred galleys was a major force. More than the sultan had gathered before. Atilo was surprised that many Mamluk galleys existed in the world.

"Fifty," Prince Alonzo said.

A respectable fleet. An entirely respectable fleet, just outnumbered four to one by its enemy. Atilo expected little of the Regent, not being in his confidence. But he was shocked Alexa had not told him of this before. "Did we know a fleet was gathering?"

"A fleet, yes," Alonzo said. "Two hundred war galleys, including hardened corsairs from Alexandria and Tunis, and an elite force of ghilman, all converging on Cyprus, no . . ."

"Ambassador Dolphino has failed," said Alexa. "Our spies in North Africa have failed. These are matters for later. I need you to leave immediately." She glanced at Alonzo, nodded slightly. "Janus has agreed you should lead his fleet."

"How?" asked Atilo. No messenger could reach Cyprus and return in the time available.

"That need not concern you."

Atilo's lips tightened. Hightown Crow, then. Unless Crucifers could talk across distances. That was possible. One Black Crucifer to another? If so, could Byzantine mages listen to the ethereal whispers? And if they could, would their emperor help or hinder Venice's ambitions? Byzantium hated the Mamluks. But it didn't love Serenissima either.

"Where does the southern emperor stand?"

A scowl crossed Alonzo's face. "Manuel Palaiologos stands with the winner. So Duchess Alexa believes. I find it hard to believe he'd support heathens."

"You're heathens to him," Alexa said.

Shrugging, the Regent smiled at Atilo. "We have our fastest galley waiting. Draw gold from the treasury. Select your staff, say your goodbyes, send Desdaio back to her father . . ."

"My lord."

"She can't stay at Ca' il Mauros alone."

"She won't go, my lord. They're estranged."

When a smirk twisted Prince Alonzo's lips, Atilo realised he'd walked straight into another trap. That made two in the same hour. The Regent was toying with him. Maybe the man was right. Atilo was getting old.

"Well," Alonzo said, "she can't stay where she is. And it seems she can't return home." He glanced at the duchess. "I guess she'll just have to come here."

"She could join my ladies-in-waiting," Alexa agreed reluctantly.

"Oh, I don't think she needs an official position. At least not yet. Let's see how it goes."

The Regent didn't expect Atilo to return. Whether he hoped he'd fail and die, win and die or simply just die was not obvious. What Atilo knew for certain was that Alonzo had just publicly staked his claim to the richest woman in Venice. In front of the man who was meant to marry her.

In front of the current duke's mother, too.

And Marco would be deposed for sure. If Alonzo got his hands on Lady Desdaio Bribanzo's fortune he'd be ruler of Venice before the year was out. An ex-*condottiero* could buy a very large army indeed with that kind of money.

54

Adif could taste the salt spray, as the wind and tides fought each other. He could feel the *Seahorse* shudder under his bare feet as her keel scraped rocks. Wince at the shriek from her already battered frame. The Mamluk could hear, taste and fear. But he couldn't see the Sicilian cliffs or the narrow gap between them.

Tycho could.

"Grip tight," Tycho said

Dizzy from water sickness and barely supported by the rope he gripped, Tycho knew his strength was draining like sand in a timer. The power and certainty that feeding on Giulietta had brought him was almost gone. Gone already were his makeshift awning and his earth-filled bag. But he could see a gap between headlands leading to a bay beyond.

And that gave him a strength he didn't expect.

What showed above the gap scared him. A thin line where darkness was turning pale. It edged the cliffs as if an artist had mixed dark and lapis blue and added a tiny trace of imperial purple.

His death written in the sky.

Grabbing the rudder from Adif, he wrenched the bar towards him, feeling crosscurrents try to kick the *Seahorse* out of true.

"We should pray," Captain Malo suggested.

Adif nodded.

"Personally," Tycho spat, "I'd hang on."

Both the men gripped a rail. The captain appeared resigned to losing control of his galley to slaves. The way he kept glancing at a sodden but ornate strapped-down bedroll suggested other worries. Although, if the inrushing tide did carry his ship on to the headland rocks, how to explain the disappearance of the owner's son would be the least of them.

Adif had experience of steering galleys.

Ten years as a sailor had been followed by three as a bosun and two as captain. He had five years as a slave after that, having been captured. Five years was a long time for a galley slave to survive. Most died in their first year. A good number of those left in the year following. He allowed their captain wasn't bad as filthy infidels went.

"The boy died in the storm," Tycho said.

"What?" Captain Malo looked surprised.

"Why not? Your ship's near collapse. It's a miracle we survived."

Pointing to its broken mast, Tycho remembered Captain Malo couldn't see the full horror of what lightning had done. Nor the number of dead slaves still to be tossed overboard. The other slaves huddled, sodden, angry and injured.

"Believe me," he said. "It's nasty."

Close up, the gap between rocks was wider than it looked.

A minute before Tycho had been wondering if the *Seahorse* would fit, now he knew two ships could pass if they didn't mind being lashed together and having their sides scraped. "Hold tight," he shouted.

Seawater heaved as it lifted the galley, carrying her with a rush across the bulging water and down to calm conditions beyond. Behind her, the sea still fought for entry. Ahead lay a low beach on which a fire burnt in front of half a dozen huts. A ramshackle jetty sank into the sea.

"It's a fishing village."

The Mamluk clapped Tycho on the shoulder.

"He can see in the dark? That's how he got us here?"

"Yes," Adif admitted.

"Get me on to dry land," Tycho said. "Cover me before daylight arrives."

"*What?*" Captain Malo demanded.

"That's my price for saving you."

"He'll give you freedom," Adif said. "You saved the *Seahorse*, you saved our lives. We'd be dead if not for you. He'll give you freedom."

"No. He won't."

And looking at the captain's face Tycho knew he was right. The owner's son was dead. Captain Malo's ship needed repairs. Captain Malo could no more risk offending Venice by freeing Tycho than Tycho could fly. He would be taken to the slave market in Cyprus and sold as Alonzo ordered.

55

Limassol's slave market was open on all four sides, roofed in crumbling clay tiles, and supported on misshapen sandstone pillars. The steps to the selling plinth were worn and dipped from years of merchandise being led before buyers.

The platform could take five at a time. Outstanding offerings were sold individually. Brothers and sisters were usually sold in pairs. The rest in bundles of three or five. No one could remember a sale to sell a single slave before.

Certainly not a sale that started at midnight.

Maybe it was the strange hour, or the fact that only one slave was on offer, that drew a huge crowd to a district most patricians tried to avoid. Mind you, most patricians, including the king, tried to avoid Limassol altogether. Squalid by day, noisy by night, stinking of animals and slaves, it was fit only for merchants.

And maybe, Sir Richard Glanville thought, the rumours of an invasion had led to the party atmosphere. A reaction to everyone's natural worry. Since returning from Venice and his time as the king's envoy he'd found himself second in command of the White Crucifers. Sometimes a tricky place to be.

Sir Richard didn't relish taking the slave to market.

The boy was filthy, dressed in a squalid doublet, with his hair braided, and swaying drunkenly as he stumbled and muttered, trying not to trip over his fetters. Sir Richard would have thought this task beneath him if the prior had not suggested it.

The price Sir Richard received was irrelevant.

What mattered was that the slave be sold within a day of arriving. And so, having been delivered last night to the Priory of the White Crucifers, the boy had been locked in a dungeon for the day, slopped down from a bucket at nightfall, and delivered to Limassol in an ox cart guarded by five men at arms.

Sir Richard would have felt better if the boy tried to escape.

"We're here," his sergeant said.

"I can see that."

The man's face tightened.

They should be preparing Cyprus against the Mamluks. Goat herds needed driving into the mountains, or slaughtering and salting against the coming siege. Swords required sharpening. Damn it, they needed making. Sir Richard commanded five hundred soldiers. What was he doing at midnight with some pretty boy slave who'd end up a merchant's catamite?

Unless the king wanted him.

Sir Richard hadn't considered that. King Janus's tastes were complicated. There was a rumour, probably false, involving the Grand Prior when both were much younger. If Janus wanted this boy that changed things.

How subtle was Venice?

Subtle enough to send an assassin disguised as a pretty slave to attract the attention of the prince he intended to kill. Sir Richard wouldn't put it past them. But why would Venice weaken Cyprus at a time like this? He took another look at the boy with the silver-grey hair.

"You," he said.

The slave turned as Sir Richard punched.

A soldier swore, Sir Richard's sergeant dropped his hand to his dagger, wondering what he'd missed, but Sir Richard's attention was on the boy. Who blocked his blow without even thinking about it and settled into a rear-foot stance, readying but not throwing an answering blow.

Looking round, Sir Richard realised enough of the crowd had seen it for rumours to raise the boy's price still further.

"No," the boy said. "I'm not."

Sir Richard's blue eyes narrowed.

"I'm not here to kill anybody. That's what you're thinking, isn't it? That I'm here to murder someone?" The boy's voice was strained. His eyes sweeping the crowd as if looking for faces he recognised.

"Let's get this over with," Sir Richard said.

Leading the slave to the steps, he passed him to the slave master.

A fat Nubian with gold earrings, proudly protruding belly and a tatty gold waistcoat that barely covered his chest, Isak collected old manuscripts, carved ivory, read three languages and spoke five. His hooped gold earrings only came out on market day, like his waistcoat and oiled belly.

"It's a good crowd," Isak said.

"Given your advertising I'm not surprised."

Proclamations had appeared on doors for those who could read. Everyone else had the words read to them or picked up the gossip in taverns. "A male slave of unsurpassing beauty, so rare his milk-white skin cannot stand sunlight, to be sold at midnight this coming Tuesday. The only sale of the day. No credit will be given."

"You know he's trained to kill?"

Isak grimaced. "Really? That'll double his price with half tonight's bidders and halve it with the rest. I need to decide what to say about that."

In the event, Isak didn't mention it.

He simply took the youth from Sir Richard, walked him to the top of the sandstone block and cut away the tatty doublet covering him. "You know what you're buying," he said. "Here he is."

Turning the half-naked boy to face the crowd hemming in all four sides of the standing stone, Isak held a lamp close to the slave's body, so they could see the whiteness of his skin, the fineness of his features, the strange silver-grey hair.

"The bidding starts at five hundred gold ducats."

A stunned silence greeted the starting price, with some bidders mentally upping the level they'd set for their final bid, and others realising the auction was too rich for them but deciding to stay, anyway, to watch.

"Here," a man said, raising his hand slightly.

Exactly who Isak expected to make the first bid. A silk merchant from Alexandria. He couldn't afford the boy but was now known to have been in the bidding war. "Any advance on five hundred?"

A hand rose, a man nodded, a second hand twitched, and then a third and a fourth; someone scratched their nose near the back. When the frenzy stopped, the bidding stood at fifteen hundred gold ducats and the Alexandria merchant was shaking his head regretfully. Hangers-on were commiserating and telling him he was wise to stop there.

The man had money worries and trouble extending his line of credit. Having been seen to bid gold on a single slave he'd find credit easier. A man with money worries wouldn't bid so highly, would he?

Isak smiled at the ways of the world.

"Any advance on fifteen hundred?"

A merchant bid an enemy up to two thousand and then dropped out, leaving his enemy to drop out two hundred ducats later. A Crucifer knight twitched his hand, and at the rear a young woman raised her whole arm, ignoring rules that suggested bidding be discreet. She was newly arrived and newly bidding.

Isak had memorised those who had bid already. And had identified a handful of those waiting for the auction to be reduced to serious bids only.

With her curling chestnut-dark hair, sweetly round face and ample bosom he would have remembered her anyway.

Glancing behind him, the previous bidder tried to discover who he was bidding against. But the woman now had her hand to her side. Obviously embarrassed to be the centre of attention of those around her.

"Your bid, my lord."

The man was a simple knight, but Isak always found it helped inflate the bids if he inflated the bidder's importance. This man, however, was not bidding for himself. No Crucifer, bound to chastity, poverty and charity, had that kind of money. Or, if they did, they were taking their vows laxly.

"Three thousand gold ducats."

The crowd gasped in admiration at the way he'd cut straight from two thousand five hundred ducats to three without bothering to hit the hundreds between. You could fit out a galley for that money. Fit out a galley, or fill a brothel with the most beautiful slaves, even buy a small palace.

"Four thousand," the young woman said.

The Crucifer knight turned to stare. She blushed, but didn't take back her bid, although she looked at the ground, before raising her eyes to meet the scowling knight's gaze, then blushed all over again.

"My lord, the bid is yours."

Around the knight the crowd held its breath.

Why would anyone pay this for a single slave? Isak knew it stopped here. He could see that in the knight's face. Either he'd reached the maximum he was ordered to bid; or he was buying for himself, which, given the fury in his eyes, seemed possible. If so, he'd reached what his forbidden purse would stand.

"Four thousand five hundred ducats."

Isak wondered if the young woman pushing frantically through the crowd knew she was bidding against herself. He looked at the knight, who shook his head. The slave was doing the same. Staring at the young woman and shaking his head as she edged towards the sandstone block and her purchase.

Pushing past Isak, the woman grabbed a blanket from the dirt and wrapped it round the slave's shoulders, covering his bare torso. The slave master noticed she was careful not to look at his body as she did so.

"My lady," the boy said. "Does Lord Atilo know?"

The woman shook her head.

"Why are you even here?" he demanded. "Why aren't you home?"

"Where's home?" she said, tears in her eyes. "With my father, who won't talk to me? Or at the Ca' Ducale, my body and fortune at the Regent's mercy, because staying alone at Ca' il Mauros isn't allowed?"

"And Pietro?" the boy asked.

The woman looked puzzled.

"The new apprentice?"

"Safe in Venice, with Iacopo and Amelia. They're allowed to stay at Ca' il Mauros, apparently." Her complaint was loud enough to carry. Those who heard it would tell those who hadn't. By morning, all Limassol would know. Although what they'd know would bear little resemblance to any truth. Isak had no idea who she was, but she worried him.

"My lady, you might want to have this conversation somewhere private. Let us settle, and you can take your purchase." He scanned the crowd for her retinue. Looking for her major domo or whoever kept her purse.

"I'm alone," she said.

Isak's smile froze. His rules were money on the nail, no credit and no taking the goods without payment. The knight's three thousand coins were better, paid now, than substantially more, paid sometime in the future, if at all . . .

"I'm Desdaio Bribanzo," she said. "This is Tycho."

The slave nodded ruefully.

Dragging a jewelled bracelet from her arm, she said. "Take this as payment. It cost five thousand ducats."

Very fine indeed. Filigree gold inlaid with cameos, carnelians, pearls, emeralds and rubies. Its weight alone made Isak wonder she didn't tire wearing the thing. "Venetian made?"

"Milanese. A present from the duke."

"Of Milan?" Isak asked, keeping his face impassive.

"As opposed to Venice, you mean?"

Isak turned the gold bracelet over in his hand, and nodded. Yes, that was exactly what he meant. And it really was very beautiful indeed. He wondered what she would have to do to earn this.

"Marco wanted to marry me too. But Alexa wouldn't let him. Well, I was told he wanted to marry me. I suspect it was Alonzo's idea."

That was the point Isak decided he needed to bring this conversation to a swift close. The bracelet had quality and was made for a duke. That would add value when it sold. All the same, the rules existed. If he broke them this time . . .

Mind you, with a Mamluk fleet approaching who knew what would happen? Mamluks needed slaves as much as the next lot. But they distrusted Nubians, and Isak had heard Byzantium was a fine place to sell slaves. Maybe even a fine place to retire. And her bracelet was portable. Useful should he need to leave in a hurry. In the time it took Isak to think this, Desdaio dragged free her earrings.

"Take these as well . . ."

And then she added a brooch to the collection. At first Isak thought the earrings were amethyst. Then he realised they were pale and flawless rubies. "Also from the Duke of Milan?"

"From Lord Dolphino."

Isak blinked.

He wanted to be away from this young woman with her impressive breasts and huge eyes, and seemingly inexhaustible supply of priceless jewellery. A woman who tossed around the names of admirals, and *condottieri*, and dukes and princes as if they were her closest neighbours.

"You should take your slave and flee."

"Why?" Desdaio asked.

"The Mamluks will be here within the week."

"Tomorrow, probably. Maybe the day after. But Cyprus is safe."

"How can it be?" asked Isak, stunned by her certainty.

"Because my future husband, Lord Atilo il Mauros, leads the fleet against them."

56

"You gave your mother's brooch? Dolphino's earrings. The bracelet Gian Maria sent you . . . ?" Atilo's mouth was a tight line. He put one hand to his dagger, although that was for Tycho, who stood to one side.

They were in an upper chamber of the Priory.

A stark and coldly decorated room, made hot by Atilo's anger and a night wind smelling of smoke and herbs. Sheep were roasting over pits outside. Food for the Crucifers who would fight tomorrow's battle.

Every ship in the Cypriot fleet would carry a mix of galley slaves and free sailors. Also Crucifer knights, crossbowmen, soldiers and pikemen. Those vessels carrying mage fire needed masters to fire the flame, work the bellows and keep the deadly mixture from killing those it should protect.

Mage fire won battles.

Stealing its secret from Byzantium had been the Crucifers' making. It also explained the hatred existing between them. Mage fire won battles and it lost them. Ships had been destroyed by the fire they carried before. They would be again.

None of that concerned Atilo now.

"How could you?" The pain in his voice was so raw that Desdaio blinked, tears filling her eyes and her bottom lip quivering. Atilo barely noticed. "I said I'd deal with it. After I talked to King Janus."

"They were selling him . . ."

"I'd have bought him back. You went *alone* to a slave market. You gave your own jewels for a disgraced slave." He shot a vicious glance at Tycho, who stayed silent.

"*You have no idea.*"

"No idea what?"

"What it feels like to be for sale."

"And you have?"

"Of course I have." Desdaio was furious. For a second, Atilo feared she would hit him. Should he let her? Or catch her wrist? How hard should he grip?

"Listen to me," she shouted. "Don't do that with your face. I don't want to know you're *thinking*. I want to know you're *listening* to me . . ."

Tears rolled down her cheeks.

"You went into his room," Atilo said, a statement of fact.

"*Yes*," she said. "*I went into his room*. To warn him about the test. *Nothing happened*. He told me to leave."

"Why didn't you tell me?"

"Look at yourself," she said. "Standing there with your hand on your dagger. Why do you think I didn't tell you?"

Tycho caught the moment the Moor's gaze shifted from Desdaio to where he stood a couple of paces behind her. Barefoot, half-starved, draped in the discarded blanket with which she'd wrapped him at the market.

"Is that all you're good for?" Atilo hissed. "Hiding behind a girl?"

"Give me a knife, old man. We'll see."

Atilo's mouth fell open.

"Even weak like this," said Tycho. "I can kill you."

"You dare . . . ?"

"You're past it." Tycho's voice was cold. "You've lost your strength, your nerve, your reflexes. All you've got left are your skills and they're not what they were, are they?" He could see the truth in Atilo's eyes. The man didn't believe all that was true. But he was worried it might be.

"Not yet ready for your grave?"

Turning his back on his old master, Tycho glanced at the darkness outside. Past midnight by an hour or so. He had two hours, maybe three, before he needed to protect himself against daylight.

And the sad thing, the thing that twisted Tycho up inside, was that he missed the sun. Missed its warmth and its brightness, its warmth on water and the smell it gave to bare skin. Memories of sunlight reminded him of the boy he used to be . . . Every time he changed the sun scared him a little more. Without his doublet and without Dr Crow's ointment he had no choice but to hide.

"Face me," Atilo said.

"Why would I bother?"

Closing the gap in three steps, Atilo slapped him.

Tycho laughed. So Atilo backhanded him hard, obviously expecting the boy to go down. But Tycho stood his ground, grinning through bloody lips. "Is that the best you can do?"

The third time Atilo struck, Tycho caught his hand, held it briefly and then tossed it away, as if discarding rubbish.

"Don't you mock me," Atilo hissed.

"Someone has to."

Drawing his dagger in a single sweep, Atilo put its point to Tycho's chin, where a blade can pass through muscle, tongue and palate, entering the cavities behind the nose to pierce the brain.

"I let you do that."

The dagger's point jabbed tighter. "No, you didn't."

"Are you sure?" The question earned Tycho the dagger point digging through skin until blood ran sluggish and black down the outside of his throat.

"Feel that?" Tycho asked.

And Atilo did. Tycho could see that from the old man's stillness and his widening eyes. Atilo's spare dagger was at his own balls. Tycho had removed it from his belt without the old man even noticing.

"Do they still work?"

"Stop it," Desdaio shouted.

Tycho had no idea which of them she was talking to. Nor did Atilo from his face. That thought only made the man angrier. The Moor's eyes were cold, his mouth above his sharp beard set hard. He wanted to hurt Tycho. Wanted to punch his blade into Tycho's brain. But the dagger at his groin froze his courage. And Desdaio's presence prevented him.

"Am I interrupting something?" said a voice from the doorway.

"*You . . . Here?*"

Tycho could have killed Atilo then. Instead, he stepped back, shooting the newcomer a twisted grin. While Atilo was still staring, Tycho returned the spare dagger to Atilo's belt with a flourish and gave their guest a bow.

Prince Leopold laughed.

"You must be Lady Desdaio. As beautiful as rumour says . . ."

She was staring from Tycho to Atilo, and then at the elegantly dressed stranger, wondering who he was and why the man she hoped to marry hated him even more than the boy he'd just wanted to kill.

"Tell me what's going on," Desdaio demanded.

Sweeping her a bow, Prince Leopold zum Bas Friedland introduced himself by name, late of Venice and recently of Cyprus. "Three killers, one innocent. Unless there are things about you I don't know . . . ?"

Prince Leopold smiled.

"No? Thought not."

"Atilo's a soldier," Desdaio protested.

"Some wars are honourable," said Prince Leopold. "Others less

368

so. He fights a darker war. As do I. If we fight the other type it's by accident. As for him . . ." He nodded towards Tycho. "His war's so dark he barely knows what it is."

"He's my slave," Atilo said dismissively.

Prince Leopold raised his eyebrows. His gaze slid to Desdaio, who'd gone tight-lipped. "I think your beloved might disagree. I hear she gave her mother's jewellery to buy him."

"Among other things," Atilo said. "I'll buy it back."

On Desdaio's face was an expression Tycho hadn't seen before. Somewhere between anger, stubbornness and irritation. Although her stance, feet planted as if she'd just stepped up to the mark on a *punta di Puglia*, suggested determination too. Meeting her eyes, Prince Leopold grinned.

"Tycho's nobody's," she said crossly. "I bought him. I freed him."

"We'll discuss this later."

Nobody saw Tycho move. One second he faced Atilo, the next he was stood behind the man, his finger drawing a line across Atilo's throat. Smiling, he stepped back and sketched another bow.

"You lose," he said.

"No," Leopold said. "He wins. He told Alonzo you had potential. Told Alexa too . . ." The prince shrugged apologetically. For mentioning Atilo's lover in front of his beloved probably.

57

A night of clarity and wonder. The kind that only comes before a major battle or the start of a siege. When everyone knows plague, fire and famine are saddling their horses and life's rules no longer apply. The end of the world will probably feel like this.

Although Bjornvin's burning, which ended his last world, felt different, Tycho hadn't known what was coming then until it did. He was someone different now. Now he could taste blood on the wind before it was spilt. Blood, and his own longing. If Prince Leopold was in Cyprus then so was Lady Giulietta. The thought made Tycho shiver.

He'd thought he'd never see her again. So the need had become a dull ache, a frostbite of the mind that ate his hope little by little, turning everything to ice. Until the hope of seeing her cracked it open.

The first surprise was King Janus sending for him.

Janus, also called John, stood in a hastily arranged chamber that had been a tower room until given grander duties. A wooden chair with a tapestry over it made do for a throne. Beside him stood the Prior of the White Crucifers. The king was thin and clean-shaven, Prior Ignacio taller and even thinner, dressed in white robes. Both men had once been handsome. Having returned Desdaio's jewellery, King Janus confirmed Tycho's freedom, commended his courage and ordered him to kneel, drawing his sword to dub him a knight.

"Your majesty!" Atilo protested.

"He will save Cyprus," Prior Ignacio explained.

Atilo looked troubled. "You've seen this, my lord?"

"We detest predivination, as we detest all forms of magic," the Prior said firmly. Which wasn't answering the question. Everyone in the tower room knew this was his stated position. No one believed it for a minute. The rumours of Crucifer power were too open and too commonplace.

"I told them," Prince Leopold said.

"Then it's a trap," Atilo's voice rose. "My slave betrayed me because of this man. The prince killed a dozen of . . . my servants," he ended, realising *followers* might invite awkward questions.

"And you a dozen of his" King Janus said.

"Oh yes," said the Prior. "We know all about that. Prince Leopold is here at the king's invitation. And under Crucifer protection." Anyone who didn't know this had just been warned. The sour expression on Atilo's face said he understood this. And knew the person being warned was him.

"This boy," King Janus said, "has done me service already."

Catching Tycho's gaze, Prince Leopold smiled, his eyes flicking to the gallery above where women watched discreetly from behind a fretworked screen.

"What is your real name?" Janus asked.

"I don't know, majesty."

"You are a Venetian foundling?" Several of the court raised their eyebrows at this question. King Janus was notorious for how little he cared about the rules governing nobility. All the same . . .

"Far from Venice. My true name was scratched on a stone thrown into Bjornvin's deepest lake to keep it hidden."

"Bjornvin?" King Janus asked.

"My home."

"You've heard of it?"

Prior Ignacio shook his head. "Never, majesty."

"And where is this home?" the king asked. "How did you reach Serenissima? By ship? Overland from the north? In a caravan across Turcoman deserts?"

"Through fire."

The Prior blanched. He glanced at Janus, who looked round the tower room, considering. A handful of knights, a German prince, Atilo il Mauros. Women on the balcony above and Desdaio standing below. And, finally, the ex-slave kneeling at his feet. The story was containable if necessary.

King Janus tightened his grip on his sword.

"Through fire?" he said lightly.

Tycho nodded. "Bjornvin burnt. I was there, then not. I fell through flames and remember nothing after that . . ."

"Nothing at all?"

"My waking memory is of being bound. Walled up in a Mamluk ship's hull and starving in the darkness until Captain Roderigo cut me free and his sergeant and men set the ship on fire."

"Is this true?" king Janus demanded.

Atilo's mouth opened, but no words emerged.

"Well?" the king demanded.

"Majesty, I know nothing of this."

"Why didn't this captain tell anyone? Surely, he would have told . . ."

"He couldn't," Tycho lied. "I bewitched him to silence."

One of the Crucifers crossed himself. *Now, Roderigo owes me*, Tycho thought. Although he doubted if he would ever collect on the debt. On King Janus's face surprise was replaced by a realisation that the Mamluks had justice on their side.

"This is not good," Janus said.

"That ship?" asked the Prior.

It seemed the sultan had every right to accuse Venice of burning one of his ships, but knowing it changed nothing. An acceptance he'd been wronged wouldn't turn back the Mamluk fleet.

"You were a prince in Bjornvin?"

"I was a slave."

King Janus laughed. "You're meant to say you're royal. At least claim nobility. It's compulsory."

"I was a slave," Tycho repeated. "My mother was an exile."

"What were her people?"

"The Fallen."

"Majesty." Prince Leopold stepped forward. Standing close to the king and the Prior, he spoke so softly that only those two men and Tycho would hear him, and Tycho shouldn't have been able to do so. "This is not something to be talked about openly. I vouch for his blood line. I owe him a life."

"As I owe you a life," King Janus said. "If you hadn't abducted Giulietta we would be married and I would be poisoned if her story is true."

"I believe it," Prince Leopold said.

"Yes," King Janus said. "So do I."

Having knighted Tycho, the king dragged him to his feet, ordered a chamberlain to find the startled youth a doublet more fitting to his new status. Janus was about to withdraw when Prince Leopold made a request of his own.

Tycho stood to one side, Desdaio to the other. In the middle was Prince Leopold, and, next to him, his bride. Lady Giulietta and Tycho had yet to look at each other.

Atilo's shock at seeing Lady Giulietta was nothing to his shock when he realised why she was there. The marriage of a Millioni to a German prince went against everything Venice stood for. He *knew* what Prince Leopold was. In a short, brutal but whispered exchange Giulietta told Atilo she did too.

And she knew Leopold had tried to abduct her that summer. But this was different. He'd saved her.

It took a direct order from King Janus for Atilo to stay in the room. And a second order to make him accept Desdaio as Lady Giulietta's maid of honour. That she chose a fellow Venetian as her maid surprised no one. That Prince Leopold zum Bas Friedland chose a newly made knight offended everybody inclined to be offended and shocked the rest.

"I do . . ."

Lady Giulietta's happiness filled the Lady chapel. Her wry smile when she looked at the stone mother was almost as sweet as her glance to the infant at her breast. Baby and bosom were shrouded by a Maltese shawl. Feeding him proved the only way to keep Leo quiet long enough to let the couple exchange vows.

"I do too," said Prince Leopold.

Then had to stand, red-faced, while Prior Ignacio insisted on asking the question which had just been answered precipitously.

The Prior's voice rolling out across the room. He was a man used to public speaking and his was a voice used to command. At the start, the congregation had been ordered to think of nothing but the wedding couple.

The Mamluk fleet did not exist.

No peasants herded sheep and goats for slaughter. No foot soldiers strengthened walls and prepared faggots of wood for burning or melting pitch to be poured from the battlements. No smiths forged new swords, no shipwrights made Cyprus's galleys seaworthy. No Crucifer knights sharpened their battle-axes.

None of these things existed.

Tycho wondered how many of the congregation realised they'd just been told exactly what was coming. What the Crucifers were doing to fight it. All under the pretence of being told not to pay it attention at all.

"Now can I say it . . . ?"

Prior Ignacio allowed himself a smile at Prince Leopold's

fervour, and the fact this was the second time he'd made his vow in less than a minute. He spoke the words, then said, "There's something else."

Prior Ignacio frowned. Wondering what came next.

"I acknowledge this child as mine." He indicated the baby. "I want him made legitimate."

"*Leopold . . .*"

"*Let me speak.*"

Giulietta shut her mouth. Not something that came naturally, and stared at the man beside her, tears in her eyes.

"This is my heir."

Prince Leopold drew back Maltese lace. As Giulietta hastily covered her breast her new husband lifted the baby from her, stared significantly at Tycho, and opened the baby's gown, exposing a scratch to its chest.

"My heir in all things."

"This is unusual," Atilo protested.

"These are unusual times." The king's voice was mild, his smile warm. But there was a rebuke in his voice.

"Yes, majesty."

Taking the baby, Prior Ignacio held it up. Maybe there was a ceremony legitimising bastards. Although Tycho suspected he was making it up as he went along. "You claim this boy as your lawful heir?"

"I do," Leopold said firmly.

"You are this boy's mother? As Prince Leopold zum Bas Friedland is his father?"

Lady Giulietta bit her lip.

"My child. We need your answer."

"The boy is mine. I went to my husband's bed a virgin. Nobody had bedded me before." Her eyes slid to Tycho. "No man has shared my bed since."

"Tell me if this is true," Janus said.

Taking the child from Leopold, the Prior stared into the

distance. The old man's face, initially blank, became increasingly puzzled.

"Well?" the king demanded.

"I sense Millioni blood in his veins."

King Janus waited impatiently for what came next. Before realising that nothing did. The Prior could sense Millioni blood. That was it. The king looked at Leopold with new interest.

"I swear I tell the truth," Giulietta said hastily.

In a handful of Latin, which was enough for the surrounding knights, Prior Ignacio named the boy Leopold's heir, confirmed the marriage of his parents, named him Leo di Millioni de zum Bas Friedland, and offered a prayer for his future.

58

"You knew?" Atilo demanded.

An hour before dawn. To the others it was still dark. For Tycho it had long since become light. He'd watched the horizon change colour. Mountains edge through shades of black. Windmills standing stark on the plain. This was a country of squat stone towers with wide sails, on slopes so barren there was as much dirt as scrub. He could have liked it here.

It obviously hurt Atilo to approach his last apprentice.

The old man's voice was as stiff as his shoulders, his question as cropped as his hair. He knew half the court watched them from a distance.

"I knew," Tycho said.

"She was there in Ca' Friedland?"

"In his bed, suckling his child." The last was a lie; she'd been in her own chamber until the battle above disturbed her. But there was no need for the old man to know that.

"Why didn't you tell me?"

"And get my throat cut? A Millioni princess in bed with the bastard of her family's enemy? You sent me to kill the prince.

Chances were, you'd kill me for failing. But returning to say that? I might as well stand naked in the sun . . ."

"You think that idea didn't cross my mind?"

"Maybe, but you'd be doing it to me. Telling you about Lady Giulietta and Leopold was doing it to myself."

"*Leopold* . . . ? He's really a friend?"

In as much as anyone could be. Tycho didn't bother to explain that bit of it. Besides, in any sensible world, Leopold and he would be enemies. Giulietta loved her husband. Tycho loved Giulietta. What better reason to hate a man than the very thought of his wife made your guts knot with longing?

"Where does that leave us?" Atilo said.

"There is no us. I could kill you but Janus wouldn't approve. So I'm going to let the Mamluks do it instead. That way you die a hero . . ."

Turning his back, Tycho threaded his way between Crucifer knights and Cypriot courtiers. Finally reaching an alcove where Prince Leopold stood with his arm round his new wife.

"Look after Leopold," she said.

"My lady . . ."

"I mean it. Protect him if you can."

"Two things," Tycho said, smiling. "One, does Leopold look like a man who lets others look after him? And two . . ." He indicated the coming dawn. "The battle will be over before I join it."

"Your eyes get no better?"

"They get worse," Tycho said.

"You're changing," Prince Leopold said. "Now, if you'd excuse us . . ."

Lady Giulietta pulled a face, but she let herself be steered towards the door, courtiers moving aside and bowing as she passed. As she disappeared under an arch, Leopold slapped her buttocks and laughed at her protest.

"The best of his family."

Turning, Tycho found King Janus at his side.

"I wouldn't know, majesty."

"Take it from me. You fight beside him?"

"With luck."

"If the battle lasts until dark?"

"You know about that?"

Janus shrugged. "Too delicate to face daylight. That's what Isak boasted on his posters. Delicate isn't the word I'd choose." His grey eyes searched Tycho's face. "Magically unable to face daylight, maybe. How did you and Leopold meet?"

"In battle, majesty."

"You've fought together before?"

"I was sent to kill him. Giulietta asked for his life. I gave it."

Glancing round, King Janus checked who might have heard the answer. His courtiers had dropped back. The Prior of the White was watching, his expression unreadable behind his beard.

"Walk with me."

The battlements were overcrowded, The air still cold, but ready to warm with the approaching day. A sergeant, in rusting breast-plate, turned to curse their pushing past and stopped, suddenly apologetic. He was old, one-eyed and crooked where his leg had once been badly broken.

Janus clapped him on the shoulder and kept walking towards a corner turret. A huge catapult had been dragged into position, and its plaited ropes were being tied to huge steel rings on the turret floor.

"The plaiting takes the shock?"

King Janus nodded his appreciation of Tycho's guess.

"You beat Prince Leopold. A famous duellist. Then gave him his life because a woman asked you. And were, it seems, banished for so doing."

Maybe the king was talking to Tycho. Maybe to himself. When Janus nodded, then nodded again, Tycho knew his second guess was correct and he'd been right to remain silent. "Tomorrow," said the king, "decides everything."

"Everything, majesty?"

"Until the next time. Of course, if tomorrow goes badly there will be no next time. No Cyprus. No Crucifer stronghold. No me, probably. No Giulietta or Desdaio except as slaves."

"Leopold will take Giulietta. I imagine Atilo intends to do the same . . ."

"Into battle?" King Janus looked aghast.

"Would you leave your woman to be defiled? If you knew defeat made that certain? Leopold won't. I doubt Atilo will either."

"My wife was poisoned."

"Majesty?"

"She died a year ago. No, two years now."

The king's gaze unfocused. Such bleakness flooded his face it was like looking at a Greek mask, right down to the hollow space behind the eyes and the drag of his mouth. A single tear said this mask belonged to a man.

"It feels like yesterday."

They stood in the near-dawn. On hastily fortified battlements. With a Mamluk fleet somewhere over the dark horizon. The men at arms had fallen back, unsure if the king's grief involved Tycho or just the situation in general. Few of those in the castle expected to be alive next month.

The peasants would change sides.

Why not? No one asked them if they wanted to be ruled over. And the cost to them was much the same whoever did. Taxes and tithes, daughters taken, sons drafted into militias. A ruler who was strong but harsh was better than one who was kind but weak. Strong rulers gave stability.

"Can you really make a difference tomorrow?"

"I have a question of my own."

King Janus sucked his teeth. "Maybe the Prior is right. I should have executed you and be done with it."

"Answering my question might be simpler."

"So like Atilo," the king said. "Perhaps that's the problem.

The Moor trained you too well. So now he has no reason to exist."

"He tried to kill me earlier."

"If he wanted to kill you, then you'd be dead." Janus caught Tycho's expression. "And so would he, perhaps. So maybe he didn't think his own life was a price worth paying to take yours. What's your question?"

"Why were you troubled when I mentioned fire?"

"Ah, yes," said King Janus, "the reason Prior Ignacio thinks I should execute you. Part of me fears he is right. "

It was, Janus told him, how Charlemagne, the greatest of the Frankish emperors, sent reinforcements from the Rhine to Roncevaux. Though his loup garou arrived too late to save Count Roland. And Prior Ignacio had told King Janus the Four Horsemen of the Apocalypse would arrive through just such a circle. Tycho could see how the Prior might be worried.

"This is instant?" Tycho asked.

"I'm not sure I understand your question."

"You step into a fire in one place and arrive instantly in the other?"

The king scratched his stubble and sighed. "We're talking heresy," he said. "Dangerous heresy at that. But, yes, I imagine it's quick. Why?"

"I was wondering if it might take longer in some cases."

"How much longer?"

"A hundred years," Tycho said, and then shrugged at the king's expression. "It was just an idea."

59

"Prince Leopold says now would be a good time, Sir Tycho."

Knuckles tapped at a box lid, then a soldier apologised roughly for his rudeness, cursed himself for cowardice and rapped harder.

"If you're done sleeping, Prince Leopold says . . ." Atilo led the fleet, but Prince Leopold represented the king. From the bitterness in the soldier's voice, Tycho took it the battle went badly. How badly he discovered when he reached deck and found himself surrounded by a broken fleet under a darkening sky.

Sailors were lashing Leopold's ship, the *Lionheart*, to Atilo's own.

Grinding into her sides, a Mamluk galley had buckled the *Lionheart*'s planks and widened her seams enough to flood the bilges. Archers who should be fighting were bailing. Just not fast enough to keep her afloat unless tied to another.

The sullen sun sinking into the far horizon was mirrored and mimicked by two dozen fires dotting the wine-dark sea around them. Mamluk ships burnt, but so did Cypriot and Venetian ones. The screams of shackled slaves could be heard across the water.

"Enjoy your sleep?"

There was strain in Leopold's voice.

His jest was forced, almost insulting. His expression grim, and his face grimed with soot and his beard with blood. More blood oozed from an arrow's gash on his arm, which had been tied above the elbow. The dark eyes that had melted Giulietta's heart looked desperate. "Where is she?" Tycho demanded.

"You love her, don't you?"

"Yes," he said simply.

"She's below. I should probably kill you, but . . ." Prince Leopold indicated the smoke and flames, the sinking ships being slowly swallowed by the sea's flat surface. "There doesn't seem much point. But I still want an honest answer."

"To what?"

"My question. You knew Giulietta before that night, didn't you? On the roof at Ca' Friedland, you recognised her from somewhere else . . ."

Tycho nodded.

"Is the child yours?"

"*What?*"

Answer enough. Simply asking obviously left a taste in Leopold's mouth because he turned his attention back to the burning wrecks around them. "Suggest something," he said. "Suggest it quick. We can't afford losses like this."

The numbers were brutal. The Mamluks needed Atilo's ship, the *San Marco*, sunk or captured. The Great Lion flying from her mast was prize enough to make a pauper rich, a soldier an officer, an officer a noble of rank.

The Mamluk's pennant held the same value.

Sultans feared their sons, generals feared their staff. Their admiral's second in command would be good at provisioning but useless in battle. His third in command would be a fighter, hated by his immediate boss, viewed with suspicion by his admiral. Hindered from treason by the fact he was the admiral's nephew, second cousin or bastard son.

Although bastards were risky.

They hated their fathers as much as their legitimate brothers. To destroy the Mamluk admiral's flagship would weaken his fleet.

News of his death would strengthen those Crucifers remaining on Cyprus to defend it. Knights, should they survive, would gain titles, captains become knights, sergeants become captains if they fought well. Four to one at the battle's start. The odds against Atilo now stood at six to one. Both sides having lost twenty vessels.

The odds could only get worse.

"Here they come again." Prince Leopold's voice was weary.

A huge Mamluk galley, its prow a castle, its copper-bound ram snaking a wake through dark water, was turning towards them, the oars along its side rising and falling in time to the beat of a drum.

"Their admiral." Tycho pointed.

An ornate galley waited on their far side.

The Mamluk admiral's aim was to crush the *Lionheart* and *San Marco* – one already damaged and lashed to the other – with one of his far larger galleys. There was a risk, obviously. That the Mamluk galley would become trapped. But if the enemy aimed right, it would smash Sir Leopold's ships to tinder, without destroying itself. Fine for mage fire.

At Prince Leopold's nod, a thickset man cuffed a boy, sending him towards a huge bellows. Another leather-aproned boy followed quickly after. The two apprentices worked a handle to pump air into a copper cylinder, where a return valve stopped it escaping. When the pressure was high enough, the firemaster stepped forward as Prince Leopold moved back.

"Try it and hide it," the prince ordered.

"Yes, sir."

Arcing over the *Seahorse*'s stern, a thin jet of fire sizzled as it hit the waves, breaking into sticky globules of flame. Although the Mamluk admiral on Atilo's far side could see this, the mage fire was hidden from the galley bearing down on Prince Leopold's own vessel.

"Fire ready, sir."

"Hold . . . Hold . . . Hold."

The enemy's prow was a wall hurtling towards them.

As the drumbeat drove faster, the ship's ram cut more water. A white wake high and visible to Tycho in the cloud-shrouded night

"Sir . . ."

"*Wait*," Leopold barked.

The firemaster waited, brass nozzle in gloved hand, his head helmeted, his torso protected by a hog-hide jerkin. Below this, a singed and tar-stained apron told of near misses and lessons learnt. There were old firemasters and bad firemasters; there were no old bad firemasters.

"Fast, wide and high. *Now.*"

Sweeping his flame up and over, the man undid his valve and fire whooshed into the air, blossoming into rain that soaked the enemy. Nothing would stop the Mamluk ship, but in that moment – as mage fire fell – its slaves panicked, and their oars lost their rhythm and the screaming began.

"Sweet gods." Wrapped in a cloak, Lady Giulietta stood next to Tycho. She was clutching a dagger in one hand.

"Where did you get that?"

"From Leopold." She glanced from her weapon to where her husband stood, his whole attention fixed on the galley bearing down on them.

Her pride was almost painful to see.

"*Brace*," Prince Leopold shouted.

Time slowed. Inside the stretched seconds Tycho turned, took the blade from Giulietta's hand, discarded it, and moved to take her fall.

Tumbling hard, she drove the breath from her body. Too stunned to be embarrassed at finding him under her. Not aware yet she'd pissed herself with shock. Barely aware his arms held her and his face inhaled her scent.

As timbers ripped, the Mamluk ram skewered the *Lionheart*, smashing emptied rowing benches and tearing the deck above. The trick now was to stop it escaping.

"Grapple hooks," Leopold ordered.

Two land anchors curved towards the Mamluk prow, the first catching fast, the second falling back. Grabbing the rope of the first, sailors flung the rope's end round the *Lionheart*'s main mast and tied it tight.

"Your highness."

The grappling irons had chains spliced to their ropes to make them hard to cut free from the enemy side. High above, Mamluk axemen were hacking at the point where the rope joined chain.

"Deal with it," Leopold ordered.

A Cypriot archer shot and missed.

Grabbing his bow, Tycho saw the man's shock turn to anger, then caution as he registered the richness of Tycho's new doublet.

"He'll give it back," Giulietta promised.

Pulling an arrow from the man's quiver, Tycho shot a Mamluk through the eye slits of his helmet and heard him tumble. The second joined the first moments later, followed by a third.

In answer, iron bars thrown by Mamluks on a walkway behind their prow came raining down. One killed a firemaster's apprentice, another injured an archer, several cracked the deck when they landed.

"*Tycho, where's Giulietta?*"

"With me. Safe enough."

Leopold laughed. His laugh deep and loud.

"Take her somewhere safer," he said. "Understand me?" The prince had promised his wife he'd keep her at his side. Now he was breaking his promise and only Tycho knew it.

"That's an order, Sir Tycho."

Prince Leopold grinned in the darkness, his teeth white and his beard lit crimson by the flames around them. His gaze swept the deck, finding Giulietta. When she looked at him he blew her a kiss.

The man expected to die.

Before he did he would pass responsibility for his wife to a man who'd beaten him in battle, savaged his woman and driven him into exile . . . Tycho wondered if Giulietta understood what was happening.

"And take the child," Leopold shouted.

"I'll get him," Tycho told Giulietta. "You give Leopold courage."

"How could he think I'd leave my . . . ?"

"He didn't, his words were for me. He's saying keep you and Leo safe until after the battle." *And beyond*, Tycho thought grimly.

The iron bars had stopped raining down, flame licked up the Mamluk prow and the grappling hooks still held. Around him, knights and men at arms were holding their breath, preparing for the real battle. What came next would be worse.

"Go," Tycho ordered, pushing her.

He realised his mistake when she swung round, and a group of archers stared. "Please," he said. "Let Prince Leopold know you love him beyond anyone else. That you'll never love another like him."

Lady Giulietta covered her mouth with her hand.

Mounting the steps from below two at a time, Tycho hit the main deck in time to see Giulietta throw her arms round Leopold and whisper something. Then she headed towards Tycho, her mouth twisted in grief, tears streaming down her face.

When Tycho tried to comfort her, she yanked free, anger replacing her misery. "You'll never be the man he is."

"I know," Tycho said.

"Leopold's going to die."

"Gloriously."

"That's meant to make a difference?"

"It will to him. He's fighting for you. For your baby. Whosever it is."

"*He told you?*"

"He wanted to know if it was mine."

"I didn't even kn-know you before . . ." Her words were fierce, her face set in fury, but there was a stumble, a looking away. That night in the basilica remained with them both.

"Turn," Tycho said. "Wave to him."

Giulietta did.

60

"Your orders, highness?"

Prince Leopold looked at the Crucifer knight. Sir Richard was no fool. In his pale blue eyes, and lined, sun-battered English face the answer to his question was already written. He simply wanted it confirmed.

"Die well."

Sir Richard grinned, hefted his hand-and-a-half sword, checked the war hammer at his hip and looked up at the unbroken wall of the Mamluk ship's prow. "When do we start?"

"Impatient to die?"

"If we're going to do it," Sir Richard said, "we might as well do it while our courage is up and our strength still holds."

Half his men would lose control of their bladders or bowels. Not through fear, but because bodies could only handle so much at once. A man in half-armour can fight full pitch for five minutes before exhaustion sets in. Staying alive and blocking blows comes well ahead of natural functions.

Clapping Sir Richard on his shoulder, Prince Leopold made his round of the others, joking with some, clasping the hands of others, gripping one apprentice by the shoulders, telling him he'd find courage when the moment came.

The boy was in tears but stood straighter when Leopold stopped to talk to his master. Their talk was short and intense. There was no disagreement. Master Theobald simply wanted to check he understood what the prince required.

At an order from Master Theobald, his apprentices began rolling red-painted barrels across the deck, stacking them below the enemy ship's prow. They did so in the face of a shower of arrows, loosed up and over from the enemy side. Luckily, gusting night winds and the Mamluk archers' own fear protected them.

As the apprentices worked, Prince Leopold's archers kept loosing their own arrows to stop Mamluk axemen cutting the grapple free. And the ship's carpenter, a balding man, bad-tempered and stout, but good at what he did and not one to suffer fools, began to hammer a nail into the Mamluk ship.

He worked quickly, ignoring those around him. Ignoring everyone. Even Sir Richard, who went to see what he was doing.

"Ask the prince."

Sir Richard decided he'd wait and see.

Once the nail was fixed, the carpenter forced it free with a long, split-tongued pry bar, working it so hard muscles ridged across the man's back, his face turned red and sweat broke out across his forehead. "Done," he said. Into the hole he fixed a hook, using his pry bar to twist it tight. "Time for another, my lord?"

The prince shook his head. So the carpenter fixed a chain to the single hook and began to wrap it round the mast.

"Help him," Leopold ordered.

Once the chain was locked in place, Leopold nodded to Master Theobald, who widened his valve nozzle, and swept flame up the Mamluk bow.

"And beyond."

The last of the mage fire fell on to their enemy.

Men screamed, axe-wielding Mamluks tried to cut the grapple, not knowing they'd been chained to their doom. They died bathed in the flames, turned to arrow-stuck candles, filling the air with the stink of meat burning.

"Now," said Leopold.

Stepping forward, Master Theobald smashed a red-painted barrel and thick sticky black tar oozed around his boots. He smashed another, then another, until the deck became slick. Slivers of silvery metal in the mix began to smoke, gently at first.

"Out of my way . . ."

When Prince Leopold began to push towards Atilo's ship, Sir Richard looked appalled, then met his gaze and felt shamed instead. It went without saying the prince would stay with those about to die. But someone had to cut the *Lionheart* free from the *San Marco*. Old enemies looked at each other.

"Help me, and hurry."

"No," Atilo said. "Move your men to my ship."

"They stay," Leopold said. "It's the only way to stop the Mamluks freeing themselves. I'm not losing the *Lionheart* without reason . . . Help keep my wife safe. And trust Sir Tycho's instincts."

He grinned at the youth next to Atilo. "We'll never get that rematch."

"Be grateful," said Tycho.

Prince Leopold laughed, and jumped on to the rail of his ship, raising his sword to begin cutting the ropes that lashed their galleys together. After a second, Tycho joined him.

61

Around Tycho the ocean was dotted with burning ships. The fleet King Janus and Venice had provided Atilo burnt, listed and sank. As for their crews, the lucky ones were dragged down by armour or the whirlpool around their dying vessels, the unlucky drowned more slowly.

The Mamluk galleys stood off in a ring,

Only the *San Marco*, Atilo's own ship, remained. The Mamluks were waiting, Tycho was unsure for what. A whole day's worth of hard-fought battle had passed. Steady attrition wearing down the Christian fleet, although they died one for one, sometimes better, the result was always going to be the same.

And Giulietta and Tycho watched it all from under the shadow of an awning. It had been a day of thunderclouds and hidden sun, and for that Tycho had been grateful. Even wearing smoked glass spectacles his eyes had burnt at the brightness. Even coated with ointment, belatedly provided by Atilo. (Dr Crow had given both to the old man. *Just in case you meet that pretty boy again.* Not daring to risk the alchemist's anger by throwing them away, Atilo had still been slow to offer Tycho this protection.)

Now the thick clouds that provided shelter had thinned to

reveal the last rays of the setting sun. From his place under the awning, Tycho examined the wreckage of Atilo's fleet, which carried in its burning hulks the ruin of the old man's reputation. It was hard to separate the Atilos he knew.

The man betrothed to Desdaio. The *magister militum* who carried a history of battles won. The head of the Assassini. He might understand the old man better if he could work out where his loyalties really lay.

With his adopted city?

With the duchess he'd taken as a lover?

To the rules of the Assassini? Rules so rigid they begged for abuse from the likes of Prince Alonzo. The Regent would greet the news of this defeat with public fury and private ambivalence. The duchess's lover dead, her faction at court suffering humiliation, the youth he'd wanted executed also dead. Only Giulietta would be denied to him. And she'd be dead too.

"Tycho," Giulietta said.

He glanced back at her.

"You're crying." She sounded surprised. Leaning forward, she touched her fingertip to his face, examining the proof glistening on her finger like oil.

"Everyone has to die," she said.

Away to one side stood Desdaio, her head bowed and shoulders shaking with fright. She was fighting not to let fear engulf her body. Being killed would be better than being captured. At best being captured meant slavery, probably in some Mamluk's harem. At worst, torture and a slow death.

"You made Leopold a promise."

"What of it?" asked Tycho, already knowing the answer and wondering why he made her put it into words. Because he didn't want what came next on his conscience, probably. Assuming someone like him, some *thing* like him had a conscience.

"When the time comes . . ."

"What?" he demanded. "When the time comes *what*?"

"You're going to make me say it?"

Tycho nodded.

"Kill me. Promise?"

"I promise." And then he realised Desdaio had come to join them, because she was there in front of him, shaking her head fiercely.

"You can't," she said desperately. "What about her baby?"

Turning to Giulietta, she said, "Do you want him to kill your baby too? It's wrong. You'll go to hell."

"We're here already," Tycho said.

Giulietta slapped him so hard it shocked all three of them into silence, and make Atilo glance back from where he stood on the prow. "That's heresy," she hissed. "Cathars have burnt for saying that."

"You think hell is worse than this?"

She opened her mouth to say yes, then shut it again. Grief filled her eyes, for the man who abducted, married and then abandoned her, all for the best of reasons. But abandoned her all the same.

"He knows," Desdaio said.

Giulietta looked at her.

"About hell. Tycho's been there."

The Mamluk admiral's own ship turned slowly. There were other galleys closer to the *San Marco*, but a message must have gone out to hold off. The sultan's admiral wanted the honour of destroying Atilo for himself. Atilo was a Moorish traitor and turncoat, after all. If it took time to turn the admiral's galley so be it. This was a waiting game. And the Mamluks had time on their side.

"You love her, don't you?" Atilo said.

The second time in twenty-four hours Tycho had been asked that question. Glancing to where Lady Giulietta stood, her back turned and the baby at her breast, he answered, "From the moment I saw her."

"At Ca' Friedland?"

"Long before that. In the basilica."

Atilo looked at him. "You love Desdaio also?"

"I like her. She makes me . . . feel easy. But there it ends."

"*I cannot do it.*"

Such was the anguish in Atilo's voice, Tycho's guts tightened. "Nor can I," he said. "Giulietta is my responsibility, however much you hate that fact. And she has asked me to take her life already. Desdaio is your responsibility. And she has not."

"Desdaio mustn't fall into Mamluk hands."

"They might ransom her," said Tycho. "If she says she's Lord Bribanzo's daughter. He'd pay extra to get her back untouched."

"And I would be dead." Atilo's voice was dry. "In time, I would be forgotten, and other suitors would appear. Ones Bribanzo likes better. But, still . . . I would give anything. Surrender this ship if I thought it would guarantee her safety."

"My lord . . ."

"*I meant it, Tycho.* Have you never loved like that?"

The question jolted Tycho's memory. And the coldness inside his mind, and the flames eating the hulks on the ocean around him, and his residual fear of the sinking sun's crimson ball were not enough to banish it. He could taste Atilo's anguish, Lady Giulietta's unnatural calmness, Desdaio's despair. Try as he might, he could not keep their pain from mocking his refusal to act.

"How long do we have?"

"How long?"

"Before that reaches us." The Mamluk galley had finished turning. Both banks of oarsmen now working together, no longer fighting the deep keel's drag, and the strong currents that swept this part of the Middle Sea.

"A few minutes at most."

On the Mamluk galley's prow, boys were filling braziers and oil jars so archers could dip their rag-wrapped arrows when the time came.

"I'm going to tell Giulietta that I love her."

Atilo's shoulders stiffened at Tycho's words. "She's a Millioni princess."

"And I'm a knight, albeit a poor and new one. I need the courage that saying this will give me."

"To do what?"

"Become something else," Tycho said sadly.

Giulietta looked at him, her eyes wide. At her side, Desdaio stood frozen in shock, the hurt in her eyes as extreme as the shock in those of the Millioni princess.

"You loved Leopold," Tycho said. "This I know."

The young woman nodded slightly, her gaze rising to his face. "Why tell me you love me now?"

"Because," Tycho said, knowing that was no answer to anything.

And he turned away from Giulietta's scowl and the barely hidden hurt in Desdaio's eyes. Walking to the prow, he ignored the oncoming ship and spoke the words he'd told A'rial he'd never say.

"Help me."

For a few seconds nothing happened.

Then the air rippled, and static flowed around him, touching his body with intimate fingers, only to vanish. He heard mocking laughter in his head, then a bulkhead door opened behind him and he heard Atilo swear.

"I thought using a door might be more discreet."

Grinning, A'rial climbed a short ladder to stand beside him. Her shoulders, seen through rips in her dress, were as scrawny as ever. Her hair was filthy. Her toes black with dirt. But her green eyes, when they examined him, looked as old as the ocean, and more dangerous than anything found in its depths.

"Ask," she demanded.

"Save us from that." Tycho nodded to the admiral's ship and the ring of Mamluk vessels around them, beyond arrow's distance. As if Atilo's crew had any arrows left or the strength to fire them.

"You think it's that simple?"

"Isn't it? You said I'd call. You were right."

"You're saying it took a reputation in ruins, a victory for the Mamluks, soldiers preparing to die, a dead friend, and your loved ones preparing to be raped or killed, and not knowing which to hope for, before you'd accept help?" Her voice was mocking. "Tell me exactly what you want."

"Giulietta saved."

"Who knows what that means? Giulietta safely back in Venice? Ensconced as the chief wife to the sultan, bearing his heir and commanding his seraglio? Cleanly dead, and removed from the coming horror? What do you *want*?"

"I've told you."

"No," she hissed, voice hard. "You haven't. So I'm going to ask one final time. *What do you want?*"

"The Mamluk fleet destroyed," Tycho answered without thought. "The Mamluk ship destroyed and our ship safe. With all in her," he added, suspecting the *stregoi* would trick him if he worded his wish badly.

"What will you pay?"

"Anything," Tycho said.

A'rial grinned. "Right answer."

62

As the Mamluk kettledrum grew louder, and their galley slaves worked the oars to its rhythm, A'rial grabbed Tycho's hand, holding it in a vice-like grip. Her nails were black, her knees scraped and bare. Around her neck hung a yellowing bird's skull, with large eyeholes and a dagger-sharp beak.

"You pay the price freely? This you must state."

"I'm still waiting for you to tell me what it is," he said, flinching as the red-haired child turned on him, her eyes sharp as broken glass.

"You know my price," she hissed. "Pay it, or not."

Tycho looked at her.

"State you pay it, or let me return home. You cannot summon me, and then quibble." There was a fury to her words far more dangerous than shouting. He wondered, not for the first time, how old A'rial really was.

Whether she was human.

But who was he to ask those questions? And she was right. He knew her price. Although he imagined it was Alexa who really wanted it, and A'rial was simply her instrument.

"Take my life instead," he begged.

A'rial shook her head dismissively.

"My soul then."

Pushing her face close to his, she mocked, "What makes you think you have one? Or ever had one? Swear it by the goddess or Giulietta dies . . ."

He should have remembered there would be a full moon.

Pale as his skin, huge and poised just above the horizon. The sun might be sunk in its glory, firing a final sliver of horizon with sullen flames, but the moon had a whole night ahead of her, and a red-haired acolyte on the deck of a losing ship, taking promises in both her mistresses' names.

"I will make Alexa an army," Tycho said. "I will embrace who I am."

Stepping on to the prow of Atilo's ship, A'rial stood tall, brought her clenched fists to her forehead in a strange salute, then flung them back, with her fingers still clenched, her arms angled back and down like the wings of a bird.

Winds whistled around her.

Lightning cracked from an unbroken sky.

The storm began instantly. Clouds gathering on the dark horizon, banking and racing at impossible speeds towards the Mamluk armada like heavenly cavalry. Mamluk archers blinked to find spray in their faces. The crescent pennant above their admiral's galley flapped so hard it sounded like cannon fire. Beneath Tycho's feet, he felt the *San Marco* lurch as wind filled her sails and she listed dangerously.

"Lower the sails," he shouted.

Atilo stared at him.

"My lord, drop the sails. Hack down the masts if you must. But get the canvas down and get Giulietta and Desdaio below . . . Please." Maybe the final word helped. Because Atilo snapped out orders to cut the sails free, and hurried the women towards a hatch. Only returning to his post when they were below.

"What have you done?"

Thunder rolled across the sky, lightning lanced seawards. A Mamluk ship in the ring around them lost its mainmast as jagged fire split the wood, and sails tumbled before anyone had time to lower them.

"My lord, go below."

"Tycho . . ."

"I must do this."

"*What have you done?*"

"Paid the price demanded to save those I love."

Tears rolled down Tycho's face, harried by the wind. He could taste their sourness in his throat, and feel emptiness under his ribs where someone had cut open his chest and was replacing his heart with ice.

"Go," he ordered.

Atilo looked shocked.

"Or stay," Tycho growled. "And die. Those are your choices."

"Those are my . . . ?"

"You think we will distinguish between friend and enemy when the killing grows fierce?" He indicated A'rial in the prow; fierce winds gusting away the arrows aimed at her, her arms stretched back, her face raised to the sky.

She was mouthing incantations. Her fingers dancing as she pulled clouds across the sky and split ships in two with strikes of lightning. A lift of her chin produced a cliff-sized wave that crushed three ships, and faded just as quickly. In a flurry of waves and thunder she'd set about reducing the Mamluk fleet to a single vessel. There had never been a storm like it. And right in the middle, red hair streaming, stood the little *stregoi*, her face running with rain that filled her mouth and dashed from her chin like a million tears. She was laughing.

When he looked back, Atilo had gone.

Tycho wanted to be there, on the Mamluk galley, facing his enemy, ripping out the bastard's guts. To think it was to be there.

Stumbling, he glanced down, seeing the waves behind him. Fear filled his throat as he fought to balance on the rail.

How he got there didn't matter.

"*Over there . . .*" A Mamluk archer shouted warning.

And Tycho stopped his arrow in mid-air, wrapped his fingers around it before the arrow could fall, and stabbed hard and fast into the neck of a man-at-arms who was advancing, short sword in hand. Twisting, Tycho felt barbs turn before he ripped the arrow free, tossed the dying man aside and hurled the arrow at the chest of the archer who'd fired it.

The arrow flew so fast it disappeared.

And then the archer was staring in shock at the shaft jutting from his mail coat. Tycho killed him, almost as an afterthought. The crack of the archer's neck lost under the howl of the wind, the crash of the waves and the roar of blood in Tycho's head.

He could feel hunger inside him. It stared through his eyes. Filled his mind. Its vision sharpening as the western horizon darkened, the final traces of daylight drowning below the waves. The Mamluk ship with its galley slaves, slave master and admiral became a frieze of red. Frozen, as time hiccuped and the sea slowed to a sullen roil, and the beast tested the bars of its cage.

"*Do it,*" said a voice in his head.

A'rial, Tycho decided. Unless he was talking to himself.

So many people to kill. So many throats to tear out, so much blood. He could drown himself in the red he'd spill on this one ship. They were firing arrows at him. The wind took most of them. The few that came close he swatted away, not even bothering to return them.

"*I said do it.*" Definitely A'rial. She sounded crosser this time.

Should he? Could he, and remain who he was? He knew the answer to that. The few times he'd embraced the moon's rays he'd felt a sliver of ice enter his heart. Enough of those slivers and his heart would freeze. He couldn't unlearn the lessons that changing taught him. And after he became himself again, the

401

memories of what he'd been remained. But how could he save Giulietta without changing? He would have to accept his destiny.

Become the last of the Fallen. The last of his line.

Or perhaps the first . . .

Raising his face to the full moon, Tycho let its rays wash over him and felt his dog teeth descend. Sinews tightened, bones twisted, muscles tore, his throat filling with his own blood. Touching fingers to his face, he found his ears had shrunk away and left knotted holes in their place. His nose was flatter, his nostrils wide like a hunting animal. However bad the *krieghund* looked, he looked far worse.

Inside Tycho's chest his heart froze, locking him into panic. Its beat was gone, his lungs were static, his breath disappearing. Only fear kept him upright. He was alive and dead in the same second.

"Sweet gods . . ."

Changing hurt more than he could imagine. A remorseless shriek of pain washing away his last dregs of being human.

This monstrous creature was what he'd become eventually. Tycho knew that for a fact. In the end, no matter how many times he reverted, this was how he would end. Monstrous and ugly. The world he'd been born into long dead. A new world in its place he could hardly bear.

His price for finally letting the beast free was that he'd spare the slaves. Because sparing them would prove to himself something human remained somewhere. And then Tycho stopped pretending he didn't want what came next and – as A'rial let her storm subside – became himself.

The Mamluk galley had double rows of benches on both sides. The top row open to the sky, with a raised walkway used by the whip master. Tycho swallowed this information in a single second.

"Die, demon."

You had to give the Mamluk sergeant credit for courage. He must have known he was about to perish. Lobbing his head over the side, Tycho kicked his body into the slave well, and faced the soldier beyond. Spiked helmet, chain mail, a wickedly curved scimitar. Tycho noted and dismissed his armour and weaponry.

The man's first blow almost landed. His second one did, slicing Tycho's lower arm to the bone and sticking fast. Grabbing the man, Tycho squeezed; throat armour buckling as Tycho crushed his voice box.

Shock, then pain. Tycho knew the sequence.

Ripping free the scimitar, he hurled it at the next man and watched him stagger back, the weapon protruding from his chest. The cut on Tycho's arm was a memory. So he gave it to a man with a spear instead. The spear man gasping as Tycho touched a hand to his face. Staggering back, he clutched his healthy arm, screaming loudly. Tycho threw him over the side. The kettle drummer died as simply.

Tycho kept moving.

It was a whip that stopped him eventually.

An iron-tipped lash spun out of nowhere and slashed his face, blood dripping into his mouth. Sword deep, he could feel his teeth where his cheek should be. Turning swiftly, to protect himself from a second blow, he held his cheek's upper and lower edges together and jagged flesh begin to mend.

The third blow he was ready for.

Catching the weighted end, he wrapped the thong around his fist and yanked, dragging the whip master to his knees on the walkway in front of him. The Mamluk never stood a chance. As Tycho moved for the kill, a slave grabbed the whip master's ankle from below. Another hand snaked upwards, chains clanking.

The slaves held the man in place while Tycho popped his eyes with taloned thumbs and tossed him sideways into the slave pit.

He tossed the whip after.

Behind Tycho were archers he didn't remember killing. Mamluk sailors, their heads twisted so far they stared in the wrong direction. A ship's mate dead on the walkway, his throat torn out, eyes missing, his guts in a pile between his knees. Tycho's thumbs dripped blood, his doublet was sticky. At no point did it occur to him to use a dagger. At no point had there been a need.

The red edges of the world faded with that realisation.

And inside Tycho's chest his heart started beating, and his lungs shuddered and drew breath. Bones twisted and muscles contracted. As stars lost their brightness in the sky, the full moon changed from scarlet to a rose-pink, and the waves began to ebb and flow at close to their normal speed.

Tycho checked behind him.

Atilo's ship stood there. A'rial still on the prow. But her arms were no longer flung back and her face no longer turned to the sky. She was staring between ships, and Tycho saw her smile as their gazes locked.

Around them lay wreckage. Broken masts and spars, vast canvas jellyfish made from sails that held pockets of air. A rudder floated with a man at arms slumped across it, an arrow in his neck. Bodies bobbed like stunned fish, rising and falling with the swell. Most were ordinary sailors, Mamluk, Cypriot or Venetian. Those rich enough to own mail were on the seabed already.

Apart from Tycho, only one free man remained alive on the ship.

And maybe he was the only one really. Because Tycho doubted he was human, and was certainly not free. A slave to his hunger if nothing else.

The Mamluk admiral was young, tall, thin and brave.

He had to be brave to stand in the door of his tiny cabin. Elegant riveted mail glinted silvery gold in the moonshine, the brand he clutched highlighted the gold-filled etching of his helmet. He wore a rich helm with a jutting nose-piece, steel cheek protectors and a gilded spike at the top. A silver crescent arched up over his eyes. It was the armour of a Mamluk prince.

"Demon," the man said.

Firelight from his flaming brand rippled along the sharpened edge of his sword, revealing tightly hammered damascene. Steel had entered the young man's soul and stiffened his spine. It was revealed in his steady gaze. Tycho was impressed.

"What are you?"

The changes Tycho had fought against became less savage as his face finished shifting shape, his ears regrew, his nostrils closing. His teeth were the last to go, retreating into his upper jaw. They hurt as viciously as ever, but this time it was less frightening. Taking a step back, the Mamluk appeared more terrified by the man than he had been by Tycho's shifting shape only moments earlier.

"*It can't be you*," he protested.

In that second Tycho decided to spare him. At least for a while. "You know me?" he said. "You know who I am?"

A brief nod was his answer.

"Then you know more than I do," Tycho said. "Because I don't know you." Slowly the Mamluk undid his helmet.

And it was Tycho's turn to step back. Because the last time he'd seen that face, Sergeant Temujin was cutting its throat before burning an entire ship. At the start of Tycho's time in Venice, with no moon over the lagoon, and a Mamluk vessel freshly boarded by Dogana guards.

"You recognise me now?"

"I watched you die," Tycho said. "Saw your ship go up in flames."

The Mamluk closed his eyes, and his lips opened in prayer. He touched his hands to his heart, his mouth and his forehead in turn; in formal goodbye to someone. And then told Tycho who.

"My twin," he said. "She insisted."

"Insisted on what?"

"Accompanying your ship. It was stupid. But she was my father's favourite and he indulged her. Until you spoke, no one knew for certain she was dead. I could feel an emptiness in my heart but

I couldn't lose hope. My father will be upset." From the way the young man said those words, much went unspoken.

Unbuckling his armour, the Mamluk dropped it at his feet, barely noticing it clatter down steps to fall into the slave well where oarsmen watched in silence. A single tug pulled fine mail over his head and he let that drop too. Reversing his scimitar, he offered it hilt first with a slight bow.

"Make it clean," he said. "And when I reach paradise I will beg for your release from the curse that afflicts you."

Tycho swung the scimitar experimentally.

A beautiful weapon, with its handle wrapped in a strand of gold wire, and a blade weighted so it carried on the down stroke, whistling as it cut through the air.

"My curse is forever," he said, lowering the blade.

"Forever?"

"Anyway, you must live."

"*Why?*"

"So you can take news of this defeat to the sultan. So I can discover why your sister was on that ship. Because enough brave men have died . . ."

Tycho felt so tired his bones ached at the thought of it. Atilo had once spoken of sadness after battle being like the sadness that comes after sex, only bleaker. Tycho had not dared say he had no knowledge of either. This was worse than he feared. A desolation that carried the taste of carrion.

In disgust, he rolled a dead archer into the well with the scimitar's tip. The following thud made him feel sadder still. Where was the elation? Atilo said some men felt that.

"I am Sir Tycho. Once an apprentice blade."

The Mamluk bowed slightly. "I am Osman. My father is the sultan. My sister, nicknamed Jasmine, was his favourite. But I am his heir."

Tycho bowed in return.

"You can kill me," said Prince Osman. "Keep me for ransom

406

or free me. Even, it seems, send me as a messenger to announce my own defeat to my father if that is the load you put on me. Although he will not believe my tale."

"Why not . . . ?

"A storm-summoning witch? A ravening, shape-shifting demon? My fleet destroyed by waves, wind and lightning? My archers' arrows swatted aside? The Venetians do not have that kind of power. My father would believe I made excuses."

"So what will you say?"

"My slaves refused to row. That I commanded poorly. The bowstrings of my archers were wet. That I surrender my command and accept my fate."

Prince Osman's eyes were bleak. His father had a reputation for cruelty. He also had enough sons, by both wives and favoured concubines, to sacrifice one if an example need be made.

"Stay here," Tycho ordered.

As if the Mamluk prince had anywhere else to go.

Atilo crossed himself when Tycho appeared from the door behind him. He opened his mouth to say something and left his mouth open as Tycho stalked past, only stopping when he reached A'rial. "I need something."

"Favours cost." Her green eyes were sharp. "You know that."

"Name your price."

"One kill. At my choosing."

"Your mistress's choosing?"

"Mine," the little *stregoi* said, her voice hard. "One time, when the hunger is on you I will ask for a kill. You will grant it without question."

"Not Giulietta, not Desdaio, not Pietro."

A'rial's smile was sour. "You're not in a position to bargain. But all the same, I agree. None of those three."

Tycho told her what he required.

A few dozen people were to forget what they'd seen and

remember what they believed they saw. As Tycho stepped back, A'rial drew herself upright and a shimmering wrapped itself around her. Once the space between her hands shone bright enough she began to chant the true history of the battle. The one the Mamluk slaves would remember.

"*Tycho . . .*"

"We'll talk later," Tycho said.

Atilo il Mauros opened his mouth and closed it once again. He was a man fond of saying the world held more than one could know. He just hadn't expected to come face to face with its strangeness that night.

"The duchess knows?" he managed finally.

Knows what? Tycho wondered. *About my hunger? About the changes that come with it?*

"Yes," he said. "Undoubtedly."

Tycho took the smoky brand from Prince Osman's hand and thrust it close to the face of a red-bearded slave, who recoiled from its flame. "No one's going to hurt you," the prince promised. Although the whip scars on the man's shoulders said he'd been hurt already, many times and brutally.

"What did you see?" Tycho asked.

The slave looked at him.

"During the battle. What did you see?"

A nod from Osman told the man he could answer.

"The Venetian fleet. It was vast. Masts like a forest circling us. So many ships, my lord, I've never seen so many. I thought we'd never escape."

Tycho could see bodies and broken spars, upturned ships and bobbing flotsam, the spreading aftermath of a naval battle. The slave could not. But when the man shivered Tycho knew he realised what was out there.

"What happened?"

For all the man had been Western once, a northerner to judge from his hair and the red in his beard, he answered as if the Mamluk fleet's fate and his were inextricably entwined.

As they were, of course.

"We were encircled. Their archers slaughtered our sailors. They had mage fire. It spread across our decks, burning everything it touched." The man's eyes were bleak as he remembered what never happened. "It was only his highness's skill that saved us. In the middle of a terrible storm he fought the Venetians to a standstill. Their entire fleet destroyed at a terrible cost."

Prince Osman's eyes were saucers. His glaze flicked between Tycho and the slave, unable to believe what he was hearing.

"Ask any of them," Tycho said.

"What will he say?" asked Prince Osman, jerking his head towards Atilo's flagship.

"That you lie. What do you expect him to say?"

"And I say he lies?" Prince Osman nodded. He was beginning to understand how this worked.

Tycho smiled.

"Your price is I tell you how I know you?"

"And a favour given without hesitation. Not involving a death in your family," said Tycho, remembering the price A'rial had extracted in her turn. "Beyond that I can't say, because I don't know."

The prince looked up sharply.

"Start with how you know me . . ."

63

In the far shallows of the night, with the darkest hours long behind him and the moon a low ghost on the horizon awaiting the sun's exorcism, Tycho crawled from his pallet to wash himself in buckets of water Giulietta had earlier ordered drawn for him. He carried the weight of Osman's answer in his heart.

Although his skin was now clean, he washed himself one final time, rinsing his mouth and spitting salty water back into a bucket, before tipping the lot over the deck. His torn doublet was over a rope in the hot pre-dawn breeze. It was now almost dry enough to wear.

Atilo slept in the captain's cabin.

Ladies Giulietta and Desdaio had the other. Denied his own bed, the *San Marco*'s original captain was at the rudder. He refused to meet Tycho's gaze. There was nothing strange about that. Everyone refused to meet Tycho's gaze, finding reasons to be somewhere else.

A'rial was gone. Already forgotten.

A storm had come from nowhere. A miracle from God, heavenly proof that San Marco, Venice's patron saint, had the ear of the divine. The only strangeness was Tycho's single-handed battle against Osman's ship.

A mighty leap, the sailors were saying. Heroic bravery, a madman's luck, sheer stupidity. Few admitted seeing anything. And those who had kept their thoughts to themselves. The newly made knight had leapt a near-impossible distance and been lucky. Everyone knew why Prince Osman had been allowed to leave. Atilo had told them it was to take news of his defeat to his father.

"Are you all right?"

Turning, Tycho found Giulietta behind him. She was dressed as no widowed woman should be, in a thin undersmock, which clung damply to her body. The garment was laced at her neck with a ribbon; loosely closed and loosely tied. "I could hear you prowling the decks."

"How did you know it was me?"

Lady Giulietta flushed.

The absolute clarity of his night vision was a secret from her, Tycho realised. A secret from everyone except Dr Crow, and perhaps Prior Ignacio of the White Crucifers. Although Atilo must be close to guessing by now.

"Just guessed," she said brightly.

"Right."

"It's hot down there."

"And up here," Tycho said.

"At least there's breeze here," said Giulietta, facing the night wind. All it did was paste her undergown more tightly to her body. She must have known, because she turned to tug discreetly at the neck.

"I'm sorry," Tycho said, looking away. "About Leopold. I would like to have known him properly."

"We can talk about him later. Right now . . ." Her voice broke. "I can't bear to think about . . . I thought you were going to die too."

"So did I."

"Really?" She sounded thoughtful.

No, not really. The thought never occurred to him. From the

411

moment he appeared on the deck of Osman's ship he'd known he was the strongest and fastest and most deadly creature aboard. Until now, he hadn't really thought about how intoxicating that was. How it would be to let that go.

"Yes," he lied. "Really."

Lady Giulietta rested her head against his shoulder.

Somehow his hand came up to stroke her hair and he felt her melt into him, then pull away. "Leo's asleep. Desdaio also. Atilo too, I imagine."

"The wind's best higher up."

She smiled sadly.

All war galleys were built to an old design. Some said the Romans invented them. Others that it was the Greeks before them. In the old days galleys had two, sometimes three rows of oars, one above the other. Tradition gave Venetian galleys a single row. Although that could change.

The cabins on this were at the stern, with a space below for the tiller, and steps up to a small deck, made from the roof of the cabins fenced in for safety. It was here a huge arbalest could be fitted, one of those vast crossbows with arrows that would pierce an enemy's sides. And it was here Tycho led Giulietta. Although she seemed uncertain why they were there when she reached the top.

"What are you thinking?" she demanded. Only to grab for a rail as the *San Marco* shifted on the swell beneath them. He saw her hit the rail and caught her before she could stumble. "How come you can balance?"

"Sheer skill," Tycho said.

Giulietta stepped away from him. "You haven't answered my question."

"Just did."

"No. About what you were thinking."

"A'rial," he said. "She's . . ." Tycho hesitated. "One of your aunt's ladies-in-waiting, I suppose." From her scowl, Giulietta thought his hesitation was about more than how to describe her. "A'rial is eleven. She looks like a starved cat."

"Some men like . . ."

"Well, I don't."

"So why think about her now?"

There was a question. The kind he should expect from a Millioni princess, who kept a good head behind those watchful eyes. "Because I owe her a debt," Tycho said. "One I will need to repay."

"What?" she said.

"Nothing important. Why?"

"You shivered." Giulietta leant her head against his shoulder. After a moment, when he said nothing, she wrapped her arms tight around him, and he found himself stroking her hair as she clung to him. "This means nothing," she muttered.

"You're upset," he agreed. And felt her freeze. "I mean it," he said hastily. "This means nothing and you're upset about . . ."

"Don't you dare say his name."

Her face was wet beneath his fingers. Her thoughts a jumble of fears, sadness and anger he tasted and then let go. So much desperation. So much emptiness. These were what had brought her up here. "You know things," he said, tugging the ribbon at the neck of her undergown. "What lies beyond Al Andalus?"

"A great sea," she whispered. "Stretching further than any ship can sail. Everyone knows that. Filled with monsters."

"And beyond that?"

His fingers caressed her throat, opened her gown and smoothed down her warm skin until he felt her nipple harden as he cupped her breast in his hand. "Some say a void," she said, her voice shaky. "That the world ends like a cliff, with the ocean spilling into nothing. If you draw too close the current sweeps you over."

Kneeling like a knight at her feet, he opened her gown further and bit softly into the underside of one breast, hearing her whimper.

413

"Then how do the seas refill?"

She frowned down as if he was a child.

"Rivers, of course. The way a fountain bowl refills from the water spilling into it. I'm not sure it's true about the cliff. Aunt Alexa says the world is round. You start there," she nodded towards the prow, and you finish here . . ." The *San Marco*'s foaming wake stretched behind her.

Lifting her gown to her hips, Tycho kissed the darkness between her thighs, feeling her shiver and tasting wetness as salt as any ocean. They stayed that way for a long time. When Giulietta finally took her fingers from his hair, she was sobbing, tears for her dead lover rolling down her face, and Tycho had another question.

"What does Aunt Alexa say is beyond this sea?"

"The far edge of the Khan's empire."

Tycho nodded sadly. He'd thought maybe Bjornvin was there.

Epilogue

Tycho woke abruptly. Aware the sun was about to break over the horizon and Dr Crow's ointment was in Atilo's cabin below. Ever since Tycho had been freed from behind the *Quaja*'s bulkhead, he'd been tortured by ignorance of why he was a prisoner in the first place. No memories existed between Withered Arm's fire circle and being walled up in a ship, where waves sickened him and silver shackles burnt his wrists.

All he'd wanted was to know who he was.

That was all anyone wanted. Why shouldn't he know? And now he did. At least, he knew part of it, and the knowledge drove all happiness from his body. He would not rest easy until he'd told the girl asleep beside him.

Reaching over, he drew the neck of Giulietta's gown together to hide her pale breasts, and gently tied its ribbon, smoothing straggles of hair from her face. She looked strange asleep, younger and less tough. Her red hair spread in a flaming halo around her. Had Leopold looked at her like this? If so, Tycho wondered what he had seen that Tycho missed.

They were not lovers, Giulietta said. Never lovers.

At least not like that. Prince Leopold zum Bas Friedland had protected her. He had snatched her from those who first abducted her, keeping her secure without her knowing, and, when she escaped, hunted her down again and introduced himself.

They were *friends*, she told Tycho fiercely.

You were allowed to cry for friends, to miss them and love them and wish everything could have been different. As to who fathered Leo, she was unable to answer that. Literally unable.

Anyway, she was intact.

Lady Giulietta had to touch his finger to a scar on her abdomen before he understood what she meant. She had *never*, and she told him this with brutal fierceness, lain with a man. And she would not lie with him now. The only man she might have lain with was dead . . .

And Tycho had held her, and dried her tears, letting her settle when crying for Leopold, the lover who wasn't, finally exhausted her enough for sleep to rescue her from sadness. Now Tycho had something to tell her of his own.

The question was how much truth could she stand?

And how much truth could he stand to tell her? The full truth? That he'd been a ragged, wizened, nameless creature, never sleeping, little more than a living skeleton when he was hunted down in the Eastern deserts? That he still had no memory of how he got there, how long he'd been in the desert or who he was before?

The bleakness of Osman's description weighed on Tycho.

To the hideousness of what Tycho could make himself become had been added the monstrousness of what he'd once been. He had speed, strength and courage. All of these came at a price. And Tycho knew, because he knew himself better now, it was a price he would pay.

This too he needed to tell her.

If Osman spoke the truth, Tycho had been almost animal when trapped by Tīmūrid mercenaries on the borders of the Mamluk empire. He'd been sold to the sultan's vizier, in a trade that saw one old enemy deal with another on behalf of Venice, a third. The sultan's mages had emptied Tycho's head of nightmares, dreams and memories. They'd emptied it of everything except a need to carry out one single task. If he hadn't drowned in Venice's lagoon – or almost drowned, whichever it was – Bjornvin's memories would never have crept back.

The bribes must have been huge and the promised rewards enormous. Prince Osman's sister had held words of power. Words designed to bind Tycho to carry out her order. He was to kill Duchess Alexa. And the man who asked for this death, offering to deliver gold and territories to the Mamluks when he finally became duke, was Alexa's brother-in-law, Lady Giulietta's uncle, Prince Alonzo.

The Regent hadn't know when it would be done. Simply that it would be. When Alonzo discovered the plan had failed, his revenge on the Mamluk *fontego* had been terrible. Had he succeeded in killing Alexa, Duke Marco IV would have been next. Prince Osman had little doubt about that. Quite possibly Lady Giulietta after that. Unless the Regent had other plans for her.

Kneeling up, Tycho stroked the sleeping girl's face until she woke, looking puzzled and still sleepy. "You should return to your cabin," he said. "But first there's something I need to tell you . . ."

Acknowledgements

You know where you are with a publisher who drags you off to the Porterhouse pub in London's Maiden Lane for a six-hour editorial meeting – and waits with good grace while you go through the script page by page. So heads up to Darren Nash, lapsed Australian, Orbit UK editorial director and good friend . . .

And a big tip of the hat to Orbit supremo Tim Holman, who filled me with food and alcohol when I flew out to New York – running a temperature and fever – to pitch him *The Fallen Blade*. Having asked me to pass the one-page synopsis to Devi Pillai, senior editor and Orbit US's self-styled Eye of Sauron, he waited while she read it. Devi nodded significantly and that was it. We were in business on both sides of the Atlantic.

To my agent Mic Cheetham for doing the real work that made this happen. Joanna Kramer for keeping me sane during the copy-edit process. Darren Nash and Devi Pillai again for thoughtful and occasionally stern editorial notes (that's you, Devi). The book's much better for them.

As always the ex-lunchtime collective of, variously, Paul McAuley, Kim Newman, China Mieville, Chris Fowler, Barry

Forshaw, Nick Harkaway, Pat Cadigan, for drinks, food, bitching sessions, general chat and sanity. If there was any justice, Rob Holdstock would still be on that list (and he is in spirit).

My son Jamie, who might have buggered off half way round the world but still calls regularly for all that he's rubbish at answering emails. Hearing from you always makes my day.

And finally, Sam Baker. Eighteen years married. More than twenty years together. Pretty good for what was meant to be a quick drink. Thank you.

extras

www.orbitbooks.net

about the author

Jon Courtenay Grimwood was born in Malta and christened in the upturned bell of a ship. He grew up in the Far East, Britain and Scandinavia. For five years he wrote a monthly review column for the *Guardian*. He has also written for *The Times*, the *Telegraph* and the *Independent*.

Shortlisted for the Aruther C. Clarke Award twice and the BSFA seven times, he won the BSFA Award for best novel with *Felaheen* featuring Asraf Bey, his half-Berber detective. He won it again with *End of the World Blues*, about a British ex-sniper running an Irish bar in Tokyo.

His work is published in French, German, Spanish, Polish, Czech, Hungarian, Russian, Turkish, Japanese, Finnish and American among others. He is married to the journalist and novelist Sam Baker, currently editor-in-chief of *Red* magazine. They divide their time between London and Winchester.

Find out more about Jon Courtenay Grimwood and other Orbit authors by registering for the free monthly newslettter at www.orbitbooks.net

interview

In recent years the depiction of the vampire in popular literature has often been more romantic than bloodthirsty. To what extent with Tycho were you deliberately attempting to return to the more savage incarnation found in European folklore?

The early fifteenth century was fairly bloodthirsty so even something non-human would probably need to toughen up to survive the humans! But yes, I wanted Tycho to be distinctly non-sparkly. It seems an insult to offer readers twenty-first-century characters with a cheap historical overlay so I've grounded his character in the times in which he finds himself. Plague is commonplace. Starvation is commonplace. Stealing bread will see you hung. Upsetting the wrong people will see you tortured. It's less than a hundred years after the Black Death killed a third of those alive in Europe. Society is brutal, sexist, cruel and unforgiving. Tycho arrives knowing none of the rules and has a hard time learning them.

But he is a romantic hero in the proper sense. And one reviewer – a philosophy professor, bizarrely – picked up something I'd missed. The two characters who sacrifice most for love – and so live up to what we consider to be human values – are both non-human. That wasn't conscious on my part. I did, however, want Tycho to feel not just the physical pain of the trials he undertakes but human emotional and spiritual pain as well. So yes, he's a return to the vampire as monster. And acceptance that the times in which we live can make monsters of us all. The secret is to overcome that monstrousness.

Of course, he's also the first vampire in Europe, a generation before Dracula, so he's the basis on which later myths and legends are founded, and some of them inevitably are misunderstandings of what Tycho is and represents.

Tycho is a complex protagonist, struggling against the dual onslaught of the hormones of puberty and the savage lusts of vampirism, not to mention being a stranger in a strange city. How challenging was it to write his character?

Hugely! Adolescence is the point at which we look in two directions at once: backwards to being a child and forwards to being an adult. God knows that's hard enough. Throw in not knowing if you're even human, and if you're not human, what kind of "not human" you are, and that makes for a tough mix for the young character to live with, and any writer to create.

Also, since Tycho doesn't even know at the beginning what he is hungering for he can't feed his addiction to blood. There's an obvious analogy with early sexuality. He knows he wants something. He hasn't quite worked out what it is. Just that he wants it very, very badly. I was really tempted to make him able to handle daylight, since it would have made writing him so much easier. So I compromised on a limited supply of alchemist's ointment, which once gone is gone (making bigger problems for the second and third book).

Being a stranger in Venice is hard on Tycho whose memories of growing up came from a hundred years earlier and half a world away (Bjornvin is in North America), but I know Venice reasonably well so that bit was less hard for me!

You have explored the significance of memories in your work before and do so again in *The Fallen Blade* as Tycho gradually remembers his past. What is it about this theme that makes it so appealing?

We are our memories. Our identity turns on where we think we come from, what we think we've done and what type of person we think that makes us. Regret is remembering having done one thing and wanting to have done another. It takes courage to regret, and even greater courage to regret and learn from the regret. Tycho's problem is: what if his memories are lies? What if he remembers incorrectly or simply makes memories up because he has no others? None of us have any proof that what we remember is true. We simply think it's true because we remember it. I think we're each probably single moments in time, only really existing in an endless succession of presents. I also think identity is fluid and how we behave is changed by what is happening around us. The big question is: is there something central and unchanging at the core (what people would once have called souls, and some still do)?

Tycho's in too much of a mess and facing too many odds to give that question real thought, but he knows the question is there. And since he's not human, he also knows the other question is: what is he? That's why the memories matter so much to him and he revisits and revisits trying to find a clue.

The Venice depicted in *The Fallen Blade* is as much a character as any of the human (and inhuman) protagonists. What research did you do to achieve this atmosphere and historical depth?
I made three trips to the city inside eighteen months: the first to get a fresh sense of the place, the second to sketch and photograph locations and the third to fill in the final gaps and write one of the really difficult scenes. I wanted to do that while I was there, so I could see the city and my monsters on an overlay inside my head. That way I got to see the *krieghund* coming out of the night fog.

The amazing thing about Venice is how little it has changed over the centuries. As always, I bought old maps and they showed that some back canals had been filled in with earth to become Rio Terra, and several islands around San Pietro at the eastern end of the island city had been joined to make a bigger island, but much of Venice is as it would have looked six hundred years ago. That's hugely helpful when writing fictional history.

It's a cliché to say Venice is the city of sex and death – but it is. Venice is dying and has been dying for over a thousand years. It's layered with history, one era on top of another. And it's made with pillars and windows and statues stolen from other cities the Venetians looted. To write Venice I just had to open my eyes and carry a notebook.

The map of Venice featured at the start of the book is fascinating. Could you tell us more about its origin?
The map is based on a five-hundred-year-old map of Venice printed in Basle. I bought the original after I signed the contract to write the three Assassini novels and sent it to Orbit, who gave it to a cartographer who used it to draw a new version, with some changes I wanted made, and with a key that showed essential locations in the book. I have both the original and a large copy of the new version out on my desk at home so I can check them whenever I need. I love the map, and I love that the city we visit in real life and Tycho's city are still so close you could use *The Fallen Blade* map to guide yourself round Venice today.

You do a lot of your writing in coffee shops – why is that? Do you find that the background noise is conducive to concentration, or is it the proximity to caffeine that's more important?
I'm trying to limit my caffeine to a jug of coffee a day! I have two reasons for writing in cafés. Actually, three . . . The first is that writing can be done anywhere (that's the real joy of it). I used to write on trains, planes and in bars. Now I

write in cafés because that's where I spend most of my time. The second is it's become a habit. I'm used to going to work by dropping down to a café for breakfast and sitting there writing until lunchtime, then I go for a long walk to think through the next section, and start work again when I get back to the house. Although @GenghisKat usually has something to say about that. The third is probably the most important: I find it much easier to get lost inside myself when surrounded by people and noise. Most of the writers I know get out of the house at some point during the day to work, otherwise there's always something to distract you!

Obviously enough, I write on my research trips (I wrote in Venice for *The Fallen Blade*, in North Africa for the Ashraf Bey crime novels, in Tokyo for *End of the World Blues*). Locking down once a year in a hotel for two or three weeks also helps me get a *lot* of words written!

The Fallen Blade marks your first foray into historical fantasy, after having written a number of SF novels. How difficult was this transition and was there anything you particularly enjoyed about writing in a different genre?
Getting proper monsters into the plot was great . . . I knew who and what Tycho was from the very first time he opened his eyes inside my head and I realised I had a new book (and remember – nowhere do I use the word vampire!). The *krieghund*, the Emperor Sigismund's shock troop of what we'd call werewolves, came out of nowhere, almost literally. I hadn't realised Prince Leopold was a *krieghund* until I wrote his battle against Tycho on the roof at Ca' Friedland, then I had to go back and include the *krieghund* attack on the Assassini that opens *The Fallen Blade* because I suddenly knew why Lord Atilo's forces were so weakened. That attack had killed their best men and the man Atilo had intended as his successor.

Magic was also a big attraction. In Tycho's time people really believed in demons and witches, alchemists and sorcerers . . . So I wanted to make them real. Not to explain them or codify them any more than I'd explain pie sellers or tavern keepers – simply make them real.

If you could go back in time and give yourself one piece of advice before you started writing this book, what would it be? And would it be different from the advice you would give yourself before you started writing your very first book?

Okay, for my first book it would be, 'Stop trying to run away; they're always going to catch you.' I was seven and locked down in an English boarding school and my first novel was about a monkey that escaped from a zoo, stole a NASA space-ship and went to live on the moon (paging Dr Freud . . .).

The first book I had published I wrote at a table in a flat in a very poor area of north London the summer I was made redundant from a publishers. I wouldn't give myself any advice because it was only sheer stupidity – and blind luck – that made me write it and send it off to an agent and have a phone call that went, 'We've sold the book and its sequel. You are writing a sequel, aren't you?'

This book? I don't know . . . I'm not big on giving advice or taking it, and people need to find their own voices and their own way of working. It took me three published novels before I came close to thinking I'd maybe learnt how to write. And like most writers I know – and I know a hell of a lot – I still doubt it most days. The best advice I could have given myself would probably have been drink less coffee and write faster!

if you enjoyed
THE FALLEN BLADE

look out for

THE EDINBURGH DEAD

by

Brian Ruckley

I

The Demonstration

Glasgow, 1818

The corpse sat in a simple, high-backed chair. A band had been tied around its stomach to keep it upright. The man – young, perhaps no more than twenty-five – had as peaceable a look to him as death might permit. A relaxed face, hands resting quite naturally, in lifelike manner, upon his knees. He was naked, but a pure white sheet had been laid across his legs and groin, for the preservation of modesty.

A few paces behind the dead man's chair, a fire burned with vigour in a metal brazier. It gave out prodigious amounts of light and heat, the latter of which in particular was hardly needed. Though the streets of Glasgow outside were awash with freezing rain and stinging winds, the air within was already close and warm and a touch stale, by virtue of the enormous audience the corpse had attracted.

They were packed in to the raked galleries of benches that occupied some three-quarters of the room's circumference. This great wooden amphitheatre had never seen quite so many beneath its domed roof. They were standing in the aisles, sitting on the steps between the blocks of benches, crowding the very highest and furthest of the doorways, craning their necks to get a view of proceedings. For all their numbers, though, and all their slightly febrile anticipation, a remarkable quiet prevailed. There was the occasional shuffling of a foot, a cough, now and again a faintly nervous laugh. But all in all the fragile, expectant silence held.

The corpse was not alone, down on the floor of the amphitheatre. Figures in long white robes moved about him, like a flock of bishops preparing a sacramental rite. The instruments of their devotion were not, however, chalice or cross or censer. Rather, a stack of metal discs, threaded on to a tall central pillar, stood on a wheeled trolley. Flat strips of copper ran from the top and bottom discs to long rods that stood upright in a glass jar. Beside this odd machinery, a man was laying out knives on a cloth. Dozens of them. And saws, and shears.

"Ladies and gentlemen," said one of the robed men, and at the first, startling sound of his voice a collective shiver of excitement thrilled its way around the whole assembly.

"Ladies and gentlemen," he said again once that tremor had passed, "you will this evening be witness to a display of true medical Prometheanism. This," he gestured towards the corpse strapped to the chair, "is Mathew Clydesdale, murderer. Executed this very day, in accordance with the sentence passed upon him by the court. And his presence here, the service he is about to perform, is also in accordance with that sentence.

"I am Professor Andrew Ure, and it is my privilege to be your guide in the first part of our explorations this evening: a demonstration of galvanic effects."

He turned and nodded to the younger men, the assistants, who had been waiting beside the gleaming and ordered array of knives. At his sign, they took up their blades. This was greeted by a swelling murmur of conversation around the theatre, and waves of shuffling and shifting as the assembled host sought a clear line of sight. But all sound, all distraction and interruption, dwindled away as the knives went to work.

A lengthwise cut was made along the inner face of the forearm, followed by two transverse incisions across the wrist and the elbow. The skin was peeled open, the two flaps of it pinned to ensure it did not slip back into place. Thus invited, the people of Glasgow looked into the meat of Mathew Clydesdale's arm, and as they did so they whispered to one another, and trembled in fascination, or horror, or wonder.

The muscles were raw, a brownish red; the bone, overlaid by them and by the straps of pale tendon, yellowish. There was little blood, for his heart had been stilled some time ago.

"Expose the cervical vertebrae, if you would," Ure murmured to his assistants, and while they tipped Clydesdale's head forward and went to work on the back of his neck, Ure bent over the exposed machinery of the arm. He probed with a short rod, and used it to elevate slightly from amongst the meat and the gristle a set of cord-like structures, somewhat grey beneath the scraps of tissue and congealed blood that adhered to them.

"Here are the nerves," he proclaimed to his rapt audience. He shifted his hand a little, letting all but one of the nerves fall back into their corporeal bed. "And this is the ulnar, the first to which we shall direct our attentions."

At Ure's instruction, the trolley that carried the tall pile of metal plates was wheeled into position beside the corpse. Ure took up one of the long metal rods attached to the apparatus and inserted it through the new opening in the back of Clydesdale's neck. Once satisfied of its position, he held it there, and raised the second rod. He looked up to the crowded benches with a grave expression.

"Now, ladies and gentlemen. Observe."

He slipped the second rod into Clydesdale's gaping arm; adjusted it, eased it into contact with the ulnar nerve.

And Clydesdale's arm spasmed. The dead hand that rested palm up on his knee twitched, the fingers clenched. There were gasps, and screams, and a shuddering of alarm. A few cheers. A few hands clapped. Ure withdrew the rod, then reinserted it. Again the fingers trembled and closed, as if trying to grasp at the life so recently extinct.

A woman near the end of one of the rows, midway up the auditorium, fainted away. She was half-carried, half-dragged from her seat and through the crowd to one of the doors, in search of reviving air.

Satisfied, Ure pushed back Clydesdale's head and turned it to one side. He nodded to his colleagues, and they set to work, cutting open the skin of the lower neck, pulling it away from the underlying structure of veins and muscles. Once they stood back, Ure delicately set the tip of a rod against a deep-buried fibrous thread.

"The phrenic nerve," he announced.

And the corpse's chest heaved. Clydesdale's whole inanimate form shifted as his ribcage rose and fell in a dreadful parody of breathing. More exclamations of amazement, and of horror. Some of those watching averted their eyes, or closed them, their morbid fascination exceeded by repulsion and unease.

"You see," Ure said calmly and clearly, "that the mechanism of breathing remains intact after death, lacking only the animating force by which it was formerly enlivened."

Though his voice was steady, his face was flushed with excitement, for he was as captivated as any by the wonders he performed.

And so the demonstration proceeded. The leg was made to straighten, jerking and kicking as if during a fit. A rod inserted into a notch cut above the orbit of Clydesdale's left eye made his face contort and convulse in a mad dance of lopsided expression. At that, another woman was overcome, and helped from the chamber. Two men departed, one after the other, each pale of visage and with a hand pressed over his mouth. One was already gagging as he made for the door.

At the conclusion of Ure's work, another white-clad figure, Professor Jeffray, took charge. He had the dead man laid out on a flat trolley, where he dissected out his every inner working, breaking open the ribcage to reveal the organs beneath, carving away until Mathew Clydesdale was rendered down to so many dissociated, exposed parts.

A state of numb shock settled across many of the observers. They shuffled out more slowly than many of them would have wished, constrained by the crowding to essay a patience few felt. Some lingered, though, after the corpse had been covered up with winding sheets, as the medical men busied themselves with tidying away the tools of their trade.

One – a tall, thin-faced and well-dressed man with a dispassionate intelligence alive in his eyes – descended from the steep slope of benches.

"Professor Ure," the man said, and Ure looked up from his rolling of the knives into their cloth parcel.

"Sir?"

"A remarkable demonstration. Fascinating."

"I am delighted you found it so. One hopes to inform and educate. Are you a medical man, sir? You have the look."

One of the attendants was damping down the brazier behind them. It hissed and crackled, spinning a few sparks up into the air.

"No, not strictly a medical man. I have some slight experience in that field, but my researches have followed a rather different course in recent years. Still, the equipment you use is most interesting."

He extended a languid arm towards the stack of discs, with all their panoply of wires and rods.

"Ah, the Voltaic pile?" Ure smiled.

"I have heard them described, of course, and seen illustrations, but this is my first opportunity to observe the thing itself. Copper and zinc plates, separated by plasterboard soaked in brine. Am I correct?"

"I believe it is charged with acid rather than brine, but in principle you are correct, yes. A quite remarkable contraption. I confess my facility with the construction and care of the things is somewhat limited. Carlyle there, on the other hand: an invaluable man. A natural and subtle talent when it comes to the machinery, whether electrical or mechanical, with which our world is becoming so crowded. He is employed here for that sole purpose, and I dare to think there is none in Scotland to match his expertise."

"Carlyle, you say?" the other man murmured, staring with acute intensity at the indicated attendant, white-clad as the others, who was examining the Voltaic pile with proprietorial concern.

"Indeed. Edward Carlyle."

"Tell me, Professor Ure – if the question is not unwelcome, of course – tell me, have you had any success in stimulating the heart?"

"No, no. Not as yet. The heart remains unresponsive. I have to say, I believe it is through stimulation of the phrenic nerve that the greatest successes will be achieved: it is my hope that it might one day even be possible to thereby restore life and its functions to the victims of drowning, suffocation. Even hanging. But we are scientists, you and I, eh? We must have a realistic view of these things. Our ignorance is reduced with every passing day – how could it be otherwise, when so many great minds are applied to the task? – but it remains prodigious.

"I rather fancy, if you will forgive me an aphorism, that we live not in the Age of Reason, as so many proclaim, but in that of Ignorance; for there is nothing reason so readily proclaims to the attentive mind as the extent of our ignorance. It transforms what were once mysteries, for ever inaccessible to human comprehension, into merely phenomena we have not yet explained, and thereby at once increases what we know and what we do not. Do you see?"

"Very astute, I am sure."

"Yes. Well. If you are interested in natural philosophy, you should consider attending some of my evening lectures. Every Tuesday and Thursday at seven o'clock. All the most recent developments are explained."

"I am an Edinburgh man. I am seldom in Glasgow, unfortunately; we came today only for your demonstration."

"Oh, I see. I am flattered. I did not catch your name, sir."

"No? Well, forgive me, I must have a word with my man Blegg over there. Do excuse me."

Blegg cut a slight figure in comparison to his master, and at that master's approach he was already sinking his head in obsequious expectation of instruction.

"Do you see the man beside the pile, Blegg? His name is Edward Carlyle. We require him, and his services, so you get yourself over there and give him my compliments. Convey my admiration of his work, and ask whether he would hear a proposal I have for him. One that could be of the utmost mutual benefit. Do you understand?"

"Yes, sir," Blegg dipped his head once more, his hands clasped as if in submissive prayer.

"And make some enquiries. We will be requiring rooms for the night. It is too late to return to Edinburgh now."

Blegg hesitated, unsure whether further commands would be forthcoming.

"Be about it, then," his employer snapped.

"Yes, sir. Yes, sir"

And Blegg scampered away to deliver the message.

II

The Dead Man

Edinburgh, 1828

The castle had colonised its craggy perch over centuries, embracing the contours of the rock with a network of angular walls, yards and barracks and gun platforms. Spilling eastwards from it, encrusting the long ridge that trailed down to the royal palace, was the Old Town of Edinburgh. There – packed inside the strict confines once set by the city's defensive wall – soaring tenements vied for space, crowding one another, making labyrinths of the narrow spaces they enclosed. It was an aged place; not designed but accreted over centuries. Thickened and tangled by the passage of years.

A multitude of gloomy and overshadowed alleyways projected, like ribs, from the great street running down the spine of the ridge. They descended into the shallow valleys to north and south, sinking away from the cleansing breezes. Through these closes and wynds the people of this ancient Edinburgh moved, and in them they lived. And died.

Down there, where one of those closes gave out on to the Cowgate, a low and grimy thoroughfare, dawn revealed a dead man curled in the doorway of a shuttered whisky shop, his blood crusted in black profusion upon his clothes and on the cobblestones around him. Looking like something forgotten, or spent and casually discarded, by the departing night.

"Who is he?" asked Adam Quire, staring down at the corpse with a faint wince of distaste.

It was not the sight of it that disturbed him, but the smell. The body stank of sour whisky and blood, and the man had soiled himself in the last moments of his life. There was a less easily identifiable dank, musty strand to the symphony, too. It all made for a noisome aura that discomfited Quire, particularly since the stale flavours of last night still lingered rather queasily in his own mouth: all the beer he had drunk and the smoke-thick air he had breathed.

"No name for him, Sergeant," said the young nightwatchman at his side. Lauder, but Quire was unsure of his forename; Gordon, perhaps.

"Who found him?"

"One of the scavengers. Grant Carstairs."

"I know him. Shake?"

"Aye. Some folk call him that. Got a bit of the palsy."

Quire kneeled at the side of the body, his knee slipping into a tiny, cold puddle couched in the crease between two cobblestones. He grimaced as the chill water soaked through his trousers.

"Nothing left of his throat," Lauder said, gesturing with the extinguished lantern still clasped in his right hand. "Look at that. What a mess."

Quire could see well enough. A ragged hole in the front of the dead man's neck exposed gristle and meat. One sleeve of his jacket was torn to shreds, as was the arm beneath. Material and flesh were barely distinguishable in the morning gloom. Furrows had been gouged in his scalp, too, the skin torn; one ear was no more than a tattered rag.

"I've not seen the like," the watchman murmured.

Quire had – and much worse – but not for a long time, and not outside the confines of a battlefield. He thought he heard as much wonder as horror in Lauder's voice. The man was young, after all; not long employed. Perhaps he had never seen at such close quarters what havoc could be wrought upon the human body. He looked a little pale, though it might be but the watery light of the winter morning making him appear so.

"He'd not have died quietly," Quire said, preoccupied now by the uncharitable fear that Lauder might empty his stomach, or faint, or otherwise complicate an already unpleasant situation.

He looked east and west along the Cowgate, then northwards up the gloomy length of Borthwick's Close. The Old Town's inhabitants were stirring from their dark tenements and gathering in silent huddles, distracted from the start of the day's business by this gruesome spectacle.

"I'll get some more men down here to help you," Quire muttered to Lauder. "Once they're here, you can start asking questions. See who heard what, and if anyone can put a name on him."

The younger man's scepticism was evident.

"Probably Irish. Cut loose once the canal was dug. Maybe he's working on that new bridge."

It was a lazy but not entirely foolish suggestion. The Old Town was full of Irish labourers bereft of labour, and Highlanders bereft of their high lands for that matter, all of them washed up here by the tides of ill fortune and poverty. More than a few had indeed found some escape from their poverty and lassitude in the building of the huge new bridge being thrown over the Cowgate, and to be named in honour of the king, George the Fourth.

But: "No," Quire said. "He's no navvy or builder."

He lifted the man's arm, turning it against the dead stiffness of the muscles to expose his palm.

"See his hand? No rougher than your own. He's not been digging earth or breaking rock. And his clothes ... might not have been a rich man, but he's no pauper either. He'll go in a pauper's grave, though, if we can't find him a name and a family. Don't want that, if we can help it. It's no way for a man to end his days."

The dead man's jacket had fallen open a little as Quire moved his arm. A flap of material there caught his eye now, and he reached gingerly in, felt the loose ends of torn stitching. He had to bend his weaker left hand at a sharp angle to do so, and felt a twinge of stiff pain in his forearm. His old wounds misliked the cold.

"Did you find anything in his pockets?" he asked.

"Nothing," Lauder grunted.

"Did you ask Shake if there was anything?"

Lauder shrugged, his cape shifting heavily. Standing watch over a corpse, on a cold dawn at the end of a long night, in the Cowgate where the city's police had no surfeit of friends ... these were not the ingredients of contentment. At the best of times, few of Quire's colleagues – the miserably paid nightwatchmen perhaps least of all – shared his notions of justice and dignity for the dead. Those things could be hard to find in the Old Town, even for the living. Easier not to try, sometimes.

"Just wait here until I get you some help," Quire said as he rose to his feet. "It'll not be long."

He began to ascend the stinking ravine of Borthwick's Close, pushing through the knot of onlookers that had gathered a short way up the alley.

"Anyone know him?" he asked as he went, but no one replied. They averted their eyes, on the whole. Only a child, holding the rough linen of his mother's skirt with one tight hand, yesterday's dirt still smudged over his cheeks, met Quire's gaze fully. The boy parted his lips in an unappealing grin, and sucked air in through the corners of his mouth. It was an idiot sort of sound.

Quire was jostled as he made his way through the crowd, but no more than he would have expected. He was a big man, wide-shouldered and wide-chested, and he knew that his angular face, framed by dense, wiry hair, suggested ill humour more often than not. Though that appearance – enhanced by his grey greatcoat, the baton at his belt and the military boots he often wore out of ancient habit – deterred most troublemakers, no assembly in the Old Town was without one or two who thought themselves above such concerns. The place had a truculent state of mind.

Quire climbed up and up the close, careful on the rough and uneven cobbles, passing dozens of small windows, only a few of them lit by oil or candle or fire. He heard someone above him, leaning out from the third or fourth storey, hawk and spit; but when he looked, there was no one to be seen, just the man-made cliff faces blocking out the sky. The close narrowed as it rose towards the High Street – if he had extended both arms, Quire could have encompassed its whole width – before burrowing through the overarching body of a tenement to disgorge him on to the Old Town's great thoroughfare.

It was akin to emerging from the Stygian depths of some mal-odorous tunnel into another world: one filled with bustle and light and all the energy and breezes that the closes did not permit within their tight confines. Scores of people moved this way and that, avoiding the little mounds of horse dung that punctuated their paths, flowing around the hawkers and stall-holders ready-ing their wares, dodging the carts and carriages that clattered up the cobble-clad road. The air shivered to a cacophony of trade and greeting and argument.

Quire advanced no more than a pace or three before a salesman sought to snare him.

"A tonic of universal efficacy, sir," the man cried, with an excess of unsolicited enthusiasm. He swept up a small, neat glass bottle from his barrow and extended it towards Quire. "No affliction of the lung or liver can withstand its beneficial application."

Quire paused, and examined the dress of the man who thus accosted him. A short stovepipe hat, a neat and clean waistcoat tightly buttoned over a paunch of some substance. The loose cuffs of an expensive shirt protruding from the jacket sleeves. Clearly the uniform of one who made a tolerable profit from the ill health and gullibility of others.

The bottle Quire was invited to examine held a pale liquid of yellowish hue.

"Looks like piss."

"Oh no, sir. Not at all," exclaimed the affronted hawker, peering with a disbelieving frown at the flask in his hand. "A miraculous elixir, rather."

Quire leaned a touch closer, gave the tonic his full attention.

"Horse's piss," he concluded, and left the man, still protesting, in his wake.

The police house was very near, on the far side of the High Street at Old Stamp Office Close. Quire cut across the currents of humanity towards it. He refused a flyer advertising a course of phrenological lectures that someone tried to thrust into his hand; narrowly avoided a crushed toe as a handcart piled high with half-finished shoes ground past.

It was all a little too much for one who had already been awake for longer than he would have wished, and he entered the abode of Edinburgh's city police with a certain relief.

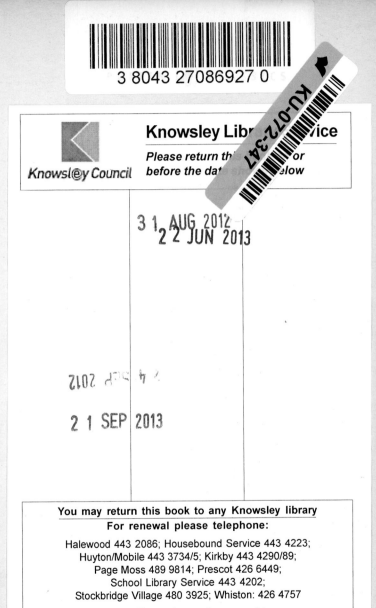

It is wonderful how quickly you get used to things, even the most astonishing. Five minutes before, the children had had no more idea than you that there was such a thing as a Sand-fairy in the world, and now they were talking to it as though they had known it all their lives.

E. NESBIT

Five Children and *It*

INTRODUCED BY
QUENTIN BLAKE

Illustrations by H. R. MILLAR

PUFFIN

PUFFIN BOOKS

Published by the Penguin Group
Penguin Books Ltd, 80 Strand, London WC2R ORL, England
Penguin Group (USA) Inc., 375 Hudson Street, New York, New York 10014, USA
Penguin Group (Canada), 90 Eglinton Avenue East, Suite 700, Toronto, Ontario, Canada M4P 2Y3
(a division of Pearson Penguin Canada Inc.)
Penguin Ireland, 25 St Stephen's Green, Dublin 2, Ireland (a division of Penguin Books Ltd)
Penguin Group (Australia), 250 Camberwell Road, Camberwell, Victoria 3124, Australia
(a division of Pearson Australia Group Pty Ltd)
Penguin Books India Pvt Ltd, 11 Community Centre, Panchsheel Park, New Delhi – 110 017, India
Penguin Group (NZ), 67 Apollo Drive, Rosedale, North Shore 0632, New Zealand
(a division of Pearson New Zealand Ltd)
Penguin Books (South Africa) (Pty) Ltd, 24 Sturdee Avenue, Rosebank, Johannesburg 2196, South Africa

Penguin Books Ltd, Registered Offices: 80 Strand, London WC2R ORL, England

puffinbooks.com

First published by T. Fisher Unwin 1902
First published in Puffin Books 1959
Reissued in this edition 2008
9

Introduction copyright © Quentin Blake, 2008159
Endnotes copyright © Penguin Books, 2008
All rights reserved

Set in Minion by Palimpsest Book Production Limited, Grangemouth, Stirlingshire
Printed in Great Britain by Clays Ltd, St Ives plc

British Library Cataloguing in Publication Data
A CIP catalogue record for this book is available from the British Library

ISBN: 978-0-141-32161-5

www.greenpenguin.co.uk

MIX
Paper from
responsible sources
FSC
www.fsc.org   FSC™ C018179

Penguin Books is committed to a sustainable
future for our business, our readers and our
planet. This book is made from paper certified
by the Forest Stewardship Council.

INTRODUCTION BY
QUENTIN BLAKE

E. Nesbit was a woman: Edith Nesbit, or Mrs Hubert Bland. A hundred years or so ago, when she was writing (books for adults as well as children), she may have felt it was an advantage to use a name that made it sound as though you were a man. After all, it was a world largely run by men. She might also have thought that someone just called E. Nesbit might not expect you to be as extremely well-behaved as someone called Mrs Hubert Bland.

This is important because E. Nesbit belongs with those writers of children's books (you will easily think of others) who are successful because of their skills as *storytellers*. Indeed, she was one of the first. She *speaks* to the reader, and it's almost as though you can hear her voice. She doesn't mind making observations that could only come from an adult, but she respects her readers, and she is not *bossy* (even if she may have been sometimes in life). I suspect that the main purpose of many books written in the nineteenth century was to *improve* their young readers; with E. Nesbit, by contrast, you feel that she was eager to tell you something interesting and entertaining.

Five Children and It was first published in 1902, so that what children wore then, and the way they spoke, and what was expected of them, all that was rather different from life today. But because E. Nesbit is very good at describing the five children and we feel that we know them, it's no surprise to discover that they are largely based on her own family.

Some of E. Nesbit's books – such as *The Railway Children* – depend on her ability to remember what it is like being a child and to give a convincing account of a family of children in difficult circumstances. *Five Children and It* goes further by introducing the possibilities of fantasy. The idea of people making wishes, and how they may go wrong or turn out not to be what was expected, isn't a new one – it comes in folk tales and fairy tales. But when our storyteller had to supply a fairy to grant the wishes, she had the brilliant idea of inventing the Psammead (with its authentic-sounding Greek name), who is almost the opposite of what you would expect of a benevolent fairy. He's bizarre in appearance, really very like a temperamental and difficult adult; the children have to learn how to humour him and there's a sort of special zest in the wishes being granted *grudgingly*.

Once given the opportunity of wishes, E. Nesbit is very good at imagining remarkable things that might happen. Suppose . . . suppose we were as beautiful as the day; suppose we had wings; suppose our brother was huge; suppose . . . And, I can't help noticing that what I find additionally attractive is that, for instance, when they go back in time to some not-very-well-specified earlier period, it's in terms of the books *they* have read. It's almost as though they were imagining it all themselves.

To John Bland

My Lamb, you are so very small,
You have not learned to read at all.
Yet never a printed book withstands
The urgence of your dimpled hands.
So, though this book is for yourself,
Let mother keep it on the shelf
Till you can read. O days that pass,
That day will come too soon, alas!

Contents

1

Beautiful as the Day

The house was three miles from the station, but before the dusty hired fly had rattled along for five minutes the children began to put their heads out of the carriage window and to say, 'Aren't we nearly there?' And every time they passed a house, which was not very often, they all said, 'Oh, *is* this it?' But it never was, till they reached the very top of the hill, just past the chalk-quarry and before you come to the gravel-pit. And then there was a white house with a green garden and an orchard beyond, and mother said, 'Here we are!'

'How white the house is,' said Robert.

'And look at the roses,' said Anthea.

'And the plums,' said Jane.

'It is rather decent,' Cyril admitted.

The Baby said, 'Wanty go walky'; and the fly stopped with a last rattle and jolt.

Everyone got its legs kicked or its feet trodden on in the scramble to get out of the carriage that very minute, but no one seemed to mind. Mother, curiously enough, was in no hurry to get out; and even when she had come down slowly and by the step, and with no jump at all, she seemed to wish to see the boxes carried in, and even to pay the driver, instead of joining in that first glorious rush round the garden and the orchard and the thorny, thistly, briery, brambly wilderness beyond the broken gate and the dry fountain at the side of the house. But the children were wiser, for once. It was not really a pretty house at all; it was quite ordinary, and mother thought it was rather inconvenient, and was quite annoyed at there being no shelves, to speak of, and hardly a cupboard in the place. Father used to say that the ironwork on the roof and coping was like an architect's nightmare. But the house was deep in the country, with no other house in sight, and the children had been in London for two years, without so much as once going to the seaside even for a day by an excursion train, and so the White House seemed to them a sort of Fairy Palace set down in an Earthly Paradise. For London is like prison for children, especially if their relations are not rich.

Of course there are the shops and the theatres, and Maskelyne and Cook's, and things, but if your people are rather poor you don't get taken to the theatres, and you can't buy things out of the shops; and London has none of those nice things that children may play with without hurting the things or themselves – such as trees and sand and woods and waters. And nearly everything in London is the wrong sort of shape – all straight lines and flat streets, instead of being all sorts of odd shapes, like things are in the country. Trees are all different, as you know, and I am sure some tiresome person must have told you that there are no two blades of grass exactly alike. But in streets, where the blades of grass don't grow, everything is like everything else. This is why so many children who live in towns are so extremely naughty. They do not know what is the matter with them, and no more do their fathers and mothers, aunts, uncles, cousins, tutors, governesses, and nurses; but I know. And so do you now. Children in the country are naughty sometimes too, but that is for quite different reasons.

The children had explored the gardens and the out-houses thoroughly before they were caught and cleaned for tea, and they saw quite well that they were certain to be happy at the White House. They thought so from the first moment, but when they found the back of the house covered with jasmine, all in white flower, and smelling like a bottle of the most expensive scent that is ever given for a birthday present; and when they had seen the lawn, all green and smooth, and quite different from the brown grass in the gardens at Camden Town; and when they had found the stable with a loft over it and some old hay still left, they were almost certain; and when Robert had found the broken swing and tumbled out of it and got a lump on his head the size of an egg, and Cyril had nipped his finger in the door of a hutch that seemed made to keep rabbits in, if you ever had any, they had no longer any doubts whatever.

The best part of it all was that there were no rules about not going to places and not doing things. In London almost everything is labelled 'You mustn't touch,' and though the label is invisible, it's just as bad, because you know it's there, or if you don't you jolly soon get told.

The White House was on the edge of a hill, with a wood behind it – and the chalk-quarry on one side and the gravel-pit on the other. Down at the bottom of the hill was a level plain, with queer-shaped white buildings where people burnt lime, and a big red brewery and other houses; and when the big chimneys were smoking and the sun was setting, the valley looked as if it was filled with golden mist, and the limekilns and oasthouses glimmered and glittered till they were like an enchanted city out of the *Arabian Nights*.

Now that I have begun to tell you about the place, I feel that I could go on and make this into a most interesting story about all the ordinary things that the children did – just the kind of things you do yourself, you know – and you would believe every word of it; and when I told about the children's being tiresome, as you are sometimes, your aunts would perhaps write in the margin of the story with a pencil, 'How true!' or 'How like life!' and you would see it and very likely be annoyed. So I will only tell you the really astonishing things that happened, and you may leave the book about quite safely, for no aunts and uncles either are likely to write 'How true!' on the edge of the story. Grown-up people find it very difficult to believe really wonderful things, unless they have what they call proof. But children will believe almost anything, and grown-ups know this. That is why they tell you that the earth is round like an orange, when you can see perfectly well that it is flat and lumpy; and why they say that the earth goes round the sun, when you can see for yourself any day that the sun gets up in the morning and goes to bed at night like a good sun as it is, and the earth knows its place, and lies as still as a mouse. Yet I daresay you believe all that about the earth and the sun, and if so you will find it quite easy to believe that before Anthea and Cyril and the others had been a week in the country they had found a fairy. At least they called it that, because that was what it called itself; and of course it knew best, but it was not at all like any fairy you ever saw or heard of or read about.

It was at the gravel-pits. Father had to go away suddenly on business, and mother had gone away to stay with Granny, who was not very well. They both went in a great hurry, and when they were gone the house seemed dreadfully quiet and empty, and the children wandered from one room to another and looked at the bits of paper and string on the floors left over from the packing, and not yet cleared up, and wished they had something to do. It was Cyril who said:

'I say, let's take our Margate spades and go and dig in the gravel-pits. We can pretend it's seaside.'

'Father said it was once,' Anthea said; 'he says there are shells there thousands of years old.'

So they went. Of course they had been to the edge of the gravel-pit and looked over, but they had not gone down into it for fear father should say they mustn't play there, and the same with the chalk-quarry. The gravel-pit is not really dangerous if you don't try to climb down the edges, but go the slow safe way round by the road, as if you were a cart.

Each of the children carried its own spade, and took it in turns to carry the Lamb. He was the baby, and they called him that because 'Baa' was the first thing he ever said. They called Anthea 'Panther', which seems silly when you read it, but when you say it it sounds a little like her name.

The gravel-pit is very large and wide, with grass growing round the edges at the top, and dry stringy wildflowers, purple and yellow. It is like a giant's wash-hand basin. And there are mounds of gravel, and holes in the sides of the basin where gravel has been taken out, and high up in the steep sides there are the little holes that are the little front doors of the little sand-martins' little houses.

The children built a castle, of course, but castle-building is rather poor fun when you have no hope of the swishing tide ever coming in to fill up the moat and wash away the drawbridge, and, at the happy last, to wet everybody up to the waist at least.

Cyril wanted to dig out a cave to play smugglers in, but the others thought it might bury them alive, so it ended in all spades going to work to dig a hole through the castle to Australia. These children, you see, believed that the world was round, and that on the other side the little Australian boys and girls were really walking wrong way up, like flies on the ceiling, with their heads hanging down into the air.

The children dug and they dug and they dug, and their hands got sandy and hot and red, and their faces got damp and shiny. The Lamb had tried to eat the sand, and had cried so hard when he found that it was not, as he had supposed, brown sugar, that he was now tired out, and was lying asleep in a warm fat bunch in the middle of the half-finished castle. This left his brothers and sisters free to work really hard, and the hole that was to come out in Australia soon grew so deep that Jane, who was called 'Pussy' for short, begged the others to stop.

'Suppose the bottom of the hole gave way suddenly,' she said, 'and you tumbled out among the little Australians, all the sand would get in their eyes.'

'Yes,' said Robert; 'and they would hate us, and throw

stones at us, and not let us see the kangaroos, or opossums, or blue-gums, or Emu Brand birds, or anything.'

Cyril and Anthea knew that Australia was not quite so near as all that, but they agreed to stop using the spades and go on with their hands. This was quite easy, because the sand at the bottom of the hole was very soft and fine and dry, like sea-sand. And there were little shells in it.

'Fancy it having been wet sea here once, all sloppy and shiny,' said Jane, 'with fishes and conger-eels and coral and mermaids.'

'And masts of ships and wrecked Spanish treasure. I wish we could find a gold doubloon, or something,' Cyril said.

'How did the sea get carried away?' Robert asked.

'Not in a pail, silly,' said his brother. 'Father says the earth got too hot underneath, like you do in bed sometimes, so it just hunched up its shoulders, and the sea had to slip off, like the blankets do off us, and the shoulder was left sticking out, and turned into dry land. Let's go and look for shells; I think that little cave looks likely, and I see something sticking out there like a bit of wrecked ship's anchor, and it's beastly hot in the Australian hole.'

The others agreed, but Anthea went on digging. She always liked to finish a thing when she had once begun it. She felt it would be a disgrace to leave that hole without getting through to Australia.

The cave was disappointing, because there were no shells, and the wrecked ship's anchor turned out to be only the broken end of a pickaxe handle, and the cave party were just making up their minds that the sand makes you thirstier when it is not by the seaside, and someone had suggested going home for lemonade, when Anthea suddenly screamed:

'Cyril! Come here! Oh, come quick! It's alive! It'll get away! Quick!'

They all hurried back.

'It's a rat, I shouldn't wonder,' said Robert. 'Father says they infest old places – and this must be pretty old if the sea was here thousands of years ago.'

'Perhaps it is a snake,' said Jane, shuddering.

'Let's look,' said Cyril, jumping into the hole. 'I'm not afraid of snakes. I like them. If it is a snake I'll tame it, and it will follow me everywhere, and I'll let it sleep round my neck at night.'

'No, you won't,' said Robert firmly. He shared Cyril's bedroom. 'But you may if it's a rat.'

'Oh, don't be silly!' said Anthea; 'it's not a rat, it's *much* bigger. And it's not a snake. It's got feet; I saw them; and fur! No – not the spade. You'll hurt it! Dig with your hands.'

'And let *it* hurt *me* instead! That's so likely, isn't it?' said Cyril, seizing a spade.

'Oh, don't!' said Anthea. 'Squirrel, *don't*. I – it sounds silly, but it said something. It really and truly did.'

9

'What?'

'It said, "You let me alone." '

But Cyril merely observed that his sister must have gone off her nut, and he and Robert dug with spades while Anthea sat on the edge of the hole, jumping up and down with hotness and anxiety. They dug carefully, and presently everyone could see that there really was something moving in the bottom of the Australian hole.

Then Anthea cried out, '*I'm* not afraid. Let me dig,' and fell on her knees and began to scratch like a dog does when he has suddenly remembered where it was that he buried his bone.

'Oh, I felt fur,' she cried, half laughing and half crying. 'I did indeed! I did!' when suddenly a dry husky voice in the sand made them all jump back, and their hearts jumped nearly as fast as they did.

'Let me alone,' it said. And now everyone heard the voice and looked at the others to see if they had too.

'But we want to see you,' said Robert bravely.

'I wish you'd come out,' said Anthea, also taking courage.

'Oh, well – if that's your wish,' the voice said, and the sand stirred and spun and scattered, and something brown and furry and fat came rolling out into the hole and the sand fell off it, and it sat there yawning and rubbing the ends of its eyes with its hands.

'I believe I must have dropped asleep,' it said, stretching itself.

The children stood round the hole in a ring, looking at the creature they had found. It was worth looking at. Its eyes were on long horns like a snail's eyes, and it could move them in and out like telescopes; it had ears like a bat's ears, and its tubby body was shaped like a spider's and covered with thick soft fur; its legs and arms were furry too, and it had hands and feet like a monkey's.

'What on earth is it?' Jane said. 'Shall we take it home?'

The thing turned its long eyes to look at her, and said: 'Does she always talk nonsense, or is it only the rubbish on her head that makes her silly?'

It looked scornfully at Jane's hat as it spoke.

'She doesn't mean to be silly,' Anthea said gently; 'we none of us do, whatever you may think! Don't be frightened; we don't want to hurt you, you know.'

'Hurt *me!*' it said. '*Me* frightened? Upon my word! Why, you talk as if I were nobody in particular.' All its fur stood out like a cat's when it is going to fight.

'Well,' said Anthea, still kindly, 'perhaps if we knew who you are in particular we could think of something to say that wouldn't make you cross. Everything we've said so far seems to have. Who are you? And don't get angry! Because really we don't know.'

'You don't know?' it said. 'Well, I knew the world had changed – but – well, really – do you mean to tell me

seriously you don't know a Psammead when you see one?'

'A Sammyadd? That's Greek to me.'

'So it is to everyone,' said the creature sharply. 'Well, in plain English, then, a *Sand-fairy*. Don't you know a Sand-fairy when you see one?'

It looked so grieved and hurt that Jane hastened to say,

'Of course I see you are, *now*. It's quite plain now one comes to look at you.'

'You came to look at me, several sentences ago,' it said crossly, beginning to curl up again in the sand.

'Oh – don't go away again! Do talk some more,' Robert cried. 'I didn't know you were a Sand-fairy, but I knew directly I saw you that you were much the wonderfullest thing I'd ever seen.'

The Sand-fairy seemed a shade less disagreeable after this.

'It isn't talking I mind,' it said, 'as long as you're reasonably civil. But I'm not going to make polite conversation for you. If you talk nicely to me, perhaps I'll answer you, and perhaps I won't. Now say something.'

Of course no one could think of anything to say, but at last Robert thought of 'How long have you lived here?' and he said it at once.

'Oh, ages – several thousand years,' replied the Psammead.

'Tell us all about it. Do.'

'It's all in books.'

'*You* aren't!' Jane said. 'Oh, tell us everything you can about yourself! We don't know anything about you, and you *are* so nice.'

The Sand-fairy smoothed his long rat-like whiskers and smiled between them.

'Do please tell!' said the children all together.

It is wonderful how quickly you get used to things,

even the most astonishing. Five minutes before, the children had had no more idea than you that there was such a thing as a Sand-fairy in the world, and now they were talking to it as though they had known it all their lives.

It drew its eyes in and said:

'How very sunny it is – quite like old times. Where do you get your Megatheriums from now?'

'What?' said the children all at once. It is very difficult always to remember that 'what' is not polite, especially in moments of surprise or agitation.

'Are Pterodactyls plentiful now?' the Sand-fairy went on.

The children were unable to reply.

'What do you have for breakfast?' the Fairy said impatiently, 'and who gives it you?'

'Eggs and bacon, and bread-and-milk, and porridge and things. Mother gives it us. What are Mega-what's-its-names and Ptero-what-do-you-call-thems? And does anyone have them for breakfast?'

'Why, almost everyone had Pterodactyl for breakfast in my time! Pterodactyls were something like crocodiles and something like birds – I believe they were very good grilled. You see it was like this: of course there were heaps of sand-fairies then, and in the morning early you went out and hunted for them, and when you'd found one it gave you your wish. People used to send their little boys down to the seashore early in the morning before breakfast to get the day's wishes, and very often the eldest boy in the family would be told to wish for a Megatherium, ready jointed for cooking. It was as big as an elephant, you see, so there was a good deal of meat on it. And if they wanted fish, the Ichthyosaurus was asked for – he was twenty to forty feet long, so there was plenty of him. And for poultry there was the Plesiosaurus; there were nice pickings on that too. Then the other children could wish for other things. But when people had dinner-parties it was nearly always Megatheriums; and Ichthyosaurus, because his fins were a great delicacy and his tail made soup.'

'There must have been heaps and heaps of cold meat left over,' said Anthea, who meant to be a good housekeeper some day.

'Oh no,' said the Psammead, 'that would never have done. Why, of course at sunset what was left over turned into stone. You find the stone bones of the Megatherium and things all over the place even now, they tell me.'

'Who tell you?' asked Cyril; but the Sand-fairy frowned and began to dig very fast with its furry hands.

'Oh, don't go!' they all cried; 'tell us more about it when it was Megatheriums for breakfast! Was the world like this then?'

It stopped digging.

'Not a bit,' it said; 'it was nearly all sand where I lived, and coal grew on trees, and the periwinkles were as big as tea-trays – you find them now; they're turned into stone. We Sand-fairies used to live on the seashore, and the children used to come with their little flint-spades and flint-pails and make castles for us to live in. That's thousands of years ago, but I hear that children still build castles on the sand. It's difficult to break yourself of a habit.'

'But why did you stop living in the castles?' asked Robert.

'It's a sad story,' said the Psammead gloomily. 'It was because they *would* build moats to the castles, and the nasty wet bubbling sea used to come in, and of course as soon as a Sand-fairy got wet it caught cold, and generally died. And so there got to be fewer and fewer, and, whenever you found a fairy and had a wish, you used to wish for a Megatherium, and eat twice as much as you wanted, because it might be weeks before you got another wish.'

'And did *you* get wet?' Robert inquired.

The Sand-fairy shuddered. 'Only once,' it said; 'the end of the twelfth hair of my top left whisker – I feel the place still in damp weather. It was only once, but it was quite enough for me. I went away as soon as the sun had dried my poor dear whisker. I scurried away to the back of the beach, and dug myself a house deep in warm dry sand, and there I've been ever since. And the sea changed its lodgings afterwards. And now I'm not going to tell you another thing.'

'Just one more, please,' said the children. 'Can you give wishes now?'

'Of course,' said it; 'didn't I give you yours a few minutes ago? You said, "I wish you'd come out," and I did.'

'Oh, please, mayn't we have another?'

'Yes, but be quick about it. I'm tired of you.'

I daresay you have often thought what you would do if you had three wishes given you, and have despised the old man and his wife in the black-pudding story, and felt certain that if you had the chance you could think of three really useful wishes without a moment's hesitation. These children had often talked this matter over, but, now the chance had suddenly come to them, they could not make up their minds.

'Quick,' said the Sand-fairy crossly. No one could think of anything, only Anthea did manage to remember a private wish of her own and Jane's which they had never told the boys. She knew the boys would not care about it – but still it was better than nothing.

'I wish we were all as beautiful as the day,' she said in a great hurry.

The children looked at each other, but each could see that the others were not any better-looking than usual. The Psammead pushed out its long eyes, and seemed to be holding its breath and swelling itself out till it was twice as fat and furry as before. Suddenly it let its breath go in a long sigh.

'I'm really afraid I can't manage it,' it said apologetically; 'I must be out of practice.'

The children were horribly disappointed.

'Oh, *do* try again!' they said.

'Well,' said the Sand-fairy, 'the fact is, I was keeping back a little strength to give the rest of you your wishes with. If you'll be contented with one wish a day amongst the lot of you I daresay I can screw myself up to it. Do you agree to that?'

'Yes, oh yes!' said Jane and Anthea. The boys nodded. They did not believe the Sand-fairy could do it. You can always make girls believe things much easier than you can boys.

It stretched out its eyes farther than ever, and swelled and swelled and swelled.

'I do hope it won't hurt itself,' said Anthea.

'Or crack its skin,' Robert said anxiously.

Everyone was very much relieved when the Sand-fairy, after getting so big that it almost filled up the hole in the sand, suddenly let out its breath and went back to its proper size.

'That's all right,' it said, panting heavily. 'It'll come easier tomorrow.'

'Did it hurt much?' asked Anthea.

'Only my poor whisker, thank you,' said he, 'but you're a kind and thoughtful child. Good day.'

It scratched suddenly and fiercely with its hands and

feet, and disappeared in the sand. Then the children looked at each other, and each child suddenly found itself alone with three perfect strangers, all radiantly beautiful.

They stood for some moments in perfect silence. Each thought that its brothers and sisters had wandered off, and that these strange children had stolen up unnoticed while it was watching the swelling form of the Sand-fairy. Anthea spoke first –

'Excuse me,' she said very politely to Jane, who now had enormous blue eyes and a cloud of russet hair, 'but have you seen two little boys and a little girl anywhere about?'

'I was just going to ask you that,' said Jane. And then Cyril cried:

'Why, it's *you*! I know the hole in your pinafore! You *are* Jane, aren't you? And you're the Panther; I can see your dirty handkerchief that you forgot to change after you'd cut your thumb! Crikey! The wish has come off, after all. I say, am I as handsome as you are?'

'If you're Cyril, I liked you much better as you were before,' said Anthea decidedly. 'You look like the picture of the young chorister, with your golden hair; you'll die young, I shouldn't wonder. And if that's Robert, he's like an Italian organ-grinder. His hair's all black.'

'You two girls are like Christmas cards, then – that's all – silly Christmas cards,' said Robert angrily. 'And Jane's hair is simply carrots.'

It was indeed of that Venetian tint so much admired by artists.

'Well, it's no use finding fault with each other,' said Anthea; 'let's get the Lamb and lug it home to dinner. The servants will admire us most awfully, you'll see.'

Baby was just waking when they got to him, and not one of the children but was relieved to find that he at least was not as beautiful as the day, but just the same as usual.

'I suppose he's too young to have wishes naturally,' said Jane. 'We shall have to mention him specially next time.'

Anthea ran forward and held out her arms.

'Come to own Panther, ducky,' she said.

The Baby looked at her disapprovingly, and put a sandy pink thumb in his mouth. Anthea was his favourite sister.

'Come, then,' she said.

'G'way long!' said the Baby.

'Come, to own Pussy,' said Jane.

'Wants my Panty,' said the Lamb dismally, and his lip trembled.

'Here, come on, Veteran,' said Robert, 'come and have a yidey on Yobby's back.'

'Yah, narky narky boy,' howled the Baby, giving way altogether. Then the children knew the worst. *The Baby did not know them!*

They looked at each other in despair, and it was terrible to each, in this dire emergency, to meet only the beautiful eyes of perfect strangers, instead of the merry, friendly, commonplace, twinkling, jolly little eyes of its own brothers and sisters.

'This is most truly awful,' said Cyril when he had tried to lift up the Lamb, and the Lamb had scratched like a cat and bellowed like a bull. 'We've got to *make friends* with him! I can't carry him home screaming like that. Fancy having to make friends with our own Baby! – it's too silly.'

That, however, was exactly what they had to do. It took over an hour, and the task was not rendered any easier by the fact that the Lamb was by this time as hungry as a lion and as thirsty as a desert.

At last he consented to allow these strangers to carry him home by turns, but as he refused to hold on to such new acquaintances he was a dead weight and most exhausting.

'Thank goodness, we're home!' said Jane, staggering through the iron gate to where Martha, the nursemaid, stood at the front door shading her eyes with her hand and looking out anxiously. 'Here! Do take Baby!'

Martha snatched the Baby from her arms.

'Thanks be, *he*'s safe back,' she said. 'Where are the others, and whoever to goodness gracious are all of you?'

'We're *us*, of course,' said Robert.

'And who's *us*, when you're at home?' asked Martha scornfully.

'I tell you it's *us*, only we're beautiful as the day,' said

Cyril. 'I'm Cyril, and these are the others, and we're jolly hungry. Let us in, and don't be a silly idiot.'

Martha merely dratted Cyril's impudence and tried to shut the door in his face.

'I know we *look* different, but I'm Anthea, and we're so tired, and it's long past dinner-time.'

'Then go home to your dinners, whoever you are; and if our children put you up to this play-acting you can tell them from me they'll catch it, so they know what to expect!' With that she did bang the door. Cyril rang the bell violently. No answer. Presently cook put her head out of a bedroom window and said:

'If you don't take yourselves off, and that precious sharp, I'll go and fetch the police.' And she slammed down the window.

'It's no good,' said Anthea. 'Oh, do, do come away before we get sent to prison!'

The boys said it was nonsense, and the law of England couldn't put you in prison for just being as beautiful as the day, but all the same they followed the others out into the lane.

'We shall be our proper selves after sunset, I suppose,' said Jane.

'I don't know,' Cyril said sadly; 'it mayn't be like that now – things have changed a good deal since Megatherium times.'

'Oh,' cried Anthea suddenly, 'perhaps we shall turn into

stone at sunset, like the Megatheriums did, so that there mayn't be any of us left over for the next day.'

She began to cry, so did Jane. Even the boys turned pale. No one had the heart to say anything.

It was a horrible afternoon. There was no house near where the children could beg a crust of bread or even a glass of water. They were afraid to go to the village, because they had seen Martha go down there with a basket, and there was a local constable. True, they were all as beautiful as the day, but that is a poor comfort when you are as hungry as a hunter and as thirsty as a sponge.

Three times they tried in vain to get the servants in the White House to let them in and listen to their tale. And then Robert went alone, hoping to be able to climb in at one of the back windows and so open the door to the others. But all the windows were out of reach, and Martha emptied a toilet-jug of cold water over him from a top window, and said:

'Go along with you, you nasty little Eyetalian monkey.'

It came at last to their sitting down in a row under the hedge, with their feet in a dry ditch, waiting for sunset, and wondering whether, when the sun *did* set, they would turn into stone, or only into their own old natural selves; and each of them still felt lonely and among strangers, and tried not to look at the others, for, though their voices were their own, their faces were so radiantly beautiful as to be quite irritating to look at.

'I don't believe we *shall* turn to stone,' said Robert, breaking a long miserable silence, 'because the Sand-fairy said he'd give us another wish tomorrow, and he couldn't if we were stone, could he?'

The others said 'No,' but they weren't at all comforted.

Another silence, longer and more miserable, was broken by Cyril's suddenly saying, 'I don't want to frighten you girls, but I believe it's beginning with me already. My foot's quite dead. I'm turning to stone, I know I am, and so will you in a minute.'

'Never mind,' said Robert kindly, 'perhaps you'll be the only stone one, and the rest of us will be all right, and we'll cherish your statue and hang garlands on it.'

But when it turned out that Cyril's foot had only gone to sleep through his sitting too long with it under him, and when it came to life in an agony of pins and needles, the others were quite cross.

'Giving us such a fright for nothing!' said Anthea.

The third and miserablest silence of all was broken by Jane. She said: 'If we *do* come out of this all right, we'll ask the Sammyadd to make it so that the servants don't notice anything different, no matter what wishes we have.'

The others only grunted. They were too wretched even to make good resolutions.

At last hunger and fright and crossness and tiredness – four very nasty things – all joined together to bring one nice thing, and that was sleep. The children lay asleep in a row, with their beautiful eyes shut and their beautiful mouths open. Anthea woke first. The sun had set, and the twilight was coming on.

Anthea pinched herself very hard, to make sure, and when she found she could still feel pinching she decided that she was not stone, and then she pinched the others. They, also, were soft.

'Wake up,' she said, almost in tears of joy; 'it's all right, we're not stone. And oh, Cyril, how nice and ugly you do look, with your old freckles and your brown hair and your little eyes. And so do you all!' she added, so that they might not feel jealous.

When they got home they were very much scolded by Martha, who told them about the strange children.

'A good-looking lot, I must say, but that impudent.'

'I know,' said Robert, who knew by experience how hopeless it would be to try to explain things to Martha.

'And where on earth have you been all this time, you naughty little things, you?'

'In the lane.'

'Why didn't you come home hours ago?'

'We couldn't because of *them*,' said Anthea.

'Who?'

'The children who were as beautiful as the day. They kept us there till after sunset. We couldn't come back till they'd gone. You don't know how we hated them! Oh, do, do give us some supper – we are so hungry.'

'Hungry! I should think so,' said Martha angrily; 'out all day like this. Well, I hope it'll be a lesson to you not to go picking up with strange children – down here after measles, as likely as not! Now mind, if you see them again, don't you speak to them – not one word nor so much as a look – but come straight away and tell me. I'll spoil their beauty for them!'

'If ever we *do* see them again we'll tell you,' Anthea said; and Robert, fixing his eyes fondly on the cold beef that was being brought in on a tray by cook, added in heartfelt undertones –

'And we'll take jolly good care we never *do* see them again.'

And they never have.

2

Golden Guineas

Anthea woke in the morning from a very real sort of dream, in which she was walking in the Zoological Gardens on a pouring wet day without any umbrella. The animals seemed desperately unhappy because of the rain, and were all growling gloomily. When she awoke, both the growling and the rain went on just the same. The growling was the heavy regular breathing of her sister Jane, who had a slight cold and was still asleep. The rain fell in slow drops on to Anthea's face from the wet corner of a bath-towel which her brother Robert was gently squeezing the water out of, to wake her up, as he now explained.

'Oh, drop it!' she said rather crossly; so he did, for he was not a brutal brother, though very ingenious in apple-pie beds, booby-traps, original methods of awakening sleeping relatives, and the other little accomplishments which make home happy.

'I had such a funny dream,' Anthea began.

'So did I,' said Jane, wakening suddenly and without

warning. 'I dreamed we found a Sand-fairy in the gravel-pits, and it said it was a Sammyadd, and we might have a new wish every day, and –'

'But that's what *I* dreamed,' said Robert. 'I was just going to tell you – and we had the first wish directly it said so. And I dreamed you girls were donkeys enough to ask for us all to be beautiful as the day, and we jolly well were, and it was perfectly beastly.'

'But *can* different people all dream the same thing?' said Anthea, sitting up in bed, 'because I dreamed all that as well as about the Zoo and the rain; and Baby didn't know us in my dream, and the servants shut us out of the house because the radiantness of our beauty was such a complete disguise, and –'

The voice of the eldest brother sounded from across the landing.

'Come on, Robert,' it said, 'you'll be late for breakfast again – unless you mean to shirk your bath like you did on Tuesday.'

'I say, come here a sec,' Robert replied. 'I didn't shirk it; I had it after brekker in father's dressing-room, because ours was emptied away.'

Cyril appeared in the doorway, partially clothed.

'Look here,' said Anthea, 'we've all had such an odd dream. We've all dreamed we found a Sand-fairy.'

Her voice died away before Cyril's contemptuous glance. 'Dream?' he said, 'you little sillies, it's *true*. I tell you it all happened. That's why I'm so keen on being down early. We'll go up there directly after brekker, and have another wish. Only we'll make up our minds, solid before we go, what it is we do want, and no one must ask for anything unless the others agree first. No more peerless beauties for this child, thank you. Not if I know it!'

The other three dressed, with their mouths open. If all that dream about the Sand-fairy was real, this real dressing seemed very like a dream, the girls thought. Jane felt that Cyril was right, but Anthea was not sure, till after they had seen Martha and heard her full and plain reminders about their naughty conduct the day before. Then Anthea was sure. 'Because,' said she, 'servants never dream anything but the things in the *Dream-book*, like snakes and oysters and going to a wedding – that means a funeral, and snakes are a false female friend, and oysters are babies.'

'Talking of babies,' said Cyril, 'where's the Lamb?'

'Martha's going to take him to Rochester to see her cousins. Mother said she might. She's dressing him now,' said Jane, 'in his very best coat and hat. Bread-and-butter, please.'

'She seems to like taking him too,' said Robert in a tone of wonder.

'Servants *do* like taking babies to see their relations,' Cyril said. 'I've noticed it before – especially in their best things.'

'I expect they pretend they're their own babies, and that they're not servants at all, but married to noble dukes of high degree, and they say the babies are the little dukes and duchesses,' Jane suggested dreamily, taking more marmalade. 'I expect that's what Martha'll say to her cousin. She'll enjoy herself most frightfully.'

'She won't enjoy herself most frightfully carrying our infant duke to Rochester,' said Robert, 'not if she's anything like me – she won't.'

'Fancy walking to Rochester with the Lamb on your back! Oh, crikey!' said Cyril in full agreement.

'She's going by carrier,' said Jane. 'Let's see them off, then we shall have done a polite and kindly act, and we shall be quite sure we've got rid of them for the day.'

So they did.

Martha wore her Sunday dress of two shades of purple, so tight in the chest that it made her stoop, and her blue hat with the pink cornflowers and white ribbon. She had a yellow-lace collar with a green bow. And the Lamb had indeed his very best cream-coloured silk coat and hat. It was a smart party that the carrier's cart picked up at the Cross Roads. When its white tilt and red wheels had slowly vanished in a swirl of chalkdust –

'And now for the Sammyadd!' said Cyril, and off they went.

As they went they decided on the wish they would ask for. Although they were all in a great hurry they did not try to climb down the sides of the gravel-pit, but went round by the safe lower road, as if they had been carts. They had made a ring of stones round the place where the Sand-fairy had disappeared, so they easily found the spot. The sun was burning and bright, and the sky was deep blue – without a cloud. The sand was very hot to touch.

'Oh – suppose it was only a dream, after all,' Robert said as the boys uncovered their spades from the sandheap where they had buried them and began to dig.

'Suppose you were a sensible chap,' said Cyril; 'one's quite as likely as the other!'

'Suppose you kept a civil tongue in your head,' Robert snapped.

'Suppose we girls take a turn,' said Jane, laughing. 'You boys seem to be getting very warm.'

'Suppose you don't come shoving your silly oar in,' said Robert, who was now warm indeed.

'We won't,' said Anthea quickly. 'Robert dear, don't be so grumpy – we won't say a word, you shall be the one to speak to the Fairy and tell him what we've decided to wish for. You'll say it much better than we shall.'

'Suppose you drop being a little humbug,' said Robert, but not crossly. 'Look out – dig with your hands, now!'

So they did, and presently uncovered the spider-shaped brown hairy body, long arms and legs, bat's ears and snail's eyes of the Sand-fairy itself. Everyone drew a deep breath of satisfaction, for now of course it couldn't have been a dream.

The Psammead sat up and shook the sand out of its fur.

'How's your left whisker this morning?' said Anthea politely.

'Nothing to boast of,' said it, 'it had rather a restless night. But thank you for asking.'

'I say,' said Robert, 'do you feel up to giving wishes today, because we very much want an extra besides the regular one? The extra's a very little one,' he added reassuringly.

'Humph!' said the Sand-fairy. (If you read this story aloud, please pronounce 'humph' exactly as it is spelt, for that is how he said it.) 'Humph! Do you know, until I heard you being disagreeable to each other just over my head, and so loud too, I really quite thought I had dreamed you all. I do have very odd dreams sometimes.'

'Do you?' Jane hurried to say, so as to get away from the subject of disagreeableness. 'I wish,' she added politely, 'you'd tell us about your dreams – they must be awfully interesting.'

'Is that the day's wish?' said the Sand-fairy, yawning.

Cyril muttered something about 'just like a girl,' and the rest stood silent. If they said 'Yes,' then good-bye to the other wishes they had decided to ask for. If they said 'No,' it would be very rude, and they had all been taught manners, and had learned a little too, which is not at all

32

the same thing. A sigh of relief broke from all lips when the Sand-fairy said:

'If I do I shan't have strength to give you a second wish; not even good tempers, or common sense, or manners, or little things like that.'

'We don't want you to put yourself out at all about *these* things, we can manage them quite well ourselves,' said Cyril eagerly; while the others looked guiltily at each other, and wished the Fairy would not keep all on about good tempers, but give them one good rowing if it wanted to, and then have done with it.

'Well,' said the Psammead, putting out his long snail's eyes so suddenly that one of them nearly went into the round boy's eyes of Robert, 'let's have the little wish first.'

'We don't want the servants to notice the gifts you give us.'

'Are kind enough to give us,' said Anthea in a whisper.

'Are kind enough to give us, I mean,' said Robert.

The Fairy swelled himself out a bit, let his breath go, and said –

'I've done *that* for you – it was quite easy. People don't notice things much, anyway. What's the next wish?'

'We want,' said Robert slowly, 'to be rich beyond the dreams of something or other.'

'Avarice,' said Jane.

'So it is,' said the Fairy unexpectedly. 'But it won't do

33

you much good, that's one comfort,' it muttered to itself. 'Come – I can't go beyond dreams, you know! How much do you want, and will you have it in gold or notes?'

'Gold, please – and millions of it.'

'This gravel-pit full be enough?' said the Fairy in an off-hand manner.

'Oh *yes*!'

'Then get out before I begin, or you'll be buried alive in it.'

It made its skinny arms so long, and waved them so frighteningly, that the children ran as hard as they could towards the road by which carts used to come to the gravel-pits. Only Anthea had presence of mind enough to shout a timid 'Good-morning, I hope your whisker will be better tomorrow,' as she ran.

On the road they turned and looked back, and they had to shut their eyes, and open them very slowly, a little bit at a time, because the sight was too dazzling for their eyes to be able to bear it. It was something like trying to look at the sun at high noon on Midsummer Day. For the whole of the sand-pit was full, right up to the very top, with new shining gold pieces, and all the little sand-martins' little front doors were covered out of sight. Where the road for the carts wound into the gravel-pit the gold lay in heaps like stones lie by the roadside, and a great bank of shining gold shelved down from where it lay flat and smooth between the tall sides of the gravel-pit. And all the gleaming heap was minted gold. And on the sides and edges of these countless coins the midday sun shone and sparkled, and glowed and gleamed till the quarry looked like the mouth of a smelting furnace, or one of the fairy halls that you see sometimes in the sky at sunset.

The children stood with their mouths open, and no one said a word.

At last Robert stopped and picked up one of the loose coins from the edge of the heap by the cart-road; and looked at it. He looked on both sides. Then he said in a low voice, quite different to his own, 'It's not sovereigns.'

'It's gold, anyway,' said Cyril. And now they all began to talk at once. They all picked up the golden treasure by handfuls, and let it run through their fingers like water, and the chink it made as it fell was wonderful music. At first they quite forgot to think of spending the money, it was so nice to play with. Jane sat down between two heaps of gold and Robert began to bury her, as you bury your father in sand when you are at the seaside and he has gone to sleep on the beach with the newspaper over his face. But Jane was not half buried before she cried out, 'Oh, stop, it's too heavy! It hurts!'

Robert said 'Bosh!' and went on.

'Let me out, I tell you,' cried Jane, and was taken out, very white, and trembling a little.

'You've no idea what it's like,' said she; 'it's like stones on you – or like chains.'

'Look here,' Cyril said, 'if this is to do us any good, it's no good our staying gasping at it like this. Let's fill our pockets and go and buy things. Don't you forget, it won't last after sunset. I wish we'd asked the Sammyadd why things don't turn to stone. Perhaps this will. I'll tell you what, there's a pony and cart in the village.'

'Do you want to buy that?' asked Jane.

'No, silly – we'll *hire* it. And then we'll go to Rochester and buy heaps and heaps of things. Look here, let's each take as much as we can carry. But it's not sovereigns. They've got a man's head on one side and a thing like the

ace of spades on the other. Fill your pockets with it, I tell you, and come along. You can jaw as we go – if you *must* jaw.'

Cyril sat down and began to fill his pockets.

'You made fun of me for getting father to have nine pockets in my Norfolks,' said he, 'but now you see!'

They did. For when Cyril had filled his nine pockets

and his handkerchief and the space between himself and his shirt front with the gold coins, he had to stand up. But he staggered, and had to sit down again in a hurry.

'Throw out some of the cargo,' said Robert. 'You'll sink the ship, old chap. That comes of nine pockets.'

And Cyril had to.

Then they set off to walk to the village. It was more than a mile, and the road was very dusty indeed, and the sun seemed to get hotter and hotter, and the gold in their pockets got heavier and heavier.

It was Jane who said, 'I don't see how we're to spend it all. There must be thousands of pounds among the lot of us. I'm going to leave some of mine behind this stump in the hedge. And directly we get to the village we'll buy some biscuits; I know it's long past dinner-time.' She took out a handful or two of gold and hid it in the hollows of an old hornbeam. 'How round and yellow they are,' she said. 'Don't you wish they were ginger-bread nuts and we were going to eat them?'

'Well, they're not, and we're not,' said Cyril. 'Come on!'

But they came on heavily and wearily. Before they reached the village, more than one stump in the hedge concealed its little hoard of hidden treasure. Yet they reached the village with about twelve hundred guineas in their pockets. But in spite of this inside wealth they looked quite ordinary outside, and no one would have thought they could have more than a half-crown each at the outside. The haze of heat, the blue of the wood smoke, made a sort of dim misty cloud over the red roofs of the village. The four sat down heavily on the first bench they came to. It happened to be outside the Blue Boar Inn.

It was decided that Cyril should go into the Blue Boar and ask for ginger-beer, because, as Anthea said, 'It is not wrong for men to go into public houses, only for children. And Cyril is nearer to being a man than us, because he is the eldest.' So he went. The others sat in the sun and waited.

'Oh, hats, how hot it is!' said Robert. 'Dogs put their tongues out when they're hot; I wonder if it would cool us at all to put out ours?'

'We might try,' Jane said; and they all put their tongues out as far as ever they could go, so that it quite stretched their throats, but it only seemed to make them thirstier than ever, besides annoying everyone who went by. So they took their tongues in again, just as Cyril came back with the ginger-beer.

'I had to pay for it out of my own two-and-seven-pence, though, that I was going to buy rabbits with,' he said. 'They wouldn't change the gold. And when I pulled out a handful the man just laughed and said it was card-counters. And I got some sponge-cakes too, out of a glass jar on the bar-counter. And some biscuits with caraways in.'

The sponge-cakes were both soft and dry and the biscuits were dry too, and yet soft, which biscuits ought not to be. But the ginger-beer made up for everything.

'It's my turn now to try to buy something with the money,' Anthea said; 'I'm next eldest. Where is the pony-cart kept?'

It was at The Chequers, and Anthea went in the back way to the yard, because they all knew that little girls ought not to go into the bars of public-houses. She came out, as she herself said, 'pleased but not proud'.

'He'll be ready in a brace of shakes, he says,' she remarked, 'and he's to have one sovereign – or whatever it is – to drive us into Rochester and back, besides waiting there till we've got everything we want. I think I managed very well.'

'You think yourself jolly clever, I daresay,' said Cyril moodily. 'How did you do it?'

'I wasn't jolly clever enough to go taking handfuls of money out of my pocket, to make it seem cheap, anyway,' she retorted. 'I just found a young man doing something to a horse's leg with a sponge and a pail. And I held out one sovereign, and I said, "Do you know what this is?" He said, "No," and he'd call his father. And the old man came, and he said it was a spade guinea; and he said was it my own to do as I liked with, and I said "Yes"; and I asked about the pony-cart, and I said he could have the guinea if he'd drive us in to Rochester. And his name is S. Crispin. And he said, "Right oh".'

It was a new sensation to be driven in a smart ponytrap along pretty country roads; it was very pleasant too (which is not always the case with new sensations), quite apart from the beautiful plans of spending the money which each child made as they went along, silently of course and quite to itself, for they felt it would never have done to let the old innkeeper hear them talk in the affluent sort of way they were thinking. The old man put them down by the bridge at their request.

'If you were going to buy a carriage and horses, where would you go?' asked Cyril, as if he were only asking for the sake of something to say.

'Billy Peasemarsh, at the Saracen's Head,' said the old man promptly. 'Though all forbid I should recommend any man where it's a question of horses, no more than I'd take anybody else's recommending if I was a-buying one. But if your pa's thinking of a turnout of any sort, there ain't a straighter man in Rochester, nor a civiller spoken, than Billy, though I says it.'

'Thank you,' said Cyril. 'The Saracen's Head.'

And now the children began to see one of the laws of nature turn upside down and stand on its head like an acrobat. Any grown-up persons would tell you that money is hard to get and easy to spend. But the fairy money had been easy to get, and spending it was not only hard, it was almost impossible. The tradespeople of Rochester seemed to shrink, to a tradesperson, from the glittering fairy gold ('furrin money' they called it, for the most part). To begin with, Anthea, who had had the misfortune to sit on her hat earlier in the day, wished to buy another. She chose a very beautiful one, trimmed with pink roses and the blue breasts of peacocks. It was marked in the window, 'Paris Model, three guineas'.

'I'm glad,' she said, 'because, if it says guineas, it means guineas, and not sovereigns, which we haven't got.'

But when she took three of the spade guineas in her hand, which was by this time rather dirty owing to her not having put on gloves before going to the gravel-pit, the black-silk young lady in the shop looked very hard at her, and went and whispered something to an older and uglier lady, also in black silk, and then they gave her back the money and said it was not current coin.

'It's good money,' said Anthea, 'and it's my own.'

'I daresay,' said the lady, 'but it's not the kind of money that's fashionable now, and we don't care about taking it.'

'I believe they think we've stolen it,' said Anthea, rejoining the others in the street; 'if we had gloves they wouldn't think we were so dishonest. It's my hands being so dirty fills their minds with doubts.'

So they chose a humble shop, and the girls bought cotton gloves, the kind at sixpence three-farthings, but when they offered a guinea the woman looked at it through her spectacles and said she had no change; so the gloves had to be paid for out of Cyril's two-and-sevenpence that he meant to buy rabbits with, and so had the green imitation crocodile-skin purse at nine-pence-halfpenny which had been bought at the same time. They tried several more shops, the kinds where you buy toys and scent, and silk handkerchiefs and books, and fancy boxes of stationery, and photographs of objects of interest in the vicinity. But nobody cared to change a guinea that day in Rochester, and as they went from shop to shop they got dirtier and dirtier, and their hair got more and more untidy, and Jane slipped and fell down on a part of the road where a water-cart had just gone by. Also they got very hungry, but they found no one would give them anything to eat for their guineas. After trying two pastrycooks in vain, they became so hungry, perhaps from the smell of the cake in the shops, as Cyril suggested, that they formed a plan of campaign in whispers and carried it out in desperation. They marched into a third pastrycook's – Beale his name was – and before the people behind the counter could interfere each child had seized three new penny buns, clapped the three together between its dirty hands, and taken a big bite out of the triple sandwich. Then they stood at bay, with the twelve buns in their hands and their mouths very full indeed. The shocked pastrycook bounded round the corner.

'Here,' said Cyril, speaking as distinctly as he could, and holding out the guinea he got ready before entering the shop, 'pay yourself out of that.'

Mr Beale snatched the coin, bit it, and put it in his pocket.

'Off you go,' he said, brief and stern like the man in the song.

'But the change?' said Anthea, who had a saving mind.

'Change!' said the man. 'I'll change you! Hout you goes; and you may think yourselves lucky I don't send for the police to find out where you got it!'

In the Castle Gardens the millionaires finished the buns, and though the curranty softness of these were delicious, and acted like a charm in raising the spirits of the party, yet even the stoutest heart quailed at the thought of venturing to sound Mr Billy Peasemarsh at the Saracen's Head on the subject of a horse and carriage. The boys would have given up the idea, but Jane was always a hopeful child, and Anthea generally an obstinate one, and their earnestness prevailed.

The whole party, by this time indescribably dirty, therefore betook itself to the Saracen's Head. The yard-method of attack having been successful at The Chequers was tried again here. Mr Peasemarsh was in the yard, and Robert opened the business in these terms –

'They tell me you have a lot of horses and carriages to sell.' It had been agreed that Robert should be spokesman, because in books it is always the gentlemen who buy horses, and not ladies, and Cyril had had his go at the Blue Boar.

'They tell you true, young man,' said Mr Peasemarsh. He was a long lean man, with very blue eyes and a tight mouth and narrow lips.

'We should like to buy some, please,' said Robert politely.

'I daresay you would.'

'Will you show us a few, please? To choose from.'

'Who are you a-kiddin of?' inquired Mr Billy Peasemarsh. 'Was you sent here of a message?'

'I tell you,' said Robert, 'we want to buy some horses and carriages, and a man told us you were straight and civil spoken, but I shouldn't wonder if he was mistaken.'

'Upon my sacred!' said Mr Peasemarsh. 'Shall I trot the whole stable out for Your Honour's Worship to see? Or shall I send round to the Bishop's to see if he's a nag or two to dispose of?'

'Please do,' said Robert, 'if it's not too much trouble. It would be very kind of you.'

Mr Peasemarsh put his hands in his pockets and laughed, and they did not like the way he did it. Then he shouted, 'Willum!'

A stooping ostler appeared in a stable door.

'Here, Willum, come and look at this 'ere young dook! Wants to buy the whole stud, lock, stock, and bar'l. And ain't got tuppence in his pocket to bless hisself with, I'll go bail!'

Willum's eyes followed his master's pointing thumb with contemptuous interest.

'Do 'e, for sure?' he said.

But Robert spoke, though both the girls were now pulling at his jacket and begging him to 'come along'. He spoke, and he was very angry; he said:

'I'm not a young duke, and I never pretended to be. And as for tuppence – what do you call this?' And before the others could stop him he had pulled out two fat handfuls of shining guineas, and held them out for Mr Peasemarsh to look at. He did look. He snatched one up in his finger and thumb. He bit it, and Jane expected him to say, 'The best horse in my stables is at your service.' But the others knew better. Still it was a blow, even to the most desponding, when he said shortly:

'Willum, shut the yard doors,' and Willum grinned and went to shut them.

'Good-afternoon,' said Robert hastily; 'we shan't buy any of your horses now, whatever you say, and I hope it'll be a lesson to you.' He had seen a little side gate open, and was moving towards it as he spoke. But Billy Peasemarsh put himself in the way.

'Not so fast, you young off-scouring!' he said. 'Willum, fetch the pleece.'

Willum went. The children stood huddled together like frightened sheep, and Mr Peasemarsh spoke to them till the pleece arrived. He said many things. Among other things he said:

'Nice lot you are, aren't you, coming tempting honest men with your guineas!'

'They *are* our guineas,' said Cyril boldly.

'Oh, of course we don't know all about that, no more we don't – oh no – course not! And dragging little gells into it too. 'Ere – I'll let the gells go if you'll come along to the pleece quiet.'

'We won't be let go,' said Jane heroically; 'not without the boys. It's our money just as much as theirs, you wicked old man.'

'Where'd you get it, then?' said the man, softening

slightly, which was not at all what the boys expected when Jane began to call names.

Jane cast a silent glance of agony at the others.

'Lost your tongue, eh? Got it fast enough when it's for calling names with. Come, speak up! Where'd you get it?'

'Out of the gravel-pit,' said truthful Jane.

'Next article,' said the man.

'I tell you we did,' Jane said. 'There's a fairy there – all over brown fur – with ears like a bat's and eyes like a snail's, and he gives you a wish a day, and they all come true.'

'Touched in the head, eh?' said the man in a low voice, 'all the more shame to you boys dragging the poor afflicted child into your sinful burglaries.'

'She's not mad; it's true,' said Anthea; 'there is a fairy. If I ever see him again I'll wish for something for you; at least I would if vengeance wasn't wicked – so there!'

'Lor' lumme,' said Billy Peasemarsh, 'if there ain't another on 'em!'

And now Willum came back with a spiteful grin on his face, and at his back a policeman, with whom Mr Peasemarsh spoke long in a hoarse earnest whisper.

'I daresay you're right,' said the policeman at last. 'Anyway, I'll take 'em up on a charge of unlawful possession, pending inquiries. And the magistrate will deal with the case. Send the afflicted ones to a home, as likely as not, and the boys to a reformatory. Now then, come

along, youngsters! No use making a fuss. You bring the gells along, Mr Peasemarsh, sir, and I'll shepherd the boys.'

Speechless with rage and horror, the four children were driven along the streets of Rochester. Tears of anger and shame blinded them, so that when Robert ran right into a passer-by he did not recognize her till a well-known voice said, 'Well, if ever I did! Oh, Master Robert, whatever have you been a doing of now?' And another voice, quite as well known, said, 'Panty; want go own Panty!'

They had run into Martha and the Baby!

Martha behaved admirably. She refused to believe a word of the policeman's story, or of Mr Peasemarsh's either, even when they made Robert turn out his pockets in an archway and show the guineas.

'I don't see nothing,' she said. 'You've gone out of your senses, you two! There ain't any gold there – only the poor child's hands, all over crock and dirt, and like the very chimbley. Oh, that I should ever see the day!'

And the children thought this very noble of Martha, even if rather wicked, till they remembered how the Fairy had promised that the servants should never notice any of the fairy gifts. So of course Martha couldn't see the gold, and so was only speaking the truth, and that was quite right, of course, but not extra noble.

It was getting dusk when they reached the police-station. The policeman told his tale to an inspector, who

sat in a large bare room with a thing like a clumsy
nursery-fender at one end to put prisoners in. Robert
wondered whether it was a cell or a dock.

'Produce the coins, officer,' said the inspector.

'Turn out your pockets,' said the constable.

Cyril desperately plunged his hands in his pockets,

stood still a moment, and then began to laugh – an odd sort of laugh that hurt, and that felt much more like crying. His pockets were empty. So were the pockets of the others. For of course at sunset all the fairy gold had vanished away.

'Turn out your pockets, and stop that noise,' said the inspector.

Cyril turned out his pockets, every one of the nine which enriched his Norfolk suit. And every pocket was empty.

'Well!' said the inspector.

'I don't know how they done it – artful little beggars! They walked in front of me the 'ole way, so as for me to keep my eye on them and not to attract a crowd and obstruct the traffic.'

'It's very remarkable,' said the inspector, frowning.

'If you've quite done a-browbeating of the innocent children,' said Martha, 'I'll hire a private carriage and we'll drive home to their papa's mansion. You'll hear about this again, young man! – I told you they hadn't got any gold, when you were pretending to see it in their poor helpless hands. It's early in the day for a constable on duty not to be able to trust his own eyes. As to the other one, the less said the better; he keeps the Saracen's Head, and he knows best what his liquor's like.'

'Take them away, for goodness' sake,' said the inspector crossly. But as they left the police-station he said. 'Now then!' to the policeman and Mr Peasemarsh, and he said it twenty times as crossly as he had spoken to Martha.

Martha was as good as her word. She took them home in a very grand carriage, because the carrier's cart was gone, and, though she had stood by them so nobly with the police, she was so angry with them as soon as they were alone for 'traipsing into Rochester by themselves', that none of them dared to mention the old man with the pony-cart from the village who was waiting for them in Rochester. And so, after one day of boundless wealth, the children found themselves sent to bed in deep disgrace, and only enriched by two pairs of cotton gloves, dirty inside because of the state of the hands they had been put on to cover, an imitation crocodile-skin purse, and twelve penny buns, long since digested.

The thing that troubled them most was the fear that the old gentleman's guinea might have disappeared at sunset with all the rest, so they went down to the village next day to apologize for not meeting him in Rochester, and to *see*. They found him very friendly. The guinea had *not* disappeared, and he had bored a hole in it and hung it on his watch-chain. As for the guinea the baker took, the children felt they *could* not care whether it had vanished or not, which was not perhaps very honest, but on the other hand was not wholly unnatural. But afterwards this preyed on Anthea's mind, and at last she secretly sent twelve stamps by post to 'Mr Beale, Baker, Rochester'. Inside she wrote, 'To pay for the buns.' I hope the guinea did disappear, for that pastrycook was really not at all a nice man, and, besides, penny buns are seven for sixpence in all really respectable shops.

3

Being Wanted

The morning after the children had been the possessors of boundless wealth, and had been unable to buy anything really useful or enjoyable with it, except two pairs of cotton gloves, twelve penny buns, an imitation crocodile-skin purse, and a ride in a pony-cart, they awoke without any of the enthusiastic happiness which they had felt on the previous day when they remembered how they had had the luck to find a Psammead, or Sand-fairy; and to receive its promise to grant them a new wish every day. For now they had had two wishes, Beauty and Wealth, and neither had exactly made them happy. But the happening of strange things, even if they are not completely pleasant things, is more amusing than those times when nothing happens but meals, and they are not always completely pleasant, especially on the days when it is cold mutton or hash.

There was no chance of talking things over before breakfast, because everyone overslept itself, as it happened, and it needed a vigorous and determined struggle to get dressed so as to be only ten minutes late for breakfast. During this meal some efforts were made to deal with the question of the Psammead in an impartial spirit, but it is very difficult to discuss anything thoroughly and at the same time to attend faithfully to your baby brother's breakfast needs. The Baby was particularly lively that morning. He not only wriggled his body through the bar of his high chair, and hung by his head, choking and purple, but he collared a tablespoon with desperate suddenness, hit Cyril heavily on the head with it, and then cried because it was taken away from him. He put his fat fist in his bread-and-milk, and demanded 'nam', which was only allowed for tea. He sang, he put his feet on the table – he clamoured to 'go walky'. The conversation was something like this:

'Look here – about that Sand-fairy – Look out! – he'll have the milk over.'

Milk removed to a safe distance.

'Yes – about that Fairy – No, Lamb dear, give Panther the narky poon.'

Then Cyril tried. 'Nothing we've had yet has turned out – He nearly had the mustard that time!'

'I wonder whether we'd better wish – Hullo! – you've done it now, my boy!' And, in a flash of glass and pink baby-paws, the bowl of golden carp in the middle of the table rolled on its side, and poured a flood of mixed water and goldfish into the Baby's lap and into the laps of the others.

Everyone was almost as much upset as the goldfish: the Lamb only remaining calm. When the pool on the floor had been mopped up, and the leaping, gasping goldfish had been collected and put back in the water, the Baby was taken away to be entirely redressed by Martha, and most of the others had to change completely. The pinafores and jackets that had been bathed in goldfish-and-water were hung out to dry, and then it turned out that Jane must either mend the dress she had torn the day before or appear all day in her best petticoat. It was white and soft and frilly, and trimmed with lace, and very, very pretty, quite as pretty as a frock, if not more so. Only it was *not* a frock, and Martha's word was law. She wouldn't let Jane wear her best frock, and she refused to listen for a moment to Robert's suggestion that Jane should wear her best petticoat and call it a dress.

'It's not respectable,' she said. And when people say that, it's no use anyone's saying anything. You will find this out for yourselves some day.

So there was nothing for it but for Jane to mend her frock. The hole had been torn the day before when she happened to tumble down in the High Street of Rochester, just where a water-cart had passed on its silvery way. She had grazed her knee, and her stocking was much more than grazed, and her dress was cut by the same stone which had attended to the knee and the stocking. Of course the others were not such sneaks as to abandon a comrade in misfortune, so they all sat on the grass-plot round the sundial, and Jane darned away for dear life. The Lamb was still in the hands of Martha having its clothes changed, so conversation was possible.

Anthea and Robert timidly tried to conceal their inmost thought, which was that the Psammead was not to be trusted; but Cyril said:

'Speak out – say what you've got to say – I hate hinting, and "don't know", and sneakish ways like that.'

So then Robert said, as in honour bound: 'Sneak yourself – Anthea and me weren't so goldfishy as you two were, so we got changed quicker, and we've had time to think it over, and if you ask me –'

'I didn't ask you,' said Jane, biting off a needleful of thread as she had always been strictly forbidden to do.

'I don't care who asks or who doesn't,' said Robert, 'but Anthea and I think the Sammyadd is a spiteful brute. If it can give us our wishes I suppose it can give itself its own, and I feel almost sure it wishes every time that our wishes shan't do us any good. Let's let the tiresome beast alone, and just go and have a jolly good game of forts, on our own, in the chalk-quarry.'

(You will remember that the happily situated house where these children were spending their holidays lay between a chalk-quarry and a gravel-pit.)

Cyril and Jane were more hopeful – they generally were.

'I don't think the Sammyadd does it on purpose,' Cyril

said; 'and, after all, it *was* silly to wish for boundless wealth. Fifty pounds in two-shilling pieces would have been much more sensible. And wishing to be beautiful as the day was simply donkeyish. I don't want to be disagreeable, but it *was*. We must try to find a really useful wish, and wish it.'

Jane dropped her work and said:

'I think so too; it's too silly to have a chance like this and not use it. I never heard of anyone else outside a book who had such a chance; there must be simply heaps of things we could wish for that wouldn't turn out Dead Sea fish, like these two things have. Do let's think hard, and wish something nice, so that we can have a real jolly day – what there is left of it.'

Jane darned away again like mad, for time was indeed getting on, and everyone began to talk at once. If you had been there you could not possibly have made head or tail of the talk, but these children were used to talking 'by fours', as soldiers march, and each of them could say what it had to say quite comfortably, and listen to the agreeable sound of its own voice, and at the same time have three-quarters of two sharp ears to spare for listening to what the others said. That is an easy example in multiplication of vulgar fractions, but, as I daresay you can't do even that, I won't ask you to tell me whether $3/4 \times 2 = 1^1/_2$, but I will ask you to believe me that this was the amount of ear each child was able to lend to the others. Lending ears was common in Roman times, as we learn from Shakespeare; but I fear I am getting too instructive.

When the frock was darned, the start for the gravel-pit was delayed by Martha's insisting on everybody's washing its hands – which was nonsense, because nobody had been doing anything at all, except Jane, and how can you get dirty doing nothing? That is a difficult question, and I cannot answer it on paper. In real life I could very soon show you – or you me, which is much more likely.

During the conversation in which the six ears were lent (there were four children, so *that* sum comes right), it had

been decided that fifty pounds in two-shilling pieces was the right wish to have. And the lucky children, who could have anything in the wide world by just wishing for it, hurriedly started for the gravel-pit to express their wishes to the Psammead. Martha caught them at the gate, and insisted on their taking the Baby with them.

'Not want him indeed! Why, everybody 'ud want him, a duck! with all their hearts they would; and you know you promised your ma to take him out every blessed day,' said Martha.

'I know we did,' said Robert in gloom, 'but I wish the Lamb wasn't quite so young and small. It would be much better fun taking him out.'

'He'll mend of his youngness with time,' said Martha; 'and as for his smallness, I don't think you'd fancy carrying of him any more, however big he was. Besides he can walk a bit, bless his precious fat legs, a ducky! He feels the benefit of the new-laid air, so he does, a pet!'

With this and a kiss, she plumped the Lamb into Anthea's arms, and went back to make new pinafores on the sewing-machine. She was a rapid performer on this instrument.

The Lamb laughed with pleasure, and said, 'Walky wif Panty,' and rode on Robert's back with yells of joy, and tried to feed Jane with stones, and altogether made himself so agreeable that nobody could long be sorry that he was of the party.

The enthusiastic Jane even suggested that they should

devote a week's wishes to assuring the Baby's future, by asking such gifts for him as the good fairies give to Infant Princes in proper fairy tales, but Anthea soberly reminded her that as the Sand-fairy's wishes only lasted till sunset they could not ensure any benefit to the Baby's later years; and Jane owned that it would be better to wish for fifty pounds in two-shilling pieces, and buy the Lamb a three-pound-fifteen rocking-horse, like those in the Army and Navy Stores list, with part of the money.

It was settled that, as soon as they had wished for the money and got it, they would get Mr Crispin to drive them into Rochester again, taking Martha with them, if they could not get out of taking her. And they would make a list of the things they really wanted before they started. Full of high hopes and excellent resolutions, they went round the safe slow cart-road to the gravel-pits, and as they went in between the mounds of gravel a sudden thought came to them, and would have turned their ruddy cheeks pale if they had been children in a book. Being real live children, it only made them stop and look at each other with rather blank and silly expressions. For now they remembered that yesterday, when they had asked the Psammead for boundless wealth, and it was getting ready to fill the quarry with the minted gold of bright guineas – millions of them – it had told the children to run along outside the quarry for fear they should be buried alive in the heavy splendid treasure. And they had run. And so it happened that they had not had time to mark the spot where the Psammead was, with a ring of stones, as before. And it was this thought that put such silly expressions on their faces.

'Never mind,' said the hopeful Jane, 'we'll soon find him.'

But this, though easily said, was hard in the doing. They looked and they looked, and though they found their seaside spades, nowhere could they find the Sand-fairy.

At last they had to sit down and rest – not at all because they were weary or disheartened, of course, but because the Lamb insisted on being put down, and you cannot look very carefully after anything you may have happened to lose in the sand if you have an active baby to look after at the same time. Get someone to drop your best knife in the sand next time you go to the seaside, and then take your baby brother with you when you go to look for it, and you will see that I am right.

The Lamb, as Martha had said, was feeling the benefit of the country air, and he was as frisky as a sandhopper. The elder ones longed to go on talking about the new wishes they would have when (or if) they found the Psammead again. But the Lamb wished to enjoy himself.

He watched his opportunity and threw a handful of sand into Anthea's face, and then suddenly burrowed his own head in the sand and waved his fat legs in the air.

Then of course the sand got into his eyes, as it had into Anthea's, and he howled.

The thoughtful Robert had brought one solid brown bottle of ginger-beer with him, relying on a thirst that had never yet failed him. This had to be uncorked hurriedly – it was the only wet thing within reach, and it was necessary to wash the sand out of the Lamb's eyes somehow. Of course the ginger hurt horribly, and he howled more than ever. And, amid his anguish of kicking, the bottle was upset and the beautiful ginger-beer frothed out into the sand and was lost for ever.

It was then that Robert, usually a very patient brother, so far forgot himself as to say:

'Anybody would want him, indeed! Only they don't; Martha doesn't, not really, or she'd jolly well keep him with her. He's a little nuisance, that's what he is. It's too bad. I only wish everybody *did* want him with all their hearts; we might get some peace in our lives.'

The Lamb stopped howling now, because Jane had suddenly remembered that there is only one safe way of taking things out of little children's eyes, and that is with your own soft wet tongue. It is quite easy if you love the Baby as much as you ought to.

Then there was a little silence. Robert was not proud of himself for having been so cross, and the others were not proud of him either. You often notice that sort of silence when someone has said something it ought not to

– and everyone else holds its tongue and waits for the one who oughtn't to have said it to say sorry.

The silence was broken by a sigh – a breath suddenly let out. The children's heads turned as if there had been a string tied to each nose, and someone had pulled all the strings at once.

And everyone saw the Sand-fairy sitting quite close to them, with the expression which it used as a smile on its hairy face.

'Good-morning,' it said; 'I did that quite easily! Everyone wants him now.'

'It doesn't matter,' said Robert sulkily, because he knew he had been behaving rather like a pig. 'No matter who wants him – there's no one here to – anyhow.'

'Ingratitude,' said the Psammead, 'is a dreadful vice.'

'We're not ungrateful,' Jane made haste to say, 'but we didn't *really* want that wish. Robert only just said it. Can't you take it back and give us a new one?'

'No – I can't,' the Sand-fairy said shortly; 'chopping and changing – it's not business. You ought to be careful what you *do* wish. There was a little boy once, he'd wished for a Plesiosaurus instead of an Ichthyosaurus, because he was too lazy to remember the easy names of everyday things, and his father had been very vexed with him, and had made him go to bed before tea-time, and wouldn't let him go out in the nice flint boat along with the other children – it was the annual school-treat next day – and

65

he came and flung himself down near me on the morning of the treat, and he kicked his little prehistoric legs about and said he wished he was dead. And of course then he was.'

'How awful!' said the children all together.

'Only till sunset, of course,' the Psammead said; 'still it was quite enough for his father and mother. And he caught it when he woke up – I can tell you. He didn't turn to stone – I forget why – but there must have been some reason. They didn't know being dead is only being asleep, and you're bound to wake up somewhere or other, either where you go to sleep or in some better place. You may be sure he caught it, giving them such a turn. Why, he wasn't allowed to taste Megatherium for a month after that. Nothing but oysters and periwinkles, and common things like that.'

All the children were quite crushed by this terrible tale. They looked at the Psammead in horror. Suddenly the Lamb perceived that something brown and furry was near him.

'Poof, poof, poofy,' he said, and made a grab.

'It's not a pussy,' Anthea was beginning, when the Sand-fairy leaped back.

'Oh, my left whisker!' it said; 'don't let him touch me. He's wet.'

Its fur stood on end with horror – and indeed a good deal of the ginger-beer had been spilt on the blue smock of the Lamb.

The Psammead dug with its hands and feet, and vanished in an instant and a whirl of sand.

The children marked the spot with a ring of stones.

'We may as well get along home,' said Robert. 'I'll say I'm sorry; but anyway if it's no good it's no harm, and we know where the sandy thing is for tomorrow.'

The others were noble. No one reproached Robert at all. Cyril picked up the Lamb, who was now quite himself again, and off they went by the safe cart-road.

The cart-road from the gravel-pits joins the road almost directly.

At the gate into the road the party stopped to shift the Lamb from Cyril's back to Robert's. And as they paused a very smart open carriage came in sight, with a coachman and a groom on the box, and inside the carriage a lady – very grand indeed, with a dress all white lace and red ribbons and a parasol all red and white – and a white fluffy dog on her lap with a red ribbon round its neck. She looked at the children, and particularly at the Baby, and she smiled at him. The children were used to this, for the Lamb was, as all the servants said, a 'very taking child'. So they waved their hands politely to the lady and expected her to drive on. But she did not. Instead she made the coachman stop. And she beckoned to Cyril, and when he went up to the carriage she said:

'What a dear darling duck of a baby! Oh, I *should* so like to adopt it! Do you think its mother would mind?'

'She'd mind very much indeed,' said Anthea shortly.

'Oh, but I should bring it up in luxury, you know. I am Lady Chittenden. You must have seen my photograph in the illustrated papers. They call me a beauty, you know, but of course that's all nonsense. Anyway –'

She opened the carriage door and jumped out. She had the wonderfullest red high-heeled shoes with silver buckles. 'Let me hold him a minute,' she said. And she took the Lamb and held him very awkwardly, as if she was not used to babies.

Then suddenly she jumped into the carriage with the Lamb in her arms and slammed the door and said, 'Drive on!'

The Lamb roared, the little white dog barked, and the coachman hesitated.

'Drive on, I tell you!' cried the lady; and the coachman did, for, as he said afterwards, it was as much as his place was worth not to.

The four children looked at each other, and then with one accord they rushed after the carriage and held on behind. Down the dusty road went the smart carriage, and after it, at double-quick time, ran the twinkling legs of the Lamb's brothers and sisters.

The Lamb howled louder and louder, but presently his howls changed by slow degree to hiccupy gurgles, and then all was still and they knew he had gone to sleep.

The carriage went on, and the eight feet that twinkled

through the dust were growing quite stiff and tired before
the carriage stopped at the lodge of a grand park. The
children crouched down behind the carriage, and the lady
got out. She looked at the Baby as it lay on the carriage
seat, and hesitated.

'The darling – I won't disturb it,' she said, and went into the lodge to talk to the woman there about a setting of Buff Orpington eggs that had not turned out well.

The coachman and footman sprang from the box and bent over the sleeping Lamb.

'Fine boy – wish he was mine,' said the coachman.

'He wouldn't favour *you* much,' said the groom sourly; 'too 'andsome.'

The coachman pretended not to hear. He said:

'Wonder at her now – I do really! Hates kids. Got none of her own, and can't abide other folkses'.'

The children, crouching in the white dust under the carriage, exchanged uncomfortable glances.

'Tell you what,' the coachman went on firmly, 'blowed if I don't hide the little nipper in the hedge and tell her his brothers took 'im! Then I'll come back for him afterwards.'

'No, you don't,' said the footman. 'I've took to that kid so as never was. If anyone's to have him, it's me – so there!'

'Stow your gab!' the coachman rejoined. 'You don't want no kids, and, if you did, one kid's the same as another to you. But I'm a married man and a judge of breed. I knows a first-rate yearling when I sees him. I'm a-goin' to 'ave him, an' least said soonest mended.'

'I should a' thought,' said the footman sneeringly, 'you'd a'most enough. What with Alfred, an' Albert, an'

Louise, an' Victor Stanley, and Helena Beatrice, and another –'

The coachman hit the footman in the chin – the footman hit the coachman in the waistcoat – the next minute the two were fighting here and there, in and out, up and down, and all over everywhere, and the little dog jumped on the box of the carriage and began barking like mad.

Cyril, still crouching in the dust, waddled on bent legs to the side of the carriage farthest from the battlefield. He unfastened the door of the carriage – the two men were far too much occupied with their quarrel to notice anything – took the Lamb in his arms, and, still stooping, carried the sleeping baby a dozen yards along the road to where a stile led into a wood. The others followed, and there among the hazels and young oaks and sweet chestnuts, covered by high strong-scented bracken, they all lay hidden till the angry voices of the men were hushed at the angry voice of the red-and-white lady, and, after a long and anxious search, the carriage at last drove away.

'My only hat!' said Cyril, drawing a deep breath as the sound of wheels at last died away. 'Everyone *does* want him now – and no mistake! That Sammyadd has done us again! Tricky brute! For any sake, let's get the kid safe home.'

So they peeped out, and finding on the right hand only

lonely white road, and nothing but lonely white road on the left, they took courage, and the road, Anthea carrying the sleeping Lamb.

Adventures dogged their footsteps. A boy with a bundle of faggots on his back dropped his bundle by the roadside and asked to look at the Baby, and then offered to carry him; but Anthea was not to be caught that way twice. They all walked on, but the boy followed, and Cyril and Robert couldn't make him go away till they had more than once invited him to smell their fists. Afterwards a little girl in a blue-and-white checked pinafore actually followed them for a quarter of a mile crying for 'the precious Baby', and then she was only got rid of by threats of tying her to a tree in the wood with all their pocket-handkerchiefs. 'So that the bears can come and eat you as soon as it gets dark,' said Cyril severely. Then she went off crying. It presently seemed wise, to the brothers and sisters of the Baby, who was wanted by everyone, to hide in the hedge whenever they saw anyone coming, and thus they managed to prevent the Lamb from arousing the inconvenient affection of a milkman, a stone-breaker, and a man who drove a cart with a paraffin barrel at the back of it. They were nearly home when the worst thing of all happened. Turning a corner suddenly they came upon two vans, a tent, and a company of gipsies encamped by the side of the road. The vans were hung all round with wicker chairs and cradles, and flower-stands and feather brushes. A lot of ragged children were industriously making dust-pies in the road, two men lay on the grass smoking, and three women were doing the family washing in an old red watering-can with the top broken off.

In a moment all the gipsies, men, women, and children, surrounded Anthea and the Baby.

'Let *me* hold him, little lady,' said one of the gipsy women, who had a mahogany-coloured face and dust-coloured hair; 'I won't hurt a hair of his head, the little picture!'

'I'd rather not,' said Anthea.

'Let me have him,' said the other woman, whose face was also of the hue of mahogany, and her hair jet-black, in greasy curls. 'I've nineteen of my own, so I have.'

'No,' said Anthea bravely, but her heart beat so that it nearly choked her.

Then one of the men pushed forward.

'Swelp me if it ain't!' he cried, 'my own long-lost cheild! Have he a strawberry mark on his left ear? No? Then he's my own babby, stolen from me in hinnocent hinfancy. 'And 'im over – and we'll not 'ave the law on yer this time.'

He snatched the Baby from Anthea, who turned scarlet and burst into tears of pure rage.

The others were standing quite still; this was much the most terrible thing that had ever happened to them. Even being taken up by the police in Rochester was nothing to

this. Cyril was quite white, and his hands trembled a little, but he made a sign to the others to shut up. He was silent a minute, thinking hard. Then he said:

'We don't want to keep him if he's yours. But you see he's used to us. You shall have him if you want him.'

'No, no!' cried Anthea – and Cyril glared at her.

'Of course we want him,' said the women, trying to get the Baby out of the man's arms. The Lamb howled loudly.

'Oh, he's hurt!' shrieked Anthea; and Cyril, in a savage undertone, bade her, 'Stow it!'

'You trust to me,' he whispered. 'Look here,' he went on, 'he's awfully tiresome with people he doesn't know very well. Suppose we stay here a bit till he gets used to you, and then when it's bedtime I give you my word of honour we'll go away and let you keep him if you want to. And then when we're gone you can decide which of you is to have him, as you all want him so much.'

'That's fair enough,' said the man who was holding the Baby, trying to loosen the red neckerchief which the Lamb had caught hold of and drawn round his mahogany throat so tight that he could hardly breathe. The gipsies whispered together, and Cyril took the chance to whisper too. He said, 'Sunset! We'll get away then.'

And then his brothers and sisters were filled with wonder and admiration at his having been so clever as to remember this.

'Oh, do let him come to us!' said Jane. 'See we'll sit down here and take care of him for you till he gets used to you.'

'What about dinner?' said Robert suddenly. The others looked at him with scorn. 'Fancy bothering about your beastly dinner when your br– I mean when the Baby' – Jane whispered hotly. Robert carefully winked at her and went on:

'You won't mind my just running home to get our

dinner?' he said to the gipsy; 'I can bring it out here in a basket.'

His brother and sisters felt themselves very noble, and despised him. They did not know his thoughtful secret intention. But the gipsies did in a minute.

'Oh yes!' they said; 'and then fetch the police with a pack of lies about it being your baby instead of ours! D'jever catch a weasel asleep?' they asked.

'If you're hungry you can pick a bit along of us,' said the light-haired gipsy woman, not unkindly. 'Here, Levi, that blessed kid'll howl all his buttons off. Give him to the little lady, and let's see if they can't get him used to us a bit.'

So the Lamb was handed back; but the gipsies crowded so closely that he could not possibly stop howling. Then the man with the red handkerchief said:

'Here, Pharaoh, make up the fire; and you girls see to the pot. Give the kid a chanst.' So the gipsies, very much against their will, went off to their work, and the children and the Lamb were left sitting on the grass.

'He'll be all right at sunset,' Jane whispered. 'But, oh, it is awful! Suppose they are frightfully angry when they come to their senses! They might beat us, or leave us tied to trees, or something.'

'No, they won't,' Anthea said. ('Oh, my Lamb, don't cry any more, it's all right, Panty's got oo, duckie!') 'They aren't unkind people, or they wouldn't be going to give us any dinner.'

'Dinner?' said Robert. 'I won't touch their nasty dinner. It would choke me!'

The others thought so too then. But when the dinner was ready – it turned out to be supper, and happened between four and five – they were all glad enough to take what they could get. It was boiled rabbit, with onions, and some bird rather like a chicken, but stringier about its legs and with a stronger taste. The Lamb had bread soaked in hot water and brown sugar sprinkled on the top. He liked this very much, and consented to let the two gipsy women feed him with it, as he sat on Anthea's lap. All that long hot afternoon Robert and Cyril and Anthea and Jane had to keep the Lamb amused and happy, while the gipsies looked eagerly on. By the time the shadows grew long and black across the meadows he had really 'taken to' the woman with the light hair, and even consented to kiss his hand to the children, and to stand up and bow, with his hand on his chest – 'like a gentleman' – to the two men. The whole gipsy camp was in raptures with him, and his brothers and sisters could not help taking some pleasure in showing off his accomplishments to an audience so interested and enthusiastic. But they longed for sunset.

'We're getting into the habit of longing for sunset,' Cyril whispered. 'How I do wish we could wish something really sensible, that would be of some use, so that we should be quite sorry when sunset came.'

The shadows got longer and longer, and at last there were no separate shadows any more, but one soft glowing shadow over everything; for the sun was out of sight – behind the hill – but he had not really set yet. The people who make the laws about lighting bicycle lamps are the people who decide when the sun sets; he has to do it, too, to the minute, or they would know the reason why!

But the gipsies were getting impatient.

'Now, young uns,' the red-handkerchief man said, 'it's time you were laying of your heads on your pillowses – so it is! The kid's all right and friendly with us now – so you just hand him over and sling that hook o' yours like you said.'

The women and children came crowding round the Lamb, arms were held out, fingers snapped invitingly, friendly faces beaming with admiring smiles; but all failed to tempt the loyal Lamb. He clung with arms and legs to Jane, who happened to be holding him, and uttered the gloomiest roar of the whole day.

'It's no good,' the woman said, 'hand the little poppet over, miss. We'll soon quiet him.'

And still the sun would not set.

'Tell her about how to put him to bed,' whispered Cyril; 'anything to gain time – and be ready to bolt when the sun really does make up its silly old mind to set.'

'Yes, I'll hand him over in just one minute,' Anthea began, talking very fast – 'but do let me just tell you he has a warm bath every night and cold in the morning, and he has a crockery rabbit to go into the warm bath with him, and little Samuel saying his prayers in white china on a red cushion for the cold bath; and if you let the soap get into his eyes, the Lamb –'

'Lamb kyes,' said he – he had stopped roaring to listen.

The woman laughed. 'As if I hadn't never bath'd a babby!' she said. 'Come – give us a hold of him. Come to 'Melia, my precious.'

'G'way, ugsie!' replied the Lamb at once.

'Yes, but,' Anthea went on, 'about his meals; you really *must* let me tell you he has an apple or a banana every morning, and bread-and-milk for breakfast, and an egg for his tea sometimes, and –'

'I've brought up ten,' said the black-ringleted woman, 'besides the others. Come, miss, 'and 'im over – I can't bear it no longer. I just must give him a hug.'

'We ain't settled yet whose he's to be, Esther,' said one of the men.

'It won't be you, Esther, with seven of 'em at your tail a'ready.'

'I ain't so sure of that,' said Esther's husband.

'And ain't I nobody, to have a say neither?' said the husband of 'Melia.

Zillah, the girl, said, 'An' me? I'm a single girl – and no one but 'im to look after – I ought to have him.'

'Hold yer tongue!'

'Shut your mouth!'

'Don't you show me no more of your imperence!'

Everyone was getting very angry. The dark gipsy faces were frowning and anxious-looking. Suddenly a change swept over them, as if some invisible sponge had wiped away these cross and anxious expressions, and left only a blank.

The children saw that the sun really *had* set. But they were afraid to move. And the gipsies were feeling so muddled, because of the invisible sponge that had washed all the feelings of the last few hours out of their hearts, that they could not say a word.

The children hardly dared to breathe. Suppose the gipsies, when they recovered speech, should be furious to think how silly they had been all day?

It was an awkward moment. Suddenly Anthea, greatly daring, held out the Lamb to the red-handkerchief man.

'Here he is!' she said.

The man drew back. 'I shouldn't like to deprive you, miss,' he said hoarsely.

'Anyone who likes can have my share of him,' said the other man.

'After all, I've got enough of my own,' said Esther.

'He's a nice little chap, though,' said Amelia. She was the

only one who now looked affectionately at the whimpering Lamb.

Zillah said, 'If I don't think I must have had a touch of the sun. *I* don't want him.'

'Then shall we take him away?' said Anthea.

'Well, suppose you do,' said Pharaoh heartily, 'and we'll say no more about it!'

And with great haste all the gipsies began to be busy about their tents for the night. All but Amelia. She went with the children as far as the bend in the road – and there she said:

'Let me give him a kiss, miss – I don't know what made us go for to behave so silly. Us gipsies don't steal babies, whatever they may tell you when you're naughty. We've enough of our own, mostly. But I've lost all mine.'

She leaned towards the Lamb; and he, looking in her eyes, unexpectedly put up a grubby soft paw and stroked her face.

'Poor, poor!' said the Lamb. And he let the gipsy woman kiss him, and, what is more, he kissed her brown cheek in return – a very nice kiss, as all his kisses are, and not a wet one like some babies give. The gipsy woman moved her finger about on his forehead, as if she had been writing something there, and the same with his chest and his hands and his feet; then she said:

'May he be brave, and have the strong head to think with, and the strong heart to love with, and the strong hands to work with, and the strong feet to travel with, and always come safe home to his own.' Then she said something in a strange language no one could understand, and suddenly added:

'Well, I must be saying "so long" – and glad to have made your acquaintance.' And she turned and went back to her home – the tent by the grassy roadside.

The children looked after her till she was out of sight. Then Robert said, 'How silly of her! Even sunset didn't put *her* right. What rot she talked!'

'Well,' said Cyril, 'if you ask me, I think it was rather decent of her –'

'Decent?' said Anthea; 'it was very nice indeed of her. I think she's a dear.'

'She's just too frightfully nice for anything,' said Jane.

And they went home – very late for tea and unspeakably late for dinner. Martha scolded, of course. But the Lamb was safe.

'I say – it turned out we wanted the Lamb as much as anyone,' said Robert, later.

'Of course.'

'But do you feel different about it now the sun's set?'

'*No*,' said all the others together.

'Then it's lasted over sunset with us.'

'No, it hasn't,' Cyril explained. 'The wish didn't do anything to *us*. We always wanted him with all our hearts when we were our proper selves, only we were all pigs this morning; especially you, Robert.' Robert bore this much with a strange calm.

'I certainly *thought* I didn't want him this morning,' said he. 'Perhaps I was a pig. But everything looked so different when we thought we were going to lose him.'

4
Wings

The next day was very wet – too wet to go out, and far too wet to think of disturbing a Sand-fairy so sensitive to water that he still, after thousands of years, felt the pain of once having had his left whisker wetted. It was a long day, and it was not till the afternoon that all the children suddenly decided to write letters to their mother. It was Robert who had the misfortune to upset the ink-pot – an unusually deep and full one – straight into that part of Anthea's desk where she had long pretended that an arrangement of gum and cardboard painted with Indian ink was a secret drawer. It was not exactly Robert's fault; it was only his misfortune that he chanced to be lifting the ink across the desk just at the moment when Anthea had got it open, and that that same moment should have been the one chosen by the Lamb to get under the table and break his squeaking bird. There was a sharp convenient wire inside the bird, and of course the Lamb ran the wire into Robert's leg at once; and so, without anyone's meaning to, the secret drawer was flooded with ink. At the same time a stream was poured over Anthea's half-finished letter.

So that her letter was something like this:

Darling Mother,
I hope you are quite well, and I hope Granny is better. The other day we . . .

Then came a flood of ink, and at the bottom these words in pencil –

It was not me upset the ink, but it took such a time clearing up, so no more as it is post-time. –
From your loving daughter,
Anthea.

Robert's letter had not even been begun. He had been drawing a ship on the blotting-paper while he was trying to think of what to say. And of course after the ink was upset he had to help Anthea to clean out her desk, and he promised to make her another secret drawer, better than the other. And she said, 'Well, make it now.' So it was post-time and his letter wasn't done. And the secret drawer wasn't done either.

Cyril wrote a long letter, very fast, and then went to set a trap for slugs that he had read about in the *Home-made Gardener*, and when it was post-time the letter could not be found, and it never was found. Perhaps the slugs ate it.

Jane's letter was the only one that went. She meant to tell her mother all about the Psammead – in fact they had all meant to do this – but she spent so long thinking how to spell the word that there was no time to tell the story properly, and it is useless to tell a story unless you *do* tell it properly, so she had to be contented with this –

My dear Mother Dear,

We are all as good as we can, like you told us to, and the Lamb has a little cold, but Martha says it is nothing, only he upset the goldfish into himself yesterday morning. When we were up at the sand-pit the other day we went round by the safe way where carts go, and we found a –

Half an hour went by before Jane felt quite sure that they could none of them spell Psammead. And they could not find it in the dictionary either, though they looked. Then Jane hastily finished her letter.

We found a strange thing, but it is nearly post-time, so no more at present from your little girl,
    Jane.
    P.S. – *If you could have a wish come true, what would you have?*

Then the postman was heard blowing his horn, and Robert rushed out in the rain to stop his cart and give him the letter. And that was how it happened that, though all the children meant to tell their mother about the Sand-fairy, somehow or other she never got to know. There were other reasons why she never got to know, but these come later.

The next day Uncle Richard came and took them all to Maidstone in a wagonette – all except the Lamb. Uncle Richard was the very best kind of uncle. He bought them toys at Maidstone. He took them into a shop and let them choose exactly what they wanted, without any restrictions about price, and no nonsense about things being instructive. It is very wise to let children choose exactly what they like, because they are very foolish and inexperienced, and sometimes they will choose a really instructive thing without meaning to. This happened to Robert, who chose, at the last moment, and in a great hurry, a box with pictures on it of winged bulls with men's heads and winged men with eagles' heads. He thought there would be animals inside, the same as on the box. When he got it home it was a Sunday puzzle about ancient Nineveh! The others chose in haste, and were happy at leisure. Cyril had a model engine, and the girls had two dolls, as well as a china tea-set with forget-me-nots on it, to be 'between them'. The boys' 'between them' was a bow and arrows.

Then Uncle Richard took them on the beautiful Medway in a boat, and then they all had tea at a beautiful pastry-cook's, and when they reached home it was far too late to have any wishes that day.

They did not tell Uncle Richard anything about the Psammead. I do not know why. And they do not know why. But I daresay you can guess.

The day after Uncle Richard had behaved so handsomely was a very hot day indeed. The people who decide what the weather is to be, and put its orders down for it in the newspapers every morning, said afterwards that it was the hottest day there had been for years. They had ordered it to be 'warmer – some showers', and warmer it certainly was. In fact it was so busy being warmer that it had no time to attend to the order about showers, so there weren't any.

Have you ever been up at five o'clock on a fine summer morning? It is very beautiful. The sunlight is pinky and yellowy, and all the grass and trees are covered with dew-diamonds. And all the shadows go the opposite way to the way they do in the evening, which is very interesting and makes you feel as though you were in a new other world.

Anthea awoke at five. She had made herself wake, and I must tell you how it is done, even if it keeps you waiting for the story to go on.

You get into bed at night, and lie down quite flat on your little back with your hands straight down by your sides. Then you say 'I *must* wake up at five' (or six, or seven, or eight, or nine, or whatever the time is that you want), and as you say it you push your chin down on to your chest and then bang your head back on the pillow. And you do this as many times as there are ones in the time you want to wake up at. (It is quite an easy sum.) Of course everything depends on your really wanting to get up at five (or six, or seven, or eight, or nine); if you don't really want to, it's all of no use. But if you do – well, try it and see. Of course in this, as in doing Latin proses or getting into mischief, practice makes perfect.

Anthea was quite perfect.

At the very moment when she opened her eyes she heard the black-and-gold clock down in the dining-room strike eleven. So she knew it was three minutes to five. The black-and-gold clock always struck wrong, but it was all right when you knew what it meant. It was like a person talking a foreign language. If you know the language it is just as easy to understand as English. And Anthea knew the clock language. She was very sleepy, but she jumped out of bed and put her face and hands into a basin of cold water. This is a fairy charm that prevents your wanting to get back into bed again. Then she dressed, and folded up her night-gown. She did not tumble it together by the sleeves, but folded it by the seams from the hem, and that will show you the kind of well-brought-up little girl she was.

Then she took her shoes in her hand and crept softly

down the stairs. She opened the dining-room window and climbed out. It would have been just as easy to go out by the door, but the window was more romantic, and less likely to be noticed by Martha.

'I will always get up at five,' she said to herself. 'It is quite too awfully pretty for anything.'

Her heart was beating very fast, for she was carrying out a plan quite her own. She could not be sure that it was a good plan, but she was quite sure that it would not be any better if she were to tell the others about it. And she had a feeling that, right or wrong, she would rather go through with it alone. She put on her shoes under the iron veranda, on the red-and-yellow shining tiles, and then she ran straight to the sand-pit, and found the Psammead's place, and dug it out; it was very cross indeed.

'It's too bad,' it said, fluffing up its fur like pigeons do their feathers at Christmas time. 'The weather's arctic, and it's the middle of the night.'

'I'm so sorry,' said Anthea gently, and she took off her white pinafore and covered the Sand-fairy up with it, all but its head, its bat's ears, and its eyes that were like a snail's eyes.

'Thank you,' it said, 'that's better. What's the wish this morning?'

'I don't know,' said she; 'that's just it. You see we've been very unlucky, so far. I wanted to talk to you about it. But – would you mind not giving me any wishes till after breakfast? It's so hard to talk to anyone if they jump out at you with wishes you don't really want!'

'You shouldn't say you wish for things if you don't wish for them. In the old days people almost always knew whether it was Megatherium or Ichthyosaurus they really wanted for dinner.'

'I'll try not,' said Anthea, 'but I do wish –'

'Look out!' said the Psammead in a warning voice, and it began to blow itself out.

'Oh, this isn't a magic wish – it's just – I should be so glad if you'd not swell yourself out and nearly burst to give me anything just now. Wait till the others are here.'

'Well, well,' it said indulgently, but it shivered.

'Would you,' asked Anthea kindly – 'would you like to come and sit on my lap? You'd be warmer, and I could turn the skirt of my frock up round you. I'd be very careful.'

Anthea had never expected that it would, but it did.

'Thank you,' it said; 'you really are rather thoughtful.' It crept on to her lap and snuggled down, and she put her arms round it with a rather frightened gentleness. 'Now then!' it said.

'Well then,' said Anthea, 'everything we have wished has turned out rather horrid. I wish you would advise us. You are so old, you must be very wise.'

'I was always generous from a child,' said the Sand-fairy. 'I've spent the whole of my waking hours in giving. But one thing I won't give – that's advice.'

'You see,' Anthea went on, 'it's such a wonderful thing – such a splendid, glorious chance. It's so good and kind and dear of you to give us our wishes, and it seems such a pity it should all be wasted just because we are too silly to know what to wish for.'

Anthea had meant to say that – and she had not wanted to say it before the others. It's one thing to say you're silly, and quite another to say that other people are.

'Child,' said the Sand-fairy sleepily, 'I can only advise you to think before you speak –'

'But I thought you never gave advice.'

'That piece doesn't count,' it said. 'You'll never take it! Besides, it's not original. It's in all the copybooks.'

'But won't you just say if you think wings would be a silly wish?'

'Wings?' it said. 'I should think you might do worse. Only, take care you aren't flying high at sunset. There was a little Ninevite boy I heard of once. He was one of King Sennacherib's sons, and a traveller brought him a Psammead. He used to keep it in a box of sand on the palace terrace. It was a dreadful degradation for one of us, of course; still the boy *was* the Assyrian King's son. And one day he wished for wings and got them. But he forgot that they would turn into stone at sunset, and when they did he fell slap on to one of the winged lions at the top of his father's great staircase; and what with *his* stone wings and the lions' stone wings – well, it's not a pretty story! But I believe the boy enjoyed himself very much till then.'

'Tell me,' said Anthea, 'why don't our wishes turn into stone now? Why do they just vanish?'

'*Autres temps, autres mœurs*,' said the creature.

'Is that the Ninevite language?' asked Anthea, who had learned no foreign language at school except French.

'What I mean is,' the Psammead went on, 'that in the old days people wished for good solid everyday gifts – Mammoths and Pterodactyls and things – and those could be turned into stone as easy as not. But people wish such high-flying fanciful things nowadays. How are you going to turn being beautiful as the day, or being wanted by everybody, into stone? You see it can't be done. And it would never do to have two rules, so they simply vanish. If being beautiful as the day *could* be turned into stone it would last an awfully long time, you know – much longer than you would. Just look at the Greek statues. It's just as well as it is. Good-bye. I *am* so sleepy.'

It jumped off her lap – dug frantically, and vanished.

Anthea was late for breakfast. It was Robert who quietly poured a spoonful of treacle down the Lamb's frock, so that he had to be taken away and washed thoroughly directly after breakfast. And it was of course a very naughty thing to do; yet it served two purposes – it delighted the Lamb, who loved above all things to be completely sticky, and it engaged Martha's attention so that the others could slip away to the sand-pit without the Lamb.

They did it, and in the lane Anthea, breathless from the scurry of that slipping, panted out –

'I want to propose we take turns to wish. Only, nobody's to have a wish if the others don't think it's a nice wish. Do you agree?'

'Who's to have first wish?' asked Robert cautiously.

'Me, if you don't mind,' said Anthea apologetically. 'And I've thought about it – and it's wings.'

There was a silence. The others rather wanted to find fault, but it was hard, because the word 'wings' raised a flutter of joyous excitement in every breast.

'Not so dusty,' said Cyril generously; and Robert added, 'Really, Panther, you're not quite such a fool as you look.'

Jane said, 'I think it would be perfectly lovely. It's like a bright dream of delirium.'

They found the Sand-fairy easily. Anthea said:

'I wish we all had beautiful wings to fly with.'

The Sand-fairy blew himself out, and next moment each child felt a funny feeling, half heaviness and half lightness, on its shoulders. The Psammead put its head on one side and turned its snail's eyes from one to the other.

'Not so dusty,' it said dreamily. 'But really, Robert, you're not quite such an angel as you look.' Robert almost blushed.

The wings were very big, and more beautiful than you can possibly imagine – for they were soft and smooth, and every feather lay neatly in its place. And the feathers were of the most lovely mixed changing colours, like the rainbow, or iridescent glass, or the beautiful scum that sometimes floats on water that is not at all nice to drink.

'Oh – but can we fly?' Jane said, standing anxiously first on one foot and then on the other.

'Look out!' said Cyril; 'you're treading on my wing.'

'Does it hurt?' asked Anthea with interest; but no one answered, for Robert had spread his wings and jumped up, and now he was slowly rising in the air. He looked very awkward in his knickerbocker suit – his boots in particular hung helplessly, and seemed much larger than when he was standing in them. But the others cared but little how he looked – or how they looked, for that matter. For now they all spread out their wings and rose in the air. Of course you all know what flying feels like, because everyone has dreamed about flying, and it seems so beautifully easy – only, you can never remember how you did it; and as a rule you have to do it without wings, in your dreams, which is more clever and uncommon, but not so easy to remember the rule for. Now the four children rose flapping from the ground, and you can't think how good the air felt running against their faces. Their wings were tremendously wide when they were spread out, and they had to fly quite a long way apart so as not to get in each other's way. But little things like this are easily learned.

All the words in the English Dictionary, and in the Greek Lexicon as well, are, I find, of no use at all to tell you exactly what it feels like to be flying, so I will not try. But I will say that to look *down* on the fields and woods, instead of *along* at them, is something like looking at a beautiful live map, where, instead of silly colours on paper, you have real moving sunny woods and green fields laid out one after the other. As Cyril said, and I can't think where he got hold of such a strange expression, 'It does you a fair treat!' It was most wonderful and more like real magic than any wish the children had had yet. They flapped and flew and sailed on their great rainbow wings, between green earth and blue sky; and they flew right over

Rochester and then swerved round towards Maidstone, and presently they all began to feel extremely hungry. Curiously enough, this happened when they were flying rather low, and just as they were crossing an orchard where some early plums shone red and ripe.

They paused on their wings. I cannot explain to you how this is done, but it is something like treading water when you are swimming, and hawks do it extremely well.

'Yes, I daresay,' said Cyril, though no one had spoken. 'But stealing is stealing even if you've got wings.'

'Do you really think so?' said Jane briskly. 'If you've got wings you're a bird, and no one minds birds breaking the commandments. At least, they may *mind*, but the birds always do it, and no one scolds them or sends them to prison.'

It was not so easy to perch on a plum-tree as you might think, because the rainbow wings were so *very* large; but somehow they all managed to do it, and the plums were certainly very sweet and juicy.

Fortunately, it was not till they had all had quite as many plums as were good for them that they saw a stout man, who looked exactly as though he owned the plum-trees, come hurrying through the orchard gate with a thick stick, and with one accord they disentangled their wings from the plum-laden branches and began to fly.

The man stopped short, with his mouth open. For he

had seen the boughs of his trees moving and twitching, and he had said to himself, 'Them young varmints – at it again!' And he had come out at once, for the lads of the village had taught him in past seasons that plums want looking after. But when he saw the rainbow wings flutter up out of the plum-tree he felt that he must have gone quite mad, and he did not like the feeling at all. And when Anthea looked down and saw his mouth go slowly open, and stay so, and his face become green and mauve in patches, she called out:

'Don't be frightened,' and felt hastily in her pocket for a threepenny-bit with a hole in it, which she had meant to hang on a ribbon round her neck, for luck. She hovered round the unfortunate plum-owner, and said, 'We have had some of your plums; we thought it wasn't stealing, but now I am not so sure. So here's some money to pay for them.'

She swooped down towards the terror-stricken grower of plums, and slipped the coin into the pocket of his jacket, and in a few flaps she had rejoined the others.

The farmer sat down on the grass, suddenly and heavily.

'Well – I'm blessed!' he said. 'This here is what they call delusions, I suppose. But this here three-penny' – he had pulled it out and bitten it – '*that's* real enough. Well, from this day forth I'll be a better man. It's the kind of thing to sober a chap for life, this is. I'm glad it was only wings, though. I'd rather see birds as aren't there, and couldn't

be, even if they pretend to talk, than some things as I could name.'

He got up slowly and heavily, and went indoors, and he was so nice to his wife that day that she felt quite happy, and said to herself, 'Law, whatever have a-come to the man!' and smartened herself up and put a blue ribbon bow at the place where her collar fastened on, and looked so pretty that he was kinder than ever. So perhaps the winged children really did do one good thing that day. If so, it was the only one; for really there is nothing like wings for getting you into trouble. But, on the other hand, if you are in trouble, there is nothing like wings for getting you out of it.

This was the case in the matter of the fierce dog who sprang out at them when they had folded up their wings as small as possible and were going up to a farm door to ask for a crust of bread and cheese, for in spite of the plums they were soon just as hungry as ever again.

Now there is no doubt whatever that, if the four had been ordinary wingless children, that black and fierce dog would have had a good bite out of the brown-stockinged leg of Robert, who was the nearest. But at first growl there was a flutter of wings, and the dog was left to strain at his chain and stand on his hind-legs as if he were trying to fly too.

They tried several other farms, but at those where there were no dogs the people were far too frightened to do anything but scream; and at last when it was nearly four o'clock, and their wings were getting miserably stiff and tired, they alighted on a church-tower and held a council of war.

'We can't possibly fly all the way home without dinner *or* tea,' said Robert with desperate decision.

'And nobody will give us any dinner, or even lunch, let alone tea,' said Cyril.

'Perhaps the clergyman here might,' suggested Anthea. 'He must know all about angels –'

'Anybody could see we're not that,' said Jane. 'Look at Robert's boots and Squirrel's plaid necktie.'

'Well,' said Cyril firmly, 'if the country you're in won't *sell* provisions, you *take* them. In wars I mean. I'm quite certain you do. And even in other stories no good brother would allow his little sisters to starve in the midst of plenty.'

'Plenty?' repeated Robert hungrily; and the others looked vaguely round the bare leads of the church-tower, and murmured, 'In the midst of?'

'Yes,' said Cyril impressively. 'There is a larder window at the side of the clergyman's house, and I saw things to eat inside – custard pudding and cold chicken and tongue – and pies – and jam. It's rather a high window – but with wings –'

'How clever of you!' said Jane.

'Not at all,' said Cyril modestly; 'any born general – Napoleon or the Duke of Marlborough – would have seen it just the same as I did.'

'It seems very wrong,' said Anthea.

'Nonsense,' said Cyril. 'What was it Sir Philip Sidney said when the soldier wouldn't stand him a drink? "My necessity is greater than his".'

'We'll club our money, though, and leave it to pay for the things, won't we?' Anthea was persuasive, and very nearly in tears, because it is most trying to feel enormously hungry and unspeakably sinful at one and the same time.

'Some of it,' was the cautious reply.

Everyone now turned out its pockets on the lead roof of the tower, where visitors for the last hundred and fifty years had cut their own and their sweethearts' initials with penknives in the soft lead. There was five-and-sevenpence-half-penny altogether, and even the upright Anthea admitted that that was too much to pay for four people's dinners. Robert said he thought eighteen pence.

And half-a-crown was finally agreed to be 'handsome'.

So Anthea wrote on the back of her last term's report, which happened to be in her pocket, and from which she first tore her own name and that of the school, the following letter:

Dear Reverend Clergyman,
   We are very hungry indeed because of having to fly all day, and we think it is not stealing when you are starving to death. We are afraid to ask you for fear you should say 'No', because of course you know

about angels, but you would not think we were
angels. We will only take the nessessities of life, and
no pudding or pie, to show you it is not grediness
but true starvation that makes us make your larder
stand and deliver. But we are not highwaymen by
trade.

'Cut it short,' said the others with one accord. And Anthea hastily added:

Our intentions are quite honourable if you only
knew. And here is half-a-crown to show we are
sinseer and grateful.
Thank you for your kind hospitality.
From Us Four.

The half-crown was wrapped in this letter, and all the children felt that when the clergyman had read it he would understand everything, as well as anyone could who had not seen the wings.

'Now,' said Cyril, 'of course there's some risk; we'd better fly straight down the other side of the tower and then flutter low across the churchyard and in through the shrubbery. There doesn't seem to be anyone about. But you never know. The window looks out into the shrubbery. It is embowered in foliage, like a window in a story. I'll go in and get the things. Robert and Anthea can take them as I hand them out through the window; and Jane can keep watch – her eyes are sharp – and whistle if she sees anyone about. Shut up, Robert! she can whistle quite well enough for that, anyway. It ought not to be a very good whistle – it'll sound more natural and birdlike. Now then – off we go!'

I cannot pretend that stealing is right. I can only say that on this occasion it did not look like stealing to the hungry four, but appeared in the light of a fair and reasonable business transaction. They had never happened to learn that a tongue – hardly cut into – a chicken and a half, a loaf of bread, and a siphon of soda-water cannot be bought in shops for half-a-crown. These were the necessaries of life, which Cyril handed out of the larder window when, quite unobserved and without hindrance or adventure, he had led the others to that happy spot. He felt that to refrain from jam, apple turnovers, cake, and mixed candied peel was a really heroic act – and I agree with him. He was also proud of not taking the custard pudding – and there I think he was wrong – because if he had taken it there would have been a difficulty about returning the dish; no one, however starving, has a right to steal china pie-dishes with little pink flowers on them. The soda-water siphon was different. They could not do without something to drink, and as the maker's name was on it they felt sure it would be returned to him wherever they might leave it. If they had time they would take it

back themselves. The man appeared to live in Rochester, which would not be much out of their way home.

Everything was carried up to the top of the tower, and laid down on a sheet of kitchen paper which Cyril had found on the top shelf of the larder. As he unfolded it, Anthea said, 'I don't think *that's* a necessity of life.'

'Yes, it is,' said he. 'We must put the things down somewhere to cut them up; and I heard father say the other day people got diseases from germans in rain-water. Now there must be lots of rain-water here – and when it dries up the germans are left, and they'd get into the things, and we should all die of scarlet fever.'

'What are germans?'

'Little waggly things you see with microscopes,' said Cyril, with a scientific air. 'They give you every illness you can think of. I'm sure the paper was a necessary, just as much as the bread and meat and water. Now then! Oh, my eyes, I am hungry!'

I do not wish to describe the picnic party on the top of the tower. You can imagine well enough what it is like to carve a chicken and a tongue with a knife that has only one blade – and that snapped off short about half-way down. But it was done. Eating with your fingers is greasy and difficult – and paper dishes soon get to look very spotty and horrid. But one thing you *can't* imagine, and that is how soda-water behaves when you try to drink it straight out of a siphon – especially a quite full one. But if imagination will not help you, experience will, and you can easily try it for yourself if you can get a grown-up to give you the siphon. If you want to have a really thorough experience, put the tube in your mouth and press the handle very suddenly and very hard. You had better do it when you are alone – and out of doors is best for this experiment.

However you eat them, tongue and chicken and new bread are very good things, and no one minds being sprinkled a little with soda-water on a really fine hot day. So that everyone enjoyed the dinner very much indeed, and everyone ate as much as it possibly could: first, because it was extremely hungry; and secondly, because, as I said, tongue and chicken and new bread are very nice.

Now, I daresay you will have noticed that if you have to wait for your dinner till long after the proper time, and then eat a great deal more dinner than usual, and sit in the hot sun on the top of a church-tower – or even anywhere else – you become soon and strangely sleepy. Now Anthea and Jane and Cyril and Robert were very like you in many ways, and when they had eaten all they could, and drunk all there was, they became sleepy, strangely and soon – especially Anthea, because she had got up so early.

One by one they left off talking and leaned back, and before it was a quarter of an hour after dinner they had all curled round and tucked themselves up under their large soft warm wings and were fast asleep. And the sun was sinking slowly in the west. (I must say it was in the west, because it is usual in books to say so, for fear careless people should think it was setting in the east. In point of fact, it was not exactly in the west either – but that's near enough.) The sun, I repeat, was sinking slowly in the west, and the children slept warmly and happily on – for wings are cosier than eiderdown quilts to sleep under. The shadow of the church-tower

fell across the churchyard, and across the Vicarage, and across the field beyond; and presently there were no more shadows, and the sun had set, and the wings were gone. And still the children slept. But not for long. Twilight is very beautiful, but it is chilly; and you know, however sleepy you are, you wake up soon enough if your brother or sister happens to be up first and pulls your blankets off you. The four wingless children shivered and woke. And there they were – on the top of a church-tower in the dusky twilight, with blue stars coming out by ones and twos and tens and twenties over their heads – miles away from home, with three-and-three-half-pence in their pockets, and a doubtful act about the necessities of life to be accounted for if anyone found them with the soda-water siphon.

They looked at each other. Cyril spoke first, picking up the siphon:

'We'd better get along down and get rid of this beastly thing. It's dark enough to leave it on the clergyman's doorstep, I should think. Come on.'

There was a little turret at the corner of the tower, and the little turret had a door in it. They had noticed this when they were eating, but had not explored it, as you would have done in their place. Because, of course, when you have wings, and can explore the whole sky, doors seem hardly worth exploring.

Now they turned towards it.

'Of course,' said Cyril, 'this is the way down.'

It was. But the door was locked on the inside!

And the world was growing darker and darker. And they were miles from home. And there was the soda-water siphon.

I shall not tell you whether anyone cried, nor, if so, how many cried, nor who cried. You will be better employed in making up your minds what you would have done if you had been in their place.

5
No Wings

Whether anyone cried or not, there was certainly an interval during which none of the party was quite itself. When they grew calmer, Anthea put her handkerchief in her pocket and her arm round Jane, and said:

'It can't be for more than one night. We can signal with our handkerchiefs in the morning. They'll be dry then. And someone will come up and let us out –'

'And find the siphon,' said Cyril gloomily; 'and we shall be sent to prison for stealing –'

'You said it wasn't stealing. You said you were sure it wasn't.'

'I'm not sure *now*,' said Cyril shortly.

'Let's throw the beastly thing slap away among the trees,' said Robert, 'then no one can do anything to us.'

'Oh yes' – Cyril's laugh was not a lighthearted one – 'and hit some chap on the head, and be murderers as well as – as the other thing.'

'But we can't stay up here all night,' said Jane; 'and I want my tea.'

'You *can't* want your tea,' said Robert; 'you've only just had your dinner.'

'But I *do* want it,' she said; 'especially when you begin talking about stopping up here all night. Oh, Panther – I want to go home! I want to go home!'

'Hush, hush,' Anthea said. 'Don't, dear. It'll be all right, somehow. Don't, don't –'

'Let her cry,' said Robert desperately; 'if she howls loud enough, someone may hear and come and let us out.'

'And see the soda-water thing,' said Anthea swiftly. 'Robert, don't be a brute. Oh, Jane, do try to be a man! It's just the same for all of us.'

Jane did try to 'be a man' – and reduced her howls to sniffs.

There was a pause. Then Cyril said slowly, 'Look here. We must risk that siphon. I'll button it up inside my jacket – perhaps no one will notice it. You others keep well in front of me. There are lights in the clergyman's house. They've not gone to bed yet. We must just yell as loud as ever we can. Now all scream when I say three. Robert, you do the yell like the railway engine, and I'll do the coo-ee like father's. The girls can do as they please. One, two, three!'

A fourfold yell rent the silent peace of the evening, and a maid at one of the Vicarage windows paused with her hand on the blind-cord.

'One, two, three!' Another yell, piercing and complex,

startled the owls and starlings to a flutter of feathers in the belfry below. The maid fled from the Vicarage window and ran down the Vicarage stairs and into the Vicarage kitchen, and fainted as soon as she had explained to the man-servant and the cook and the cook's cousin that she had seen a ghost. It was quite untrue, of course, but I suppose the girl's nerves were a little upset by the yelling.

'One, two, three!' The Vicar was on his doorstep by this time, and there was no mistaking the yell that greeted him.

'Goodness me,' he said to his wife, 'my dear, someone's being murdered in the church! Give me my hat and a thick stick, and tell Andrew to come after me. I expect it's the lunatic who stole the tongue.'

The children had seen the flash of light when the Vicar opened his front door. They had seen his dark form on the doorstep, and they had paused for breath, and also to see what he would do.

When he turned back for his hat, Cyril said hastily:

'He thinks he only fancied he heard something. You don't half yell! Now! One, two, three!'

It was certainly a whole yell this time, and the Vicar's wife flung her arms round her husband and screamed a feeble echo of it.

'You shan't go!' she said, 'not alone. Jessie!' – the maid unfainted and came out of the kitchen – 'send Andrew at once. There's a dangerous lunatic in the church, and he must go immediately and catch it.'

'I expect he *will* catch it too,' said Jessie to herself as she went through the kitchen door. 'Here, Andrew,' she said, 'there's someone screaming like mad in the church, and the missus says you're to go along and catch it.'

'Not alone, I don't,' said Andrew in low firm tones. To his master he merely said, 'Yis, sir.'

'You heard those screams?'

'I did think I noticed a sort of something,' said Andrew.

'Well, come on, then,' said the Vicar. 'My dear, I *must* go!' He pushed her gently into the sitting-room, banged the door, and rushed out, dragging Andrew by the arm.

A volley of yells greeted them. As it died into silence Andrew shouted, 'Hullo, you there! Did you call?'

'Yes,' shouted four far-away voices.

'They seem to be in the air,' said the Vicar. 'Very remarkable.'

'Where are you?' shouted Andrew, and Cyril replied in his deepest voice, very slow and loud:

'CHURCH! TOWER! TOP!'

'Come down, then!' said Andrew; and the same voice replied:

'*Can't! Door locked!*'

'My goodness!' said the Vicar. 'Andrew fetch the stable lantern. Perhaps it would be as well to fetch another man from the village.'

'With the rest of the gang about, very likely. No, sir; if this 'ere ain't a trap – well, may I never! There's cook's cousin at the back door now. He's a keeper, sir, and used to dealing with vicious characters. And he's got his gun, sir.'

'Hullo there!' shouted Cyril from the church-tower; 'come up and let us out.'

'We're a-coming,' said Andrew. 'I'm a-going to get a policeman and a gun.'

'Andrew, Andrew,' said the Vicar, 'that's not the truth.'

'It's near enough, sir, for the likes of them.'

So Andrew fetched the lantern and the cook's cousin; and the Vicar's wife begged them all to be very careful.

They went across the churchyard – it was quite dark now – and as they went they talked. The Vicar was certain a lunatic was on the church-tower – the one who had written the mad letter, and taken the cold tongue and things. Andrew thought it was a 'trap'; the cook's cousin alone was calm. 'Great cry, little wool,' said he; 'dangerous chaps is quieter.' He was not at all afraid. But then he had a gun. That was why he was asked to lead the way up the worn steep dark steps of the church-tower. He did lead the way, with the lantern in one hand and the gun in the other. Andrew went next. He pretended afterwards that this was because he was braver than his master, but really it was because he thought of traps, and he did not like the idea of being behind the others for fear someone should come softly up behind him and catch hold of his legs in the dark. They went on and on, and round and round the little corkscrew staircase – then through the bell-ringers' loft, where the bell-ropes hung with soft furry ends like giant caterpillars – then up another stair into the belfry, where the big quiet bells are – and then on, up a ladder with broad steps – and then up a little stone stair. And at the top of that there was a little door. And the door was bolted on the stair side.

The cook's cousin, who was a gamekeeper, kicked at the door, and said:

'Hullo, you there!'

The children were holding on to each other on the other side of the door, and trembling with anxiousness – and very hoarse with their howls. They could hardly speak, but Cyril managed to reply huskily:

'Hullo, you there!'

'How did you get up there?'

It was no use saying 'We flew up', so Cyril said:

'We got up – and then we found the door was locked and we couldn't get down. Let us out – do.'

'How many of you are there?' asked the keeper.

'Only four,' said Cyril.

'Are you armed?'

'Are we what?'

'I've got my gun handy – so you'd best not try any tricks,' said the keeper. 'If we open the door, will you promise to come quietly down, and no nonsense?'

'Yes – oh YES!' said all the children together.

'Bless me,' said the Vicar, 'surely that was a female voice?'

'Shall I open the door, sir?' said the keeper. Andrew went down a few steps, 'to leave room for the others' he said afterwards.

'Yes,' said the Vicar, 'open the door. Remember,' he said through the keyhole, 'we have come to release you. You will keep your promise to refrain from violence?'

'How this bolt do stick,' said the keeper; 'anyone 'ud

117

think it hadn't been drawed for half a year.' As a matter of fact it hadn't.

When all the bolts were drawn, the keeper spoke deep-chested words through the keyhole.

'I don't open,' said he, 'till you've gone over to the other side of the tower. And if one of you comes at me I fire. Now!'

'We're all over on the other side,' said the voices.

The keeper felt pleased with himself, and owned himself a bold man when he threw open that door, and, stepping out into the leads, flashed the full light of the stable lantern on to the group of desperadoes standing against the parapet on the other side of the tower.

He lowered his gun, and he nearly dropped the lantern.

'So help me,' he cried, 'if they ain't a pack of kiddies!'

The Vicar now advanced.

'How did you come here?' he asked severely. 'Tell me at once.'

'Oh, take us down,' said Jane, catching at his coat, 'and we'll tell you anything you like. You won't believe us, but it doesn't matter. Oh, take us down!'

The others crowded round him, with the same entreaty. All but Cyril. He had enough to do with the soda-water siphon, which would keep slipping down under his jacket. It needed both hands to keep it steady in its place.

But he said, standing as far out of the lantern light as possible:

'Please do take us down.'

So they were taken down. It is no joke to go down a strange church-tower in the dark, but the keeper helped them – only, Cyril had to be independent because of the soda-water siphon. It would keep trying to get away. Half-way down the ladder it all but escaped. Cyril just caught it by its spout, and as nearly as possible lost his footing. He was trembling and pale when at last they reached the bottom of the winding stair and stepped out on to the flags of the church-porch.

Then suddenly the keeper caught Cyril and Robert each by an arm.

'You bring along the gells, sir,' said he; 'you and Andrew can manage them.'

'Let go!' said Cyril; 'we aren't running away. We haven't hurt your old church. Leave go!'

'You just come along,' said the keeper; and Cyril dared not oppose him with violence, because just then the siphon began to slip again.

So they were all marched into the Vicarage study, and the Vicar's wife came rushing in.

'Oh, William, *are* you safe?' she cried.

Robert hastened to allay her anxiety.

'Yes,' he said, 'he's quite safe. We haven't hurt him at all. And please, we're very late, and they'll be anxious at home. Could you send us home in your carriage?'

'Or perhaps there's a hotel near where we could get a

carriage from,' said Anthea. 'Martha will be very anxious as it is.'

The Vicar had sunk into a chair, overcome by emotion and amazement.

Cyril had also sat down, and was leaning forward with his elbows on his knees because of that soda-water siphon.

'But how did you come to be locked up in the church-tower?' asked the Vicar.

'We went up,' said Robert slowly, 'and we were tired, and we all went to sleep, and when we woke up we found the door was locked, so we yelled.'

'I should think you did!' said the Vicar's wife. 'Frightening everybody out of their wits like this! You ought to be ashamed of yourselves.'

'We *are*,' said Jane gently.

'But who locked the door?' asked the Vicar.

'I don't know at all,' said Robert, with perfect truth. 'Do please send us home.'

'Well, really,' said the Vicar, 'I suppose we'd better. Andrew, put the horse to, and you can take them home.'

'Not alone, I don't,' said Andrew to himself.

'And,' the Vicar went on, 'let this be a lesson to you . . .' He went on talking, and the children listened miserably. But the keeper was not listening. He was looking at the unfortunate Cyril. He knew all about poachers of course, so he knew how people look when they're hiding something.

The Vicar had just got to the part about trying to grow up to be a blessing to your parents, and not a trouble and a disgrace, when the keeper suddenly said:

'Arst him what he's got there under his jacket'; and Cyril knew that concealment was at an end. So he stood up, and squared his shoulders and tried to look noble, like the boys in books that no one can look in the face of and doubt that they come of brave and noble families and will be faithful to the death, and he pulled out the soda-water siphon and said:

'Well, there you are, then.'

There was a silence. Cyril went on – there was nothing else for it:

'Yes, we took this out of your larder, and some chicken and tongue and bread. We were very hungry, and we didn't take the custard or jam. We only took bread and meat and water – and we couldn't help its being the soda kind – just the necessaries of life; and we left half-a-crown to pay for it, and we left a letter. And we're very sorry. And my father will pay a fine or anything you like, but don't send us to prison. Mother would be so vexed. You know what you said about not being a disgrace. Well, don't you go and do it to us – that's all! We're as sorry as we can be. There!'

'However did you get up to the larder window?' said Mrs Vicar.

'I can't tell you that,' said Cyril firmly.

'Is this the whole truth you've been telling me?' asked the clergyman.

'No,' answered Jane suddenly; 'it's all true, but it's not the whole truth. We can't tell you that. It's no good asking. Oh, do forgive us and take us home!' She ran to the Vicar's wife and threw her arms round her. The Vicar's wife put her arms round Jane, and the keeper whispered behind his hand to the Vicar:

'They're all right, sir – I expect it's a pal they're standing by. Someone put 'em up to it, and they won't peach. Game little kids.'

'Tell me,' said the Vicar kindly, 'are you screening someone else? Had anyone else anything to do with this?'

'Yes,' said Anthea, thinking of the Psammead; 'but it wasn't their fault.'

'Very well, my dears,' said the Vicar, 'then let's say no more about it. Only just tell us why you wrote such an odd letter.'

'I don't know,' said Cyril. 'You see, Anthea wrote it in such a hurry, and it really didn't seem like stealing then. But afterwards, when we found we couldn't get down off the church-tower, it seemed just exactly like it. We are all very sorry –'

'Say no more about it,' said the Vicar's wife; 'but another time just think before you take other people's tongues. Now – some cake and milk before you go home?'

When Andrew came to say that the horse was put to,

and was he expected to be led alone into the trap that he had plainly seen from the first, he found the children eating cake and drinking milk and laughing at the Vicar's jokes. Jane was sitting on the Vicar's wife's lap.

So you see they got off better than they deserved.

The gamekeeper, who was the cook's cousin, asked leave to drive home with them, and Andrew was only too glad to have someone to protect him from the trap he was so certain of.

When the wagonette reached their own house, between the chalk-quarry and the gravel-pit, the children were very sleepy, but they felt that they and the keeper were friends for life.

Andrew dumped the children down at the iron gate without a word.

'You get along home,' said the Vicarage cook's cousin, who was a gamekeeper. 'I'll get me home on Shanks' mare.'

So Andrew had to drive off alone, which he did not like at all, and it was the keeper that was cousin to the Vicarage cook who went with the children to the door, and, when they had been swept to bed in a whirlwind of reproaches, remained to explain to Martha and the cook and the housemaid exactly what had happened. He explained so well that Martha was quite amiable the next morning.

After that he often used to come over and see Martha, and in the end – but that is another story, as dear Mr Kipling says.

Martha was obliged to stick to what she had said the night before about keeping the children indoors the next day for a punishment. But she wasn't at all snarky about it, and agreed to let Robert go out for half an hour to get something he particularly wanted.

This, of course, was the day's wish.

Robert rushed to the gravel-pit, found the Psammead, and presently wished for –

But that, too, is another story.

6

A Castle and no Dinner

The others were to be kept in as a punishment for the misfortunes of the day before. Of course Martha thought it was naughtiness, and not misfortune – so you must not blame her. She only thought she was doing her duty. You know grown-up people often say they do not like to punish you, and that they only do it for your own good, and that it hurts them as much as it hurts you – and this is really very often the truth.

Martha certainly hated having to punish the children quite as much as they hated to be punished. For one thing, she knew what a noise there would be in the house all day. And she had other reasons.

'I declare,' she said to the cook, 'it seems almost a shame keeping of them indoors this lovely day; but they are that audacious, they'll be walking in with their heads knocked off some of these days, if I don't put my foot down. You make them a cake for tea tomorrow, dear. And we'll have Baby along of us soon as we've got a bit forrard with our work. Then they can have a good romp with them beds. Here's ten o'clock nearly, and no rabbits caught!'

People say that in Kent when they mean 'and no work done'.

So all the others were kept in, but Robert, as I have said, was allowed to go out for half an hour to get something they all wanted. And that, of course, was the day's wish.

He had no difficulty in finding the Sand-fairy, for the day was already so hot that it had actually, for the first time, come out of its own accord, and it was sitting in a sort of pool of soft sand, stretching itself, and trimming its whiskers, and turning its snail's eyes round and round.

'Ha!' it said when its left eye saw Robert; 'I've been looking out for you. Where are the rest of you? Not smashed themselves up with those wings, I hope?'

'No,' said Robert; 'but the wings got us into a row, just like all the wishes always do. So the others are kept indoors, and I was only let out for half an hour – to get the wish. So please let me wish as quickly as I can.'

'Wish away,' said the Psammead, twisting itself round in the sand. But Robert couldn't wish away. He forgot all the things he had been thinking about, and nothing would come into his head but little things for himself, like toffee, a foreign stamp album, or a clasp-knife with three blades and a corkscrew. He sat down to think better, but it was no use. He could only think of things the others would not have cared for – such as a football, or a pair of leg-guards, or to be able to lick Simpkins minor thoroughly when he went back to school.

'Well,' said the Psammead at last, 'you'd better hurry up with that wish of yours. Time flies.'

'I know it does,' said Robert. '*I* can't think what to wish for. I wish you could give one of the others their wish without their having to come here to ask for it. Oh, *don't!*'

But it was too late. The Psammead had blown itself out to about three times its proper size, and now it collapsed like a pricked bubble, and with a deep sigh leaned back against the edge of its sand-pool, quite faint with the effort.

'There!' it said in a weak voice; 'it was tremendously hard – but I did it. Run along home, or they're sure to wish for something silly before you get there.'

They were – quite sure; Robert felt this, and as he ran home his mind was deeply occupied with the sort of wishes he might find they had wished in his absence. They might wish for rabbits, or white mice, or chocolate, or a fine day tomorrow, or even – and that was most likely – someone might have said, 'I do wish to goodness Robert would hurry up.' Well, he *was* hurrying up, and so they would have their wish, and the day would be wasted. Then he tried to think what they could wish for – something that would be amusing indoors. That had been his own difficulty from the beginning. So few things are amusing indoors when the sun is shining outside and you mayn't go out, however much you want to.

Robert was running as fast as he could, but when he turned the corner that ought to have brought him within sight of the architect's nightmare – the ornamental iron-work on the top of the house – he opened his eyes so wide that he had to drop into a walk; for you cannot run with your eyes wide open. Then suddenly he stopped short, for there was no house to be seen. The front-garden railings were gone too, and where the house had stood – Robert rubbed his eyes and looked again. Yes, the others *had* wished – there was no doubt about that – and they must have wished that they lived in a castle; for there the castle stood black and stately, and very tall and broad, with battlements and lancet windows, and eight great towers; and, where the garden and the orchard had been, there were white things dotted like mushrooms. Robert walked slowly on, and as he got nearer he saw that these were tents, and men in armour were walking about among the tents – crowds and crowds of them.

'Oh, crikey!' said Robert fervently. 'They *have*! They've wished for a castle, and it's being besieged! It's just like that Sand-fairy! I wish we'd never seen the beastly thing!'

At the little window above the great gateway, across the

moat that now lay where the garden had been but half an hour ago, someone was waving something pale and dust-coloured. Robert thought it was one of Cyril's handkerchiefs. They had never been white since the day when he had upset the bottle of 'Combined Toning and Fixing Solution' into the drawer where they were. Robert waved back, and immediately felt that he had been unwise. For his signal had been seen by the besieging force, and two men in steel-caps were coming towards him. They had high brown boots on their long legs, and they came towards him with such great strides that Robert remembered the shortness of his own legs and did not run away. He knew it would be useless to himself, and he feared it might be irritating to the foe. So he stood still – and the two men seemed quite pleased with him.

'By my halidom,' said one, 'a brave varlet this!'

Robert felt pleased at being *called* brave, and some-how it made him *feel* brave. He passed over the 'varlet'. It was the way people talked in historical romances for the young, he knew, and it was evidently not meant for rudeness. He only hoped he would be able to understand what they said to him. He had not always been able quite to follow the conversations in the historical romances for the young.

'His garb is strange,' said the other. 'Some outlandish treachery, belike.'

'Say, lad, what brings thee hither?'

Robert knew this meant, 'Now then, youngster, what are you up to here, eh?' – so he said:

'If you please, I want to go home.'

'Go, then!' said the man in the longest boots; 'none

hindereth, and nought lets us to follow. Zooks!' he added in a cautious undertone, 'I misdoubt me but he beareth tidings to the besieged.'

'Where dwellest thou, young knave?' inquired the man with the largest steel-cap.

'Over there,' said Robert; and directly he had said it he knew he ought to have said 'Yonder!'

'Ha – sayest so?' rejoined the longest boots. 'Come hither, boy. This is a matter for our leader.'

And to the leader Robert was dragged forthwith – by the reluctant ear.

The leader was the most glorious creature Robert had ever seen. He was exactly like the pictures Robert had so often admired in the historical romances. He had armour, and a helmet, and a horse, and a crest, and feathers, and a shield, and a lance, and a sword. His armour and his weapons were all, I am almost sure, of quite different periods. The shield was thirteenth-century, while the sword was of the pattern used in the Peninsular War. The cuirass was of the time of Charles I, and the helmet dated from the Second Crusade. The arms on the shield were very grand – three red running lions on a blue ground. The tents were of the latest brand and the whole appearance of camp, army, and leader might have been a shock to some. But Robert was dumb with admiration, and it all seemed to him perfectly correct, because he knew no more of heraldry or archaeology than the gifted artists who usually drew the pictures for the historical romances. The scene was indeed 'exactly like a picture'. He admired it all so much that he felt braver than ever.

'Come hither, lad,' said the glorious leader, when the men in Cromwellian steel-caps had said a few low eager words. And he took off his helmet, because he could not see properly with it on. He had a kind face, and long fair hair. 'Have no fear; thou shalt take no scathe,' he said.

Robert was glad of that. He wondered what 'scathe' was, and if it was nastier than the senna tea which he had to take sometimes.

'Unfold thy tale without alarm,' said the leader kindly. 'Whence comest thou, and what is thine intent?'

'My what?' said Robert.

'What seekest thou to accomplish? What is thine errand, that thou wanderest here alone among these rough men-at-arms? Poor child, thy mother's heart aches for thee e'en now, I'll warrant me.'

'I don't think so,' said Robert; 'you see, she doesn't know I'm out.'

The leader wiped away a manly tear, exactly as a leader in a historical romance would have done, and said:

'Fear not to speak the truth, my child; thou hast nought to fear from Wulfric de Talbot.'

Robert had a wild feeling that this glorious leader of

the besieging party – being himself part of a wish – would be able to understand better than Martha, or the gipsies, or the policeman in Rochester, or the clergyman of yesterday, the true tale of the wishes and the Psammead. The only difficulty was that he knew he could never remember enough 'quothas' and 'beshrew mes', and things like that, to make his talk sound like the talk of a boy in a historical romance. However, he began boldly enough, with a sentence straight out of *Ralph de Courcy; or, The Boy Crusader*. He said:

'Grammercy for thy courtesy, fair sir knight. The fact is, it's like this – and I hope you're not in a hurry, because the story's rather a breather. Father and mother are away, and when we were down playing in the sand-pits we found a Psammead.'

'I cry thee mercy! A Sammyadd?' said the knight.

'Yes, a sort of – of fairy, or enchanter – yes, that's it, an enchanter; and he said we could have a wish every day, and we wished first to be beautiful.'

'Thy wish was scarce granted,' muttered one of the men-at-arms, looking at Robert, who went on as if he had not heard, though he thought the remark very rude indeed.

'And then we wished for money – treasure, you know; but we couldn't spend it. And yesterday we wished for wings, and we got them, and we had a ripping time to begin with –'

'Thy speech is strange and uncouth,' said Sir Wulfric de Talbot. 'Repeat thy words – what hadst thou?'

'A ripping – I mean a jolly – no – we were contented with our lot – that's what I mean; only, after that we got into an awful fix.'

'What is a fix? A fray, mayhap?'

'No – not a fray. A – a – a tight place.'

'A dungeon? Alas for thy youthful fettered limbs!' said the knight, with polite sympathy.

'It wasn't a dungeon. We just – just encountered un-deserved misfortunes,' Robert explained, 'and today we are punished by not being allowed to go out. That's where I live,' – he pointed to the castle. 'The others are in there, and they're not allowed to go out. It's all the Psammead's – I mean the enchanter's fault. I wish we'd never seen him.'

'He is an enchanter of might?'

'Oh yes – of might and main. Rather!'

'And thou deemest that it is the spells of the enchanter whom thou hast angered that have lent strength to the besieging party,' said the gallant leader; 'but know thou that Wulfric de Talbot needs no enchanter's aid to lead his followers to victory.'

'No, I'm sure you don't,' said Robert, with hasty courtesy; 'of course not – you wouldn't, you know. But, all the same, it's partly his fault, but we're most to blame. You couldn't have done anything if it hadn't been for us.'

'How now, bold boy?' asked Sir Wulfric haughtily. 'Thy speech is dark, and eke scarce courteous. Unravel me this riddle!'

'Oh,' said Robert desperately, 'of course you don't know it, but you're not *real* at all. You're only here because the others must have been idiots enough to wish for a castle – and when the sun sets you'll just vanish away, and it'll be all right.'

The captain and the men-at-arms exchanged glances, at first pitying, and then sterner, as the longest-booted man said, 'Beware, noble my lord; the urchin doth but feign madness to escape from our clutches. Shall we not bind him?'

'I'm no more mad than you are,' said Robert angrily, 'perhaps not so much – only, I was an idiot to think you'd understand anything. Let me go – I haven't done anything to you.'

'Whither?' asked the knight, who seemed to have believed all the enchanter story till it came to his own share in it. 'Whither wouldst thou wend?'

'Home, of course.' Robert pointed to the castle.

'To carry news of succour? Nay!'

'All right then,' said Robert, struck by a sudden idea; 'then let me go somewhere else.' His mind sought eagerly among his memories of the historical romance.

'Sir Wulfric de Talbot,' he said slowly, 'should think foul scorn to – to keep a chap – I mean one who has done him no hurt – when he wants to cut off quietly – I mean to depart without violence.'

'This to my face! Beshrew thee for a knave!' replied Sir Wulfric. But the appeal seemed to have gone home. 'Yet thou sayest sooth,' he added thoughtfully. 'Go where thou wilt,' he added nobly, 'thou art free. Wulfric de Talbot warreth not with babes, and Jakin here shall bear thee company.'

'All right,' said Robert wildly. 'Jakin will enjoy himself, I think. Come on, Jakin. Sir Wulfric, I salute thee.'

He saluted after the modern military manner, and set off running to the sand-pit, Jakin's long boots keeping up easily.

He found the Fairy. He dug it up, he woke it up, he implored it to give him one more wish.

'I've done two today already,' it grumbled, 'and one was as stiff a bit of work as ever I did.'

'Oh, do, do, do, do, *do*!' said Robert, while Jakin looked on with an expression of open-mouthed horror at the strange beast that talked, and gazed with its snail's eyes at him.

'Well, what is it?' snapped the Psammead, with cross sleepiness.

'I wish I was with the others,' said Robert. And the Psammead began to swell. Robert never thought of wishing the castle and the siege away. Of course he knew they had all come out of a wish, but swords and daggers and pikes and lances seemed much too real to be wished away. Robert lost consciousness for an instant. When he opened his eyes the others were crowding around him.

'We never heard you come in,' they said. 'How awfully jolly of you to wish it to give us our wish!'

'Of course we understood that was what you'd done.'

'But you ought to have told us. Suppose we'd wished something silly.'

'Silly?' said Robert, very crossly indeed. 'How much

sillier could you have been, I'd like to know? You nearly settled *me* – I can tell you.'

Then he told his story, and the others admitted that it certainly had been rough on him. But they praised his courage and cleverness so much that he presently got back his lost temper, and felt braver than ever, and consented to be captain of the besieged force.

'We haven't done anything yet,' said Anthea comfortably; 'we waited for you. We're going to shoot at them through these little loopholes with the bow and arrows uncle gave you, and you shall have first shot.'

'I don't think I would,' said Robert cautiously; 'you don't know what they're like near to. They've got *real* bows and arrows – an awful length – and swords and pikes and daggers, and all sorts of sharp things. They're all quite, quite real. It's not just a – a picture, or a vision, or anything; they can *hurt us* – or kill us even, I shouldn't wonder. I can feel my ear all sore still. Look here – have you explored the castle? Because I think we'd better let them alone as long as they let us alone. I heard that Jakin man say they weren't going to attack till just before sundown. We can be getting ready for the attack. Are there any soldiers in the castle to defend it?'

'We don't know,' said Cyril. 'You see, directly I'd wished we were in a besieged castle, everything seemed to go upside down, and when it came straight we looked out of the window, and saw the camp and things and you – and of course we kept on looking at everything. Isn't this room jolly? It's as real as real!'

It was. It was square, with stone walls four feet thick, and great beams for ceiling. A low door at the corner led to a flight of steps, up and down. The children went down; they found themselves in a great arched gatehouse – the enormous doors were shut and barred. There was a window in a little room at the bottom of the round turret up which the stair wound, rather larger than the other windows, and looking through it they saw that the drawbridge was up and the portcullis down; the moat looked very wide and deep. Opposite the great door that led to the moat was another great door, with a little door in it. The children went through this, and found themselves in a big paved courtyard, with the great grey walls of the castle rising dark and heavy on all four sides.

Near the middle of the courtyard stood Martha, moving her right hand backwards and forwards in the air. The cook was stooping down and moving her hands, also in a very curious way. But the oddest and at the same time most terrible thing was the Lamb, who was sitting on nothing, about three feet from the ground, laughing happily.

The children ran towards him. Just as Anthea was reaching out her arms to take him, Martha said crossly, 'Let him alone – do, miss, when he is good.'

'But what's he *doing*?' said Anthea.

'Doing? Why, a-setting in his high chair as good as gold, a precious, watching me doing of the ironing. Get along with you, do – my iron's cold again.'

She went towards the cook, and seemed to poke an invisible fire with an unseen poker – the cook seemed to be putting an unseen dish into an invisible oven.

'Run along with you, do,' she said; 'I'm behind-hand as it is. You won't get no dinner if you come a-hindering of me like this. Come, off you goes, or I'll pin a dishcloth to some of your tails.'

'You're *sure* the Lamb's all right?' asked Jane anxiously.

'Right as ninepence, if you don't come unsettling of him. I thought you'd like to be rid of him for today; but take him, if you want him, for gracious' sake.'

'No, no,' they said, and hastened away. They would have to defend the castle presently, and the Lamb was safer even suspended in mid-air in an invisible kitchen than in the guardroom of a besieged castle. They went through the first doorway they came to, and sat down helplessly on a wooden bench that ran along the room inside.

'How awful!' said Anthea and Jane together; and Jane added, 'I feel as if I was in a mad asylum.'

'What does it mean?' Anthea said. 'It's creepy; I don't like it. I wish we'd wished for something plain – a rocking-horse, or a donkey, or something.'

'It's no use wishing *now*,' said Robert bitterly; and Cyril said:

'Do dry up a sec; I want to think.'

He buried his face in his hands, and the others looked about them. They were in a long room with an arched roof. There were wooden tables along it, and one across at the end of the room, on a sort of raised platform. The room was very dim and dark. The floor was strewn with dry things like sticks, and they did not smell nice.

Cyril sat up suddenly and said:

'Look here – it's all right. I think it's like this. You know, we wished that the servants shouldn't notice any difference when we got wishes. And nothing happens to the Lamb unless we specially wish it to. So of course they don't notice the castle or anything. But then the castle is on the same place where our house was – is, I mean – and the servants have to go on being in the house, or else they would notice. But you can't have a castle mixed up with our house – and so we can't see the house, because we see the castle; and they can't see the castle, because they go on seeing the house; and so –'

'Oh, *don't*!' said Jane; 'you make my head go all swimmy, like being on a roundabout. It doesn't matter! Only, I hope we shall be able to see our dinner, that's all – because if it's invisible it'll be unfeelable as well, and then we can't eat it! I *know* it will, because I tried to feel if I could feel the Lamb's chair, and there was nothing under him at all but air. And we can't eat air, and I feel just as if I hadn't had any breakfast for years and years.'

141

'It's no use thinking about it,' said Anthea. 'Let's go on exploring. Perhaps we might find something to eat.'

This lighted hope in every breast, and they went on exploring the castle. But though it was the most perfect and delightful castle you can possibly imagine, and furnished in the most complete and beautiful manner, neither food nor men-at-arms were to be found in it.

'If only you'd thought of wishing to be besieged in a castle thoroughly garrisoned and provisioned!' said Jane reproachfully.

'You can't think of everything, you know,' said Anthea. 'I should think it must be nearly dinner-time by now.'

It wasn't; but they hung about watching the strange movements of the servants in the middle of the court-yard, because, of course, they couldn't be sure where the dining-room of the invisible house was. Presently they saw Martha carrying an invisible tray across the court-yard, for it seemed that, by the most fortunate accident, the dining-room of the house and the banqueting-hall of the castle were in the same place. But oh, how their hearts sank when they perceived that the tray was invisible!

They waited in wretched silence while Martha went through the form of carving an unseen leg of mutton and serving invisible greens and potatoes with a spoon that no one could see. When she had left the room, the children looked at the empty table, and then at each other.

'This is worse than anything,' said Robert, who had not till now been particularly keen on his dinner.

'I'm not so very hungry,' said Anthea, trying to make the best of things, as usual.

Cyril tightened his belt ostentatiously. Jane burst into tears.

7

A Siege and Bed

The children were sitting in the gloomy banqueting-hall, at the end of one of the long bare wooden tables. There was now no hope. Martha had brought in the dinner, and the dinner was invisible, and unfeelable too; for, when they rubbed their hands along the table, they knew but too well that for them there was nothing there *but* table.

Suddenly Cyril felt in his pocket.

'Right, *oh*!' he cried. 'Look here! Biscuits.'

Rather broken and crumbled, certainly, but still biscuits. Three whole ones, and a generous handful of crumbs and fragments.

'I got them this morning – cook – and I'd quite forgotten,' he explained as he divided them with scrupulous fairness into four heaps.

They were eaten in a happy silence, though they tasted a little oddly, because they had been in Cyril's pocket all the morning with a hank of tarred twine, some green fir-cones, and a ball of cobbler's wax.

'Yes, but look here, Squirrel,' said Robert; 'you're so

clever at explaining about invisibleness and all that. How is it the biscuits are here, and all the bread and meat and things have disappeared?'

'I don't know,' said Cyril after a pause, 'unless it's because *we* had them. Nothing about us has changed. Everything's in my pocket all right.'

'Then if we *had* the mutton it would be real,' said Robert. 'Oh, don't I wish we could find it!'

'But we can't find it. I suppose it isn't ours till we've got it in our mouths.'

'Or in our pockets,' said Jane, thinking of the biscuits.

'Who puts mutton in their pockets, goose-girl?' said Cyril. 'But I know – at any rate, I'll try it!'

He leaned over the table with his face about an inch from it, and kept opening and shutting his mouth as if he were taking bites out of air.

'It's no good,' said Robert in deep dejection. 'You'll only – Hullo!'

Cyril stood up with a grin of triumph, holding a square piece of bread in his mouth. It was quite real. Everyone saw it. It is true that, directly he bit a piece off, the rest vanished; but it was all right, because he knew he had it in his hand though he could neither see nor feel it. He took another bite from the air between his fingers, and it turned into bread as he bit. The next moment all the others were following his example, and opening and shutting their mouths an inch or so from the bare-looking table. Robert captured a slice of mutton, and – but I think I will draw a veil over the rest of this painful scene. It is enough to say that they all had enough mutton, and that when Martha came to change the plates she said she had never seen such a mess in all her born days.

The pudding was, fortunately, a plain suet roly-poly, and in answer to Martha's questions the children all with one accord said that they would *not* have treacle on it – nor jam, nor sugar – 'Just plain, please,' they said. Martha said, 'Well, I never – what next, I wonder!' and went away.

Then ensued another scene on which I will not dwell, for nobody looks nice picking up slices of suet pudding from the table in its mouth, like a dog.

The great thing, after all, was that they had had dinner; and now everyone felt more courage to prepare for the attack that was to be delivered before sunset. Robert, as captain, insisted on climbing to the top of one of the towers to reconnoitre, so up they all went. And now they could see all round the castle, and could see, too, that beyond the moat, on every side, the tents of the besieging party were pitched. Rather uncomfortable shivers ran down the children's backs as they saw that all the men were very busy cleaning or sharpening their arms, re-stringing their bows, and polishing their shields. A large party came along the road, with horses dragging along the great trunk of a tree; and Cyril felt quite pale, because he knew this was for a battering-ram.

'What a good thing we've got a moat,' he said; 'and what a good thing the drawbridge is up – I should never have known how to work it.'

'Of course it would be up in a besieged castle.'

'You'd think there ought to have been soldiers in it, wouldn't you?' said Robert.

'You see you don't know how long it's been besieged,' said Cyril darkly; 'perhaps most of the brave defenders were killed quite early in the siege and all the provisions eaten, and now there are only a few intrepid survivors – that's us, and we are going to defend it to the death.'

'How do you begin – defending to the death, I mean?' asked Anthea.

'We ought to be heavily armed – and then shoot at them when they advance to the attack.'

'They used to pour boiling lead down on besiegers when they got too close,' said Anthea. 'Father showed me the holes on purpose for pouring it down through at Bodiam Castle. And there are holes like it in the gate-tower here.'

'I think I'm glad it's only a game; it *is* only a game, isn't it?' said Jane.

But no one answered.

The children found plenty of strange weapons in the castle, and if they were armed at all it was soon plain that they would be, as Cyril said, 'armed heavily' – for these swords and lances and crossbows were far too weighty even for Cyril's manly strength; and as for the longbows, none

147

of the children could even begin to bend them. The daggers were better; but Jane hoped that the besiegers would not come close enough for daggers to be of any use.

'Never mind, we can hurl them like javelins,' said Cyril, 'or drop them on people's heads. I say – there are lots of stones on the other side of the courtyard. If we took some of those up? Just to drop on their heads if they were to try swimming the moat.'

So a heap of stones grew apace, up in the room above the gate; and another heap, a shiny spiky dangerous-looking heap, of daggers and knives.

As Anthea was crossing the courtyard for more stones, a sudden and valuable idea came to her. She went to Martha and said, 'May we have just biscuits for tea? We're going to play at besieged castles, and we'd like the biscuits to provision the garrison. Put mine in my pocket, please, my hands are so dirty. And I'll tell the others to fetch theirs.'

This was indeed a happy thought, for now with four generous handfuls of air, which turned to biscuit as Martha crammed it into their pockets, the garrison was well provisioned till sundown.

They brought up some iron pots of cold water to pour on the besiegers instead of hot lead, with which the castle did not seem to be provided.

The afternoon passed with wonderful quickness. It was very exciting; but none of them, except Robert, could feel all the time that this was real deadly dangerous work. To the others, who had only seen the camp and the besiegers from a distance, the whole thing seemed half a game of make-believe, and half a splendidly distinct and perfectly safe dream. But it was only now and then that Robert could feel this.

When it seemed to be tea-time the biscuits were eaten with water from the deep well in the courtyard, drunk out of horns. Cyril insisted on putting by eight of the biscuits, in case anyone should feel faint in stress of battle.

Just as he was putting away the reserve biscuits in a sort of little stone cupboard without a door, a sudden sound made him drop three. It was the loud fierce cry of a trumpet.

'You see it *is* real,' said Robert, 'and they are going to attack.'

All rushed to the narrow windows.

'Yes,' said Robert, 'they're all coming out of their tents and moving about like ants. There's that Jakin dancing about where the bridge joins on. I wish he could see me put my tongue out at him! Yah!'

The others were far too pale to wish to put their tongues out at anybody. They looked at Robert with surprised respect. Anthea said:

'You really *are* brave, Robert.'

'Rot!' Cyril's pallor turned to redness now, all in a minute. 'He's been getting ready to be brave all the afternoon. And I wasn't ready, that's all. I shall be braver than he is in half a jiffy.'

'Oh dear!' said Jane, 'what does it matter which of you is the bravest? I think Cyril was a perfect silly to wish for a castle, and I don't want to play.'

'It *isn't*' – Robert was beginning sternly, but Anthea interrupted –

'Oh yes, you do,' she said coaxingly; 'it's a very nice game, really, because they can't possibly get in, and if they do the women and children are always spared by civilized armies.'

'But are you quite, quite sure they *are* civilized?' asked Jane, panting. 'They seem to be such a long time ago.'

'Of course they are.' Anthea pointed cheerfully through the narrow window. 'Why, look at the little flags on their lances, how bright they are – and how fine the leader is! Look, that's him – isn't it, Robert? – on the grey horse.'

Jane consented to look, and the scene was almost too pretty to be alarming. The green turf, the white tents, the flash of pennoned lances, the gleam of armour, and the bright colours of scarf and tunic – it was just like a splendid coloured picture. The trumpets were sounding, and when the trumpets stopped for breath the children could hear the cling-clang of armour and the murmur of voices.

A trumpeter came forward to the edge of the moat, which now seemed very much narrower than at first, and blew the longest and loudest blast they had yet heard. When the blaring noise had died away, a man who was with the trumpeter shouted:

'What ho, within there!' and his voice came plainly to the garrison in the gate-house.

'Hullo there!' Robert bellowed back at once.

'In the name of our Lord the King, and of our good lord and trusty leader Sir Wulfric de Talbot, we summon this castle to surrender – on pain of fire and sword and no quarter. Do ye surrender?'

'No,' bawled Robert, 'of course we don't! Never, *Never*, NEVER!'

The man answered back:

'Then your fate be on your own heads.'

'Cheer,' said Robert in a fierce whisper. 'Cheer to show them we aren't afraid, and rattle the daggers to make more noise. One, two, three! Hip, hip, hooray! Again – Hip, hip, hooray! One more – Hip, hip, hooray!' The cheers were rather high and weak, but the rattle of the daggers lent them strength and depth.

There was another shout from the camp across the moat – and then the beleaguered fortress felt that the attack had indeed begun.

It was getting rather dark in the room above the great gate, and Jane took a very little courage as she remembered that sunset *couldn't* be far off now.

'The moat is dreadfully thin,' said Anthea.

'But they can't get into the castle even if they do swim over,' said Robert. And as he spoke he heard feet on the stair outside – heavy feet and the clank of steel. No one breathed for a moment. The steel and the feet went on up the turret stairs. Then Robert sprang softly to the door. He pulled off his shoes.

'Wait here,' he whispered, and stole quickly and softly after the boots and the spur-clank. He peeped into the upper room. The man was there – and it was Jakin, all dripping with moat-water, and he was fiddling about with the machinery which Robert felt sure worked the drawbridge. Robert banged the door suddenly, and turned the great key in the lock, just as Jakin sprang to the inside of the door. Then he tore downstairs and into the little turret at the foot of the tower where the biggest window was.

'We ought to have defended *this*!' he cried to the others as they followed him. He was just in time. Another man had swum over, and his fingers were on the window-ledge. Robert never knew how the man had managed to climb up out of the water. But he saw the clinging fingers, and hit them as hard as he could with an iron bar that he caught up from the floor. The man fell with a plop-plash into the moat-water. In another moment Robert was outside the little room, had banged its door and was shooting home the enormous bolts, and calling to Cyril to lend a hand.

Then they stood in the arched gate-house, breathing hard and looking at each other.

Jane's mouth was open.

'Cheer up, Jenny,' said Robert – 'it won't last much longer.'

There was a creaking above, and something rattled and shook. The pavement they stood on seemed to tremble. Then a crash told them that the drawbridge had been lowered to its place.

'That's that beast Jakin,' said Robert. 'There's still the portcullis; I'm almost certain that's worked from lower down.'

And now the drawbridge rang and echoed hollowly to the hoofs of horses and the tramp of armed men.

'Up – quick!' cried Robert. 'Let's drop things on them.'

Even the girls were feeling almost brave now. They followed Robert quickly, and under his directions began to drop stones out through the long narrow windows. There was a confused noise below, and some groans.

'Oh dear!' said Anthea, putting down the stone she was just going to drop out. 'I'm afraid we've hurt somebody!'

Robert caught up the stone in a fury.

'I should just hope we *had*!' he said; 'I'd give something for a jolly good boiling kettle of lead. Surrender, indeed!'

And now came more tramping, and a pause, and then the thundering thump of the battering-ram. And the little room was almost quite dark.

'We've held it,' cried Robert, 'we *won't* surrender! The sun *must* set in a minute. Here – they're all jawing underneath again. Pity there's no time to get more stones! Here, pour that water down on them. It's no good, of course, but they'll hate it.'

'Oh dear!' said Jane; 'don't you think we'd better surrender?'

'Never!' said Robert; 'we'll have a parley if you like, but we'll never surrender. Oh, I'll be a soldier when I grow up – you just see if I don't. I won't go into the Civil Service, whatever anyone says.'

'Let's wave a handkerchief and ask for a parley,' Jane pleaded. 'I don't believe the sun's going to set tonight at all.'

'Give them the water first – the brutes!' said the bloodthirsty Robert. So Anthea tilted the pot over the nearest lead-hole, and poured. They heard a splash below, but no one below seemed to have felt it. And again the ram battered the great door. Anthea paused.

'How idiotic,' said Robert, lying flat on the floor and putting one eye to the lead hole. 'Of course the holes go straight down into the gate-house – that's for when the enemy has got past the door and the portcullis, and almost all is lost. Here, hand me the pot.' He crawled on to the three-cornered window-ledge in the middle of the wall, and, taking the pot from Anthea, poured the water out through the arrow-slit.

And as he began to pour, the noise of the battering-ram and the trampling of the foe and the shouts of 'Surrender!' and 'De Talbot for ever!' all suddenly stopped and went out like the snuff of a candle; the little dark room seemed to whirl round and turn topsy-turvy, and when the children came to themselves there they were safe and sound, in the big front bedroom of their own house – the house with the ornamental nightmare iron-top to the roof.

They all crowded to the window and looked out. The moat and the tents and the besieging force were all gone – and there was the garden with its tangle of dahlias and

marigolds and asters and late roses, and the spiky iron railings and the quiet white road.

Everyone drew a deep breath.

'And that's all right!' said Robert. 'I told you so! And, I say, we didn't surrender, did we?'

'Aren't you glad now I wished for a castle?' asked Cyril.

'I think I am *now*,' said Anthea slowly. 'But I wouldn't wish for it again, I think, Squirrel dear!'

'Oh, it was simply splendid!' said Jane unexpectedly. 'I wasn't frightened a bit.'

'Oh, I say!' Cyril was beginning, but Anthea stopped him.

'Look here,' she said, 'it's just come into my head. This is the very first thing we've wished for that hasn't got us into a row. And there hasn't been the least little scrap of a row about this. Nobody's raging downstairs, we're safe and sound, we've had an awfully jolly day – at least, not jolly exactly, but you know what I mean. And we know now how brave Robert is – and Cyril too, of course,' she added hastily, 'and Jane as well. And we haven't got into a row with a single grown-up.'

The door was opened suddenly and fiercely.

'You ought to be ashamed of yourselves,' said the voice of Martha, and they could tell by her voice that she was very angry indeed. 'I thought you couldn't last through the day without getting up to some doggery! A person can't take a breath of air on the front doorstep but you must be emptying the wash-hand jug on to their heads! Off you go to bed, the lot of you, and try to get up better children in the morning. Now then – don't let me have to tell you twice. If I find any of you not in bed in ten minutes I'll let you know it, that's all! A new cap, and everything!'

She flounced out amid a disregarded chorus of regrets and apologies. The children were very sorry, but really it was not their faults. You can't help it if you are pouring water on a besieging foe, and your castle suddenly changes into your house – and everything changes with it except the water, and that happens to fall on somebody else's clean cap.

'I don't know why the water didn't change into nothing, though,' said Cyril.

'Why should it?' asked Robert. 'Water's water all the world over.'

'I expect the castle well was the same as ours in the stable-yard,' said Jane. And that was really the case.

'I thought we couldn't get through a wish-day without a row,' said Cyril; 'it was much too good to be true. Come on, Bobs, my military hero. If we lick into bed sharp she won't be so frumious, and perhaps she'll bring us up some supper. I'm jolly hungry! Good-night, kids.'

'Good-night. I hope the castle won't come creeping back in the night,' said Jane.

'Of course it won't,' said Anthea briskly, 'but Martha

will – not in the night, but in a minute. Here, turn round, I'll get that knot out of your pinafore strings.'

'Wouldn't it have been degrading for Sir Wulfric de Talbot,' said Jane dreamily, 'if he could have known that half the besieged garrison wore pinafores?'

'And the other half knickerbockers. Yes – frightfully. Do stand still – you're only tightening the knot,' said Anthea.

8

Bigger Than the Baker's Boy

'Look here,' said Cyril. 'I've got an idea.'

'Does it hurt much?' said Robert sympathetically.

'Don't be a jackape! I'm not humbugging.'

'Shut up, Bobs!' said Anthea.

'Silence for the Squirrel's oration,' said Robert.

Cyril balanced himself on the edge of the water-butt in the backyard, where they all happened to be, and spoke.

'Friends, Romans, countrymen – and women – we found a Sammyadd. We have had wishes. We've had wings, and being beautiful as the day – ugh! – that was pretty jolly beastly if you like – and wealth and castles, and that rotten gipsy business with the Lamb. But we're no forrader. We haven't really got anything worth having for our wishes.'

'We've had things happening,' said Robert; 'that's always something.'

'It's not enough, unless they're the right things,' said Cyril firmly. 'Now I've been thinking –'

'Not really?' whispered Robert.

'In the silent what's-its-names of the night. It's like

159

suddenly being asked something out of history – the date of the Conquest or something; you know it all right all the time, but when you're asked it all goes out of your head. Ladies and gentlemen, you know jolly well that when we're all rotting about in the usual way heaps of things keep cropping up, and then real earnest wishes come into the heads of the beholder –'

'Hear, hear!' said Robert.

'– of the beholder, however stupid he is,' Cyril went on. 'Why, even Robert might happen to think of a really useful wish if he didn't injure his poor little brains trying so hard to think. – Shut up, Bobs, I tell you! – You'll have the whole show over.'

A struggle on the edge of a water-butt is exciting, but damp. When it was over, and the boys were partially dried, Anthea said:

'It really was you began it, Bobs. Now honour is satisfied, do let Squirrel go on. We're wasting the whole morning.'

'Well then,' said Cyril, still wringing the water out of the tails of his jacket, 'I'll call it pax if Bobs will.'

'Pax then,' said Robert sulkily. 'But I've got a lump as big as a cricket ball over my eye.'

Anthea patiently offered a dust-coloured handkerchief, and Robert bathed his wounds in silence. 'Now, Squirrel,' she said.

'Well then – let's just play bandits, or forts, or soldiers, or any of the old games. We're dead sure to think of something if we try not to. You always do.'

The others consented. Bandits was hastily chosen for the game. 'It's as good as anything else,' said Jane gloomily. It must be owned that Robert was at first but a half-hearted bandit, but when Anthea had borrowed from Martha the red-spotted handkerchief in which the keeper had brought her mushrooms that morning, and had tied up Robert's head with it so that he could be the wounded hero who had saved the bandit captain's life the day before, he cheered up wonderfully. All were soon armed. Bows and arrows slung on the back look well; and umbrellas and cricket stumps stuck through the belt give a fine impression of the wearer's being armed to the teeth. The white cotton hats that men wear in the country nowadays have a very brigandish effect when a few turkey's feathers are stuck in them. The Lamb's mail-cart was covered with a red-and-blue checked tablecloth, and made an admirable baggage-wagon. The Lamb asleep inside it was not at all in the way. So the banditti set out along the road that led to the sand-pit.

'We ought to be near the Sammyadd,' said Cyril, 'in case we think of anything suddenly.'

It is all very well to make up your minds to play bandits – or chess, or ping-pong, or any other agreeable game – but it is not easy to do it with spirit when all the wonderful wishes you can think of, or can't think of, are waiting for you round the corner. The game was dragging a little, and some of the bandits were beginning to feel that the others were disagreeable things, and were saying so candidly, when the baker's boy came along the road with loaves in a basket. The opportunity was not one to be lost.

'Stand and deliver!' cried Cyril.

'Your money or your life!' said Robert.

And they stood on each side of the baker's boy. Unfortunately, he did not seem to enter into the spirit of the thing at all. He was a baker's boy of an unusually large size. He merely said:

'Chuck it now, d'ye hear!' and pushed the bandits aside most disrespectfully.

Then Robert lassoed him with Jane's skipping-rope, and instead of going round his shoulders, as Robert intended, it went round his feet and tripped him up. The basket was upset, the beautiful new loaves went bumping and bouncing all over the dusty chalky road. The girls ran to pick them up, and all in a moment Robert and the baker's boy were fighting it out, man to man, with Cyril to see fair play, and the skipping-rope twisting round their legs like an interested snake that wished to be a peace-maker. It did not succeed; indeed the way the boxwood handles sprang up and hit the fighters on the shins and ankles was not at all peace-making. I know this is the second fight – or contest – in this chapter, but I can't help it. It was that sort of day. You know yourself there are days when rows seem to keep on happening, quite without your meaning them to. If I were a writer of tales of adventure such as those which used to appear in *The Boys of England* when I was young, of course I should be able to describe the fight, but I cannot do it. I never can see what happens during a fight, even when it is only dogs. Also, if I had been one of these *Boys of England* writers, Robert would have got the best of it. But I am like George Washington – I cannot tell a lie, even about a cherry-tree, much less about a fight, and I cannot conceal from you that Robert was badly beaten, for the second time that day. The baker's boy blacked his other eye, and, being ignorant of the first rules of fair play and gentlemanly behaviour, he also pulled Robert's hair, and kicked him on the knee. Robert always used to say he could have licked the butcher if it hadn't been for the girls. But I am not sure. Anyway, what happened was this, and very painful it was to self-respecting boys.

Cyril was just tearing off his coat so as to help his brother in proper style, when Jane threw her arms round his legs and began to cry and ask him not to go and be beaten too. That 'too' was very nice for Robert, as you can imagine – but it was nothing to what he felt when Anthea rushed in between him and the baker's boy, and caught that unfair and degraded fighter round the waist, imploring him not to fight any more.

'Oh, don't hurt my brother any more!' she said in floods

of tears. 'He didn't mean it – it's only play. And I'm sure he's very sorry.'

You see how unfair this was to Robert. Because, if the baker's boy had had any right and chivalrous instincts, and had yielded to Anthea's pleading and accepted her despicable apology, Robert could not, in honour, have done anything to him at a future time. But Robert's fears, if he had any, were soon dispelled. Chivalry was a stranger to the breast of the baker's boy. He pushed Anthea away very roughly, and he chased Robert with kicks and unpleasant conversation right down the road to the sand-pit, and there, with one last kick, he landed him in a heap of sand.

'I'll larn you, you young varmint!' he said, and went off to pick up his loaves and go about his business. Cyril, impeded by Jane, could do nothing without hurting her, for she clung round his legs with the strength of despair. The baker's boy went off red and damp about the face; abusive to the last, he called them a pack of silly idiots, and disappeared round the corner. Then Jane's grasp loosened. Cyril turned away in silent dignity to follow Robert, and the girls followed him, weeping without restraint.

It was not a happy party that flung itself down in the sand beside the sobbing Robert. For Robert was sobbing – mostly with rage. Though of course I know that a really heroic boy is always dry-eyed after a fight. But then he always wins, which had not been the case with Robert.

Cyril was angry with Jane; Robert was furious with Anthea; the girls were miserable; and not one of the four was pleased with the baker's boy. There was, as French writers say, 'a silence full of emotion'.

Then Robert dug his toes and his hands into the sand and wriggled in his rage. 'He'd better wait till I'm grown up – the cowardly brute! Beast! – I hate him! But I'll pay him out. Just because he's bigger than me.'

'You began,' said Jane incautiously.

'I know I did, silly – but I was only rotting – and he kicked me – look here –'

Robert tore down a stocking and showed a purple bruise touched up with red.

'I only wish I was bigger than him, that's all.'

He dug his fingers in the sand, and sprang up, for his hand had touched something furry. It was the Psammead, of course – 'On the look-out to make sillies of them as usual,' as Cyril remarked later. And of course the next moment Robert's wish was granted, and he was bigger than the baker's boy. Oh, but much, much bigger. He was bigger than the big policeman who used to be at the crossing at the Mansion House years ago – the one who was so kind in helping old ladies over the crossing – and he was the biggest man *I* have ever seen, as well as the kindest. No one had a foot-rule in its pocket, so Robert could not be measured – but he was taller than your father would be if he stood on your mother's head, which I am sure he would never be unkind enough to do. He must have been ten or eleven feet high, and as broad as a boy of that height ought to be; his Norfolk suit had fortunately grown too, and now he stood up in it – with one of his enormous stockings turned down to show the gigantic bruise on his vast leg. Immense tears of fury still stood on his flushed giant face. He looked so surprised, and he was so large to be wearing an Eton collar, that the others could not help laughing.

'The Sammyadd's done us again,' said Cyril.

'Not us – *me*,' said Robert. 'If you'd got any decent feeling you'd try to make it make you the same size. You've no idea how silly it feels,' he added thoughtlessly.

'And I don't want to; I can jolly well see how silly it looks,' Cyril was beginning; but Anthea said:

'Oh, *don't*! I don't know what's the matter with you boys today. Look here, Squirrel, let's play fair. It is hateful for poor old Bobs, all alone up there. Let's ask the Sammyadd for another wish, and, if it will, I do really think we ought to be made the same size.'

The others agreed, but not gaily; but when they found the Psammead, it wouldn't.

'Not I,' it said crossly, rubbing its face with its feet. 'He's a rude violent boy, and it'll do him good to be the wrong size for a bit. What did he want to come digging me out with his nasty wet hands for? He nearly touched me! He's a perfect savage. A boy of the Stone Age would have had more sense.'

Robert's hands had indeed been wet – with tears.

'Go away and leave me in peace, do,' the Psammead went on. 'I can't think why you don't wish for something sensible – something to eat or drink, or good manners, or good tempers. Go along with you, do!'

It almost snarled as it shook its whiskers, and turned a sulky brown back on them. The most hopeful felt that further parley was vain.

They turned again to the colossal Robert.

'Whatever shall we do?' they said; and they all said it.

'First,' said Robert grimly, 'I'm going to reason with that baker's boy. I shall catch him at the end of the road.'

'Don't hit a chap littler than yourself, old man,' said Cyril.

'Do I look like hitting him?' said Robert scornfully. 'Why, I should *kill* him. But I'll give him something to remember. Wait till I pull up my stocking.' He pulled up his stocking, which was as large as a small bolstercase, and strode off. His strides were six or seven feet long, so that it was quite easy for him to be at the bottom of the hill, ready to meet the baker's boy when he came down swinging the empty basket to meet his master's cart, which had been leaving bread at the cottages along the road.

Robert crouched behind a haystack in the farmyard, that is at the corner, and when he heard the boy come whistling along, he jumped out at him and caught him by the collar.

'Now,' he said, and his voice was about four times its usual size, just as his body was four times its, 'I'm going to teach you to kick boys smaller than you.'

He lifted up the baker's boy and set him on the top of the haystack, which was about sixteen feet from the ground, and then he sat down on the roof of the cowshed and told the baker's boy exactly what he thought of him. I don't think the boy heard it all – he was in a sort of

trance of terror. When Robert had said everything he could think of, and some things twice over, he shook the boy and said:

'And now get down the best way you can,' and left him.

I don't know how the baker's boy got down, but I do know that he missed the cart, and got into the very hottest of hot water when he turned up at last at the bakehouse. I am sorry for him, but, after all, it was quite right that he should be taught that English boys mustn't use their feet when they fight, but their fists. Of course the water he got into only became hotter when he tried to tell his master about the boy he had licked and the giant as high as a church, because no one could possibly believe such a tale as that. Next day the tale was believed – but that was too late to be of any use to the baker's boy.

When Robert rejoined the others he found them in the garden. Anthea had thoughtfully asked Martha to let them have dinner out there – because the dining-room was rather small, and it would have been so awkward to have a brother the size of Robert in there. The Lamb, who had slept peacefully during the whole stormy morning, was now found to be sneezing, and Martha said he had a cold and would be better indoors.

'And really it's just as well,' said Cyril, 'for I don't believe he'd ever have stopped screaming if he'd once seen you the awful size you are!'

Robert was indeed what a draper would call an 'out-size' in boys. He found himself able to step right over the iron gate in the front garden.

Martha brought out the dinner – it was cold veal and baked potatoes, with sago pudding and stewed plums to follow.

She of course did not notice that Robert was anything

but the usual size, and she gave him as much meat and potatoes as usual and no more. You have no idea how small your usual helping of dinner looks when you are many times your proper size. Robert groaned, and asked for more bread. But Martha would not go on giving more bread for ever. She was in a hurry, because the keeper intended to call on his way to Benenhurst Fair, and she wished to be dressed smartly before he came.

'I wish *we* were going to the Fair,' said Robert.

'You can't go anywhere that size,' said Cyril.

'Why not?' said Robert. 'They have giants at fairs, much bigger ones than me.'

'Not much, they don't,' Cyril was beginning, when Jane screamed 'Oh!' with such loud suddenness that they all thumped her on the back and asked whether she had swallowed a plum-stone.

'No,' she said, breathless from being thumped, 'it's – it's not a plum-stone. It's an idea. Let's take Robert to the Fair, and get them to give us money for showing him! Then we really *shall* get something out of the old Sammyadd at last!'

'Take me, indeed!' said Robert indignantly. 'Much more likely me take you!'

And so it turned out. The idea appealed irresistibly to everyone but Robert, and even he was brought round by Anthea's suggestion that he should have a double share of any money they might make. There was a little old pony-trap in the coach-house – the kind that is called a

governess-cart. It seemed desirable to get to the Fair as quickly as possible, so Robert – who could now take enormous steps and so go very fast indeed – consented to wheel the others in this. It was as easy to him now as wheeling the Lamb in the mail-cart had been in the morning. The Lamb's cold prevented his being of the party.

It was a strange sensation being wheeled in a pony-carriage by a giant. Everyone enjoyed the journey except Robert and the few people they passed on the way. These mostly went into what looked like some kind of standing-up fits by the roadside, as Anthea said. Just outside Benenhurst, Robert hid in a barn, and the others went on to the Fair.

There were some swings, and a hooting tooting blaring merry-go-round, and a shooting-gallery and coconut shies. Resisting an impulse to win a coconut – or at least to attempt the enterprise – Cyril went up to the woman who was loading little guns before the array of glass bottles on strings against a sheet of canvas.

'Here you are, little gentleman!' she said. 'Penny a shot!'

'No, thank you,' said Cyril, 'we are here on business, not on pleasure. Who's the master?'

'The what?'

'The master – the head – the boss of the show.'

'Over there,' she said, pointing to a stout man in a dirty linen jacket who was sleeping in the sun; 'but I don't advise you to wake him sudden. His temper's contrary, especially these hot days. Better have a shot while you're waiting.'

'It's rather important,' said Cyril. 'It'll be very profitable to him. I think he'll be sorry if we take it away.'

'Oh, if it's money in his pocket,' said the woman. 'No kid now? What is it?'

'It's a *giant*.'

'You *are* kidding?'

'Come along and see,' said Anthea.

The woman looked doubtfully at them, then she called

to a ragged little girl in striped stockings and a dingy white petticoat that came below her brown frock, and leaving her in charge of the 'shooting-gallery' she turned to Anthea and said, 'Well, hurry up! But if you *are* kidding, you'd best say so. I'm as mild as milk myself, but my Bill he's a fair terror and –'

Anthea led the way to the barn. 'It really *is* a giant,' she said. 'He's a giant little boy – in Norfolks like my brother's there. And we didn't bring him up to the Fair because people do stare so, and they seem to go into kind of standing-up fits when they see him. And we thought perhaps you'd like to show him and get pennies; and if you like to pay us something, you can – only, it'll have to be rather a lot, because we promised him he should have a double share of whatever we made.'

The woman murmured something indistinct, of which the children could only hear the words, 'Swelp me!', 'balmy', and 'crumpet', which conveyed no definite idea to their minds.

She had taken Anthea's hand, and was holding it very firmly; and Anthea could not help wondering what would happen if Robert should have wandered off or turned his proper size during the interval. But she knew that the Psammead's gifts really did last till sunset, however inconvenient their lasting might be; and she did not think, somehow, that Robert would care to go out alone while he was that size.

When they reached the barn and Cyril called 'Robert!' there was a stir among the loose hay, and Robert began to come out. His hand and arm came first – then a foot and leg. When the woman saw the hand she said 'My!' but when she saw the foot she said 'Upon my civvy!' and when, by slow and heavy degrees, the whole of Robert's enormous bulk was at last completely disclosed, she drew a long breath and began to say many things, compared with which 'balmy' and 'crumpet' seemed quite ordinary. She dropped into understandable English at last.

'What'll you take for him?' she said excitedly. 'Anything in reason. We'd have a special van built – leastways, I know where there's a second-hand one would do up handsome – what a baby elephant had, as died. What'll you take? He's soft, ain't he? Them giants mostly is – but I never see– no, never! What'll you take? Down on the nail. We'll treat him like a king, and give him first-rate grub and a doss fit for a bloomin' dook. He must be dotty or he wouldn't need you kids to cart him about. What'll you take for him?'

'They won't take anything,' said Robert sternly. 'I'm no more soft than you are – not so much, I shouldn't wonder. I'll come and be a show for today if you'll give me' – he hesitated at the enormous price he was about to ask – 'if you'll give me fifteen shillings.'

'Done,' said the woman, so quickly that Robert felt he had been unfair to himself, and wished he had asked thirty. 'Come on now – and see my Bill – and we'll fix a price for the season. I dessay you might get as much as two quid a week reg'lar. Come on – and make yourself as small as you can, for gracious' sake!'

This was not very small, and a crowd gathered quickly, so that it was at the head of an enthusiastic procession that Robert entered the trampled meadow where the Fair was held, and passed over the stubbly yellow dusty grass to the door of the biggest tent. He crept in, and the woman went to call her Bill. He was the big sleeping man, and he did not seem at all pleased at being awakened. Cyril, watching through a slit in the tent, saw him scowl and shake a heavy fist and a sleepy head. Then the woman went on speaking very fast. Cyril heard 'Strewth,' and 'biggest draw you ever, so help me!' and he began to share Robert's feeling that fifteen shillings was indeed far too little. Bill slouched up to the tent and entered. When he beheld the magnificent proportions of Robert he said but little – 'Strike me pink!' were the only words the children could afterwards remember – but he produced fifteen shillings, mainly in sixpences and coppers, and handed it to Robert.

'We'll fix up about what you're to draw when the show's over tonight,' he said with hoarse heartiness. 'Lor' love a duck! you'll be that happy with us you'll never want to leave us. Can you do a song now – or a bit of a breakdown?'

'Not today,' said Robert, rejecting the idea of trying to sing 'As once in May', a favourite of his mother's, and the only song he could think of at the moment.

'Get Levi and clear them bloomin' photos out. Clear the tent. Stick up a curtain or suthink,' the man went on. 'Lor', what a pity we ain't got no tights his size! But we'll have 'em before the week's out. Young man, your fortune's made. It's a good thing you came to me, and not to some chaps as I could tell you on. I've known blokes as beat their giants, and starved 'em too; so I'll tell you straight, you're in luck this day if you never was afore. 'Cos I'm a lamb, I am – and I don't deceive you.'

'I'm not afraid of anyone's beating *me*,' said Robert, looking down on the 'lamb'. Robert was crouched on his knees, because the tent was not big enough for him to stand upright in, but even in that position he could still look down on most people. 'But I'm awfully hungry – I wish you'd get me something to eat.'

'Here, 'Becca,' said the hoarse Bill. 'Get him some grub – the best you've got, mind!' Another whisper followed, of which the children only heard, 'Down in black and white – first thing tomorrow.'

Then the woman went to get the food – it was only bread and cheese when it came, but it was delightful to the large and empty Robert; and the man went to post sentinels round the tent, to give the alarm if Robert should attempt to escape with his fifteen shillings.

'As if we weren't honest,' said Anthea indignantly when the meaning of the sentinels dawned on her.

Then began a very strange and wonderful afternoon.

Bill was a man who knew his business. In a very little while, the photographic views, the spy-glasses you look at them through, so that they really seem rather real, and the lights you see them by, were all packed away. A curtain – it was an old red-and-black carpet really – was run across the tent. Robert was concealed behind, and Bill was standing on a trestle-table outside the tent making a speech. It was rather a good speech. It began by saying that the giant it was his privilege to introduce to the public that day was the eldest son of the Emperor of San Francisco, compelled through an unfortunate love affair with the Duchess of the Fiji Islands to leave his own country and take refuge in England – the land of liberty – where freedom was the right of every man, no matter how big he was. It ended by the announcement that the first twenty who came to the tent door should see the giant for threepence apiece. 'After that,' said Bill, 'the price is riz, and I don't undertake to say what it won't be riz to. So now's yer time.'

A young man squiring his sweetheart on her afternoon out was the first to come forward. For that occasion his was the princely attitude – no expense spared – money no object. His girl wished to see the giant? Well, she should see the giant, even though seeing the giant cost threepence each and the other entertainments were all penny ones.

The flap of the tent was raised – the couple entered. Next moment a wild shriek from the girl thrilled through all present. Bill slapped his leg. 'That's done the trick!' he whispered to 'Becca. It was indeed a splendid advertisement of the charms of Robert. When the girl came out she was pale and trembling, and a crowd was round the tent.

'What was it like?' asked a bailiff.

'Oh! – horrid! – you wouldn't believe,' she said. 'It's as big as a barn, and that fierce. It froze the blood in my bones. I wouldn't ha' missed seeing it for anything.'

The fierceness was only caused by Robert's trying not to laugh. But the desire to do that soon left him, and before sunset he was more inclined to cry than to laugh, and more inclined to sleep than either. For, by ones and twos and threes, people kept coming in all the afternoon, and Robert had to shake hands with those who wished it, and allow himself to be punched and pulled and patted and thumped, so that people might make sure he was really real.

The other children sat on a bench and watched and waited, and were very bored indeed. It seemed to them that this was the hardest way of earning money that could have been invented. And only fifteen shillings! Bill had taken four times that already, for the news of the giant had spread, and tradespeople in carts, and gentlepeople in carriages, came from far and near. One gentleman with an eyeglass, and a very large yellow rose in his buttonhole, offered Robert, in an obliging whisper, ten pounds a week to appear at the Crystal Palace. Robert had to say 'No'.

'I can't,' he said regretfully. 'It's no use promising what you can't do.'

'Ah, poor fellow, bound for a term of years, I suppose! Well, here's my card; when your time's up come to me.'

'I will – if I'm the same size then,' said Robert truthfully.

'If you grow a bit, so much the better,' said the gentleman.

When he had gone, Robert beckoned Cyril and said:

'Tell them I must and will have an easy. And I want my tea.'

Tea was provided, and a paper hastily pinned on the tent. It said:

CLOSED FOR HALF AN HOUR
WHILE THE GIANT GETS HIS TEA

Then there was a hurried council.

'How am I to get away?' said Robert. 'I've been thinking about it all the afternoon.'

'Why, walk out when the sun sets and you're your right size. They can't do anything to us.'

Robert opened his eyes. 'Why, they'd nearly kill us,' he said, 'when they saw me get my right size. No, we must think of some other way. We *must* be alone when the sun sets.'

'I know,' said Cyril briskly, and he went to the door, outside which Bill was smoking a clay pipe and talking in a low voice to 'Becca. Cyril heard him say – 'Good as havin' a fortune left you.'

'Look here,' said Cyril, 'you can let people come in again in a minute. He's nearly finished his tea. But he *must* be left alone when the sun sets. He's very queer at that time of day, and if he's worried I won't answer for the consequences.'

'Why – what comes over him?' asked Bill.

'I don't know; it's – it's a sort of a *change*,' said Cyril candidly. 'He isn't at all like himself – you'd hardly know him. He's very queer indeed. Someone'll get hurt if he's not alone about sunset.' This was true.

'He'll pull round for the evening, I s'pose?'

'Oh yes – half an hour after sunset he'll be quite himself again.'

'Best humour him,' said the woman.

And so, at what Cyril judged was about half an hour before sunset, the tent was again closed 'whilst the giant gets his supper'.

The crowd was very merry about the giant's meals and their coming so close together.

'Well, he can pick a bit,' Bill owned. 'You see he has to eat hearty, being the size he is.'

Inside the tent the four children breathlessly arranged a plan of retreat.

'You go *now*,' said Cyril to the girls, 'and get along home as fast as you can. Oh, never mind the beastly pony-cart; we'll get that tomorrow. Robert and I are dressed the same. We'll manage somehow, like Sydney Carton did. Only, you girls *must* get out, or it's all no go. We can run, but you can't – whatever you may think. No, Jane, it's no good Robert going out and knocking people down. The police would follow him till he turned his proper size, and then arrest him like a shot. Go you must! If you don't, I'll never speak to you again. It was you got us into this mess really, hanging round people's legs the way you did this morning. *Go*, I tell you!'

And Jane and Anthea went.

'We're going home,' they said to Bill. 'We're leaving the giant with you. Be kind to him.' And that, as Anthea said afterwards, was very deceitful, but what were they to do?

When they had gone, Cyril went to Bill.

'Look here,' he said, 'he wants some ears of corn – there's some in the next field but one. I'll just run and get it. Oh, and he says can't you loop up the tent at the back a bit? He says he's stifling for a breath of air. I'll see no one peeps in at him. I'll cover him up, and he can take a nap while I go for the corn. He *will* have it – there's no holding him when he gets like this.'

The giant was made comfortable with a heap of sacks and an old tarpaulin. The curtain was looped up, and the brothers were left alone. They matured their plan in whispers. Outside, the merry-go-round blared out its comic tunes, screaming now and then to attract public notice.

Half a minute after the sun had set, a boy in a Norfolk suit came out past Bill.

'I'm off for the corn,' he said, and mingled quickly with the crowd.

At the same instant a boy came out of the back of the tent past 'Becca, posted there as sentinel.

'I'm off after the corn,' said this boy also. And he, too, moved away quietly and was lost in the crowd. The front-door boy was Cyril; the back-door was Robert – now, since sunset, once more his proper size. They walked quickly through the field, and along the road, where Robert caught Cyril up. Then they ran. They were home as soon as the girls were, for it was a long way, and they ran most of it. It was indeed a *very* long way, as they found when they had to go and drag the pony-trap home next morning, with no enormous Robert to wheel them in it as if it were a mail-cart, and they were babies and he was their gigantic nursemaid.

I cannot possibly tell you what Bill and 'Becca said when they found that the giant had gone. For one thing, I do not know.

9
Grown Up

Cyril had once pointed out that ordinary life is full of occasions on which a wish would be most useful. And this thought filled his mind when he happened to wake early on the morning after the morning after Robert had wished to be bigger than the baker's boy, and had been it. The day that lay between these two days had been occupied entirely by getting the governess-cart home from Benenhurst.

Cyril dressed hastily; he did not take a bath, because tin baths are so noisy, and he had no wish to rouse Robert, and he slipped off alone, as Anthea had once done, and ran through the dewy morning to the sand-pit. He dug up the Psammead very carefully and kindly, and began the conversation by asking it whether it still felt any ill effects from the contact with the tears of Robert the day before yesterday. The Psammead was in a good temper. It replied politely.

'And now, what can I do for you?' it said. 'I suppose you've come here so early to ask for something for

yourself, something your brothers and sisters aren't to know about, eh? Now, do be persuaded for your own good! Ask for a good fat Megatherium and have done with it.'

'Thank you – not today, I think,' said Cyril cautiously. 'What I really wanted to say was – you know how you're always wishing for things when you're playing at anything?'

'I seldom play,' said the Psammead coldly.

'Well, you know what I mean,' Cyril went on impatiently. 'What I want to say is: won't you let us have our wish just when we think of it, and just where we happen to be? So that we don't have to come and disturb you again,' added the crafty Cyril.

'It'll only end in your wishing for something you don't

really want, like you did about the castle,' said the Psammead, stretching its brown arms and yawning. 'It's always the same since people left off eating really wholesome things. However, have it your own way. Good-bye.'

'Good-bye,' said Cyril politely.

'I'll tell you what,' said the Psammead suddenly, shooting out its long snail's eyes – 'I'm getting tired of you – all of you. You have no more sense than so many oysters. Go along with you!'

And Cyril went.

'What an awful long time babies *stay* babies,' said Cyril after the Lamb had taken his watch out of his pocket while he wasn't noticing, and with coos and clucks of naughty rapture had opened the case and used the whole thing as a garden spade, and when even immersion in a wash-hand basin had failed to wash the mould from the works and make the watch go again. Cyril had said several things in the heat of the moment; but now he was calmer, and had even consented to carry the Lamb part of the way to the woods. Cyril had persuaded the others to agree to his plan, and not to wish for anything more till they really did wish it. Meantime it seemed good to go to the woods for nuts, and on the mossy grass under a sweet chestnut-tree the five were sitting. The Lamb was pulling up the moss by fat handfuls, and Cyril was gloomily contemplating the ruins of his watch.

'He does grow,' said Anthea. 'Doesn't oo, precious?'

'Me grow,' said the Lamb cheerfully – 'me grow big boy, have guns an' mouses – an' – an' . . .' Imagination or vocabulary gave out here. But anyway it was the longest speech the Lamb had ever made, and it charmed everyone, even Cyril, who tumbled the Lamb over and rolled him in the moss to the music of delighted squeals.

'I suppose he'll be grown up some day,' Anthea was saying, dreamily looking up at the blue of the sky that showed between the long straight chestnut-leaves. But at that moment the Lamb, struggling gaily with Cyril, thrust a stoutly-shod little foot against his brother's chest; there was a crack! – the innocent Lamb had broken the glass of father's second-best Waterbury watch, which Cyril had borrowed without leave.

'Grow up some day!' said Cyril bitterly, plumping the Lamb down on the grass. 'I daresay he will – when nobody wants him to. I wish to goodness he would –'

'*Oh*, take care!' cried Anthea in an agony of apprehension. But it was too late – like music to a song her words and Cyril's came out together –

Anthea – 'Oh, take care!'

Cyril – 'Grow up now!'

The faithful Psammead was true to its promise, and there, before the horrified eyes of its brothers and sisters, the Lamb suddenly and violently grew up. It was the most terrible moment. The change was not so sudden as the wish-changes usually were. The Baby's face changed first. It grew thinner

and larger, lines came in the forehead, the eyes grew more deep-set and darker in colour, the mouth grew longer and thinner; most terrible of all, a little dark moustache appeared on the lip of one who was still – except as to the face – a two-year-old baby in a linen smock and white open-work socks.

'Oh, I wish it wouldn't! Oh, I wish it wouldn't! You boys might wish as well!' They all wished hard, for the sight was enough to dismay the most heartless. They all wished so hard, indeed, that they felt quite giddy and almost lost consciousness; but the wishing was quite vain, for, when the wood ceased to whirl round, their dazzled eyes were riveted at once by the spectacle of a very proper-looking young man in flannels and a straw hat – a young man who wore the same little black moustache which just before they had actually seen growing upon the Baby's lip. This, then, was the Lamb – grown up! Their own Lamb! It was a terrible moment. The grown-up Lamb moved gracefully across the moss and settled himself against the trunk of the sweet chestnut. He tilted the straw hat over his eyes. He was evidently weary. He was going to sleep. The Lamb – the original little tiresome beloved Lamb often went to sleep at odd times and in unexpected places. Was this new Lamb in the grey flannel suit and the pale green necktie like the other Lamb? or had his mind grown up together with his body?

That was the question which the others, in a hurried council held among the yellowing bracken a few yards from the sleeper, debated eagerly.

'Whichever it is, it'll be just as awful,' said Anthea. 'If his inside senses are grown up too, he won't stand our looking after him; and if he's still a baby inside of him how on earth are we to get him to do anything? And it'll be getting on for dinner-time in a minute –'

'And we haven't got any nuts,' said Jane.

'Oh, bother nuts!' said Robert; 'but dinner's different

– I didn't have half enough dinner yesterday. Couldn't we tie him to the tree and go home to our dinners and come back afterwards?'

'A fat lot of dinner we should get if we went back without the Lamb!' said Cyril in scornful misery. 'And it'll be just the same if we go back with him in the state he is now. Yes, I know it's my doing; don't rub it in! I know I'm a beast, and not fit to live; you can take that for settled, and say no more about it. The question is, what are we going to do?'

'Let's wake him up, and take him into Rochester or Maidstone and get some grub at a pastrycook's,' said Robert hopefully.

'Take him?' repeated Cyril. 'Yes – do! It's all my fault – I don't deny that – but you'll find you've got your work cut out for you if you try to take that young man anywhere. The Lamb always was spoilt, but now he's grown up he's a demon – simply. I can see it. Look at his mouth.'

'Well then,' said Robert, 'let's wake him up and see what *he'll* do. Perhaps *he'll* take us to Maidstone and stand Sam. He ought to have a hat of money in the pockets of those extra-special bags. We *must* have dinner, anyway.'

They drew lots with little bits of bracken. It fell to Jane's lot to waken the grown-up Lamb.

She did it gently by tickling his nose with a twig of wild

honeysuckle. He said 'Bother the flies!' twice, and then opened his eyes.

'Hullo, kiddies!' he said in a languid tone, 'still here? What's the giddy hour? You'll be late for your grub!'

'I know we shall,' said Robert bitterly.

'Then cut along home,' said the grown-up Lamb.

'What about your grub, though?' asked Jane.

'Oh, how far is it to the station, do you think? I've a sort of notion that I'll run up to town and have some lunch at the club.'

Blank misery fell like a pall on the four others. The Lamb – alone – unattended – would go to town and have lunch at a club! Perhaps he would also have tea there. Perhaps sunset would come upon him amid the dazzling luxury of club-land, and a helpless cross sleepy baby would find itself alone amid unsympathetic waiters, and would wail miserably for 'Panty' from the depths of a club armchair! The picture moved Anthea almost to tears.

'Oh no, Lamb ducky, you mustn't do that!' she cried incautiously.

The grown-up Lamb frowned. 'My dear Anthea,' he said, 'how often am I to tell you that my name is Hilary or St Maur or Devereux? – any of my baptismal names are free to my little brothers and sisters, but *not* "Lamb" – a relic of foolish and far-off childhood.'

This was awful. He was their elder brother now, was

he? Well, of course he was, if he was grown up – since they weren't. Thus, in whispers, Anthea and Robert.

But the almost daily adventures resulting from the Psammead wishes were making the children wise beyond their years.

'Dear Hilary,' said Anthea, and the others choked at the name, 'you know father didn't wish you to go to London. He wouldn't like us to be left alone without you to take care of us. Oh, deceitful beast that I am!' she added to herself.

'Look here,' said Cyril, 'if you're our elder brother, why not behave as such and take us over to Maidstone and give us a jolly good blow-out, and we'll go on the river afterwards?'

'I'm infinitely obliged to you,' said the Lamb courteously, 'but I should prefer solitude. Go home to your lunch – I mean your dinner. Perhaps I may look in about tea-time – or I may not be home till after you are in your beds.'

Their beds! Speaking glances flashed between the wretched four. Much bed there would be for them if they went home without the Lamb.

'We promised mother not to lose sight of you if we took you out,' Jane said before the others could stop her.

'Look here, Jane,' said the grown-up Lamb, putting his hands in his pockets and looking down at her, 'little girls should be seen and not heard. You kids must learn not to make yourselves a nuisance. Run along home now – and perhaps, if you're good, I'll give you each a penny tomorrow.'

'Look here,' said Cyril, in the best 'man to man' tone at his command, 'where are you going, old man? You might let Bobs and me come with you – even if you don't want the girls.'

This was really rather noble of Cyril, for he never did care much about being seen in public with the Lamb, who of course after sunset would be a baby again.

The 'man to man' tone succeeded.

'I shall just run over to Maidstone on my bike,' said the new Lamb airily, fingering the little black moustache. 'I can lunch at The Crown – and perhaps I'll have a pull on the river; but I can't take you all on the machine – now, can I? Run along home, like good children.'

The position was desperate. Robert exchanged a despairing look with Cyril. Anthea detached a pin from her waistband, a pin whose withdrawal left a gaping chasm between skirt and bodice, and handed it furtively to Robert – with a grimace of the darkest and deepest meaning. Robert slipped away to the road. There, sure enough, stood a bicycle – a beautiful new free-wheel. Of course Robert understood at once that if the Lamb was grown up he *must* have a bicycle. This had always been one of Robert's own reasons for wishing to be grown up. He hastily began to use the pin – eleven punctures in the back tyre, seven in the front. He would have made the total twenty-two but for the rustling of the yellow hazel-leaves, which warned him of the approach of the others. He hastily leaned a hand on each wheel, and was rewarded by the 'whish' of what was left of the air escaping from eighteen neat pin-holes.

'Your bike's run down,' said Robert, wondering how he could so soon have learned to deceive.

'So it is,' said Cyril.

'It's a puncture,' said Anthea, stooping down, and

standing up again with a thorn which she had got ready for the purpose. 'Look here.'

The grown-up Lamb (or Hilary, as I suppose one must now call him) fixed his pump and blew up the tyre. The punctured state of it was soon evident.

'I suppose there's a cottage somewhere near – where one could get a pail of water?' said the Lamb.

There was; and when the number of punctures had been made manifest, it was felt to be a special blessing that the cottage provided 'teas for cyclists'. It provided an odd sort of tea-and-hammy meal for the Lamb and his brothers. This was paid for out of the fifteen shillings which had been earned by Robert when he was a giant – for the Lamb, it appeared, had unfortunately no money about him. This was a great disappointment for the others; but it is a thing that will happen, even to the most grown-up of us. However, Robert had enough to eat, and that was something. Quietly but persistently the miserable four took it in turns to try to persuade the Lamb (or St Maur) to spend the rest of the day in the woods. There was not very much of the day left by the time he had mended the eighteenth puncture. He looked up from the completed work with a sigh of relief, and suddenly put his tie straight.

'There's a lady coming,' he said briskly – 'for goodness' sake, get out of the way. Go home – hide – vanish somehow! I can't be seen with a pack of dirty kids.' His brothers and sisters were indeed rather dirty, because, earlier in the day, the Lamb, in his infant state, had sprinkled a good deal of garden soil over them. The grown-up Lamb's voice was so tyrant-like, as Jane said afterwards, that they actually retreated to the back garden, and left him with his little moustache and his flannel suit to meet alone the young lady, who now came up the front garden wheeling a bicycle.

The woman of the house came out, and the young lady spoke to her – the Lamb raised his hat as she passed him – and the children could not hear what she said, though they were craning round the corner by the pig-pail and listening with all their ears. They felt it to be 'perfectly fair', as Robert said, 'with that wretched Lamb in that condition'.

When the Lamb spoke in a languid voice heavy with politeness, they heard well enough.

'A puncture?' he was saying. 'Can I not be of any assistance? If you could allow me –?'

There was a stifled explosion of laughter behind the pig-pail – the grown-up Lamb (otherwise Devereux) turned the tail of an angry eye in its direction.

'You're very kind,' said the lady, looking at the Lamb. She looked rather shy, but, as the boys put it, there didn't seem to be any nonsense about her.

'But oh,' whispered Cyril behind the pig-pail, 'I should have thought he'd had enough bicycle-mending for one day – and if she only knew that really and truly he's only a whiny-piny, silly little baby!'

'He's *not*,' Anthea murmured angrily. 'He's a dear – if people only let him alone. It's our own precious Lamb still, whatever silly idiots may turn him into – isn't he, Pussy?'

Jane doubtfully supposed so.

Now, the Lamb – whom I must try to remember to call St Maur – was examining the lady's bicycle and talking to her with a very grown-up manner indeed. No one could possibly have supposed, to see and hear him, that only that very morning he had been a chubby child of two years breaking other people's Waterbury watches. Devereux (as he ought to be called for the future) took out a gold watch when he had mended the lady's bicycle, and all the onlookers behind the pig-pail said 'Oh!' – because it seemed so unfair that the Baby, who had only that morning destroyed two cheap but honest watches, should now, in the grown-upness Cyril's folly had raised him to, have a real gold watch – with a chain and seals!

Hilary (as I will now term him) withered his brothers and sisters with a glance, and then said to the lady – with whom he seemed to be quite friendly:

'If you will allow me, I will ride with you as far as the Cross Roads; it is getting late, and there are tramps about.'

No one will ever know what answer the young lady

intended to give to this gallant offer, for, directly Anthea heard it made, she rushed out, knocking against the pig-pail, which overflowed in a turbid stream, and caught the Lamb (I suppose I ought to say Hilary) by the arm. The others followed, and in an instant the four dirty children were visible, beyond disguise.

'Don't let him,' said Anthea to the lady, and she spoke with intense earnestness; 'he's not fit to go with anyone!'

'Go away, little girl!' said St Maur (as we will now call him) in a terrible voice. 'Go home at once!'

'You'd much better not have anything to do with him,' the now reckless Anthea went on. 'He doesn't know who he is. He's something very different from what you think he is.'

'What do you mean?' asked the lady not unnaturally, while Devereux (as I must term the grown-up Lamb) tried vainly to push Anthea away. The others backed her up, and she stood solid as a rock.

'You just let him go with you,' said Anthea, 'you'll soon see what I mean! How would you like to suddenly see a poor little helpless baby spinning along down-hill beside you with its feet up on a bicycle it had lost control of?'

The lady had turned rather pale.

'Who are these very dirty children?' she asked the grown-up Lamb (sometimes called St Maur in these pages).

'I don't know,' he lied miserably.

'Oh, Lamb! how *can* you?' cried Jane – 'when you know perfectly well you're our own little baby brother that we're so fond of. We're his big brothers and sisters,' she explained, turning to the lady, who with trembling hands was now turning her bicycle towards the gate, 'and we've got to take care of him. And we must get him home before sunset, or I don't know whatever will become of us. You see, he's sort of under a spell – enchanted – you know what I mean!'

Again and again the Lamb (Devereux, I mean) had tried to stop Jane's eloquence, but Robert and Cyril held him, one by each leg, and no proper explanation was possible. The lady rode hastily away, and electrified her relatives at dinner by telling them of her escape from a family of dangerous lunatics. 'The little girl's eyes were simply those of a maniac. I can't think how she came to be at large,' she said.

When her bicycle had whizzed away down the road, Cyril spoke gravely.

'Hilary, old chap,' he said, 'you must have had a sunstroke or something. And the things you've been saying to that lady! Why, if we were to tell you the things you've said when you are yourself again, say tomorrow morning, you wouldn't even understand them – let alone believe them! You trust to me, old chap, and come home now, and if you're not yourself in the morning we'll ask the milkman to ask the doctor to come.'

The poor grown-up Lamb (St Maur was really one of his Christian names) seemed now too bewildered to resist.

'Since you seem all to be as mad as the whole worshipful company of hatters,' he said bitterly, 'I suppose I *had* better take you home. But you're not to suppose I shall pass this over. I shall have something to say to you all tomorrow morning.'

'Yes, you will, my Lamb,' said Anthea under her breath, 'but it won't be at all the sort of thing you think it's going to be.'

In her heart she could hear the pretty, soft little loving voice of the baby Lamb – so different from the affected tones of the dreadful grown-up Lamb (one of whose names was Devereux) – saying, 'Me love Panty – wants to come to own Panty.'

'Oh, let's get home, for goodness' sake,' she said. 'You shall say whatever you like in the morning – if you can,' she added in a whisper.

It was a gloomy party that went home through the soft evening. During Anthea's remarks Robert had again made play with the pin and the bicycle tyre and the Lamb (whom they had to call St Maur or Devereux or Hilary) seemed really at last to have had his fill of bicycle-mending. So the machine was wheeled.

The sun was just on the point of setting when they arrived at the White House. The four elder children would have liked to linger in the lane till the complete sunsetting turned the grown-up Lamb (whose Christian names I will not further weary you by repeating) into their own dear tiresome baby brother. But he, in his grown-upness, insisted on going on, and thus he was met in the front garden by Martha.

Now you remember that, as a special favour, the Psammead had arranged that the servants in the house should never notice any change brought about by the wishes of the children. Therefore Martha merely saw the usual party, with the baby Lamb, about whom she had been desperately anxious all the afternoon, trotting beside Anthea on fat baby legs, while the children, of course, still saw the grown-up Lamb (never mind what names he was christened by), and Martha rushed at him and caught him in her arms, exclaiming:

'Come to his own Martha, then – a precious poppet!'

The grown-up Lamb (whose names shall now be buried in oblivion) struggled furiously. An expression of intense horror and annoyance was seen on his face. But Martha was stronger than he. She lifted him up and carried him into the house. None of the children will ever forget that picture. The neat grey-flannel-suited grown-up young man with the green tie and the little black moustache – fortunately, he was slightly built, and not tall – struggling in the sturdy arms of Martha, who bore him away helpless, imploring him, as she went, to be a good boy now, and come and have his nice bremmilk! Fortunately, the sun set as they reached the doorstep, the bicycle disappeared, and Martha was seen to carry into the house the real live darling sleepy two-year-old Lamb. The grown-up Lamb (nameless henceforth) was gone for ever.

'For ever,' said Cyril, 'because, as soon as ever the Lamb's old enough to be bullied, we must jolly well begin to bully him, for his own sake – so that he mayn't grow up like *that*.'

'You shan't bully him,' said Anthea stoutly; 'not if I can stop it.'

'We must tame him by kindness,' said Jane.

'You see,' said Robert, 'if he grows up in the usual way, there'll be plenty of time to correct him as he goes along. The awful thing today was his growing up so suddenly. There was no time to improve him at all.'

'He doesn't want any improving,' said Anthea as the voice of the Lamb came cooing through the open door, just as she had heard it in her heart that afternoon:

'Me loves Panty – wants to come to own Panty!'

10

Scalps

Probably the day would have been a greater success if Cyril had not been reading *The Last of the Mohicans*. The story was running in his head at breakfast, and as he took his third cup of tea he said dreamily, 'I wish there were Red Indians in England – not big ones, you know, but little ones, just about the right size for us to fight.'

Everyone disagreed with him at the time, and no one attached any importance to the incident. But when they went down to the sand-pit to ask for a hundred pounds in two-shilling pieces with Queen Victoria's head on, to prevent mistakes – which they had always felt to be a really reasonable wish that must turn out well – they found out that they had done it again! For the Psammead, which was very cross and sleepy, said:

'Oh, don't bother me. You've had your wish.'

'I didn't know it,' said Cyril.

'Don't you remember yesterday?' said the Sand-fairy, still more disagreeably. 'You asked me to let you have your wishes wherever you happened to be, and you wished this morning, and you've got it.'

'Oh, have we?' said Robert. 'What is it?'

'So you've forgotten?' said the Psammead, beginning to burrow. 'Never mind; you'll know soon enough. And I wish you joy of it! A nice thing you've let yourselves in for!'

'We always do, somehow,' said Jane sadly.

And now the odd thing was that no one could remember anyone's having wished for anything that morning. The wish about the Red Indians had not stuck in anyone's head. It was a most anxious morning. Everyone was trying to remember what had been wished for, and no one could, and everyone kept expecting something awful to happen every minute. It was most agitating; they knew, from what the Psammead had said, that they must have wished for something more than usually undesirable, and they spent several hours in most agonizing uncertainty. It was not till nearly dinner-time that Jane tumbled over *The Last of the Mohicans* – which had, of course, been left face downwards on the floor – and when Anthea had picked her and the book up she suddenly said, 'I know!' and sat down flat on the carpet.

'Oh, Pussy, how awful! It was Indians he wished for – Cyril – at breakfast, don't you remember? He said, "I wish there were Red Indians in England," – and now there are, and they're going about scalping people all over the country, like as not.'

'Perhaps they're only in Northumberland and Durham,' said Jane soothingly. It was almost impossible to believe that it could really hurt people much to be scalped so far away as that.

'Don't you believe it!' said Anthea. 'The Sammyadd said we'd let ourselves in for a nice thing. That means they'll come *here*. And suppose they scalped the Lamb!'

'Perhaps the scalping would come right again at sunset,' said Jane; but she did not speak so hopefully as usual.

'Not it!' said Anthea. 'The things that grow out of the wishes don't go. Look at the fifteen shillings! Pussy, I'm going to break something, and you must let me have every penny of money you've got. The Indians will come *here*, don't you see? That spiteful Sammyadd as good as said so. You see what my plan is? Come on!'

Jane did not see at all. But she followed her sister meekly into their mother's bedroom.

Anthea lifted down the heavy water-jug – it had a pattern of storks and long grasses on it, which Anthea never forgot. She carried it into the dressing-room, and carefully emptied the water out of it into the bath. Then she took the jug back into the bedroom and dropped it on the floor. You know how a jug always breaks if you happen to drop it by accident. If you happen to drop it on purpose, it is quite different. Anthea dropped that jug three times, and it was as unbroken as ever. So at last she had to take her father's boot-tree and break the jug with that in cold blood. It was heartless work.

Next she broke open the missionary-box with the poker. Jane told her that it was wrong, of course, but Anthea shut her lips very tight and then said:

'Don't be silly – it's a matter of life and death.'

There was not very much in the missionary-box – only seven-and-fourpence – but the girls between them had nearly four shillings. This made over eleven shillings, as you will easily see.

Anthea tied up the money in a corner of her pocket-handkerchief. 'Come on, Jane!' she said, and ran down to the farm. She knew that the farmer was going into Rochester that afternoon. In fact it had been arranged that he was to take the four children with him. They had planned this in the happy hour when they believed that they were going to get that hundred pounds, in two-shilling pieces, out of the Psammead. They had arranged to pay the farmer two shillings each for the ride. Now Anthea hastily explained to him that they could not go, but would he take Martha and the Baby instead? He agreed, but he was not pleased to get only half-a-crown instead of eight shillings.

Then the girls ran home again. Anthea was agitated, but not flurried. When she came to think it over afterwards, she could not help seeing that she had acted with the most far-seeing promptitude, just like a born general. She fetched a little box from her corner drawer, and went to find Martha, who was laying the cloth and not in the best of tempers.

'Look here,' said Anthea. 'I've broken the toilet-jug in mother's room.'

'Just like you – always up to some mischief,' said Martha, dumping down a salt-cellar with a bang.

'Don't be cross, Martha dear,' said Anthea. 'I've got enough money to pay for a new one – if only you'll be a dear and go and buy it for us. Your cousins keep a china-shop, don't they? And I would like you to get it today, in case mother comes home tomorrow. You know she said she might, perhaps.'

'But you're all going into town yourselves,' said Martha.

'We can't afford to, if we get the new jug,' said Anthea; 'but we'll pay for you to go, if you'll take the Lamb. And I say, Martha, look here – I'll give you my Liberty box, if you'll go. Look, it's most awfully pretty – all inlaid with real silver and ivory and ebony like King Solomon's temple.'

'I see,' said Martha; 'no, I don't want your box, miss. What you want is to get the precious Lamb off your hands for the afternoon. Don't you go for to think I don't see through you!'

This was so true that Anthea longed to deny it at once. Martha had no business to know so much. But she held her tongue.

Martha set down the bread with a bang that made it jump off its trencher.

'I *do* want the jug got,' said Anthea softly. 'You *will* go, won't you?'

'Well, just for this once, I don't mind; but mind you don't get into none of your outrageous mischief while I'm gone – that's all!'

'He's going earlier than he thought,' said Anthea eagerly. 'You'd better hurry and get dressed. Do put on that lovely purple frock, Martha, and the hat with the pink cornflowers, and the yellow-lace collar. Jane'll finish laying the cloth, and I'll wash the Lamb and get him ready.'

As she washed the unwilling Lamb, and hurried him into his best clothes, Anthea peeped out of the window from time to time; so far all was well – she could see no Red Indians. When with a rush and a scurry and some deepening of the damask of Martha's complexion she and the Lamb had been got off, Anthea drew a deep breath.

'*He's* safe!' she said, and, to Jane's horror, flung herself down on the floor and burst into floods of tears. Jane did not understand at all how a person could be so brave and like a general, and then suddenly give way and go flat like an air-balloon when you prick it. It is better not to go flat, of course, but you will observe that Anthea did not give way till her aim was accomplished. She had got the dear Lamb out of danger – she felt certain the Red Indians would be round the White House or nowhere – the farmer's cart would not come back till after sunset, so she could afford to cry a little. It was partly with joy that she cried, because she had done what she meant to do. She cried for about three minutes, while Jane hugged her miserably and said at five-second intervals, 'Don't cry, Panther dear!'

Then she jumped up, rubbed her eyes hard with the corner of her pinafore, so that they kept red for the rest of the day, and started to tell the boys. But just at that moment cook rang the dinner-bell, and nothing could be said till they had all been helped to minced beef. Then cook left the room, and Anthea told her tale. But it is a mistake to tell a thrilling tale when people are eating minced beef and boiled potatoes. There seemed somehow to be something about the food that made the idea of Red Indians seem flat and unbelievable. The boys actually laughed, and called Anthea a little silly.

'Why,' said Cyril, 'I'm almost sure it was before I said that, that Jane said she wished it would be a fine day.'

'It wasn't,' said Jane briefly.

'Why, if it was Indians,' Cyril went on – 'salt, please, and mustard – I must have something to make this mush go down – if it was Indians, they'd have been infesting the place long before this – you know they would. I believe it's the fine day.'

'Then why did the Sammyadd say we'd let ourselves in for a nice thing?' asked Anthea. She was feeling very cross.

She knew she had acted with nobility and discretion, and after that it was very hard to be called a little silly, especially when she had the weight of a burglared missionary-box and about seven-and-fourpence, mostly in coppers, lying like lead upon her conscience.

There was a silence, during which cook took away the mincy plates and brought in the treacle-pudding. As soon as she had retired, Cyril began again.

'Of course I don't mean to say,' he admitted, 'that it wasn't a good thing to get Martha and the Lamb out of the light for the afternoon; but as for Red Indians – why, you know jolly well the wishes always come that very minute. If there was going to be Red Indians, they'd be here now.'

'I expect they are,' said Anthea; 'they're lurking amid the undergrowth, for anything you know. I do think you're most beastly unkind.'

'Indians almost always *do* lurk, really, though, don't they?' put in Jane, anxious for peace.

'No, they don't,' said Cyril tartly. 'And I'm not unkind, I'm only truthful. And I say it was utter rot breaking the water-jug; and as for the missionary-box, I believe it's a treason-crime, and I shouldn't wonder if you could be hanged for it, if any of us was to split –'

'Shut up, can't you?' said Robert; but Cyril couldn't. You see, he felt in his heart that if there *should* be Indians they would be entirely his own fault, so he did not wish to believe in them. And trying not to believe things when in your heart you are almost sure they are true, is as bad for the temper as anything I know.

'It's simply idiotic,' he said, 'talking about Indians, when you can see for yourselves that it's Jane who's got her wish. Look what a fine day it is – *OH* –'

He had turned towards the window to point out the fineness of the day – the others turned too – and a frozen silence caught at Cyril, and none of the others felt at all like breaking it. For there, peering round the corner of the window, among the red leaves of the Virginia creeper, was a face – a brown face, with a long nose and a tight mouth and very bright eyes. And the face was painted in coloured patches. It had long black hair, and in the hair were feathers!

Every child's mouth in the room opened, and stayed open. The treacle-pudding was growing white and cold on their plates. No one could move.

Suddenly the feathered head was cautiously withdrawn, and the spell was broken. I am sorry to say that Anthea's first words were very like a girl.

'There, now!' she said. 'I told you so!'

Treacle-pudding had now definitely ceased to charm. Hastily wrapping their portions in a *Spectator* of the week before the week before last, they hid them behind the crinkled-paper stove-ornament, and fled upstairs to reconnoitre and to hold a hurried council.

'Pax,' said Cyril handsomely when they reached their mother's bedroom. 'Panther, I'm sorry if I was a brute.'

'All right,' said Anthea, 'but you see now!'

No further trace of Indians, however, could be discerned from the windows.

'Well,' said Robert, 'what are we to do?'

'The only thing I can think of,' said Anthea, who was now generally admitted to be the heroine of the day, 'is – if we dressed up as like Indians as we can, and looked out of the windows, or even went out. They might think we were the powerful leaders of a large neighbouring tribe, and – and not do anything to us, you know, for fear of awful vengeance.'

'But Eliza, and the cook?' said Jane.

'You forget – they can't notice anything,' said Robert. 'They wouldn't notice anything out of the way, even if they were scalped or roasted at a slow fire.'

'But would they come right at sunset?'

'Of course. You can't be really scalped or burned to death without noticing it, and you'd be sure to notice it next day, even if it escaped your attention at the time,' said Cyril. 'I think Anthea's right, but we shall want a most awful lot of feathers.'

'I'll go down to the hen-house,' said Robert. 'There's one of the turkeys in there – it's not very well. I could cut its feathers without it minding much. It's very bad – doesn't seem to care what happens to it. Get me the cutting-out scissors.'

Earnest reconnoitring convinced them all that no Indians were in the poultry-yard. Robert went. In five minutes he came back – pale, but with many feathers.

'Look here,' he said, 'this is jolly serious. I cut off the feathers, and when I turned to come out there was an Indian squinting at me from under the old hen-coop. I just brandished the feathers and yelled, and got away before he could get the coop off the top of himself. Panther, get the coloured blankets off our beds, and look slippy, can't you?'

It is wonderful how like an Indian you can make yourselves with blankets and feathers and coloured scarves. Of course none of the children happened to have long black hair, but there was a lot of black calico that had been got to cover school-books with. They cut strips of this into a sort of fine fringe, and fastened it round their heads with the amber-coloured ribbons off the girls' Sunday dresses. Then they stuck turkeys' feathers in the ribbons. The calico looked very like long black hair, especially when the strips began to curl up a bit.

'But our faces,' said Anthea, 'they're not at all the right colour. We're all rather pale, and I'm sure I don't know why, but Cyril is the colour of putty.'

'I'm not,' said Cyril.

'The real Indians outside seem to be brownish,' said Robert hastily. 'I think we ought to be really *red* – it's sort of superior to have a red skin, if you are one.'

The red ochre cook used for the kitchen bricks seemed to be about the reddest thing in the house. The children mixed some in a saucer with milk, as they had seen cook do for the kitchen floor. Then they carefully painted each other's faces and hands with it, till they were quite as red as any Red Indian need be – if not redder.

They knew at once that they must look very terrible when they met Eliza in the passage, and she screamed aloud. This unsolicited testimonial pleased them very much. Hastily telling her not to be a goose, and that it was only a game, the four blanketed, feathered, really and truly Redskins went boldly out to meet the foe. I say boldly. That is because I wish to be polite. At any rate, they went.

Along the hedge dividing the wilderness from the garden was a row of dark heads, all highly feathered.

'It's our only chance,' whispered Anthea. 'Much better than to wait for their blood-freezing attack. We must pretend like mad. Like that game of cards where you pretend you've got aces when you haven't. Fluffing they call it, I think. Now then. Whoop!'

With four wild war-whoops – or as near them as English children could be expected to go without any previous practice – they rushed through the gate and struck four warlike attitudes in face of the line of Red Indians. These were all about the same height, and that height was Cyril's.

'I hope to goodness they can talk English,' said Cyril through his attitude.

Anthea knew they could, though she never knew how she came to know it. She had a white towel tied to a walking-stick. This was a flag of truce, and she waved it, in the hope that the Indians would know what it was. Apparently they did – for one who was browner than the others stepped forward.

'Ye seek a pow-wow?' he said in excellent English. 'I am Golden Eagle, of the mighty tribe of Rock-dwellers.'

'And I,' said Anthea, with a sudden inspiration, 'am the Black Panther – chief of the – the – the – Mazawattee tribe. My brothers – I don't mean – yes, I do – the tribe – I mean the Mazawattees – are in ambush below the brow of yonder hill.'

'And what mighty warriors be these?' asked Golden Eagle, turning to the others.

Cyril said he was the great chief Squirrel, of the Moning Congo tribe, and, seeing that Jane was sucking her thumb and could evidently think of no name for herself, he added, 'This great warrior is Wild Cat – Pussy Ferox we call it in this land – leader of the vast Phiteezi tribe.'

'And thou, valorous Redskin?' Golden Eagle inquired suddenly of Robert, who, taken unawares, could only reply that he was Bobs, leader of the Cape Mounted Police.

'And now,' said Black Panther, 'our tribes, if we just whistle them up, will far outnumber your puny forces; so resistance is useless. Return, therefore, to your own land, O brother, and smoke pipes of peace in your wampums with your squaws and your medicine-men, and dress yourselves in the gayest wigwams, and eat happily of the juicy fresh-caught moccasins.'

'You've got it all wrong,' murmured Cyril angrily. But Golden Eagle only looked inquiringly at her.

'Thy customs are other than ours, O Black Panther,' he said. 'Bring up thy tribe, that we may hold pow-wow in state before them, as becomes great chiefs.'

'We'll bring them up right enough,' said Anthea, 'with their bows and arrows, and tomahawks, and scalping-knives, and everything you can think of, if you don't look sharp and go.'

She spoke bravely enough, but the hearts of all the children were beating furiously, and their breath came in shorter and shorter gasps. For the little real Red Indians were closing up round them – coming nearer and nearer with angry murmurs – so that they were the centre of a crowd of dark, cruel faces.

'It's no go,' whispered Robert. 'I knew it wouldn't be. We must make a bolt for the Psammead. It might help us. If it doesn't – well, I suppose we shall come alive again at sunset. I wonder if scalping hurts as much as they say.'

'I'll wave the flag again,' said Anthea. 'If they stand back, we'll run for it.'

She waved the towel, and the chief commanded his followers to stand back. Then, charging wildly at the place where the line of Indians was thinnest, the four children started to run. Their first rush knocked down some half-dozen Indians, over whose blanketed bodies the children leaped, and made straight for the sand-pit. This was no time for the safe easy way by which carts go down – right over the edge of the sand-pit they went, among the yellow and pale purple flowers and dried grasses, past the little sand-martins' little front doors, skipping, clinging, bounding, stumbling, sprawling, and finally rolling.

Yellow Eagle and his followers came up with them just at the very spot where they had seen the Psammead that morning.

Breathless and beaten, the wretched children now awaited their fate. Sharp knives and axes gleamed round them, but worse than these was the cruel light in the eyes of Golden Eagle and his followers.

'Ye have lied to us, O Black Panther of the Mazawattees – and thou, too, Squirrel of the Moning Congos. These also, Pussy Ferox of the Phiteezi, and Bobs of the Cape Mounted Police – these also have lied to us, if not with their tongue, yet by their silence. Ye have lied under the cover of the Truce-flag of the Pale-face. Ye have no followers. Your tribes are far away – following the hunting trail. What shall be their doom?' he concluded, turning with a bitter smile to the other Red Indians.

'Build we the fire!' shouted his followers; and at once a dozen ready volunteers started to look for fuel. The four children, each held between two strong little Indians, cast despairing glances round them. Oh, if they could only see the Psammead!

'Do you mean to scalp us first and then roast us?' asked Anthea desperately.

'Of course!' Redskin opened his eyes at her. 'It's always done.'

The Indians had formed a ring round the children, and now sat on the ground gazing at their captives. There was a threatening silence.

Then slowly, by twos and threes, the Indians who had gone to look for firewood came back, and they came back empty-handed. They had not been able to find a single stick of wood, for a fire! No one ever can, as a matter of fact, in that part of Kent.

The children drew a deep breath of relief, but it ended in a moan of terror. For bright knives were being brandished all about them. Next moment each child was seized by an Indian; each closed its eyes and tried not to scream. They waited for the sharp agony of the knife. It did not come. Next moment they were released, and fell in a trembling heap. Their heads did not hurt at all. They only felt strangely cool! Wild war-whoops rang in their ears.

When they ventured to open their eyes they saw four of their foes dancing round them with wild leaps and screams, and each of the four brandished in his hand a scalp of long flowing black hair. They put their hands to their heads – their own scalps were safe! The poor untutored savages had indeed scalped the children. But they had only, so to speak, scalped them of the black calico ringlets!

The children fell into each other's arms, sobbing and laughing.

'Their scalps are ours,' chanted the chief; 'ill-rooted were their ill-fated hairs! They came off in the hands of the victors – without struggle, without resistance, they yielded their scalps to the conquering Rock-dwellers! Oh, how little a thing is a scalp so lightly won!'

'They'll take our real ones in a minute; you see if they don't,' said Robert, trying to rub some of the red ochre off his face and hands on to his hair.

'Cheated of our just and fiery revenge are we,' the chant went on – 'but there are other torments than the scalping-knife and the flames. Yet is the slow fire the correct thing. O strange unnatural country, wherein a man may find no wood to burn his enemy! – Ah, for the boundless forests of my native land, where the great trees for thousands of miles grow but to furnish firewood wherewithal to burn our foes. Ah, would we were but in our native forest once more!'

Suddenly, like a flash of lightning, the golden gravel shone all round the four children instead of the dusky figures. For every single Indian had vanished on the instant at their leader's word. The Psammead must have been there all the time. And it had given the Indian chief his wish.

Martha brought home a jug with a pattern of storks and long grasses on it. Also she brought back all Anthea's money.

'My cousin, she give me the jug for luck; she said it was an odd one what the basin of had got smashed.'

'Oh, Martha, you are a dear!' sighed Anthea, throwing her arms round her.

'Yes,' giggled Martha, 'you'd better make the most of me while you've got me. I shall give your ma notice directly the minute she comes back.'

'Oh, Martha, we haven't been so *very* horrid to you, have we?' asked Anthea, aghast.

'Oh, it ain't that, miss.' Martha giggled more than ever. 'I'm a-goin' to be married. It's Beale the game-keeper. He's been a-proposin' to me off and on ever since you come home from the clergyman's where you got locked up on the church-tower. And today I said the word an' made him a happy man.'

Anthea put the seven-and-fourpence back in the missionary-box, and pasted paper over the place where the poker had broken it. She was very glad to be able to do this, and she does not know to this day whether breaking open a missionary-box is or is not a hanging matter.

11

The Last Wish

Of course you, who see above that this is the eleventh (and last) chapter, know very well that the day of which this chapter tells must be the last on which Cyril, Anthea, Robert, and Jane will have a chance of getting anything out of the Psammead, or Sand-fairy.

But the children themselves did not know this. They were full of rosy visions, and, whereas on other days they had often found it extremely difficult to think of anything really nice to wish for, their brains were now full of the most beautiful and sensible ideas. 'This,' as Jane remarked afterwards, 'is always the way.' Everyone was up extra early that morning, and these plans were hopefully discussed in the garden before breakfast. The old idea of one hundred pounds in modern florins was still first favourite, but there were others that ran it close – the chief of these being the 'pony each' idea. This had a great advantage. You could wish for a pony each during the morning, ride it all day, have it vanish at sunset, and wish it back again next day. Which would be an economy of litter and stabling. But at breakfast two things happened. First, there was a letter from mother. Granny was better, and mother and father hoped to be home that very afternoon. A cheer arose. And of course this news at once scattered all the before-breakfast wish-ideas. For everyone saw quite plainly that the wish for the day must be something to please mother and not to please themselves.

'I wonder what she *would* like,' pondered Cyril.

'She'd like us all to be good,' said Jane primly.

'Yes – but that's so dull for us,' Cyril rejoined; 'and, besides, I should hope we could be that without sand-fairies to help us. No; it must be something splendid, that we couldn't possibly get without wishing for.'

'Look out,' said Anthea in a warning voice; 'don't forget yesterday. Remember, we get our wishes now just wherever we happen to be when we say "I wish". Don't let's let ourselves in for anything silly – today of all days.'

'All right,' said Cyril. 'You needn't jaw.'

Just then Martha came in with a jug full of hot water for the teapot – and a face full of importance for the children.

'A blessing we're all alive to eat our breakfasses!' she said darkly.

'Why, whatever's happened?' everybody asked.

'Oh, nothing,' said Martha, 'only it seems nobody's safe from being murdered in their beds nowadays.'

'Why,' said Jane as an agreeable thrill of horror ran down her back and legs and out at her toes, '*has* anyone been murdered in their beds?'

'Well – not exactly,' said Martha; 'but they might just as well. There's been burglars over at Peasmarsh Place – Beale's just told me – and they've took every single one of Lady Chittenden's diamonds and jewels and things, and she's a-goin' out of one fainting fit into another, with hardly time to say "Oh, my diamonds!" in between. And Lord Chittenden's away in London.'

'Lady Chittenden,' said Anthea; 'we've seen her. She wears a red-and-white dress, and she has no children of her own and can't abide other folks's.'

'That's her,' said Martha. 'Well, she's put all her trust in riches, and you see how she's served. They say the diamonds and things was worth thousands of thousands of pounds. There was a necklace and a river – whatever that is – and no end of bracelets; and a tarrer and ever so many rings. But there, I mustn't stand talking and all the place to clean down afore your ma comes home.'

'I don't see why she should ever have had such lots of diamonds,' said Anthea when Martha had flounced off. 'She was rather a nasty lady, I thought. And mother hasn't any diamonds, and hardly any jewels – the topaz necklace, and the sapphire ring daddy gave her when they were engaged, and the garnet star, and the little pearl brooch with great-grandpapa's hair in it – that's about all.'

'When I'm grown up I'll buy mother no end of diamonds,' said Robert, 'if she wants them. I shall make so much money exploring in Africa I shan't know what to do with it.'

'Wouldn't it be jolly,' said Jane dreamily, 'if mother could find all those lovely things, necklaces and rivers of diamonds and tarrers?'

'*Ti – aras*,' said Cyril.

'Ti – aras, then – and rings and everything in her room when she came home? I wish she would.'

The others gazed at her in horror.

'Well, she *will*,' said Robert; 'you've wished, my good Jane – and our only chance now is to find the Psammead, and if it's in a good temper it *may* take back the wish and give us another. If not – well – goodness knows what we're in for! – the police, of course, and – Don't cry, silly! We'll stand by you. Father says we need never be afraid if we don't do anything wrong and always speak the truth.'

But Cyril and Anthea exchanged gloomy glances. They remembered how convincing the truth about the Psammead had been once before when told to the police.

It was a day of misfortunes. Of course the Psammead could not be found. Nor the jewels, though every one of the children searched their mother's room again and again.

'Of course,' Robert said, '*we* couldn't find them. It'll be mother who'll do that. Perhaps she'll think they've been in the house for years and years, and never know they are the stolen ones at all.'

'Oh yes!' Cyril was very scornful; 'then mother will be a receiver of stolen goods, and you know jolly well what *that's* worse than.'

Another and exhaustive search of the sand-pit failed to reveal the Psammead, so the children went back to the house slowly and sadly.

'I don't care,' said Anthea stoutly, 'we'll tell mother the truth, and she'll give back the jewels – and make everything all right.'

'Do you think so?' said Cyril slowly. 'Do you think she'll believe us? Could anyone believe about a Sammyadd unless they'd seen it? She'll think we're pretending. Or else she'll think we're raving mad, and then we shall be sent to Bedlam. How would you like it?' – he turned suddenly on the miserable Jane – 'how would you like it, to be shut up in an iron cage with bars and padded walls, and nothing to do but stick straws in your hair all day, and listen to the howlings and ravings of the other maniacs? Make up your minds to it, all of you. It's no use telling mother.'

'But it's true,' said Jane.

'Of course it is, but it's not true enough for grown-up people to believe it,' said Anthea. 'Cyril's right. Let's put flowers in all the vases, and try not to think about diamonds. After all, everything has come right in the end all the other times.'

So they filled all the pots they could find with flowers

– asters and zinnias, and loose-leaved late red roses from the wall of the stable-yard, till the house was a perfect bower.

And almost as soon as dinner was cleared away mother arrived, and was clasped in eight loving arms. It was very difficult indeed not to tell her all about the Psammead at once, because they had got into the habit of telling her everything. But they did succeed in not telling her.

Mother, on her side, had plenty to tell them – about Granny, and Granny's pigeons, and Auntie Emma's lame tame donkey. She was very delighted with the flowery-boweryness of the house; and everything seemed so natural and pleasant, now that she was home again, that the children almost thought they must have dreamed the Psammead.

But, when mother moved towards the stairs to go up to her bedroom and take off her bonnet, the eight arms clung round her just as if she only had two children, one the Lamb and the other an octopus.

'Don't go up, mummy darling,' said Anthea; 'let me take your things up for you.'

'Or I will,' said Cyril.

'We want you to come and look at the rose-tree,' said Robert.

'Oh, don't go up!' said Jane helplessly.

'Nonsense, dears,' said mother briskly, 'I'm not such an old woman yet that I can't take my bonnet off in the proper place. Besides, I must wash these black hands of mine.'

So up she went, and the children, following her, exchanged glances of gloomy foreboding.

Mother took off her bonnet – it was a very pretty hat, really, with white roses on it – and when she had taken it off she went to the dressing-table to do her pretty hair.

On the table between the ring-stand and the pincushion lay a green leather case. Mother opened it.

'Oh, how lovely!' she cried. It was a ring, a large pearl with shining many-lighted diamonds set round it. 'Wherever did this come from?' mother asked, trying it on her wedding finger, which it fitted beautifully. 'However did it come here?'

'I don't know,' said each of the children truthfully.

'Father must have told Martha to put it here,' mother said. 'I'll run down and ask her.'

'Let me look at it,' said Anthea, who knew Martha would not be able to see the ring. But when Martha was asked, of course she denied putting the ring there, and so did Eliza and cook.

Mother came back to her bedroom, very much interested and pleased about the ring. But, when she opened the dressing-table drawer and found a long case containing an almost priceless diamond necklace, she was more interested still, though not so pleased. In the wardrobe, when she went to put away her 'bonnet', she found a tiara and several brooches, and the rest of the jewellery turned up in various parts of the room during the next half-hour. The children looked more and more uncomfortable, and now Jane began to sniff.

Mother looked at her gravely.

'Jane,' she said, 'I am sure you know something about this. Now think before you speak, and tell me the truth.'

'We found a Fairy,' said Jane obediently.

'No nonsense, please,' said her mother sharply.

'Don't be silly, Jane,' Cyril interrupted. Then he went on desperately. 'Look here, mother, we've never seen the things before, but Lady Chittenden at Peasmarsh Place lost all her jewellery by wicked burglars last night. Could this possibly be it?'

All drew a deep breath. They were saved.

'But how could they have put it here? And why should they?' asked mother, not unreasonably. 'Surely it would have been easier and safer to make off with it?'

'Suppose,' said Cyril, 'they thought it better to wait for – for sunset – nightfall, I mean, before they went off with it. No one but us knew that you were coming back today.'

'I must send for the police at once,' said mother distractedly. 'Oh, how I wish daddy were here!'

'Wouldn't it be better to wait till he *does* come?' asked Robert, knowing that his father would not be home before sunset.

'No, no; I can't wait a minute with all this on my mind,' cried mother. 'All this' was the heap of jewel-cases on the bed. They put them all in the wardrobe, and mother locked it. Then mother called Martha.

'Martha,' she said, 'has any stranger been into my room since I've been away? Now, answer me truthfully.'

'No, mum,' answered Martha; 'leastways, what I mean to say –'

She stopped.

'Come,' said her mistress kindly; 'I see someone has. You must tell me at once. Don't be frightened. I'm sure you haven't done anything wrong.'

Martha burst into heavy sobs.

'I was a-goin' to give you warning this very day, mum, to leave at the end of my month, so I was – on account of me being going to make a respectable young man happy. A gamekeeper he is by trade, mum – and I wouldn't deceive you – of the name of Beale. And it's as true as I stand here, it was your coming home in such a hurry, and no warning given, out of the kindness of his heart it was, as he says, "Martha, my beauty," he says – which I ain't, and never was, but you know how them men will go on – "I can't see you a-toiling and a-moiling and not lend a 'elping 'and; which mine is a strong arm and it's yours, Martha, my dear," says he. And so he helped me a-cleanin' of the windows – but outside, mum, the whole time, and me in; if I never say another breathing word it's the gospel truth.'

'Were you with him the whole time?' asked her mistress.

'Him outside and me in, I was,' said Martha; 'except for fetching up a fresh pail and the leather that that slut of a Eliza 'd hidden away behind the mangle.'

'That will do,' said the children's mother. 'I am not pleased with you, Martha, but you have spoken the truth, and that counts for something.'

When Martha had gone, the children clung round their mother.

'Oh, mummy darling,' cried Anthea, 'it isn't Beale's fault, it isn't really! He's a great dear; he is, truly and honourably, and as honest as the day. Don't let the police take him, mummy! Oh, don't, don't, don't!'

It was truly awful. Here was an innocent man accused of robbery through that silly wish of Jane's, and it was absolutely useless to tell the truth. All longed to, but they thought of the straws in the hair and the shrieks of the other frantic maniacs, and they could not do it.

'Is there a cart hereabouts?' asked mother feverishly. 'A trap of any sort? I must drive into Rochester and tell the police at once.'

All the children sobbed, 'There's a cart at the farm, but, oh, don't go! – Don't go! – Oh, don't go! – wait till daddy comes home!'

Mother took not the faintest notice. When she had set her mind on a thing she always went straight through with it; she was rather like Anthea in this respect.

'Look here, Cyril,' she said, sticking on her hat with long sharp violet-headed pins, 'I leave you in charge. Stay in the dressing-room. You can pretend to be swimming boats in the bath, or something. Say I gave you leave. But stay there, with the landing door open; I've locked the other. And don't let anyone go into my room. Remember, no one knows the jewels are there except me, and all of you, and the wicked thieves who put them there. Robert, you stay in the garden and watch the windows. If anyone tries to get in you must run and tell the two farm men that I'll send up to wait in the kitchen. I'll tell them there are dangerous characters about – that's true enough. Now, remember, I trust you both. But I don't think they'll try it till after dark, so you're quite safe. Good-bye, darlings.'

And she locked her bedroom door and went off with the key in her pocket.

The children could not help admiring the dashing and decided way in which she had acted. They thought how useful she would have been in organizing escape from some of the tight places in which they had found themselves of late in consequence of their ill-timed wishes.

'She's a born general,' said Cyril – 'but I don't know what's going to happen to us. Even if the girls were to hunt for that beastly Sammyadd and find it, and get it to take the jewels away again, mother would only think we hadn't looked out properly and let the burglars sneak in and nick them – or else the police will think *we've* got them – or else that she's been fooling them. Oh, it's a pretty decent average ghastly mess this time, and no mistake!'

He savagely made a paper boat and began to float it in the bath, as he had been told to do.

Robert went into the garden and sat down on the worn yellow grass, with his miserable head between his helpless hands.

Anthea and Jane whispered together in the passage downstairs, where the coconut matting was – with the hole in it that you always caught your foot in if you were not careful. Martha's voice could be heard in the kitchen – grumbling loud and long.

'It's simply quite too dreadfully awful,' said Anthea. 'How do you know all the diamonds are there too? If they aren't, the police will think mother and father have got them, and that they've only given up some of them for a kind of desperate blind. And they'll be put in prison, and we shall be branded outcasts, the children of felons. And it won't be at all nice for father and mother either,' she added, by a candid afterthought.

'But what can we *do*?' asked Jane.

'Nothing – at least we might look for the Psammead again. It's a very, *very* hot day. He may have come out to warm that whisker of his.'

'He won't give us any more beastly wishes today,' said Jane flatly. 'He gets crosser and crosser every time we see him. I believe he hates having to give wishes.'

Anthea had been shaking her head gloomily – now she stopped shaking it so suddenly that it really looked as though she were pricking up her ears.

'What is it?' asked Jane. 'Oh, have you thought of something?'

'Our one chance,' cried Anthea dramatically; 'the last lone-lorn forlorn hope. Come on.'

At a brisk trot she led the way to the sand-pit. Oh, joy! – there was the Psammead, basking in a golden sandy hollow and preening its whiskers happily in the glowing afternoon sun. The moment it saw them it whisked round and began to burrow – it evidently preferred its own company to theirs. But Anthea was too quick for it. She caught it by its furry shoulders gently but firmly, and held it.

'Here – none of that!' said the Psammead. 'Leave go of me, will you?'

But Anthea held him fast.

'Dear kind darling Sammyadd,' she said breathlessly.

'Oh yes – it's all very well,' it said; 'you want another wish, I expect. But I can't keep on slaving from morning till night giving people their wishes. I must have *some* time to myself.'

'Do you hate giving wishes?' asked Anthea gently, and her voice trembled with excitement.

'Of course I do,' it said. 'Leave go of me or I'll bite! – I really will – I mean it. Oh, well, if you choose to risk it.'

Anthea risked it and held on.

'Look here,' she said, 'don't bite me – listen to reason. If you'll only do what we want today, we'll never ask you for another wish as long as we live.'

The Psammead was much moved.

'I'd do anything,' it said in a tearful voice. 'I'd almost burst myself to give you one wish after another, as long as I held out, if you'd only never, never ask me to do it after today. If you knew how I hate to blow myself out with other people's wishes, and how frightened I am always that I shall strain a muscle or something. And then to wake up every morning and know you've *got* to do it. You don't know what it is – you don't know what it is, you don't!' Its voice cracked with emotion, and the last 'don't' was a squeak.

Anthea set it down gently on the sand.

'It's all over now,' she said soothingly. 'We promise faithfully never to ask for another wish after today.'

'Well, go ahead,' said the Psammead; 'let's get it over.'

'How many can you do?'

'I don't know – as long as I can hold out.'

'Well, first, I wish Lady Chittenden may find she's never lost her jewels.'

The Psammead blew itself out, collapsed, and said, 'Done.'

'I wish,' said Anthea more slowly, 'mother mayn't get to the police.'

'Done,' said the creature after the proper interval.

'I wish,' said Jane suddenly, 'mother could forget all about the diamonds.'

'Done,' said the Psammead; but its voice was weaker.

'Wouldn't you like to rest a little?' asked Anthea considerately.

'Yes, please,' said the Psammead; 'and, before we go further, will you wish something for me?'

'Can't you do wishes for yourself?'

'Of course not,' it said; 'we were always expected to give each other our wishes – not that we had any to speak of in the good old Megatherium days. Just wish, will you, that you may never be able, any of you, to tell anyone a word about *Me*.'

'Why?' asked Jane.

'Why, don't you see, if you told grown-ups I should have no peace of my life. They'd get hold of me, and they wouldn't wish silly things like you do, but real earnest things; and the scientific people would hit on some way of making things last after sunset, as likely as not; and they'd ask for a graduated income-tax, and old-age pensions and manhood suffrage, and free secondary education, and dull things like that; and get them, and keep them, and the whole world would be turned topsy-turvy. Do wish it! Quick!'

Anthea repeated the Psammead's wish, and it blew itself out to a larger size than they had yet seen it attain.

'And now,' it said as it collapsed, 'can I do anything more for you?'

'Just one thing; and I think that clears everything up, doesn't it, Jane? I wish Martha to forget about the diamond ring, and mother to forget about the keeper cleaning the windows.'

'It's like the "Brass Bottle",' said Jane.

'Yes, I'm glad we read that or I should never have thought of it.'

'Now,' said the Psammead faintly, 'I'm almost worn out. Is there anything else?'

'No; only thank you kindly for all you've done for us, and I hope you'll have a good long sleep, and I hope we shall see you again some day.'

'Is that a wish?' it said in a weak voice.

'Yes, please,' said the two girls together.

Then for the last time in this story they saw the Psammead blow itself out and collapse suddenly. It nodded to them, blinked its long snail's eyes, burrowed, and disappeared, scratching fiercely to the last, and the sand closed over it.

'I hope we've done right?' said Jane.

'I'm sure we have,' said Anthea. 'Come on home and tell the boys.'

Anthea found Cyril glooming over his paper boats,

and told him. Jane told Robert. The two tales were only just ended when mother walked in, hot and dusty. She explained that as she was being driven into Rochester to buy the girls' autumn school-dresses the axle had broken, and but for the narrowness of the lane and the high soft hedges she would have been thrown out. As it was, she was not hurt, but she had had to walk home. 'And oh, my dearest dear chicks,' she said, 'I am simply dying for a cup of tea! Do run and see if the kettle boils!'

'So you see it's all right,' Jane whispered. 'She doesn't remember.'

'No more does Martha,' said Anthea, who had been to ask after the state of the kettle.

As the servants sat at their tea, Beale the game-keeper dropped in. He brought the welcome news that Lady Chittenden's diamonds had not been lost at all. Lord Chittenden had taken them to be re-set and cleaned, and the maid who knew about it had gone for a holiday. So that was all right.

'I wonder if we ever shall see the Psammead again,' said Jane wistfully as they walked in the garden, while mother was putting the Lamb to bed.

'I'm sure we shall,' said Cyril, 'if you really wished it.'

'We've promised never to ask it for another wish,' said Anthea.

'I never want to,' said Robert earnestly.

They did see it again, of course, but not in this story. And it was not in a sand-pit either, but in a very, very, very different place. It was in a – But I must say no more.

PUFFIN ⊕ CLASSICS

Five Children and *It*

With Puffin Classics, the adventure isn't
over when you reach the final page.
Want to discover more about your favourite
characters, their creators and their worlds?
Read on . . .

CONTENTS

NAME: Edith Nesbit, better known as E. Nesbit (as an author); Daisy (as a nickname)
BORN: 15 August 1858
DIED: 4 May 1924
NATIONALITY: British
LIVED: born in London, E. Nesbit lived all over Europe during her childhood, then as an adult lived in Kent and London
MARRIED: to Hubert Bland, 1880–1914, and to Thomas Tucker, from 1917 onwards
CHILDREN: Paul, Iris and Fabian (Bland) were her own children, but she brought up Hubert Bland's other children – Rosamund and John – also as her own.

What was she like?

Edith Nesbit was a mischievous, tomboyish child who grew into an unconventional adult. Known as Daisy by her friends, she was constantly looking for fun and adventure with her siblings. She was unable to settle at any of the boarding schools that her mother sent her to and ran away on more than one occasion. She refused to act as society expected her to. Instead, she wore what she liked, cut her hair as she liked and didn't hesitate to voice her opinion on a whole range of subjects. Although she was outspoken, she was always very sociable and well liked. Despite her life being dogged by financial difficulties she was very generous and gave so much away that she was almost bankrupt when she died.

Where did she grow up?

Because Edith's sister Mary was a sickly child, the family lived in many different places in an effort to improve her health. While she was growing up, Edith lived in Brighton, Paris, Bordeaux (and a number of other French towns), Spain and Germany. They finally settled in Kent after Mary died and spent three idyllic years in a place called Halstead Hall. Edith spent some of her happiest childhood days there, playing with her brothers beside a railway, writing poetry and swinging in a hammock, and it was, without doubt, the source of inspiration for many of the books that she wrote in later life. When Edith was seventeen years old, they moved to London.

What did she do apart from writing books?

Edith and her husband were keen socialists. This meant that they believed property and wealth should be shared fairly. They were among the founding members of the Fabian Society – a forerunner of the Labour Party – and edited the society's journal. They even named their son Fabian! Their home became a centre for socialist and literary discussion. Their friends included some of the greatest writers and thinkers of the time, including George Bernard Shaw and H. G. Wells.

Where did E. Nesbit get the idea for Five Children and It?

E. Nesbit only began to write children's fiction after years as a successful writer for adults. Thanks to her success, she was approached by a popular children's magazine of the time to write pieces about her childhood. But Edith turned from describing the literal facts of her childhood to capturing in fictional form the happy and relaxed atmosphere she had known as a girl. The result was a bestselling series of children's books that have remained firm favourites for over a hundred years.

What did people think of Five Children and It *when it was first published?*

Five Children and It was published in 1902 – E. Nesbit's third novel for children in just four years. The speed with which her books were released shows the demand there must have been for them. And the number of titles that are still in print shows how popular they are still. Since they were published, E. Nesbit's books have inspired a number of fantasy authors, including C. S. Lewis, who wrote of how she influenced his *Narnia* series.

What other books did she write?

E. Nesbit was a prolific author, who published about forty children's books and worked on many others. As well as novels and short stories, she wrote plays and collections of verse. Apart from *Five Children and It*, her most famous books include *The Story of the Treasure Seekers*, *The Wouldbegoods* and *The Railway Children*. Many have been adapted for film and television.

Cyril – the eldest of the five children. Known as Squirrel, because that's what his name sounds like.

Anthea – the elder sister, also known as Panther, because that sounds like her name. She means to be a good housekeeper some day and always likes to do the right thing.

Jane – the younger sister, also known as Pussy.

Robert – the middle brother. He likes being in charge and although he is not unkind he loves to play practical jokes.

The Lamb – the youngest of the five children, the baby is known as the Lamb because 'Baa' was the first thing he ever said. His real name is Hilary St Maur Devereux.

Mother – the children's mother. She appears only briefly, spending most of the novel looking after Granny.

Father – the children's father. He goes away suddenly on business and misses out on all the excitement.

Martha – the children's nursemaid; she is responsible for them while their parents are away.

It – the Psammead or Sand-fairy that the five children meet in the gravel-pit.

E. Nesbit often speaks directly to the reader, like this:

Now that I have begun to tell you about the place, I feel that I could go on and make this into a most interesting story about all the ordinary things that the children did – just the kind of things you do yourself, you know . . . (page 4)

Why do you think she writes in this style?

The author has some controversial opinions. For example: 'You can always make girls believe things much easier than boys.' (page 18) Do you think she would have written the same if the book had been published today instead of in 1902? Can you spot any other comments like this?

E. Nesbit mentions a 'Mr Kipling' on page 123 of this novel. Can you guess his full name? (Clue: he's another author in the Puffin Classics series.)

Edith Nesbit always wrote under the name of E. Nesbit instead of using her full name. Why do you think she did this? Are there any other authors who use their initials instead of their first name(s)?

Here's a description of the Psammead from page 11:

Its eyes were on long horns like a snail's eyes, and it could move them in and out like telescopes; it had ears like a bat's ears, and its tubby body was shaped like a spider's and covered with thick soft fur; its legs and arms were furry too, and it had hands and feet like a monkey's.

If you were lucky enough to find your own Sand-fairy, what do you think it would look like? Draw your own Sand-fairy!

The Psammead has an awful habit of twisting the children's wishes, so they never get exactly what they were hoping for. Can you think of three of your own wishes and imagine how the Psammead might interpret these in an awkward way? Better still, can you think of a foolproof wish that would turn out exactly as you expected?

Five Children and It was first published over a hundred years ago. Robert, Anthea, Cyril, Jane and the Lamb are different in many ways to children today, for example, in the clothes that they wear. How many more differences can you spot? And in how many ways are these Edwardian children the same as children in the twenty-first century?

The five main characters from *Five Children and It* appear in two other books by E. Nesbit. These are *The Phoenix and the Carpet* and *The Story of the Amulet*. So if you've enjoyed reading about Robert, Anthea, Cyril, Jane and the Lamb, you can catch up with them again in two more magical children's books.

The 1991 TV adaptation of *Five Children and It* was called *The Sand-fairy* when it was shown in the USA.

In 1992, Helen Cresswell wrote a sequel to E. Nesbit's *Five Children and It*. Called *The Return of the Psammead*, it tells the story of a new family of children. They discover the Sand-fairy and ask it to grant even more wishes. Helen Cresswell later adapted this book for television.

The 2004 film version of *Five Children and It* starred Freddie Highmore, Kenneth Branagh, Zoë Wannamaker and Norman Wisdom. Eddie Izzard provided the voice of the Psammead. However, the film was slightly different to the book. The children's father does not go away on business, but to war, and their mother works as a nurse, looking after wounded soldiers. The five children are sent to stay at their cousin's house.

GLOSSARY

Assyrian – someone who lived in the ancient country of Assyria in the Middle East

asylum – an old-fashioned name for a psychiatric hospital

Bedlam – an old nickname for Bethlem Royal Hospital in London, the world's first psychiatric hospital, and now meaning a place or state of uproar and chaos

belfry – the part of a bell tower where the bells are kept

caraway – the seed of a plant of the parsley family

coping – the top of a row of bricks or a wall, usually sloped or curved

cuirass – a piece of armour made up of a breastplate and a backplate fastened together

damask – a beautiful fabric with a pattern showing on both sides

doubloon – a Spanish gold coin

Eton collar – a broad, stiff white collar worn outside the coat collar, once worn by pupils of Eton College

farthing – an old UK coin, worth a quarter of an old penny

fender – a fireguard used to stop coals falling out of the fireplace

florin – an old UK coin, worth two shillings (10p)

fly – an old-fashioned one-horse carriage

guinea – an old UK coin, worth twenty-one shillings (£1.05)

half-crown – an old UK coin, worth two shillings and sixpence (12.5p)

heraldry – an old-fashioned system of coats of arms that are used to represent different families

hornbeam – a type of tree with oval leaves, tough nuts and pale wood

knickerbockers – short, loose trousers that are gathered at the knee

limekiln – a type of oven where quicklime is produced; quicklime is used to make building materials

megatherium – an extinct giant ground sloth

oasthouse – a building that contains a kiln (a type of oven)

ostler – someone who once looked after the horses of people staying at an inn

parley – a conversation between two opposing sides in a dispute

pax – what children used to say when they wanted to make friends after an argument

pennoned – something that has a flag attached

plaid – checked or tartan cloth

Psammead – a Sand-fairy

reconnoitre – to check out an area before doing something there

reformatory – a place where young offenders used to be sent instead of prison

sago pudding – a old-fashioned sweet dessert

sandhopper – a small shellfish found on the seashore

soda-siphon – a special bottle used to make fizzy soda water

smelting furnace – a type of oven used to take metals from ore

sovereign – an old UK coin, worth one pound

suffrage – the right to vote in political elections

varlet – a good-for-nothing rogue

varmint – a troublesome or naughty person

wagonette – a four-wheeled horse-drawn vehicle, used for pleasure trips

If you have enjoyed *Five Children and It* you may like to read *Peter Pan*, in which Peter leads the three Darling children over the rooftops and away to Neverland:

The Flight

'Second to the right, and straight on till morning.'

That, Peter had told Wendy, was the way to the Neverland; but even birds, carrying maps and consulting them at windy corners, could not have sighted it with these instructions. Peter, you see, just said anything that came into his head.

At first his companions trusted him implicitly, and so great were the delights of flying that they wasted time circling round church spires or any other tall objects on the way that took their fancy.

John and Michael raced, Michael getting a start.

They recalled with contempt that not so long ago they had thought themselves fine fellows for being able to fly round a room.

Not so long ago. But how long ago? They were flying over the sea before this thought began to disturb Wendy seriously. John thought it was their second sea and their third night.

Sometimes it was dark and sometimes light, and now they were very cold and again too warm. Did they really feel hungry at times, or were they merely pretending because Peter had such a jolly new way of feeding them? His way was to pursue birds who had food in their mouths suitable for humans and snatch it from them; then the birds would follow and snatch it back; and they would all go chasing each other gaily for miles, parting at last with mutual expressions of good-will. But Wendy noticed with gentle concern that Peter did not seem to know that this was rather an odd way of getting your bread and butter, nor even that there are other ways.

Certainly they did not pretend to be sleepy, they were sleepy; and that was a danger, for the moment they popped off, down they fell. The awful thing was that Peter thought this funny.

'There he goes again!' he would cry gleefully, as Michael suddenly dropped like a stone.

'Save him, save him!' cried Wendy, looking with horror at the cruel sea far below. Eventually Peter would dive through the air, and catch Michael just before he could strike the sea, and it was lovely the way he did it; but he always waited till the last moment, and you felt it was his cleverness that interested him and not the saving of human life. Also he was fond of variety, and the sport that engrossed him one moment would suddenly cease to engage him, so there was always the possibility that the next time you fell he would let you go.

He could sleep in the air without falling, by merely lying on his back and floating, but this was, partly at least, because he was so light that if you got behind him and blew he went faster.

'Do be more polite to him,' Wendy whispered to John, when they were playing 'Follow my Leader'.

'Then tell him to stop showing off,' said John.

When playing Follow my Leader, Peter would fly close to the water and touch each shark's tail in passing, just as in the street you may run your finger along an iron railing. They could not follow him in this with much success, so perhaps it was rather like showing off, especially as he kept looking behind to see how many tails they missed.

'You must be nice to him,' Wendy impressed on her brothers. 'What would we do if he were to leave us?'

'We could go back,' Michael said.

'How could we ever find our way back without him?'

'Well, then, we could go on,' said John.

'That is the awful thing, John. We should have to go on, for we don't know how to stop.'

Peter Pan is available in Puffin Classics